TURTLE, COYOTE, RAVEN and RINGO:
Mystical Journeys

A novel

By Lon Seymour

Dedication:

To Carol Sampson who, a long while ago, read and critiqued the first troublesome draft of the novel. And to Shanda Plock, who aided and abetted with this latest version.

Turtle, Coyote, Raven and Ringo is a work of fiction in the tradition of satire and lampoon. As fiction, names, characters, businesses, places, events, locales, and incidents are either the products of the author's imagination or used in a fictitious manner. For the purpose of story, historical events are likewise fictionalized. Any resemblance to actual persons, living or dead, or actual events is purely coincidental.

BrandED Publishing

A Division of
BrandED Consultants Group
5713 Teller Street #503
Arvada, CO 80002

Phone: 303.264.7930
E-mail: info@BrandEDus.net

TABLE OF CONTENTS

Part 3: The Future—Three Rivers

The history of a place is made up of four things: first there is the land, then there are the people, consider also the influence of the land over the people, and last, the impact of the people upon the land. To seek harmony between oneself and Mother Earth in the name of the people creates heroes—those who serve others. To seek to conquer the land, our Mother, or to conquer the people, our fathers, for fame or greed, profits one not. To willfully seek to influence the history of a place leads to folly.

Tarhe, Wyandotte Sachem

PRELUDE

I am the narrator of this tale. I am Turtle. As you will hear me say often: It is upon my shell that you live and it is I, Turtle, who is the father of you all, although all of you—save the indigenous— have forgotten me. I am Turtle the beguiler and confederate of the tricksters Raven and Coyote, and it is we who manipulate the plot of this tale. Plot, character, setting—through us are all three one. The setting is a character; thus, the place, the land, which is me, Turtle, furthers the plot, and confounds the cabal.

I begin with a poem.

> *Past, present, future*
> *Each manifest by*
> *One little ...*
> *Two little ...*
> *Three little Indians.*

> *If Wolf Song is the past*
> *Then is Hands of the Bear the present*
> *Then is Three Rivers is the future*

> *Pay you attention to all three.*

PREFACE: Fact and Fiction

The following are facts. The adventures and tall tales inhabiting the pages of this novel between these random facts are fiction and imaginative manipulations, historical liberties; or at least, events much more difficult to prove.

Many ancient cultures believed the world was created on the carapace of the deity Turtle.

65 to 45 million years ago, as the present Rocky Mountains folded and faulted their way into existence, great red slabs of Pennsylvanian and Permian sedimentary rocks—300 million-year-old sandstone and shale, originally the bottom of a great sea, shallow and half a continent wide, but long, long gone—were tilted and eroded into dramatic red monoliths west of what was to be the location of Denver, Colorado, the Queen City of the Plains and gateway to the Rockies. Wind and rain carved a bowl with perfect acoustical attributes. Taking advantage of the gift from Mother Nature, the Civilian Conservation Corps and citizens of Denver built an amphitheater completed in 1941, and have since entertained tens of thousands of concertgoers, warmed by the rocks, mesmerized by the rising moon, and dazzled by the stars.

Colonel William Fredrick Remington Cody (1846-1917), was proprietor, manager, master of ceremonies, and performer extraordinaire in the frontier extravaganza Buffalo Bill's Wild West and Congress of Rough Riders of the World, which traveled throughout America and Europe, including a command performance at Windsor Castle (June 26, 1892) to celebrate Queen Victoria's Golden Jubilee.

Sitting Bull, Tatanka-Iyotanka, performed briefly in Buffalo Bill's Wild West, but did not travel to perform for Mother England, Queen Victoria. On December 15, 1890, while being arrested by a group of authorities made up of a few US soldiers and forty-six Indian policemen, Sitting Bull was unceremoniously executed. The Indian slayers were fellow Sioux. Sergeant Red Tomahawk fired the fatal bullet into the back of the head of the legendary Hunkpapa chief.

The famous Oglala sage and oracle, Black Elk, accompanied the Wild West to England, where he and several other Indians were lost and wandered for two years through Britain, France, and Germany, until finally returned to America and ultimately reunited with the touring Buffalo Bill troupe.

At exactly five minutes past noon on January 10, 1917, Buffalo Bill Cody, Colonel Fredrick Remington Cody, the famous frontier scout and American showman, hero of the dime-novel, died in Denver, Colorado, while visiting his sister May. Harry H. Tammen, the publisher of The Denver Post newspaper, paid the widow Louisa Cody a tidy sum to keep the earthly remains of the old Indian fighter near Denver. Buffalo Bill was buried on Lookout Mountain, the western wall of Golden, Colorado, and a scenic perch just west of the Queen City of the Plains, much to the consternation of Cody's Wyoming kinsmen, friends, and Wild West zealots.

In the summer of 1948 the American Legion Post of Cody, Wyoming, offered a $10,000 reward for the return of Buffalo Bill's remains from Lookout Mountain, Golden, Colorado, to the town in Wyoming, which is his namesake. In response, the Denver Chapter of the American Legion, the Leyden-Chiles-Wickersham Post, rallied a squad of Denver Legionnaires to race up the mountain and guard the tomb. In support, the National Guard drove two antique tanks up Lariat Trail, a winding mountainous road, dominated by narrow curves, tight switchbacks, and lethal drop-offs. Yes, it's true—tanks. (It was just such "overkill" that motivated this tale.)

In 1950, or there about, an eccentric entrepreneur, who had obviously visited (and been enamored with) Taos and Santa Fe, New Mexico, (300 hundred miles south of Golden) built an out of place construct in the Northern New Mexican adobe style at the junction of Colorado Highway 40 (known as Mount Vernon Canyon Road) and the entrance to Mount Vernon Country Club on Lariat Trail. The building, which still sits at the southernmost end of the notorious Lariat Loop, has gone through a variety of alpine purposes, but for several decades has maintained its unique "Pueblo Revival" identity. Mount Vernon Country Club has for an equal number of decades been a private gourmet establishment, nestled on Lookout Mountain, with elegant views of Denver and the Great Plains to the east. Many a high school prom couple has passed through its portals previous to prom night debauchery.

In August of 1964, The Beatles, fondly known as the Fab-Four, preformed a summer concert at Red Rocks Amphitheater, just west of Denver, between Morrison and Golden. Red Rocks has been called the greatest outdoor venue by entertainment luminaries from Glenn Miller to Ray Charles, from Joan Baez to Nora Jones. The Beatles, it has often been said, introduced a new age in music, social awareness, and spiritual revival. While visiting The Rockies, they stayed at the celebrated Brown Palace Hotel, the hostel of choice for the "mighty and the affluent." In the old times (and good times), when the country was young, The Brown hosted the spawn of wild cat'rs—gamblers, cheats, bandits, speculators, mountain men, cowpoke, and pioneers—authentic frontier folk. Politicians also felt right at home. Since the glory days of gold and silver, The Brown Palace has put out the red carpet for royalty and presidents, including Teddy Roosevelt, Herbert Hoover, and F.D.R. It served as the pre-convention headquarters for General Dwight D. Eisenhower. No politicos spent more time in The Brown than Mamie and Ike. And, oh yes, Zsa Zsa Gabor was a frequent guest.

The mountains of New Mexico are said to be enchanted. Confirmation of this spectral allure is embossed, stamped with pneumatic vigor by felons on the state's license plates. Nuevo Méjico is also a land of paradox—enchanted contrasts and contradictions, if not always ludicrous, then witty. Although the local Anglo citizens and tax payers give myth little credence, the indigenous Pueblo People and the Hispanic martyrs immortalize the deities and denizens of the mountain ranges that radiate firedog red in the rising and the setting sun. Who but the phantasmagoria could live among the summits named after the blood of Christ—the Sangre de Christos— or the refreshing, bewitching, and mystical watermelon—the Sandias.

Ancient frontier spirits, a trio of tricksters, were awakened into paranormal action by the suburbanization and consequent gentrification of the foothills above Golden, Colorado. Sensing the opportunity for skullduggery, they trekked from the land of enchantment and north along the ridges of the Rocky Mountains. They bivouacked near Red Rocks Park and Amphitheater. Turtle, Coyote, and Raven formed a loose alliance based on chicanery. Wayfaring from New Mexico to Colorado begot a great thirst.

TURTLE, COYOTE, RAVEN and RINGO:
Mystical Journeys

Part One: Wolf Song is the Past

"Promises in the past portend the future."—Wolf Song, Lakota

"Only by acceptance of the past, can you alter it."—T.S. Elliot, author

Chapter One

America According to John

Summer, 1964

And the nonbelievers thought I could not fly. Well, the jokes on them.
— Turtle

"It's a vast country," said Ringo as the airliner jetted past the Mississippi River and over the Great American Plains.

"Vast and wide," said George. "I flew to Saint Louis once, to see me sister. She's nearly a bloody Yank by now, don't cha know, but it didn't seem this far. It's vast."

"I've never been awake in a plane this long," said Paul, pulling his seatbelt tighter. "Doesn't feel safe to be in the sky this long, wings or no wings. Wings . . . hmmm, interesting thought . . . anyway, it's bloody vast."

"Dry," said John.

"Vast and dry," repeated Ringo.

"No," said John. "I'm dry. I'm getting thirsty listening to all this brilliant geographical observation. I need another bloody drink."

"I'll have another drink meself," said Paul. "I've never been awake this long on a bloody plane."

"We have to arrive sober in Denver, boys," said Brian. "There'll be reporters and a crowd at the airport."

"Judging from the vastness so brilliantly described by young Ringo here, I'd say we have plenty of time. Stewardess," called out John. "Bring me and me chum, Paul here, another drink."

"Endless," said George.

"Vast and endless," repeated Ringo.

"John?" asked George, "Do you suppose we'll see any Indians?"

"Does Ravi have relatives over here?" asked Ringo. "They have huge families those Indians."

"He's asking about American Indians, you bugger," said Paul.

"Just being a skiver, George. Bit of blarney, trifling wit ya. I know the difference. Well, come ta think of it, maybe the mots on me. What *is* the difference?" asked Ringo.

"That's a tough question," said George. "John?"

"It's an unfortunate mistake that we call the indigenous people of America: *Indians*. It's the fault of bloody Columbus. When the wanker sailed west from Spain and landed in the Caribbean, he thought he had hit India, so he called the people he found *Indians*. Pretty bloody stupid, if you ask me."

"What did he think happened to Japan and China and the bloody Philippines on the way to India I wonder?" said George.

"Pretty bloody stupid is right," said Paul. "I've never thought the Spaniards very bright."

"Italian," said John.

"What?" asked Paul.

"Columbus," said John. "He was Italian. He was only working for the Spaniards."

"Well, there you are," said Paul.

"The indigenous American people came from China originally. Up through Russia and over a land bridge to Alaska," said John.

"Alaska is one of the colonies now," said Ringo. "I hear it's huge."

"Vast," said John.

"Stewardess, hurry," called Paul.

"It was Vasco da Gama discovered India for the Spanish," said George.

"Portuguese," said John.

The three novices looked at each other perplexed, but none asked the obvious follow-up question. They sat for a time, Ringo staring out the oval window at the flat terrain below. He noticed the slight undulation of the ground. Here and there large circles of green were centered in larger brown squares creating a quilted pattern to the plain. He guessed that roads created the grid but he wondered what made the green circles. Finally he spoke, "John," he asked, "If he thought he was in India, why did Columbus call it *America*?"

"He didn't," answered John sipping a rum and Coke.

Ringo waited. Paul opened his eyes. George turned toward John. John sat and sipped.

"It was another Spaniard called it *America*," said Brian. "Named it after his bloody self."

"Italian," said John.

"Well, there you are," said Paul and closed his eyes.

"How much farther?" asked Ringo.

Paul appeared to drift into a nap. John and Brian quietly discussed the logistics of the Denver concert. Ringo knew better than to insert himself into that confab. George leaned his seat as far back as it would go, stared at the ceiling and hummed a tune he was composing in his head. "Probably never get performed," he mumbled.

"What?" asked Ringo.

"Nothing, nothing to get on about," he continued composing.

Ringo stared out the window for several minutes then searched the pocket on the back of the seat in front of him. His search disturbed John and Brian.

They both looked at him through the crack between the seats. "If there's anything I can do; if there's anything that you want," said John.

"Sorry," he half-heartedly apologized. He turned in his seat and looked up and down the aisle. His fidgeting got a glance from George. Ringo figured now was as good a time as any, so he struggled out of his seatbelt and tried to step over George into the aisle. He ended up stepping on George's foot.

"Well," said George, "that's the end of that song."

"What song?" asked Ringo, finally standing in the aisle.

"Not to worry, lad. It'll never get a play."

"What are you two going on about?" grumbled Paul. "Ringo, me boy, it's not safe to be walking about in a plane that's thirty thousand feet above sweet Mother Earth."

"Nothing to fret about," said George. "Paul, let Ringo do as he pleases. Go back to sleep. Don't let us disturb you, by any means. Probably contemplating a tune, were ya. Well, far be it from us to interrupt. A catchy new ditty is it? When will we be privileged to hear it? No? . . . just nodding off are we, ignoring our responsibilities? Well, you've earned some time to relax; don't let us perturb. There'll be plenty of time to create once we've landed."

"George," asked Paul, "have you gone daft?"

"No, it's not me. Ringo's in a tweak, that's all."

"So what's got you undone, Ringo?"

"Searching," he answered.

"For what, may I ask?" said George.

"Knowledge," he answered. "What else is worth knowing?"

"Can't you take it someplace else?" said Paul. "Sod off."

"Done," said Ringo and walked to the front of the plane where the attendants were conversing. They twittered as he approached.

"You've hurt his feelings," said George and sat back in his seat.

"I don't mean to," answered Paul. "I just thought I'd catch a few winks, that's all. Does he need some comforting? Do you want me to hold 'is hand?"

"Funny," said George. "Well, I'll tell you something I think you'll understand. You know he hates being left out; how he hates being alone."

"That's not true. The little minim is always wandering off by hisself. No harm done. The stewardesses can guide him along."

Ringo lit up like a holiday as he approached the trio of attentive women, his search abandoned to admiration. The four of them laughed and giggled, and generally disturbed everyone else in first class. Paul stirred and looked as if he were going to give up the nap.

George, on the other hand, faded from song to light sleep. Half an hour later, a bubbling Ringo returned. He woke George as he struggled past him to the window seat. George opened only one chastising eye. Ringo grinned apologetically and plopped into his chair. Once landed, he offered George a nut from a bag he was holding. George ignored him. "Cashews," he tempted with a shake of the bag, "Got 'um from the old gentleman up front." He watched as George opened one eye, confirmed that he didn't want a nut and then looked toward the cockpit and the bevy of frenzied hostesses. George turned just enough to give Ringo a look of disbelief.

"What old gentleman?" he asked.

Ringo answered, "The old geezer standing next to the loo waving at me." He waved back and lifted the bag of nuts. "Tar," he mouthed an exaggerated thank you.

George looked again but acted disgusted. He closed both eyes and turned his back toward his mate. "Ringo, lad, you've been locked up in this re-circulating air for too bloody long. I don't see any codger up front."

"He's right there next to the stewardesses, going in the bog. Don't tell me you can't spy him. He says he knows Red Rocks, where we're playing the concert, he knows it very well. He said his people are very excited that we're coming. Seems they've been waiting a long time. See, he's waving again. Nice old gaffer. He's even darker and more crinkled than Ravi. Well, he's gone now; back inside, probably turning the blue water green again. I'll introduce you when he walks by."

"Ringo," said George, "just eat your bloody cashews and let me catch a nod, would ya. I'll meet him later. Lots later," he said under his breath.

Ringo waited, watching George until he felt he had returned to slumber. Ringo leaned over and whispered toward John.

"Then who discovered South America?"

"The North Americans," answered John.

Ringo sat back and looked out the window. He started to lean forward with another question.

"They were the bloody Chinese-Russian-Eskimo-Indian blokes what crossed the great Bering land bridge, Ringo," said George with his eyes still closed.

This satisfied him, but only for a minute. "It seems to me," Ringo began talking louder now that George was awake. "That the Indians probably don't like being called *Indians* if it was a mistake by Columbus and all. What do they call themselves?"

"By their first name probably," said Paul, now also awakened. "Hello, lads. I'm Paul, Paul the Bloody Hostile." He smiled, anticipating a laugh. The others were silent.

"By their tribal names, I suppose," George broke the lull.

"The People," answered John.

"I beg your pardon?" asked Ringo.

"Most tribal names for America's indigenous citizenry translates to mean *The People*. It's being ethnocentric."

"Well, there you are," mumbled Paul. "Do I smell nuts? Thanks, Ringo, thanks for sharing."

"I don't believe I've ever seen an Eskimo," said Ringo, leaning across George and offering Paul a cashew.

"You've seen the bloody Chinese haven't you?" asked Paul, taking the bag.

Ringo nodded to Paul to keep the nuts. "Sure, they look like the bleedin' Mongols, now don't they?"

There was a pause. Ringo stirred again.

"No, Ringo, I don't know who discovered bloody Mongolia," said John.

There was another pause.

"Probably the bleeding Chinese on their way to becoming the bloody Mongols on their way across the land bridge to become the Eskimos on their bloody way to becoming the Indians discovered by an Italian-Spaniard who thought he was in bloody China, but the people were already gone to Mongolia," Ringo whispered.

George laughed and mussed Ringo's hair.

"Hey!" said Ringo. He straightened his hair and looked out the window. "Do you suppose we will ever play back in the USSR?" he asked into the glass.

"Maybe in football," answered Paul. "Why are you fretting over all this?"

"I'm curious that's all. Inquisitive, like. It's an ethnocentric trait of my people."

"Your people?"

"Percussionists," answered Ringo.

"How much bloody farther?" asked Paul, making sure his belt was tight.

Chapter Two

Gyah'-wish Atak-ía: Turtle Tells the Story of Creation

Summer, 1964

Put your ear to the earth and listen to the song of your birth and being; lift yourself away from her, your Mother, forget the song, and invite ruin. — Turtle

A turtle, a coyote, and a raven walked into a bar . . . They were thirsty for margaritas. Actually, they were The Turtle, The Coyote, and The Raven. The Coyote was telling a joke.

"So the rabbi says . . ."

"Heard it," interrupted Raven.

"Raven's right, Coyote. It's a howl," said Turtle, "but you told that same joke the last time we met for a deities drink."

"Don't be rude, old bird," said Coyote. "Do I interrupt you when you're telling a story?"

"All the time," said Raven, his feathers ruffled.

Coyote changed the subject. "Since my jokes are not appreciated, and I've got places to go and people to trick . . ."

"Now, don't go all she-wolf on us," Raven interrupted again. "We all like your jokes. You're acting a bit *peckish*, old dog. Is anything wrong?"

"Nothing I can put my paw on. Oh, I hate to complain . . ."

Turtle and Raven exchanged doubtful looks.

". . . but it seems lately that I'm losing my touch, or at least, there are certainly fewer opportunities for serious trickery. Something's changed. Haven't you fellows noticed? There's a lack of something in the air." He lifted his sharp snout and sniffed. "Nothing. Wait a minute . . . there is the faintest odor of duplicity wafting this way. Turtle, if ancient memory serves me right, that's your aroma? "

"I know exactly what you are wailing about," said Raven, ignoring Coyote's question. "Why, if Turtle had not invited me, and if I didn't love his margaritas so, I never would have left the deep woods and come this close to a city at this time of year. Summers are too hot. This is August, old cards . . . but, honestly, there's nothing to keep me in the hills. Chicanery is at an all time low. Don't you agree, Turtle?"

"I'm glad you said something, Coyote. You, too, Raven. The truth is, I'm feeling greatly underappreciated since returning to the foothills. I enjoy visiting here and you know that Red Rocks is one of my favorite haunts, but things are too quiet for my reptilian taste and I've decided to do something about it. The planets are coming together, some dubious characters have moved nearby, it's summer, yes, but the concert season is well underway at Red Rocks, and, I don't know if you have been paying attention to the music scene, but I sense that something is afoot. These Beatles characters are coming to Red Rocks and a couple of local natives are due for an adventure. I think the time is ripe for some pettifoggery."

"I'm hoping there's nothing 'petty' about it, Turtle, old friend," said Raven. "What's up?"

"Oh, I don't know," whined Coyote. "It seems that people just don't appreciate us like they used to. Honestly, I'm feeling a little blue."

"'Honestly?' 'Honestly!' Do we look that gullible, Coyote? You've never had an honest day in your perpetual life," said Raven. "But I do understand your plight. A blue coyote? We know exactly what you mean, moon dog. Haven't we all been to Santa Fe? Look what they've done with your image. There are blue coyotes in every damn gift shop and on every menu in town. You've become a cute little pet. Doesn't that raise your dander? Doesn't that bristle your fur?"

"Well, it's got *me* hot under the shell," said Turtle.

"A slow burn?" asked Raven.

Coyote laughed, "A slow burn, I get it, Raven. Good one. Yep, that's you, Turtle . . . slow to burn."

"Not anymore I'm not. I am Turtle, Gyah'-wish, and I am still here. They have forgotten me. They have forgotten us, eh Raven, ehya Coyote? This mystifies me. After all these eons humankind has forgotten that I am responsible for their being," he took a sip of his margarita, "and you two are responsible for most of their woes."

"Now wait a minute, old hard noggin, as I recall your son had something to do with human folly."

"And human success. Well, at least one of them did. But I repeat, humans have not remembered that it is upon my shell, my back, that Sky Woman fell. The world was covered with sea; she would have surely drowned had the waterfowl not slowed her fall, had Muskrat not brought mud from the depths and piled it on my back, and had I not been there for her to land upon. It is thus that Sky Woman, Aataentsic, became the grandmother of them all."

"Could I get a little more salt?" asked Coyote. "I can never get enough salt."

"Yes, please," said Raven. "I too love the salt. That's not to say the margarita is not good, Turtle. It's delicious."

"I'm glad you like it," answered Turtle. "As you know, it's an ancient family recipe. Personally, I think too much salt spoils the delicate flavors, but each trickster to his own, I suppose."

Coyote and Raven acknowledged their amusement at vexing their old friend.

Turtle passed the flat bowl of salt and continued. "I remember when salt was more valuable than gold to these humans. How times have changed. They have forgotten that my sister, Little Turtle, made the Sun and the Moon, his wife, to light the darkness so Aataentsic could see this new world.

"Few remember that Aataentsic dwelt originally in regions above the world and was among those human-like beings who had never wept and knew nothing of death. They have forgotten that such a thing had to change in order for humans to appear, that one supernatural being had to experience death for their sake."

"That sounds familiar," said Raven.

"Salt in the wound," added Coyote. "More salt, Turtle?" he teased.

Turtle ignored the jibe, "Of course this sacrifice for creation sounds familiar, but humans have forgotten, or never acknowledged, that it was the teacher of Aataentsic who made such a sacrifice. In seeking medicine for the elder, and the first to die in the sky region,

Aataentsic fell through a hole in the sky left by an uprooted tree. The hole was created by the elder himself, and who, it turns out, was her brother and her father and her husband at different times and all together. But these simple-minded humans are taken aback with concerns about petty morality. It never dawns on them that we are supernatural beings and they owe their existence to such miracles and such contradictions."

"Contradictions!" barked Coyote. "Now you're talking my craft." His quick tongue danced around his muzzle and squeegeed the salt and tequila. He howled in delight.

"I'm glad you're pleased," said Turtle. "But if I may continue: The fall was particularly harrowing because Aataentsic was pregnant. Loon cried out for all waterfowl to fly in unison and upon their winged backs catch the falling woman-being. They did so, lowered her safely, and placed her upon my carapace. It was then that Loon called for all deep divers to swim below and bring forth mud from which an earth could be built upon my back and provide a place for Aataentsic to dwell. All died in their attempts until at last Muskrat made his dive and although he floated to the surface drowned, in searching his paws and his mouth, the needed mud was found. And the world was built—upon me."

"It's not about just you, Turtle," challenged Raven. "We all know the story, or at least your version of creation. Yes, we know, and you never hesitate to remind us, that Coyote and I came later. Humans created our persona once they were established on 'your' world, but, frankly, it gets a little tiring. We know that Aataentsic gave birth to a daughter and that the child grew quickly and it was not long until Aataentsic noticed that her daughter, too, was pregnant. I hope you're not going to blame Coyote or me for that?"

"Relax, Raven. Have another drink. No one is blaming you for anything. Although this is a long and complex tale, suffice it to say that it was I, Turtle, who was the father of the twin sons soon born. And it was I who mourned the death in childbirth of their mother, my bride. It was however Aataentsic who sought retribution for the death of her daughter. She asked of the boys, 'Which of you two destroyed my child?' The second born, Tawiskaron, also called Tah'-weh-skah', and known as Flint, answered, 'Truly I believe it was he.' He blamed the first, his brother, Iouskeha or Sapling."

"I always liked Flint," said Coyote. "He was a great liar."

"My son, Sapling," said Turtle, "was of the appearance of mankind for it was he in birth who turned himself around, up-side-down, and entered the world so that his mother would live. Thus did he establish the manner in which all humans would be born."

"Yes," said Raven, "and they have acted up-side-down ever since."

"It was Flint," added Coyote, "who refused to be born appropriately and thus caused the death of his mother. Flint convinced the grandmother that it was his goody-two-shoed brother who had caused the death. Quite the trickster."

"Flint was not of the appearance of humankind for he looked as if he was ice-coated and his flesh was stone," said Turtle. He continued.

"Aataentsic cast out the first born. She grabbed him by the leg and flung him far from her. Do not be taken aback, these are not human beings, they are mystical. It was I, Turtle, who raised the outcast son for I witnessed that he was the truthful twin."

"And Flint, the little bamboozler," laughed Coyote, "the little fox, who was raised by wolves."

"No, no," interrupted Raven. "You're thinking of two other brothers, those Mediterranean chaps. Come to think of it, this two-brother-caper, one good and one bad, again sounds awfully familiar."

"It should," said Turtle, trying to regain control. "But you're right: Thus it was that the brothers took opposite paths—one good and the other evil. Thus it was that I, Turtle, became a witness to all things.

"As time went on, Sapling, my ward, made the earth to grow. He was preparing the place for humans. Flint created the mountains to impede the travel of man. Sapling created a climate that was warm and hospitable, Flint invented winter. It was to Sapling that I, Turtle, gave the secret of fire, and he in turn gave it to the humans. Thus he is called by the Huron: Tseh'-stah, Made of Fire.

"Flint threatened humankind with ice. Sapling gave humans corn and Flint gave them ashes and famine."

"You're being a little hard on the lad, are you not?" asked Coyote. "After all, it is having a choice between good and evil that makes humans so interesting, is it not? And is it not the fact that they so often choose the wrong path that gives us, well at least Raven and I, a calling?" He howled again.

Turtle filled Coyote's glass with more margarita. "Quiet down, you old hyena. I know you favor Flint, but recall: Sapling created rain and Flint snow. Sapling instilled humans with heart and hope; Flint forces them to dwell in darkness and folly. And it was Sapling, Tseh-stah, the good twin, who promised to be the eternal guardian of humankind. This I witnessed. It was Flint wrestling with Sapling that made the world, my carapace, uneven. And as I am the earth upon which they dwell, so are Flint and Sapling uncles to all humans. Do not be taken aback . . .

"Oh, how you turtles appreciate that saying, since the back is your most evident asset and your most obvious burden," said Raven. "We know you harbor jealousy of my ability to fly."

"And my swiftness afoot," interrupted Coyote.

"But old friend," said Raven to Turtle, "We all dwell in paradox. No wonder you feel a kinship to these people, and you are disappointed that they have forgotten you, forgotten us, for if you look closely you will see that slumbering within them are both Sapling and Flint, Fire and Ice, wisdom and folly."

"Affinity and irreverence," added Turtle.

"It has been this way since your creation and it continues today," Raven changed his tone. "Unless this is leading to another enterprise, something fun, let's change the subject. If, however, you have a point; if this is leading to a plan and some mayhem, by all means continue, and make another batch of your savory margaritas."

"I'll drink to that," said Coyote.

"Oh, I, Turtle, have they long forgotten in these modern times, and I am aware that the legacy of Sapling and Flint lives on. I watch and I see it is so."

"Forgive me for saying so, Turtle," said Raven, "but you're sounding a little pedestrian, pedantic, even. You're becoming a kernel self-indulgent. Did you have a few margaritas before we got here?"

"Yea, Turtle, why so glum?" asked Coyote. "Sure . . . human folks are irreverent. But you forget, there are a few people who still pay respect, limited as it is, to Turtle and Raven and me. Oh, sure, the dominate culture of their world has done its best to eliminate these folks who remember, who have clans named in honor of forest deities. You know: the *Indians*."

Turtle interrupted, "A misnomer instigated by an exploration leading to carnage, another tale about good versus evil, the quest for heroism, and human folly. Native American brothers have not yet been won over to the indifference of the white folks, the nonobservant and impious."

Coyote, apparently miffed at being interrupted or impatient for action, said, "We're all getting preachy; are we going to initiate some mayhem or not. I'm all about trickery, you know . . ." He licked his muzzle again and his eyes sparkled, either from finding more salt or the idea of impending skullduggery.

"You're right, Coyote. Most have forgotten me, but the spirits of our Indian brothers vivify me, give me energy, revive my being; therefore, their struggle is relevant to me and to you, my kin. Their saga is symbolic of the plight and dangers caused by the human assumption that I no longer exist." He took a long, thoughtful drink and allowed the cold agave juice to cool his thoughts.

"Turtle," asked Raven, "can you do frozen margaritas? That could prove a special treat, eh, Coyote?"

"Or do they believe that I slumber and do not see their world? I am here, I am Turtle, and I tell you now, mine is a restless sleep for when Turtle tosses and turns earthquakes and tidal waves result and the world changes. Be aware, it is when they, and they are still my children, follow the way of Flint that I stir. Suddenly they remember me by other names—Dragon, Destroyer, and The Beast!"

Raven spoke to Coyote, "I love his margaritas, but honestly, I think tequila makes him loco."

"I'll drink to that," answered Coyote.

"I am aware that when I am quiet," continued Turtle, not caring if his drinking partners were listening, "when I am nurturing and benevolent, they call me Gaea, Tierra Madre, and Mother Earth. Do I mind being referred to as female? They forget, I am mythical, we are mythical; therefore, titles mean little; call me Mother Earth or Father Turtle, pillager or protector, creator or destroyer, benefactor or The Beast."

"Call me irresponsible," said Coyote.

"However, when they are irreverent and disrespectful of the gifts bestowed by me and by Sapling . . ."

"Call me inconceivable," continued Coyote.

". . . their actions cause me to rumble and cause Flint and folly to emerge, and cause Coyote and Raven to awaken, ehya. They should recall, if they are wise, that I slumber beneath them and you, my friends, linger in the shadows."

"Unless he has a plan for some shenanigans, I think it's time to cut old Turtle off the tequila," said Raven. "Next thing you know, he'll think he can fly."

"Look at that smile," Coyote howled and licked his muzzle in anticipation. "He has a plan.

Chapter Three

COYOTE

Summer, 1886

Morning Dove spoke to me, Turtle, of the Indian theory of existence: "...everything on the earth has a purpose, every disease an herb to cure it, and every person a mission."

It was a matinee demise. For the hundredth time, Wolf Song feigned death and rolled off the rump of the galloping pony. He bellyflopped on the arena floor creating an explosion of dust, leaving the ashen outline of a volcano victim in the arena dirt, bringing to mind a fossilized victim of ancient Pompeii. Of course, Wolf Song had no knowledge of Mediterranean disasters; as yet, he had never traveled across The Great Waters. A shadowy remnant of troubled soul rose with the dust, swirling in the winds, lost to the heavens. The theatrical debasement of his soul began in 1883. It was at the hands of Buffalo Bill and Cody's self-proclaimed "extravaganza," *The Wild West and Congress of Rough Riders of the World.*

First came The Deadwood Stage Coach, the team of horses at full gallop, staged fear on the faces of the driver, the passengers, and the guard riding shotgun. Next it was the Indians to enter, giving chase at full tilt, and it was he, Wolf Song, Lakota, who was the first to drop at the curtain-open report from the rifle. He had barely a chance to enter the enclosure before he had to roll backwards off the haunches of his speeding mount and crash full-faced to the earth. Only at the last moment was he permitted to roll out of the way of the stampeding entrance of the heroic cavalry led by the Colonel himself—William Frederick Cody—Buffalo Bill.

The staccato hooves of the charging horses obliterated the soil silhouette left by Wolf Song. The veloce charge of the bugle went unheard by the young Sioux; his head was still ringing from the choreographed fall. From the wings, where he stood slumped and trying to find his breath, he watched as *Pahaska*, Long-Hair, led his equestrian troop to the rescue of The Deadwood Stage. Once again, the soldiers were heroic and his Indian brothers foiled in their savage pursuit of the innocent. The fakery humiliated and haunted Wolf Song. The histrionics were insulting as well as impious. He shook his head and another particle of his spirit made a dusty exit. He swore revenge on Cody.

"To be the first to die in battle should be an honor, my young Oglala friend," said Black Elk, the Lakota oracle. "But to do so as a sham does not enrich your spirit. It ties heavy rocks to your ankles as you try to swim the river of life. Are you giving due consideration to the potential folly of this performance?"

"It is not my fault, Wichasha Wakan. You were there. You witnessed the first fall. It was during a rehearsal. It was an accident. It was not my fault that Pahaska, this pompous Buffalo Bill, liked what he saw and told me to do it for every show. It was not my intention to die a false death, to die a hundred deaths and never take a scalp, it is not of my choosing to never count coup. Shall I never become a warrior, a hero?"

"Seeking to be the hero, young brother, is often a road to folly."

"I followed you and Sitting Bull to this place of perversity, of contrariness, because I was too young and too clumsy to be a warrior. I did not fight at Greasy Grass, at Custer's Last Stand as Buffalo Bill calls it, Custer and for that I have felt shame." He brushed more dust from his legs and arms. "It is well known that I was thrown from a pony as we Oglala mounted a charge to repulse Custer and his infamous Seventh Cavalry. I did not *fight* at Little Big Horn because I lay in the dirt." He continued to dust himself. "And this arena dirt looks much the same. No, I stayed in the camp and stood outside the teepee of Sitting Bull as he recovered from his wounds—wounds inflicted at the Sun Dance."

"There is some honor in that, Wolf Song."

"Honor? If I only believed that it was so. There were no heroics—no scalps, no coup, no blood shed for The People. In truth, I stood outside the tent petrified that the *Wasichus* might break through our ranks and attack the village. I stood like the child I am, cowardly and uninitiated, and prayed that the soldiers were all wiped out before they could cross the river." He slapped his thighs, clapped his hands to blast away the last of the day's dust, and turned to walk away when he saw Sitting Bull approaching. He stood, hanging his head, looking at the ground, cursing it. "Even you, Mother Earth, have with Pahaska conspired against me." He thought he heard a rumbling beneath him. It must be the pounding of the horses. The shadow of Sitting Bull crossed over him. His shame would not allow him to acknowledge his chief.

"Is he hurt?" asked the Hunkpapa legend.

"The boy still suffers, Tatanka-Iyotanka. I should be more careful not to rub in the folly of his feigned deaths. It is I who has upset him."

"I too have caused frustration for you, young Wolf Song, and for the others. Perhaps it was a mistake to join Buffalo Bill in this 'extravaganza' rather than sit with the old chiefs and reminisce about past heroics and our victory at Greasy Grass. I felt I could learn something of these Wasichus—something to help us, The People, in our struggle."

"We have both learned much, Tatanka-Iyotanka. We have learned that there are too many whites to fight," said Black Elk.

"If we each killed ten, a hundred would take their place."

"And a hundred more for each of those hundred," mumbled Wolf Song still looking at the ground.

"It boggles the mind. So many! It portends the undoing of The People. I have seen as much in my dreams. No longer do I see the Wasichus coming into our village upside down." Sitting Bull paused. He shook his head as if trying to rattle the boggles back in a row. "Well, it is time for me to mount the fine horse Pahaska has given me and ride around the arena. He laughed as he mimicked the introduction Buffalo Bill barked through the huge megaphone, "The Great Hero of His People and Respected General of a Noble Enemy."

"I do not feel noble," mumbled Wolf Song.

"I enjoy the dancing horse," said Sitting Bull. "I think he enjoys the music and all the noise. I think the horse enjoys the cheers and the gunshots and the Wasichu music. For me it is not so much. I like giving coins to the children." He mounted the circus horse and waited for the soldiers, the stagecoach, and the other Indians to exit the arena.

Wolf Song stood where he was, desperately trying to look taller.

The large group of performers milled around the wide opening in the curtain walls. From his elevated perch John Duffey, riding shotgun on the stage, pointed his rifle at Wolf Song and made a popping noise with his tongue and lips. "Got'cha again, boy! I never miss!"

John Y. "Squaw Man" Nelson, the driver, coughed a good-hearted laugh. Wolf Song almost forced a self-effacing smile. He liked Nelson. He knew Squaw Man would never intentionally insult him. Nelson had a half-dozen children of his own by his Indian wife. Squaw Man was an "almost Indian" white man. Wolf Song knew that Squaw Man laughed as a father might, remembering *his* first fall and recollecting the worst of a errant pony ride. But then a group of three Cheyenne warriors echoed the laughter, and their intent was clearly mocking. Their laughter struck Wolf Song with the force of an actual bullet. The salt of insult burned in the Wasichu wound initiated by Buffalo Bill.

"*Wihili*," jibed the Cheyenne, pointing at Wolf Song. Ordinarily it would be an honor to be called a *Coyote,* for the coyote is a trickster, a spirit of wit, and a god who in many Indian religions created humans. But this "little dog" remark was a clear insult. "Wihili," repeated another of the three.

Wolf Song knew that they were stealing coup by making fun of his small stature. They insult my namesake and my Oglala blood. They think me arrogant to have such a beautiful name, but too small to be the wolf. And being the first to die at the hands of the Wasichu in this sham, they think they can embarrass me in front of my brothers and these Wasichu strangers. They will learn that even the little coyote has a nasty bite.

Wolf Song could hear the introduction for Sitting Bull through the off-stage noise, ". . . respected general of a noble enemy . . ." He saw Pahaska exit the stage and then Buffalo Bill's voice changed in his direction. His heart sunk into the depth of his dusty soul.

"Where is the kid who does that great fall off the pony?" bellowed Buffalo Bill above the backstage crowd. "Where is the kid that is the first one shot?" The Colonel and a man wearing a press pass in his hatband pushed through the mob. "I need to show this reporter here that there ain't nobody really shot in this extravaganza. Ha, ha."

Wolf Song thought about running, but when he saw the Cheyenne pointing at him, he stood his ground.

"Wihili," all three sung and pointed, getting Bill's attention.

Buffalo Bill grinned, "Here he is." He slapped Wolf Song on the back and a small cloud of dust rose from his shoulders toward the sky, carrying with it another speck of spirit. "I told you he was all right!"

The reporter pulled a small tablet out of his pocket and a pencil from behind his ear. "That was quite a fall you took there, laddy. Are you still in one piece?"

Wolf Song didn't understand the question.

"Well you seem to be tolerable," said the reporter as he patted Wolf Song on the back and another dust phantom took flight.

Wolf Song tensed, things were embarrassing enough without this Wasichu stranger touching him. The familiarity put him off. He looked toward Buffalo Bill and then to Black Elk for an explanation.

"What is your name, son?" asked the newsman.

"Wihili," repeated the Cheyenne.

"Wolf Song," mumbled the youth.

"That's it," interrupted Buffalo Bill, perhaps embarrassed at not knowing the youngster's name. "It's Willie, Willie Wolf Song."

The young Oglala stood dumbfounded. This was insult heaped upon injury. How could Buffalo Bill be so ignorant as to twist the Cheyenne affront into a name?

"That *is* quite a spectacular fall he takes. He's the best, ol' Willie is." Buffalo Bill pulled the reporter toward the corral. "Ain't no way we're gonna let young Willie get hurt. None of my Indians are in any danger from the theatrics. Of course, there is real frontier peril at every turn, but I just won't take any chances with my Indians in the exhibition." He called out to a wrangler on horseback who was leaning from his saddle to open the corral fence.

"Damn, Bob, I told you some of the Indian ponies was still too rank for the theatrics, cut that little beauty out and put her with the rodeo stock." The Colonel noticed the reporter seemed fascinated by the horses, the frontier palaver, and the apparently genuine danger. Bill raised his voice even louder, "Now listen, Bob, I don't want any of these young braves hurt. As I have said a hundred times, the Indians are the most important part of this show. It's them the public will come out to see. I want to treat my Indians like something special." He turned to the reporter, "I can put a pair of boots, a big hat and a red shirt on any man, and call him a cowboy, but I cannot dress anyone up and call him an Indian."

The reporter was writing feverishly.

"Say Willie," Buffalo called from a short distance, just loud enough so that everyone in the vicinity could hear. "I've got a great idea. We are thinking about adding Custer's Last Stand as part of the performance. In addition to being the first dropped in the Deadwood Stage extravaganza, you could be the first one shot at the Little Big Horn." He turned to the reporter for a reaction to the Buffalo Bill brilliance, and then back toward where Wolf Song had stood. "What do you think about that, Willie? How would you like to be the first shot by General George Armstrong Custer, Willie boy? Would you like that? It could make you famous." Wolf Song disappeared behind the stagecoach and listened through the windows. "Well now, where the hell did he get off to? Just shy, I guess."

"Indians are like that," said the reporter, acting as if he knew.

Wolf Song learned two vices from his internship with the *Wild West*. He had his first experience with liquor, a destructive experiment, and he acquired an obsessive taste for roasted cashews, a habit that caused him more trouble than the alcohol. He would use these vices for comfort when things were going poorly, such as when the name *Willie* stuck and everyone, friend and foe alike, began using the accidental indignity.

When he realized that his theatrical career was to be enhanced by being the first Indian to die additional deaths at the hands of the shade of the greatest of Sioux enemies—Custer—he sought an escape through liquor and legume. The unsettling insult was exacerbated by the fact that it was not actually Custer, but another who so resembled the zealot that an ominous ghoulishness dismayed him. He knew that what whites consider supernatural, Indians accepted as a dark intrinsic element of the real world. As a protégé of sorts of the mystic Black Elk, Wolf Song was particularly sensitive to the metaphysical.

Because Buffalo Bill would have fired him had he caught him drunk again, Wolf Song stole a pound of hot nuts from a concessionaire and hid away in the quarters of Black Elk. He listened half-heatedly as the elder tried to counsel him.

"Folly," preached the shaman, "divides humankind into two camps: those who create folly as do the Wasichus, and those, though not instigators, whom it follows despite their ignorance of it. Perhaps," he thought further, "because of their ignorance of it. Folly can make of one the hero or the fool, but only the fool pursues folly, allows himself to be wooed.

"Custer . . ." said Black Elk.

Wolf Song squirmed at the mention of the name and devoured several nuts.

"Custer—wanting greatly to be the hero was so wooed into folly. Our proud brother, Sitting Bull, must be careful not to let fame among the whites cloud his destiny and force a journey from heroism to folly. You too must carefully consider your actions among this race of daft people." He reached into the sack Willie held, "Choices can be made to redeem yourself. Son of my brothers, it is known to me that your spirit has suffered at the hands of the whites." Black Elk took a cashew from the paper bag and ate it. His eyebrows rose in subtle delight. "But I have dreamed that he who daily is the opossum, shall revenge himself, so shall you wreak havoc on the world of the Wasichu, so shall you be greater than Pahaska, He-With-Long-Hair."

Both were silent for a moment. Black Elk looked at Wolf Song, expecting a reply. Getting none, he continued.

"Pahaska endangers his soul, do you not see that? He has chosen a contrary direction. He is a hero to his people, but he now travels from true heroism to an unreal performance of heroics. His rebirth is false. There lay the danger. To be a hero you must find yourself. In order to find yourself, and thereby provide yourself with the opportunity to become a hero, a person of principle, you must journey from the false to the real. Heroes, warriors, substantial people must be born, must die, and must be reborn. This is why we send our youth on a vision quest—to be reborn. You, Wolf Song have not yet had the initiation. The war and now this 'extravaganza' have distracted you. Be careful how you proceed. The opportunity to return to the Circle is still there for you, if you choose wisely."

Dubious and only somewhat relieved, Willie offered Black Elk another nut.

Chapter Four

Nuts

Summer, 1886

I, Turtle, observed that in the stillness of night, when nature seems asleep, there comes a gentle rapping at the door of the human heart. Open it and a voice will inquire, "Brothers, what of your people? From whom do they come? What will their future be?"

Simon Pokagon, Pottawatomie, answered me thus: "Mortal man has not the power to draw aside the veil of unborn time. That gift belongs of the Divine alone. But it is given to a few to closely judge the future by the present, and the past."

"I dreamed of turtles," said Willie Wolf Song.

"Was it an informative dream? Much of my wisdom," said Black Elk, "comes through dreams. The People place great countenance in dreams." He turned toward John Y., Squaw Man, Nelson, who with his children sat by the campfire. "Indian people believe that the dream state is the immanent part of living. I dreamt that all the world is a dance and all the men and women merely dancers. They move within the circle and sometimes outside the circle, and one man in his time hears many drums . . ."

"Very funny," said John Y.

"What's funny?" asked one of the six children climbing from lap to crown on the old stage driver.

"I believe our friend Black Elk is pulling our Yankee' legs a bit, boys."

"He's not pulling your legs, Pa, but I will!" The boy jumped from Squaw Man's shoulder to his foot and began pulling on his boot.

The campfire in front of Black Elk's teepee was warm and the conversation cordial, but Wolf Song was troubled by his dream.

"Usually your metaphors inform and enlighten me, Black Elk. But that one escapes me. I am fighting against those rocks tied 'round my ankles. I am dreaming of bizarre beasts. Have you no other counsel for me?"

"Of course I do, my brother. Do not concern yourself with that particular narrative, I heard it recently, and it inadvertently became a part of a dream. So, Squaw Man, you know this story teller: Shakes Spear?"

"Being as we are in the same business—show business—I have over the years become acquainted with the Bard."

"I would like to meet this Wasichu. There seems to be a wisdom in him which is painfully absent from most other whites."

"Present company excepted I hope," said John Y. "Although you might not find him to home these days, I did overhear that the *Wild West* is goin' to jolly Old England."

"Boating—across the Great Waters?" asked Wolf Song.

"Less'n you can fly," answered Nelson.

"I dreamed of great waters and giant turtle beasts," said Willie. He took another cashew and waited patiently while the salt dissolved. He split the halves apart with his teeth and stored one half in his cheek as does the chipmunk and consumed the other. He then slowly enjoyed the last half. "I dreamt of a great beast, a turtle as large as the world, and this great turtle divided itself into seven and The People emerged upon one of these seven and the white man upon another. Although she was now one of many, ours was still a great beast—a spirit snapping turtle so large that her cragged shell stretched beyond the horizon of the rising sun and beyond that of the setting sun as well. She was a sister among seven such beasts, each different but the same, each drifting on a great sphere of liquid fire."

"Seven did ya say?" asked Nelson.

"Seven, eight, nine, ten," proudly recited the eldest of Nelson's brood.

"Seven," repeated Wolf Song. "Each sleeping and drifting. Often they would bump into one another and their great weight would force new crags and spikes as tall as mountains along their rugged shells. Sometimes the edge of one of the shells would dip below the colliding sister and great huge lakes would form—as wide as the oceans spoken of by the whites. And their water was bitter."

"You been reading some white man's geography books, Willie? Ol' Black Elk here obviously been eaves dropping on some theatrical events? I don't know nothing about what 'drifting on fire' could mean, but seven great landmasses sounds about right."

"I do not read the Wasichu writing, Squaw Man. I believe it makes you contrary."

"I had a turtle once," said Nelson's youngest. "It crawled under a wagon and got squeeshed."

"Tell me more of your dream, Wolf Song," said Black Elk.

"Far to the north and to the south the great ocean lakes would freeze and it was under such a frozen expanse that the head of the great turtle upon which we dwell slumbered. The crags on its back rose above the water, the wide spaces in between created the plains upon which buffalo ran. Her tail, as craggy as her back, curved to the south and the east and her southern sister bit and clung to the tip of her tail making a connected pair of sacred siblings and their backs a great chain of mountains. It was then I knew that She was at once our Mother Earth and provider, but also Mother Beast, prone to anger."

"You know," said Squaw Man, "a long time ago, before Columbus proved 'um different, the Europeans believed the world was flat and a floatin' on the back of this giant turtle. They believed you could sail right off the edge of the earth. I seen drawings."

Wolf Song and Black Elk looked at each other, Willie confirming that his kinsman also thought that maybe the earlier whites were smarter than this contemporary bunch. Willie offered Squaw Man a cashew.

"But you're right. A long time ago we whites lost contact with Mother Earth. We forgot her."

"You forgot mommy?" asked a child.

"Not your mommy, ya scamp," he answered. "I could never forget your mommy." He turned to Wolf Song. "One of the reasons I took me an Indian wife and stuck around with Ol' Bill here is that I never cared none about getting rich. There are, as I am sure you know, fella's who would sell their mother for a pocket of gold. They have no respect for Mother Earth or Mother Beast, as you call it. They consider only the turf upon which they stand; they claim it as something to own; they wrench gold from it. They are single minded."

"Wasichus do not comprehend that the Mother is at once the terrain and the unifying spirit of the kinship of all living things," said Black Elk.

"Present company excluded, I hope," answered Nelson.

Black Elk nodded.

"I have seen that the back of the great snapping turtle goes far beyond the borders of our lands, beyond the sacred Black Hills, across other mountains both East and West of Lakota lands." said Wolf Song.

"Your dreams tell me that you are a person of the earth, Wolf Song. Others are of the water, fire, and the sky. I believe your destiny is tied to the Mother. Sad, but these whites only consider her as ripe for conquering," said Black Elk. "They risk awakening an angry earth. Quakes, fires, floods and droughts shall be the proxy of an angry Mother—The Beast. To tempt such reprisal, whether through the innocence of The People or the arrogance of the whites is folly."

"It's a sad statement, but true, brothers," said Squaw Man. "Well, I appreciate the history lesson, but I had better get these children to bed. Thanks for the cashews. Your fire was warm."

All six kids clambered onto Nelson. One clung to each leg. Two hung from his arms. The eldest jumped onto his back and the smallest hung from his belly.

"Now he looks more like the opossum than you, Wolf Song."

The joke brought Wolf Song back from interpreting his dream. He thought again about Buffalo Bill. "Pahaska is such a man."

"What kind of man?"

"One of those who desires only riches. One of those who insults our Mother."

"You allow your anger to speak for you, Little Brother. How is it that you believe Pahaska is so?"

"I know you think the insults are unintentional, but they continue to pile up. I have tallied the humiliations on a coup stick. A pole which may never tap an enemy, never reclaim respect, and which I know the Shyelas, the Cheyenne, joke and call *The Impotent*

Pole of the Opossum." He paused and stewed in his resentment. "What of my picture on the poster for the show. Dozens of posters were done, hundreds of photographs. There was even a moving picture of the Deadwood Stage attack shot by the Wasichu, Mister Thomas Edison. The only time I was in a poster the caption named me as *Rain-In-The-Face.* Is this not an insult?" Willie wallowed in cashew consolation. "He uses us to make money. We are the most important part of his show. He has said that himself. He pays us very little. He invites those dogs, the Shyelas, the Blue Clouds, Sioux enemies, to partake in the 'extravaganza.'"

"What do you need with the white man's money? You are fed well. You have a place to sleep, a pony to ride; although, they won't let you ride it all the way around the arena."

"You take advantage of your older age, Wichasha Wakan, with such jibes."

Black Elk smiled, being all of twenty—just a few years older that Wolf Song—and took a nut from the bag.

"I need the white man's money to send home to my family," said Wolf Song. "I am not there to provide for them. This way they can purchase food from the agent. He charges much more than the goods are worth. I send all of my money home. It is the one thing that gives me pride."

Buffalo Bill suddenly appeared within the ring of fire light. "I don't understand too much Sioux palaver, just enough that I'm glad to hear you two are talking about money. Willie boy, we got a problem."

"It is customary for one approaching from the dark to announce himself, Pahaska," challenged Wolf Song.

"It is customary for an employee to show a little respect to his employer, Willie. It is also appropriate for a kid to show a little respect for his elders, and a scalawag to show remorse to his betters."

Wolf Song felt the sting of another insult.

"I'm looking at the report I get on supplies we use to keep this *extravaganza* running and all of you people fed. But there is something that has been brought to my attention and it isn't in Johnny Baker's report." He rattled the several sheets of paper at Wolf Song. "Do you know what that might be?"

"I do not read the Wasichu writing."

"Well then, I'll tell ya. It says here that in one week *The Buffalo Bill Wild West Show* consumed 7,000 pounds of meat, 2,100 loaves of bread, 3,200 quarts of milk, 3 barrels of sugar, 200 pounds of jelly, 225 pounds of coffee, 100 pounds of salt, 4 barrels of flour, and 500 pies. But ya know what ain't here? I'll tell ya. He forgot to report on the 10 pounds of cashews disappearing every week."

Wolf Song looked down at the brown sack of nuts he held, but said nothing.

"Tell ya what I'm gonna do, Willie boy. I'm gonna garnish your wages and pay off your nut debt."

"I do not understand."

"I'm not paying you anymore. I'm taking your money and giving it to the cashew concessionaire. And if I find out your stealing anymore nuts, I'm gonna let John Duffey use real bullets in the Deadwood Stage extravaganza. Do you understand that?"

Wolf Song went into his opossum routine. He sat silently.

"Although it is against my better judgment, I'm gonna keep you on through our trip to Europe. In fact I am taking only you Sioux. I am trying to talk Sitting Bull into going and for some reason I cannot comprehend, he likes you. Besides you owing me money, I need all the Indians I can muster; seems the Crow, Pawnee, and Cheyenne are fighting all the time. Seems some little coyote has been stirring up trouble. Now I wonder who the hell that could be; don't you? Anyway, I'm sending the other tribes home. It just breaks my heart to do this. As far as I'm concerned it is your fault the *Wild West* is losing authenticity by me having to eliminate the vast variety of MY aboriginal exhibits." He stomped off into the darkness.

Wolf Song had no way of knowing that night but it was because of this new Sioux policy that most uninitiated Americans and Europeans would come to think of all Indians as having long headdresses, wearing fringe buckskins, living in teepees, and hunting buffalo from racing ponies. Little did he know that he was indirectly responsible for another injustice forced upon his kindred—the Hollywood Indian stereotype.

"I am thinking," said Wolf Song. "If I can go across the great water to this other land, the home land of the Wasichu, then maybe I can sacrifice Pahaska to this other great turtle. Maybe in this ancient land they will understand my desire for coup and revenge."

"That is doubtful," said Black Elk. "Is this not the land from which they came? Would not the laws be the same? I believe this is the home of the Queen Mother spoken of in Canada. Is she not an admirer of Buffalo Bill?"

Wolf Song grinned at Black Elk and placed a cashew between his lips. It looked like a single tusk. He sucked it inside his mouth, making a small popping noise. He split the halves and sucked the salt off the half in his teeth. "Since these foolish whites do not believe in it, maybe I could surprise Pahaska and push him over the edge of the earth."

Chapter Five

Continental Drift

Autumn, 1886

I, Turtle, have heard over the eons an unfathomable number of prayers to Mother Earth and innumerable curses of The Beast. What irony that the faithful pray and plead to the same spirit, or, as it may be, spirits: sung about in songs and called upon as guardians by children and adults alike. Black Elk was correct: we are all, each of us, elements of the Great Mystery, dancers seeking entry into the Circle. Flint and Sapling inhabit me, as do I them; inhabit you and the world . . . both worlds: that of darkness and that of light.

"Prepare your death song," screamed Wolf Song above the thunder of the waves on the big water. "Sitting Bull was wrong. We shall never live through this journey. The fire-boat will take us to our deaths."

"I cannot sing," yelled Black Elk. "Everything I ate has come up and still more tries to come up 'though there is nothing left. I cannot get enough breath to sing."

"The women cry. The men are dressing for death, Black Elk. I am too weak. I cannot look my best to meet the Great Spirit. We will never see our homes again. I fear that I shame our ancestors dying on these waters, an enemy I cannot fight. I blame Pahaska for this!"

"It is my fault, Wolf Song. I thought the journey could help us close the break in the hoop. Look, now even the Wasichus have stopped their laughter and they cling to the rail. They have turned from pink to green."

"Wichasha Wakan, forgive me, but you yourself have turned from red to white."

"And you to gray, Wolf Song. We are wiped out." The young oracle began to sing his death chant.

Wolf Song thought back to the days before they took the iron road through the big cities, before they walked up the plank to the fireboat and felt the turtle move beneath them.

"I do not believe I will travel with you across the big waters," Sitting Bull said to them. "I believe it is time for me to return to the Black Hills, to Grand River. I will miss Little Annie Sure Shot, but I will not miss these rude Americans who shout insults at me. I will take the dancing horse Pahaska gave to me."

Wolf Song knew that his chief was disenchanted. It was a sad commentary that although Buffalo Bill introduced Sitting Bull as a great hero to his people and as a respected general of a noble enemy, American audiences would often *boo* the chief. The booing confused Sitting Bull.

"We hold our enemies in respect," complained Sitting Bull. "In fact, the strength of a man is determined by the power and the magic of his enemies. If we insult a member of another tribe, it is done with humor or wit."

Black Elk added, "Until it comes time for the scalping."

They all laughed.

"A ceremony we Indians learned from the white settlers of the Great Lakes," added Wolf Song. "Booing and belittling an enemy shows weakness and contains no honor. Heckling is an art, and these Wasichu are artless."

"The Canadians, people of Grandmother's Country, are more sociable. They cheer," said Sitting Bull.

"They, my chief, have never lost kin or property to The People." said Wolf Song.

The chief looked at him sternly. "Why are you rude to me, Wolf Song?"

"Wolf Song has become cranky since he can no longer pilfer cashews," explained Black Elk.

"I am sorry, Tatanka-Iyotanka. I am out of sorts."

"Is he drunk again, Black Elk?"

"It is my fault. I remind him of his farcical dying. I have also asked that he come along across the big waters instead of running away from his debt to Pahaska. I think I can find something in the

Wasichu's cities to help us close the hoop and return our people to the center of the world and the flowering tree."

"Do you share the vision of the Wichasha Wakan, Wolf Song?" asked Sitting Bull.

"I go for a different reason, Tatanka-Iyotanka."

"We must each follow our own path, younger brothers. And I fear your journey will be long. I fear Wolf Song that your hatred for Pahaska will make your course longer still—beyond the big water. I fear also that your quest, Black Elk, of fulfilling the promise of your great vision will not be aided by this journey, but I hope I am wrong. I dreamed of a great turtle last night. He shifted in his slumber and created huge waves on the big waters. I thought I had foreseen your demise, but then I knew it was not so, for I saw you dancing for Grandmother England. It was confusing for the aura of death was in my dream. And then, just before I woke, I saw a bull buffalo enter my lodge upside down. Our Lakota brothers ate of his liver. I am saddened and I will return home. Be safe, and most of all, be wise on your journey, little brothers."

The departure of Sitting Bull and several others was a sad day for those remaining with *The Wild West*. The dream of the great chief hung over Wolf Song and Black Elk like a dark cloud rolling in from a cold sea. After all, had not Tatanka-Iyotanka foretold of the death of Custer and the Wasichu disaster at Greasy Grass?

Besides being a great warrior and statesman, Sitting Bull was also a holy man, a Wichasha Wakan, he who could prophesy. Although *wichasha* literally meant *man*, when used in conjunction with *wakan,* it referred to a special spirituality, to a unique leadership, to a worldly wisdom. It meant he had the gift of visions. The only consolation for Wolf Song was that Sitting Bull had indeed said he saw them both dancing for the Great Grandmother of England. He had said "both," had he not?

It was not too long after the departure of Sitting Bull that news of the death of Crazy Horse reached Black Elk and Wolf Song.

"Perhaps it is this murder of Crazy Horse by his Sioux brothers that was the subject of the dream of Tatanka-Iyotanka." said Wolf Song.

"Perhaps," answered Black Elk. "We must prepare for our journey."

Back in the reality of the storm at sea, Wolf Song cried out, "How does one prepare for this watery hell? How can one find the trail to the Great Mystery when one is at the bottom of the big water? I think you were right, Black Elk, when you said I was a being of the earth, how I long for solid ground!"

Black Elk continued to sing his death song.

"I was a fool to try to stay near Pahaska, to seek an opportunity for revenge. His 'extravaganza' will be my undoing." He joined the chorus of the doomed.

Eight days later, as it turns out, Wolf Song admitted that Sitting Bull was indeed clairvoyant. They approached a shore with many fire-boats nearby and the houses built close together.

"Great news," bellowed Buffalo Bill to the gathering of the Wild West company. "We have been here for nearly six months and now, at last, Her Majesty will be attending the exhibition. It will be *The Golden Jubilee Command Performance.* I expect everything to be perfect." All of the Wasichus applauded and buzzed about with great excitement. "Willie," said Cody, "We need to talk." Buffalo Bill pulled Wolf Song away from the crowd. John Y., Squaw Man, Nelson accompanied them. "I need you to translate, Squaw Man, in case Willie boy here doesn't understand my Sioux and signing."

"You bet, Colonel. Me and Willie get along fine."

"Willie," said Buffalo Bill with seriousness, "your dying has become farcical, overly melodramatic, and I don't appreciate it."

Wolf Song looked at John Y. not understanding.

Nelson tried to explain melodramatic. Wolf Song mumbled something in response.

"What did he say?" asked Bill.

"He's a bit confused, Colonel. Says somebody read him one of your dime novels the other night and he thought you would appreciate this kind of showing off."

"Tell him I will not have him making a mockery of the performance!"

Willie knew he had tried to upstage, make a sham of the Custer battle, but now he made the mistake of saying in clearly understandable English, "It's only a show."

Cody hated the word *show*.

"It's a genuine educational exhibition of the American West, you nut thief." He stormed away.

Insult was added to injury at the Royal reception after *The Golden Jubilee Command Performance* when Colonel William F. "Buffalo Bill" Cody proudly introduced Black Elk as "an exotic example of the Indian character" to Queen Victoria; the Queen turned her back on Cody and responded to the Indians, Willie among them, by saying, ". . . today, I have seen the best-looking people I know . . . and if you belonged to me, I would not let them take you around in a *show* like this."

The story in the American newspapers stated that later that day Black Elk and several "other Indians" lost their way in the confusing Manchester streets and missed the boat for home. European journalists said an offended Cody abandoned Black Elk and Willie and the others. With the exception of Willie's severely limited skills with "American," none of the troupe knew any European languages. They blundered through England, France, and Germany for three years, finally hitching their booty to another wild west show touring the Continent. *Pawnee Bill's Great Far East* used them as a headliner for a short period and then gave them a ride back to the states.

When they finally returned to Cody's show—to Cody's educational exhibition—Buffalo Bill welcomed Black Elk like a long lost brother and had the troupe give three rousing cheers for his safe return. He fired Willie on the spot.

Chapter Six

Dirge

Winter, December 18, 1890

The great Suquamish chief, Seattle wisely said to me, "There is no death, only a change of worlds."

A migrant wind rattled the pine boughs. A raven cried out. The morning was cold and Wolf Song could see his breath as he stepped from his lodge to investigate why, before the sun was up, the dogs were barking. He saw the group of tin stars, the ceska maza, gathering around the lodge of Sitting Bull. He could make out the silhouettes of rifles and revolvers in the hands of the hated Indian police. "What mischief is this?" he called out to the dark group of intruders.

The rifle butt rammed just below his diaphragm, slamming the air from his lungs, stealing his voice. He looked up from where he had collapsed and recognized his assailant. It was Bull Head, a rival chief of Sitting Bull and a leader among the tin stars. Through his tears—caused by the cold, the gun butt battering, and his struggle to breathe—Wolf Song helplessly watched as twenty more Sioux, many dressed in a partial uniform of White soldiers, crept from the shadows to take cover behind trees. "There must be forty of these traitors skulking about," he said to himself. "What is to become of Sitting Bull?"

"Brother," a taunting bellow could be heard above the ruckus of the dogs. "We came after you."

Wolf Song recognized the harbinger as Shave Head. He identified several others as they forced their way into the small cabin. Two old men and Red Whirlwind, the wife of Chief One Bull, ran out into the confusion. The interlopers let them pass. Wolf Song could see Crow Foot, the fourteen-year-old son of Sitting Bull, in the doorway. Two ceska maza pushed him out of the way. And then to his horror, Wolf Song saw several of the traitorous tin stars wrestle a naked Sitting Bull to the door. Bull Head, the dog who had assaulted him, was now among them.

"This is a great way to do things," pleaded Sitting Bull, his sarcasm and disdain obvious "not to give me a chance to put on my clothes in the wintertime."

Bull Head appeared embarrassed by the rebuke. He looked through the door and saw that a crowd was gathering. Bull Head barked something to Sitting Bull's wife about organizing clothing. It was inaudible to Wolf Song who finally was able to get to his feet. He pushed closer to the doorway.

Bull Head had taken Sitting Bull's right arm and Shave Head his left. Red Tomahawk, another sergeant, followed immediately, holding a pistol at the back of the captive chief.

Catch-the-Bear, armed with a Winchester, pushed through the crowd and challenged the police, "You think you are going to take him? You shall not do it!" He pleaded to the others who stood lifeless, numbed by the cold, stunned by the audacity of the ceska maza. "Come on now," yelled Catch-the-Bear, "let us protect our chief!"

From the cabin door young Crow Foot admonished Sitting Bull, "You call yourself a brave chief, now you allow yourself to be taken by the ceska maza."

Sitting Bull stopped suddenly. His captors paused, as if allowing the chief to contemplate Crow Foot's challenge. They too must have been surprised that there was not a bigger struggle. Looking deeply into the eyes of Wolf Song, Sitting Bull declared, "Then I shall not go."

The gaze of Sitting Bull triggered in Wolf Song the remembrance of when he fell from the pony just before the battle at Greasy Grass. It was the same look of disappointment, tempered with understanding and forgiveness, but it allowed the heart-wrenching disappointment of missing the battle with Custer to well up inside him once again. He was crushed by the realization that his inability to serve his chief was about to be repeated. The emotional implosion was legible across his face. Sitting Bull's expression turned from one of forgiveness directed at Wolf Song to one of defiance directed at his captors. The chief raised his face to the crowd and looked directly at Bull Head and repeated, "Then I shall not go."

Some in the crowd pleaded with Sitting Bull to accompany the police and avoid trouble. Others cursed the transgressors. Bull Head and Shave Head lost patience and pulled on Sitting Bull. Red Tomahawk pushed. The physical manhandling of Sitting Bull enraged the crowd. Wolf Song heard a policeman he knew as Lone Man, a kinsman of Bull Head, try to shout commands to restore order. It was ineffective.

Catch-the-Bear called out above the voice of Lone Man, "You shall not take our chief!" He leveled his rifle and fired at Bull Head.

Wolf Song watched the mayhem evolve as if in a dream. All motion was slowed, every action was observed in grisly detail, each sound was a rumble of dark thunder and doom. The death songs of his ancestors rang in a nightmarish, nasal crescendo. Bullets in flight spun past him, mimicking the tweedle of reed flutes.

Wolf Song witnessed Bull Head pull his revolver as he crumbled from the impact of a bullet slamming into his body, expelling in a report of bloody air. Dying, Bull Head fired into Sitting Bull's chest. Red Tomahawk, either in panic or vengeance, fired his pistol into the back of the wounded chief's head. Brain and blood exploded across Wolf Song's face, the sudden warmth was as shocking as the horror. The gaze Sitting Bull now cast toward Wolf Song was empty and cold; there was no evidence of surprise. Strikes-the-Kettle, a villager and friend, fired his vindictive message into the stomach of Shave Head.

Lone Man, seeing his kinsman crumble, grabbed the rifle of Catch-the-Bear. It jammed as Bear tried again to fire. Lone Man struck Catch-the-Bear with the butt of the Winchester and used it as a club to wreak *his* vendetta.

The latent torment of decades suddenly energized Wolf Song. He joined in the angry battle, knowing it was too late to save his chief, aggravating that it may also be too late to save his own soul. Although he survived—physically unwounded and unscathed—his spirit joined that of his mentor on the frozen bloody ground.

It was several months later when Willie Wolf Song sat eating cashews with his comrade Black Elk. He split the halves with his front teeth and crushed each in turn. They proved to be little consolation as Wolf Song continued to tell his friend the tragedy of the death of Sitting Bull.

"Five more followers of Sitting Bull died, some armed, some not. Four more tin stars perished. The wounded from both sides crawled for cover. I do not know how I ended up near the banks of the Grand River but a man I was fighting, I believe his name was *Middle*, lost a foot in a gory explosion of ice, bone, and blood. I left him there, screaming, and ran back toward Sitting Bull's cabin. The ceska maza were seeking sanctuary in the cabin, dragging Bull Head with them. He had taken more bullets and was near death." Wolf Song unconsciously selected one of the largest cashews he could see near the top of the bag and placed it between his front teeth. He held it there momentarily, remembering the carnage, sitting wide-eyed, apparently emotionless.

"What happened then?" asked Black Elk.

Wolf Song tongued the cashew into his cheek where he stored it as he slowly came back to the moment. "They found young Crow Foot hiding in the cabin." Wolf Song took on the character of Sitting Bull's terrified son and in a youth's voice, combined with the high pitch of a death chant, he cried out, "Uncles, do not kill me. I do not wish to die." He dropped the characterization and looked directly at Black Elk. "But Bull Head was still full of rancor, he knew by now he had been wiped out. The others voiced threats against the youth. He told the others to do what they like with Crow Foot for he was one of them who has caused all this trouble. I heard later that it was Lone Man who clubbed young Crow Foot in the head."

He paused, unconsciously sucked the cashew from its hiding place and crushed it with his molars, the crunch echoing in his skull. He sensed little satisfaction from its earthy taste.

"Crow Foot stumbled from the lodge and into my view. It was Lone Man who fired first. Two others joined him. I suppose they thought they were avenging the death of Bull Head when they murdered the boy. Crow Foot died near his father.

"I saw the men in the cabin weep. I do not know whether they cried because of the death of their police comrades or because of the irreconcilable carnage they inflicted on kinsmen and neighbors. I wonder if they sensed that in the venomous world they had created, in wiping out so many, in killing their greatest chief, that they had inadvertently aided in the ruin of their own people. Did the dawning of their self-inflicted doom move them to tears, or did the bitter taste of vengeful hearts insulate them from murderous deeds. What folly."

"What folly indeed," whispered Black Elk.

"Did you hear of the horse?" Wolf Song asked.

"No, what of the horse?" answered Black Elk.

"An eerie irony," said Wolf Song. "Sitting Bull's circus horse, the one given him by the coward Buffalo Bill, must have thought that the loud voices and the ring of pistol shots were part of *The Wild West* show. The crazy old horse began to dance, just as he did in the 'extravaganza.' The sarcasm of the quoted word from Cody was obvious. "Many loyal to Sitting Bull swore it was a Ghost Dance, that the horse was possessed by the fleeting spirit of Tatanka-Iyotanka."

"What do you feel?"

"I feel that the greatest chief of the Hunkpapa was stolen from us and that I did nothing to prevent it. I feel the coward. I do not know if the spirit of Sitting Bull was put upon his journey through the horse, but I do know that I am doomed to never trek upon the hero's path. To take the heroic journey, the good red road, I must avenge the death of Sitting Bull with the death of Buffalo Bill."

"I do not understand Buffalo Bill's part in this, Wolf Song."

"I have been told by many, by soldiers, even by several ceska maza among the many, that Buffalo Bill could have saved Sitting Bull."

"How is this so? It seems remote."

"You know of the Wasichus agent McLaughlin?"

"Yes, the reservation agent, of course."

"And of the Wasichus chief soldier, Colonel Drum?"

"Yes, I know of him, too"

"And of the long knife general, Miles."

"General Miles is known to many."

"Each of them and many stay-by-the-fort Sioux, including Bull Head and Grey Eagle conspired to arrest Sitting Bull. They feared that he would inspire another uprising because of Sitting Bull's interest in the Ghost Dance."

Black Elk noticed that Wolf Song had used the white man's term for The People—a tribal name that connoted *enemy*. "Yes, Sitting Bull and Big Foot talked of the dance. He often said that such a miracle could restore our greatness, could return us to the circle."

"They feared Sitting Bull. He was a powerful Wichasha Wakan, a spiritual leader still. They were jealous of him being a dreamer of sacred dreams and an interpreter of life."

"This could well be," said Black Elk. "Tatanka-Iyotanka was indeed a noble man and a prophet."

"The fear of Sitting Bull and the Ghost Dance also cost Big Foot and his people their lives. It almost took you, my brother."

"The shielding tree was shattered," said Black Elk, "as if by lightning. The hoop was broken. So many lives lost. The vision of their wailing deaths haunts me every night. I am lessened, diminished by their loss, disheartened."

"How did you survive, old friend?" asked Wolf Song.

"I did not run, rather I stood my ground and it was as if the bullets could not find me. Those who ran, mostly women and children, they were cut down by the Hotchkiss carbine guns. Many of the soldiers sat on the hills above Chankae Opi Wakpala with the horrible Hotchkiss guns. There was no honor in the fighting. The soldiers had earlier collected all of the rifles from the men. A few braves also ran to try and reclaim their rifles. They too were cut down, wiped out by the repeating thunder of the Hotchkiss. Big Foot was wiped out as he waved a white flag of surrender. He was ill and weak. His frozen face haunts me. Three hundred Minneconjous died that morning."

"And the Wasichus have the gall to call this massacre the Battle at Wounded Knee. I have heard that the contorted and frozen bodies of men, women, and children were shoved into a mass grave."

"Big Foot's body was frozen with his arms raised, pleading for justice and mercy for his people. We had been talking of the Ghost Dance. Yellow Bird was speaking about this Paiute named

Wavoka. It is said that he could be a messiah and that the Ghost Dance would bring back the buffalo and that our killed brothers and uncles would return to us. Yellow Bird and Big Foot said that the Ghost Shirts could render the white man's bullets harmless. Many among us had danced the Ghost Dance and wore the shirts. The drum song of the Hotchkiss tore out the hearts of the Minneconjous. The Ghost Dancers died and their bodies froze in the red snows along with the innocent. The waters of the Chankae Opi Wakpala ran dark with blood and the cold gray sky of Pine Ridge echoed with cries of the dying. These dishonorable, heinous Wasichus, how did we live among these savages?"

"And Buffalo Bill is the most disreputable."

Black Elk sat silently. The sharp raven calls of those murdered at Wounded Knee filled the room and then eventually faded through the walls. "Continue," he said to Wolf Song.

"When I witnessed the execution of Sitting Bull and the hateful murder of Crow Foot I dropped to my knees and mourned life. I began my death song, for I had no desire to live further. Several soldiers who accompanied the ceska maza mocked me and surrounded me. I wished for them to end the agony then and there, but they continued to taunt me. One of them knew me from *The Wild West*. I don't know why. But it was he who laughed as he told me that the long knife general called Miles had not fully agreed to the arrest of Sitting Bull and it was Miles who beseeched Buffalo Bill to intercede before the arrest. Cody was to meet with Sitting Bull and warn him. He would have listened to Cody because Sitting Bull and Big Foot had reconciled themselves to protect their starving people. But the meeting never took place."

"Why?"

"Because agent McLaughlin and Colonel Drum sent their men to waylay Buffalo Bill."

"How was this done?"

"All they had to do was offer the old fool a drink of whiskey and ask him to tell them about his exploits as a great Indian scout and pony rider. They worked in relays to get the Great American Hero drunk. This gave agent McLaughlin time to send a message over the high-strung wire to the great father in Washington and repeal Chief General Miles' plan. Buffalo Bill played into their hands. He spent the whole night boasting about himself and collapsed drunk before dawn. The same morning Sitting Bull collapsed at my feet, his brains blown out upon my face, blinding me with hate—a thousand lifetimes of hate for Buffalo Bill. I have suffered a thousand deaths because of this man. I will suffer one more life in order to achieve his death, or I will haunt him from the lightless world until revenge is mine." He threw the bag of cashews against the wall and covered his eyes with his palms to prevent the burning tears from exploding into sight and embarrassing his friend.

Chapter Seven

Lament

Winter, 1917

"Like pound, please," said the lone Indian to a hot-nut concessionaire on Broadway and Colfax, near the Colorado capitol building.

"A pound? Yes, sir. That's a lot of cashews for one man."

"Like cashews."

"Yes, sir, a pound it is. Excuse me for asking, but you do have the money to pay for a full pound don't 'cha?"

"Have money." He threw down several coins onto the counter.

"That's fine, chief. I was just checking."

"Not chief. Not warrior, not hero, not nobody."

"Whatever you say. Here's your nuts. You here for the funeral of Buffalo Bill or just seeing the sights?"

"Am here 'cause I'm very sad."

"Well, I can understand that. The death of Old Bill has upset us all."

"Yes, sad 'cause I not the hawk. I have no wings of the air. Heartsick 'cause I not do it."

"Well, chief, that's very poetic. But none of us had a chance to say a proper goodbye. You can go through the procession line to give your farewell, if you're a mind to."

"Yes, I going through."

"That's nice, chief."

"Going through to make sure Pashaka dead."

Tricksters often have a great appreciation for those who also possess the gift of chicanery. Just such a character plays a major role in the burial of Buffalo Bill. You Denverites dug a deep hole into my carapace in which to intern William F. Cody; it is only appropriate that I, Turtle, have the opportunity to tell you this part of the saga as I saw it. I told you before, I watch. The culprit of whom I speak is Harry Tammen, the owner of The Denver Post, the most powerful newspaper of the region. Oh, yes, I watch and I read. Did you think that we timeless ones do not change with the times?

Tammen aggravated the fiscal (and resulting physical) ruin of Cody. Cody was in debt. He was about to lose The Wild West. Tammen loaned him money for a percentage of ownership and the opportunity to play a role in the production of the extravaganza. Tammen had aspirations to be in show business, but only those closest to him knew this. Your human egos rival those of us gods. So, through financial skullduggery, behind the scenes, Tammen accelerated the bankruptcy of Cody and ended up as the majority owner of the Wild West. Celebrating duplicity, or at least raising it to new Western heights, he convinced a naïve Cody to sign away years of trust and friendship with his legitimate partners, Pawnee Bill Gordon Lillie and Johnny Baker. Now that's some trick.

The local press, owned by Tammen, while singing his praises often spoke unkindly of The Beast. They attributed to yours truly territorial earthquakes, mine cave-ins, droughts, and even floods. I was blamed when the gold around Denver petered out. I, therefore, do not have great affection for the fourth estate, and risk their wrath when pontificating about Tammen. But believe me, I am misunderstood. Yes, I profess that Mr. Harry Tammen was a corporate scoundrel of paramount magnitude. He was the pinnacle, the Pike's Peak of trickery. (I enjoy using metaphors that refer to my physical attributes.) But in pointing out such foibles, I too sing the praises of the sneaky SOB.

When poor old Buffalo Bill passed away, Tammen and his Denver cronies saw great advantage to Bill's remains remaining in Colorado. This was a contentious contradiction according to Bill's brethren in Wyoming. When they tell the story, the widow Louisa Cody and the people of Wyoming all agreed that the location of Bill's final "couch," as stated in Bill's will, was to be atop Cedar

Mountain, a magnificent Wyoming view. I've done great work up north as well. You need to visit. But, I digress.

That Mrs. Cody would not speak to the scourge Tammen was also well documented and often observed. Therefore, being the clever opportunist he was, Tammen coerced Edgar McMechen, curator of the Colorado Historical Society, to temp the Widow Cody with a ten thousand dollar bribe. She was to report that Buffalo Bill, upon his deathbed, had changed his mind about Wyoming and requested to be buried on "Mount Lookout." She obliged the exploiter, and much to the chagrin of Wyoming, there Buffalo Bill lies. My colleague Coyote would be proud. Our coconspirator Raven would be raucous.

History fascinates me. Perhaps my interest is based on having participated in numerous historical events, if not as an observer, then as an accomplice, and oftentimes as an instigator. History fascinates me, but trickery nourishes.

Through human trickery Buffalo Bill thus became the most famous and most perpetual citizen of Golden, Colorado. His Lookout Mountain gravesite is nestled at 7,375 feet of altitude above the town. Golden, originally named Golden City, squats in a valley separated from Denver, the Queen City of the Plains, by two flat mesas, North and South Table Mountain, and a treeless bump of a hill called Green Mountain—not my most picturesque mound. The west shoulder of the town rests below the first of the nearby foothills, the infamous Lookout Mountain. Golden was the original capital of Colorado. Her founding fathers were enterprising and ambitious men of pioneer vision. General George West, William Austin Hamilton Loveland, Edward Lewis Berthoud, entrepreneurs all, began a variety of businesses, including a local newspaper and general retail outlets, but culminated in courageous railroad ventures. Each served a variety of governmental, educational, and altruistic roles. Golden began to blossom while Denver and Auraria remained rather squalid mining camps on the banks of Cherry Creek. Eventually, however, Denver grew and was made the state capital through political high jinx, economic maneuvering, and the corrupt power of railroad barons. Our friend Tammen, of course, played a role.

To this day there remains the remnant of resentment from the prodigy of Golden's founding fathers, which has manifested itself in a bitter oxymoronic reversal of town mission and parish philosophy. The attitude of the citizenry has evolved from civic optimism to: if you can't beat the corrupt bastards; isolate yourself from the citified sons-of-bitches.

I have observed that current natives of Golden wear an expression reminiscent, centuries past, of the physiognomy of reclusive mountain men, who once annually drifted out of their deep-woods isolation and reluctantly attended a rendezvous at some semi-civilized site such as Golden. They were (and are) suspicious, cynical, incredulous, guarded, provincial, maybe even a bit prejudice, not necessarily racial, but definitely "holdin' to their own." They are the perfect quarry for chicanery.

Somehow, by losing the battle for supremacy with Denver, many of the townsfolk lost their zest and zeal and their farsightedness. Therefore, to the rest of Colorado, Goldenites were quaint foothill folk. However, because the citizens of Golden refused to see past the Tabletops (in the direction of Denver), they considered themselves authentic mountain people, and boasted about the innate characteristics of an insular population: recalcitrance, nonconformity, resistance, ungovernability, but with that frontier charm that made them interesting.

Today, Golden takes great pride in serving as the gateway to the Continental Divide. There is a huge sign that says so. "Howdy Folks. Welcome to GOLDEN: Where the West Begins." It was a gift to the city from the Holland family, of The Holland House hotel fame. Recently, with dubious wisdom, the city fathers changed the wording of the sign to read: Where the West Remains. Such is my point. It arches, like a rainbow, across the entire width of Washington, the main street. One might suspect a satiric wit were it not for the obvious pride the locals take in dressing like cowpokes and drinking like miners. Other folks, tourists and travelers, those less sedentary than the locals and wishing to explore the Rockies, must pass through Golden to reach the dizzying heights of either Berthoud or Loveland Pass, two of the most scenic summits on my spine. Both routes over the Continental Divide are named after founders of Golden. George West, historically considered the first citizen of Golden, is buried nearby, his grave much less splendid than Buffalo Bill's. It is a unique phenomenon among you humans to give more tribute to entertainers, tricksters, and rogues than to solid citizens. I thank you. You have helped to keep my brethren and me around all these centuries.

Trekking north out of Golden on a back road that runs past the flatirons, a dramatic series of distinctive vertical stone fins, shaped like Gothic windows, or vandalized tombstones, one can get to Boulder, that bastion of liberal thinking, a town out of place when considering the characteristics of its neighbors. However, traveling due south out of Golden, along the toes of the foothills, following the crevasse running parallel to the hogbacks, the alligator dorsal spines on the back of The Beast, for about eight miles one winds his or her way into the tiny town of Morrison, gateway to Pine, Evergreen, and Indian Hills. This is the way to South Park and a variety of other mountain passes in the San Juan and Sangre de Cristo Mountains. We'll travel there later.

Morrison has a restaurant known for Mexican food and Golden has one famous for biscuits. Both are quick-to-the-draw in defense of their respective cuisine.

Coyote informs me that most of the women of Golden shave their armpits and a few of the men put down the toilet seat. Such superfluous grooming is rare in Morrison.

While Morrison is famous for dinosaur fossils imbedded in the surrounding red and ochre sandstone hills named after the town, Golden is famous for beer. The Coors brewery bubbles its hops between the two mesas at the east boundary of the town on Clear Creek, a stream trickling east from the snow-capped peaks of the Great Divide. Both towns have had their historical share of miners, outlaws, gamblers, hooligans, and generally colorful characters. Their progeny still infest the surrounding valleys. Golden is also the home of the highly respected School of Mines which graduates geological engineers, but these somewhat sensible and often intelligent young people are claimed by neither community, although I hold a particular and obvious affection for them.

Smack-dab-halfway between the two towns is Red Rocks Park: a singular, phenomenal, improbable, unparalleled, memorable, outdoor amphitheater. It is one of my best creations. It is the reason I inhabit this area as a timeless deity and often visit in the guise of a mortal. Anyone who visits Red Rocks understands how a magical setting can influence humankind. I would think it is obvious why I, Turtle, would have an interest here.

Red Rocks is a natural concert arena formed between huge sedimentary rock outcroppings, sienna in color, made of rugged Morrison sandstone, sitting like a separated bow and stern of a giant ark. A rugged ship, designed by a Neanderthal rather than a pious family man, it split in half during its prehistoric sinking, the points of both bow and stern protruding upward and westward. Now petrified, the ark resembles an exposed vertebra, a barnacle burrowing to the bone of The Beast below. Tender to the touch, I awaken.

And overlooking this entire scenic spender, atop Lookout Mountain, is the grave of America's most famous Westerner, Buffalo Bill. Could he sit up, he would have a wonderful view of Denver to the east and the miles of plains beyond. If he could turn around, he would view the majestic Continental Divide to the west: tall, snow capped, cragged, the pinnacle of the jagged back of the sacred snapping turtle. According to Bill himself before his demise, "one can see four states from this perch."

The Lookout Mountain burial site above Golden proved to be a deep bone of contention, several bones actually—a skeleton of contention for the clan and kin in Cody. Cody, Wyoming, is the town founded by the Colonel and named in his honor. Bill's burial highjacking was such a disharmony for these Wyoming folk that the local American Legion posted a ten-thousand-dollar-cold-cash reward for the return of William Fredrick's body from Colorado to Cody. Anticipate if you will, a localized irritation, a mosquito bite on my earthen rump. I stir.

How can one blame Mrs. Cody for planting poor Bill in Colorado? Although they reconciled late in life, earlier W. F. was a notorious womanizer. He spent less time at home than Ulysses and he left her impoverished. Tammen accelerated Bill's poor business principles into a state of destitute indigence. She had suffered along with the showman as he evolved through American royalty immersed in financial ignorance to, as Bill would lament, "poverty, penury, pennilessness, pauperism, and now beggary." The woman needed some operating capital and if it meant switching the plot of the old dupe, so be it. Ironically, as trickery will have it, in 1921 Louisa was buried next to Bill on Lookout.

But as for Bill's funeral, I remember the headlines in the Denver Post, Tammen's paper:

"25,000 JOURNEY TO LOOKOUT MOUNTAIN TOP TO PAY FINAL TRIBUTE AT ROCK HEWN SHRINE OF 'COL. W. F. CODY,' NATIONS BELOVED HERO."

Sub-headlines declared:
"PAHASKA RESTS AT CREST OF PEAK IN RUGGED HILLS," and,
"ALL NATURE BOWS IN HOMAGE AS CASKET IS OPENED TO VIEW OF PILGRIMS OF SUNSET TRAIL."

All in all, despite the involvement of Harry Tammen, and that his sunset took four long months, the melodramatic Old Scout would have been pleased with the pomp.

Willie Wolf Song and a companion, Rides Tall, waited until after the sun went down, the band left, and the twenty-five thousand disbanded. Both reeked of alcohol. The taller of the figures cast off the aromatic scent of cashews.

"You cannot hide, Colonel," said Wolf Song, "from my vengeance in the womb of Mother Earth. I will pray to Her and to the Great Grandfather to cast you out and to help me. Even if I have to pursue you in the spirit world, I will force you to pay your debt to Sitting Bull. I will trek the dark road, march through hell, enter the catacombs of The Beast to find your shade and cripple your soul."

They both took a swig from a bottle. Rides Tall returned it to its hiding place under his jacket.

"Buffalo Bill," slurred Wolf Song. His voice echoed disdain, he mimicked the puffed out chest of the Wasichu politician who spoke earlier.

"Alias, William Cody," said Rides Tall.

"Colonel William Frederick Cody." The contempt remained.

"The f-a-a-amous Buffalo Bill." Rides Tall exaggerated the adjective and made large arching circles as he gestured with both arms.

"The famous Pony Express Rider."

"The famous frontier scout."

"The famous international showman," Wolf Song bent in a mocking bow.

"The famous sharpshooter!" Rides Tall mimed aiming a rifle.

"Victor over Yellow Hand." Wolf Song sounded melancholy.

"Famous friend of Texas Jack and Ned Buntline." He almost laughed.

"Kit Carson and Wild Bill Hickok."

"Sitting Bull . . ."

"And," said a new voice as a dark figure emerged from the shadows, "Black Elk." It was the Wichasha Wakan.

"Welcome, Black Elk," said Rides Tall.

"Brother," acknowledged Wolf Song.

"Friends, you seem to be foolishly involved in some sort of folly. Have I interrupted your celebration?"

"Not at all, old friend. We were simply paying homage . . ."

"Lamenting," interrupted Rides Tall.

Black Elk spoke: "The life of an Indian is like the wings of the air. That is why you notice the hawk knows how to get his prey. The Indian is like that. The hawk swoops down on its prey; so does the Indian. In his lament he is like an animal. For instance, the coyote is sly; so is the Indian. The eagle is the same. That is why the Indian is always feathered up; he is a relative to the wings of the air."

"Well said, wise brother," said Wolf Song. "You have no idea of the irony."

"Perhaps I know more than you think, old friend."

Wolf Song flushed with embarrassment, and, taking the bottle from Rides Tall pocket, changed the subject with a sarcastic toast, "To our past benefactor, the famous instructor of the American character, the Honorable William F. Cody."

Rides Tall pitched a small paperback book onto the grave, "Buffalo Bill, hero of the Washacus ten cent novel."

"Cody is dead. Did you have a hand in this, Wolf Song?" asked Black Elk.

Wolf Song became less bellicose, and in a ghostly calm replied, "Not yet."

Chapter Eight

Elegy

Winter, 1930

Although not a Lakota, nor a friend of Wolf Song,
Toohoolhoolzote, a Nez Percé, once spoke a sentiment to me, Turtle,
that recounts the discontentment with unsuited death, such as that of
Sitting Bull—witnessed by Wolf Song. The old Nez Percé chieftain
said, "I saw that . . . life went out with . . . blood. This taught me for
what purpose I am here. I came into this world to die. My body is
only to hold a spirit life. Should my blood be sprinkled, I want no
wounds from behind. Death should come fronting me."

In a world of winters Wolf Song had quit counting the
passing of years. He vaguely knew that in the white man's world it
was sometime in the middle of the years numbered 1930. He was
much more aware that it had been many winters since he had seen
his brother Black Elk at the gravesite of Buffalo Bill. It had been ten
since the death of Pahaska. It was over forty years since they had
talked of Sitting Bull and since Wounded Knee. The current event
that drove home his plaint was that Wolf Song stumbled across a
book written by a Wasichus called John Neihardt. The title was
BLACK ELK SPEAKS, and although Wolf Song had never learned
to read the white man's language, as did Rides Tall, he did recognize
several words. Not enough, however, to read Niehardt's writing. He
took the book from the window. He held it and turned it from side to
side as if some sort of understanding would fall out if he turned it the
right way. He contemplated the weight of the object. He thumbed
through it looking for pictures. After a few minutes he noticed that
the clerk and a customer were staring at him. He walked the book to
the clerk behind the heavy desk and asked him to read a passage near
the end that Wolf Song recognized as a prayer supposedly spoken by

the old oracle and his life-long brother. The clerk sighed; his impatience and disgust were obvious. However, the customer, a woman dressed in furs said she would read it. Wolf Song nodded his thanks, crossed his hands and looked at the floor. What he heard he believed could indeed have been the words of his old friend.

She read, "With tears running, O Great Spirit, Great Spirit, my Grandfather—with running tears I must say now that the tree has never bloomed. A pitiful old man, you see here, and I have fallen away and have done nothing. Here at the center of the world, where you took me when I was young and taught me; here, old, I stand, and the tree is withered, Grandfather, my Grandfather!

"Again, and maybe the last time on this earth, I recall the great vision you sent me. It may be that some little root of the sacred tree still lives. Nourish it then, that it may leaf and bloom and fill with singing birds. Hear me, not for myself, but for my people; I am old. Hear me that they may once more go back into the sacred hoop and find the good red road, the shielding tree!"

Wolf Song recalled his friend's deep disappointment in not being able to lead his people out of the disaster begun by the whites. He remembered how an elderly Black Elk had in desperation turned his back on the faith of the Lakota.

"He became one of those who worshipped with the Black Robes," said Wolf Song quietly.

"I'm sorry?" asked the woman.

"I was sorry, too," Wolf Song said firmly. "I was very disappointed. It was difficult talking to him after he converted to Jesus-the-Father-and-the-Son and did mass at the white father's church. He was disappointed that I was never as spiritual or religious because I was bitter. He tried to help me find the red road. I was resistant, angry, vengeful. He became disappointed in Wakantanka, the great grandfather. He became ill and the white man's medicine and prayers cured him." Wolf Song wanted to say that Black Elk had assimilated the white man's religion, but did not know the words and was embarrassed that he had already said too much. He thought but did not speak, *Black Elk will die and his spirit will be as frozen and contorted as the cadaver of Big Foot. And he will wander the other world of the unaccomplished and unfulfilled as aimlessly as the spirits of Crazy Horse and Sitting Bull. And this, too, shall be my fate if I cannot somehow cripple and mutilate the soul of Buffalo Bill and force him to join us in our dark place of no sacred directions.*

"You knew Black Elk?" the woman asked.

"Is he dead now? Is that why there is this book?"

"No, I believe he is still alive. Do you want to see him? Is there something I can do?"

"I shall see him in the next world. Catholics who are alive are too difficult to talk to. Do you know where I can buy cashews?"

She stood wide-eyed and shook her head, no.

He walked out of the store.

Chapter Nine

The Hero's Journey

Summer, 1964

After a dozen rounds of margaritas Raven and Coyote fell into a stupor. Coyote looked as if he had passed out; he lay his head on the bar. Raven, although still upright, leaned against a thick pine post holding up both the roof and the inebriated bird. Later the two deities would complain that it was the altitude. They were not used to drinking on the top of a mountain. Turtle knew it was just an excuse. The fact was: they couldn't hold their liquor, not like the old days, not since Christian and other folks had weakened them through indifference. They had all drunk together many times here at the peak of Lookout Mountain. Buffalo Bill Cody's Bar Grill and Texaco Station was Turtle's favorite haunt when they were all haunting the Colorado foothills. Their torpor, however, was not going to stop Turtle from his intended pontificating. He had a presentation to make. He had visual aids, for crying out loud. Coyote unconsciously licked his salt incrusted muzzle and whined in comatose delight. That was all the cue Turtle needed. He went on with his lengthy introduction to the explanation of his planned skullduggery.

"As I am sure you already know, my friends, my colleagues in mayhem . . ." Turtle watched as Raven cooed an asymmetrical rhythm of soft cackles. His beady eyes blinked in synchronous coincidence. "The hero's journey mirrors the epic of humankind," Turtle spoke to no one in particular now that his audience had apparently abandoned him, "which in turn reflects the chronicle of the Earth. I, Turtle, in dreams informed Wichasha Wakan and his cohort Wolf Song, our pawn, of this parallelism, and the Lakota oracle in turn translated for The People that each saga requires birth, death, and rebirth. Three key ingredients.

"He dreamed of the birth of a continent, of which we have spoken; the death of a great hero, thus far there are several likely candidates besides Tatanka Iotonka; and rebirth within a new spiritual age. And that is why I have brought you here today, to define this new spiritual age, to point out that it is through the coming of this new age that we shall again find potency. We need only to support the instigators." He paused and sipped the last of his margarita. *Needs salt.* "And pull a little trick now and then.

"Recall, in his prophecy, Wichasha Wakan intermingled global, human, and transcendental elements. And he spoke of the importance of caverns to the heroic quest. I stand in full agreement." He looked to his drinking partners; they exhibited only the slightest sign of life. Raven turned his head toward Turtle. Turtle couldn't tell if it was in interest to what he was saying or in anger at being woken. Coyote opened one eye, looked toward Turtle, pulled his tongue off the bar and back into his muzzle. His facial expression projected an exhausted disgust with the taste of whatever his tongue transported into his head. "Let's review," said Turtle. "Thus far we have birth, death, rebirth, the potential of a new era, and caves."

"Consider first the painted prehistoric caves of Lascaux and Altamira." He turned his back to the others and strolled up stage in dramatic fashion. "While they support the point, they are too far away to impact our tale," he made an exaggerated turn and pointed at his friends who only now began to shift with attention, "and unknown to the Oglala shaman. The Front Range, however, here, just west of Denver, is an area peppered with caves and mines, a region on my dorsum with a local history rich in geological transformations, human epic, and ripe for a spiritual conversion." He pointed at an easel and an illegible illustration portraying a simplified version of continental drift. "A tectonic tug of war gave birth to the region. The great shallow sea that submerged me subsided under the uprising pressure of the Pacific plate pushing for more room on the bed of Mother Earth."

"Turtle, old chum," interrupted Raven, still leaning on the post for support, "you're not going to give the roadside geography lecture again, are you?"

Turtle ignored him. "Mountainous cousins of the Front Range emerged—parallel ripples, crocodilian ridges on the shell of Turtle."

"I hate it," said Coyote, "when he refers to himself in the third person." He closed his one attentive eye and smacked his dry lips. "Wake me when it's over."

Turtle continued, "They include the Park Range, the Gore, the Mosquito, and the Sawatch, as well as the San Juan Mountains and, of course, the Sangre de Cristo—your stomping grounds, Coyote, you uninformed Philistine."

"Now I always liked the Philistines," mumbled Coyote. "They and their neighbors, the Egyptians, worshiped my cousins the jackals. Those were the days. Then those blasted sons of Abraham came alone and made doggy dirt of that gig."

"Isn't that the point Turtle is trying to make," said Raven, pushing away from the pine post. "Isn't he talking about getting some payback. This new era . . . isn't he saying our time is coming again."

"Well," said Coyote, "why the Hounds of Hades doesn't he just say so? All I'm hearing is mountains this and mountains that."

"All were formed through folding and faulting," Turtle continued to ignore them, "and great volcanic hiccups. And now, Wind, River, Rain, and human kind work tirelessly to reduce mountains to hills and hills to plains and return them eventually to the sea. The sea, in turn, creates new mountains. We've gone full circle: the circle of life, the sacred hoop of which Wichasha Wakan so elegantly spoke."

"And those within the hoop walk the good road under one sky from youth to age to death, thus invite renaissance by returning to the earth, from the earth to the sea, from the light to the dark. I get it," said Raven.

"And here's the part you'll like, Coyote," said Turtle. "From across the sea, to sow the new age, come four sages. They are journeying from a cavern in an ancient port on an ancestral island once visited by our Lakota medicine man. Except for one, their names were reminiscent of saints, and his was the appellation of a monarch: John, Paul, George and the king——Richard, also known as Ringo. There is an irony here that is intoxicating, because none are saints, quite the contrary, although brought up as Christians, they are entertaining Hinduism and that plethora of animal deities. Our brothers call to us."

"Yes, yes, yes," said Coyote. "I've heard of the Fab Four, a fine pack of wolfish rogues, but isn't their new age about music?"

"Theirs is a spiritual revolution," answered Turtle "a cultural and generational conflict, instigated by youth and bolstered by music whose original rumblings owe their roots to the gospel harmonics of the disenfranchised. It was the Rock'n'Roll revolution——you can't sit down, oh no, you can't sit down." Turtle danced a finger-waving jig, "The disenfranchised! Feel a kinship?" Raven shook his head at Turtle's lack of rhythm and blatant theatrics.

"It was the pandemonium created by the invading Mersey marauders that opened the floodgates for the electrical-pharmacological avatar. Fueled by hallucinogens, Fender guitars, a heavy backbeat, a celebration of bass and base, the lads from Liverpool conquered and demolished two-hundred years of provincial funk."

Raven spoke up, "Much to the surprise of one of the main players, John Lennon, who when asked in interview after interview why their music held such power——and what was it the Beatles were doing differently?——replied, 'I dun' know. It's only Rock'n'Roll.'"

"As the Rock'n'Roll revolution grew and evolved into the Age of Aquarius, many members of the majority race adopted an archetype for enhanced spiritualism from the very people the Establishment had tried to annihilate or violently assimilate——our Native Americans. So, yes, Coyote," said Turtle. "We have again come full circle."

Coyote seemed unimpressed. He asked, "Any chance of getting another drink. I'm parched. Is there anything worse than starting to sober up in the daylight?"

"It's night, you old hound," said Raven. "Look outside. It's dark. As dark as a cave."

Turtle took his cue, "The Fab Four began in a cavern—The Cavern—just below the streets of Liverpool. Many Indians believe that humankind emerged from holes, small caverns, in Mother Earth, sipapu."

"By the way," said Coyote, finally joining in, "the spelling of the appellation *Beatle* is based on the word *beat*, as in *downbeat* or the beating of the heart."

"A rhythm," added Turtle, "mirrored in the dance of Native Americans when awakening Mother Earth. Of this we have spoken."

Coyote continued, "Before the downbeat of the rascal Richard Starkey enriched their local skittle band, the original group——John, Paul, and George——called themselves 'The Moon Dogs.' Am I the only scoundrel who knew that?"

" Hardly," said Turtle, "but did you know that this summer—1964—John, Paul, George, and Ringo have crossed the ocean and a continent to play a concert at Red Rocks Park and Amphitheater, right here in our backyard?"

"Yes, so?" said Coyote. "Do you have tickets?"

"Tickets," said Raven. "Tickets. We don't need no stinking tickets."

"Is it not relevant," asked Turtle, "to the premonition of the shaman, that the original 'Moon Dogs,' musicians with long hair, born in a cavern, would come to visit the lair of Pahaska, meaning Long Hair? And that Pahaska, Buffalo Bill, is buried in a deep hole in the ground above Red Rocks Amphitheater, the site of the concert? And, irony or all ironies, Buffalo Bill's sworn enemy is Willie Wolf Song——Wolf Song!——a synonymy with the musical affectation: 'Moon Dog.'"

"Eerie, isn't it?" said Raven.

"What's your point?" asked Coyote. Turtle started again. Coyote interrupted, "No, no, never mind, Turtle, I was only teasing. But, if you want me to join in on this vendetta of yours, I need another margarita, a batch of margaritas, and this time, don't scrimp on the salt."

Ringo peered out the window while the plane taxied toward the gate. He saw the limousine on the tarmac adjacent to the airport concourse. He could hear the high pitched roar of the screaming fans through the fuselage of the plane and over the noise of the engines. By now, it was a familiar sound, like the largest angry flock of birds ever assembled, approaching in a fury from a distance. He looked around; everyone could hear the chants and while John and Paul looked amused, other passengers appeared petrified. Outside and above the window of the plane he saw thousands of red, sweaty, pre-pubescent faces pressed against the glass of the huge picture windows of the concourse. A temporary fence and police line had been set-up near the runway to contain the zealous, fanatic *ingénues* ("Do you speak French?" "Non.") wanting a closer look and, Ringo feared, a personal souvenir. Paul was the first off the plane. He paused in the bright Rocky Mountain sun. The throngs screamed. He smiled, waved and scurried down the mechanical stairs toward the car. George was next, the screams continued. John and Brian exited together followed by Ringo. Ringo paused at the top of the stairs and bobbed his head back and forth. His hair did a hula. The thunderous screams rattled the windows and shook the car.

"Well, there you are," said Paul as he got in the limo.

"They sound like a bunch of wild Indians," said Brian.

"That's an unfair stereotype," said John.

"Not according to Rudyard Kipling," commented George.

"Now, don't go confusing Ringo," said Paul.

"Tar," said Ringo.

They watched as sporadic fanatics slipped through the police line and rushed the limo.

"Like lemmings determined to fly," said John. "If many more get through, we could die smiling. Watch this."

One particularly agile girl had dodged several diving tackles made by the police and grabbed the door handle of the limo. It was locked. Two policemen were trying to pull her off, but she stuck like a barnacle. John pushed the button to open the window. "Hello, Love," he said to her face. She hit the ground like Icarus, fanatic wings melting in the heat of passion, dust and feathers flying. A sea of fans flooded through the break in the police dam made by the failed tackles for the first girl. They surrounded the limo.

"It's pandemonium out there," said Ringo.

"Total pandemonium; it's bedlam" agreed George.

"Vast pandemonium," said Paul.

"I don't care for it," started John. "It's not about the music anymore. It's about the *Beatles*. All this screaming, they can't even hear the music. It's bonkers."

"Pandemonium and bonkers," said Ringo. A buxom young girl had her breasts pressed up against the car window next to Ringo. The crowd pushed from behind; she flattened and filled the glass. "It's tintamarre," said Ringo, "but it does present some rare opportunities." He reached for the window button on his armrest.

"Well, aren't you the lyrical one," said John

"Don't you dare, Ringo," said George, "or we'll be having Pandora's pandemonium in here."

The police had pulled several of the frantic fans from in front of the limo. The car began to accelerate past the crowd.

"With their red faces and all, and the police in uniform," said Ringo. "It looks like the calvary and the Indians in hand-to-hand combat."

"Cavalry," corrected John.

"If Ringo opens that window," said George, "we may all have a religious experience."

"I wonder," Ringo asked, "with all these wild heathens about, where's Buffalo Bill or General Custard?"

John said nothing. Ringo watched. He made faces at the girls running next to the limo. It so shocked the lead runner, she tripped and fell; a hundred followers tumbled first over her and then over each other.

"Like a herd of stampeding wildebeest," said John.

"Who gnu?" said Paul.

"I hope no one is hurt," said Ringo.

"I believe a couple of the policemen have been crushed into ecstasy," said Paul.

"Smothered by an avalanche of adolescent boobies," said George.

"You're very lyrical too, aren't ya," said John.

"Poetic," said Ringo.

"Vastly poetic," said Paul.

"Stop that," said John.

"Look!" pointed Ringo. "That chubby one is about to jump from the terrace onto the limo."

"If she hits us we could be crushed," cringed George.

"She's huge," yelled Ringo.

"Vast," said John.

"I thought we were going to stop," said Paul.

"I hope the driver doesn't stop," said Ringo.

"She missed us," said George.

"That poor policeman," said Ringo.

"My god, she's up and chasing us," George was turned looking out the back.

"Gear," said John.

"Really, please," asked Paul, "how much farther?"

"It won't be long," sang John.

Ringo bobbed his head to John's cadence.

Chapter Ten

A Roasted Aroma

Summer, 1948

I, Turtle, love the Rocky Mountains. Among the undulations upon my earthly shell, they are the most spectacular. At their heights, the summits are unconquerable. Man does not modify these peaks; they transform him. However, below the tree line, nestled in the foothills and the valleys, humankind leaves their mark. It is in these transition areas where the conflicts between man and nature, another of my aliases, are most likely to spark.

There is a distinct aroma of summer in the Rockies. Pine is an obvious element, but not the kind of scent canned as air freshener or squeezed into jiffy cakes, a sweet and tamed pine—an illusion, a poor trick, perpetuated by men of bad taste. The true pine is an aged aroma, fermented and warmed by the summer sun. It has an edge, a hearty, independent tree smell that boasts of centuries of survival beyond time, past the days of the great buffalo herds, back to the dawning of the creation of the world upon the back of Turtle. It's an aroma discontented with the genteel life of providing shelter for chickadees and tuft-eared squirrels. It reeks of danger, not from predators such as the puma or bear, whose harm is piddling and individual. Rather, it's as if all the trees are in destructive collusion, if they can just get organized. It's a foreshadowing of inflammable danger, one lightning strike away. The pine forest smells differently in winter, blanketed in deep snow. It's asleep. In the summer, near the ground, where man can walk, there is a definite combustible aroma.

A middle-aged Willie, long retired from the Wild West Show, was the recent, past proprietor of Wolf Song's Hot Nut Emporium. He'd gone bankrupt. Sales were fair, but he ate more stock than he sold. His new occupational goal was to extend his tenure as the Cody, Wyoming, town-drunk.

A Major emeritus in the Wyoming American Legion approached Wolf Song with an opportunity to redeem his drowned soul.

"I hear you used to know Buffalo Bill," asked the Major.

"Knew him," answered Wolf Song. "Died for him many times."

"Then you are the right man for the job," said the old soldier. "And I hear you been to Denver and the town west of there—Golden."

"Been there. Died once."

The Major appeared pulsed, but continued with his questioning. "And I suppose you heard what those damn Denverites have done with the body of Buffalo Bill? Buried him atop Lookout Mountain and published the lie that that's where he chose to rest eternally. We in the Legion believe Bill belongs here, near Cody, on Cedar Mountain. Have you seen their heretical and irreverent crypt?"

"Saw," said Willie, proud that he was never much for words.

"Well, man, we need someone to guide us to Golden to steal back the remains of our town's sake. Are you interested? Can you keep a secret? Are you up to the task? Have I found the right man? Say Something. Man, I'm waiting."

A sudden and surprising dawn lifted Wolf Song's melancholy. A thought galloped across his mind. After all these years his plan for revenge on the old showman could reach fruition by leading these fools to the grave, helping them steal the old buffalo hunter, in turn steal him from his rescuers, and then secretly dispose of the remains in different places, forcing the spirit of Buffalo Bill to wander eternity in shame. By hiding his bones in several locales, Willie could prevent the spirit of Cody from uniting in the afterlife. This is why The People often mutilated the bodies of their enemies, so that they would have to drift eternally in the Great Hunting Grounds—crippled, disjointed, and vanquished.

"Can do," said Willie.

"Enough said," whispered the Major.

Willie Wolf Song led the group of Wyoming grave robbers through the thick pine of, if he understood their cursing, the steepest sloped forest they had ever trekked. They grumbled that the wide, open spaces and polished glass sky of Wyoming was more majestic, and "frankly" more damn comfortable. This Colorado sky, they complained, seemed to be closing in on them. "In Wyoming," said a lanky fellow at the back of the group, "forests are hiked only long enough to get to a trout stream. We've been hiking straight up this steep mountainside for more than two hours."

Willie liked it; the summer aroma reminded him of roasted cashews. He had them park their trucks far below on Highway 6, parallel to Clear Creek at the bottom of the steep valley. They were climbing up the backside, the west slope of Lookout and had slunk across the switchbacks on Lariat Trail several times. Each time, someone in the group complained that they could have driven up at least this far. But Willie felt it was smarter to reconnoiter the gravesite from the cover of the woods rather than drive a bunch of pickup trucks with Wyoming license plates up Lariat. Parading anywhere near the gravesite could alert the locals.

"Damn, it's hot down here in Colorado," complained a raider named Luther. "Are we going to try to steal Bill in broad day light?"

"No," answered Willie. "See better in day. Steal at night."

"Yea, and I can shoot better in the daylight," snarled a young cowboy-type they called: *Kid.*

"They won't be any shooting today, Kid," said the Major. "I can't believe you packed that six-shooter all the way up this mountain."

"Where my guns go, I go," said Kid.

"That's a lot of weight to be packing for a fella not much taller than a toilet seat," laughed Luther.

Willie watched as Kid spun in a blink and had his pistol pointing at the source of the insult.

"Damn, Kid, put that thing away," ordered the Major. "We've got a job to do here, think about that. Nothing is going to stop us from our determined objective. And you, Luther ..."

Luther had scampered and was hiding behind a tree.

"And you, Luther, had better quit razing Kid and keep your mind on business, or I may shoot you myself when we get back to Cody with Bill."

Luther slunk meekly from behind the tree, "Well, it is pretty damn hot. And these woods smell funny."

"We are all hot, Luther. Quit your complaining," said the Major. "How much farther is it, Wolf Song?"

"Not far."

"Can we stop and rest a bit?"

"Not far."

"Damn," said Luther.

"Damn is right," said another of the troop, and he sat down on a stool-sized granite rock in the shade of an ancient Ponderosa pine. All of the others followed suit except Kid.

Willie knew he was never as patient and stoic as the stereotypical Indian of fiction; who was? But he had over the past several decades shown considerable patience under a variety of strenuous situations. This lot of complainers, however, was quickly wearing thin. He was beginning to question whether or not his vendetta against Buffalo Bill was worth this aggravation. *How in the name of the Great Grandfather did we lose the war to these Wasichu. Only Kid and I do not complain. I am an old man and I live mostly on nuts.* Willie and Kid continued for another hundred yards and then stood at the crest of a ridge. The sun came from behind a large cumulus cloud and ricocheted off Willie's hair, damp from perspiration, and silver from age. He pushed it back along his temples and felt a slight sprinkle of remorse about the metallic color.

"Here," he motioned with his hand, pointing over the ridge. He watched Kid sit down, out of breath, and pull his kerchief from around his thick pine tree of a neck, mop his brow and then pull out his pistol. He rubbed it lovingly with the damp bandanna. *He is not much older than I was when I left for the Buffalo Bill 'extravaganza.'*

He heard the others struggle to their feet and labor up the hill. It was as he remembered: just to the east, down a short slope, across a parking lot, sat a log building with a green tar roof. A large, hand-painted sign read PA-HA-SKA TEE PEE."

"What now," asked the Major. "Do we wait here until dark?"

"No," said Willie, "we tour museum, have a drink. I'm thirsty."

"But you said we had to be secretive."

"I said trucks attract attention. No one knows who we are. We have to be careful, not stupid. Let's get a beer."

"I'll drink to that," said Luther and he began walking down the hill and across the parking lot. Several others followed.

"Now wait a minute, men," barked the Major. "I don't like this one bit."

Willie and the Kid waited with the Major as he watched the raiders ignore his concerns and parade into the museum.

"Well, what the hell," the Major moaned and began down the hill. As he and Willie approached the entrance, the screen door squeaked open and Luther stepped out.

"They only sell cokes and lemonade in there. Just right for you, Kid," he grinned. "The girl said there is a bar just up the road."

"Well, then let's tour the museum," pleaded the Major. "See how they have done by Buffalo Bill."

The others filed past Luther and the Major, and walked toward the road.

"Don't you want to see the displays?" asked the Major.

"We'll see 'um after," answered Luther.

"I look," said Willie.

"I should hope so," said the Major as he entered the building.

"Me, too," said Kid. "If I was dying of thirst, I wouldn't drink with that bunch of buffalo farts."

The building had the smell of old pine, but Willie could also detect the lilac perfumes of the thousands of grandmothers and the bubblegum pops of their grandsons. The dust of human occupation stirred the cigarette odors of past visits. The aroma of thousands of Sunday-shined shoes lingered, as did the bouquet of mothballs and dry cleaning. Willie visualized the aromatic shadows of the latest patrons. At times he felt he could deduce what they had eaten for their Sunday brunch. He instinctively scouted for the fragrance of roasting nuts.

The architecture was typical Wasichu—more rustic Alpine than American West, but the memorabilia inside was definite Wild West. A large portrait of Buffalo Bill proudly mounted on his great white steed, Isham, dominated the room. Dozens of framed posters advertising *Buffalo Bill's Wild West and Congress of Rough Riders of the World* hung throughout the building. The posters were colorful, bright, and animated. Bucking broncos arched toward the sky in exaggerated attempts to launch their riders; who stuck fast with frontier fortitude. He looked for his image in scenes of Indians riding bareback in reenacted attacks on the Deadwood Stage, but figured he had already been shot off his pony. There were other pictures of gauchos launching bolas at stampeding cattle, Bedouins in there white desert robes mounted on magnificent Arabian stallions, and vaqueros doing rope tricks from the backs of their racing Mexican thoroughbreds. There were portrait posters of Buffalo Bill as scout, horseman, pony express rider, and master showman. Two of his saddles were mounted in displays along with other tack and paraphernalia. One of his famous Stetson sombreros hung next to a pair of fancy, hip-high boots.

Annie Oakley took aim at an unseen target in a faded photograph. Goldie Griffith Cameron angelically smiled at the viewer, her hat and fringed gloves too big for her petite demeanor. She was one of five women who rode broncos. The Indians were always amazed. Wolf Song resented that she was allowed to stay on her horse. No one shot her.

Several displays had "Authentic Indian Artifacts." There were prehistoric arrowheads, ancient and modern baskets, and a Crow cradleboard. There was a picture of Iron Tail, the Sioux chosen as the model for the Indian Head Nickel; because, said the sign, he looked so "typically like an American Indian." And there was a photograph of a black cowboy actually riding an elk. The photo had a hand written caption, "Master Voter Hall, a Feejee Indian from Africa." Wolf Song grumbled at the misinformation, a false trail, although he was pleased that he recognized several of the White man's words.

Many photos, however, needed no caption. He knew the subjects, for example, a pudgy fourteen year old sharp shooter named Lillian Smith posed in a fringed skirt, a Winchester lever action leaning against her knee.

A model of a new building sat on a pedestal of pine bark near the snack bar. The sign below read:

HELP US BUILD A GRAND FIREPROOF MUSEUM
FOR THIS FABULOUS COLLECTION OF THE OLD WEST
BUFFALO BILL MEMORIAL MUSEUM
CITY AND COUNTY OF DENVER
HON. JOHNNY BAKER, MGR.

A portrait of Baker, Buffalo Bill's protégé, hung nearby. Wolf Song recognized "Young Johnny," and remembered the speech he gave at Buffalo Bill's funeral. But Wolf Song also remembered hearing that Young Johnny had died in a spring snow storm on Lookout Mountain around 1931. Always the promoter, Johnny Baker had often preached that Denver needed a museum next to the grave. Today a huge water jug filled with coins and folded dollar bills still sat next to the model and Young Johnny's pitch.

Kid crammed a five dollar bill into the jug. The Major gave him a look of what-the-hell-are-you-doing. Kid shrugged and shook his head in dismay, probably realizing that it was a bit contradictory to be participating in a mission to steal the remains of Buffalo Bill and contributing to the sons-of-bitches who robbed Wyoming of their favorite son. Willie liked Kid—he had a generous nature, and was not afraid to give tribute to his enemy.

"He's not the sharpest arrow in the quiver," said the Major, but Willie didn't understand.

It all looked too familiar to Wolf Song. He stood quietly in front of a photo of Sitting Bull. The Major and Kid tried to ask him questions but he simply grunted in response. There were dozens of photographs of groups of cowboys and scores of Indians. Willie tried to find himself. He spotted a group picture and noticed that his face was blocked out by a Cheyenne leaning into his space. He remembered that either he was absent or covered or misnamed in every image of the Wild West in which he appeared, like a ghost whose only claim to fame was a hundred deaths. He looked to see if the concession stand was selling nuts. No luck. "Time to go now," grumbled Willie. "Thirsty."

Luther and the boys were six sheets and nine rounds to the wind when the Major entered the Robin's Nest Bar. Luther laughed and pointed at the three unlikely companions. Two pitchers of cold

Coors beer and six empties sat on the tabletops where the band of raiders had spread out. Luther picked the spot near the picture windows so they could enjoy the panorama view of the cities of Golden and Denver just to the east.

"Hey," said one of the troopers, "you can see the brewery from here."

"I'll drink to that," answered Luther.

"We are going up to look at the grave," the Major interrupted. "You men will stop this joviality and join us. That's an order. We shall all now pay our respects to Colonel Cody. Put that pitcher down and fall in."

"Can I use the bathroom first, Major, or do you want me pissing in the woods?" Luther laughed, stumbled to his feet, and meandered toward the bathroom.

Several of the other men, closer to the facilities, jumped up and beat Luther to the conveniences because he took the time to turn and give the Major a sarcastic salute. He pantomimed shooting Kid with his finger. When he entered the bathroom, his cohorts occupied the single toilet stall and both urinals.

"Could be a while, Luther," one fellow joked.

"Got to go," Luther laughed. "This America's Fine Light brewed with Rocky Mountain spring water is going right through me. You only rent a beer, ya know."

He stood in front of the sink and unzipped his fly. "This'll do just fine." As he let go with a sigh, then growled, "Do you believe the Major? Who died and made him captain?"

Just as he finished and adjusted himself the large, burly bartender pushed open the door to the bathroom.

"You can't be thinking about pissing in the sink, you asshole," yelled the bartender.

"Too late," grinned Luther.

The bartender lifted Luther off the ground by his collar. "I'm throwing your butt out'a here, smart ass."

"You can't throw me out, you SOB., just cause you ain't got enough pissers to accommodate the Wyoming Legionnaires the first time we got'ta pass water."

"Yeah," said another, "you can't throw us out. This here is our contribution to the Colorado River."

The bartender held Luther off the floor a good eight inches. Luther wiggled and kicked the air to no avail. "You are all out of here, you bunch of Wyoming hicks." He turned toward the exit carrying Luther at arm's reach.

"It's all right, young man," pleaded the Major. "We were just leaving anyway. I'll take care of my friend here. You don't have to throw him out."

"Oh, it's my pleasure," said the bartender as he pushed open the door with his left hand and made ready to pitch Luther into the parking lot with his right.

"You can't treat a veteran like that," squawked one of the drunks.

"Yeah, we're Legionaires, you can't treat us like some kind of bums," said another.

"Major, tell this gorilla to put me down," choked Luther. "Kid, don't just stand there laughing, shoot the son-of-a-bitch."

"Silence!" yelled the Major. He turned apologetically to the bartender. "Sorry about the ruckus. I'll establish order, sir, I assure you."

"O.K., Major," acknowledged the bartender. "The nearest American Legion bar is down at the bottom of Lariat Trail in Golden. The drinks are a lot cheaper there and the bathroom is large enough to accommodate all you war heroes. Don't come back here." He dropped Luther on the floor.

"Oh, I'll be back all right," slurred Luther as his companions helped him off the ground. "We got business for now, but I'll be back."

"I assure you, sir, I'll take charge," repeated the Major. "And we will definitely be on our way. No business; we'll be heading home now." He turned toward Luther. "Sergeant, you will compose yourself and come to attention. You will apologize to this young man."

"Piss off, *Sir*" rebutted Luther and stumbled toward the street. The others followed, each mumbling their own exit insults.

All were out of ear shot when the bartender returned inside and grabbed the phone. "Hazel, get me the Sheriff, there is a band of Wyoming crazies on the mountain. They're all drunk and I think one of them is armed."

Sheriff Alan Sweet took the call himself even though he had three deputies under his supervision. He was young, energetic, ambitious, and loved police work. This was his first administrative position. He was a careerist. Underlings assumed he still enjoyed the day-to-day and was humble enough to do clerical or whatever was needed. In reality, he was a control freak.

"Well, I tell you, Bart, as a matter of coincidence I'm on my way to the Mayor's office as we speak, but if those Wyoming boys show up, call here and one of my deputies will get there lickety-split. Meanwhile, I'll have a car start up Lariat and take a look-see. You say you thought one of 'um, a kid, might be carrying a pistol? And another one is an Injun, right. That does sound a bit peculiar. I'll send a car around." He hung up the phone and thought *I'm hoping that this actually could be a problem. We could use a little excitement around here; after all, this is an election year.*

Sweet was surprised that there were several of the local muckety-mucks at the Mayor's office, including the Commandant of the National Guard at Camp George West just south of town.

"Have you seen this?" asked the Mayor as he thrust a paper toward the Sheriff.

Sweet read. It was a leaflet from the Wyoming American Legion offering a ten thousand dollar reward for the return of the remains of Buffalo Bill to Cody. No questions asked.

"Well, what do you think?" asked the Mayor.

"I think we may have a problem," answered Sweet. He purposefully kept his poker face, hiding a grin of anticipation.

"No one would take this seriously, do you think, Sheriff?" asked the Commandant.

"I've been on the phone with the editor of The Denver Post," said the editor of the local Golden Transcript. Sweet thought the editor's staccato rhythm of speech must come from being too long around the rat-a-tat-tat of the presses. "He says the Post is ready to declare war! You know, he's the Grand Poo-Bah of the Leyden-Chiles-Wickersham Post of the American Legion. I tell you, they're extremely vexed!"

"War! What kind of war? A range war? A feudal war? Florence versus Sienna? Golden versus Cody?" The Commandant, obviously amused by the hysterics of the editor, grinned at Sweet.

They both despised the Editor's propensity to name-drop.

"Well, as Commandant of an active military post, it is my professional *combat* opinion," he made quote marks in the air with his fingers, "that we allow cooler heads to prevail. I've never feared pamphlets or propaganda. Oh, I know a paper cut is the worst, but sorry, Ernie, as far as I'm concerned, the sword cuts deeper than the press."

"Pen!" shouted the editor. "Wars have been started based on a lot less than this, Commandant. This isn't the first time Cody and Wyoming have threatened to steal Old Bill. They have never admitted that Bill begged to be buried on Lookout. They have always professed that my old friend Tammem and the Post stole Bill from Cody. Bought him as a tourist attraction; paid-off the bereaved widow. Don't you read the papers?"

"I think we may have a problem, sir," repeated Sweet, "I just got a call from Bart, the bartender at the Robin's Nest. He had to throw out several drunken Legionnaires. I think he said they were from Wyoming."

"Holy shit," cried the Mayor.

Coolly, the Commandant took long strides to the phone. "This is Commandant Murphy, get me the officer of the day. I don't care where he is, get him. Well, go and get him. I want that camp on alert in five minutes, son. Get him off his butt, and back into his uniform. Tell him this could be war!"

"Holy shit," cried the Mayor,

"This is Commandant Murphy, Colonel Campbell, Alex, do I have your full attention? We may have a serious situation on Lookout Mountain. I want you to rev up two tanks and a full squad of men and get them the hell up Lariat Trail and set up a post at Buffalo Bill's grave. Use my parade tank."

The Commandant's tank was more of a parade float than a weapon of war. To make it look more formidable, it was equipped with an extra-long barrel that was actually plastic PVC pipe painted to look like hard steel. Soldiers serving under the Commandant weren't fooled but gullible parade spectators may have, as was the point, had a more positive opinion of the Commandant's virility as symbolized by the "cannon." The unenhanced tank had a functional 37mm gun. It was snub-nosed and too short and nonthreatening in appearance for the Commandant to ride in frequent parades, but it could actually fire forearm-sized shells.

"Yes, soldier, at the grave. And I want the appropriate unit fully armed, if you get my meaning." He paused, waiting for a response. He didn't get the answer he expected, "What the hell do you mean we've got no one to pilot the tanks? What about those two transfers from California? I don't give a damn if you haven't had a chance to check them out. Mount up and get your khaki butts up that mountain A.S.A.P. Hop to it, son!"

"Commandant, are you sure that's necessary? I can send a squad car up there," said Sweet. "Sending tanks up Lariat seems a bit radical?"

"Are you questioning my judgment, Chief?" asked the Commandant.

"Yeah, Sweet, are you questioning the Commandant's orders?" asked the editor. "For the record, I mean? Maybe I should call the Governor, he's a friend of mine; he probably has a statement. This is an election year. I should call the Post. They're *extremely* vexed! I've got a scoop here. Where's the phone?"

"Holy shit," cried the Mayor.

Chapter Eleven

Cactus Face

Summer, 1948

Upon my back you humans have cut circuitous scars. Roads and byways winding to isolated destinations, places where you trespassed into the realm of the spirits, Elysian places, the haunts of Turtle and Tierra Madre. You tread upon them and in so doing, turned them from sacred to secular. Just such a blemish have you scribed on Lookout Mountain and named it Lariat Trail. The ancient and pious Ute have been supplanted by utility vehicles.

    I have ridden the uplift from the vast plains and soared above this road; I have walked this serpentine path. In seven miles it climbs two thousand feet in altitude. On my lorica are thirty-six tight curves, including thirteen switchbacks, turns so dramatic that the road loops back upon itself and runs parallel to its own path at a slightly higher elevation, looking from above like ribbon candy.

    In more quiet times, before Buffalo Bill was buried at the peak of Lariat Trail and the summit of Lookout, when Denver was a small town nestled gently on my apron and recovering from the shenanigans of the gold rush, I would take delight in observing buckboards and wagons full of Sunday celebrants meander up Lariat Trail and picnic in quiet spots with magnificent views of Golden below and Denver to the east. Lately, however, since the invention of the automobile, I watch tourists and flat-land drivers risk life and limb venturing on Lariat Trail, trying to navigate the curves while enjoying the views. Children and grandmothers lean from one side of the car to the other as they progress around the tight switchbacks, as if shifting their piddling weights could save them from drifting over the edge.

    Seniors from Golden High School, located at the base of Lookout, often pull a colorful prank, you know I love trickery, and adolescence is a fertile stream in which to recruit. They jump in their jalopies and speed up Lariat, following a car full of tourists. They laugh at the rubberneck choreography: lean-left-lean-right; don't look down. The local students recklessly tailgate the tourists, flash their lights to unhinge the already nervous sightseers, pass them on a hairpin curve, being as bellicose as possible, and heckling them from paranoia to panic.

The youth consider it great fun, and it can be repeated while blasting both up and down the mountain. I am aware of only a few teenagers killed annually, and the number of oglers forced over the precipice is a deeply kept secret of the local chamber of commerce and their member merchants and bar owners.

Just when I thought I had seen everything, the most incongruous sight in decades has drawn me back to Lookout. Even if I had not seen it for myself, the noise would have awakened me and brought me near. You humans are so entertaining. You tempt disaster with such finesse. I must observe more closely; perhaps I can finally help my neophyte Wolf Song in his quest. I see a stage hereabout, ready to set with a scene or two for the foolhardy. I have become the playwright. The saga continues.

Army Reserve Captains William T. Rudolph and Alonzo P. Doogan were of the same mind. They knew immediately that there was something extremely dangerous and utterly ludicrous about driving these antiquated tanks up this narrow and winding mountain road.

Doogan grew up in the area. As a teenager, he and his hooligan friends took great delight in harassing tourists, scaring the sweet bejeezus out of them as they tried to negotiate the numerous sharp turns and precarious drop-offs.

"What's the name of this road?" Captain Rudolph, Doogan's cohort in the second tank, yelled above the Triassic clamber of the treads.

"Lariat Trail, why, what difference does it make?"

Rudolph answered, "I want to know what folks are going to read in our obituaries."

"These tanks are prehistoric," Doogan yelled at Rudolph. A brief daydream eased past his adrenaline attentiveness. He envisioned two triceratops trying to escape extinction by clawing their way up a steep, sandy dune. Claw as they might, gravity sucked them down. In the end they rotated slowly at the bottom of the gigantic sand bowl, in a slow-motion flush, a final pirouette, their smallish forelegs extended in a futile effort to slow the spin or hold them aloft. The last whirling image was of their fierce, beak-like jaws, snapping a curse as their huge maws filled with the suffocating sand.

He was jerked out of his fantasy by a sudden jolt of the tank as it jostled around a hairpin turn. Doogan could see the wreckage of an old car several hundred feet below, crushed and crammed between some rocks. He knew that kids often pushed old cars over the edge for fun, but he also knew that, once in a while, drivers—usually drunks, sometimes tourists—missed a turn. He gestured to get Rudolph's attention and then pointed downward at the wreck.

"What a horrible way to go," Rudolph yelled.

Rudolph and Doogan had opened the emergency exit doors in the back of the turrets of their WWI, Renault designed tanks. Each sat through the double doors, outside the turret on the roof of the engine housing, with their feet dangling inside the tanks. Ordinarily, they would stand in the gunner's position, but the idea of standing, enclosed in the claustrophobic canister, blind to the world except for peering through the gun sight, crawling at two miles per hour—three on a straightaway—for seven miles and a dozen hairpin switchbacks, seemed more like punishment than command. It reminded Rudolph of solitary confinement in the hot box of a Southern chain-gang prison. "Put your feet on the bunk; it's a night in the box."

"Did you say something, sir?" asked the pilot of his tank. He sat in a confined space at the front of the tank, under another pair of double, hinged doors, peering through a tiny window propped open more for air than visibility.

"If this is some kind of a joke, some kind of initiation for the new officers, it isn't funny. It's dangerous. Is there someone in the company who knows Captain Doogan from high school? Did Doogan piss off some teacher who's become a general? Did he get somebody's sister pregnant? The commandant's daughter?" Rudolph noticed his voice had an edge of anger tinged with fright. He was leaning over and yelling through the interior of the tank.

"Sir?"

"A joke—is this some kind of an initiation for new guys, or are you Colorado clowns just crazy? Having someone drive an old tank like this M1917 up this road?"

"Sir?"

"Pilot, do you think this is funny?" He yelled again through the turret emergency door and past his feet.

He knew he wouldn't be heard if he tried to yell past the turret, which blocked his view of the road straight ahead. However, he could see the shoulder to the right and noticed that the tank was approaching the edge. He could see the town of Golden a thousand feet below.

Because the radios and headsets were not functional—FUBAR since the last parade and forgotten, the pilot opened his two entrance plates, hung like tilted cabinet doors, and pulled himself up, but the vertical hung doors kept closing on him as he leaned forward through his view port and entry. He had turned back counterclockwise, opposite the shoulder of the road and the drop-off. His contortion and being bounced back into his driver's seat by the rattling doors had inadvertently generated a slight pull on the right ball-capped steering lever. He was looking up toward Rudolph trying to hear.

"Watch where you're going, son!"

"Sir?" The driver tried to turn and face his captain, but the space was too confining.

"The road, soldier, the road! Watch the road!"

The driver looked forward, fell back into his seat and quickly jerked the tank back onto Lariat Trail.

"Sir, yes, sir." he barked, and then sheepishly said, "Sorry, sir."

"You know, Doogan," Rudolph yelled above the noise, "my ex-wife is still miffed about me leaving California."

"Yeah, you told me. She's afraid you'll forget to mail the alimony checks."

"She always thought you were a bad influence; led me down the wrong road."

"She's a smart girl, Rudi. I always liked Nancy Jane, but you didn't need my help making wrong turns. Sorry, but what has this got to do with our current predicament? You're blaming all this on me, aren't you?"

"When I'd get caught coming home at sunrise and she'd ask where the hell I'd been and I always said, 'With Doogan,' she'd accuse me of following you everywhere. I remember just before we left Pendleton, she carped, 'If Doogan drove over a cliff . . . ?' Well, if you go over at the next curve, Captain, you're going to force me to make my ex a liar. I ain't following you this time."

"I knew Nancy Jane didn't like me, Rudi, but I had no idea it was because you blamed your philandering on me. Bad influence my ass; if I go over, I'm taking you with me."

"And leave poor Nancy Jane a widow? Haven't you hurt her enough?"

"You're divorced, ya nitwit. I don't think technically she can be called a widow." Doogan turned toward the second tank, his back to the road ahead. "Besides, Captain Rudolph, Nancy Jane was right. You're dumb enough to follow me off this cliff. You can't do anything without me. How many times have I bailed you out of trouble?"

"One for all . . .," laughed Rudolph, "wasn't that our motto?"

"That was our creed while drinking beer and slugging it out in bar fights, Rudi, not for making life-changing decisions, not for career goals. I have to admit, I was a little surprised when you volunteered for duty in Colorado, a California beach boy like yourself. No wonder Nancy Jane hates me."

"She'll really be pissed if you get us killed, Doogan. She'll probably never speak to you again. Me neither." Rudolph paused. He was smiling.

Doogan interpreted Rudi's grin as a bulls eye, that his jibe had hit its target and that he, Doogan, was indeed concerned that Rudi's ex-wife blamed him for her husband's rambunctious behavior. He felt sad about their divorce, but knowing Rudi as well as he did; honestly, the marriage never had a chance. Rudolph yelled something and brought Doogan back. "What?"

"I said," said Rudolph, "I never realized before that I'm afraid of heights and I'm really starting to hate the smell of pine."

"Well, you better get used to it; we're stuck here for our last hitch, ya prevaricating ass hole. Now quit your bitching and enjoy the beautiful mountain scenery."

"Back at ya', Captain Doogan; time to take your eye off the mountains; you're drifting toward the scenery."

Doogan looked to see that Rudolph was right and yelled down, "Pilot, watch the damn road. Are you trying to get us killed?" He laughed to himself that the youngster was still wearing his helmet with the defunct earphones. It had to make it harder to hear, which was their most looming problem and Doogan doubted the flimsy helmet would save the lad if they did indeed drive over the edge.

"Sorry, Captain, but the slope is so steep I'm having trouble seeing the road past the bow of the tank. When we take a curve or get near the edge, all I can see is the tops of the trees and the sky."

"That's an affirmative, soldier, but if I stand inside the turret in the gunner position, my view is even worse than yours. Sitting back here, I'll try to watch the road past the turret, and if it looks like we're going over, I'll drum loudly on the turret. By the way, what's your name, son?"

"Earl, sir, and may I say: Welcome to the Forty-second Armored, Colorado National Guard, Camp George West, sir."

"We'll shake hands later, Earl. Thanks for the welcome. For now, just keep your eyes trained forward."

"Sir, yes, sir. It will be a lot easier to see on the way down, sir."

It had not crossed Doogan's mind that, yes—indeed, they were going to have to drive these seven ton monstrosities back down this hellish road. He mumbled, "As you were, Earl. I hope our brakes are good."

Rudolph yelled, "Seriously, Doogan, you heard the orders, what are we doing on this sidewinder?"

"The commandant simply said to hustle two tanks ASAP to the top of the mountain and post guard at the gravesite."

"Gravesite? What gravesite. Who'd be crazy enough to get buried up here? Who's grave are we talking?"

"Buffalo Bill."

"Who?" asked Rudolph, almost to himself. "Bill who? I'm Bill." He asked his pilot. "Who's grave? Some Bill's grave?" He looked back toward the leading tank. "Doogan, you know I'm superstitious. I don't like a grave nearby with the name Bill on it. Is this some kind of a joke?"

The voice from below in his tank said, "Buffalo, Sir."

"Where?" barked Rudolph as he rotated, the turret obstructing his pivot. "There's buffalo up here?"

"Actually, yes, sir, but not on this side of the mountain. On the south side, about twelve or thirteen clicks from here, sir. We have a buffalo pasture. But that's not where we're going, sir. We're going to guard Buffalo Bill's grave, sir. We're not protecting the bison, sir; you know, buffalos, the animal. We're posting guard for Buffalo, as in Bill, sir. He's on this side. That is, his grave is on this side. Sir."

"You are trying to be funny, aren't you, soldier?"

"Sir, no, sir!"

"Then what the hell are you talking about?"

"Buffalo Bill, sir. He's buried on Lookout Mountain."

"This mountain?"

"Sir, yes, sir."

"Stop that."

"Yes, sir."

"Soldier."

"Sir?"

"Watch the road. I'll be right back."

The tank jerked back toward the middle of the pavement. Rudolph climbed out of his tank, slid down the engine housing, rode sidesaddle on the skid tail for a moment, adroitly got his footing, and walked uphill to Doogan's tank. It wasn't much of a race. He climbed aboard the extended tail housing and lounged comfortably behind Doogan. He looked forward and laughed at the six-foot cannon barrel on Doogan's tank. Rudolph's tank was equipped with the historical 37mm, short-nosed cannon. "Ooo, Cactus Face, yours is bigger than mine."

"According to my pilot, Earl," said Doogan. "the Commandant uses this tank for parades and carnivals. That's why mine has a new camouflaged paint job and yours looks like an old dying, stegosaurus. Jealous?"

"I tell you seriously, Captain Doogan, I'm not looking forward to meeting our new commander, not if taking tanks up this miserable road is his idea of defensive strategy. We may have made a mistake thinking our last hitch would be a snap here in Colorado. We may not live to see retirement."

"You might be right, Rudolph. I thought if we got to Colorado we could pool our pensions and buy ourselves a little piece of the bourgeoning ski business. It's going to boom soon and there is a fortune to be made. I've got friends from the old Tenth Mountain Ski Division. They're begging me to get involved."

"I got nothing against getting rich, Cactus Face, but to tell you the truth, more than money, my motivation was that there would be a lot of playing tag with ski-bunnies."

"I know what motivates you, Rudi. Chasing tail: ski bunnies, surfer girls, strippers, coeds, nurses, waitresses, nurses. Hell, I've even witnessed you hustling a dog catcher."

"I like a woman who loves animals. That's why Nancy Jane and I get along. Well . . . used to get along. Besides, poontang is not a bad motivator. Of course, we have to live long enough to meet some local girls. Soldier," he yelled to the trailing tank, "do you see this curve coming up?"

"Sir, yes, sir," came the muffled answer.

"So, Captain Rudolph, have you deserted your post?"

"Seriously, Doogan—sir—if I see a break in these woods, I may make a run for it. AWOL or no AWOL, court-martial be damned. They're going to have a hell of a time finding me in this forest."

"They'd find you in an hour, Rudi, probably in the nearest bar. What makes you think you can hide in these mountains? This isn't California, it's Colorado, Captain, the Wild West. We're crawling in bounty hunters, Indian scouts, professional trackers. Hell, you couldn't hide from our local boy scouts."

"Hey, don't sell my skills at hide and seek short, Doogan. I just need a quick refresher. After all, there's no place to hide on the beach. Besides, I think I've got a little Indian blood in me."

"You've got salt water in your veins, Rudi. Everybody thinks there's a Cherokee princess in their past. But trust me, Captain, you haven't got enough Indian blood in you to survive a nosebleed."

"Look, Doogan, you know I'm behind you all the way. Who else would put up with your harebrained schemes? But, seriously, I *am* a sea level, Redondo Beach kind of guy, you know what I mean. Look over the edge, CF, that's one serious wipeout. If we go much higher, I'm going to get that nosebleed."

"If you do, Rudi, I'll put you in for a Purple Heart."

The pilot below yelled, "Did you say something, sir?".

"Keep your eyes on the road, soldier," the two Captains barked in duet.

"Sir, yes, sir. Sorry, sir, sorry. Sirs, sorry, sirs." He corrected his cadence.

Rudolph laughed, "Your puppy is housebroke even better than mine," and slid off the back of the lead tank. "Returning to duty, Captain Cactus Face, Sir, yes, Sir." It was an easy downhill jog and climb to remount his dinosaur.

If he tried, Doogan could see his old house below the winding road and sheer slope. He had driven the Lariat Loop many times as a teenager, both the safe south side, Mount Vernon Canyon, and this slithering serpent, Lariat Trail. Both ways will eventually get you to Buffalo Bill's grave. One, only somewhat perilous, you are in the mountains after all, and this route, as dangerous as a coiled viper. The southern route skirted Golden and climbed a gentler, less curvy two-lane highway, US 40, up Mount Vernon Canyon. This northern trek, this rattler of a road started not far from his old house on the western edge of Golden. Memories, mimicking the meandering road, curled into his mind.

In high school he dated a girl who lived in Mount Vernon Country Club, a genteel foothills suburb on the southern slope of Lookout Mountain. To get to her house he sometimes drove Lariat Trail as part of the wild bunch, scaring tourists, but more often took the long way, the southern loop. Just before the gated entrance to Mount Vernon Country Club was an old, flat-roofed adobe building. It was totally out of place for the mountains of Colorado. Local builders usually imitated Alpine architecture, even here in the foothills. This building borrowed its blueprint from Northern New Mexico. He had seen similar designs during visits with his parents to Santa Fe and Taos. It appeared earthy with a low ceiling; its height was based on human proportions. Rather than sliding off steep sloped trusses, the weighty winter snows were supported via the girth of the walls and the simple post and beam structure. Large logs, vigas, supported the roof and interior ceiling and the blunt ends stuck out of the exterior walls along the roofline. The door was painted turquoise. He wondered what possessed the builder to snuggle a cozy, old adobe onto this hairpin exit from a canyon highway in the foothills of Colorado. But he liked the building; it was unique and somehow inviting. He often took this longer way to Sharon's because of the adobe and, despite the greater mileage, because it had fewer curves and was faster—Sharon waited in the woods at the end of the road.

Once in the car, riding shotgun, Sharon, however, insisted they exit Lookout the other way—Lariat Trail. She liked that it had more curves than a boa constrictor, was a driver's challenge, a dare devil's dream, and filled with danger and adventure. Sharon loved Lariat Trail. She particularly liked it at night. There was little or no traffic, and she could view the lights of Denver. She would murmur in Doogan's ear that there was something romantic about being so high that you felt airborne, and she loved the way the distant lights of a big city beckoned her. Riding a tank up Lariat would have tickled her roller coaster sense of adventure.

The clambering of the tank became almost rhythmical; he allowed it to take him back to a happier and less dangerous time. Doogan almost pulled away as Sharon's soft, amorous hands reached to hold his chin in an affectionate cup. Ever since puberty, he was self-conscious about his abrasive beard. It had always been difficult for him to accept that she found his prickly-pear complexion attractive. Later, a great number of other women thought it intriguing, and more than a few considered it inviting. Even in the dim light of his bedroom he could see that his date's face, particularly around her full mouth, was red and raw with the love rash for which he was infamous. Despite his embarrassment, he was fond of his nickname—Cactus Face. There was a semi-famous football player from Oklahoma with the same nickname. He and his dad played ball together. Doogan had played football. For jocks, a moniker is important, and he liked the frontier, macho connotation that *Cactus Face* conjured. Doogan was still a large athletically built man. His full head of hair was thick and black with only a trace of gray at the temples. He unconsciously touched his temple and thought again about Sharon.

His stubble had proved to be a problem even in high school. There was no hiding the fact from Sharon's father that she and Doogan had been amorous. That was obviously not an innocent blush on the young girl's cheeks. He remembered prom night and the party after the dance, when all the graduating seniors changed from their formal wear to shorts and cutoff jeans. Several girls noticed Doogan's cholla needle rash on the inside of Sharon's thighs. He remembered how she sidestepped the embarrassment. "He's a real fun date—affectionate as hell," she giggled, took his hand and swung it playfully, exaggerating innocence, "but you definitely need time to heal."

He remembered a bit of envy in the laughing responses of the girls, and how the cupidity of the boys was visible and obvious.

The tank and his dreams rumbled on until a squeaky voice came from the pilot below, "Sir? Is there a curve ahead? All I can see is the sky. We're not on a cliff, are we, sir? Sir?"

Doogan returned to the road and heard the loud ka-chug-a-chug-a-chugging of the ancient tanks fighting gravity. The Budha HV, four-cylinder, forty-two horses were under gunned for the incline of Lariat Trail. "Go left until you see the trees, Earl." Doogan was only half conscious as they lumbered, their great weight taking bites out of the pavement as they pivoted around a switchback. Rumbling, like rejects from the Cretaceous, they continued their slow meandering climb up Lariat Trail. Doogan let his memories slip behind him. He pictured them coasting downhill, around the dangerous curves, going too fast, no brakes, seeking adventure, risking an airborne leap off the edge, exploding like fireworks, the remnants glittering and showering his hometown.

He turned around to see if Rudolph had noticed his daydreaming. He watched Rudi's tank maneuver the tight curve. It had been a couple of decades since he had seen these old models, let alone driven one. The Renault FT17, the M1917 copy, manufactured in America, was a World War I relic. They were originally designed for one person. The poor Frog had to pilot the clumsy machine, load and fire the canon himself. No wonder the French got their antique-loving asses kicked by the Germans. These tanks looked more like a concept from a designer of toys than an engineer of war machinery. The profile of their treads was egg shaped, a dinosaur egg with a huge fat end toward the front and a small, pointed end rolling up the rear. A primitive design, the tuna can turret sat between the ancient reptilian eggs, dwarfed by the treads. The gunner-captain stood like Jack trapped in his box, and the pilot wrestled to maneuver the unwieldy turtle using two levers that reigned in or freed the treads.

"It must be saboteurs," yelled Rudolph.

"What?" called Doogan, not totally recovered from his reminiscences.

"That's got to be the real reason we are tanking up this road. Sabotage. Maybe someone is trying to blow up those radio towers I see on top. Cactus Face, Sir, there are more twists and turns in this road than a bate worm just hooked, and I'd rather be trolling just now—know what I mean."

Before Doogan could answer, his tank took a large slab out of the shoulder on the drop off side of the road. A cloud of dust and spitting gravel filled the air. "Pilot," called Doogan, "let's try to keep her somewhere near the middle of the road. How long have you been driving tanks?"

"This is my third weekend, Sir."

"You're kidding, right? Right?"

"Right it is, Sir."

Doogan panicked—he was starting to turn. "As you were, soldier, as you were. Do not go starboard. Is that clear? Let's keep her in the center."

"Center it is, Sir."

Rudolph yelled across, "It must be saboteurs, otherwise this is total looney tunes. You suppose any of them are women? We may have to force some information out of 'um, if you know what I mean."

"I know what you mean, Rudolph. I always know what you mean, and you always mean the same thing. Keep your mind on the driving, Casanova, you're drifting toward the edge. This is a hell of a view, Bill. You can see the Coors Brewery down there in the valley, and I believe that bright spot, way over there, just below the horizon, is the capitol building in Denver. It's amazing how the gold dome lights up in the sun."

"Yep, it's a great view all right, but you better keep your eye on the road, yourself, scout."

"Hard to port, Earl. Let's be careful here."

"Sorry, Captain, but the road is so steep I'm steering by staring at the tree tops."

"Roger that, Earl. I'll be more help. Just been enjoying the view. Brings back old memories. Guess I've missed this part of the country. Let's take a slight turn port and get us in the middle of this twister. We've got a serious switchback coming up to the left. I'll take you around."

The tank scuffed its way left. Rudolph's tank followed. A pick-up truck descending the trail rounded the hidden curve and suddenly met the tanks face to face.

"Halt, Earl!" Doogan screamed. "Holy hell, halt!" He pounded on the drum of a turret.

The tank convulsed as it tried to shake off its momentum. It made a prehistoric groan.

The truck skidded, its grill stopping just inches from the protruding tank treads. It made a modern scream.

The cosmetic barrel of the tank cannon crashed through the windshield of the pick-up.

The driver of the truck looked for a long moment at the huge gun filling his cab. He eased open the door and unfurled on the pick-up running board. "Boy howdy." he said calmly as he looked at the cannon's intrusion into his truck. "I almost lost an eye."

"You almost lost a head," yelled Doogan. "Is anyone hurt?"

Slowly, shyly, a young girl's face emerged from under the canon and into view through the shattered windshield. Her complexion was white from fright, her eyes large and dark.

"Are you OK, Flora?" asked the driver. "Boy howdy." He leaned inside the truck, reached over the canon barrel and turned off the radio. He stood back on the running board, lifted his cowboy hat, scratched his head, and looked over the edge of the cliff to his left. "I did the right thing, huh? Not swerving I mean. That's one hellacious precipice." He looked to Doogan as if expecting some kind of congratulations for not killing himself. "I knew ya'll were coming up the trail, but I didn't expect to meet ya so soon. Boy howdy!"

"Well, it's nice to meet you, too, cowboy," said Doogan, amazed at the driver's calm. "Is she all right?"

"Oh, yeah, she's okey-dōkey," he answered. "She don't talk much." The girl waved meekly at Doogan. "I'm just glad I was driving or someone could'a got hurt."

"I said, back her up slowly," Doogan heard Rudolph yelling frantically behind him. Relief turned to alarm when he saw that the second tank had swerved to the right to avoid rear-ending his tank, and hung precariously over the shoulder of the road. The drop-off looked like the entrance to a ski jump, the city of Golden squatted below looking like an anthill.

"Pilot," said Rudolph, "now don't panic, but I'm going to get out and move to the stern of the tank. Redistribute the weight, get it? Pilot, you stay put and let's get this coffin into reverse. Sorry, bad choice of words. And don't worry, boy, I'm with you all the way."

Doogan watched Rudolph climb from the canister and stand on the skid tail of the tank. He looked back at Cactus Face, shook his head "no-way", clapped his hands together and pantomimed as if he were going to dive head first off the rear of the tank.

"You okay?" Rudolph yelled, but looked at Doogan. Now he thumbed toward the housing and with his other hand, pointed a finger, and circled his ear in a gesture that clearly communicated: he-must-be-crazy-if-he-thinks-I'm-staying-with-this-tank.

"I think so, sir," a meek voice echoed from the canister. "Captain Rudolph, are you still there?"

"I'm here, son," he said as he looked behind the tank for an appropriate spot to jump.

The tank lurched as the pilot shifted it into reverse. Rudolph jumped, Doogan bit his lip, the quiet girl screamed, the cowboy tried to talk but fright closed his throat. "Bo...," was all that squeaked out.

It seemed an eternity, but finally the treads stopped slipping and grabbed the gravel shoulder. In sporadic leaps backward the tank inched its way onto the road and parked.

The pilot threw open the double doors and nervously stuck his head out of the housing. "How did I do, sir? Sir?" He couldn't spot Rudolph.

"You did great, kid," came Rudolph's voice from the shoulder of the road, exactly at the spot where they almost went over. Rudolph was apparently calming himself or castigating the gods by urinating over the cliff, his yellow stream arching into the wild blue just beyond the point of potential disaster. "You did great. Couldn't have done better myself." He looked toward Doogan with an expression that sought a confirmation that he was still alive and remained an irreverent friend.

"That was close", grinned the driver of the pick-up. "We heard you guys might actually be coming up, so I was sent down to look for you."

"Well you found us," said Doogan. "Who are you anyway?"

"I live on Lookout. I'm part of the local militia. We heard that some sons-a-bitches from Wyoming was trying to steal Old Bill."

"Old Bill?" asked Doogan.

"Buffalo Bill, you know . . ."

"Why would anyone want to steal Old Bill? He's still dead isn't he?"

"Well, now you're just joshing me. 'Course he's dead. Buried even. I believe those Wyoming sons-a-bitches want to excavate him and take his earthy remains back to Cody, Wyoming, the sons-a-bitches."

"You mean exhume, don't you, cowboy?"

"No, I mean they want dig him up and steal his bones."

"Those sons-a-bitches," said Doogan.

"Boy howdy," said Rudolph.

"I'm OK," said the pale girl.

Chapter Twelve

Lariat Trail

Summer, 1948

Many of you humans have a propensity for folly, self-destructive mayhem, but others of you simply have a creative knack for entertaining pandemonium. You're catalysts. This Doogan seems to enjoy the tumult and the danger; he appears receptive. There's promise here. Despite his tendencies to attract bedlam, his calm reminds me of a tenet by Joseph Brant, Thayendanegea, a Mohawk. He says, "No person among us desires any other reward for performing a brave and worthy action, but the consciousness of having served his nation."

"Lead on, Captain Doogan," said Captain Rudolph, "but next time you stop that prehistoric monster, give a signal; your brake lights are out."

Doogan watched the pick-up back away from his tank and off the faux cannon. He could see and hear pieces of shattered windshield fill the seat and bounce over the hood of the truck. He could not hear what the cowboy was mumbling to the big-eyed girl. They both had their heads turned around watching the way as he backed the old Chevy, but Doogan guessed that "boy howdy" was in there somewhere.

By this time several other pick-up trucks and half a dozen sedans had pulled behind the wounded truck. People leaned out the windows for a better view of the other absurd machines. Several parked their cars on the narrow shoulders of the road and began walking next to the incongruous monsters. A line of a dozen vehicles had appeared behind Rudolph's tank. More vehicles quickly joined the queue.

"What the hell is going on," Doogan said aloud, "Going to be one hell of a traffic jam."

"I don't think so, Sir," said Earl the pilot, "Look at those cars turning around. I think its going to be a parade."

Earl was right. Cars and trucks on the up-side of the tanks took turns turning around and pulled over to make room for Doogan to pass. The cars on the downhill side behind Rudolph continued lining up, honking their horns and flashing their lights. The drivers and passengers gave a Bronx hurrah.

Doogan mumbled to himself, "I believe we've lost the element of surprise."

The tanks passed so closely to the parked cars that passengers put their hands out the windows to touch the slow ceratopsians. Females blew kisses to Doogan and Rudolph. One coed opened her blouse and flashed her ample cleavage.

Rudolph yelled, "I'm changing my mind, Captain Doogan. You're right about the view. Them there are some kind of hills, if you know what I mean. I think I'm going to like it here in Colorado."

"Try not to hit the cars," answered Doogan.

The parade progressed at a titanic, mechanical snail's pace. Doogan remained careful, skeptical, and somewhat confused by the bedlam. Rudolph lifted his shirt several times and flashed his chest to young ladies parked along the roadway.

Twenty minutes and four miles later, up the meandering road, a carload of college kids were pushing their rumple seat Model T. It had patches of red and gray primer and several Greek letters painted in a variety of gaudy colors, representing both fraternities and sororities.

"It just died on us," yelled a young coed kneeling backwards in the passenger seat.

Rudolph raised his shirt for her, but she took no notice.

"Boy howdy, gal, you are holding up the military," yelled the cowboy through his glassless windshield.

"Get that jalopy out of the way," another driver yelled from behind the tanks.

Rudolph lifted his shirt again and whistled loudly. Doogan grinned, but there was still no acknowledgment from the coed.

A loud impatient avalanche of horns and complaints piled up on the slippery slope.

"Push it over," someone yelled.

Doogan noticed an ominous linear progression as the idea dawned, like falling dominoes, on the lads pushing the car. Each grinned as the destructive suggestion hit him and then turned his head to see if the idea had sunk in with his nearest cohort.

"Yea, let's push it over."

"No," said the girl kneeling in the passenger seat. "I've got a better idea." She stood up in the seat and began leading a sideline cheer, "Have the tank push it over! Have the tank push it over!"

All joined in. The horns grew louder and the crowd began chanting, "Push it over, push it over, push it over."

"That's a negative," Doogan rebutted.

The girl from the jalopy jumped from the car, ran to the first tank and climbed up next to Doogan. She wrapped her arms around his neck and pleaded, "Yeah, come on, Cap-ee-tan, Sir. You can do it. Just push the old clunker over the edge. It'll be jake."

The crowd cheered reinforcement: "Push it over, push it over, push . . ."

She rubbed her hand along his cheek, "Come on, man, you can . . ." She paused and rubbed his chin again and in a more private and sultry voice said, "My, you are *quite* a man aren't you."

"Let me do it, Cactus Face," yelled Rudolph. "Hey, Girlie, I'll do it. You can ride on my tank."

"Cactus Face," she cooed. "Come on, Captain Cactus Face. I'll bet you *can* do it."

"Yeah . . . well," he blushed. "You better jump down, Miss. This is the property of the U. S. Army National Guard. We don't need anyone hurt. You kids just push your car over to the shoulder and we can probably get by."

"Come on, Captain," yelled the boy who was driving the car and was now next to the tank.

"Yea, please, Cactus Face," hummed the young girl and she rubbed his chin again.

"Captain Doogan, Captain Doogan," yelled Earl from inside the tank. " I keep getting broken messages on the radio. There's a lot of static but I thinks it's the Commandant. Sir, I think he's caught in the traffic jam behind us. It's huge. He sounds pissed, sir. He wants to know what's holding things up. What should I tell him?"

"Tell him we have an old jalopy blocking the curve."

"Captain, the Commandant says it may be an attempt by the Wyoming guys to detain the tanks. He says proceed at all costs, posthaste, but get up this mountain."

"It's no Wyoming plot," said Doogan. "Tell the Commandant that . . ."

The girl cut him off, "Now's your chance Captain Doogan. You can do it." She suddenly stood up and yelled to the crowd, "The Commandant says it's okay to push it off!"

The crowd renewed its chants, "Push it off, push it off, push the car off . . ."

"Well, maybe . . .," said Doogan more to himself than in response. Before he could finish his thought the girl jumped up and down, pulled off her white sweater with a large Delta Gamma embroidered in red and twirled it over her head. Horns and cheers of appreciation reverberated off the mountain.

"We can do it, sir," said Earl, a gleeful voice from below. He was holding his thumb up, mimicking a pilot's affirmative gesture. "It could be, like she said—'jake'."

Doogan looked down into the tank and had to laugh aloud at Earl's mischievous grin.

"What the hell," said Doogan. "Put her in gear, Earl. We'll back the old clunker off. Use the skid tail. The tracks extend too far beyond the bow; they'll just eat the rumble seat. Let's get this zoo on the road. Or, off the road, should I say. The animals are getting restless."

"I think I'm going to love it here," screamed Rudolph as he raised his shirt again.

The girl grabbed Doogan's face and rubbed it between her breasts. As he pulled away he could see the instant rash above her bra. "Yeah, it might be O.K. at that," he chirped.

The girl dove from the tank, did a quick tuck and landed in a cheerleading seat drop into the arms of the college kid. He flung her in the air; she landed with a bounce and chorus-line kick, as she raised her arms in a victory salute.

The boys guided the old auto down the edge of the switchback toward the narrow shoulder. Earl pulled the tank into the space just vacated with Doogan calling out from above. As Doogan yelled directions down through the tight cabin, Earl slowly backed the tank toward the car. Doogan pounded on the turret when the two machines met. The coed jumped on the back of the tank and led a cheer dedicated to destruction. The kid who was driving the jalopy checked to make sure the skid plate of the tank was up against the rear of the car. The trunk bowed under the misfit but began to roll forward.

"Push it over, push it over . . . ," chanted the crowd. Doogan thought the chant was deeper, less frantic, more determined, with a Lord-of-the-Flies tone to it. "Push it over, push it over . . ."

The old Model T was no burden for the tank. Doogan warned the cheerleader to jump off; she was in danger of taking a fall. He offered his hand to help her down. Earl couldn't see; he was taking his cue from another of the college kids standing upslope and in front of the tank. The undergraduate gave him the okay. Earl gave the car one last nudge. The girl gave Doogan a questioning smile that seemed to say that she interpreted his order as flirtatious, as if she suddenly became demure. Instead of grabbing his extended hand, she took a coquettish pose: hands on her hips. Before Doogan could yell, the tank halted with a lurch. He saw the car lunge forward and roll toward the cliff. When the tank floundered, the coed lost her balance and slipped off the side, past the turret, in a running tumble toward the car. The old car eased over the edge into the air; the girl spun her arms like a whirligig in a hurricane, attempting to regain her precarious balance as the old wreck arched into a swan dive, seemed momentarily to gain the ability to fly, then nosed into an explosive dance of demolishment. The crowd gasped as the girl stumbled along the same path.

"Oh, hell," yelled Doogan.

"Oh, hell no . . . ," yelled Rudolph.

The driver of the jalopy grabbed at her sweater that was waving like a flag as she gained momentum. It slipped from her hand and he stood dumfounded and helpless. At the very last second, sprinting from near the pick-up, the cowboy ran up behind her, reached around her just below shoulder height and, with a technique learned from bulldogging calves, grabbed her—saving the day. His eyes were now as huge as his partner's back in the pick-up. It was difficult to tell if his expression was from the surprised satisfaction of having just saved a life or getting ample handfuls of coed. Doogan heard the parade go berserk with joy.

"Boy howdy," the cowboy cooed and hung on.

"On to the grave," the DG yelled as she pushed out from his hold. She gave Doogan an embarrassed smile as she straightened her skirt, and her boyfriend gave her back the sweater she had lost. The boyfriend looked at the rash still evident on her cleavage. It was as red as her blushing face. He also gave Doogan a sheepish grin.

The cowboy was smiling more broadly than anyone as he returned to his pick-up and started the engine. His girlfriend leaned over and, hugging his neck, gave him a huge kiss on the cheek. Doogan thought he heard the words ". . . my hero," sometime during the smooch.

The rest of the spectators scrambled for their cars. Several walked beside the tanks with the college kids. Doogan noticed his pilot straining to get a look at the cute girl from his narrow, confining seat.

"Keep her between the cars, Earl," said Doogan.

"Aye, aye, Cactus Face," gleefully responded the pilot.

"Call me Captain, Earl."

Chapter Thirteen

Best Laid Plans

Summer, 1948

I am pleased to find that you humans illustrated me, Turtle, in historical documents. I often see myself on old maps along with daunting images of sea serpents and monsters. I don't mind. I also found my likeness in religious documents, most often holding up some other beast—an elephant, for example—which holds up the world. Close enough. My favorite affectation is when I am placed on old navigation charts next to the edge of the world over which an unfortunate ship is cascading to its destruction. Seems right.

I discovered also that over the centuries you humans love documenting yourselves via photography. Although Wolf Song was portrayed in several historical photographs of The Wild West, he was never correctly named or captioned. He, of course, believes that these mistakes are purposeful insults perpetuated by Buffalo Bill.

Historical photographs often show great explorers, adventurers, exploiters sometimes, Napoleon's soldiers, for example, standing atop great monuments and natural wonders. They are usually in silhouette, dwarfed by the vastness of nature and history. Huge skies filled with dramatic sunsets, even in black and white photos, usually serve as a histrionic background.

Captain Alonzo P. Doogan wished that people would stop taking pictures of him sitting on top of his tank. The sky was beginning to fill with what would probably prove to be a theatrical sunset. Huge anvils of cumulus nimbus floating above the distant horizons caught the last of the sun as it slide behind the hills, creating giant fiery curtains to the end of day. He would have liked to enjoy it, but the flash of the cameras was hurting his eyes. He thought he was going blind. Doogan was disgusted with the melee.

Captain Rudolph, on the other hand, looked as if he was trying to duplicate those archived images seen in every book about war. "Captain William Rudolph," the caption would read, "hero, silhouetted and majestic." He sat on the top of his tank posing. Doogan watched the pandemonium from his perch next to the crystalline monument tombstone of Colonel William Frederick Cody: Buffalo Bill.

The commandant had radioed orders that he wanted a tank parked literally "on top" of the grave. Doogan had Earl maneuver the bogus rhino, the impotent parade pachyderm, as close to the monument as he could, without knocking it over. Rudolph's tank, with its functioning thirty-seven millimeters of firepower, parked on the opposite side of the grave, facing the other direction. Doogan sent Earl and the other pilot to scout some grub while he awaited further orders. Doogan and Rudolph sat the watch.

"Who would be crazy enough to try to steal this old coot's bones in the middle of this circus?" Doogan asked no one in particular.

"You talking to me, Cactus Face?" Rudolph asked, posing for a top-heavy tomato.

"I'm saying this is insane. No one is going to try to rob this grave with these tanks sitting here and half of Colorado cavorting just down the road. Look at that nonsense. Talk about killing the fatted calf." He looked toward the grandstand. "Holy Moses! Look, Rudi! Some old geezer *is* setting up to make a speech. Tell me it's not D. W. Griffith."

"Well, Cactus Face, don't look now but that old fart is wearing a uniform, and I believe I see a bird on his collar."

Doogan waited for his eyes to adjust; he still saw spots from the flash bulbs. "You don't suppose? You're right. That's probably our Commandant.

"This is my fault, Rudolph, I should never have convinced you that Colorado was the place to finish our hitch. I don't blame you if you pull your side arm and pump a .45 slug in me right now. You could plead insanity—mine."

"Oh, I don't know, Cactus Face. I kind'a like it."

"This madness, you like this?"

"I don't know, it's kind'a exciting. You have to admit pushing that old jalopy over the edge was fun."

"Fun?"

"And some of these mountain women, slap a little make-up on 'um and they'd be presentable. I love this mountain air. The view from up here is great, the people are very friendly, and I think driving a tank up a mountain in the middle of a parade with girls flashing their tits at me . . . well, I may have found my niche."

"That little coed from the car was kind of cute, wasn't she?"

"Cute? You got me, Doogan. I wasn't looking at her face."

They both laughed and perused the crowd—a frenzied kinetic mass overflowing the street, the parking lot, and the local bars. It looked like the scene in De Mille's *Ten Commandments* when the wandering Jews, tired of waiting for Moses to return from Mt. Sinai, and under the dubious influence of Edward G. Robinson, celebrate the pagan revival of the Golden Calf with an orgy. Rudolf was thinking of going tribal and joining the bacchanal.

Sheriff Sweet of Golden hitched a ride with the Mayor. They came up the back way, the south loop, to avoid the turns and traffic on Lariat Trail. Sweet was miffed that the Colonel pulled rank and insisted that the military could oversee the event and keep order. His Golden Police were relegated to traffic control on Lariat Trail, on the opposite side of the grave, the dark side of the mountain, the side away from the spotlights and publicity. Sweet's limited number of squad cars had their hands full on Lariat, so he took advantage of the mayor's offer to ride along in his limo. Both agreed that The Loop road, Mount Vernon Canyon, would be a faster route, but just past the gate to Mount Vernon Country Club the climate changed. Traffic grew heavy, crowds of boisterous people walked along the shoulders of the narrow two-lane road, slowing the long line of cars. The frivolity of a county fair filled the air. Sweet didn't like it but the mayor commented how fortuitous it was to have a crowd like this with elections just around the bend. Although he had only recently admitted his own ambitions, he knew the mayor was in a constant state of political heat—arousal and response. As a rookie patrolman things were simple—you were hired for the job, you kept physically fit, kept your nose clean, kept your side arm clean, and didn't piss off your supervisor. However, as chief, life became more complex. Whether you liked it or not, you were suddenly immersed in politics. You glad-handed right and left, kissed a little ass, demanded a little posterior smooch now and then, watched your back, and kept your enemies close. Too many dinner meetings and cocktail receptions robbed you of your svelte physique and too many back room deals stained your karma. Your "sweet" disposition suffered. Surprisingly, the Chief found out he was good at politics and the little burg of Golden was beginning to feel professionally constraining. The Colonel was, of course, an old campaigner. Advancing in the military was no different from gaining favor in the public sector. And the longer Sweet and the mayor were stuck in traffic, the larger and more unruly the crowd got, the more comfortable Sweet became with the Guard being in charge. He'd wait and see—another skill he had only recently developed.

By the time they arrived at the parking lot of The Robin's Nest and fought the crowd to the open space south of the grave, the Colonel and his army boys had set up a speakers stand. At the sight of a podium and microphone the mayor beamed. Sweet recalled an axiom often spouted by the Colonel, that clever old warhorse: Never miss an opportunity to tell the masses you're doing the right thing, right. The Colonel was preparing to address the ocean of celebrants. Sweet and the Mayor approached the platform, but were halted by a couple of guardsmen. At a pretentious signal from the Colonel they were permitted to climb aboard. Not until they stood at the elevated height could they judge the vastness of the flock.

"Holy shit," was the mayor's assessment.

Sheriff Sweet whispered to the Mayor, "Voters, Mayor, every one of them." He smiled and waved to the crowd. They reacted with wild howls.

The Colonel turned his back on the audience to say something to another dignitary walking up the steps to the platform. The Mayor saw an opening and instinctively stepped to the microphone.

"Golden!" said the Mayor. He paused to make sure he had their attention, and then his volume climbed to a yell, "Golden, where the West Begins; where Westerners remain!" The people hooted their delight.

The Colonel grabbed the microphone putting his hand over the spherical screen, "What the hell do you think you're doing, Mayor, I was supposed to speak first."

"Relax, Colonel," he replied, turning to face the crowd but speaking in a tone only those on the podium could hear, "you got your job; I'm up for re-election this fall." He stepped in front of the Colonel and leaned into the mic again, "Golden, am I right? Ain't no sons-o-bitches from Wyoming going to steal our Buffalo Bill. Not while I'm Mayor they're not." The cheers exploded.

"Now listen you little show-boating, holy-shiting, son-of-a-goat, let's stick to the planned agenda, or I might just have to take my tanks and go home."

"Not unless you want to be hung as a traitor, you won't." He waved again, and again they cheered. "You think this crowd will let you leave Old Bill unguarded and not ship your military derriere off to Alaska? Or worse, Wyoming!" He turned again to the microphone, yelling into it, "A great American hero, a man of frontier courage, a son of the West, and a friend of our fathers in Golden . . ."

"Not to mention an A-number-one tourist attraction," mumbled the Sheriff to the Colonel.

". . . a friend to the red man and his white brothers, " the Mayor continued, "and a man after my own heart. Old Bill didn't mind taking a snort once in a while, getting into a brawl, and bringing to bear the big guns if necessary, if forced into a corner. Well, as you good people can see, just look up that hill behind you. We have brought the big guns for Bill, and if those unholy sheep ranchers in the Cody Legion want a war, by god, Golden is going to give them one."

"Jesus," mumbled the Colonel.

"Christ," mumbled Doogan.

"Lord," mumbled the Sheriff.

"Hallelujah," cried Rudolph, "will you look at the big guns on that blonde next to the speakers' platform."

"May I?" asked the Sheriff of the Colonel.

"Why the hell not," acknowledged the Commandant, shaking his head at the bedlam, and gestured toward the microphone.

"I love my job," Sheriff Sweet yelled into the microphone. "And I love this town, and I love the story of Buffalo Bill."

"Sweet, Sweet, Sweet," they chanted in a burgeoning and primordial rumble from the depths of the congregation.

"Bill, Bill, Bill," another group to the north began.

"Sweet," those to the south took their impromptu cue.

"Bill", those to the north repeated in turn.

"Sweet, Bill, Sweet, Bill, Sweet, Bill," each group answered the other in alternating rhythm.

"Holy shit," mumbled the Mayor. "This son-o-bitch is after my job."

Sweet turned to the Mayor and covered the mic, "Oh, I've got bigger aspirations than the mayor of Golden, ole friend. You're job is safe, but, if you're smart, you'll let me scratch your ambitious back tonight." He turned to face the crowd, and chanted with the mantra: *Bill, Bill, Bill.*

From the trees behind the tanks, but with a clear view of the mob, Luther and the contingent of Wyoming Legionaries watched the proceedings and listened to the chant with trepidation.

"How the hell did I let you talk me into this," said Luther out loud.

"How the hell did we get talked into this?" every adventurer from Wyoming asked, except two: Kid and Willie.

"This may be a little more difficult than we originally planned," said the Major Emeritus.

"If I can just get off one good shot," said Kid, "I'll be happy when they hang me."

Luther gave him a look.

"Trouble, maybe," muttered Wolf Song, never much for words.

The ranger next to Luther whispered, "That chant is scaring the piss out me."

"You ain't lying," said Luther. "This waiting and watching is killing me. I'm thinking serious about take'n a piss and going home."

They stood quietly in the shadows. Luther heard the Major address Kid and Wolf Song. "I hate to admit it, but I'm trapped by indecision—fight or flee?"

"Well, sir," said Luther, "I think the question is actually, how do we flee—fast or slow? Well, actually—how fast and which way?"

"Do you know the way out of here, Wolf Song?" asked the Major.

"At least it will be downhill," said Luther

"Too soon to leave," answered Willie.

"What the hell is he talking about?" asked Luther.

"How in the name of Iwo Jima should I know," answered the Major.

"Maybe not so bad," said Willie. "Maybe we should join party. No one know us." He smiled and looked at the Major. Luther thought the smile was demonic, and the idea ludicrous. He turned and walked toward the forest behind them.

"And where do you think you're going, Luther?"

"To give back some pure Rocky Mountain spring water. These Ponderosa look dry."

"Well, be careful. We sure don't want to be discovered."

"No shit, Major," answered Luther as he staggered deeper toward the northern darkness.

Luther leaned against a tree and unbuttoned his Levi's. As he began to relieve himself he thought there was something peculiar about the sound. He had always bragged to anyone who would listen that his stream sounded like "cow piss hitting a flat rock." But in this strange and dangerous forest it seemed to echo—stereo. "Damn, strangest mountains I even been in," he said aloud.

"Oh, I don't know," came a voice from the darkness, "I kind'a like 'um."

Luther felt the adrenaline surge through his body with the force of a flush from an eighty-story toilet. He panicked, lost control and sprayed the nearby rocks, trees, and all over his boots.

"Sorry, man, didn't mean to startle you," said a huge guy in an Army captain's uniform. His nametag read: Rudolph. He was zipping up his khakis.

"Hell fire, man, you didn't scare me," stuttered Luther. "I just didn't expect to find no perv out here while I was taking a piss." He prematurely put himself away and soiled his jeans. He rushed back to the sanctuary of his Wyoming companions.

"Yeah, well," called out Rudolph, "like I said, sorry. I can see you weren't scared." He laughed, "That was a pretty messy marking of your territory there, Hoss."

"Where the hell have you been?" the Major asked Luther.

"I told you, damn it; I had to take a piss."

"Maybe you should have opened your pants first," giggled Kid.

"Shut up, you runt," Luther moved aggressively toward his heckler.

The Kid pulled his pistol in a blink of an eye and had it pointed against Luther's crotch, "I can dry this out for you real quick, Luther, but you will be singing soprano for the rest of your. . ."

"As you were, gentlemen. And I mean: now!" interrupted the Major. "Kid, put that revolver away."

Both men held their ground until several of the others smirked and guffawed under their breath. Embarrassed, the sham combatants separated.

"Piss off," yelled Luther as he finally turned and walked toward the dark.

Captain Rudolph, upon returning to the tanks, climbed up next to Doogan on the same mound of steel. "Cactus Face, who do you suppose those guys are, the ones arguing over there in the woods?" He pointed toward the man he had startled and the others.

"More of the local crazies, I suppose. Why?"

He laughed and offered a cigarette to Doogan, "Nothing. Just scared the piss out of one of 'um, that's all."

Doogan took one from the pack, Rudolph lit Doogan's, then his own. He shook the match and tossed it cavalierly.

"Whoa, Rudi, be careful this place is a tender box."

"Sorry, didn't mean to startle you," Rudolph laughed loudly.

Doogan looked at him and asked, "What the hell is so funny about that?"

"Well, if I start a fire, I know a guy with a hose who could put it out, no problem."

"What in the hell are you talking about, Captain Rudolph?"

"Nothing, Cactus Face, you had to be there."

"Is it those guys in the woods over there?"

"Yeah, but I don't think they are anything to worry about. Besides, I think that's them coming our way." He pointed toward the west as the group sauntered from the forest, trying to look nonchalant.

"Captains," saluted the leader in an old major's uniform as he led the procession past the tanks. "I see you're on point tonight. Keep up the good work."

"Evening," said Willie, never much for words.

"Great guns," said Kid. "What caliber are those hummers?"

"Keep walking, Kid," buzzed Luther.

"Sorry again, Pal, didn't mean to give you a jolt," said Rudolph as Luther passed beneath him.

"Piss off," mumbled Luther under his breath.

"Friends of yours?" Doogan asked his colleague.

"We only just met," laughed Rudolph.

"Who is the grumpy one with the wet stains," asked Doogan.

"That's the fire marshal I was telling you about."

Doogan watched the rag-tag group mingle with the crowd. He saw the Indian stand in the shadow of a building on the periphery of the pandemonium. Something didn't smell right.

After a few moments he asked, "Rudi, did that kid have a holster strapped to his leg?"

"I didn't see it if he did, Cactus Face. You think something's funny about those guys?"

"Oh, hell Rudi, not those guys, nor half the inmates yelling for that duffus sheriff. No, there is nothing funny about any of this Colorado crowd: pushing cars off mountains, flashing boobs, parading behind antique tanks up a tittie-twister road, using government time and money to guard the grave of some white-haired, show biz, booze-head, buffalo hunter. No, Rudi, why would I think there was something funny about those guys?"

"Yeah, me neither."

They sat quietly for several minutes, Doogan trying to find the kid in the crowd and also watch the Indian in the shadows. He thought he spotted the kid near the speakers stand. He thought to himself that if the youngster was carrying a gun, could he possibly be planning to assassinate one of the speakers? *Who? Which one? The Mayor, the Sheriff, the Commandant? Why? None of them seemed that important.* Then he thought*: and so what if the kid did plan to shoot one of them. Good riddance. Go for the idiot commandant first. He's the one who ordered me up this mountain. Then the sheriff; he's looks the most ambitious.*

He continued to try to keep tabs on both the dubious characters. The moon drifted from behind some tin colored clouds, adding an eerie light to the ruckus, the frenzy becoming even more staged—a B movie crowd scene. Shadows from the surrounding pine trees drifted across the tanks with a boding glide, contorting with the metal contours.

"Once you get used to the crowd noise," said Rudolph, "it seems quiet. Too quiet, if you know what I mean."

"Cut the crap, Rudi. Did that kid, or did he not, have a holster. Do you suppose he's carrying a gun?"

"Doogan, I didn't see anything, but if you're worried, I'll go check him out."

"I think we better, but I'll check out the kid. See him working his way toward the speakers? There. You keep an eye on the old Indian. He is standing in the shadow of that . . ."

"I know where he is, I've been watching too. But I'll take the kid; I should have been more observant. Tally ho, Captain."

In unison they dismounted Doogan's tank, straightened their side arms, tucked in their shirts in the back of their pants as they marched toward the crowd. Both noticed their synchronized ritual. Doogan could tell that Rudolph was amused by the theatrical choreography and was fantasizing another movie or historical photo op. "Damn-it, Rudi, get serious. Be careful; this isn't the O. K. Corral and you're not Victor Mature."

"Are you calling me *immature*, Cactus Face? That hurts."

He laughed as they split up near the edge of the jumble, Rudolph forcing his way toward the platform, Doogan subtly moving to a vantage where he could watch the Indian without being obvious. He knew the Indian saw him, although the sly old fox acknowledged nothing. His quarry stayed put.

The crowd noise was a background roar—laughing, cheering, yelling jokes, and trading good-humored insults with those at the podium.

"You can tell those Wyoming hoodlums for me," yelled an audience member, "we'll be a sending them back to where the buffalo roam and the antelope play!"

"Yeah, with more than a discouraging word," added another.

"Now folks," said Sheriff Sweet still at the microphone, "we don't want any violence. Of course, we here in Golden don't consider tar and feathering as violence, now do we!"

"Sweet, Bill, Sweet, Bill, Sweet," they rumbled again.

Rudolph pushed up next to the kid and looked down at his hip. Sure enough, he had a holster strapped to his leg, but there was no gun in it. "Excuse me, son," yelled out Rudolph so he could be heard above the Sheriff and the crowd; the kid jumped but did not panic. "Why do you have that holster?"

It was the guy with the wet pants, standing next to the kid who panicked at the sound of Rudi's voice.

Rudolph almost laughed and started to say, "I didn't mean to startle you," when the guy pulled a revolver from under the kid's shirt and pointed it at Rudolph.

"Now take it easy, partner, I didn't mean to . . ."said Rudolph, thinking better of finishing his statement.

"Luther, don't be a fool," yelled the major.

"Gi'me back my gun," yelled the kid.

"Piss off, all of you," yelled Luther. "Back up, give me some room." He fired the gun into the air.

"Holy shit," cried the Mayor as he ducked behind the Sheriff.

"Now remain calm," yelled the Sheriff into the mic as all hell broke loose.

Rudi risked a quick look to see if Doogan had responded to the shot. Doogan was looking his way, and Rudolph caught a glimpse of the Indian slipping away.

Wolf Song took advantage of the shot and the captain's distraction to slip from his shadow into the deeper darkness behind the Pahaska Tee Pee building. He slowly pulled on the screen door to the back exit. As careful as he was, it squeaked. By this time the captain was rounding the corner to the museum's dark side. Wolf Song surmised he heard the door. Willie closed the door as quietly as he could, and leaned against the building.

The captain walked right past him in the alpine dark. In the dim light Wolf Song watched him feel for the door. He pulled on the screen, it squeaked loudly. He tried the inside door. It was locked.

"I like cashews," Wolf Song said as calmly as he could, not wanting to panic the captain.

Startled but controlled, the soldier replied, "What?"

"I like cashew nuts," Wolf Song repeated.

"I'll bet you do. Shopping for some now, are ya? Maybe you should wait 'till the place is open." He was looking toward where he heard the voice, but obviously could not see Willie. He stepped in the direction of the voice.

As silent as his namesake, Willie the Wolf stepped aside and was gone. As he slipped between some trees, he heard the captain move in a frenzy. Wolf Song couldn't believe it, but the captain was coming right toward him.

Rudolph stood and tried to gather his wits while the crowd stampeded in all directions. The Luther clown was waving the gun and trying to clear an exit for himself. His friends lined up behind him like a dormitory of frightened orphans being led to corporal punishment.

Rudi watched the Sheriff, the Mayor, and the Commandant fight for the microphone. The Mayor was at a distinct disadvantage because he refused to give up his protected spot behind the Sheriff while he insisted on pushing the Commandant out of the way. The Commandant was yelling orders and calling for the tanks.

"That's great, Colonel," Rudi heard the sheriff say, "you want to see some real wide-eyed panic, have those tanks pull into this crowd." The sheriff won the fight for the mic. "Now everybody just stay where you are," he yelled. "Let the gentleman with the gun go his way, and everybody else just sit down!"

No one heard, no one listened, no one sat.

"Oh my god the tanks are coming; look out for the tanks; we'll be crushed," some idiot screamed.

Panic griped the crowd, but not Rudolph. Judging from the direction Luther was heading Rudolph figured the gunman was trying to escape the same way he entered, in the woods behind the tanks. Rudolph skirted the crowd and briskly walked to the same tree where he first frightened Luther. He was right. Coming from behind the tree, Rudolph reached out and disarmed Luther with one swift coordinated grab of the gun-hand and a knee to Luther's pride.

The pistol fired as Luther crumbled to the ground. The bullet rocketed just a few yards, ricocheting off a granite boulder. Hot chips of rock flew in every direction.

Rudolph, feeling a bit cocky at his deductive reasoning in figuring out the escape of these outlaws, but being too boastful at having overpowered the villain, suddenly realized that he had forgotten the number one rule of combat—cover your flank. The major, with what could only be called a rather charming judo chop, smacked Rudolph on the back of his neck. The blow was not fatal, neither was it debilitating, annoying is what it was, but it did get Rudolph's attention and he turned to chastise the major. The major wore an expression of apology. Rudolph felt his own expression metamorphosing from now-what-the-hell-was-that, to you-silly-old-fart, to I'm-going-to-knock-the-shit-out-of-you when, ignoring the rule twice, and much to his surprise, the Luther villain smacked him in the back of the head with a rock.

Rudolph dropped to his knees and also dropped the gun. "Sorry," snarled Luther, "I didn't mean to startle you." He picked up the revolver and pointed it at Rudolph.

"As you were, Luther." cried the major. "Put that gun away. There will be no killing on this endeavor." He stepped between them. "You heard me, Luther. Now put that damn thing away. Tomorrow is another day. Back to Wyoming!"

Luther pushed Rudolph over with the heel of his boot and ran into the darkness beyond. The others followed, cheering like the vanquished suddenly reprieved and yelling gibes at a semiconscious Rudolph.

He rose, rubbing the back of his head, checking his hand for blood. There was some, but it was not as bad as it could have been. "I wonder if I'll get a Purple Heart for this?"

Once he assessed he was not going to die from his wounds he became astutely concerned that he did not recall seeing the kid with the holster in the group that just escaped. Maybe the human fire hose got away, but he might still be able to catch the boy who started it all.

Kid was thinking he was the only true hero among the Wyoming vigilantes. With the cunning of a young soldier trapped behind enemy lines, he devised a different kind of retaliation. He wanted to wreak as much destruction as possible before hightailing it. In the panic that followed the gunshot, he ran to the tanks. They were abandoned. He slipped inside one. Although he had never been in the military, he recognized the old crank starter in the rear of the tight cabin, midway up from the floor. He would have no trouble starting the monster, after all, he had driven a dozen different tractors and heavy farm equipment before moving to Cody. Although cow punchers have few opportunities to drive tanks, he immediately recognized the two-lever steering system and the three pedals on the floor—brake on the right, gas in the middle, and clutch on the left. He also identified the breach-loading canon, and . . . there were live rounds, big cartridges, about the size of a porno dildo, lined up in a holder on the wall. He lifted one from its mount. It weighed about a pound. "I can do some damage with this big dick." He thrust it into the barrel and pulled down the lever, closing the breach. Pleased with himself, he pivoted from the cannon, bent down, and gave the starter crank a turn.

Willie slunk through the pine forest using all the skills he learned as a youth hunting deer and skulking for ponies to steal from his Arapahoe and Cheyenne neighbors. He scrambled to the eastern slope of Lookout, making his way toward the hogbacks south of the failed body snatch. Willie moved as secretly as the wind, but periodically the lights from Golden and Denver cast him as a ghostly silhouette. He knew these brief luminous moments informed his pursuer of his location. That was fine; Willie saw Kid sneak into the tank. The way he figured it: the best that could happen is Kid might get lucky and somehow vandalize Buffalo Bill's tomb, crush the insulting monument under the iron tread of the tank, maybe even blow a great canon hole in the museum. To dream is to live. The worst that could happen: Kid might get caught before he can do any damage. According to Lakota tradition, regardless of any destruction, Kid could still celebrate first-touch coup. Willie would keep this tank captain busy long enough to give Kid a fair shot. He trusted that the Major and the idiot Luther were keeping the other captain entertained.

Chapter Fourteen

Pahaska

Summer, 1948 and later

*The terrain south and east of Buffalo Bill's grave was much
more open, fewer trees, but the ground was less predictable. Here
lay the exposed sedimentary layer of the Permian beach that once
bordered the ancient inland sea, a vacation spot of dinosaurs. Oh
yes, I, Turtle was there. It was here (and on the hogbacks near
Morrison) when the spike-tailed stegosaurus lumbered in a fatigued
escape attempt from the ferocious Tyrannosaurus. Although the
tracks of the dinosaur chase, forever embedded in the sandstone,
were going the opposite direction of the contemporary pursuit,
Doogan was, I saw, overconfident and thought he was playing the
role of the predator. What folly.*

Wolf Song skipped agilely between the prehistoric footprints,
recognizing them as the trail of great monsters before the time of
Wakan Tanka, before the time of the White Buffalo Woman and the
creation of The People. His avoidance of them resembled a graceful
dance in homage of the earth and the sleeping beast.

He watched the captain in pursuit, making sure he did not
lose him. The captain was having trouble keeping up. It was obvious
that it had been a long time since he had played hide-and-seek.
Although, his natural athleticism aided him in his quest, he lacked
the grace of Wolf Song and the respect for The Beast. Willie
watched: the captain avoided stepping in a stone print to his left, but
as he passed by it he looked too long, probably wondering what
could make a tri-cloven hole like that. In looking to his left, he did
not see the partner print of the terrible king lizard. He stumbled into
it.

Willie heard the loud snap of the bone and the anguished groan that followed. He turned to see the captain in the dim light of the distant city as he tried to rise, but fell painfully to the ground. The game had changed. This was not good coup, causing a clumsy white to cripple himself, not too much of a challenge, no bravery involved, little risk to himself. He sat for a moment and watched the Wasichu captain in the cool dimness. Bats flew erratically overhead, and a refreshing breeze slid up the diagonal slope on which their chase had ended. The growing anvil of a building thunder storm was drawing air. Willie considered leaving the careless man where he lay; the Wasichu could probably struggle or limp his way back to the gravesite; the embarrassment would serve him right. He watched the man try to get up again. When he fell this time he let out a terrible cry. Willie sat thinking and watching a while longer. And then, as silently as the spirit it represented, as smoothly as the breeze drifting up the slope, an owl glided over the white man and landed above in a Ponderosa. Wolf Song pondered this evil omen, a death spirit. Willie looked to the sky and read the moon. It flew in crescent, behind a cloud of clear-water-blue smoothness. And then the shimmering brother star came out from behind the cloud. It flashed brightly and then dimmed quickly, disappearing again.

This clumsy Wasichu will die here. Maybe that's as it should be, but the moon did tell me to help. Sometimes the Great One makes strange requests of us. He walked to the side of his fallen pursuer. Wolf Song could see the white of the jagged bone sticking through the side of the man's leg. He saw that the man had not only tripped, but had jammed the toe of his boot into the narrow angle of the toe of the petrified print, and this had caused the unholy twisting of the leg and the spiral, compound fracture. The Wasichu appeared unconscious. Willie sat next to him on the lip of the thunder track and watched for a moment. He looked into the tree at the owl. "Not tonight sister, for some reason, I cannot comprehend and do not question, the Mother of us all wants this one to live." The owl silently took off. Willie watched her glide into what seemed to be a night growing into sunrise. This did not make sense, the sky tinted orange at the wrong time and in the wrong direction. Then his nose confirmed his fears—it was fire. Above them, near where the chase had started, the forest was burning.

Rudi was moving slowly, nursing the pain in his head with small steps and repeated curious touches to the wound with alternating hands, as if one hand would discover something different from the other. Perhaps the right hand could find enhanced drama. The blood flow did not increase as he walked. This was somewhat disappointing; he was thinking seriously about the Purple Heart. The sound of someone trying to start the tank; however, quickened his pace, and he suddenly forgot about his injury. *Now what the hell is going on? Did the crew get back? Where the hell is Doogan?*

Kid was getting nowhere. He remembered from a war movie he saw that tanks were like his "pap's" antique tractor—lever driven. Obviously, there was no steering wheel. He knew that you clamp down on one tread and the other one drives you around in the opposite direction. This pair of levers was for steering, but which of these other damn levers puts this cuss in gear? He felt for the clutch pedal. He pulled the nearest lever and popped the clutch. The tank lurched forward but the engine died. He struggled to find neutral. He put the gear lever back in its original position and fought his way backwards, out of the driver's seat, into the tight cabin. He cranked the starter again. The tank rumbled to life.

Rudolph knew now it was not the crew, nor could it be Doogan, killing and restarting the tank. He began to run. As he came out of the woods he saw his tank heading due east a few yards, and then pivot in a port turn, spitting rock and dirt from under the gyrating tread at the crowd standing nearby in dumfounded amazement at how fast a tank could spin. It suddenly turned south, causing that section of the audience to panic and part like the waters. It leveled three small pine trees, and proceeded toward the speaker platform in an uncoordinated, jerky, zigzag path.

Sheriff Sweet, urging everyone to stay calm, remained at the microphone until the very last second when he grabbed the Mayor who was still hiding behind him. The Sheriff and his ward jumped out of the path of the charging tank, the Mayor yelling on their way to the pavement, "Holy shit!"

The Commandant, in an incredibly agile move for an old soldier, jumped from the platform in front of the tank. "I command you to stop this machine," he yelled into the open pilot's window. "Who the hell are you?" he said to a kid with a menacing grin. The tank lurched forward, heedless of his rank. He jumped out of way and landed near the Sheriff and Mayor.

"Not one of your boys, I take it?" asked the Sheriff as Rudi ran by.

After demolishing the speaker stand the tank continued east between two buildings and toward the edge of the mountain. It would have tumbled off had not the driver finally pivoted it, but in his panicked turn he again stalled the engine.

"One shot, just give me one damn shot," he yelled loud enough for the others to hear.

Rudi stopped to help the Commandant to his feet.

"Sweet," yelled the Commandant, "Where are your policemen? Someone has got to rush that tank and pull that punk out of there."

"Well, Colonel, as you may recall, this was to be the military's show. You didn't want the presence of cops making it look like a police action. 'This is War,' I believe that is what I heard. My boys, the unwashed and unwanted, are still doing traffic control. Where are your boys?"

"That's a damn good question, Chief," muttered the Mayor. "Where are the soldiers who are supposed to be manning those tanks?"

Rudi and the Commandant looked at each other.

"Holy shit," screamed the Mayor when he noticed the turret was turning in their direction, "I think that little bastard is loading the cannon. Colonel, is he loading the cannon? What's that noise? I think he's loading the cannon."

"That punk can't load that cannon. It might be old, but that is a technical piece of equipment. Some punk kid is not able to figure out how to load that cannon." He looked again at Rudolph for confirmation, and said with his eyes: *Get your army ass over there and do something about that tank!*

Rudolph started toward the tank just as the roar of the gun and muzzle flash shattered the night. The kid figured out how to load the cannon. And fire it. But he was having trouble aiming it and controlling the turret. The projectile took the tops off a pair of ancient lodge pole pines. Anyone present could hear the ordinance sing as it raced toward the moon, things were quiet when it reached it's apex but the banshee song hummed even louder as it gained speed in its descent. An explosion, just down slope on the northwest side of the mountain illuminated the night.

It was Captain's Rudolph's good intentions and heroic nature that enticed him to jump and hug the short barrel. He wrapped his arms around the cannon in an attempt to force the gun downward. If, whoever was in there, got off another shot, it would harmlessly fire into the ground. The next step in Rudolph's plan was to jump inside and put an angry end to this tank joy ride. His intent was honorable, but the results were disappointing. He forced the barrel downward as planned, but not down far enough before the vandal got off his second ceremonial shot. The recoil bounced Rudolph six feet, straight up in the air, the concussion knocked him semiconscious while in flight, and the eventual splash down, interrupted by a splayed bodily ricochet off the cannon, nearly ruptured his spleen.

This shot, with Rudolph's help, found pay dirt, actually tomb dirt. It up-rooted the huge obelisk monument made of large quartz boulders.

Other than the berserk cheering inside the tank, the silence was eerie. Rudolph thought for a moment that his concussion had deafened him. But then he heard the hailstorm. It was the quartz fragments from the grave returning to earth. The surreal shower of diamonds painfully pelted Rudi. The brass plaque, that moments ago marked the grave, rang loudly as it hit the pavement near the trio of VIP's.

"Holy shit; that was close," mumbled the Mayor.

Rudolph sat up and checked to see if he was now bleeding more. As the thought of a second purple heart crossed his mind he saw his pilot and Earl rush the tank; Earl threw open the front driver's door and Rudi's pilot dived through the emergency doors on the turret. They restrained the maniac in a you-take-him-high; I'll-take-him-low tackle. It was the kid with the holster. As they pulled him from the machine he gurgled in a demented laugh, "Sorry, Old Bill, but we had to show these sons-of-bitches they can't steal from your town's folk and not face the wrath of the Wyoming American Legion, the Cody Rotary, and the Benevolent Order of the fuckin' Elks."

Captain Rudolph, as he stumbled toward the tank, was the first to notice. He was familiar with the smell of cannon fire, but an unaccustomed aroma rose beyond the black powder fragrance. He asked, "What's burning?"

They all turned in unison to the glowing sky behind them, to the northwest.

"Holy . . .," said the Mayor.

"Shit" said Sweet.

With practiced precision Sweet was on the radio in the mayor's limo informing the Golden, Lookout Mountain, Genesee, Mount Vernon, and Morrison Fire Departments they had an event on Lookout at the Buffalo Bill gravesite. The Colonel informed his base on one of the tank radios that their fire squad should go on stand-by alert, and begin the phone tree calling the other Guard units to the ready state, should the municipal fire departments need backup. The Mayor, an old volunteer firefighter himself, ran to the trunk of his car and pulled out shovels, picks, and hardhats.

The Commandant continued calmly, "You boys in the tanks be on the ready, we'll use you to create a fire break before the fire departments get here. There is bound to be a hell of a lot of traffic impeding them; people trying to get off this damn mountain and away from this fiasco."

Sweet followed, "We have routed all the neighboring fire units up Mount Vernon Canyon and in the back door, avoiding Lariat Trail and the heaviest traffic."

The Mayor added, "I called the weather people at National Atmospheric in Boulder, the winds are expected to be mild and blowing northwest. That makes Lariat the best evacuation for the remaining civilians, and if she spreads, it will be away from the buildings up here and toward open space. Oh, yeah, Holy shit, I almost forgot, there is a good chance of thunderstorms and heavy rains. The wind could be a problem but the rain might help."

"It'll have to be a hell of a lot of rain," commented Sweet. "Let's have a look see at this baby. I think I hear sirens to the south."

Wolf Song knew that if he tried to reset the compound fracture of this Wasichu's right leg, the white man would pass out again. From the position of the foot he confirmed it was a spiral break, and although Willie felt himself strong for his age, this was a bear-sized white man. He knew he could not carry him far. Then there was the fire. Judging by the wind and because they were down slope, they might be OK.

The tank captain was delirious with pain. He was nauseous, faint, but weakly asked Wolf Song, "Why did you come back?"

"I like cashews," answered Willie. "Remember, if we live."

"Judging from the glow on the top of the hill, we're about to get our nuts roasted," said the captain.

The old Indian smiled for the first time in years. "I can tie your leg so you can bounce using me as crutch. Going to hurt a lot, but you must stay awake. Too big for me to carry far."

"I'll do my best, chief. It's going to get too warm to stick around here."

"Not chief, not even warrior—opossum."

"Whatever. My name is Alonzo Doogan," he stuck out his hand.

Wolf Song took his hand and pulled it over his own shoulders, "Not proper to ask Indian his name. Wasichus call me Willie."

Doogan struggled to stay conscious. "Yeah," he grimaced, "and I know. You like cashews."

Rudolph was too rattled to be much good to the fire fighters. He sat near his tank trying to shake some sense into his head. The pilots stood nearby waiting for orders from the Commandant, but the Colonel and his colleagues, Sweet and the Mayor, were busy with shovels clearing a firebreak just west of the grave as fire crews hooked up hoses to their pump trucks.

"The parking lot of the Pa-Ha-Ska Museum will keep the fire from going north, but we need to use the roads to contain the fire from moving south," yelled Sweet. "We can use the wide, paved patches to make a stand. Lariat Trail will protect the buildings on the east side of the road. That should isolate the fire on the west side.

There are no buildings on that slope and no body would be foolish enough to try to flee in that direction, ya' think?"

Before they could implement their plan, the fickle nature of the Colorado weather changed things. Every native knew about the climate; the going joke was: If you don't like the weather, just wait ten minutes; it'll change. The anticipated thunderstorm let loose to the south with hail the size of baseballs. It was a mixed blessing. The rain and hail would prevent the fire from racing south toward residences, but the violent downdraft created by the falling hail stones generated swift winds that pushed the fire down both the east and west slopes of the mountain. The tops of the tall trees exploded and fire jumped Lariat Trail. The fire was being pushed by the microburst winds. A downburst occurs as heavier hail and rain-cooled air rushes out from the bottom of the thunderstorm. Downburst winds can exceed one hundred miles an hour.

As far as the Wyoming militia was concerned, the fire had an avenging mind of its own. It was following them down slope—with the rage of the Erinyes.

Luther, never one for ceremony, pulled ahead of the Major in a downhill sprint that was outrunning the rolling rocks he and the others knocked loose as they stumbled down the northwest face of Lookout.

Of course, their original intention was to avoid the crazed Colorado crowd, but the complication of explosion and the resultant fire at their flank added enthusiasm to their escape.

"I can't believe they fired the tank at us. They're trying to kill us, the crazy Colorado sons-of-bitches."

Just when they seemed to gain a few yards on the fire, and they could take advantage of the luxury of looking where they were going, the smoke would tumble up behind them, the smell of burning pine would again force its way past them, and the heat would broil at their backs. Despite the panic, a few of them made a courier comment chastising Luther for shooting the kid's gun in the air. All the threats were impotent, however, because Luther was out distancing them one and all.

Luther thought he caught sight of the road far below, he ran up onto a pyramid-shaped rock formation to see above the thick bottoms of the trees. "I can see the trucks," he yelled with excitement down hill. As he turned to inform his companions he saw for the first time the true immensity of the wall of flames following the troupe—twice the height of the trees. There was no hint of the top of the mountain from which they had just raced. "Who the hell did we piss-off?" he yelled as he jumped off the downhill side of the rocks. He was not about to run down and around the rock formation, not with Pele's curtain rolling toward him. He hit the ground hard and pitched forward loosing his balance, he tumbled face first toward the forest floor, tucking in his head at the last moment, did a forward somersault, and came back to his feet without losing a step. "Don't matter if the fire don't get you, Luther," yelled one of his cohort—soon caught and passed, "we are going to roast your swine's ass on a spit when we get home and sell your charred gristle to tourists for jerky." The insult was lost in the wind of Luther's speed and the crackle of the fire closing behind them.

Luther soon caught another pair of stragglers in the downhill derby. Their plight slowed him only for a moment.

A cowboy acquaintance sported a long, frontier mullet, tied back with rawhide. It began to smolder. He slowed as he sensed that something was amiss. Another rancher-type paced behind him hitting the burning hair with his wide brimmed cowboy hat.

"I'm going as fast as I can, Bufford, quit hitting me with that damn hat."

"It's either this or dumping dirt on your head, you dullard. Your hair is on fire!"

The man could not stop, of course, but he kept looking around as if by seeing the burning ponytail he could somehow aid his plight. Bufford continued to smack him but was in reality fanning the flames. It was an impossible task: first, because he had a running target, and second, because their timing was off, and he kept whacking the guy's face instead of his hair.

"Quit looking around, ya idgit, I'm gonna put out your eye."

Luther lost interest and sprinted ahead just as the terrorized team burst out of the trees into the opening on the bank of Clear Creek and splashed headlong into the chilling waters.

Like a Brahma bull bored now that it had thrown its rider, the wind changed its direction and began blowing up the canyon instead of down the slope. The fire began to stall, turning back upon itself. Crews above sensed the change for the better and attacked with renewed vigor, knowing the fire could be contained within the loose triangle of Clear Creek to the west, Lariat Trail to the north, and several dirt roads intersecting the area on the east side. The rains soaked the south side.

Several dozens of cars lined Highway 6, paralleling Clear Creek. Many were those of volunteers, knowing the creek and highway would be the place to make a stand against the fire. Many also belonged to those sufferers of that unforgivable plague of mankind: gawking at disasters. They were there, possibly in harms way, fascinated by the destruction of the forest. You could register the disappointment on their faces when one asked a bone-tired and waterlogged Luther, exiting from the stream and climbing the steep bank, "Was any one killed?"

"Piss off," he replied.

He saw their trucks tucked safely, inconspicuously, among the cars lining the road. No one noticed the Wyoming license plates; their interest was on the flames on the opposite side of the creek.

A policeman walked up to them, ignoring their scorched appearance and barked," You civilians have got to clear the area. There is serious danger here!"

"No shit," mumbled the cowboy with the scorched hair.

The policeman continued, "We have got to make room for emergency vehicles. Please, move your cars and get out of this area."

"No problem," answered the Major.

Willie had traversed back to the museum by skirting blazing areas and trekking through burned out patches. There were only a few times when he had to carry Doogan over burned out terrain. Nevertheless, the trek had been a struggle. Smoke continuously covered them, and Doogan could not stay conscious in his pain. Because of Doogan's size and Willie's age, he could only go a few yards before he had to set the titan on a rock formation or a charred stump or a fallen, ashen trunk. The trek back took so long that the original fire crew, at the top of the mountain near the museum, was cleaning up when Willie walked out of the charcoal forest with Doogan across his shoulder. He collapsed to the pavement of the parking lot before anyone cold rush to his aid, but it made a dramatic entrance worthy of *The Wild West* extravaganza, and Willie knew good theater.

Doogan opened his eyes when they tumbled to the blacktop. The other tank captain and the crews arrived just in time to hear Doogan say with surprise, "My god, you've saved my life," He smiled at the others and passed out again.

The odyssey covered both Willie and Doogan with dirt and soot, but neither suffered any serious burns. Doogan's uniform had several burned spots on the fanny where Willie had to set him down on a charred tree trunk, knowing he would never get him up again if he had to lift him from the ground. So, he figured a few minor burns would not be too bad. Life is pain. He could have left the clumsy Wasichu in the dinosaur track. Perhaps, now—at last—Wolf Song would be recognized as a hero. There was no Buffalo Bill to embarrass and insult him. Perhaps now he would fulfill the prophecy of Black Elk, gain great coup, and get his picture in the white man's papers.

Before they had even washed their faces of the ash from the fire, the Mayor, the Sheriff, and the Commandant had hatched the plan for the cover up of the bungled Buffalo Bill debacle.

The Commandant would boast that his unit had responded to threats and sightings of potential grave robbers from Wyoming by sending two tanks and their crackerjack crews to guard the monument. He had to spin the obvious presence of the tanks because half of Colorado paraded up Lookout Mountain with them.

Yes, they would admit, a crazed Wyoming culprit actually drew a gun in a desperate attempt to avoid arrest, and threatened the crowd around the gravesite. But the culprit was apprehended immediately. He was consequently shipped off to a neutral jurisdiction within Colorado because the foothills officials knew there was no way he could receive a fair trial in Golden. Thus, as far as the public was concerned, the generous authorities were being judiciously neutral. Only the tank crews, the VIP's, and the damn Indian knew it was bullshit.

Yes, it was true: the rest of his gang started a fire in an attempt to distract the authorities while they vandalized Buffalo Bill's monument. And, yes the monument would be repaired.

In fact, in the coming weeks the remains of Buffalo Bill would be exhumed, solid granite would be blasted away to a depth of thirty feet, the remains re-entombed, crisscrossed with rebar, and thirty tons of concrete poured on top. A new quartz obelisk was replaced at the tomb, and a thick-iron-picket fence would surround the entire monument. In the future, unless the grave robbers were equipped with nuclear explosives, Bill was going nowhere.

There was to be no mention of a highjacked tank and a wayward cannon shot. The Kid was in custody and was to serve as the scapegoat for the whole untidy affair. He was never to be given access to the press. The maximum security prison at Canyon City was to be his new home. He would be quietly tried and convicted of reckless endangerment and malicious vandalism. The attempted murder charge would be dropped if Kid promised to go home after serving his time for the more minor offenses, and if he never told anyone what had actually happened.

Sweet was particularly persuasive when he enlightened Kid that senior and more veteran criminals would, in all likelihood, initiate the kid as their new cellblock "boy-toy." Kid gladly agreed to any deal that would shorten his stay in Colorado and provide him isolation.

Although returning to Cody and pistol-whipping Luther was a repetitive dream, he headed south to Texas rather than return to Wyoming when his time was served.

Sadly, there could be no mention of Willie's heroism in the news accounts. Again he felt Buffalo Bill had somehow cheated him of his spiritual due. He vowed to stay on Lookout Mountain and wait until the time was right for an appropriate vendetta on the spirit of the "Great American Hero."

As for Doogan and Rudolph, there were major consequences for their misguided heroics. They were forced to accept early retirement—all benefits would be paid *if* they said nothing about the tank nabbing and the fiasco that followed. Any word leaking out to the press, or anyone else, and they would spend the remainder of their enlistment in the brig and lose all retirement benefits. They agreed to the former despite the reduced retirement package. Early retirement and the results of Doogan's injury put an end to their plans to get involved in the burgeoning skiing business.

"The doctors say I'm probably going to limp around like a coyote what gnawed his foot out of a trap," said Doogan as they sat in the Robin's Nest Bar just down the road from the Buffalo Bill Memorial Museum. They had returned to the scene of the crime to reminisce their ruin. "I'm going to have one leg shorter than the other, if I ever get out of this cast. It itches like hell. The sooner we get back to California, the better."

"Oh, I dunno, Cactus Face. Despite all our trouble, I kind of like it around here."

"You what?"

"I don't know," pondered Rudolph, "I had a lot of time to look around while you where in the hospital and I kind'a like it. Golden especially. I took several tours of the brewery. Did you know they give you all you can drink after one of those tours, and if you're smart, you can drop out of the tour as they turn the first corner and go straight to the hospitality bar? Anyway, I . . ."

Doogan interrupted, "You got laid!"

"Well, yes, and there is the brewery."

"Horse-pockey, Rudolph. You got laid and now you think you belong here."

"It ain't just that. I mean that's a major part of it, but I really do like it around here and, to be honest with you, I was never that thrilled about the skiing thing in the first place. I was talking to the manager of the museum there," he thumbed toward the Buffalo Bill Memorial building, "and he said he thinks I actually look a little like old Bill. He thinks if I grew my hair and a beard, I could be Old Bill's double. We put on a hat and looked in a mirror," he held his finger to his upper lip mimicking a mustache, "and, you know, I do kind of look like the geezer. The manager said he'd pay me to impersonate Buffalo Bill at special events, and a friend of his is opening a restaurant just down the hill. It's going to look like an old stucco-walled fort, like Bent's Fort from the mountain man days, and he will pay me just to greet people coming to the restaurant; me dressed as Buffalo Bill, of course."

"That's great Rudolph, but what about our deal? A partnership, you and me going into business together. What about that?'

"That's the good part. Mr. Baker has this building he wants to sell. It's an old adobe he had planned to turn into a restaurant or trading post. It's right down at the bottom of the back road to Lookout, the easy part of the Lariat Loop, not that winding nightmare we drove up in the tanks. Just down from Mount Vernon Country Club; you've seen it. Anyway, it's right on Highway 40, going up to the hills. Ninety percent of the people going up to the mountains drive right by this place and there are rumors of an Interstate Highway being built right on top of 40. If we put our money together, we can probably swing this place and go into the souvenir shop and lunch counter business. Hell, you're the business mind, but I could greet customers as Buffalo Bill. I mean, I don't have to work the front door at The Fort Restaurant until night time, dinner, and all."

"You been doing a lot of planning, Old Scout."

"I ain't been doing any planning, Cactus Face. I'm just telling you what I been thinking about since you been in the hospital. I haven't made any commitments to anyone. Like you said, I've just been scouting, so to speak. Anyway, there is nothing for me in California; we don't have the money to be skiing tycoons, and like I said, mostly I just been touring the brewery and trying to get laid."

"Who is she?" Doogan asked.

"They, Cactus Face. Who are they," he smiled largely.

The residents of Lookout Mountain and the townsfolk of Golden considered Doogan and Rudolph as local heroes. They felt the military and local authorities gave them a bum deal, so they made the two intrepid paragons feel welcome wherever they went. By the time Rudolph had grown a beard, they had a deal on paper for the building on Highway 40. For Doogan it seemed like preordained symmetry. This was the building he often passed, and which peaked his curiosity, when he drove into Mount Vernon to pick up his high school sweetheart.

And while Doogan was gaining quite a reputation for the rashes he was leaving on the local ladies, Rudolph seemed to do best with gullible female tourists, many actually believed he was *The* Buffalo Bill. There was a remarkable resemblance, and Rudi enjoyed his celebrity to the fullest. If not found at The Fort, or at the Bar of the Holland House, or at the Morrison Inn, or the Robin's Nest, or the Golden Eagle Lounge, or once in a while at his own business— Buffalo Bill Cody's Grill and Trading Post, one could usually find him at the Hospitality Room of the Coors Brewery.

Doogan slowly gained a sincere interest in the arts and crafts of the Southwest and the Plains, becoming an astute collector and dealer in Native American art and antiques. It was the gallery and Trading Post that kept the business afloat. Food service was not Doogan's forte. He enjoyed the buying trips to Taos and Santa Fe, the wilds of Arizona, and the Navajo Lands. He scoured the Dakotas, Montana, and even Minnesota. He dabbled for awhile in Anglo western artists such as George Catlin, Frederic Remington, and Charlie Russell, photographs from Curtis, painters from the Taos School—Sharp, Blumenschein, Hennings, Ufer, Fetchin, Dasburg, even Sloan. But eventually, and because of the economics involved, he focused on his particular expertise: Indian arts. To gain operating capital and focus on Native crafts, he ended up selling many of his finest Southwest landscape paintings to, of all people, The Boy Scouts of America and the Koshari Kiva in La Junta, Colorado.

Rudolph would often complain that the place looked more like a museum than a "gift shop." As he recalled, retailers were supposed to sell something "once in a while". His concerns were appropriate. That Doogan hated parting with his handpicked treasures was a local anecdote. He kept the important and historical pieces hidden away in the back of the gallery, and tried his best to peddle the more common pieces. "The good stuff" was brought out only for fellow collectors and experts.

His collection of horse effigy batons was one of the finest south of the Dakotas. These three foot carved canes with a portrait of a revered horse were done by warriors to commemorate favorite mounts fallen in battle. The braves often decorated the cane with mane or tail hair from the eulogized steed. Warrior shields, Ghost shirts, buckskin leggings, and jackets were carefully wrapped in moisture proof packages; a few were rotated on display to keep the tourists entertained, as were authentic war bonnets. He had an enticing stock of lances, tomahawks, war clubs, arrows, and both modern and ancient arrowheads. But more important to Doogan were the effigy clubs carried in various dances and ceremonies. Many depicted historical characters, heroes of particular fame, or animals of important protective spiritual significance. Moccasins, tobacco bags, vests, pipe bags, and cradleboards decorated with glass beads, or with the more historical porcupine quills, were among some of the most beautiful pieces. Doogan even had several buffalo robes and hide paintings. He pitched an authentic teepee in the front of the Trading Post for several years.

He also collected buffalo calf bone pipes— *Ptehinčala Hubu Canunpa*. Indian men carved individual pipes and held them as sacred. It is only because of Doogan's thorough knowledge and reverence that such objects were left *temporarily* in his custodial care.

His collection of Southwestern arts was just as impressive. Polychrome, black on black, and incised pottery, modern and historical, lined the upper shelves of the trading post. Baskets— Apache, Pima, Papago, and others sat next to the ceramics. Jewelry and rugs done by Navajo people filled display cases and hung from the walls. Again, the best pieces were stored in the back room; the more commercial pieces displayed for the tourists. Periodically and begrudgingly, Cactus Face was forced to sell a rare piece to maintain the trading post.

Quite a while after the business was established, on a night sharp with the chill of an early fall, Willie Wolf Song was found sitting in a dark corner. If a tourist had passed by the window, he would have thought Willie was a wooden Indian.

"Jesus, man, you scared the bejeebers out of me," cried Doogan upon discovering Willie.

"Like cashews," was Wolf Song's reply.

"I wondered if I would ever see you again," said Doogan. "Come in here," he pointed toward the cafe side of the business, "I've something to show you."

There, near the cash register, was a hot cashew machine. "I put this in hoping you might show up." He looked with pride to see Willie's reaction.

"Like cashews," Willie repeated and opened his hand to reveal several nuts he had previously taken.

"That's OK, you old coyote. This is for you. And you are welcome to stay as long as it suits you. It's the least I can do. You have my promise on that, as long as I'm alive, you have a home." He opened the door to the nut machine, the aroma of warmed cashews drifted out. He smiled and ate one and said, "You know you old Lakota, I think I too like cashews."

Willie smiled, put a nut between lips, and sucked it into his head with a popping sound.

Rudolph spent less and less time at the trading post and more and more time toasting to his local celebrity in the bars of Golden and Morrison. He and Doogan had discussed an amiable buyout of Rudolph's share of the business. Doogan needed the flexibility to expand the trading post, and Rudolph needed the cash.

The night of Willie's return Doogan was looking for Rudi to pay him off, but Rudolph had not been seen on Lookout for a week or more. Doogan figured he could find him in Golden. Willie accompanied Doogan down the mountain. Rumors in the Golden bars were that Rudi was in Morrison, probably at the Morrison Inn, washing down his favorite burritos with boilermakers. The rumors were right. Rudi was hunkered over a plate of the Inn's famous burros when Cactus Face and Wolf Song walked up.

"Rudi," started Doogan, "I brought your check. It's what we agreed on and a touch more for friendship. What say you sign the papers here and we drink to it? Oh, by the way you'll never guess who showed up at the trading post."

Rudolph laid down his fork and turned, all smiles, to greet Doogan, "I'll bet it's that old cauterized Indian you been searching for, Cactus Face."

Willie staggered backwards at the sight sitting in front of him. His eyes went wide and he dropped the handful of nuts he was carrying.

"Buenos noches, Amigo," Rudolph stood and stuck out his hand.

It was the same face, the same gesture as when Buffalo Bill asked Wolf Song to be the first to die in each and every show. Never much for words, in his shock, Willie Wolf Song simply mumbled aloud, "Pahaska!"

Chapter Fifteen

Wild Billy

Summer, 1964

I don't enjoy destruction. Despite my reputation as The Beast, I prefer the association as Turtle. Emotions, like "enjoy," are difficult to define for us "mythologicals," us animistic figures. I say "mythological," but I would rather you were convinced that "spiritual" was a more accurate term—anima mundi, even better. Either way, as I am sure you realize, our existence is dependent on your, well—for lack of a better term—worship of us. At least, your continued recognition, superstition will do. Our need of you humans, dubious as it might be, creates an interesting paradox. We have the power to destroy because you worship us; stop worshiping and we lose our powers. For example, in my more ill tempered times an earth quake or two may generate some peril; oh, all right, some outright destruction. I couldn't do it if you humans didn't allow me to. The irony doesn't escape me; you falter in your "recognition," worship, if you will, and I get impatient and all hell breaks loose. You could resent me if you wished and in your anger refuse to, well, again—for lack of a better term—worship, and end my days. The irony goes even deeper. You see, for us otherworldly denizens, even your anger is recognition of sorts, and it keeps us alive. We don't need your love and devotion, although we gain greater strength from positive affection. Hate is OK, but we prefer answering prayers. Hey, this wasn't our plan. You have only yourselves to blame. Regardless, I don't necessarily enjoy destruction. I use it to remind you that I'm still here, but I much prefer folly and mayhem— trickery. Remember, I fathered both Flint and Sapling, both winter and summer, both night's darkness and the light of day. I much prefer being the catalyst in your self-destruction (or your triumphs). I don't need humankind to help level mountains and sink islands, or to build beautiful landscapes, but I do use you to further the plot in my chicanery. Hey, it's a long existence; one gets bored. Therefore, I am always scouting for talent. The foothills west of Denver are currently well populated with fools. If I had human emotions, I'd have to admit a bit of dubious joy at the plethora of potential collaborators. By the way, I can take on a human form whenever I wish, whenever it is advantageous in my recruiting for folly.

I don't usually admit these things, Mr. Turtle, you say your name is Turtle, right? *Repeat the name twice and you will always remember it.* Well, Mr. Turtle, as I was saying, I don't usually talk about my past and how I became the proprietor of *Cody's*, and, I don't mind saying, a leading citizen here in Golden. But there is something about you that makes me want to talk. You have a mystical, almost spiritual air. You're not a man of the cloth are you? Well, never mind, now you'll think I'm trying to flatter my way into your pocketbook. I'm not, really. Of course, I sell for a living, but the hard sell is not my way. It's not the way of the West. My past is not exactly a secret, you know, but I don't advertise it. It might be bad for business. I mean, if the tourists thought I wasn't really from the West, if they thought I wasn't really a grizzled old mountain man, Cody's might suffer a loss of Western authenticity. This Old West persona is a profitable image for me as the proprietor of a trading post and rustic old tavern. I'm sure you understand.

I always believed my destiny was bound to the West. More cowboys, than one might imagine, have finagled their way from New Jersey to Colorado. That is, more jaspers from New Jersey, than one might imagine, have finagled their way out West to become cowboys. I know dozens, right here in Golden. We should start a club. We could call ourselves the *Golden Jersey Boys.* Have a bowling team; wear gold team shirts. Sorry, I'm digressing, the plague of a creative mind. Always the entrepreneur. Anyway, it does not take long for pretenders to acquire the affectations of native-born Westerners. It usually begins with a name change. Mine for example, Mischa Swarz becomes Wild Billy. George Leroy becomes Butch, James Henry is known as Doc, Bartholomew is shortened to Bat, Richard becomes Ringo, add to this Waco, Pecos, Sundance, Tex, Nevada, the Oklahoma Kid, the Colorado Kid, the Arizona Kid, the California Kid, the Comanche Kid, the Apache Kid, Pawnee Bill, Billy the Kid, Bronco Billy, Wet Willy, Will, Gil, Indian Joe, Little Joe, just plain Joe, José, Moe, Mosey, Calamity, Catastrophe, Storm, Red, Blue, Whitey, Goldie, 'you're Yeller,' Shorty, Slim, Sam, Sandy, Slick, Partner, Pard, Pete, Laredo, Laramie, Toledo, Tulsa, Wichita, Cookie, Preacher, Dale, Ned, Bob, Bill, Bart, Boone, Bum, Bronco, Bubbles and Bull. Holy cow! Well, I digress.

Next is a costume alteration with the two most important accouterments placed on opposite ends of the galoot—hat and boots. And blue jeans on the bottom—three most important ends. The first problem posed by these new items is: does one wear the jeans in or over the boot? If one phrases their questions using, "does one," it's already a mute point—Westerners don't say, "one." And one does not tuck one's jeans into one's boots. Trust me. Vests are always an enhancement, and large belt buckles are a must. Shirts with snaps or lots of extra buttons are good, as are yards of extra ticking that outline the shoulders, the pockets, and the cuffs. I have all these items in stock, if you're interested. Pointy collars and pointy-toed boots are basic, and can be made graniloquent with silver and bejeweled collar and toe cups. Expensive, but very classy. Round-toed boots are for dancing; they're too difficult to get into a stirrup. Only cabróns wear round-toed boots. Now I *can* fix you up with any of these items. But the hat is the most important and telling piece of equipment for a *true* cowpoke. Large brims, even exaggerated brims, manifest authenticity. Cute, small-brimmed, Mouseketeer cowboy hats are a dead giveaway of an Eastern impersonator, a dude, a greenhorn. The image is enriched by sweat, range wear-and-tear, and a worn-out hatband—no feathers. I sell a lot of feathered hatbands to tourists and city folk. Straw hats in the summer and felt beginning in fall, and if you don't understand what that means, your hat is probably too damn cute. Black, brown or beige; get it?

A wooden match or toothpick clenched between the teeth and constantly interfering with appropriate articulation is a traditional finishing touch. A lump of chew in the cheek or a circular can of snuff wearing a ring through the wallet pocket separates the wrangler from the wanna-be.

One last point: if you dress like this in Colorado, the locals will think you're a Texas tourist; if you dress like this in Texas, they think you're from Oklahoma; if *one* dresses like this in Oklahoma, folks will think you're an Indian.

My paternal grandfather was named Mischa Pietrov Alexandrovsk Swarznikopopulartarschink, Senior. Affectionately called Mischa. Grandfather was an expert in fine porcelain, both the Oriental originals and the Eastern European pieces derived from Asian techniques. He had a high appreciation for quality ceramics which he passed on to his sons, and his sons, in turn, tried to pass on to their sons. At one time the Czar's Curator of the Arts held him in great favor, but the climate in pre-war Russia turned colder for Jews.

I was named after my grandfather. Therefore, my real name is Mischa Pietrov Alexandrovsk Swarznikopopulartarschink, the Second. Grandfather, Mischa the First, an original by anyone's book, sold several pieces of prized porcelain to avoid Czarist persecution of our family. There were beautiful pieces: a cobalt blue-and-white vase from the Ming dynasty's Wan-li reign, other Kraak ware, a matched pair of tri-color camels, a kendi pouring vessel with ornate carp. Using the proceeds from the sale, he packed up the entire extended family: cousins, nephews, nieces, as well as his children, and shipped twenty-seven people to America. Our freight included the remainder of the exquisite ceramic and rug collection. In America grandfather shortened the family name to Swarznik, and my father, when he became family patriarch, shortened it further to Swarz. Mischa, II, that's me, was born in Teaneck, New Jersey, but grew up in Manhattan. Sadly, I never knew my grandfather and namesake. Most of the family settled somewhere in the five boroughs.

However, my Uncle Max, the black sheep of all my father's brothers, seven in total, decided to try his luck in a wild town to the south called Miami Beach. With gregarious charm and indefatigable energy, he quickly shmoozed his way up the ladder of success in the hotel and resort business.

"I started as a bellboy," he would tell anyone who would listen, "but I was good looking then, and clever. I remembered everybody's name. It didn't matter who: the big shots, their wives, their children, their dogs even. I knew the name of everyone who worked in the hotel and those of the deliverymen, the maids, the guy who sold papers and candy in the lobby—Fidel Sanchez, was his name. People like that. They like you to call them by their name. It makes them feel important. Mischa, remember this."

I was impressed with Uncle Max because he was the first to lose his Russian and Jewish accent. Max worked very hard to acquire an American manner of speaking. However, because the people with whom he most often spoke in Miami were the other bellmen, the bartenders, the maids, and the hired personnel in the hotel, his new manner of speaking had a slight hint of Cuba. But, like he said, he was good looking then. So he progressed from bellboy to bartender, to assistant manager, to manager of the Eden Rocke, to partner in a new hotel. "People thought my speech was sexy," he would say, "like a royal European expatriate hiding out in the States via South America. The women especially liked it."

I also liked it. Max didn't sound Orthodox and Old World, an accent which embarrassed me. I was a typical, self-conscious *American* teenager. So, I used Max as a mentor and worked hard to remember peoples' names and to sound American. Uncle Max had been my favorite since I was a toddler. He would pull coins from behind my ears. He would do the same trick with my sister and cousins. It was a neat trick and the kids always got to keep the quarters. The best summers of my youth were spent in Florida with Uncle Max. When things got busy in the hotel Max would let me put on a bellman's uniform and schlep luggage. I got to keep the tips. Max would say, "This is your own little private account, Kiddo, for a rainy day. No need to bother your father with knowing what a rich guy you're becoming. So, what is the name of the guy who hands out towels at the pool, third shift? Right! You're a smart kid." Max would pull a silver dollar from my ear and plant it squarely in my palm. He would close my hand around the coin and pinch my cheek. "And good looking, too."

I spent a lot of time around the pool and got very tan. I let my hair grow long and even learned a bit of Cuban profanity. I felt Hispanic people had more energy and zest for living than my family in Manhattan—a typical adolescent attitude. I've come to find out how the sagas of both families, Jews and Cubans, are coalesced by tragedy and struggle.

When I was about seventeen, Max returned to Manhattan from a trip to "The Great American West." He was investigating a rustic place called Phoenix, Arizona, as a possible resort hotel location. "Too dry, and too hot," he decided. "And there is no ocean. I would miss the ocean. But, I drove from Phoenix, north to a place called New Mexico and I visited a charming old town called Santa Fe and, my brother, Moisha, there are ceramics there I think you should see."

Max unwrapped a large shinny black pot. It had the polished surface of a black pearl and near the top were what looked like gray incised dragons. Anyway that's what my father called them—dragons. Actually they were snakes, feathered serpents, an ancient rain symbol, intertwined along the rim. I think he interpreted the sacred serpents as dragons because he had always worked with Asian pottery. Regardless, as the patriarch, he did not like being corrected. Things were off to a bad start when Max corrected his mistake, "Dragon schmagon, Moisha, this is America! This vessel came from the desert, a place where the Indians live in mud houses. It's called a Pueblo—San Ildephonso—some Catholic saint, I don't know what he did, but they name their villages after such saints. Anyway, a handsome young woman named Maria Martinez makes these pots by hand—the coil method, you know. None are thrown on the wheel and none are poured in molds. She burnishes them with stones, river rocks, and fires them in cow dung. Can you believe anything this beautiful comes from cow shit?"

Being a teenager, I laughed at the profanity; my mother frowned. My father sulked.

"Sorry, but I'm so excited to show you," Max went on. "The West is full of such beautiful things, and I wondered, would you want to sell such prizes in Papa's shop?"

Perhaps it was that my father was still sensitive about the antique store being called, "Papa's shop," since he had inherited it several years ago, and to be honest, greatly improved the cash flow. Regardless, whether he was responding to the unintentional insult or truly did not care for the pot, he barked out, "Feh! It is crude. And no people of taste will have such a pot in their homes, done by savages, and smelling of dreck. Aroysgevorfeneh gelt, wasted money! Whatever you paid for that black shtik of mud was too much. Next you will be telling me you want us to wear cowboy boots and lazlo our women."

"It's *lasso*, Moisha," my Uncle Max answered, "No, I can see The Wild West is not for you."

I, of course, was immediately dazzled by the pot. I saw the wildness, the ruggedness of the West in its dark depths. I imagined the smell of campfires and dreamed of the vast horizon exploding in sunsets of red, orange, and gold.

"But think about this," Max continued. "I also visited Denver, Colorado and a friend of mine from Florida now is the dean of a hotel and resort college at Denver University. Mischa loves the resort business. I will pay for him to go to this school, if you will allow him to work for me later. He is a good kid, he remembers everybody's names, a gaon, and he is a good-looking guy. He can go very far in this business. He can take care of his parents when his father, Moisha, is too old to work and too old to see new ideas."

My father immediately saw the excitement in my eyes. "What harm could it do," he said. "I have the whole family to look after now. Children and grand children, wives and sisters. I'm one man, what can I do. A mess I inherited. Better my zun, the loksh, becomes a hotel tycoon, a good rug salesman he is not. A good student he is not, a smart kid, I don't think so. A bellboy, a grinning hotel clerk, a golom—maybe. Is this schmontses? Look at you, Max, my brother. It's a nice suit you're wearing, a diamond ring on your hand. Not bad, but for me diamonds are for women to wear. But you do well, and a ganef, you are not. Worse could happen to this kid. Besides, a college graduate we do not have yet in the family. Maybe it could work. Dos gefelt mir. Considering all the kids I'm responsible for, him I won't miss."

He spoke for all to hear, "The boy can do what he likes. He is no good in the antique business anyhow. He breaks more than he sells. But the first time I see him on a horse, home he comes."

It was from that moment, and for the next year, while I finished high school, I wore black, pointy-toed cowboy boots. It drove my father crazy and forced my mother to tears as I clomped around the house. I watched—at least ten times—every Western movie that hit Manhattan. My father beat me silly one evening when I came home wearing a cowboy hat and refused, in a forced frontier accent, to remove it in the house and put on a proper yarmulke for the Sabbath. "A man don't remove his hat, 'cept far a wedding or a funeral, pard."

"Its going to be your funeral, you shlump, if you don't take off that stupid hat—shmatteh—cover your head properly. The sooner you go this Denber, the better. Meshugener, you are making your mother and me crazy. Oi, g'vald with the cowboys."

"The other students at my high school mocked me. They called me Tex and Roy and Hoppy. The girls thought I looked like a hood, a juvenile delinquent, "Marlon Brando he is not," and the boys thought I looked like a schlemiel. "Hey," they would yell. "Roy Schlemiel Rogers, where did you park your horse?" I hated them, and the day after school was out I was on the train west.

I actually thought I would see Indians on the streets and buffalo on the front lawns of Denver. I was greatly disappointed and a bit concerned when the students at Denver University had similar disparaging things to say about my Western dress. They were no more forgiving than were my Manhattan high school chums. "Hey, Hopalong Schlemiel Cassidy, where did you get those boots?" The problem was that although most of my professors and colleagues liked me, I remembered everybody's names, I couldn't pass a class, nor could I get a date. I dreamed of the Old West, Tombstone, Dodge City, and Santa Fe. I loved the mountains and learned more about the Ute Indians and miners than I did about hotel accounting and restaurant management. My fate was sealed when I attended a Glen Miller concert at a new outdoor amphitheater just west of Denver called Red Rocks Park.

I remember this night. He didn't have a ticket. So, he—Wild Billy Swarz—actually he wasn't Wild Billy yet; sorry, time means little to us mythologicals. I often hung out atop the northern rock formation because it was here that people often fell. Like moths to a flame, dozens of teenagers, college students, tourists, macho boys, and drunks climbed the rocks and took a tumble off the North face. No serious disasters, but humorous folly often followed—a broken arm or two, a cracked skull, skinned knees and elbows—kid stuff. So, he, Mischa Swarz, along with a dozen other foolish souls, climbed the giant red monolith that formed the north wall of the natural amphitheater. The stage sat snugly between two behemoth

*primordial pyramids, surrounded by numerous lesser monuments
and diagonal slabs of sedimentary sandstone, pushed skyward by
folding and faulting, geological waves in my terrestrial blanket,
wrinkled and rolled while I tossed and turned during slumber.
Sitting atop the formation, dangerously perched like a puffin on the
cliffs, Mischa and his cohorts watched a leviathan, summer moon
undulate in the soupy evening over Denver to the east. One of my
favorite moons, it swam in the shallows of reflected city lights
beneath a midnight blue sky congested with stars, luminous on the
nocturnal tide. I remember this night; it was then that I first
considered him as a recruit. He mumbled something to one of the
other gate-crashers about feeling submerged "in potential discovery
and eminent adventure." No wonder most his friends thought him
odd. He scanned the chiffon silhouette of the northern horizon and
spotted a lone twinkling light in the dark distance, near the middle of
a two-dimensional, purple-shadow foothill. It was as if one of the
stars had fallen from the sky and nestled in the middle of this violet
triangle. He vowed he would hike the few miles in the dark to
investigate that lone starry light. At the intermission of the concert,
he began his trek. I followed in the shadows. After about a mile or
two the orchestra started again, and the muffled but mellow sounds
of Big Band music softly filled the valley as Mischa walked toward
Lookout Mountain, the grounded star, and his decree with destiny.*

*Although Mischa did not know it, great prehistoric beasts
walked this same trek ten million years before. Then, however, the
land was flat, swampy, and adjacent to a giant shallow inland sea.
In the dark he passed right over their footprints and unconsciously
kicked the petrified fossils of fist sized squid and ancient nautilus. I
remember; the light drew him on. Eventually, he had to cross
Highway 40 and climb uphill along its shoulders. There was very
little traffic and the twittering light beckoned him. He often lost sight
of the light behind hills, but if he continued long enough it would
reappear around a curve or between slopes. I, Turtle, silently urged
him on.*

I walked past a sign that said, "Mount Vernon Country Club
2 Miles, Lookout Mountain 6 Miles." I thought to myself, "Mischa,
if this light turns out to be a country club, I'm going to smack myself

for my credulity. I finally walked around the last curve and through
the pine trees I saw the source of the light. An old neon sign
sputtered in rhythmic death throngs its fading message: " CO Y
GRIL & RA IN   PO T."

"I wondered: did they misspell, "Girl?" What the hell was a
'Coy Girl Rain Pot?' No, it didn't make sense, although the visual
image of a bevy of girls waiting in the rain smoking pot was
intriguing. It had been a long walk, after all. As I got closer I could
read the letters that had long ago dwindled—CODY'S BAR GRILL
& TRADING POST. It sat on top of an old adobe building. The
building looked as if it had crawled in penance all the way from the
pueblos of New Mexico. An old man was hanging a sloppily painted
sign below the neon from an extending viga. "FOR SALE," it read. I
felt the cold shutter of goose flesh and a chilling dip of my
consciousness: somehow I knew, I was home.

"You look like a puppy what just lost its wean," said the old
man hanging the sign. "There is hot coffee inside." He nodded
toward the door. Even in the dark and distorted light of the neon sign
I could see the door was painted as bright a turquoise as modern
pigment science would allow. I cautiously entered. It was as if
suddenly walking into a dream—the musky smell of harsh tobacco
smoke and piñon, of old buffalo robes and wet horse hide, of
gunpowder and campfire coffee. A fire that needed tending
smoldered in the huge rock fireplace, and a lone green, bankers lamp
on a desk near the entrance dimly illuminated an interior, which was
filled with the silhouettes of shelves and counters cluttered with
Indian and frontier paraphernalia. Toward the back of the building, a
red and yellow Hot Nut machine cast a weak light on the cafe
counter and a row of red-topped, chrome stools. Like a ghost, a
slumped figure drifted between the light of the nut machine. I stood
paralyzed. The old spirit reached slowly and opened the doors of the
machine; ethereally reached inside. He turned his weathered face
toward me and grinned an evil toothless smile. He raised the
forefinger of his other hand to his leathery lips and signaled for
silence. His eyes demonically sparkled in the red light of the Hot
Nuts machine.

"Damn it, Willie," florescent light suddenly blinked on and
filled the room with an unnatural white-green flood, "You old addict,

you gummed away a pound of those things already today. You're going to make yourself sick." The old man had finished hanging his sign and entered behind me. "Coffee?" he asked.

I sat on a stool; the ancient Indian strolled behind the counter and sat in a rocker near the entrance to the grill. The old white man stood behind the counter and poured three cups of coffee. The Indian placed a cashew between his lips. It sat there like a yellowed tusk pointing toward his corrugated nose. When he saw me watching he wiggled the nut up and down, and got that same demonic twinkle in his eyes. When he was sure he had my attention on the legume tusk, he suddenly sucked it inside his mouth with a pop.

The white man walked around the counter to the fireplace and lifted a split pine log from the woodbox. I turned on the stool and visually drank in the interior. Even in the unpleasant green cast of the florescent light I was still mesmerized. Here was the Dakotas and the New Mexico of Uncle Max's tales, the west of the Hollywood films, all those frontier things I had anticipated in Denver that had been paved over and citified.

"How much?" I heard myself ask. I didn't even recognize my voice.

The old man threw the log on the fire and reached for the poker to stir the embers, "The coffee? It's ten cents, usually, but I already closed the books today. It's on me. Have another, if you like. That's the last pot and it will just keep me up and make old Willie there wet his bed."

The old Indian placed another cashew between his lips and twinkled.

"No, sir," I asked, still in a dream. "How much for the trading post?"

The old man laughed as he rubbed his hands together to shake off the pine bark and the Indian sucked the nut into his head. "Well, I don't rightly know. I haven't figured that out just yet. You know somebody who might be interested?"

"Me." I still couldn't believe I said it.

He laughed again and I thought I heard another pop of an inhaled nut tusk.

"Sorry, son," he said, "but you don't look exactly prosperous at the moment."

"Well, I'm not, prosperous," I said, "but I can come up with a little cash for a down payment. How big of a hurry are you in to sell?"

"No hurry. How much is a *little cash*?" he asked

I added quickly in my head. I had over the years saved about five thousand dollars from tips as a bellman in Florida—a secret stash I told no one about. With the anticipated tuition check from Uncle Max, books and materials, rent in the dorm, plus the small check my father sent to curb living expenses, I figured I could probably put together an additional two thousand illicit dollars and another thousand in nine weeks, and for several nine-week intervals until Max and the family caught on that I wasn't going to school. I concluded that I could fool them for at least a year and a half, maybe two.

I excitedly gave the sum of my calculations, "Six, maybe seven thousand, to start with. How much?"

"That's not an awful lot, kid," he said. "But have another cup of java and let's talk."

"My name is Mischa Swarz, sir. May I ask your name?" I was feeling confident.

"Sure, son, thanks for asking. It's Doogan. But most people call me Cactus Face." He rubbed his chin with roughish delight and grinned. I immediately knew where he got his nickname. The white whiskers on his jaw were as prickly as nettle.

"That over there," the old man pushed a thumb toward the Indian. "That's Willie, Willie Wolf Song."

I quivered with excitement. *It's the West, the real West.*

The deal we struck was this: seven thousand dollars down; a thousand every nine weeks at tuition time for three years; Cactus Face would continue to run the place for the next three years and split the net seventy-five percent to twenty-five percent held in escrow for me. I would work for room and board and what was to be my wages would be applied to paying toward the principal of the sale. At the end of the three years, the place was mine, or at least fifty-one percent. I would then be the manager/owner, lock-stock-and-cashews, but would have to keep on old Wolf Song until the ancient indigenous American died or decided to move of his own accord. The remaining forty-nine percent could be paid off at an annual amount agreed upon at the beginning of each fiscal year, "so as not to shrink your sphincter and give me enough to buy cigarettes, beer, and bate worms. I figure I'd like to drown about a hundred of the little wagglers a month." said Doogan.

In the years that followed I fooled my Uncle Max and my father into thinking I was attending Denver University. Anticipating the day I took over, I planned a dozen improvements. But I had to admit, the best times were while I was learning the trading post aspects of the business. This included traveling in the winter with Doogan to Northern New Mexico and Arizona; purchasing the pottery, basketry, and weavings from the Indians. I studied the various histories of both Plains and Pueblo Indian people, of desert tribes, and mountain clans, and eventually became an expert in their arts and crafts. I studied like I was possessed, something, I'm sad to say, I could never do at D. U. even though I'd made a promise to Uncle Max.

At last, for legitimate reasons, I got to dress in Western garb, and, as is necessary for any good merchant of the Southwest, I became an entertaining storyteller and an expert liar. Don't you agree?

Doogan was the first to call me: Billy. It was after he coaxed me onto a horse for the first time. The fall to the ground was longer than the ride, and all of the attempts that followed resulted in the same painful conclusion. "Mischa, my boy," he grumbled. "I don't believe you could ride a wild *billy* goat. I better teach you to drive."

Wolf Song smiled, he never laughed, and grunted some incoherent Indian/English mumble that sounded like, "Been there, done that."

Despite my painful riding lessons, I took great glee in finding my niche on Lookout Mountain, and now—at last—had acquired an occidental nickname: Wild Billy. I was very proud of this nom de guerre, a pseudonym which I first thought combined two famous characters from Western lore—Buffalo Bill Cody, of course, considering the name of the business, and *Wild* Bill Hickok. I silently hoped that locals and tourists alike associated me with these frontier characters. I warmly assumed that they gave credence to my new name. I mentioned before how Easterners change their monikers. The nickname becomes a symbol of acceptance into the frontier fraternity. Buffalo Bill's real name was William Frederick Cody, and that of Wild Bill was James Butler Hickok. Both were originally from the East. You understand my point. Doogan, a rare Colorado native, Captain Alonzo P. Doogan, retired, often teased me mercilessly that my nickname had nothing to do with either frontiersman.

There was, I hate to admit, neighborly doubt about my nom de plume. And I also hate to admit, but at first I, Wild Billy and soon-to-be-proprietor of a trading post, was confused as to which frontier hero was which. I'd been studying hard to learn about Indian crafts. My knowledge of frontier lore came from the movies I had frequented in Manhattan. So, rather than admit ignorance and admit I was a name-usurper, I started lying about my background. I needed a Western nickname—for the business and for my newly acquired vaquero pride. After all, who ever heard of a cowboy called *Mischa*?

Buffalo Bill, now there was a hero with whom I wouldn't mind being associated. I found out later that Wild Bill Hickok was a good friend of Buffalo Bill's. The two old frontier fables had brawled and debauched nearby in Denver as they spent raucous nights at the Buckhorn Exchange, a frontier bar serving buffalo and rattlesnake. Every inch of wall sprouts the trophy heads of big game, much of it bagged by Buffalo Bill himself. Or there was Billy the Kid, the infamous New Mexican outlaw. It wouldn't be so bad if people associated me with a rough and tough hombre like Billy the Kid. So, I didn't mind when Doogan started calling me Billy, and when asked my name by locals and tourists alike, I would answer, "Billy, Wild Billy. Ask me again and I'll slap ya' silly."

From the first day I fell off that horse, I hated the dumb animals. Not good for someone named Wild Billy and trying to look every bit the plainsman. It's okay not to ride a horse if you are a New Jersey Jew boy named Mischa, but not for the proprietor of a Western bar and grill. They have a blind spot right in the middle of their head. Horses not Jews. Well, maybe my father. So anything that moves from the right and past the blind spot to the left, surprises the stupid beast. Yes, I know they're beautiful animals, but mine would jump—every time. I never understood why the four-legged idiot couldn't remember that whatever was moving there on the right would in all likelihood reappear on the left. He'd buck and I'd fall off.

Regardless of the danger, I was forced to learn to ride so I could participate in parades on Buffalo Bill Days in Golden. It's a huge, annual celebration and attracts crowds from all over the Foothills and Denver. There are food booths, beer stands, a rodeo; the whole town is lit up. Cactus Face would insist that we ride in the annual parade. He would say, "It's good advertising, and it is the only time I can get old Willie to come out in the day light."

True to his lycanthropic totem, Wolf Song did most of his marauding after sundown. I always thought, because of the way his eyes twinkled in the dimmest of light, that the old Indian could see in the dark.

It wasn't until after the second or third Buffalo Bill Days parade that I was informed about the legend of the real and actual William F. Cody. Everyone just assumed I knew. Buffalo Bill, I found out, had his grave and a museum right on Lookout Mountain. I felt like one of those typical locals who never enjoyed those things that bring visitors to their realms; I had never toured the museum. Oh, I knew where it was, I had to: so I could give directions. If customers or lost tourists asked, I even knew the price of admission and the hours it was open. But, I was so busy learning the business; I never dropped into the place. I didn't know the fate of William Frederick Cody. So, needless to say, I was surprised to learn that it was not the real Buffalo Bill leading the parade. The old silver-haired and buckskinned rider looked authentic. I made the mistake of asking Cactus Face to introduce me to Buffalo Bill. It was only after twelve rounds of drinks, all of which I paid for, that Doogan confessed the lie. We were not drinking with the real Buffalo Bill. The old geezer dressed as Buffalo Bill was a long-time friend of Doogan's named *Rudi*. They had a great laugh at my expense. I felt as dumb as my horse. And after so many drinks, *I* was jumping when someone crossed from my left to my right.

"Damn-it, Billy Goat, you are as gullible as the hick tourists we sell our goods. Now tomorrow, I want you to drive, don't ride, over to the Pa-Ha-Ska Teepee Gift Shop and buy yourself a book on Buffalo Bill. While you are there, you should visit his grave." They laughed and laughed until Rudi threw-up.

I didn't mind Doogan's joviality; it's the code of the West to take good-natured ribbing. So, I decided to take his advice and do some research. But I was too late.

Both Doogan and Rudi were drunk from all the rounds bought by "Billy Goat." They continued to drink. More rounds were weaseled from other customers while they told and retold the story of my mistaking Rudi for the real Buffalo Bill. You know, I'm not totally clear, but I think it was Willie Wolf Song who first put the idea in my head that Rudi was the real Buffalo Bill.

Regardless, they finally stumbled arm-in-arm from the bar and together mounted the horse that the sham Buffalo Bill rode in the parade earlier that day. I remember . . . Captain in the Reserves, Bill Rudolph, mounted with a flare and a wide wave of his Stetson to the appreciative crowd on Washington Street. Cactus Face ran and pounced over the hindquarters like a Pony Express rider to the cheers of the celebrants on the crowded sidewalk. The horse reared in a postcard pose, with Doogan hugging Rudolph's middle. The white-haired, old cowboy turned the horse in a pirouette and spurred it into a gallop. For three blocks they raced with the wind, a nose ahead of the clomping of the shoed hooves echoing down the street. It was at the intersection of Washington and Thirteenth that the Coors Beer truck propelled the trio through the plate glass windows of Foss Drug Store.

I was the first to the scene of the accident. "I never saw them coming," the driver pleaded for understanding. "I had the green light. I was looking for cars, not horses!"

No one blamed the driver—the parade was over hours ago; who but Cactus Face and Rudi would be riding a horse on a city street? The silent crowd gathered around my fallen heroes.

Doogan was cut and bleeding badly. He stumbled to his feet and mumbled, "Captain Rudolph, I believe we have killed this horse."

The old cowboy coughed blood as he laughed, waved his hat in a departing gesture, and with his dying breath said, "That's OK, Cactus Face, he's borrowed."

Doogan was rushed to the hospital where I wept at his bedside, "Like a puppy what lost it's wean."

"Now, now, Billy Goat, don't you fret," he said to me. "I have lived as I wished for a long time, and, son, no movie cowboy could ask for a better exit."

He had me bring in the papers to the trading post the next day and signed everything over to me. I wept again.

"Now you must promise me," said Cactus Face, "that you will watch after old Willie, and I believe it is appropriate you learn a little something about the real Buffalo Bill. By the way, they will be needing a replacement for the parade. And besides," he said as he patted my hand, "it's good advertising." With that, Cactus Face Doogan, my mentor, a true frontier hero, and the best friend a man could ever have, drifted over the Great Divide.

It took a few days for me to take care of the funeral details. I published an inquiry in The Denver Post and the Rocky Mountain News for any possible relatives or family survivors. No one answered. After the funeral I returned to the trading post in the dark. There was an unexplained summer chill. The old neon beckoned me as it did that first night years ago.

Willie Wolf Song was gone, as was most of the good merchandise—the Martinez pots, the Luci Lewis ceramics, the best Navajo rugs. I remembered thinking that it was probably the right time for the old thief to go, being the end of an era and all. The liquor storage cabinet had also been raided. A case of the best Scotch was gone, as was the entire stock of cashews. Liquor sales were my latest contribution to the cafe and trading post. I talked Doogan into applying for a liquor license and in the first month of stocking booze and beer we had nearly doubled the gross. Doogan was proud of his young protégé.

I pulled at the hair on the back of my head. It was getting fairly long since I quit being a college student. I thought it wouldn't take too long to grow to my shoulders, I said out loud, "I could bleach it white." I rubbed my chin, "I bet I could grow a beard in no time."

To keep myself from deeper sorrow, I pulled from the desk drawer some architectural plans Doogan and I had drawn up. We had planned to expand the cafe into a bar and restaurant, and maybe even add a pool table. There were rumors of an interstate highway, I-70, that may be built right on top of old US 40 in the near future. Doogan and I had discussed that those Interstate travelers are going to need something to eat and drink, and we can sell a hell of a lot of Indian trinkets to the rubes. We laughed. We knew we were the only stop between Denver and Idaho Springs. I took a large red marker from the desk that night, the night after Doogan's funeral, and I and scribbled two circles in front of the drawing of the trading post. Below them I drew two, vertical rectangles; it looked like two tall Fisher-Price people standing in front of the cafe, but then I printed a large red "T" in each circle. Above the building schematic I wrote in large letters: *BUFFALO BILL CODY'S BAR GRILL TRADING POST and TEXACO STATION—WELCOME TO THE WEST.* And here I am, Mr. Turtle, isn't it? You see, I always remember a name. How can I be of service?

Chapter Sixteen

The Brown Palace

Summer, 1964

When one has been around as long as I, Turtle, one becomes interested in history and culture. Stick around long enough and one witnesses the influence on history (and culture) by landscape. I have a particular affinity for geology.

We all know what history is—I am history. But, what is culture? Well, it's not too large a stretch to suggest that you are culture. A study of culture includes the arts, crafts, politics, costume, romance, music, and, of course—cuisine. All are human endeavors. I take particular delight in architecture and how it epitomizes history and culture.

Moreover, when in architecture the traditional, Western rectangular motif is abandoned for the triangle, the tussle between fame and folly is particularly entertaining. Take, for example, the pyramids.

All in all, the pyramids are the product of $a^2 + b^2 = c^2$ adjacent to $c^2 = b^2 + a^2$, that is, an isosceles right triangle juxtaposed in height to a reverse but equal isosceles right triangle; mirror images of one another. Confusing? Not if you're Egyptian.

The Eiffel Tower could be considered a triangle motif: linear and phallic, but a triangle nevertheless.

The Greeks would place triangles on top of their golden proportioned rectangles.

The Flatiron Building in New York, D. H. Burnham's 1902 masterpiece, sets an appropriate modern tone, and of course, so will the East Wing of the National Museum, I. M. Pei's proposed masterpiece, a celebration of the triangle with the glorious vigor that only a sovereign budget can stimulate.

In nineteenth century Denver, the triangle became an expression of the frontier, of adventure, of risk. The grand hotel, based on the triangle, became a symbol of the entrepreneurial spirit of historical and colorful Colorado. It is for that reason that The Brown Palace—while flirting with disaster in design, financing, attitude and ambiance—has become a beloved landmark of the Queen City of the Plains.

It was, is, and always will be the important place to stay in Denver, and on the Front Range. The Brown Palace has been the residence of mountain men and gamblers, hooligans and heroes, royalty and rowdies, politicians and presidents. The Brown Palace, so unique and bodacious in design, was destined to become as famous as its tenants, an establishment that brags about reflecting "the old times, the good times, when the Country was young."

Wedged, triangularly, between Broadway, Seventeenth Street, and Tremont, The Brown Palace stands as a monument to individualism. Henry C. Brown, after whom the hotel is named—not the beautiful brown colored stone exterior as is often believed—was not the sole entrepreneur. It was too big an enterprise for one man, just as the folly of the Front Range is too big a history for one character.

Frank E. Edbrooke was the architect of the Brown. And over the years, the hotel was partly owned, mortgaged to, or managed by nearly every major mover and shaker in early Denver history, including William H. Bush and his partner H. A. W. "Maxey" Tabor; W. S. Stratton, after whom the town in eastern Colorado is named; Charles Boettcher, namesake of the contemporary performing arts center, altruistic scholarship for Colorado undergrads, and numerous other public museums, wings of museums, gardens, and so on. Anyone who was anyone in Colorado and particularly Denver history, stayed, played (and probably got laid) at The Brown.

In the basic armature and exterior of the building, there was no wood. The skeleton of the building was created in steel; the steel totally hidden within hollow rectangles of stone. Even the floors and walls were made of hollow blocks of porous terra cotta.

The entire infrastructure—the ventilation, wiring, plumbing—were hidden in stone covered shafts running the height of the building.

The exterior was (is) primarily Arizona sandstone and Colorado red granite. Most of the stone was taken from quarries next to good ol' Morrison, twin city of the Front Range.

The building is basically fireproof; the second fireproof building built in America, the Brown's completion date being 1892.

The kitchen, by the way, was on the top floor in order to secure perfect ventilation and prevent any possibility of the "malodorous ghosts of dead and gone dinners" drifting unwanted into the rooms.

Ghosts and other less ethereal guests were housed in rooms, each and every one, having a street view.

Over the years, a variety of restaurants and lounges has provided entertainment and hospitality: The Ship Tavern being one of the most popular, famous, and enduring.

Long before the Beatles reserved rooms at The Brown Palace, the famous and infamous warmed the beds. These included both the Roosevelt boys and numerous other presidents. Eisenhower used the Brown as his campaign headquarters in the 1950's.

The Unsinkable Molly was a frequent guest. She was, however, no relation to H. C. Brown, the founder.

Hollywood and New York entertainment greats always choose The Brown as their home away from home. Thus, we have entered into the modern era (1964) for the royal old queen, and the stay of a rambunctious musical group from England threatens the sanctity of our cherished landmark, but somehow the manager allowed himself to be cajoled into accommodating these hooligans: The Fab Four, the harbingers of the new age. The Plaza in New York learned a difficult lesson: that celebrity does not guarantee civility.

"The furniture is a bit old," said Ringo.

"Antique," said George.

"It's an ambiance thing," said John. "You know, like when we were in New York, everything had to look worn-out."

"It's bloody Victorian," said Paul. "Like all those tired old posh places in England. Only there is a bloody stuffed buffalo head above the door, and the towels are much nicer. Worth pilfering."

"And the bathrobes, now there's a score," said George.

"What do ya need another bath robe for?" asked Ringo.

"Because it's there," said John.

"I thought the lift rather shabby," said Ringo.

"The elevator," said George. "We're in America now."

"I bloody know we're in America, George. I was on the plane with you, ya twit, the whole vast way. I was just thinking, for a rich country and famous hotel, the lift was shabby."

"Dilapidated," said Paul.

"It wasn't the bloody lift," repeated George.

"Meager," said Paul.

"If it wasn't the bloody lift, then what brought us up all this way? I'm beginning to worry about you, George."

"That's what I'm trying to tell you, Ringo. It's an elevator."

"And a seedy one at that," said Paul.

"It wasn't the lift or the bloody elevator," said John.

"Now I'm beginning to worry about you, John," said Ringo.

"Faded," said Paul.

"That's not what I meant, Ringo. I meant it wasn't the regular elevator. It was the service elevator."

"A bit down at the heel," Paul continued.

"That's what I was trying to tell him, " George was gruff.

"Did I say decayed?" asked Paul.

"Well," said Ringo, "that's a bit discouraging, now isn't it."

"Meager," repeated Paul.

"You said that already," said George.

"What's discouraging, Ringo, me Lad?" asked John.

"Well, if that's the service elevator, how good can the service possibly be?"

"Meager?" asked Paul of George.

"Meager!" answered George.

"Well, that's what I was afraid of," said Ringo, feeling justified.

"Why don't you have a look at your own rooms?" asked John.

"We're not all staying in here then?" asked Ringo.

"No, me Lad, it's a suite, got two bloody bed chambers."

"I had to stay with George in New York," said Ringo.

"They'll be starting rumors about you lads," said Paul.

"There was a door that opened to both suites," said George. "He had his own room. He just insisted I keep the doors open."

"Yeah," said Ringo. "It was Dutch doors."

"No, Ringo. They're not called Dutch doors," George began to explain.

"Now there you go again, George," Ringo interrupted. "Well, Mr. Got-All-the-Answers, do you happen to know the original name of New York?"

"Manhattan?" answered George with doubt and dread.

"No, George, they called it New Amsterdam and that's why in a New York hotel those are called Dutch doors."

"Pitiful," said Paul.

"Sorrowful," said John.

"Poignant," said George.

"Tar, George," said Ringo proudly. "Now which way is me room. I hope it's not as old as John's. What do you suppose they call Dutch doors in Colorado?" Paul and George followed Ringo into the adjacent room.

It was not long until Paul returned, "There must be five thousand teenage girls, surrounding the hotel."

"Going to make it difficult getting out tonight."

"We may have to take Ringo's shabby elevator."

"Maybe we should leave Ringo here with Bryan."

"No, we can't. Ringo will blab, then none of us will get out."

Ringo entered the room with a look of deep concern. "Is The Brown Palace supposed to be haunted," he asked.

"They're a little tormented that we're here," answered John. "The pandemonium outside and all. Why, what's wrong, laddy? You look troubled."

"The wall in me room keeps meowing."

"Meowing?"

"Yes, a bloody scary meowing."

"You're sure it wasn't caterwauling," teased Paul.

"Seriously, it was meowing, you know," he made the cat noise.

"Some sort of cat-astrophe," Paul continued.

"Paul, please," said John. "Give it a rest."

"You mean nip it?"

"Could it be the noise from outside, Ringo?" asked John.

"Yes, Ringo," said Paul, "it's quite catastrophic, a cat-cophoy."

"You're pushing it, Paul"

"No, it's not the noise outside," answered Ringo. "I'm categorically sure about that."

"Very good, Ringo," said Paul, "but you could be lion."

"Bugger both of you," said John.

"That's awfully Cat-holic, of you John."

"I'm going to catapult you right out of this room," John joined in.

George entered the room, "I'm suffering a bloody catarrh."

"I don't see your catarrh, nor your guitar, Paul. They haven't brought up the instruments yet, have they?" asked Ringo.

"That's not what I meant, Ringo, me boy," said George. "Someone has had a bloody cat in here. I'm having an allergic reaction."

"There, I told ya, didn't I?"

"This is a bloody luxury hotel," said John. "There are no cats; there are no ghosts. There are several thousand prepubescent American ingénues screaming outside." He raised his voice to a yell and looked George in the eye, "They are anything but catatonic!" He stomped off to the bathroom.

"What got into John," asked George.

"That was a bit of a catharsis, wasn't it?" said Paul.

"Listen to him in there, it sounds like a bloody cataract," giggled Ringo.

"What's happening here?" asked George. "I can't seem to cat-ch on." The three went to the windows and looked out at the crowd below. George continued, "I once had a skirt tell me my allergy to cats was a ploy to have her change the sheets before we pillowed."

"Making sure some other tomcat wasn't there first, ehh," said Paul.

Ringo seemed confused, they all starred out the window at the chaos below.

"It's getting a bit tiresome, isn't it?" asked George.

"Irksome, actually," said Paul.

They heard screaming that seemed to be much closer than the street.

"Look," called Ringo, "There is bloody bunch of them across the street on that roof. They are pointing toward the other window and screaming."

"I wonder if John pulled the curtains?" asked George.

"Girls may be getting a view of John's Celtic megalith."

"Well, he always was the most popular," said Ringo.

"Now that's irksome," challenged Paul. "Where did you hear that?"

"From John," answered Ringo.

"Speak of the devil," said George as John returned.

"Hey," said John, "There's a bloody cat in the loo!"

"Sure it wasn't just one of your many personal fans? Maybe she's hiding in the shower." said Paul.

"You mean one of those tarts across the way on the roof?" answered John. "No, I heard the cat before I shook."

"Well then," asked Ringo, "do you suppose the hotel is haunted?"

"Possessed, maybe," said Paul.

"I'm not allergic to ghosts," answered George, "only cats."

"I'm calling the bloody manager," said John and went to the phone.

"Right, give him a call," said Paul, "Maybe he's one of your many personal fans. He might be dying to hear from you."

"What's got into Paul?" asked John.

"He's finding the whole thing a bit irksome," answered Ringo.

"Well then, I agree," started John, "I said it already, it's not about the music anymore, its . . . yes, may I speak to the manager please?"

"Can we quote you on that?" said Paul.

"You're becoming a bit irksome yourself," said John. "Is there something I don't . . . yes, this is Mr. Lennon in the Presidential Suite. We seem to have a cat in the walls; either that or your hotel is haunted." He smiled, seeking confirmation of his clever remark from the others.

"So, his room is the bloody Presidential Suite. Well, he is the most popular," said Paul.

"Sometimes I find him the most irksome," said George.

"Well, I know you're a bit distracted right now with the girls and all, but we're just a bit concerned about the possibilities of a cat, you see my boy George is allergic. Really, over five thousand, and you've had to set up a hospital of sorts in the lobby, so many of them fainting and all. Well. Yes, I did see the ones on the roof across the way. Nearly bit off the policeman's finger trying to get her off, you say. Well."

"Did you tell him you gave the girls a little wag?" asked George.

"No wonder he's the most popular," said Paul.

"I hope the officer is going to be all right," continued John with the manager, "but, we are a bit concerned about this cat thing. Oh, it's OK is it? And why might that be? You know the cat." He nodded to the others and spoke above the mouthpiece. "It's OK, George, he knows the cat." He talked into receiver again, "Oh, Zsa Zsa, you say. Well, that makes all the bloody difference in the world. Tar." He hung up. "It's harmonious, lads, the cat belongs to Zsa Zsa Gabor. Seems it crawled into the ventilation system. They are sending someone up."

"A Lennon fan, no doubt," continued Paul.

"You don't look good in green, Paul," said John as he walked into the bathroom. He got down on all fours and began chanting, "Here kitty, kitty, kitty."

"Paul's not wearing any green, George," questioned Ringo. "I'm beginning to worry about all of you."

"Don't fret your little head, Ringo. Better you should worry that young girl on the roof over there doesn't try to jump all the way across that street and into this window."

"Hey that's not the girl from the airport bridge is it?"

"No, I don't think so. They are all starting to look alike."

"Here kitty, kitty, kitty," said John in the bathroom.

"You don't suppose John is teasing that girl into jumping do you?" asked Ringo. Paul stomped into the tiled room and stood above John.

"What the bloody hell did you mean telling Ringo that you're the most popular?"

"Did I tell him that, Paul?"

"So says Ringo."

"Well, to borrow your own words, 'there you are.' "

"It's true isn't it? You have always thought you were the most popular."

"Actually no, Paul, I don't. I don't think I'm the most popular. I don't know what bloody difference it makes if I am more popular than you."

"Then you do think you're the most bloody popular?"

"Here kitty, kitty . . . no, Paul, I already told you I don't think I'm the most popular,"

"Who is then?" asked Paul.

"Well, Ringo, of course." John, apparently tired of crawling on his knees rose and sat on the toilet, "Here kitty, kitty, you bloody cat."

"Ringo?" Paul was momentarily puzzled. "You're probably right." He changed the subject. "How is it we're going to get out of here tonight?"

"I've got a plan. A secret tunnel under the street, the waiter in the pub told me about. I just hope we don't end up like the bloody cat."

There was a sudden ruckus down the hall, near the service elevator. "Sounds like someone else is disappointed with the lift," said Ringo.

Zsa Zsa Gabor, trailed by two uniformed bellmen and three uniformed policemen, burst into the room.

"Darlings," she purred, "is it true, have you found my precious Foo-Foo?"

"Foo-Foo is in the loo," answered George.

She flitted toward the bathroom, "Foo-Foo, darling where are you?" She burst into the room, John still comfortable on the toilet. "Oh, excuse me, darling, have you got my Foo-Foo?"

John looked down, as if checking out his personals, "Foo-Foo is that you?"

"Foo-Foo," asked Paul, "is that what the pretty ladies call it in France?"

"Hungary," said John.

"Well, never mind then," said Paul.

She turned to Paul and repeated, "Do you have Foo-Foo?"

"New, I don't believe I *dew*," answered Paul.

Zsa Zsa looked at him and cooed, "Paul, oh, Darling, it's so nice to meet you. You're the cute one, aren't you." She gently pawed his cheek.

Ringo joined them in the bathroom, "Hi, I'm the most popular one," he beamed. "John says so."

"Hello, darling. I'm Zsa Zsa. I'm the cutest and the most popular one, too."

"I'm sorry, Mr. Lennon," apologized one of the police. "There was no stopping her."

Zsa Zsa turned to the policeman, "Oh, darling, don't be a Gestapo pooh-pooh. These lovely boys are eager to see me." She pawed Paul's cheek again, "Isn't that so?" She turned to John, "He is *sooo* cute, isn't he?"

"Lovely," said John.

"Comely," said George.

"Pleasing," said Ringo.

"Delightful," John started another round.

"Charming," said George.

"Oh, you Darlings," interrupted Zsa Zsa. "You are all so cute. I just love your hair. And those blue jackets. They are so cute, too."

"Paul looks good in green as well," said Ringo. "But I'm the most popular." He shook his head to make his hair dance.

"You're all the most popular darlings I know," she cooed. "Now you cute boys, where is my Foo-Foo?"

"Might Foo-Foo be the cat then?" asked John

"Yes, of course, Darling. The man at the desk told me as I was leaving through that revolution in the lobby that they found my darling Foo-Foo. True?"

"Well, not totally true," stammered John.

"Too true," said Paul.

"Sad but true," bemoaned Ringo. "Is there something I can do to keep you from getting blue?"

"Me, too," giggled George.

"Screw you!" pounced John. "Am I the only one hearing this?"

"What am I to do," whined Zsa Zsa.

"I think we can help you," said the taller of the bellmen.

John put his hands over his ears and just shook his head.

"I see you're not alone," said Paul, "so it must take two."

"What do you darlings plan to do?" asked Zsa Zsa.

John couldn't believe his ears.

"We brought a can of tuna," the bellman answered.

"Doesn't count, doesn't count," raved Paul. "You broke the train."

The bellman stood puzzled. John mumbled, "Thank you."

"Too late, John" said Paul. "You'll have to start a new."

"What are you talking about, Darling?" asked Zsa Zsa.

"Don't encourage him," said George to Zsa Zsa. He turned to the bellmen, "Now can we get on with the rescue. I've got allergies to bloody cats."

"Who knew?" said Ringo.

"Stop it, stop it, stop it," yelled John.

"Oh, that's silly, Darling," laughed Zsa Zsa, "Every man says that when he thinks he smells something suspicious on the pillow."

"Well," said Paul, "there you are."

The hotel bellhops went into the bathroom and opened a can of tuna. They placed it behind the toilet and near the air vent, which opened into one of the great vertical, infrastructure tunnels. Because Ringo was the first to hear the cat, they did the same in his room.

"Well, Darlings, I have to fly. It may take me forever to get through the lobby. It looks like a Russian field hospital down there. The chaos and I will probably be inundated for autographs. The price of popularity, I suppose."

"I know what you mean," said Ringo.

"If my precious Foo-Foo comes out, you are going to have to be darlings and ship her to me. I must take her sister, Moo-Moo, and shoo."

"Oh, pooh," said Paul. "I was hoping we could all go out and get something to eat. Zsa Zsa, dear, we're thinking about some good old American type food. Can't you join us? You know, venison, pheasant, wild pig. Frontier food."

"That sounds more like Ivanhoe, Darling. You know I once dated Errol Flynn, or was it Robert Taylor, such handsome darlings. They, too, tried to tell me they were allergic to cats. But sorry, no, I can't possibly. You were such a darling to ask."

"Buffalo, Biscuits, hard-tack, jerky, pioneer grub, partner," said George.

"Yes, burritos, enchiladas, tacos, beans, and something called a chimichanga," beamed Ringo.

"That's not American, Ringo. That's Mexican."

"That's ridiculous. Next you'll be telling me spaghetti isn't Italian."

"Originally: Chinese."

"You're a cheeky lot," said Ringo.

John interrupted, "What's all the fuss then? I'll just call room service and order a bit of mayonnaise. We've got tuna in the bathroom."

"And sweet pickle relish," said Ringo. "Got to have relish with me tuna."

"Actually," said John, "I relish a grilled cheese."

"Don't tease."

"Yes," agreed Ringo, "a grilled cheese if you please."

Paul joined in, "I'm on my knees."

"It all sounds so delicious, darlings, but I cannot stay. Please, send me my Foo-Foo as soon as you get her. I just can't bear to be without her. You're such darlings." She touched Paul on the cheek again and kissed Ringo on the top of the head, then turned in a flowing pirouette, grabbed the arm of one of the police and said, "Come, darling, I will need an escort of the local gendarme if I'm ever to get through that melee downstairs. Oh, you're very tall aren't you?"

The other police followed Zsa Zsa and her new escort. John and a bellman were talking quietly near the bathroom door. John slipped him some money. He smiled and put the several bills in his pocket. He looked at his watch and nodded his head in the affirmative. John got a Cheshire cat grin on his face.

"You look like you might actually try for the tuna," said Paul. "What's up?"

"Well, the bell lad and I were just confirming our escape route for this evening. Seems there is indeed a historical and secret tunnel from the Brown Palace to the Navarre building across the street. We agree that Zsa Zsa leaving could create the distraction we need to make it unseen to the infamous tunnel. Hungry, anyone?"

"I believe Hungarian is the proper term," said George

"John, you old dog," said Paul.

"What about the cat?" asked Ringo.

The tunnel smelled of darkness, history, and secrets. "It's the kind of place", thought John, "where, ever since I was a nipper, the minute I enter, I feel like I have to go the bathroom. The excitement of being where you're not supposed to, I suppose. The perverse allure that there is a chance you could get caught sneaking around. Like, when I was a tike playing hide and seek in me parents' closet."

"I have to go to the bathroom," whispered Ringo.

"It's bloody dark in here," whispered George.

"Why are we whispering?" asked Paul.

"Because it's bloody dark in here," answered George.

"What's that noise?" asked Paul.

"Bloody hell, Ringo, not now. Not here," cried John.

"I can't help it. It just come over me. I had to go. Don't believe I added anything to the musty smell of the place, and it is a dirt floor after all. Sorry, I felt guilty, like when I hide in me parents' closet."

"Are you making fun?" asked John.

"Well, don't forget to give it a wag," said Paul.

"Ringo always has all the fun," said George.

"Never do forget," smiled Ringo and he shook his head. His hair danced and he half expected to hear screams of admiration.

"The darkness is vast," said George.

"Deep and vast," mumbled Ringo as he zipped his britches.

"How much farther is it?" asked Paul.

"The darkness is immense," George repeated.

"It can't be too much farther," answered John. "The bellman said it runs under the street to the Navarre building directly across. He's supposed to be waiting for us."

"The darkness is extensive," said George. "Is the Navarre far?"

"Oh, please," said John. "Don't start. Not here. Not now."

"Boundless," said Ringo.

"Where is the torch" asked Paul. "Didn't we bring a torch?"

"A voluminous darkness," said George.

"Expansive," said Ringo.

"Burgeoning," said George.

"Burgeoning?" asked John.

"Who's got the bloody torch?" yelled Paul.

"I do," answered George.

"Well, flick the bloody thing on!" exclaimed Paul.

"Ahh, a burgeoning light," said John.

"What is this place?" asked Paul.

"It was a smugglers' tunnel during the American Prohibition —booze and broads—sight unseen," said John. "Sneaked from the fancy hotel to the scrubber house."

"Are we going to visit some chippies?" asked Ringo.

"Trollops," said George.

"Floozies," added Paul.

"Strumpets," continued George.

"Harlots," said Paul.

"Are we going to partake of paramours?" asked Ringo.

"Alas, the doxy business is long gone, Ringo, me horny little chum. We are using the tunnel as an escape from the pandemonium at the hotel."

"My disappointment is vast," said Ringo.

"Burgeoning," said George.

"Let me hold the torch," said Paul.

"Hold yourself," answered George.

"It's my turn," whined Paul.

"Children, we must learn to share," said John.

"I haven't had a turn," pouted Ringo.

"You are holding yourself," said John to Ringo.

"Oh, all right," said George handing the flashlight to Paul. "But no games!"

"I can't help it," replied Ringo. "It's spooky. This place gives me the chills."

Paul flicked out the light. "And it's daaaark. Heh, heh, heh."

"I knew you'd do some childish thing," said George. "give me back the bloody torch. You are such an adolescent."

"Juvenile," said John.

"Urchin," said George

"Whippersnapper," giggled Paul

"Enfant terrible," added John. "Enfant gate," he emphasized. He paused. "Wait a moment. What's that noise?"

Paul pointed the light toward the sound.

"Bloody hell, Ringo, not again!"

Paul refused to leave on the light. But they continued, confident they knew the way by memory. All made prankish ghost noises except Ringo.

"Minx," said George.

"Tot," added John, but suddenly yelled, "Bloody hell!"

At the end of the tunnel, there where three stairs and a concrete platform over which John tripped.

"Put on the bloody light, Paul, before I break me leg!"

Paul turned on the flashlight and shined it on the stairs, around the end of the tunnel and onto an old iron door that hung from huge riveted hinges. It was open just a tad. The dark continued beyond the door.

"We've lost Ringo," noticed George.

"Your childish noises have scared him back to the hotel," said John.

Paul shined the light all around the platform and past the door. Ringo was not to be seen.

"Look, there is his last spot," said Paul shining the light down the tunnel, "and his tinkle leaves a trail coming this way. It stops there, but no Ringo. It's a mystery. Oh, the horror."

"There's evil afoot," said George. "And Scotland Yard's an ocean away."

"A bloody film noir," said John.

"John," asked Paul, "Have you gone blooming Frog on us here in the dark?"

"Ringo," called out John. "Would you quit fooling around!" There was no answer.

"You see what you've done, Paul," said George, "with your brattish nonsense. You scared the boy, and he's bolted for who knows where."

"Or the boogey man's got him," whispered Paul.

"Give me the torch," demanded John. "I'll find him."

John grabbed the flashlight from Paul and pointed it back down the tunnel. He followed the oval of light on the floor, flashing it on the walls every few paces as he progressed into the dark.

George and Paul watched the circle of light descend away from them as the darkness grew around them.

"The darkness is encroaching," said George.

"Dramatically engulfing," whispered Paul.

"John," yelled George, "can you give us just a bit of light back here for a moment?"

John ignored him. The light grew smaller and dimmer. The darkness closed in on the pair. Suddenly a terrible groan from John echoed up the tunnel toward them. The light flashed on the distant ceiling and went out.

"There is very little humor in that," yelled Paul. "John? John?"

There was no answer.

"Now look what you've done," chastised George.

There was no sound. The damp coldness of the tunnel slowly entered them. Neither said a word. Even their breathing was silent. They waited for some sign from John. Nothing came.

"First you lose Ringo, and now John," whispered George. "I can play the bloody guitar but where the hell are we going to find a drummer at this late date?"

"Percussionist," came Ringo's voice from behind them.

Both jumped out of their skin. Their screams echoed down the tunnel, becoming a chorus of fright. They turned toward the voice but could see nothing. Suddenly, just inches away in the other direction, a face emerged from the darkness behind them. Sensing it, but not yet focusing, they turned in midair and screamed. The face was horribly lighted from below and the elongated shadows of the chin and nose made it ghoulish.

"I see you've found Ringo," chanted John. "Boogie, boogie." The light went out.

The laughter of John and Ringo filled the darkness. It went on for several minutes. Every time it seemed to die, one or the other of them would begin again and renew the merriment.

Finally, Ringo stopped and asked, "What's that noise?"

John flashed the light toward the sound and found Paul and George leaning against the tunnel wall.

"It's your fault," grinned Paul. "Bloody impish if you ask me."

"Well that's a vast improvement," said George as he zipped his pants, and turned to leave the tunnel.

"Hold on," pleaded Ringo. "I won't be a moment."

TURTLE, COYOTE, RAVEN and RINGO:
Mystical Journeys

Part Two: Hands of the Bear is the Present

"It's being here now that's important . . . All there is ever, is the now."—George Harrison, Beatle

"I live in the moment; can't seem to get past it."—Anthony Hands of the Bear, Tohono O'odham

Chapter Seventeen

Hardhat

Summer, 1964

*The Anasazi Indians, ancient ancestral architects, first
expanded caves to meet their residential needs in the south facing
walls of Mesa Verde, Chaco Canyon, and Bandelier's Frijoles
Canyon. Each landscape is a masterpiece collaboration of Earth—
me Turtle, Wind, and Rain. Today, in an attempt to be clever and to
maintain the rugged Paleolithic environment of the park, modern
planners at Red Rocks Amphitheater mimicked the* ancient ones *and
built extensions adjacent to natural vaults; thus, were bathrooms
built to augment existing caves, which were in turn used as
storerooms. The contemporary masonry echoed the Pueblo adobe
and stonework of the Anasazi who also taught the moderns to use the
caves for storage. Consider your grandmother's root cellar—cool,
dark, spooky.*

*Speaking of spooky, such is the song of unseen, dripping
water. During slumber, I allow my natural collaborators, Rain and
Wind, to sculpt my epidermal layer. Water, the more capricious of
my artistic kin, recently took an uncharted path down the steep rock
slippery-slide of the north face of the northern formation enclosing
the amphitheater and eventually disappeared into a crevasse and
darkness. Male visitors and park employees, frequent users of the
faux-adobe facilities, heard the hydro-melody echoing behind a
cinder block wall perpendicular to the urinals. Being less aesthetic
than I, they surmised aqueous damage. From the reverberating
sound of it, they deduced that there must be a natural cave, a
forgotten storeroom, beyond the man-made partition. Fearing
further damage, the current engineers decided to try and subvert the
creative efforts of Rain and in so doing, have irked her sculptural
partner, Turtle . . . me . . . when irritated or circumvented—The
Beast. What folly follows . . .*

A group of Denver-based engineers sat around a large conference table. Architectural plans covered the surface; coffee cups held down the curled paper corners.

"We've lost the original plans," said the architect near the head of the table, "They're buried in some warehouse, but I reiterate, building bathrooms adjacent to caves used as store rooms was common practice when the park was first designed. Besides," said the engineer, "we need to expand the bathrooms in anticipation of the huge crowds the upcoming Beatles concert is bound to attract. Go figure. If there is space behind that wall," he tapped the blueprint with his mechanical pencil, "the expansion can go inward rather than having to knock down the fine pseudo-Anasazi adobe of the exterior. In addition, we won't have to build over the sidewalk and can avoid widening the ramped walkway. Call that Indian guy on Lookout who screwed up the plumbing job in the concession stand, he owes us some time, and have him knock down the wall; then we can get a look-see into the cave."

It was the consensus strategy. Park administrators agreed. One added a second element to the plan, "And have that little bandy rooster, Henry Humboldt, and his Rangers keep an eye on things."

Despite the natural rock walls, the concrete floors, and urinals that looked more like huge low industrial sinks, designed in an effort to accommodate inaccuracy and historical offhand intent by males, the place still smelled like a bathroom.

I'm being punished, thought Anthony, for screwing up the job in the concession stand. He'd show them: I'm taking a break. I need a beer and a smoke. This piss-ant job, and it does smell like ant piss, will be here tomorrow.

He was born: Anthony Hands of the Bear, Antonio Nowi Ahgachug. Today, they call him *Tony Hardhat*. He earned this bumptious moniker by taking serious coup on a rather grizzly construction worker one intoxicated evening at Buffalo Bill Cody's Bar Grill Trading Post and Texaco Station. It was a fair fight, a legendary bout for the local mountain people, and after annihilating his Viking combatant with his fists-of-the-bear, Tony, instead of scalping him, ceremoniously relieved his downed enemy of his bright-yellow-plastic hardhat and has worn it to this day as a symbol of victory.

Tony considered himself a regular, "a consummate attendee," at Cody's and, when not forced into manual labor, bragged that his calling was being the in-house hustler. He knew it was not an overly impressive monarchy; there was only one pool table. However, his fiefdom had a lot of frontier ambiance—a century of pine smoke and soot ambiance, of cigar smog, tall tales, and manly laughter. The aroma was enhanced by a history of a million cigarettes smoked, 20,000 beers spilled, 10,000 hearty fires, and a chimney (and floor) never swept.

Anthony aesthetically loved that the rustic, heavy pine tables, chairs, and pioneer furniture were made dark not by wood stain, but by time. Eons of marinating in a thick interior atmosphere had turned the white pine into a comfortable, earthy umber. The dark granite, moss-rock fireplace with a flawed flue and a floor of ancient ashes was the fountainhead of the miasmal marinate. The fireplace was large enough to park a Volkswagen atop the log grill and sizzle the bug: wheels and all. The smoking tires would have added little to darken the air. But Tony's pool table was well lit. Otherwise, any ambient light came meekly through a front window; the panes of which were as dark and dirty as the mantel of the fireplace. The windows had thick wells of rough pine that mirrored the depth of the adobe walls. A weak incandescence would periodically enter the bar when a rare and unwary gift shop customer opened the door in search of the bathroom. Anthony had little respect for those hardy souls who stayed, even if they did have an obvious love of the frontier and an immunity to air pollution. It was his sepulcher and he felt they trespassed into his dark soup. Unless they naïvely drifted toward the illuminated pool table, innocently looked toward the bar, and unsuspectingly asked, "Anybody want to play?"

This was Tony's hideout. It was here at Cody's he found pleasure and sometimes peace. He was trying to avoid being found by Henry Humboldt, Chief Ranger and Superintendent in Charge of the Red Rocks Rangers. He knew that Humboldt would drive all over the mountain, and notify every storeowner and barkeep that he was looking for that lazy bastard Hardhat, and there was going to be hell to pay when he found him. He also trusted that no one would squeal his whereabouts to Humboldt.

Tony had been nursing a beer and chatting it up with Wild Billy for about an hour when the unexpected happened: the scrawny silhouette of Henry Humboldt stood in the alien light of the doorway between the bar and the gift shop. Tony was caught. Found out because he had underestimated Humboldt. What happened? He saw Henry's truck speed passed the bar, going both up the mountain and back down, exhibiting Henry's usual confusion. His plan was tried-and-true, as he had done so many times before, if he saw Henry's official Ranger, four-wheeler pull up in front of the bar, he would skedaddle out the back door and exit through the gift shop. He often bragged that any good ne'er-do-well always has two escape routes. Learned that from the prairie dogs.

Rarely could Henry boast about fooling Anthony. But this time, although Tony hated to admit it, brag he could.

"I got you, you sonsa-bitch. I knew if you saw the truck go passed the bar in a hurry, you'd get complacent. Careless, Hardhat! Ha! You thought because I was in a hurry, I had someplace to go, work to do. Not on your life, con man. I used the cunning of a Kodiak grizzly circling back onto his prey." Henry often told a redundant story about fishing salmon in Alaska and how the bears would circle back on the unwary. Henry, a man of small stature, more that of a cub than a large boar, enjoyed metaphorically comparing himself to animals. Tony and his friends also enjoyed creating animal metaphors about Henry, beasts less majestic than the grizzly, although all agreed: Henry was a large boor.

Anthony could picture Humboldt sneaking through the gift shop, like a thief among the icons of tourism, like a spoiled domestic Siamese stalking the pet canary because the cat had long ago lost its ability to actually hunt.

"Well," said Anthony, "I hate to admit it, but you caught me beer handed."

"You can't hide from me, Hard-head," grinned Humboldt. He loved blaspheming Tony's nickname. "You thought it was me driving by all those times. Well, it wasn't. Officer Jeffery Sheppard was driving, smart-ass. And he dropped me just down the hill. We knew you were in here the whole time. Now what do you think of that, boy." He also loved calling Tony, a man twice his size, "boy."

Tony didn't say it out loud but he thought Sheppard was also a horse's ass. In fact, Sheppard was worse. He was a brown-nosed, opportunist horse's ass who would sell out anybody for a promotion. "Ol' Sheep-hard and you are a clever pair, Henry. It's difficult knowing sometimes which of you is on top ... of the game."

Humboldt either didn't hear the insult or chose to ignore it. "That wall has got to come down tonight. The city architects will be here tomorrow to check out the cave and the water damage. You need to get your lazy ass over there and use that hard head of yours on the cinder block." He laughed at his own joke. "The city is still pissed about the sloppy job you did in the concession stand, and if they figure out that it was you who ate all those candy bars, you could be arrested for stealing park property. Oh, how I would love that. So I suggest that it is best you get your Indian ass moving." Humboldt looked past Tony at Billy behind the bar.

"And you, Billy, I thought we were friends. Why didn't you call me and let me know Hard Fart was here?"

"Now Henry, we are friends, but I don't believe snitching is in my job description. You and Tony here are big boys, you need to learn to play together; you don't need me as a nursemaid."

"I'll remember this, Billy. Someday, sometime you'll wish you had me on your side. Someday you'll need me. You'll wish you had my authority as an officer of the law to get you out of a tight spot. Well, just remember this: I needed a favor from you and you took the side of this lazy good-for-nothing pool shark."

Tony rose off the stool with deliberate slowness and dropped a five-dollar bill on the bar, "Thanks, Wildman. Save my seat." He turned and, while tucking in his shirttail, stood over Humboldt. "I won't be long."

Humboldt held his ground, grinned at Billy and said, "My Indian is just as insolent as that old thief who used to live here. What ever happened to that old Wolf-breath, Billy?"

"You got me, Henry. Robbed me blind and disappeared. You know how these heathens are." He winked at Tony. "Can't be trusted with our horses or our women."

Henry grimaced. Judging from his expression: he did not
know whether or not Billy had purposefully re-opened an old wound
by reminding him that Tony had once stolen away from Humboldt
the affections of a local mountain beauty.

"Let's get going, Hard-fart," Henry barked.

"You use that *fart* word three times today, Henry, and it will
become a permanent part of your vocabulary," answered Tony. He
smiled at Billy and offered his traditional exit salutation which
mixed Italian and Papago and translated as: *Good-bye, you old fox.*
He waved and said, "Ciao, ge'echu gaso."

"Oh, did I interrupt your dinner, Hardhead?" barked Henry.
"Chowing down were we? I'm so sorry. Get a move on."

Tony and Billy looked at each other incredulously, trying to
make sense of Henry.

Anthony exited the bar, but definitely did not like what was
happening outside. The sky had gone from sunny and partly cloudy
to dark and ominous. The air had cooled since he'd been hiding. He
thought of the local cliché: If you don't like the weather in Colorado,
wait ten minutes. He didn't have ten minutes. Suddenly, the cold
summer thunderstorm reminded him who was really in charge. A
quarter-sized hailstone ricocheted off his noggin. The hailstone
caught Anthony on his brow, just above his right eye. "Key-rye-sst,
I'm blinded," he yelled. Another, with a wicked whizzing *wheeee*,
whisked through the sodden air, and struck Tony on the top of his
head. It stung like an angry wasp. He wished now he hadn't left his
yellow hardhat in the truck. He ran for cover under a conifer next to
the tavern, wishing also that he had not been so clever in parking the
truck among the tourist cars. As it was, Henry saw it anyway and
surmised he was in the bar. "Why are the gods punishing me?" he
asked the tree; no answer, only the indignant wind.

"Forget the hail, Hardhead," yelled Humboldt from the
sanctuary of Cody's doorway. "Get your ass moving. This storm
won't last. You need to get that wall down. Get over to the
amphitheater, NOW!"

Up yours, Anthony mumbled as he ran from under the tall
pine and made a break for his pickup. He pulled his jacket over his
head and ran into the melee just as a lightning bolt hit the crown of a
tree a few yards from the one he vacated. The hair on his body went

horizontal; that on his head had a vertical panic. Electricity filled the air. The sweet, sickening smell of ozone surrounded him. A burst of adrenaline fueled a standing long jump of thirty feet. He covered half the distance to his truck before the profanity left his lips. When he landed he looked back at Humboldt. The lightning had knocked the Superintendent in Charge flat on his administrative ass, and blown off his ill-fitting toupee. I wish I had knocked off that cheap rug. He stood just long enough to shoot Henry the bird, thinking the Chief Ranger could not see the gesture from his prostrate position.

Henry caught a glimpse of the insult as he rolled over and crawled for cover into Cody's.

"Think it'll rain, Henry?" asked Billy.

"I'm going to rain on the parade of that insubordinate Indian. That sonsa-bitch just shot me the bird!"

"Oh, I'm sure the light was playing tricks on you, Henry. Tony would never be that disrespectful."

The roar of Anthony's truck was easily audible despite the thunder as it raced past the open doorway. In the brief illumination of a synchronized lightning flash he saw the silhouette of Anthony Hands of the Bear repeat his obscene gesture through the window of the truck. He turned to Billy to confirm the insult.

"Well maybe not," Billy said. "How 'bout a drink, Henry?"

"Forget it, Billy. I'm going to catch that sonsa-bitch and give him what for." Henry dusted himself off, picked up his toupee, and hurried toward the door. He paused as another bolt from above struck nearby. He shook a cloud of dirt out of his wig. "Jesus Christ, Billy," he continued to brush off his hair, "don't you ever sweep your floor?"

"Usually I just wait for a storm like this, Henry. I open the front and back doors at the same time, and let the wind tidy things up. Sure you don't want a drink while you're waiting for the lightning to stop?"

"I'm not afraid of any damn lightning!" He pulled his Smokey-the-Bear hat tightly down over his head, rocked back on his right foot, then sprung forward into a run. Three steps—and the next flash froze him in his tracks. He did a sudden pirouette and flew back into the bar. "Sonsa-bitch!" he yelled as he ran past Billy. "I forgot, I told Officer Sheppard to pick me up by the gift shop." He jerked open the door and ran into the tourist spot. When his wet shoes hit the linoleum floor, he began a two-legged, uncontrolled skid. A cloud of dust, carried on the abrupt breeze caused by both portals being open, followed him from the bar through the door, but even in his panic he heard Billy.

"There ya go, Henry, that's how I sweep up, but be careful, that gift shop floor gets slicker than deer guts on a door knob if your shoes are wet."

The door to the gift shop slammed shut with a bang. "Sonsabitch," he bellowed. He feebly grabbed for anything to break his fall. He did his best to protect his head as the loud crash of pottery, trinkets, and Chief Ranger hit the floor.

It was quiet for a couple of minutes as Henry took inventory of his limbs. Nothing was broken, other than several pieces of pottery. His bottom and his pride, of course, were severely bruised. Henry slunk into the bar leaving the door open behind him. Wild Billy had already poured a drink.

The vagrant dust cloud, sensing the reversal of the wind made a break for the parking lot as it followed him back into the bar. The front door banged closed. Henry dusted himself again and burped a meek cough. He leaned on the bar, sipped the bourbon, and said submissively, "Just add this and the stuff inside there to my tab, Billy. I'll settle up on the first of the month."

"No problem, Superintendent Humboldt. Thanks for shopping at Cody's."

Henry picked up his drink and sauntered to the window. He took a few slow sips; let the pungent and aged sweetness warm his belly. "I believe the storm is letting up," he said to no one in particular.

Anthony had just made it to his truck, cursing the hail and Humboldt in the same soggy breath. The sudden heat from his body, steamed by his panicked sprint, combined with the damp, cold air inside the truck and immediately fogged up his windows. He pushed the wet hair out of his eyes and raked along his temples using spread fingers on both hands. He took a deep breath and started the pickup. It growled as he gave it gas. He turned on the windshield wipers;

they didn't help clear the mist on the interior of the glass. He turned to his right and leaned over the back of the bench seat, tried to look out the rear windshield, couldn't see anything but the wavering glow of the lighted sign for Cody's. The rain and his aching eye impaired his vision. He wiped the glass with his hand; it took the sheen off the layer of fog with a squeak, but did little to clarify the view. Trusting to luck—he sensed the irony—he threw the truck into reverse and accelerated. Everything seemed benign until he tried to ease an extra, backward foot in order to lighten his struggle with the steering wheel when he pulled forward. The crunch was odious; his hands strangled the steering wheel as his anger with Humboldt and with himself seethed through his ears. He rolled down the driver's side window and peered toward the back of the truck at the suspected victim. There was no visible damage, he rationalized, and decided against a closer inspection as hailstones bounced off the truck. He looked around the parking lot, the air was opaque in the thunderstorm, "Screw it," he said aloud, dropped the three speed transmission into first and sped away, driving by the front door of the bar to salute Henry one more time.

Mr. Lucky, as he now called himself, had the uneasy feeling the storm was following him. He could see clear, blue-violet, evening skies just out of reach in every direction. An eerie Maxfield Parish glow, post sunset, surrounded him. Tony usually took the time to admire the clouds, the vaporous anvils of cumulonimbus, but not this evening. He felt an Icabod-Crane-uneasiness and kept looking in the rearview mirror for a pumpkin-headed horseman or the angry owner of a wounded sedan. Anthony had always translated current happenings into references from literature or music. Many a time, he caught himself humming the lyrics to a song that somehow related to his current situation, or recalled a quote from some obscure poem or novel. He thought he saw a large black raven leading the storm. *Nevermore*, he mumbled to himself.

It wasn't long until he noticed a speeding car approaching from the rear. Its bright lights, diffused in the glaze of interior window fog, illuminated his entire back windshield in a fervid curtain. As the vehicle got closer, too close for comfort, the foreboding bright lights ricocheted off the rearview mirror, temporarily blinding him. Hail began to pelt the windshield again.

He wished he were back in Cody's nursing a beer and hustling some pool. Why had nature turned on him? Why in the world was he out in this storm risking life and limb? He began to hum a *Wizard of Oz* tune and meekly sung the lyrics, "If I only had a brain . . ." He looked again in the rearview mirror and wondered why those lights were approaching so fast. Didn't they know it was hailing? "Courage," he muttered.

"There he is, Officer Sheppard," yelled an irate Henry Humboldt. "When you catch up, pull next to him on his driver's side. I want to repay his insubordination with a little gesture of my own—something I learned in New Orleans."

Anthony unconsciously increased his speed as the lights grew nearer. He recalled that Colorado law states that headlights must be turned on a half-hour before sunset, but not your brights, and sure the hell not while tailgating someone. He knew that most Colorado drivers ignore the law, preferring for some frontier reason, wrought with folly, to drive until they are dark gray silhouettes speeding down black opaque boulevards. "I'm blinded by the light . . .," he sang out loud.

A propane truck driver coming up the mountain, driving into the sunset, also somewhat blinded by the glare, had as per most of his fellow Colorado drivers neglected to turn on his headlights. He approached the oncoming traffic in the dark of the shadow of the undulating foothill.

Officer Sheppard slammed the four-wheel drive Dodge into a lower gear for more control and pulled alongside Anthony's truck, matching the speed. He was confused when out of the corner of his eye he saw Chief Superintendent Humboldt contort his body with his head too close to Sheppard's shoulder for heterosexual comfort, and his rump pointing toward the passenger window. Humboldt had tucked his legs under his torso and was obviously off balance as he used his hands to finish pulling down his trousers, exposing his buttocks in the direction of Hands of the Bear, forcing Officer Sheppard to take his eyes off the road, a potentially dangerous reflex for the driver of a speeding car on a storm dampened mountain highway.

"Kiss my ass, you heathen son of a . . . oh, shit!" Humboldt's well planned, bare-butt insult became precarious when he noticed the propane truck ominously emerging from the shadows. He looked up to see if Sheppard saw the truck. Sheppard was looking with total shock at his senior officer. Obviously, he had not yet seen their approaching doom.

Anthony remained temporarily blinded from looking in the rearview mirror at whoever was tailgating him. He never saw Henry's rebuttal, but was thankful that the lights of this idiot trying to pass on a curve illuminated the on-coming truck, which had carelessly drifted halfway into Anthony's lane. Tony eased his pickup over to the shoulder and tapped the accelerator to get to a wide part of the road before the propane truck. He sped past the rude six-wheeler and on down the hill. Out of the corner of his eye he noticed that whomever it was trying to pass him had suddenly slowed down and was trying to get back into the proper lane. Anthony cleared the propane truck and quickly followed the left-hand curve of the road around the slope, into shadow, leaving the car with the bright lights and the careless truck behind him, out of sight on the other side. He hummed, "She'll be coming 'round the mountain when she comes." He wasn't sure if he heard something or not, but he looked in the mirror. A strange flame-orange glow joined the reds of the sunset. A burning ribbon of light outlined the dark hillside eclipsed by the distant sky. "Man, is that pretty," he thought to himself. "You don't see that color very often."

"Sonsa-bitch," screamed Henry as he instinctively tried to turn his back on the impending collision. The waist of his pants bundled around his knees impeded a coordinated effort. His bare butt now faced the front of the Dodge and the oncoming truck. He noticed that Sheppard still stared in shock at him and not at the advancing doom. In resignation he mumbled, "Sheppard . . .?"

When Sheppard looked at the face of his chief, to fathom some sort of explanation as to why a grown man of Humboldt's rank would bare his ass, he saw the panic in the superintendent's eyes. He finally looked forward, searching for a source. He saw the truck. It dawned on him that trying to stop on a hail-covered highway usually achieves the same reaction as trying to run on a floor of marbles. As a kid he had suffered a broken arm doing just that. He remembered it very clearly; the memory was burned early in the life that just flashed before him. Too late for reason and deduction of cause and effect, he instinctively hit the brakes.

The suddenly impeded tires dove through the layer of frozen spheres searching for pavement. They screamed in protest.

The propane truck continued to lumber in their direction.

The driver of the truck was temporarily blinded by the bright lights and stupefied into inaction by what he thought he saw angrily glaring at him through the approaching car's windscreen—a bare ass. He also was late in slamming on his brakes.

The effect on the glazed road was the same. The truck turned broadside toward the tobogganing Dodge.

The Dodge struck the truck just behind the cab. Henry was thrown butt-first onto the gearshift knob of the four-on-the-floor transmission, thus sustaining the most serious injury in the wreck. The bruise and intrusion was particularly devitalizing because his britches were still around his knees. He left deep claw marks on the back of the car's seat and the right arm of Officer Sheppard.

The folly continued. The driver of the truck spun around and looked out the back cab window, involuntarily seeking confirmation that he had just seen a naked ass, that a smaller truck had hit him, and that his explosive cargo had just jumped ship. He was right about one thing: the cylindrical propane tank shot off the truck like a rocket.

He watched the white, bulbous bullet fly straight and true at eight feet above the ground; slow as it leveled the 2x4 framework of a condominium complex under construction, and then gently arched over the ledge of the mountain toward the valley below.

One hundred and thirty-seven, big-breasted, white turkeys; forty-two Mille Fluer hens; three dozen, prize, Silver Grey Dorking

Bantams; six Buff Brahma roosters; a mated pair of rare African pheasants, and a full-bloomed peacock, all boarding in Stanley Manely's poultry house heard it coming, but there was little they could do. They never even had a chance to cackle before the crackle.

Stanley Manely, Junior, the pride of his father's seed, was at the moment of impact leaning on a garden hoe sampling some of his own home grown. He had just finished weeding his secret patch of marijuana, hidden down slope and behind the barn. He stood confused and dumbfounded as he watched his father's three blue ribbon Arabian mares faint dead in their tracks and his dad's prized, breeding, palomino stallion jolt into paralysis. The blast singed and surprised him. He knew he was still alive when he smelled the butterball, holiday aroma of roast turkey filling the valley.

Stanley Manely, Senior, who fancied himself as the big man of the mountain—Stan the Man—himself, President-elect of the Country Club, was at the moment fornicating with one Miss Fleeta Meeker, divorcee and manager of a nearby Pahaska Aristocrat Trailer Court, owned by Mr. Manely, Senior, a married man. They separated momentarily when the concussion from the explosion blew out every window in the trailer park, and Stanley, Senior, muttered amidst a fit of passion, "Now I wonder what in the hell that was?" The earth literally moved for sweet Fleeta.

According to the volunteer firemen who responded (and later took great joy in telling the story of the near disaster on loud summer evenings at Buffalo Bill Cody's Bar Grill Trading Post and Texaco Station) the only additional human injury incurred because of the accident, besides the painful intrusion of Chief Ranger Henry Humboldt, happened a few hours later when a very stoned Stanley Manely, Junior, was beaten soundly by his irate father for not taking care of things while "Pop was in town picking up supplies."

The firemen went on to say that the only thing that kept the entire estate from burning down was that everything was recently soaked by a passing thunderstorm. "The Lord gives and He taketh away," one of the fire fighters was heard to say. No one else seemed to appreciate his ironic observation. After they put out the wreckage of the barn Mrs. Manely invited them for dinner. "Pass the turkey would you, Junior," asked the same prophetic fireman, "God knows there's plenty."

Anthony pulled his pickup into the parking lot on the north side of Red Rocks Park. He was curious about the strange glow visible in the distance on the backside of Lookout Mountain. The hail had stopped, but the sky remained ominous. He grabbed his tool chest out of the back of his truck and headed for the bathroom and his task of knocking down an old cinder block wall. He glided up the ramp walkway. Large strides and a familiarity of the place hastened his journey, but he kept looking at the sky. The clouds, dark-violet in the last dimming light of day, drifted with a pace quicker than his nimble gait, as if in a Disney time-lapse documentary. He made film observations as well as musical. "There's a storm out tonight. I can't tell if it's sunny or bright, but I only have eyes for. . . ." He watched the clouds percolate into giant cumulonimbus formations. Distant lightning periodically exposed the clandestine bottoms of the copious, cloud anvils. The padlock he had place on the door was unlocked. Nice of you to lockup after yourself, Cumbolt, he thought. He pushed open the door. It made an eerie grown he had never noticed before. "Well, dumbbell, you never had to work here at night before," he talked out loud in a feeble attempt to find some sort of comfort from a human voice. He reached around the door well to find the light switch. "Fudge cookies," he mumbled as he got no response from clicking the switch. He tried it again, I knew the damn electrician would leave the juice off. Anthony reached into his shirt pocket and pulled out a book of matches. They felt damp. All I need is enough light to get me inside and find my kerosene lamp. Earlier that day he had unloaded the back of his truck and stashed his kerosene heater, a lamp, some camping equipment, and his power tools. You can't leave a damn thing in your truck anymore. There are thieves on this mountain. The match ignited on the third pull, just as a lightning bolt ignited over Lookout to the north. He jumped inside the bathroom; the match blew out. Damn, he muttered. Why the hell am I so jumpy? He turned toward the door to use the dim outside light to help him see what he was doing. The matches were too wet. Swell, he said. Well, Mr. Lucky, that figures. He waited for several minutes as his eyes became more accustomed to the dark. I feel like

I'm late to a damn movie and it's too dark to find a seat. I'm standing in the aisle waiting for something bright to happen on the screen. Another lightning bolt flashed, closer this time, and with a loud retort. I'm going, I'm going. He used the brief light to get his bearings. Feeling his way cautiously, he tripped only four times over equipment left by electricians. "Pendejos!" At last he felt something familiar. He searched out the lamp, carefully pulled off the glass chimney and with his other hand reached for his matches again. His derelict, recent memory returned when he felt the dampness of the matchbook. Yes sir, Mr. Lucky, you're on a roll. He sat in the dark listening to the thunder getting closer and the water doing its mischief behind the cold, cinder block wall. A wall that, if things keep going this well, may never come down. He thought about packing it in and heading back to Cody's but he knew Henry would throw a fit. I guess I could rub a couple of sticks together, he laughed at himself. If I was a smart Indian, I'd have a damn lighter. He walked toward the dim light drifting in the open door. As he leaned against the doorsill a flash of lightning and inspiration simultaneously illuminated. I've got a propane torch and a striker in the tool box. He struggled back into the depths of the bathroom, hitting his shin only once. He found the torch and flint striker, turned the knob, and smelled the gas as he ignited the torch. Boy, that's a familiar smell. He rubbed his head, still tender from the hailstone and laughed at the vision of the lightning blowing Henry Humboldt off his feet. Well, Anthony Necessity-is-the-Mother-of-Invention-Hands-of-the-Bear, let's get that kerosene lamp lit. A kerosene odor filled the white-walled room. The light was not bright but seemed warm in contrast to the deep violet and charcoal skies outside.

By lamp light he surveyed the damage the water had done to the bottom of the cinder block wall. He decided he could get a better view from the storage room to his right. He reached for the knob. It was locked. I'm getting a little tired of this. He raised his foot and kicked the door near the knob. It sprung open with a loud crack. Sorry, Henry, he said with sarcasm. The storeroom was a mess. It looks like no one has been in here for a century, he muttered as the dust settled from his entrance. Liquid soap had long ago solidified into green muck; rolls of toilet paper had turned brown and shriveled over the years as they absorbed moisture. Large two-gallon cans of old disinfectant had rusted around their circular edges. One had rusted through and spilled out it contents, which had long ago dried or washed away.

Here was the source of the water melody that initiated the investigation. Rain, over the ages, had eaten a trench through the floor of the storeroom. The first material washed away was a bad batch of concrete poured decades ago. It was obvious that sudden thunderstorms caused mini-flash floods and did the most damage. He surmised that the rain pooled in hidden reservoirs in the massive rock formations above, gathered force and in a sudden fast flush of accumulated ordinance released the torrent and its dynamic hydraulic power. He figured that the lavatory foundation and the adjacent sandstone received the brunt of the attack because it was there that the downhill ride flattened out.

An old newspaper lay on top of the disinfectant cans. Anthony picked it up and shook off the heavy dust. It too had turned brown, but he could make out the Masthead: *The Golden Transcript, August 15, 1952.* The front-page headline said, "EQUESTRIAN MISHAP KILLS LOCAL HEROES." He read about the deaths of a Cactus Face Doogan and William, Pahaska, Rudolph, heroes of the battle over the remains of Colonel William Frederick, Buffalo Bill, Cody. It seems that a gang of outlaw Legionnaires from Cody, Wyoming, tried to rob Bill's grave. He recalled that Billy often talked about Doogan and how the Bar Grill and Trading Post came into his hands. He set the paper aside thinking it might prove to be some good reading if he had to take a break. I hope I have enough kerosene.

The dry wall, an ironic term thought Tony, under the circumstances, at the bottom of the back wall was eaten away by the transient water. The framing was warped and twisted. Tony brought the lamp closer as he leaned down and inspected the hole left by the damage. That's peculiar, he said to himself. It looks as if someone has built a masonry wall behind this dry wall. He pulled on a patina-stained piece of the sheet rock. It crumbled away from the wood, exposing the ancient rock partition. Several of the rocks fell into the water trench. What the hell is that doing there? He continued to pull away dry wall when he heard a clunk in the bathroom. He looked around the corner of the closet holding the lamp in front of him.

Several of the cinder blocks had also fallen from the bottom of the bathroom wall into the trench. Well, that will make that job easier. He returned to the storeroom. Anthony held the lamp close to the remaining wall. I don't know who the hell built this, but he was no mason. He pulled from the top and the whole tangled structure tumbled in a cloud of dust. He had to jump backward to avoid getting hit. He slammed himself against the opposite wall. Way to go, Joshua. He rubbed the back of his head. He turned and gave his attention to the mortar-less rock wall now completely exposed. Someone went to a lot of trouble to rock up an entrance here, he surmised. I've seen enough work at Chaco Canyon to recognize that this is man-made. He stepped across the ruble and touched the ancient wall. More rocks fell from the bottom and he heard another cinder block hit the trench in the bathroom. He lay down on the floor to look underneath the fragile barrier. He could see that both the antique and the newer, cinder block walls were precariously supported by a diagonal rock slab which had been undercut by the water and cracked away from the natural stone ceiling. He could also see that there seemed to be a long chamber behind the walls. He stuffed debris under the suspended rock masonry to support the ancient wall, went into the bathroom proper, and began gently tapping on the cinder blocks. He worked from the bottom up and the large gray bricks fell with ease. It didn't take long, the entire structure came tumbling down, Jericho Two, he thought as he jumped backwards to again avoided being hit by falling debris. It seemed to happen in slow motion: cinder bricks tilted downward into the space below them, falling in a domino rhythm, like the rows of a weaving being pulled apart, blocks descending to the left until the end of the row was reached, and then reversing and peeling away to the right, only to begin left again, then right, then left. He tripped over his toolbox as he retreated, a block bounced near his feet, so he crab-walked backwards grabbing for his lamp. He knocked the lamp over in the scramble. It was extinguished but not broken. A frightening rumble, more sinister than the thunder outside filled the echoing acoustic chamber of the bathroom. He knew from the sound that the rock slab had fallen and the rock wall followed suit. The dust choked him and a thought flashed through his mind: how glad he was that he had never taken a job in a mine. Through the dust and darkness he thought he saw the midnight blue of the sky to the left of where the cinder block wall had been.

He finally located the propane striker and lit the kerosene lamp. Oh, shit, Mr. Lucky, you have really screwed-up now. This is going to piss them off worse than the candy bars. At the end of the bathroom where the cinder block wall had once stood lay a huge pile of brick and rock and rubble. He accomplished opening the hidden cave, but in completing his task he had also destroyed about five feet of the front wall of the bathroom. A gaping hole let in the dim night and rain-cooled air from outside.

Tony lifted the lamp to see better. Bizarre shapes reflected the kerosene flicker in the depths of the cave. He climbed carefully over the pile of fallen refuse. Shadows, exaggerated by the angle of the light, grew on the triangular cavern walls. He saw stacks and rows of dust-covered pottery, black-on-black and polychrome Indian ceramics. There was a large slab of stone, probably the younger cousin of the one he had inadvertently dislodged. There was something lying on the slab. He approached slowly, lifting the lamp past his face and holding it above his head. It took a moment for his eyes to readjust to the contrasting dark and dim light. He still could not quite make out what the organic shape was on the slab. A flash of lightning suddenly illuminated the void, accelerated his focus, and filled him with adrenaline. In a backward leap he cleared the pile of rubble and exited the cavern through the new hole in the front wall. He stood in the rain a good ten feet beyond the building, trying to force his brain to reconstruct the image he had just seen. Oblivious to the small hail pelting his head, he closed his eyes and once again saw the skull that stared at him just a moment ago in the cave. I don't know how, but somehow that little prick Humboldt is going to blame this dead guy on me.

It took him several minutes to work up his courage and reenter the tomb. Going only as far as necessary to get another look at the grisly skull, he discovered it was still attached to its gruesome skeleton. Now, more inquisitive than frightened, he inspected the entire cave—from the periphery. He was less frightened, but a long way from courageous. He noted that the skeleton was wearing the remains of some beaded buckskins and an eagle feather war bonnet lay just above the skull. The cavern was filled with Indian artifacts:

pottery, piles of blankets, weapons, baskets, and what could be, guessing from a safe distance, jewelry. I better call Henry. This is over my head. He blew out the lamp, set it just inside the open-air bathroom, and dug deeply in his pocket for the keys to his truck.

Where is the nearest phone? he asked himself. "Screw that," he said out loud, and then thought, I'm going for the most familiar phone; phones are like bathrooms, it's worth traveling a few extra miles. I need the comfort.

He drove as fast as his pickup would carry him—straight to Buffalo Bill Cody's Bar Grill Trading Post and Texaco Station.

After throwing down a calming shot of Turkey, first things first, he grabbed the phone off the counter behind the bar and dialed the number to the office of the Red Rocks Rangers.

"You know, Anthony, we do have a pay phone," grumbled Billy.

Tony turned his back on the bartender, slumped his shoulders toward his chest in a foolish effort to create privacy and spoke into the mouthpiece. "This is Tony Hardhat, let me talk to Humboldt. It is an emergency; I need to talk to Henry."

"The Supervisor in Charge is unavailable at the moment, Hardhat. I hope you are calling from the bathroom in Red Rocks. Are you playing a radio as you work or is that a juke box I hear in the background?"

"Look, don't give me any shit. I said this was an emergency. Put Henry on."

"Then you haven't heard?"

"Heard what?"

"Superintendent in Charge Humboldt was in a serious automobile accident this evening."

Anthony had mixed feelings about his next question, "Is he dead?"

"No. Fortunately he suffered minor bruises and cuts except for . . .," he paused.

"Except for what?"

"Well, he suffered a rather serious injury to his . . .," he paused again.

"Yes?"

"I'm not sure he'd want this to be general knowledge."

"Come on. Henry is almost like family," he lied. "What the hell happened to him?"

"To his anus, actually. There, I said it. I suppose it was going to get out anyway."

"No shit," giggled Anthony. He bit his lip to keep from laughing out loud.

"Yes, and it's very serious. The doctor said it was the most bizarre injury he had ever seen. They actually had to sew stitches in the Supervisor's rectum. Internal stitches, can you imagine? They actually took photographs. The doctor wanted to document the whole thing for the medical journals. They are going to write an article with pictures and everything!"

"Well, I knew it," Anthony said with an insincere seriousness. "I was afraid something terrible would happen. There were omens, you know. Tonight, the storm and other stuff. We Indians know about things like this."

"It's true," responded the Ranger. "I've had a strange feeling all day that something big was going to happen. I had no idea it would be to the detriment of poor Supervisor Humboldt."

"Well, I think everyone on the mountain would agree," chuckled Anthony. "It was inevitable that one day Henry Humboldt, Chief Ranger and Superintendent in Charge was destined to become a world famous asshole."

Chapter Eighteen

Moon

Early summer, 1964

Wah-trohn'-yoh-noh-neh, the keeper of the heavens, is the oldest name belonging to the Little Turtle Clan of the Wyandotte People. They have given me (Big Turtle) kin with whom to create the universe and Little Turtle is important. They agreed with their Iroquois cousins that Falling Sky Woman took her perilous tumble through the clouds and was carried by the waterfowl to a soft landing and dwelled upon my back, creating the earth and you humans, but it is to Little Turtle they give credit for creating the sun and the moon—the heavens—gifts from the Animal Council to light the darkness in the new world of Falling Sky Woman, the grandmother of you all. Little Turtle created Sun from lightning and eventually gave him life and spirit so he could run around the sky. However, being independent (and cantankerous) he would often disappear for long periods and leave the world in darkness. The Council decided that to solve the night problem Sun needed a wife. How often have you humans heard this matrimonial strategy as a solution for one who runs around and shines too brightly? I digress. Little Turtle created the Moon, and together, Sun and Moon populated the heavens with their children the Stars. Typical of wanderers, and males with too much energy, Sun became angry at Moon. Perhaps he was jealous that she too had a warming light and The People worshiped her equally. Perhaps he was just irascible. Regardless, he fought with Moon. He took her warmth and almost extinguished her totally, taking pieces night by night.

Moon had to be rescued by Little Turtle, who, to make a long story short, negotiated the balance in the heavens you humans enjoy to this day. Sun wanders around the sky and lights the day. At the end of his wanderings, he sinks into a tunnel dug under the earth by another of my kinsmen, Mud Turtle, so that his bright light can reappear in the heavens from the east each tomorrow. Comes the night; however, Moon, diminished by her husband's anger and malevolence, casts a dimmer light, and is afflicted to repeat a sad pattern. After gaining her original form, with the encouragement of Little Turtle, animated with the hope that she might again win over her husband's favor, she appears full and enchanting. Alas, she begins to pine all too soon and diminishes daily from his neglect and inattention. She wanes.

Numerous human civilizations worshiped the sun and the moon. You have created calendars for both, and most often, you give sun a masculine identity and moon a feminine. You seem comfortably dwelling in dichotomy, constantly categorizing things as black and white, good and evil, light and dark, male and female. You're comfortable with this shortsightedness, and I enjoy the human folly it sows. Take for example my latest cast member, Anthony Hands of the Bear—to the authorities he is Flint: destructive, unruly, sullen, and dark. To his friends, however, he has the characteristics of Sapling: warm, creative, humorous, generous—illuminating. Friends can be important.

We tricksters have a great affinity for the shadows, for the night, and for the moon.

It was poker night at Buffalo Bill Cody's Bar Grill Trading Post and Texaco Station. Wild Billy, the proprietor, enjoyed having company on a night that would ordinarily be slow and boring. He also enjoyed the revenue, modest as it was, generated by the half-dozen regulars attending the game. They always gave *the house* its cut, so Billy gladly provided the service as dealer when six gamblers showed up. He didn't mind instructing any unexpected patrons of the bar to "help themselves." Pool and poker were generally the only attractions on Sunday night.

Anthony Hands of the Bear, better known as Tony Hardhat, was a regular. At the moment, waiting for the others to show up, he was in the back room playing pool. Regulars included the head coach of the Wheat Ridge Senior High School basketball team, Michael Patrick Shane, affectionately called MP, and his younger brother Patrick Michael Shane, known by friends as PM. Phoebe, their mother, named both after their paternal uncles.

Billy recalled that Phoebe was infamous for her vocal and adamant chastisements of any referee who unjustly called a foul on her basketball champion sons. She was brutally unprejudiced—equally just—in her commentary, however, because if one of the sons was unsportsmanlike, rude to an official or coach, took a cheap shot on an opposing player, or generally didn't play up to her expectations, she would walk out on the floor in the middle of a game and pull them off by their ear. No one knowingly risked the wrath of Phoebe.

She had not hesitated to chastise Billy about the general untidiness of his bar when PM escorted her one Sunday afternoon to Lookout. She refused to eat in the grill. She also expressed open disfavor of the abbreviated names by which Cody regulars addressed her sons.

Billy, on the other hand, thought the brother's pseudonyms fit. Michael Patrick, the older, could get somewhat authoritarian, and he often acted like the policeman or the chaperone of the group—the guy with good judgment. He was intelligent enough to foresee that certain actions by the gang could lead to trouble. He was more professional acting, organized in his thinking, formal in dress, and capitalistic in goals. He always had money and often picked up a round of drinks. Billy liked that.

PM, Patrick Michael, was the opposite. He never came out until it was dark.

Both were good-looking guys. MP was six feet four or five and broad-shouldered, bigger-boned than his brother, and had a well-coifed head of black hair. PM was smaller-framed, also over six feet, and, appropriate for his alias, had these dark bedroom eyes. Rumors around Cody's were that his droopy eyes were the result of over indulgence with drink, drugs, and debauchery. Women loved them both, the brothers, not PM's eyes.

The assistant principal of Wheat Ridge High School, Proctor Pyler, was a good friend of MP's and often sat in on the game. Everyone who knew him, or had heard of him, affectionately called him *Pies*, and lots of people had heard of him. He grew up a gregarious and witty youth in rural Oklahoma. He played football for

Denver University to local fame and later coached a number of successful high school athletic teams. He was a member of the Elks, the VFW, and any other organized or semi-organized local group of good ol' boys. Everyone liked Pies. Billy had heard comment that Pies had the unique ability for disciplining rowdy high school students, but never alienating them. He scolded the hell out of them, expelled and suspended many, but they always maintained the greatest respect for him. The same was true of their parents. A common scenario was Pies calling parents into the office because he was going to expel their son, but after a few minutes everybody exited the conference laughing and shaking hands. Billy liked him because he was always in a good mood, always friendly, bought a round when it was his turn, and tipped the bartender.

Billy did not care for an infrequent player, however, a "hanger-on" of the brothers. Billy surmised he was a friend of PM, the younger. His name was Toby Upland. He was a well-read, bright guy who never hesitated showing off his intelligence. A sarcastic, cynical, scruffy SOB as far as Billy was concerned, and—worst of all—he never seemed to have any money, was forever bumming a cigarette from the bar, and redundantly joked during the game, "Hey, isn't it Wild Billy's turn to buy a round?" He talked too much, drank too much, and celebrated too loudly about the rarely won pot. He and PM often disappeared outside the bar or into the bathroom together. People assumed they were doing drugs. Upland would return to the table all too happy and, of course, immediately bark, "Isn't it Billy's turn to buy a round?"

Tony Hardhat was usually the fifth seat, if he wasn't skinning a wayward tourist at pool. A local landowner was the sixth, an entrepreneur named Stanley Manley. Manley fancied himself quite a big shot on the mountain. At least Billy thought so. Manley would often have a few too many and brag about how he almost bought the property on which sat Buffalo Bill Cody's Bar Grill Trading Post and Texaco Station. "I would've just bulldozed this old adobe piece-of-crap and put up a condo," he would parrot twenty times a night. "Billy, how the hell did you get old Doogan to sell you this place? I know I offered him a lot more than it was worth."

Manley would often bring his son, Stanley Manley, Junior, to the games and stake him if the action wasn't too bold. Stan the Man wanted Junior to learn some *manly* activities and quit hanging around behind the barn. Stan would have become murderous if he had known that it was Toby Upland who had turned young Junior on to marijuana during one of the breaks in the game.

"The kid's not like the old man, Billy. He's got no head for numbers and irresponsible as hell. Can't even do a respectable job shoveling horseshit. You've seen my prize palomino, haven't ya' Billy. Didn't you want to borrow him for the parade? Now there is something to be proud of. That is one great horse."

"I'll drink to prize horse flesh," said Toby Upland. "Stan, my man, isn't it your turn to buy a round?"

MP, PM, Toby, Stan, the Pies, and Billy sat ready to start the game. Billy unwrapped a fresh deck, the players organized their chips and Stanley, Junior, stood behind the empty seat.

"Where's Hardhat?" asked Stan.

Billy yelled-out toward the pool room, "Anthony, we're ready for some poker. Let that poor tourist go; you've taken enough of his money."

Tony appeared in the dark doorway and leaned on the doorsill. "Been snookered so far, Wild Billy." He turned his hardhat around backwards and grinned. "How about a shot of Turkey?"

"Help yourself. You know where I keep it. So, I guess it'll be about a half-hour before you can join us?"

"Sounds about right. Let Stanley, Junior, sit in for a few hands. If his dad won't stake him, I will. This kid is a gambler; right Junior? You want to play for me for a while?"

"You bet, Tony. Can I dad?"

"If you're playing with Hardhat's money, you can do whatever you want," said Stanley, Senior.

Hands of the Bear threw down two twenty dollar bills for chips and Stanley, Junior, pulled out the chair to sit with such excitement that it jarred the table and knocked over the stacks of chips the others had just organized.

"That'll cost you a drink," complained Toby Upland.

"Sorry," Junior mumbled meekly and looked at his father.

Stanley, Senior, simply shook his head and began restacking his chips.

Pies laughed, "No problem, young man. I like an enthusiastic gambler. Hardhat, pour a drink for Upland while you're behind the bar. I'd take another of America's Fine and Light, a cold one. Anybody else, while we got such a cute waitress?"

As Tony stepped behind the bar he said, "I hope you bunch of card sharks are good tippers, 'cause I don't plan on waiting on you again. I ain't your mother."

"Speaking of mothers," said Pies. "Michael, how's your mom?"

"Still feisty, Pie Man. Thanks for asking."

"Has she caused any riots at your games?" asked Upland.

"No, but she has chewed me out for coaching mistakes at half-time, in front of everybody, before I could escape to the locker room."

"I miss Phoebe," said Pies. "Why don't we invite her to play a little poker?"

"Oh, god," mumbled PM.

"Why ruin a good thing?" said MP.

"She'd kibitz every hand," said Upland, "and scold the hell out of PM for his poor poker playing."

"Speaking of playing some poker," said Stanley, Senior. "Are we going to play or what?"

"Right you are Mr. Manley," said Billy. "I'm dealing, Junior, but we rotate the privilege of starting the bet for games where you don't need a minimum hand to open, like Texas Hold'um. In which case I place this token in front of the rotated deal. And since we are rewarding age before beauty, I'll put the token in front of your father first." Billy moved a round clay disk, an old Indian totem piece, in front of Stanley, Senior. It had a painted image, faded by age, of the full moon.

Stanley Manley, Senior, pushed the token away. "Don't put that heathen thing in front of me, Billy. You trying to kill my luck. Use a chip or something."

Tony Hardhat had just returned with the drinks. "That's a moon token, Mr. Manley. Those are for *good* luck. Luck is a lady to us heathens. My mother's name was *Moon*."

"Enough with the mother talk," complained Manley. "Are we going to play poker or not?"

"Why did they call her *Moon*?" asked Pies.

"Because she had craters," said Upland before he could stop himself.

The table went silent. Tony set down Upland's drink and purposefully spilled it in his lap.

"Christ, Tony! It was only a joke." He jumped up and brushed his wet crotch. "I'm not paying for that!"

"Your joke wasn't funny the first time you said it, and it's not funny tonight." Hardhat was not apologetic. "And when did you ever pay for anything?" He turned from the table and walked toward the dark doorway to the poolroom.

"It must be a full fucking moon tonight," said Manley. "Are we going to play or what? Time is money, boys, and I want all yours. Deal the damn cards, Billy. Since I'm the first *token* dealer, it's five-card draw, jacks or better to open, nothing wild. Let's keep it pure."

Tony Hardhat walked past the tourist who had wracked the balls for another game of eight ball and was patiently waiting, ready to break. "I'll be with you in a minute, sport," said Tony. "Go pour yourself a drink at the bar. Tell Billy it's on my tab. I've got to calm down for just a minute before I bust somebody's face. Again."

Tony could see the tourist wasn't about to argue. "Thanks for the drink; I'll watch the poker game for awhile; let me know when you want to play." He walked out and left Tony alone in the dim room.

Anthony Hands of the Bear quietly took a seat in the dark corner and looked at the pool table, the only well lit section of the room. He stared at the cue ball, a bright white sphere on the dark, aged green felt. As he stared the moon like ball grew brighter and the rest of the table and the room disappeared. The full moon filled his mind and he thought about his mother.

To her tribal kin, the Tohono O'odham Indians of southern Arizona, her rough and scarred complexion was not a problem, and the name Mashath, meaning Moon, was not a derogatory comment, it simply described her well. Her mother called her Mashath Owich in her native tongue or Luz de la Luna, Light of the Moon, or Luzita, Little Light in the Spanish language common on the reservation.

Later, as a young adult she was called, Wakon Mashath, Baptized Moon. This title did carry a bit of sarcasm, just a touch of biting wit common among her people. It subtly referred to her mother's easy conversion to Catholicism and other white ways.

Many of the Papago, as outsiders knew the O'odham, were not particularly tall. Tony was the exception; he was near six feet. Moon's height would have been considered diminutive regardless of her being Papago. Her considerable weight added to a moon-like stature, as did her quietness. Tony felt she was beautiful. He and most others saw past her rondure, particularly when she moved. She was a graceful woman and would glide more than walk. She reflected the innate beauty and grace of the O'odham people, garnered through centuries of living in harmony with their demanding and unconquerable environment.

Tony knew that although many Native Americans suffered scarred facial skin because of terrible diseases transmitted by the whites, such as small pox, Moon's blemishes were more than likely the result of unusually rich consumption, including French fries and chocolate. He was not aware of her ever suffering from fevers, pox, bane, or serious illness. Tony and his mother had led financially privileged lives because of their relationship with the only milgan, white person, on the reservation—Tony's adopted grandfather, Barlow S. Snead. According to Snead, Moon was a healthy and happy child. He saw and understood her innate gracefulness, most evident in her hand movement and smile. To Barlow and to Tony she exuded inner peace and happiness. She had the voice of a morning bird, singing eyes, and, vis-à-vis her physique, a gracile wit.

Moon, was the daughter of Isabella Dancing Feet—Isabella Pies de Baile, or Isabella Bailey as the government called her. Isabella was the original cook of the Indian Oasis Cafe in the small town of Sels, spelled by white folks as *Sells*, called Komkch'ed e Wah'osithk by the natives, and coincidently meaning: Turtle got wedged. She stayed on when the cafe ownership changed hands from a local O'odham to an eccentric Anglo. There were rumors in Sels that Moon was actually the prodigy of an illicit affair between Isabella and Barlow S. Snead, consummated not long after Snead took over the ownership of the cafe. But like most back-fence hearsay about Barlow, it wasn't true. He never bothered to repudiate tattle. Isabella was also above chin-wag.

As far as Isabella was concerned, when—as a young and very pregnant itinerant—she crossed the border from Mexico, from historical O'odham lands in the So-nohla Valley, to the reservation lands of America, she left any shame there in the south. Barlow never asked and her prominence was never a topic of conversation. One cool Sonoran evening Isabella took off her apron, quietly wandered into the desert, dug a shallow pit among a stand of mesquite, and under a full moon brought her daughter from the world of dreams to the world of pain. Isabella returned to the cafe, laid her bundle, wrapped in a blanket, on the work counter next to the coolness of the milk machine and said, "We cannot let her suffer as I have, Snead. She will have a bright life, as bright as the luz de la luna.

Isabella was an excellent cook, as Moon was to prove to be, once Isabella relinquished her throne. Isabella cooked a mean pot of beans and tortillas as light as quail feathers. She could spice up a red sauce that was sweet fire in the mouth, but her green chili paralleled the secret atomic experiments going on in Los Alamos. She also knew how to make nawait, the wine from the saguaro fruit essential for the summer celebration of Quitovac Wi:gita. Barlow loved her "native" cooking, particularly a good plate of posole, and a blast of menudo after too much nawait, but the tourists were seldom adventurous enough to partake of Isabella's comida picanta. Thus, as a child Moon had access to all those unhealthy Anglo foods Barlow added to the menu to attract tourists. Hamburgers, hot-dogs, T-bones, potatoes with gravy, chicken fried chicken, chicken fried steak, pasteurized milk, strawberry ice cream, and Hershey's chocolate—lots of milk and chocolate. Moon would stand near the large milk cooler, a four-foot high stainless steel box set on the kitchen counter, and gorge herself on the cold milk which magically filled her glass with just the pull of a lever.

In her teenage years she developed a terrible case of acne, and the medication applied by the white nurses in the nearby federal dispensary simply made things worse. Of course, Moon had no intentions of giving up her milk and candy. A local shaman who rubbed dirt on Moon's face finally cleared up the acne. The indigenous soil, taken from the floor of a nearby Ho'ok ki, witch's cave, cured her after a few weeks of diligent application. However, her earlier trials with modern medication left her face terribly scarred. Tony remembered how Barlow would laugh when he told the story about the reactions of tourists when Moon served them with dirt caked on her face. Her appearance dampened a few appetites, but no whites had the courage to ask. The locals, of course, were very familiar with the treatment, so they said nothing. White fathers and mothers would clandestinely survey the other patrons of the cafe, searching for a reaction to Moon's mud face. No one reacted; no one wanted to risk not being served. If the tourists wanted to eat, the Indian Oasis Cafe was the only place within 4,000 square miles.

How Barlow S. Snead became the sole Anglo living and owning a business in Sels, the center of the Papago reservation, is as much local conjecture and rumor as is the father of Moon. Somehow Barlow won ownership of the Sels Indian Oasis Cafe from its original Papago owner. The natives in restless moments assumed it was probably in a card game. When the Feds tried to kick old Barlow off, he got a trial administered by the tribal elders rather than a local judge; the reservation was an autonomous nation, after all. The verdict, rumored to have been influenced by gifts to the tribal council, declared that Barlow had won the business fair and square and that he did indeed own it. However, the land upon which the cafe was located remained in Papago dominion and a hefty rent was appropriately applied.

No one knew for sure what brought Barlow into the desert; he didn't talk much, but the locals claimed that he was a camp follower and gambler, drawn to Tucson by the copper boom, and he made his fortune by cheating miners at cards and pool sharking. He was a weathered character, wiry and usually dressed to the nines in Western dude apparel. With his hand-crafted, black patent leather cowboy boots; black, wide-brim, ten-gallon Stetson; a four-inch oval, gold buckled belt; and turquoise bolo tie he looked like a ring master from Buffalo Bill's Wild West. He was not a slow talker but was painfully deliberate with his verbal delivery. He often rolled his own cigarettes but loved thin panatela cigars from Cuba.

Tony knew the truth of how his adopted grandfather came by the Indian Oasis Cafe. It was in a card game. He won some prime pecan acreage from the rambunctious son of one of the landed Anglo families but became bored sitting on the porch of the farmhouse and watching pecans fall to the ground. So he offered the pecan orchard in trade for the cafe. Prime pecan land off the reservation was a rare opportunity for a Papago. To the Indian it seemed like an all too rare touch of redemption against the whites. Barlow was totally comfortable with the trade. He loved the desert and preferred the quiet simplicity of the local Indians to the boisterous miners and pretentious landowners.

In truth, Barlow refused to play cards with his Native American friends and customers. He felt they did not have the knack for lying and cheating required of a successful poker player. However, he would shoot pool with them for cokes and quarters. He had an entire shelf in the storeroom of washed, gallon-sized mayonnaise jars filled with the winnings. Not to take the two-bit bet would have insulted his pool opponent and Barlow cared too much for these friends to offend them intentionally.

Barlow enjoyed telling stories. Tony loved the tales told directly to him, but he also enjoyed eavesdropping when Barlow had a trapped audience of white friends. As Tony grew he noticed that the whites and his Papago neighbors had very different senses of humor. He recalled stories when Barlow pointed out to visiting whites how he "particularly enjoyed the literal and guileless manner in which my Papago neighbors tried to live traditional harmonious lives while interacting with uninitiated and alien Anglos. From my perch on the porch of the Indian Oasis I was often quietly amused by witnessing the subtle ironies of the human condition made evident by interactions between white government workers, tourists, sales people, and my Papago friends.

"A government man, new to the territory, once stopped his federal issue Plymouth sedan in front of the cafe. A friend and I, the local Tash Siwani, or Sun Chief, probably the person the federal man was looking for, were sitting and eating some homemade peach ice-cream.

" 'Can you tell me where the tribal headquarters building is,' called the government man, rudely yelling through his passenger window and not getting out of his car.

"I sat quiet, as was appropriate, acknowledging the rank of the chief sitting next to me with a mouth full of peach delight. It took a long time for the Papago to answer. Meanwhile, the impatient driver looked back-and-forth between the road and me, hoping the answer would materialize either from the landscape or this simpleton eating ice cream. The federal man's expression switched from frustration to a sad pleading. I offered no console; there is a protocol, after all.

"Finally the old chief spoke, 'You go up road about a quarter mile or so and turn left at the white house painted green.'

"His answer, of course, was very literal. For years the landmark house had been white, ever since I moved to Sels. Recently, however, in a radical bit of adventure for the village, the owner had painted it green. If listened to closely, the answer not only gave appropriate directions, but also some important history about where the stranger was going. The government man did not listen that closely. He sped up the street, leaving dust in his wake. We watched, quietly as he drove right past the white house painted green. A few minutes later he came back the other way and drove right past it again. He slid to a stop in the gravel on the opposite side of the street in front of the cafe. Got out and slammed his door. He almost got hit by a pickup as he crossed the street. A black and white shepherd mutt barked an insult at his stupidity in stepping into the road without looking. The pickup was of course the second vehicle to come down the road in the last two hours including his Plymouth. The man stormed past me and the chief, asking no one in particular, 'Is there a phone?'

"As proprietor, I took the initiative this time. I thumbed toward the interior with my ice cream spoon. 'Just past the brown counter painted red.'

"Although we felt a bit impolite in listening, we could hear the government man asking to speak to Ramon Lopez.

" 'He isn't in at the moment.'

" 'When do you expect him?'

" 'That's pretty hard to say.'

" 'Can you give me directions to the office. I could wait.'

" 'If you want you could. Take the main road to Javapi street and turn left. You will recognize it because there is an old white house painted green. We are about another quarter mile toward the do'ag,'

"Do'ag, of course, means *mountains*.

"The federal man thought she said dog, and mumbled to himself that it figured a goddamn dog could be a landmark in this hellhole. He stormed out of the cafe and almost crossed the highway without looking. He stopped suddenly, looked left, looked right and looked back at me and Ramon Lopez, the man for whom he was looking. We smiled and he crossed in a huff, jumped into his car and screeched into a U-turn, pulling right in front of the very same pickup truck, now on its return trip from wherever. The driver blasted his horn and the dog repeated his barking insult. The Plymouth sat for a long time in the middle of the road as the government man tried to compose himself. Eventually he sped west toward the infamous green house. This time he made the turn. Ramon, the chief, and I could see his dust cloud rise above the houses and tree line.

"After several minutes, Ramon asked me if I would like some more ice cream. He slowly sauntered into the cafe and dished up two more servings. We neighbors don't stand on much formality in the cafe, most everybody helps themselves to whatever—coffee, another helping of potatoes, a refill of ice tea. Ramon dished the ice cream and then walked over to the counter phone and picked up the receiver." Barlow held his hand to his ear as if he had a phone.

" 'Gertudres, Olla, como esta? Bien, bien tambien. Por favor, could you please connect me with my office? Gracious.' He waited. 'Margarita, olla, como esta? Could you please do me a favor? If anyone is looking for me, tell him I am up at the Indian Oasis Cafe and ask him if he wants any ice cream.' "

They all laughed. Tony laughed inwardly, amused at the sense of humor of these strange white people.

Thinking about his grandfather brought back another of Barlow's stories that had to do with the history of the green house. It was his favorite. It took place when his grandfather was still just a customer at the cafe, before he made his trade and became the owner, when Tony was just a twinkle in Moon's eye, "a sweet morning dream."

Barlow would begin, "The government, in a gesture of Federal generosity for postponing payment for land stolen from the Papago in the name of Eminent Domain, built for the tribal elders four cinder block and frame houses west on the highway, not far from the Cafe, at Javapi Road. They did this without really checking with the local chiefs. The houses were typical suburban bungalows, one story, three tiny bedrooms, typically tacky, but they did have a fireplace. Even in the desert the nights get cold. The government built them at the same time as they built the school and the tribal office building. And although they considered putting on swamp coolers, they decided against it, after all the Indians were used to the heat and it was a lot of extra expense. The local Indian agent, clergy from de Bac, and government people from as far as Phoenix attended the ribbon cutting and celebration.

"The elders, being courteous people, accepted the houses with humility and quietly took a tour. They were intrigued by the running water in the kitchen and fascinated by the toilets. The agent forced one of the chiefs to sit on the toilet, with the lid down, of course, and have his picture taken for the Tucson and Phoenix papers. An indiscreet caption ran in the Tucson paper stating, 'Papago Chiefs Find *POT* of Gold.' The chief was not insulted because he never read the white man's paper.

"A few other details the government never considered was that the old chiefs were definitely 'old school' O'odham and well conditioned and comfortable with their historical life style. For example, right angles and corners made them uncomfortable. All their lives they have lived in the open and only went indoors, so to speak, to sleep and escape the greatest heat of the day. Their lodgings were made of mud and sticks and were always round. Roundness was sacred and harmonious, symbolic of the cycles of life and the directions of the spirit. Homes were also temporary. Being people of the desert, living on a land of very fragile and limited resources, they were semi-nomadic, following the rains, traveling with the seasons, never abusing the land with too many demands. Sedentary homes were an alien concept.

"Politeness demanded that they moved into the row of houses, inappropriate and contrary as they were; so, they quietly suffered in the heat of the poorly insulated structures. None of them had ever seen glass windows, let alone learned to open one. It didn't occur to the Feds to demonstrate anything that simple. Once the officials quit dropping in to see how things were going, the Papago elders broke out the windows to try to get a little air. Several of the chiefs left the doors open to the refrigerators in order to cool things down a bit. The appliances, of course, soon burned out their compressors. The Indians did not feel it appropriate to ask for them to be fixed, thus indebting themselves even more to these strange white chiefs. They were already deeply concerned about how to repay the gift of the houses, as was the custom of their people— unquestioned generosity, sharing, and reciprocity. So the refrigerators burned out, the windows were busted out, and still the chiefs sat in discomfort rather than insult their government benefactors.

"Their wives didn't trust electricity, so avoided the stoves. They logically did their cooking in the fireplaces. They would have preferred cooking out of doors, in front of the houses, but their husbands reminded them that they would be seen by the passing whites and risked insulting them. When winter came, with the windows gone, the fireplaces could not heat the homes. Several of the inhabitants simply built fires in the occupied rooms. The ceilings turned black from soot and the air was fouled and smoky because, said the Indians, 'The white man covers the entire roof, there is no place for the smoke to exit. They close off the stars and the air. They live inside these boxes all the day, like the Ho'ok in her cave. The angles and corners invite demons to dwell in these coffins. We cannot prevent insulting these unintelligent people for much longer.'

"The chiefs brought into the houses their most prized possessions—their horses. The small bedrooms made adequate corrals and by filling the bathtub with hay and allowing the horses to drink from the toilets they could feed and water their stock. The dwellings, of course, began to smell. The people moved out and the four bungalows became what in the minds of the elders was exactly what they were best designed for—barns. The most useful element of the buildings was running water, a luxurious answer to the most pressing need of the Indians. The houses became the communal wahia, or wells. For years they were annually painted white and kept in reasonable repair so as not to insult the gift givers. Eventually the family of the corner home, in reckless abandon, painted their landmark and it became known as Ce:dagi Wahia, Green Well.

"Later that day, when the newly arrived government man finally found Ramon Lopez at the cafe, his excuse for twice missing the turn-off was that to him the building looked like a damn stable."

Tony missed his adopted grandfather and his mother, but he knew he could never return to the rez. His life had changed greatly, and while Barlow's popular stories amused him, he knew that they pointed out the unintentional dichotomy of his childhood and his life among the whites. Even Tony's upbringing was atypical of the Papago people, as was Moon's. He was raised in the cafe, listening to Western music on the jukebox, eating American junk food, and sleeping on a pool table. He was taller than the other boys, a standout in sports. He remembered his grandfather's most poignant advice: "Sure, son," Barlow would preach. "Basketball is OK for running off some horniness, but you can earn your keep anywhere in this country if you can shoot good pool." So he became an excellent pool player and he mastered the many confusing games of poker. Before he left the reservation, Tony was considered alien, outside the circle, disharmonious. Even a gentle and polite people like the O'odham could be imprudent when demanding adherence to a traditional life-style.

There were rumors from the Sels small minded, jealous neighbors, but mostly the local clergy, that Tony was Barlow's boy—Snead having wooed the mother and the daughter, but this was not true. The Church thought Barlow was a bad influence on the Indians, but even for a scoundrel as reputedly immoral as Snead, all knew that incest was not a possibility. Barlow S. Snead had fathered a son, however, in Tucson. Barlow spoke of him rarely. Tony heard he was now a famous artist in New York. He sat numbly for a moment, thinking about nothing. The fading thought that he had never been to New York or any other large city east of Denver percolated in his mind but had not reached a boil when young Stanley Manley, Junior, meekly entered the dark poolroom.

Tony could tell that Junior could not see him in the corner but knew he was somewhere in the darkness.

"Mr. Hardhat, sir? I've lost all your money, mostly to my dad. They are wondering if you are going to play. Dad gave me a chip to buy you a drink, if you're ready. Would you like a drink?"

"A drink sounds good, Junior. Would you like one?" asked Tony.

"Oh, I don't think my dad would like that. Thanks anyway."

"Tell you what. I'll sneak a couple cold beers out of Billy's cooler. You stay in here; I'll come back and we can play a game of pool."

"Oh, I don't play pool; the old man is against it. Besides, I don't have any money. My dad says you are a hustler and never get into a game with you."

"Your old man doesn't care much for Indians, does he? Or is it just me?"

"I don't know what he likes to tell you the truth. I don't think he likes my mom much anymore. I don't think he likes me much either. He's kinda hard to please. Oh, I know. He likes Fleeta Meeker over at the motel. I'm not supposed to know, but he likes her a lot."

"Fleeta is a special gal. Who wouldn't like Fleeta? What do you say? How about a little eight ball? We'll play just for fun, Junior. No bets. What do you do for fun?"

"I'm kinda in to horticulture right now," said Junior with a rye smile Tony did not comprehend. "I play a little baseball and I like this poker thing. My old man says I'm no good with numbers, but I think I could catch on to some gambling strategies well enough. I lost your forty bucks, but I nursed it quite awhile. I actually won a few hands in stud poker. I lost most of it in that damn Two-card hold'um game. The betting there gets pretty intense. I don't think it's a Sunday night kind of game. I think my old man likes it because it lets him bully people when he's got a bigger stake than the other players."

"I think you're right, Junior. I'll get the beers, but you find a cue to shoot some pool with. I'll give you a lesson for free. Baseball is OK to run off some horniness, but you can earn your keep anywhere in this country if you can shoot good pool.

Chapter Nineteen

Baton Rouge

Spring, 1959

The chants of the Tchoupitoulas call me to New Orleans. I am a tourist in the realm of my cousin Snapping Turtle, but recruiting players motivated a visit. I am enamored with the appearance of these "Black Indians."

In New Mexico, where I feel more at home, the zoqueteras, adobe plasterers, mix the blood of cattle and goats in the mud taken from Tierra Madre to use in making earthen floors, often for small family chapels. Thus, are the floors darker and more sienna than the walls. They polish and smooth the floor to a rich varnished plane, a surface as burnished as earthen skin. But the earth of New Mexico is light and brownish when compared to the rich sable mud of the Mississippi marsh, now in the early evolutionary stages of becoming petroleum. It is this rare color—fertile soil and rich blood—that imbued the Tchoupitoulas brothers.

Duets—brothers, lovers, kinsmen—often add harmony, unity, and symmetry to chronicle. "Harmony" in that their actions reflect like elements, even for those whose stories do not dominate. Their variation, slight but related, adds interest (and in this case: color). "Unity" because similar elements, pairs, create relationships— patterns within the plot. They act as catalysts "resonating" oneness. And "symmetry" to add balance—tying together loose elements and distant stories, or balancing the actions of opposing pairs, such as Flint and Sapling, good and evil, white and black, or in this case: White and Red.

The older but considerably smaller brother was called Talks Softly. He liked it when friends called him: T.S. The younger and much larger brother was known as Big Stick. His Tchoupitoulas

Indian name was Red Stick. In the town of his birth and among his Creole kinfolk his name was, of course, pronounced: *Baton Rouge.* To his brother he was known as Red.

Talks Softy, a self-admitted small and effeminate man, was Red Stick's biggest fan. T.S. would boast that his brother Red was a large and muscular man—handsome and confident—as dark as the deepest night sky above the Louisiana swamps when viewed far from the city, as dark as the midnight depths of the Mississippi between Baton Rouge and New Orleans. T.S., a self-admitted gay man, prone to rhapsodic admiration of his brother and appreciation of life, would brag to anyone who would listen that Red's eyes often sparkled with intelligence, bright, just as were the stars in that black bayou sky. His skin was smooth and reflected the same subtle luster as the soulful rift of a blues saxophone solo in the last minutes of dark, murmuring from the alleys of the French Quarter. Only it had the slightest tone of sienna. It gave his coloring the hue of dark congealed blood. Talks Softly was also a (self-admitted) handsome man. "I am as pretty as a poet should be." He was equally proud of his Indian, Negro, French heritage and his Tchoupitoulas ancestry. For the past several years he had volunteered as the central costume designer for the Dancing Magnolia "tribe" of their local troupe of Tchoupitoulas Indians, often called the Mardi Gras Indians by tourists and natives alike who couldn't be bothered to learn the indigenous title. Although the actual making of the costume was a basically individual task, Talks Softly was always there in a semi-official capacity to consult on design and aid with sewing and stitchery. His obvious homosexuality was never a problem for his family or any of his Tchoupitoulas colleagues. He was a well-respected member of the tribe because of his skills, his innate intelligence, and his general affability. A genteel man, he never had anything negative to say and never chastised his tribal friends for their lack of design or maladroit needlework. He would in a very soft voice, as his name suggests, make recommendations for costume improvement.

All too often a stranger or tourist or group of macho dockworkers wandering the French Quarter would make a disparaging crack about his voice or choice of pillowing partners, and Red would have to become the "Big Stick" protector that his name suggests. With the fury of a character from a Jim Croche song Red would violently insist upon the proper respect due his brother. In no uncertain terms he would pummel his point home, and although they were originally from Baton Rouge, they became local New Orleans legends. That their parents had the premonition of their respective brotherly roles and the relevance of their respective names was a given in the neighborhood. No one ever questioned that the mother of Talks Softly and Big Stick knew exactly what she was doing and who her sons would become. That their mother had slightly misinterpreted the famous quote referring to Roosevelt diplomacy only reinforced her neighbors' suspicions that she was indeed clairvoyant about the future of her sons.

Red's reputation, according to T.S., as a revanchist was enhanced by what witnesses recognized as wit. A violent wit, but nevertheless, whenever possible, Red would enrich his thrashing with some kind of symbolic humor. For example, when a group of rowdy sailors tried to pick on Talks Softly and some of his colleagues, Big Stick slapped the sailors silly with a wet mop. "I think you should apologize, swabby, ya' gob," was the sarcastic but humorously relevant jibe he yelled as he bludgeoned a charging midshipman across the bow with the heavy, soaked yarn mace, and then spanked the descending seaman roughly on the rump with the wooden handle he had broken off the mop. It would seem that when the drunken crew of sailors saw Red break the one inch diameter staff without using his knee—he simply held the mop in front of them and snapped it like a twig—that they would have done the smart thing: apologize to his brother, save some face, avoid a beating, and exit the bar. But no, with egos fueled by high-octane hooch and because they felt, "we outnumber the coloreds and the sissy ain't gonna hurt nobody," they allowed their stupidity and prejudices to get them into a painful and embarrassing scrubbing. Incidentally, the sissy did more than his share of mopping up. Brothers being brothers and growing up together, Talks Softly learned how to fight well, simply in the name of sibling self-defense.

"Red," said T.S., "once taught a cruising combo of country western bandy cocks a painful arsis using their own instruments as truncheons. He sang a Conway Twitty ditty as he beat them in rhythm. He thumped dockworkers using their own hard hats and pulverized carpenters with their tool belts. To the cheers of locals, Red once upon a time, well it is a French Quarter legend, lifted the rear end of a Nash Rambler to prevent an insulting car salesman from escaping his penance. The tires spun in the air about waist high as Red twisted the car toward the curb and balanced the differential on a nearby fire hydrant. The car clerk refused to leave his vehicle when invited out by Big Stick, and Red, being an avenger not a bully, let the man sit alone and contemplate his flippancy until dawn, there in his little aqua and white, two-tone, sanctuary.

"Red never did anything so cliché as using billiard cues to nightstick pool sharks, but once he did pin a hustler to a wall by pushing the ponderous walnut and slate table up against him. It took eight pool patrons to free the frightened flim-flamer."

Eventually, Talks Softly, T.S. to those who knew him well, decided it was time to go it alone and live out-from-under his younger but larger brother's protective wing.

"I'm moving to Denver," he announced one early summer evening on the verandah of a Creole bar as a Cajun downbeat made the humid air even heavier than the late spring rains. A snapping turtle as big around as a car tire poked his head above the murky water to see who was speaking in such a soft voice.

"Why Denver?" asked Red; the turtle seeing the owner of the new voice ducked for cover in the shallow, slow water.

"A friend has offered me a job in a costume shop—The American Costume Emporium of Larimer Street, can you imagine," he smiled at the somewhat pretentious title. "Besides, I'm tired to the bone of all these moss-key-toes and chiggers and swamp vermin." His gaze drifted over toward a loud group of Bayou ruffians sitting at a table at the opposite end of the wooden plank porch.

"Swatin' bugs ain't no problem, T.S., if dat's what's bothering ya."

"It's not that, Red. Really, I need a change of scene. The air of Colorado is cool and clean. It doesn't stink of fish and crawdads. There are huge mountains just out of town and the horizon is not flat. You can wear the same shirt all day long."

Red instinctively lifted his muscular arm and looked to see if a circle of perspiration had stained the underarm. It had.

"The job pays well and I'll get to design something besides headdresses and sequined skirts. People will need costumes all year long and not just for Mardi Gras. Doesn't that sound wonderful? My friend said the theater business in Denver is just about to explode, and who knows where we could go from there."

"What am I supposed to do if you leave, T.S.?"

"Just what you do now. You love your job on the streetcars. You must have some sort of seniority by now? You're well fixed." He tittered at the innuendo. "Just 'cause I move doesn't mean you have to. I can take care of myself. And, besides, you have got to be tired of always having to thrash some tourist 'cause you think he insulted me."

"I don't mind; I kind'a like it."

"Really, Red, if it hasn't grown tiresome for you, it has for me."

"What about the Magnolias? How they gonna do without you?"

"The Magnolias will be fine. How's this for an idea. Maybe I'll come home for Mardi Gras and you visit me in Denver in the summers?"

"OK, I guess."

"Look at it this way, you big lummox. I'll be a missionary for the Tchoupitoulas. Maybe we can start a new chapter."

"Is this friend someone you can trust?"

"Implicitly."

"'Cause if he isn't, I can swat bugs just as good in high altitude as I can here."

"Don't worry, he's not like that. He's more like me . . . you know, sensitive with incredibly good taste."

"Very funny, T.S."

"Red, it's an adventure. I want to do it. Besides I don't think they even have moss-key-toes in Denver. It's too cold."

"You don't even have a heavy coat."

"I'll get one. Hell's fire, I'll design one and I'll make one for each of us, I'll have it for you when you come visit."

A glazing tear wallowed below Red Stick's bright eye. "It'll be hard here without you, T.S. You'll be missed."

"You'll be fine. Besides, it's time for you to find a woman and maybe get married."

"Don't insult my intelligence just because you're leaving town, T.S."

Red reached for his beer and Talks Softly for his drink.

"I just love these Mint Tulips. Should we order another in celebration of my upcoming adventure?"

"Julip, T.S. It's Mint Julip. No one in Denver is going to think you're calling 'um Tulips is funny. Maybe you better stay around here for awhile."

"I'm not going to let you spoil it for me, Red. I'm going to have another drink, to celebrate my decision. Now call the damn waiter over here for me will you, he can never hear my voice."

They pooled some money and bought T.S. an old woody station wagon so he could take several of the Tchoupitoulas Indian costumes with him as well as a few personal possessions. With road map in hand and a flask of Mint Tulips riding shotgun, Talks Softly began his trek north, away from the swamp critters and bayou rats; leaving behind the jazz of Bourbon Street, the hot beignets and chicory coffee, and a huge, dark black brother who when he wept left fluid trails of lighter skin, like lightning bolts cutting across his stormy, smoke cheeks. Perhaps it was the salt.

It was several months before Red reinstated his wit and vigor as he conducted his streetcar past the mansions of New Orleans. He sought out blues halls rather than jazz joints for a long time, and cut a lonely figure as he walked solo on the streets of the Quarter. For the first time in twelve years he didn't finish his Indian costume and march in the Mardi Gras parade; he was content to stay behind and clean up the warehouse where the Tchoupitoulas warmed up and worked themselves into a Creole frenzy before hitting the streets. Written correspondence from Talks Softly was only a whisper.

Midway through the second year of the separation came the call. It was 1964—summer. "Red, is that you?" asked the soft voice on the phone.

"How goes it, T.S.?"

"Got your letter, it came at a good time. I've missed you, too, but been awfully busy. How would you like to come up for a visit this summer? I'll bet it's hot in New Orleans. Why don't you come? There is an extra room in the house and, Oh Red, I'm so excited— I've got Beatles tickets."

"You've got what?"

"Tickets to the Beatles concert. They are playing just outside of town. In August."

"Who?"

"The Beatles. Jesus, Mary, and Joseph you need to get out of the Quarter and away from Legion Hall once in a while. You haven't heard of the Beatles."

"Non, can't say I have. Who are they?"

"The English, the Mersey Beat boys, the Lads from Liverpool, the Fab Four? John, Paul, George and Ringo? Does that ring a bell?"

"I'm French . . . Creole . . . what the hell do I care about the puant Anglais."

Henry Benjamin Humboldt was also brought up in the town Baton Rouge, much to his consternation. He followed in his father's footsteps. Inheriting both of Pop's most blatant characteristics: an unrealized desire to be a law enforcement officer and an unreasonable but vocal hatred of the French, Blacks, Indians, drunks, rough necks, red necks, construction workers, Creole, Cajun (people, food, and music), guys who wore suits, women who wore too much make-up, women in authority, fags and administrators.

Pop prided himself about his English heritage and a mythical lineage of police constabulary kin. The story told at the dinner table (serving good solid American meat and potatoes, none of that spicy, mixed-up gumbo garbage) was that the Humboldt clan first drifted into Louisiana as merchant ship detectives, instrumental in rescuing the economics of the Delta out of the hands of the lazy French and into those of the enterprising English. It was only the great global distances and poor leadership from the Isle of Britain that finally forced his native country to sue for peace and relinquish control of the enterprising hub. The Frogs eventually sold off the lands of the Louisiana Purchase to the ingrate Americans.

Something closer to the truth was that the Humboldt clan was probably begot by a British soldier deserting his troops during the shellacking they received at the hands of Andrew Jackson at the Battle of New Orleans in 1814. After witnessing the demise of several of his colleagues from artillery fired from an alligator, if one is to believe the song, probably almost as big a lie as the heritage of the Humboldt, the soldier let out lickety-split for the swamps. Thus was initiated the disdain for administrators or officers in this case. It was probably in trying to survive as a Limey deserter in a land populated by the French, Creole, Cajun and now by boisterous Americans that generated the negative preferences for particular human kind. And it was probably in trying to survive in the swamps eating crayfish, turtle, catfish, and snake that prejudiced the Humboldt palate in favor of less exotic cuisine.

Regardless of the truth, Henry was cut from the same bolt of tweed as his father and *his* father before him. Henry carried these learned prejudices with him into early adulthood and it looked as if he would live a life of the same humid futility and stifling frustration as old Pops when, "At last I'm going to be able to leave the stench of that muddy river. I've taken a job in Colorado as the Chief Ranger and Superintendent in Charge of the Red Rocks Rangers Police Force." In considering his new title, Superintendent in Charge, and his hatred of administrators, Henry finally decided if you can't beat 'um, join 'um.

What Henry did not bother to tell his security colleagues at the petroleum plant was that the Red Rocks Rangers were technically another security staff rather than a true police unit. They were convened mainly for crowd control during concerts. Between entertainment events, they patrolled the park on horseback in an effort to keep tourists from hurting themselves while climbing the huge rock formations surrounding the amphitheater. Wearing Mounties' hats and clomping around on horses was considered the most prestigious of duties for the Red Rocks Rangers. Being the wild bunch that they were, they enthusiastically called it Picnic Patrol.

"At last," cried Henry with energetic delight, "I'm going to get my ass out of Louisiana!"

"Ass," was an ironic choice of words for two reasons. First, Ass was Henry's neighborhood nickname. His mother always called

Henry by his middle name, since his father and he had the same first name and this tended to confuse the two males of the household. Thus when she yelled, "Hen-ry," she was addressing the father. Benjamin was young Henry's middle name and his mother would affectionately call him Benny. However, to the Creole neighbors who sensed the Humboldt animosity toward their kind, "Benny," yelled by the mother into the streets at dusk sounded like *Benêt*, meaning fool or booby or in Henry's case—ass. A tad of vindictive satisfaction would be gained by the young boys and girls of French and Creole descent saying, "Bon Jour, Benêt," as they passed him on the streets or at school. Benny suspected something because of all the giggles, but could never quite deduce the joke. It only accelerated his detesting of the non-Anglos.

The second irony in Henry's choice of the word has to do with him physically putting his ass in nontraditional and unique circumstances that proved to haunt him, give him great pain, and cause his professional diminishment. It unites the coincidental fates of both of the sons of Baton Rouge.

Young Henry literally followed his father professionally. Pops was a security guard at the large petroleum plant in Baton Rouge and although he was never promoted to an administrative position, being passed over because his supervisor was a damn woman and a Cajun at that, he had accumulated enough clout and seniority to get young Henry, Benny, a job. Young Henry was more ambitious than Pops, so while working in security he also attended police science classes at Lafayette Community College. It was at college that Henry noticed that he left more hair on the shower drain than when he entered. He was going bald. Soon his head would be as smooth, according to his mother, as a baby's behind; Henry took it as another ass joke. Upon graduating with an Associate's Degree in Criminology he and several of his classmates decided to celebrate by attending the Mardi Gras in New Orleans. Henry, Benjamin, Benny, Benêt, Little Ass, Baby's Bottom Humboldt in the name of celebration allowed himself to get really drunk for the first time.

"Whoa, look at the ass on that one, Henry," said one of the drunken community college graduates as he looked over the large cigar he was lighting. He pointed with the unlit end of the long stogie at the round rump of a young female attendant throwing beads from the corner of a float. She was scantily dressed in a sequined bra and G-string and had bent over to pick up another handful of colorful plastic necklaces from a box on the bed of the float.

"Jesus, Arnold, you're drunk. She's a negra," answered Henry.

"Why I got a better ass than that," laughed another of the future criminologists.

"Say's who?" challenged Henry.

"Say's me." He turned and quickly dropped his pants below his buttocks and flashed his bare bottom at Henry and his companions. They all laughed hysterically, reinforcing the maxim about the sophisticated nature of the sense of humor of law enforcement officers.

As the next float of sparsely clad beauties rolled by the entire group of prospective policemen dropped "trou" and in unison flaunted their bare butts at the platform of girls.

The chorus of ladies laughed and threw beads at the pale butts; the costumed marchers, for the most part, laughed and pointed at the line of derogatory derrière. The graduates loved being in the spotlight so much they repeated their back-door shenanigans for several floats in a row, each giving the same raucous response.

After the series of floats passed there was a lull in the parade and then several costumed Mardi Gras marchers danced by. The bevy of butt-boys lost interest in their redundant perverse performance. All but, sorry, all except Henry who seemed to have found his unique niche in exposing his pocky podex to people for whom he had hidden disdain. Hidden, that is, until now.

"The Tchoupitoulas are coming," yelled an excited reveler in the crowd.

"The who?" asked one of Henry's companions.

"The Mardi Gras Indians," answered another of his pals.

"The niggra-Indian-fags," laughed Henry.

"Whoa, Henry, take it easy. We're having a good time here. Have a drink," he handed Henry a quart-size paper cup partially filled with the remnants of a multiple rum concoction called a Hurricane, which they all had purchased at Pat O'Brien's. Henry took a long drink.

Soon the rambunctious music and the frenetic movement of the Tchoupitoulas dancers came into view. The headdresses were huge and brightly colorful. Blue, red, orange, yellow, and violet clad Indians spun and jumped to the staccato beat of the music. The costumes were heavy with sequins and baubles. Full-length loincloths and long capes repeated the intense color schemes of the war bonnets, turning into bulky propellers of glittering hues as the dancers spun.

Into Henry's sight pranced a pink clad figure more demure than the others. His costume was even more ornate and polished. He gave an effeminate wave to friends just down from Henry and his group. "Fag," mumbled Henry. He set down his drink and turned his back to the approaching rocking frolickers, and undid his belt.

"Whoa, Henry, I'm not sure that's such a great idea right now."

It was too late. Henry dropped his britches and yelled, "Hey, fag! How do you like these apples, you little rump ranger you."

Several of the dancers stopped in their tracks, immediately understanding the gesture: this honky ass-hole was not trying to be funny and join in the bawdy celebration, he was being insulting. A particularly dark and large tribe member angrily approached Henry who remained bent over and oblivious to the impending enforcer, consumed with delight at his insolence.

"Red!" the pink Indian tried to yell but his voice was too soft to be heard above the carnival cacophony.

"Big Stick, don't!" yelled another dancer.

"Uh-oh," anticipated Henry's friend Arnold, the huge cigar he was smoking went from full to half-mast as he accurately assessed the imminent encounter.

Actually it didn't go too badly. Mr. Baton Rouge, Red to his friends, using his infamous wit, decided not to risk harming any innocent bystanders on the crowded sidewalk with flying ass-hole; so, he chose instead to remove the burning cigar from the mouth of the fool next to the offender and snubbed it out on the perpetrator's bare buttocks.

"Allow me to re-butt your insult, ass-hole," he said as the burning tobacco left its strawberry shaped brand all too near Henry's namesake.

"That's going to leave a cute little scar," said the doctor later that evening. "You're going to have to keep medicating it on your drive to Denver or it's likely to get infected."

"Infected?" asked Henry. "What would that do?"

"Make it even more uncomfortable than it is now, Mr. Humboldt. It could become somewhat dangerous. If you don't take care of it properly, I mean, it could require minor surgery or even a skin graft. That's a nasty burn you've got there. How did you say it happened?"

Henry left two days later and had to stop midway through his drive to have his blemish treated by a doctor in a clinic in Oklahoma City. The doctor was possibly of Native American ancestry, so Henry lied about how the burn happened. He said he sat on a loose piece of charcoal at a family picnic.

The doctors reply was an empathetic, "You've got to be more careful."

Several years later, Talks Softly, a respected Tchoupitoulas tribal member from the Dancing Magnolias Troupe, New Orleans Chapter, packed his woody station wagon and set out on the same long drive as had Henry Benjamin Humboldt, from New Orleans to Denver. Both incidentally stopped briefly in their respective home town of Baton Rouge to say good-bye to kinfolk. Little did either of them know, despite an Indian's providence for prophecy, they would meet again. It is never wise for one to forget one's background.

Chapter Twenty

Olivia

Summer, 1964

It wasn't so long ago that humankind, in your search for knowledge, truth, morality, and being, considered both nature and man, the rational and the empirical, night and day, good and evil, black and white, the light and the dark, both the masculine sun and the feminine moon, Mother Earth and the Father in the Heavens— gods and immortals both male and female. Ironically, you Christian Sons of Abraham have no trouble with spiritual duality as long as it deals with male deities. Catholics, for example, believe in the Father-Son-Holy Spirit, but Mary, the mother and nurturer of Jesus, and Mary Magdalene, the disciple and confidant, cause great discomfort for the clerical elite. Of equal irony is that for the common folk and the indigenous, however, the females have played a historically prominent role. Both Marys are celestial and sublime.

You're surprised I know such things. It surprises me that you're surprised. After all, have I not informed you of my duality and the learning that comes from longevity? One doesn't hang around the physical and the ethereal worlds for centuries without learning something about one's brethren. Note that I did not say, "learning about the competition." Yes, I know, many fundamental worshipers of the religions fathered by Abraham interpret a reference to Turtle and my close kin as pagan and blasphemous. No polytheists y'all: one for all and all for one; even if it kills you, even if you kill in the name of your sole deity.

We "manifestations" of the native cultures respect and celebrate the female. You heard me: "man-ifestations." The gender specificity of the term has not escaped me. We "pagans" understand that we are each male and female. We hold each as holy. Therefore, if we celebrate the feminine, it seems to me that you, our children, should accept feminist importance and give Eve and Lilith a break—

oh yes, I was around back then, too. Consider the benevolence of White Buffalo Calf Woman, Pte Ska Win. Her story is relevant. Before bestowing to The People the sacred bundle, seven ceremonies to guide living, she set the ground work, (Sorry, but I am Turtle and terra firma, after all) the ground rules by annihilating a brave with "bad" thoughts. She would not tolerate disrespect. As I recall, Jehovah cleansed the population of the irreverent several times. So, this should not shock you nor alienate you from "the female," either as a deity or as a protagonist, antagonist or catalyst.

Often, we spirits take on a physical, human identity that is either male or female (or both) in order to teach humankind, to bless you, to punish you, to be "conjugal" with you (Alleluia—a religious term), and to be a conjurer—always the trickster, don't forget. I am sure you are aware of the pagan myths, the fables, and the seductions therein. Consider that we deified are as often the debauched as the pursuer. Therefore, in accordance with myth, it is obligatory that the conflict character of a story be the opposite sex, enchanting, mutually wise, equally flawed, and devastatingly beautiful. How often you mortals, and I must admit, we gods and kings, goddesses and queens have fallen crown over footing for a handsome lad or, in this case, a local beauty.

Olivia Hotchkiss, anthropologist, botanist, and adopted member of the Onça Parda tribe of Amazonian Brazil, had forgotten that when white men speak to her they stare at her chest. It had been nine long months since she had to suffer that indignity. The fact that she was semi-nude did not make her more forgiving of this small oily trespasser. He was a messenger from her mentor and employer, Professor Edwin T. Antwerp. The fact that the messenger had found this isolated Onça Parda village and had the courage to deliver the message among these rumored headhunters should have given him some credence, but Olivia was not impressed as long as he continued to talk to her breasts.

"Nossa, Senhora," he muttered as he walked from the selva, the jungle, into the clearing while cursing the chuva grossa; the hard rain made loud pops as it pelted the filthy brim of his black baseball cap. Profuse perspiration had turned the bottom near the band an ochre color—as yellow as the mud on Olivia's bare feet.

"O Professor says if I find you I am to radio him your location. He needs to see you right away. Some kind of an emergencia." The messenger pulled a microphone from the radio backpack and began broadcasting. Olivia knew that the Onça Parda, spying from the cover of their huts and the surrounding selva, would think this was very funny—a man talking into a black rock. When the rock answered, however, she heard them run for deep cover. Even as he talked into the radio he stared at Olivia's torso.

"I will set the radio beacon for the pilot to home-in on tomorrow morning, amanha, because it will be at least half a day's flight from Brasilia for the Professor. You must immediately relay the message to him that we have found her. I will have her ready to leave by tomorrow."

"Hey, now wait just one minute," Olivia protested.

"Sim, afirmativa, amanha," he ignored her. "Acabado . . . over and out." He put away the microphone. "Professoria Olivia, the Chefe said you were about to conclude your studies here in the jungle anyway, and there is some kind of a new find in Colorado, America, your home. There is a danger an Indio tomb may be looted. He asks that you fly to Denver instead of home to Colorado Springs and apologizes it is a month early. He will give you the details tomorrow."

Leaving had not crossed her mind. The thought of an early departure upset Olivia. She felt she had become a part of the Onça Parda community. The messenger obviously thought likewise.

"Gone nativo, have we?" His bristled lips climbed into a lascivious and affected grin.

Olivia crossed her arms in front of her bare breasts, embarrassed by her nudity for the first time in decades. Perhaps she had gone a bit too "native". Adapting to the *natural,* Amazonian lifestyle had consumed more of the last few months than had serious, scientific observation. If she was indeed losing her impartial scholarly perspective, maybe it was time to leave. She turned from the messenger and strolled toward the women's barraca. Sensing that his eyes were following her, she nonchalantly dropped her hands and spread the red loincloth so it covered her naked behind.

Breasts and buttocks *a' naturel* were the uniform of the day for this tiny village. She was furious that the messenger had so rudely interjected bourgeois mores back into her life. It forced the quandary of how she would formally present the pristine and natural lives of her rainforest friends to her academic colleagues.

The Onça Parda people were one of the few relatively unspoiled tribes left in the Blue Water region of the rain forests of Brazil—between the Xingu River and the Rio da Duvida, the River of Doubt. They had rejected all of the white man's *advancements* with the exception of metal tools. These, they felt, were actually gifts from the gods. The white man had simply stolen them. So the Onça Parda stole them back; thus, returning them to appropriate hands. In the place of stolen machetes, axes, and fishhooks the Onça Parda would leave something of much more value—skulls. White victims were not particularly thrilled with the exchange. They did not know that the Onça Parda came by their skulls in a much more humane manner than that perpetuated by rumors. The skulls were those of their dearly departed and, for the most part, the relatives died of natural causes. The Onça Parda practiced a limited form of ancestor worship. They actually ground the bones of their deceased and added the powder to their soup. They saved the cranium. The skulls acted as intermediaries with the forest spirits. It was bad luck for the spirits of the departed to reenter the village. Thus, leaving a skull for a machete communicated to the gods and spirits that the trade was fair.

Swapping stuff for skulls was, however, interpreted by the whites as a discouragement to further trading or contact with the Onça Parda. The white traders and explorers, as is traditional with Western ways, mistook the tratado as a threat. In so doing, they had allowed the Onça Parda to remain isolated and basically unknown. Olivia found pleasure in the ironic humor.

Likewise, other Xingu tribes left the Onça Parda pretty much alone. Militant groups—some of whom were true headhunters—seldom attacked the Onça Parda because the Onça Parda benevolently served as jungle pharmacists. They had a vast botanical knowledge of herbs, medicines, and particularly of hallucinogens, which they smoked, chewed, drank, ground into an inhalant powder, and baked into their bread. Neighboring tribes, with whom they freely traded such drugs, called them the *Niopo People*.

Niopo (or Yopo) and Caapi are two popular hallucinogens distributed by the Onça Parda. So were a local Datura, an imported Trichocereus cactus, a Bolivian Ololiuqui, Viho for making a snuff, and half-a-dozen psilocybine and psilocine mushrooms.

Often an Onça Parda would serve as the shaman or medicine man for a more aggressive tribe, such as the Kalani and Yanomami. Because they appreciated and needed their skills, no one bothered the Niopo People, their local dealers.

Being constantly stoned left the Onça Parda fairly mellow and non-aggressive; so they, in turn, did not bother anyone else. Territory was never a source of contention because the Onça Parda were more nomadic than the other tribes due to their constant searching, collecting, and harvesting of the pharmacopoeia between the Xingu and the vast Blue Water Region of the Amazon.

No tribes raided the Onça Parda for their women because, again, being stoned most of the time left them rather sexually unresponsive. This also helped to keep the tribe small.

Olivia was proud of the fact that she was a refreshing exception to the rule when it came to Anglos. As a white person she didn't want anything from the Onça Parda except their knowledge of the drugs, which they freely gave to anyone anyway. She originally gained entrance and eventual acceptance into the realm of the Onça Parda by buying dozens of Onça Parda skulls from bewildered Brazilians, and building an altar pyramid of skulls in the rain forest near the Xingu River. She painted her face like a skull, circled the altar with machetes, and placed herself—naked—in the middle. Olivia thought her painted mask looked authentic and skull-like. However, she was told later by the shaman that the Onça Parda, watching from the cover of the forest, thought the large dark spot representing the nose hole and the large circles of dark eye make-up made her look more like a puma or cougar. In addition, being a blonde, her pubis reminded the Onça Parda of the jungle cat's fur. In fact, the puma is the animal totem of the tribe. Only the eldest had ever seen a white person, and none had ever set eyes on a blonde. The few Brazilian women they had spied were brunette and similar in coloring to themselves. They figured this woman, if not a goddess, was at least a curiosity. Besides, the Onça Parda thought that sitting on top of the skull pyramid was the funniest thing they had ever seen, and since a sense of humor was one of the prized characteristics of their people, they let this comedian into their fold.

For the past nine months, Olivia enjoyed making these gentle people laugh. The local shaman adopted Olivia and she lived a protected life under his mentorship. It was from the shaman that she learned about the indigenous medicines and spiritual herbs—drugs, actually. She experimented with the drugs. She would be sure to point out to future audiences that this was not usually allowed for women, but it was in getting stoned with them that Olivia proved to be the most entertaining. She would mime great Western literature, such as *Three Blind Mice* and *Humpty Dumpty*. The men laughed so hard they had no objections in allowing Olivia to experiment with the drogas—"one pill makes you small" and several can make you fall off the wall. It was when Olivia tried to mimic "fat" for Humpty that they laughed loudest.

Anyway, over the past several months she had categorized, personally investigated, and documented a large variety of local spiritual aids. Her collection of scientific samples was extensive. It included Virola, known as the Semen of the Sun and used most often as a snuff forced up a recipient's nose with a short blowgun. The beans of Niopo or Yopo were ground into a powder and also used as a snuff. Chewable leaves, including Coca and Jopa, were numerous. Flowers, roots, twigs, small fruits, cacti, and fungi filled a hundred plastic specimen bags in her psychoactive collection. Many were unknown to the Western world and others, although categorized, had never been investigated. Olivia was laying the groundwork to become the phytochemist extraordinaire, the psychedelic shaman of the approaching Aquarian age.

The messenger from Antwerp followed Olivia toward the women's hut trying to peak at her fanny. From the shadows, several *warriors* carrying spears suddenly stood between him and Olivia.

"Are these people dangerous? Pessoas perigosas?" He pleaded for her assistance.

She turned around and grinned at him. "No." She told him to look them directly in the eyes when speaking. "Naõ, se você olhar diretamente nos olhos deles, guardo falar com eles." This, of course was a lie.

The messenger stared intently at the closest native. "Pare, halt, amigo. I mean no harm." He grinned and opened his arms showing he had no weapons. However, what he did have was several gold teeth. Olivia knew that the Onça Parda had never seen gold teeth. Now this was a frightening skull.

The tiny, blowgun dart got him in the back of the neck. It must have felt like a bee sting. He turned and faced his attacker with a look of bewilderment. His grin became a bit feebler and less frightening. He dropped to his knees with an intoxicated smile; mumbled, "Opa," and passed out on his face.

Olivia smiled but, too late for the intruder to comprehend, she said in the native tongue, "Boy, are you going to have a headache in the morning," She heard her companions laugh. The warrior with the blowgun slapped his knee with jubilance. Olivia knew it was her sense of humor the Onça Parda loved best.

She sat that night with the old shaman. They talked through the evening and the late-night rainstorms.

"The rain disguises your tears, daughter. What has this man-who-talks-to-stones said to you to make you so sad?"

"He has come with a message from my chief, my white chief, saying I must leave the hospitality of the Onça Parda, father. It makes me very sad to leave 'The World,' and I will miss you greatly."

"It is inappropriate for you to leave at this time, daughter. You have been growing in the womb of the people for nearly nine full moons. You are not yet ready to be born. To go now would mean an inappropriate birth—feet first. This could cause death. No, this is wrong what the man-who-talks-to-stones is trying to do. We will eliminate this man and you will stay here until the time has passed for you to be properly born a person."

"It is not the fault of this man. He is a messenger, as I said, from my white chief. You should not harm this man. He, and I, will leave your world tomorrow on a great flying machine. Perhaps, one day I can return." The word machine meant nothing to the shaman, and *helicopter* proved impossible to explain.

"It is inappropriate that you make me wait to die. My time is near and your leaving means I have to wait. I cannot go until a new shaman is found. Your leaving makes these proper things very difficult."

Not quite understanding that the old man was referring to her as the new shaman, Olivia said, "If I can delay your dying, then I am glad. The world needs you, father, and it is proper that you stay with the people for a long, long time to come."

Around noon the next day Olivia worried. The Onça Parda were skittish about the distant thunder of an approaching helicopter. She had tried to explain to the tribe what to expect; they got a great laugh out of this story, but as soon as the whirlybird came into sight over the treetops the Onça Parda disappeared in a panic. The helicopter beat the air into submission just over the village. It landed loudly in the tiny plaza surrounded by huts. The mechanical winds collapsed thatched walls, blew several hammocas off their posts, and sent chickens and dogs flying.

Professor Antwerp stepped from the aircraft. Just as she had remembered, he was a tiny replica of Teddy Roosevelt—pith helmet, glasses, and full mustache. He had excellent posture and did not have to duck to avoid the rotors. His *Theodorian* ego would not allow him to slump as he approached Olivia. She was still dressed in her scanty native garb. He glanced at her nakedness, but immediately looked her in the eye and said, "Olivia, you have no shoes."

To the old shaman, spying from the rain forest, this was truly a magical event. His being under the influence of niopo only enhanced the spirituality of the occasion. He remembered this mustached man. The old sorcerer had seen Teddy Roosevelt, the real Teddy Roosevelt, who had decades ago visited the Xingu River region of Brazil. A famous Brazilian explorer, Candido Mariano da Silva Rondon, an orphan from the frontier who became an unyielding champion of the Indians, led Teddy Roosevelt on an expedition and search for a river whose very existence was questioned by the geographers at the time. They found it and Rio da Duvida—River of Doubt—now appears on maps as Rio Roosevelt. Stranger things have happened in the jungle.

The old shaman was a toddler when Roosevelt and Rondon trekked near an Onça Parda village. Children are often permitted into the male barraco or hut. Sometimes the air is rather thick with the local niopo, and even the kids can get a little wacky. The future shaman was being carried piggyback by his older brother, and his brother was hanging out with the older men in the hut smoking maconha when an excited neighbor entered yelling about the great white chief who was cruising down the river. All the tribe went to greet their respected friend Candido Mariano da Silva Rondon and see this alleged great chief of the brancos. His tiny toddler memory, with the aid of the local herb, was indelibly imprinted with the image of Teddy Roosevelt.

The shaman deduced that the man talking to Olivia was the same great chief he had seen as a youngster. His smaller size than the original vision did not bother the shaman because he knew that when one sees someone or something as a child and doesn't see that thing again until one is an adult, the thing or person looks small in comparison to their memory. Therefore, a smaller great white chief—Roo-so-velt seemed logical. The fact that he had not aged, simply added to the magic. The shaman shouted, "Beleza."

Antwerp and Olivia turned and looked at the old man. "What did he say?"

"Literally translated," answered Olivia, "He just yelled, 'Wow!' "

Antwerp signaled to the pilot to cut the engine. "I have your passport, visa, and copies of the notes you sent me are in the briefcase. Your medical records, credit cards, and the other personal items you left in the office vault are here, too. I also have proper documentation for you to take your samples out of Brazil and into the US. Have you packed?" he asked.

"I have nothing to pack, Professor. My clothes rotted and my luggage washed away months ago during the rainy season. I saved only the camera, the tape recorder, and additional notes."

"Well, your suitcase is probably drifting somewhere off Rio by now. How are we going to get you back to America? I brought no spare clothes." He looked at the messenger. He appeared groggy and terribly paranoid. "Give her your clothes," Antwerp ordered.

"But senior Professor, o que posso restir, what will I wear?" the man pleaded as he pulled his Grateful Dead tee shirt over his head. He explained to Antwerp that it was his last clean shirt. He had saved it to wear in the village. Antwerp remembered seeing the shirt weeks earlier. It had a large skull silk-screened on it. The messenger wore it at the suggestion of Antwerp, who deduced that with these natives, it couldn't hurt.

"You can borrow a loincloth," Antwerp said. "Trade them your machete, but for god's sake don't stare them in the eye when you trade. Eye contact is a threat to these people."

The messenger looked with confusion and hurt at Olivia. She shrugged. He handed her his pants and she, with a timid look of remorse, handed him her loincloth. The messenger shyly looked at the ground, avoiding a peek at Olivia, and touched the back of his neck. Antwerp, mildly embarrassed, turned toward the helicopter, but heard the pilot yell, "Gostosa!"—a comment referring to the delectability of Olivia. He looked up and saw the pilot fall out of his seat.

Olivia used the machete to cut the legs off the pants, thus creating shorts and pulled on the tee shirt. She gathered up two Onça Parda woven jute bags stuffed with her collection of herbs and her camera. She regretted that it was now impossible to say good-bye to the shaman and her friends hiding in the forest. She had tried to say good-bye this morning, but they had only laughed and laughed at her miming of a helicopter. She knew that even after the whirlybird took off they would remain hidden for a day or two.

Olivia had no idea but she had just become part of Onça Parda mythology—The Laughing Panther Woman stolen before her birth by the Ageless Roosevelt, Chief of the Giant Thunder Wasps. Several days later the Onça Parda built a shrine of skulls in her honor. And just below the skull at the very peak of the pyramid they placed a small triangle of puma fur.

She cried quietly as they flew over the green canopy of caoutchouc, the tree of weeping wood, along the cafe-con-leite route of the greatest river in the world, toward the airport in Belem, the largest city in Amazonia. Giant tapirs ran for cover from the sound of the aggressive rotors. Botos, fresh water dolphin, dived from the undulating shadow skimming over the creamed coffee-colored water.

Standing in a glass-enclosed office across the gate from her plane Olivia felt exhausted. She had just spent another hour arguing in her best Portuguese with airport officials. She had to argue her way onto the plane in Belem, and now in Rio she was trying to talk Brazilian customs agents out of a strip search. Of course, she knew it was never the custom to search departing passengers. She also knew that it was her looks and the fact she was transporting a variety of Amazonian herbs and hallucinogens, despite legal documentation, that made her vulnerable to local border guard machismo. Finally, she screamed profanities in Portuguese, Spanish, Onça Parda, and English. She chastised them for their failure when they spoke to her to look her in the eyes. The outburst forced the guards to pause in confusion just long enough that she bravely gathered her few things and flew out of the office, up the concourse, and onto the waiting plane. When she looked back Antwerp was continuing to challenge the soldiers. She could hear them arguing about who got to do the search. The impatient flight crew pulled the plane doors closed behind her and ended the debate.

Once the plane was over the gulf she tried to relax. She was not used to clothes, particularly these tight fitting ones, so she had trouble sleeping even though she had the pair of first class seats to herself. The other first class passengers seemed to be giving her a wide berth. She didn't mind. She figured that if they could afford first class that most of them were probably the decadent descendants of the bandeirantes, the marauding bands of bandit frontiersmen who originally plundered the riches of the Amazon, and seingueiros, the rubber barons who gained their wealth during the wars by bleeding the indigenous rubber trees of Amazonia and using the Indians as slaves. None bothered to introduce themselves, thus saved her the effort of being rude in return. She stared out the window at the sun setting on the ocean below and thought about her life and the world to which she was returning.

Olivia was raised in Colorado Springs, Colorado, by her maternal grandmother, an officious widow of a brigadier General, the fifth General in a bloodline of distinguished military zealots. Grandma, likewise came from a family of dedicated men of the armed forces. She bragged about ancestors dumping tea into Boston Harbor and sacrificing toes to frostbite for the Father of our Country. Although the family heritage was of strong conservative Yankee stock and Grandmamma was a tough old broad with servants and strangers, she could never control Olivia's adventurous spirit. "Adventurous spirit," that is how Grandmamma would try to explain Olivia to family friends.

Olivia lost her parents to an unfortunate food poisoning disaster. Their untimely demise was the result of a display of culinary bravado. While showing off to family and friends from Boston, they consumed tainted Rocky Mountain oysters. They inappropriately boasted that here in the Wild West gourmets scoff at citified priggishness. The General in an exaggerated gesture dispatched one of the beef testicles dripping in gravy, smacked his lips, and fed one to his wife. She feigned delight and quietly murmured that the gravy tasted funny. Olivia was fortunately a practicing vegetarian at the time. She refused to eat meat more to frustrate her parents than for any moral reason; that, and she refused to participate in her parent's theatrics. The Bostonian relatives smugly implying that one is what one eats, begged off and survived to tell of the family tragedy.

Precocious and parentless, a rebellious Olivia, while still in high school, dated Air Force Academy undergraduates, much to the consternation of Grandmamma. In college, while she worked on her Bachelor of Science in Botany, she dated professors and perpetuated Grandmamma's dismay. She had no trouble earning high grades even though Colorado College was considered a demanding school. She focused on hallucinogenic plants, both as part of her botany major and as the major recreational element of her social life. Antwerp, a family friend from Boston, had no trouble advocating a scholarship for Olivia to pursue a Masters degree at Harvard where he was the Chair of the Anthropology Department. She continued her research, academic and social, using only natural therapudants, derived from plant sources. Olivia exercised focused scientific integrity and held to rigorous standards. It was this very issue that broke off her rumored relationship with a Dr. Timothy Leary of LSD fame—LSD being a manmade chemical product. Grandmamma pleaded for help from Antwerp when the Colorado Springs paper ran an article about Leary including a photograph of the arrest of the acid guru. Olivia appeared in the background, accosting one of the arresting officers. The article also mentioned Olivia as Leary's protégé. Grandmamma phoned Antwerp.

Dr. Edwin T. Antwerp was the country's greatest authority on Indigenous Peoples of the Americas. Under the tutelage of Antwerp, Olivia began her doctoral work in anthropology. Together, they devised her thesis, an ethnographic study of indigenous native shaman rituals, particularly those using drugs, specifically, hallucinogens. In collusion with Grandmamma Antwerp figured he would keep Olivia out of trouble by shipping her off to the Amazon. South America seemed right, it was far from Boston, further from Colorado Springs, and there was a mystery tribe there about which very little was known except that they were practitioners of shaman rituals using local botanical hallucinogens. About a year ought to do it. That would give Dr. Leary time enough to self-destruct.

Mid-way through the flight from Brazil, Olivia asked the stewardess for a glass of white wine. The uniformed woman watched as Olivia took a small envelope from her pack and poured a mysterious white powder in the wine. "It's medicinal," offered Olivia and the stewardess smiled and moved on. Olivia slowly sipped the wine. When she finished she crept to the restroom trying not to attract attention. In the mirror of the bathroom, as the magic powder began to warm her, she mimed *Three Blind Mice* and laughed loudly at how silly she looked, and wept quietly at missing her cheerful companions in the rain forest. She returned to her seat, fell quietly asleep, and dreamed of multicolored macaws, red howler monkeys, soft-footed jaguars, and a gentle people who believed that in their dreams they traveled as pumas.

She saw the large cat jump from her hammock and stroll through the village to the rainforest; the feline looked over its left shoulder to glimpse the setting sun, and then jumped into the dark forest. In her dreams she followed the cougar as it scampered in the dark until it came to a wide river, and contrary to the myth of cats being afraid of water, it jumped in and began swimming as the new sun rose far to the right at the mouth of the giant river. Powerful currents seemed to carry it along, and when it finally reached the shore, it leapt in a high arching jump, but at the end of the great leap the mighty puma landed on a high rock pediment, a tall column of red sandstone. It stood and surveyed the surrounding canyons and pillars of stone, and the desert beyond. Again it leapt and this time landed in front of a dark cave entrance. The cat tilted its head and growled a banshee like scream, and then slunk into the cave. As her cat's eyes became used to the dark she saw the body of a great North American Indian chief, clad in fine beaded buckskins and war bonnet of a hundred feathers, and she knew each feather was a badge of courage symbolizing an honorable death. Again she growled and from the darkness of the cave emerged a handsome brave, naked except for a loincloth and a war bonnet that barely touched the floor. The feathers were tied to the long tails of the bonnet with red and black cloth. He held a long pipe, the bowl was of red stone, the stem and mouthpiece of wood, both incised with sacred markings, four colorful ribbons and a single eagle feather hung from the stem. The brave lifted the pipe toward the heavens and sang a prayer in a beautiful language she did not understand. The puma, whose fur seemed to thicken and appear even more luxuriously soft, rose from her bed near the proud chief, and sidled to the brave. The sleek cat rubbed her ribs along the bare legs of the prayer giver, back and forth as he continued his song, back and forth again and again, purring. Beings approached from the West; she saw a setting sun behind great thunderhead clouds. They transformed into Indians painted in black and flying toward the prayer singer. Lightning flashed from their hands and rain fell from their eyes. Their dark bodies were painted with zigzag patterns of lightning. She had never seen such spirits. They were not rainforest beings. She continued to rub back and forth on the legs of the brave, only now it was she, Olivia, nude, on her hands and knees. She looked to the north and growled. A giant Indian painted in white appeared, his hands forming a cone over his mouth, great white clouds of smoke flew from his mouth, propelled by his powerful lungs. A cold wind filled the cave and when she looked, the puma was back at the legs of the prayer giver. From the eastern darkness emerged a brave with his total body painted red; he held the morning star in his hands, extended forward as if in an offering. And from the south came an Indian in yellow, it changed from more masculine to more feminine with each step and back again, over and over. The male spirit grew strong and powerful, and she could feel heat radiating from him. The more feminine character wore a skirt of evergreen and corn flowers in his/her hair. The spirits formed a circle around the prayer giver and the puma. And the cave filled with a light too intense for her eyes.

Olivia awoke with the hot Texas sun blasting through the airplane window. The attendant leaned over her and asked her to fasten her seat belt; they were on final approach to Houston. She struggled to awaken, felt sticky from perspiration, sat up, pulled her seat belt tight, and pulled the window shade down to escape the sun. She heard the tires of the jet screech a wild cougar scream as they contacted the runway. Olivia closed her eyes; the prayer giver offered her the pipe. She opened her eyes quickly, surprised that the dream continued while she was awake. Passengers were standing in the isles ready to depart the plane.

The airport at Houston, though not crowded, seemed to close in on Olivia. It seemed urban, alien, mechanical, frantic, and loud. She prepared herself for the next round of haggling with small men wearing large badges.

"O'so!" Olivia thought to herself, "This customs agent looks like a fullback for the Longhorns or whoever the heck the football team is here in Houston. She was not much for organized sports. He was a large man, muscle-beach-brawny, blonde, tan, clean-shaven, and packing a chromed, cannon-sized magnum of some sort in a Western gunslinger holster tied low on his thigh. It's a young John Wayne, she reflected. No, this hombre is bigger. She grinned as she placed her passport and the documentation for her agricultural specimens on the tall counter. Her grin was part instinctive friendliness, but more bemusement at suddenly finding herself in front of a large blonde all-American boy. It just dawned on her how long she had been among rather short, dark-skinned, brunette people, and how long it had been since she was among crowds of people in clothes. She looked around at the people lining up for customs inspection from other flights. The skirts on the girls were shorter, she didn't mind, but they were also wearing sling-back high heel shoes.

While the cute, suggestive clothes were actually intriguing and, to her surprise, gave her a warm feeling of welcome home, she knew she could never get used to those shoes, not for walking, anyway. Now she was unconsciously grinning.

The agent was not smiling; he noticed she was looking around the terminal with a naïve expression. He coughed to get her attention, looked her in the eye, and immediately allowed his eyes to meander to her chest.

"We will have to do some checking here."

Olivia noticed his stare and mumbled out loud, "Well, since I've been away, I guess things haven't changed much."

"Pardon me, missy?" he stated more than asked. His accent was a deep Texas drawl. "We may have a few questions, if you don't mind."

She tried to keep from laughing. It had been so long since she heard such a regionalized American harmonic. It amused her. She wasn't making fun of the young man; it really was novel to experience the radical but historically familiar sing-song. An unwanted blush forced itself to her cheeks as she struggled not to laugh. She felt her grin grow ridiculously large. She knew her twitter generated another assessment of her face. He was obviously looking for a tip-off for some hidden shenanigans.

He continued to look at her documentation, periodically searched her face for an indication of criminal nervousness, glanced several times at her chest, and gruffly evaluated her casual outfit.

"I had to leave Brazil in a hurry," she smiled, noticing his negative reaction to her Grateful Dead T-shirt and cut-off shorts, and then realized that her statement could be taken out of current context and did little to further her innocence.

"Most of what you have declared is illegal to bring into this country. Comprende?"

Why was he speaking Spanish, she wondered. Was he clumsy enough to think that a perpetrator or illegal may slip and answer in their native tongue? Or was he just being Texan?

"Si, jefe, comprendo."

He raised his eyes from her chest to her face. She was still smiling. He stared again at the Grateful Dead graphic. "I get a lot of you hippies who can speak Spanish."

"Actually, I speak twelve languages," Olivia replied. She gently placed her finger under his chin and lifted his gaze to meet her eyes. She spoke in her best Boston nasal to emphasize she was American. "As you can see by the permits, I have both the permission of our Federal Government and the Brazilian authorities to bring these specimens (she purposefully did not call them drugs) into the country. I am a doctoral student of anthropology and ethnobotanical studies—indigenous herpetology. You understand? These medicines (again, she did not mention they were drugs) are part of an important scientific study. You understand about science, officer. Don't you?"

"Well, ma'am, you don't look much like a scientist, nor like many of the doctors I know. You look like just another damn hippy and I can't tell if your official documents are real or not. You're no longer in Brazil where it would appear everybody dresses like hippies. No, ma'am, this is America. Actually, it's better than just America, you are in Texas now, and we don't much cotton to anything 'official' from no foreign governments, especially no sudamericano oficiales, what try very often to smuggle beaners and other illegal contraband across our borders. And while we must act respectful to our own government officials, we don't take too much as being too serious from those carpetbaggers in Washington-comma-D-period-C-period."

"I understand your concern, officer. Had I had any choice, I would not have spent the last eighteen hours in this ridiculous T-shirt, but as I said, I had to leave Brazil in an *official* hurry. Our government and my mentor from Harvard, that's a university, maybe you've heard of it, plucked me right out of the Amazonian jungle and threw me on a plane. We, Harvard and our government from Washington-comma-D-period-C-period, and me, have an important scientific emergency in Colorado. So here I am. And I would appreciate it if you would stop staring at my chest and get me passed through customs." She had stopped smiling.

"Lady," he looked her in the eyes. "You ain't going nowhere." He picked up her passport and put it in the shirt pocket of his uniform. As he stacked her documents and tapped them on the counter top to even out the pages he said, "And for your Yankeefied information, I know Harvard is a university. It might surprise you to know that I went to college, Doctor Hotchkiss, is it? I got my . . . A-period-S-period at San Jacinto C-period-C-period, and my B-period-S-period at T-period-C-period-U-period in Fort Worth. That's a city. And I got my M-period-S-period in criminal law in Austin, the home of the U-period of T-period. That's a university, and it has a football team. You understand football, don't you? It's an American game. You're in America now, and we get to use our hands. Anymore, crap out of you and there is likely to be a strip search, ma'am."

"Not by you: Y-period-O-period-U-period." She stood defiantly with her arms across her chest. "You make fun of the Brazilians because they don't play American football and in soccer can't use their hands, but I'll tell you something, officer, in law enforcement, you all play the same damn games."

"Keep it up, lady. I'm going to enjoy this." He pantomimed putting a latex glove over his left hand and snapping the elastic around his wrist. "Rubber gloves—maybe we need 'um, maybe not. Rubber—doesn't that come from Brazil?"

"Would you call your supervisor, please? This has gone as far as it's going to with you, you S-period-O-period-B-period."

"Buena idea, I'll be glad to call my supervisor, wait here." He went to a nearby red phone. "Is Supervisor Standish available?" Olivia could hear him ask. "No, well then who the hell is on duty? Oh, no, not that perra . . . well, connect me." He waited a moment while meandering over Olivia with his eyes. "Mzzz. Hernandez, I have a hippie down here trying to get back in the country with some bullshit documentation from the Brazilian-commie-government saying she can transport drugs. Much as I hate to bother you, I'll need your authorization unless you would rather wait until Supervisor Standish gets back from the can. Yes, ma'am." He hung up the phone. He leaned against the wall next to the phone with his right hand on the butt of his revolver, but said nothing to Olivia.

Olivia felt tired, starved, and somewhat paranoid from her powered wine on the plane. She knew she could not pass a blood test. The constant stare of the agent made her uncomfortable. She thought about how gentle her jungle friends were compared to these so-called civilized people.

In a few minutes a uniformed woman approached the customs station. She was medium height, athletically built, pressed and polished. She walked with confidence straight to the officer. He handed her Olivia's passport and the other paperwork. She flipped open the passport and looked at Olivia. She quickly perused the other documents. He turned his back to Olivia and the woman disappeared between his huge torso and the wall. He said something Olivia could not make out. The uniformed woman stuck her head around the side of the officer and looked Olivia up and down. It was a comedic scene, her face appearing and disappearing like a curious but shy child hiding behind a large parent. He continued to report the situation. Her face popped out on the other side. Olivia saw the guard lift up his left hand, wiggle the fingers, and pantomime snapping on a glove again.

"You did what?" Olivia heard the woman yell. She was shaking her head in disgust as she maneuvered around the colossus and came straight to Olivia.

She spoke with a Hispanic accent, "Shall we go to my office." It was an order, not a question.

"Do you need my help?" asked Wyatt Earp.

"No, gracious, Herbert," she replied. "I don't believe I'll be needing anything from you. You have done quite enough already. Qué barbaridad!" She said something in Spanish to Olivia that appeared too quick for the agent to comprehend.

Olivia and the supervisor conversed in Spanish as they walked up the ramp.

"De nada," mumbled the agent.

It wasn't long until Olivia had told Supervisor Hernandez about the entire nine months in the jungle and her struggle getting out of Brazil.

"I know," said Hernandez, "they can never look you in the eye. But, Olivia, you cannot walk around the Houston airport in that outfit. This is Texas, where men are men and their horses have learned to say no. I'll take you shopping as soon as Supervisor Standish gets back from his break. Meanwhile, if you don't mind, I need to confirm a few things with the US Agricultural Department. It probably wouldn't hurt to call these credit card companies; I assume these credit cards in your bag are still good."

"Yes, I guess so. I really didn't have a chance to use them in the jungle, and I left in such a hurry. I would love something new to wear. I want to thank you for being cordial. Since I left the rain forest I have run into nothing but rude bufóns."

"Well, we women have to stick together, now don't we. Besides, we received a memo from Harvard University and the office of a Professor Antwerp to expect you on the flight from Brazil. He said your work was very important. Harvard, eh chica, muy impresionante!" They laughed.

After a few phone calls and a long conversation a lanky man with a rumpled uniform entered the office. Hernandez and Olivia walked toward the door. Standish stared at Olivia's chest.

"Buenos Dias," she laughed.

Hernandez told Olivia in Spanish, "I'd like to see him try to identify you from a mug shot."

Olivia's connecting flight landed at Stapleton International Airport just east of Denver, Colorado. She felt even more confined by her new clothes. Since she anticipated a trek to the site of the Indian grave she purchased very practical clothing—hiking boots, which felt heavy and clumsy; blue jeans, with full length legs this time; a blue cotton work shirt; a couple of clean tee-shirts, one she wore beneath the work shirt; and a cotton, summer weight sweater— she recalled that even summer evenings in Colorado can get cool. She bought a bra but removed it almost immediately. She felt imprisoned. This is going to take some getting used to.

On the plane she worried why Antwerp had chosen her to work on this Northern Native American site. Her background was obviously Native South American people. She had a few classes from Antwerp that addressed the Great American Plains tribes and the Southwestern Pueblo people, but she was not the expert. He had mumbled something about the need of her Spanish and that no one else could pull away on such short notice. After all, it was simply a diverted flight to Denver, and she was a native of the area. According to her notes her Brazilian study was completed; her Grandmother had become worried about her. That could possibly be the motive—Grandmamma was pulling the puppet strings again. Antwerp said it was time to come home to America. He would catch up to her in a day, two at most. Besides, there was some sort of jurisdiction dispute with the authorities, and there was a danger someone would loot the tomb. He needed a creative, take-charge person to woo the authorities. He was convinced after reviewing her skull-alter strategy that the brilliance she exhibited in gaining her access to the most isolated tribe in the New World would serve her well in handling this simple dispute and guaranteeing the safety of the site. All the flattery, of course, was the dead giveaway. There must be something secretive about the discovery; Antwerp was trying to control things and he needed someone—family—to help him in his skullduggery. He was well known for manipulating anthropological expeditions and races for discovery. Besides, he finished the conversation by saying he remembered she liked Beatle's music. Now what the hell did that have to do with anything?

Chapter Twenty-one

Pickles

Summer, 1964

*Politics have played perplexing roles in the affairs of deities,
just as they have among mortals. The foothills saga is tainted with
political intrigue. Bubble, bubble, toil, and trouble—you can thank
all who are holy that the cauldron of political trouble boiling
between Golden and Denver contains Turtle soup. The stew pot is
my recipe, and it's after the entrée that the host makes sure everyone
gets their just desserts.*

It was not Anthony Hands of the Bear's intent to eaves drop,
but he recognized some of the men at the table between the bar and
the fireplace. They used to be Friday noontime regulars to Buffalo
Bill Cody's Bar Grill Trading Post and Texaco Station, and the man
doing all the talking was Alan Sweet, past Golden and current Chief
of the Denver Police. Sweet and the laughter were loud enough to
get Tony's attention and perk his curiosity. Wild Billy the proprietor,
standing behind the bar opposite Tony, ignored the boisterous
conversation, and busied himself with bar business, but Tony
listened. Sweet was addressing the only character Tony did not
recognize.

"There were over two hundred applicants for the position of
Denver Police Chief, but only three of us were given interviews—
myself and two others. One candidate was from Atlanta—the Head
of Internal Affairs for the police department of that rebels den. He
looked great on paper, I heard, so Denver flew him in. He turned out
to be black. Later the Mayor told me that his explanation to the
search committee was, 'Well hell, no one knew—after all, he had a
honkey name.'

"The hiring committee formally stated, however, that they
believed his coming from an internal affairs background greatly

diminished his candidacy, particularly when considering the traditional lack of trust internal affairs detectives generate—generally—among the rank and file. Scuttlebutt was that they were actually less concerned with 'internal affairs' than they were with 'external appearances,' if you get my drift."

Tony couldn't help himself, when Sweet made his racial comment, he looked over at the speaker. They made immediate eye contact. Sweet was staring back, wearing a dangerous grin. Tony turned around and slumped over the bar.

"The second candidate," said Sweet, focusing again on his tablemates, "was Chuck Parsons, an honest cop who had worked his way up through the aforementioned rank and file. It didn't surprise me when I found out his unwavering honesty weakened his chances, particularly when in the interview he said he refused to show special treatment for some of Denver's more affluent citizenry. He had the makin's of a good cop, but was politically naïve. When he asked the committee whether or not he got the promotion, their answer was that they felt it was more important to have a man of his integrity closer to the heart and soul of day-to-day policing. He was demoted. Back on the beat he went, proving that in pursuing one's ambitions to improve one's station, it is sometimes better not to bring attention to the aforementioned one's self. Via the insulation of anonymity, a lot of guys have had long and rewarding careers by disappearing into the institutional shadows. When they foolishly decide to take some responsibility, or expectations are unexpectedly thrust upon them, their sudden appearance motivates their permanent disappearance."

They all laughed. Tony acted as if he didn't hear, but sneaked a peak in the mirror behind the bar.

Sweet leaned back in his heavy pine chair and looked pleased. He continued. "I, on the other hand, have always been in the spotlight and enjoyed a modicum of celebrity. It suits me. I believe the search committee regarded me as a local hero. You recall, when I was the Chief for the City of Golden, I thwarted the theft of the remains of Buffalo Bill. We ran off a mob of Wyoming Legionnaires and incarcerated the crazed young cowboy who led the gang—all this while putting out a forest fire started by the grave robbers as a distraction. Their plan failed, and here we are. I believe that if I hadn't left Golden for Denver's head job, they would have put up a statue of me somewhere here on Lookout. Now don't get me wrong, I don't want a statue; I'm just saying that's how crazy things were, that's how enthusiastic folks were to claim a hero." He called out toward the bar. "You believe that's true, Billy?"

"What's that, Chief?"

"That you mountain folk would have put up a statue—The Hero of Lookout."

"Pay your tab, Chief, I'll put up a statue."

"Ah, Billy, you know our little Friday group is good for business; why . . . seems to me you'd be willing to float a few drinks for the free public relations we're providing."

"Chief, I love ya'; I've always loved ya' but the only time my bar is mentioned in connection with you being a customer is when you're in some kind of political trouble."

"Haven't you ever heard the ol' axiom, Billy—any publicity is good publicity?"

"Good point, Chief. Another round? I'll add it to your tab."

"You're a frugal ol' Billy Goat," he said loudly and then more quietly said to the table newcomer, "and a cheap ol' bastard." Sweet laughed and continued more publicly, "Ol' Billy here is not the first owner of Cody's Bar and Grill. A local character named Cactus Face Doogan was the original owner. Ol' Cactus Face had a rambunctious friend who dressed up like Buffalo Bill himself. Those two rogues and I had different ideas about what sort of public relations was good for business here on Lookout. I obviously leaned toward law and order; Doogan and his sidekick favored local color and mischief making. I think they drank up all their profits and definitely contributed to the growth of the Coors Brewery. We had more than a few disturbing-the-peace confrontations and drunk-and-disorderly debacles to contend with; as well as, a few debates about debauchery.

"They had an ancient ol' Indian who hung out with them, named Willie Wolf Song. He was the third stooge. And although I could never catch him salty-handed, I suspected it was Willie who forced Foss Drug eventually to quit selling roasted cashews—they were losing too much to pilferage. The two right hands give to the local economy and the left takes away. But all three were, if you'll pardon the pun, nuts.

"I hate to admit it, but I sort of miss those ol' rogues," he looked toward the bar. "You, Billy?"

"What's that, Chief?"

"You miss ol' Doogan and Rudolph . . . and Willie?"

"Yeah, Chief, I miss Doogan. I miss him a lot. Rudi was entertaining. But, you never did catch Wolf Song, did ya, Chief? Old scoundrel robbed me blind—pottery, blankets, Indian jewelry, a ton of cashews, and a case of my best Scotch."

"My only unsolved crime before I left Golden for Denver. Sorry, Billy, but you know how clandestine and sneaky those Indians can be."

Tony again couldn't help himself; he turned and looked at Sweet. The penetrating eyes and I-dare-you grin were waiting.

"The army was pretty pissed at Doogan. They took away his retirement. He had to give up on his dream to open a ski resort. He broke his leg the night of the attempted grave robbery. And, of course, the army blamed him for a tank being hijacked. I liked ol' Doogan. It was a shame, but I'm afraid *they* made him the whipping boy for the fiasco. You know the army—they wanted a scapegoat worse than the citizens needed a hero. Fate keeps strange bedfellows."

No one except Tony noted the misquote.

"I became a hero and poor ol' Doogan becomes a local blemish; Rudolph—the town drunk. They were an amusing pair. I remember, every time I saw them together in a local bar I'd ask, 'We're not going to start another fire tonight are we, boys?' And Doogan would reply, 'How's it going Hero, got a match?' "

"My butt and you're face," mumbled Tony, alarmed at his reflex response, and panicked that he had spoken too loudly. He intently searched Billy's face for any sign that the Chief had heard him. Billy smiled mildly. Tony slumped over his beer, trying to disappear.

"Well, men, I hate to be a party pooper, but I got to get back to the office and clean up a couple of things before the weekend. Carson, bring the car around." Officer Carson, Sweet's driver and protégé jumped into a run. "I'll put these drinks on my tab, boys. It was another productive meeting." He stood and pushed his chair back with his calves. It squeaked on the hard floor. He set his police cap slightly off-kilter in an obviously practiced ceremony. He started to exit, but stopped directly behind Tony and talked over him, "Billy, just add today to my account; maybe we'll see you next Friday. Try to fumigate the place by then."

Tony didn't dare move.

"Always a delight, Chief," answered Billy. "It's good to see that Carson is as sprite as ever."

"Adios, Wild Man." Sweet's bulk filled the doorway and blocked the light as he left. The others sauntered out behind the Chief.

"See ya', Billy," said one of the followers. Tony thought he recognized him, but couldn't quite place the face.

"So long, Mr. Mayor."

"Until next time, Billy," said a second, a taller man, also familiar.

"Thanks, Mayor, until next time."

"Thanks for the hospitality, Billy," said a third as he approached the door.

"Anytime, Councilman."

A couple of others waved as they left.

When he was sure they had gone Tony barked, "Jeez, what a pride of assholes! Is Sweet a friend of yours, Billy?"

"No, not a friend—more a necessary evil acquaintance."

"And who were those other guys? It looked like a Mafia meeting."

"That's the FAC Committee."

"*Fact* committee?"

"Yeah, FAC—fact—Foothills Action Consortium; they profess to be a nonpartisan *fact* finding group. In truth, they are a behind-the-scenes influence-peddling and policy-making group of right wing Republicans. The tall guy is the past mayor of Golden, the one after him is the mayor of Morrison; there were a couple of city councilmen and a major landowner/car dealer. He's a main political contributor hereabouts."

"I've read about those guys. That's the group out to get the governor, Dick Lyon. Why?"

"Well, first of all, Lyon is a Democrat, and second: the Gov, better known as Richard the Lyonheart, and Chief Sweet, also known as Pickles, have been political adversaries for years. Lyon is well known for criticizing the FAC Committee. He calls them the F-A-C club, you know: Friday Afternoon Club. Lyon isn't shy about referring to them as a Republican fraternity of good ol' boys, frat rats, out getting blasted on Friday afternoons and hatching a bunch of juvenile, political pranks. I think the two guys just plain dislike each other and hate the other's politics."

Tony asked, "Sweet seemed to be the leader of the group. How did he get so powerful? He's such an ass. Did you see him trying to intimidate me? What have *I* ever done to him?"

"You remember that he used to be the head bluecoat here in Golden? Well, he's become even more unbearable since Denver made him head honcho. Obviously, he has further political ambitions. He had, and still has, several powerful supporters, influential people beyond the FAC, including the current owner of The Denver Post. The Post has always inserted itself into Denver politics, regional business, and as a matter of fact, local history. Did you know the old, original Denver Post paid off the widow of Buffalo Bill to bury him on Lookout instead of in Wyoming?"

"I've heard the stories, sure; who hasn't?"

"Well, I think it was the episode in our infamous local history that sparked Sweet's ambitions. You know the story about when the posse of Wyoming hotheads tried to steal Old Bill off Lookout. 'Course you have, who hasn't? Anyway, Sweet was the only gendarme who came out smelling like a rose. He cashed in on all the confusion and bad press for the Army and the politicos. I think The Denver Post, being appreciative that the body snatching was foiled, made Sweet out to be the hero. Why not? He was young and virile; he fit the journalistic bill for what a hero should look like—Old West handsome. Well, obviously, that was a few years back, as you can see, since the attempt at grave robbing, he's kinda' gone to seed. But, you know the news business; back then if they didn't make him out to be John Wayne, then at least, they portrayed him as fricking Andy of Mayberry.

"Otis was the only guy I could relate to in that show," said Anthony. "There was a guy you could sit around and have a drink with. So who did you identify with back then—innocent little Opey?"

"I showed up later. I was young, but not that young. But you're right, I was an innocent when I met Doogan. I kinda' loved Doogan; he became my mentor. It was Doogan I bought this bar from."

"I've heard the stories, Wild Bill."

"Doogan got a raw deal from the army. Sweet doesn't like to admit it, but he didn't help Doogan's cause any. Of course, I can't complain too much; it all worked out for me—owning Cody's, I mean."

Billy paused, apparently reminiscing. He began again, "The same powerful, behind-the-scenes hooligans who canonized Sweet, the local jingoists, held the military responsible for the clusterfuck. In turn, the brass made Doogan and Rudi the scapegoats. Doogan's resort ambitions took a downhill tumble."

"I heard," said Tony. "Sweet seemed to delight in talking about it."

"Doogan and Rudi, I'm afraid, insulated their disappointment with alcohol. Over the next few years Cactus Face and Captain Bill became local characters—barflies and boozers.

"Meanwhile, Sweet groomed notoriety as one determined John Law SOB—a head thumper. The way I see it, however, there were two flaws to his fame. First: local crime was not exactly organized by the La Cosa Nostra. Lawbreakers in Golden were jaywalkers, parking violators, speeders, bicycle thieves, an occasional drunk—usually Rudolph—and an unconvicted nut poacher. That leads to the second ding in his armor. He never caught Wolf Song. I knew it was the old nut thief who cleaned me out, but Sweet said he had no evidence . . . he had no weapon, dubious motive, and no body. Willie disappeared. 'It's all circumstantial, Wildman,' Sweet would tell me. 'I'll admit that everybody knows the old savage was a thief ... well, aren't they all,' he would say. No offence, Tony."

"None taken, Wildman. I know it was Sweet talking."

"Sweet looked at the whole episode as a big joke. He summed up his cavalier attitude by saying that he could never catch the wily desperado *red* handed.

"I'd like to think, although he'd never admit it, that it haunts Sweet . . . not that he gives a damn about the Trading Post, but that he left an unsolved crime on the books before he left for Denver."

"I've always felt that the lack of crime in Golden was due to a deficiency in the imagination and energy of her criminals," said Tony.

Well, regardless, the powers to be, all the other folk attributed the lack of crime to Sweet's iron hand. Anyway, that's the way his supporters saw it; so they made him a hero."

"I'm with you, Billy. He scares the poop out of me; I don't think he likes Indians."

"He doesn't like anybody, Hardhat, but hates the red man even more now that he's the Chief of Police in Denver. Think about it: It's a different situation in a big city; you know that. A band of braves wander off the reservation, can't get work, end up bumming quarters and begging for drinks on Larimer Street, in the skid row bars. They get drunk and start fights, and Sweet and his boys have to contend with 'um. Now you know I ain't anti-Indian, Tony. I'm just saying that big cities like Denver alienate folks, Indians most particular. Demon rum does its destruction, their world turns to shit, and your brothers feel the wrath of Sweet's nightstick."

Anthony Hands of the Bear sat quietly.

"I'm sorry, Tony. I've hurt your feelings."

"It's not that, Billy. I know you're right, but I find it upsetting—disappointing. It's one of the reasons I left Sels and the Papago reservation. I just couldn't see me falling into that fatal routine. It's happened to several of my friends. I thank my grandfather for teaching me how to play pool and hammer a nail, that way I can spend my time chasing pussy instead of lost pride. It's when I have to listen to bullies like Sweet and take their insults because they're cops that I want to strike back. And that Carson guy, talk about a Barney Fife. What's his story?"

Billy put a cold beer in front of Tony. "Carson was a deputy here in Golden when Sweet was the Chief. He's been Sweet's puppy dog for as long as I can remember. When Sweet went to Denver, Carson followed. Sweet pulled strings to get Carson in the police academy and Carson has been lathered up ever since.

Billy went baritone in a perfect imitation of Sweet's voice. "I couldn't go off and leave you in Golden, Little Buddy. Who'd fetch for me? I take your enthusiasm as a compliment, Carson, my boy. If I get the job, you damn betcha' there's a place for you on the force. Why, I'd do everything in my power to expedite the whole thing. You're a good cop, Carson, a little high spirited once in a while, but a hell of a lot better and a damn site superior to any of those Rent-A-Cop Rangers up in Red Rocks. I'd be pleased to have you accompany me into Denver, son."

"Jeez, I hate the idea," interrupted Tony, "that there is something that Sweet and I might agree on, but I scorn Henry Humboldt and the Rangers more than I do that Denver group."

Billy continued with his imitation. "Carson, I believe we're out of doughnuts. Make mine a glazed. I hate those little candy sprinkles they put on the chocolate ones; damn things get caught in your teeth." Billy chuckled at his joke. "Damn Billy, I gotta keep that boy next to me . . . so he don't get hurt."

Billy and Tony laughed.

"So," asked Tony, "what's with Sweet's nickname—Pickles?"

"Sweet quickly became a public figure in Denver; was in the news a lot. Rumors were he was being groomed for bigger things. When I asked him about his political ambitions he used to say, 'Doesn't hurt to know who you know, you know!'

"I don't know whether or not his nickname was given to him by his powerful peers or his political enemies; regardless, over the years Chief Sweet was often maliciously, or sometimes fondly, referred to as *Pickles*.

"If you asked his family, it was an affectionate term coined by his wife—'My Sweet Pickle.' But a critical newspaper reporter, from that other Denver paper, said the nickname was the result of a malapropism Sweet uttered during a presentation at Civic Center when he referred to his hate of pork barrel politics as 'pickle' barrel.

"Enemies also liked to slander Sweet by repeating that it was his proclivity for gratis oral sex from the local call girls that earned him the nickname. The Denver prostitutes tattled that Sweet suffered from genital warts; therefore, his personal apparatus resembled a large Gherkin."

Both men convulsed in laughter; Tony had to turn his back and spit his beer to prevent from choking.

After a moment of unsteady calm Billy continued. "My all-time favorite anti-Sweet story involved the Chief and Governor Lyon. I remember the headlines in the Rocky Mountain News: 'PICKLES RUIN PEANUT BUTTER.' It was a quote from the Governor and drove the political wedge between the two men even deeper. Their relationship was always tenuous—Sweet's political ambitions being rather transparent. The Foothills Action Consortium, probably at Sweet's urging, had made several public statements that were anti-Lyon and severely critical of several of the governor's pet initiatives.

"Dick and the Democratic felt the Friday Afternoon Club was a definite thorn in the Donkey's flank. In retaliation, they used every opportunity to get involved in the Denver political melee, even though their turf was the state. Here's an example: Lyon, the Governor, personally mediated a disputed contract between the Denver School Board and the DPS teachers union—a city issue. In fact, much to the chagrin of the FAC, his 'interference,' expedited an early settlement. Surprised the hell out of everybody; embarrassed Sweet and his buddy, the Denver Mayor. Later, Lyon rallied his progressive colleagues when he discovered that the free-lunch program for the inner-city schools was running out of federal funding, and at-risk of not providing a gratis lunch to several thousands of Denver's elementary students, most of whom were the kids of minority Democrats. He personally called the CEO's of King Soopers, Safeway, Albertson's, and cajoled them into donating lunch goodies: an ocean of milk, an arena of grape jelly, acres of potato chips, and an oozing glacier of peanut butter.

"Lyon had the Denver Fire and Police Departments deliver the first loads of lunchables. He figured it was a rare effort on his part at goodwill and showmanship. It was good story and he was willing to bury the political hatchet; sorry about using that old cliché . . ."

"Not a problem."

". . . and share the political wealth, so to speak. It was a great local media celebration. It even got national press play. The most redundant image from the Fourth Estate was of a policeman, a fireman, and a bevy of black youngsters sitting together on the back of a fire truck sharing peanut butter sandwiches. 'Umm, I just loves peanut butter,' a big-eyed second grader would chortle for the camera, the sticky confection making the child's statement smack with maudlin sweetness. What opportunists these guys are. I've never eaten peanut butter since.

"Unfortunately, it was later uncovered that nearly a hundred cases of Skippy Smooth and Peter Pan Chunky never got delivered. Several were found in the pantry of local fire stations and in the squad rooms of the Denver Police. Channel Seven, using a hidden camera in a van, filmed cops loading cases of Jiffy into the trunks of a long line of personal vehicles—not the black-and-white cruisers designated for the publicity event. Although Sweet was not driving, the film did show a suspicious carton being loaded into his Buick.

"Governor Lyon was outraged at the scandal. In an attempt to distance himself from the impropriety and take full political advantage of Sweet's blunder, and to take a shot at the Foothills Action Consortium, Lyon gave an anecdote as part of his press denial."

Billy looked up at the ceiling to help him remember Lyon's quote, " 'When I was a lad growing up in a poor but clean neighborhood, right here in North Denver, my parents, both working people, would once in a while have to hire a baby-sitter. And although this woman's intent was honorable, she turned out to be quite a Grinch. Every day she would give my brothers and my sister and me the same lunch. And every day she would spoil it. Somewhere, not in Colorado, somehow, for no reason I know, this crone got the idea to slice up a sour dill and place it on our Skippy sandwiches. Well, folks, you can take it from me—pickles ruins peanut butter.'

"Of course, the press and most of the public understood the reference to the scandalized police chief. It's a sticky business, politics."

Chapter Twenty-two

War of the Biscuits and Burritos

Summer, 1964

If art and architecture are inspirational elements in the study
of civilizations, then "cuisine" is a delectable ingredient. Two local
menus stand as quintessential cultural attributes.

    The cafe in The Holland House Hotel in Golden had all the
homey comfort of a small town family establishment. Although it sat
at the foot of Lookout Mountain and considered itself the last
Epicurean stop-off before the Great Divide, it exhibited the charm of
one of those western plains hasheries where the agrarians sit around
nursing several cups of java, chewing toothpicks, answering
redundant meteorological questions with monosyllable replies. The
dogma de jour was abridged to utterances of: "yup, nope, hot," and,
once in a while, going into a diatribe of prophetic and historic
relevance such as, ". . . a well digger's ass . . ." or ". . . busier than
a one legged man in a kicking contest." Their hats, baseball and
truckers' caps, rugged in style, promoted proud American farm
products such as John Deere or Haley's Seed and Feed.

    The air in The Holland House Cafe became heavy and sweet
with the perfume of freshly baked biscuits and newly brewed coffee,
triggering memories from the old timers: a bygone and busted
miner, the latest in a long string of barbers, and the last of the local
ranchers—the Bachman brothers. The aroma elicited comparisons
to the biscuits their granny used to bake, and how the "flour,"
rather than "flower" fragrance of granny's cakes and breads
blossomed in the mornings. They swapped yarns of past feasts,
lethal winters, and barefoot walks uphill both directions.

    Sadly for the old timers, the aroma and the reputation of the
biscuits eventually filled the valley and drifted east past the tabletops
toward Denver. Tourists—as far as the locals were concerned, never
thinking to call these Denver folk "neighbors"—began showing up

to partake of hot biscuits. When they dared to bring up comparisons to their grandmothers' baked goods, the locals, rather than hearing an echo and finding common ground, thought the day-trippers sounded presumptuous. On Sunday, the invaders were so thick a local could not even get a seat in the cafe—Don't these gaw-damn carpetbaggers have a home of their own?

But these grumpy old codgers were in the minority and their geriatric complaints could not hold back progress, for as the sweet soft dough of the palettes of biscuits rose daily, so did the pride of the progressive citizens of Golden.

Down the street, Coors Brewery had tours, which were capped off with a cold one at their hospitality room. And cold it was. The beer tasted as if it was chilled by glaciers in the local mountains and transported by the often-touted "pure Rocky Mountain Spring Water."

Foss Drug became the souvenir capital of the Front Range. In Golden there were more friendly bars per block than Boston, and it was great fun for the big city folk to take pictures of one another under the famous arching sign declaring they were "WELCOME" and were indeed standing at the very spot "Where The West Remains," despite the fact that a century had past since Loveland and Berthoud and General West had founded the burg. Golden was a burgeoning hamlet struggling to maintain a balance between modern convenience and Victorian charm. It was a tedious balance at best, one ripe with potential conflict. Several annual, street celebrations exasperated the combustibility. One can see why Golden is among my favorite haunts.

A sister city, Morrison, sits nestled in the Foothills a few miles south of Golden. The natural stone amphitheater, Red Rocks, my greatest sculptural achievement, sits dead center between the two. Morrison was likewise working diligently to capitalize on Victorian ambiance, a boisterous miner's past, and frontier pugnaciousness. But Morrison was more tightly packed into a confining, yet picturesque, valley. There was no room for large hotels. While Golden could historically brag of The Bella Vista, the Astor House, the Omaha House, and eventually The Holland House, Morrison had no such luxurious accommodations. Golden also trumpeted about the Colorado School of Mines, the Coors Brewery, and the Jefferson County seat of government. Morrison's tight valley could never oblige such enhancements.

Regardless of the differences, perhaps because of the differences, tourists and Denverites flocked to both towns for a dose of nostalgia. The mistake these visitors made, however, was talking openly in restaurants and shops about the "delightful" meal or "enchanting" souvenir they "discovered" in the other town. "Oh, you've got to go to Golden next Sunday," they would chatter at the antique lunch table in Morrison, "for breakfast or brunch at The Holland House. They serve the best biscuits in the world. I'm telling you, they are to die for—better than my Nana used to make." They would gossip in the souvenir aisles of Foss Drug, "That's an interesting trinket, but you must drive over to Morrison, it's just a short way from here; they have a shop there with real fossils. Very rare, and frankly," they would say under their breath but still irritatingly loud enough to be heard by the shop proprietor, "their prices are much better." Among the entrepreneurs of both Golden and Morrison a subtle and unwritten competitive resentment emerged.

Golden, however, held an undisputed growth lead considering those blessings mentioned before: the brewery, the school, the county government, and most of all, those ambrosial biscuits. But by the early sixties Morrison launched a serious gourmet challenge. It drifted up from south of the border, winding its way through Texas, Arizona and with a unique flavorful deviation, New Mexico. It was energized with fiery spices and romantic utterances such as: tore-tee-ya, so-pa-pee-ya, een-chee-laa-da, ray-yeah-no and, of course, burr-ee-toe. The cuisine of Mexico had invaded the Foothills with a picante energy that raised a new and intriguing aroma, whiffing along the hogbacks toward the valley of Golden and spilling over into the Queen City of the Plains. The Morrison Inn, fast becoming famous for its smothered burritos, had dropped a gauntlet filled with fresh salsa.

Then these Morrison upstarts had the gall to rent a street booth at the August celebration in Golden—Buffalo Bill's Days. This was Golden's biggest party of the year and the Morrison Inn had the audacity to sell their foreign fare right across the street from The Holland House, and allowing—hell: encouraging—the aroma of

their pungent condiments to compete with the historical and
maternal fragrance of the biscuits.

"I don't bloody know what it is," said Ringo, "but something smells delicious."

"Delectable," said George.

"Savory," said John.

"Appetizing," answered Paul.

"I'm bloody hungry," said Ringo.

"Agreed," said John. "What is that delightful spicy aroma?"

"Spicy?" asked Paul, "It smells like freshly baked bread. It reminds me when I was a youth and the hot buns me granny would bake."

"You're bonkers, Paul," said George. "I smell cayenne or some other spicily spice. It reminds me of East Indian food me granny refused to fix."

"Bread," said Ringo.

"Acrid," repeated George. "Pungent, tangy, peppery, piquant, curried, bloody nippy." He kept impatiently on, ruining the game for the others.

"Wait a moment," interrupted John. "Turn this way," he said twisting his head to the east and raising his nose. "Now smell." Ringo started to say something. "Bugger it, Ringo. Now turn this way." He turned his head to the west and took a great whiff.

"Bloody hell," said Paul. "It's both, now isn't it?"

"Well, that complicates things," said George.

"I'm still hungry," said Ringo.

"As am I," said John.

"Well, which is it?" asked George. "Something basic or something adventurous?"

"Baked goods," said Ringo and Paul in unison.

"Spice," answered John at the same time.

"We may have to split up," said George.

"Part company," said Ringo.

"Take different roads," said Paul.

"The sooner the bloody better," said John.

"There are rumors about, John, of disenchantment. You're being very prophetic," said George.

John ignored the query and indulged himself, "To partake of the peppery is the path I ponder."

"He's very pretentious," said Paul.

"Redundant," criticized Ringo.

"That's the cooking kettle calling the pepper pot black," said John, sensing a touch of offense. "Well, we are a bit conspicuous, lolling about like a group of gelada baboons on Gibraltar. It's trouble if anyone recognizes us. We should definitely separate."

"Perhaps we should get out of these togs and purchase some Western ware," suggested Paul.

"That's a good idea," said Ringo. "John, why didn't you think of that? I think I'd look mod in one of those ten-gallon Stetsons. Hats suit me. And the cowboy boots might add an inch or two in height."

"It'd take about ten gallons to set off your profile," said John. "And I don't think cowboy boots are any taller than those Mercy Mods you're wearing. Maybe some stilts . . ."

"That's a low blow, John," said George. "Ringo can't help if he's *pinnacle-ly* challenged."

"Elevation deprivation," said Paul.

"That's hurtful," said Ringo.

"I didn't say it," said George. "It was bloody John now wasn't it?"

"I'm not enjoying these games," said Ringo. "Not when they suddenly take a turn and leave me the target. Sod off about my nose. Besides, I thought America's gone metric. I'd therefore have a ten liter nose; I mean hat ... I'd purchase a ten liter chapeau. Drat!"

"Rumors . . . it's nothing but rumors, laddy. Never happen. Thought we wasn't gonna' cater to rumors, lads. And enough about your nose, Ringo. No rumor there."

"I'd entertain an apology," said Ringo.

"Is he talking about rumors regarding American measurements or the latest tidings sniffed out by the press about our quarreling?" asked Paul.

"And I don't apologize, Ringo," said John, "You yourself have always said your nose is nothing to sneeze at."

"Yeah, and it was you that answered that daft reporter asking about getting conceited by saying every time you feel your head is swelling you just look at Ringo for proof we're not supermen. My feelings are hurt. I don't believe I want to dine with the likes of you, John Winston Lennon."

"Ringo, mate, you know I'm just joshing. Don't be mad; it makes me sad; come on, lad: Give us a wink and let us think of you," sang John.

"Piss off, Winston," said Ringo. "Enough of the argy-bargy. Paul, if you're hungry, me stomach is rumbling as loud as me drums. Let's spend a shilling or two on some buns; let's eat."

"Dollars and cents," said John.

"Make's sense," said George. "He's acting purposefully dense."

"And they're biscuits, Richard Starkey," added John. "You're in America, lad. Soft rolls like those you're savoring are called *biscuits,* not like in Liverpool where *biscuits* are . . ."

"Crackers," said Ringo. "I know . . . I'm not totally daft, John; however, I think you've gone utterly *crackers*. By the by, could I borrow a small boodle, Paul?" asked Ringo, "I'm ignoring John's persistence."

"I wouldn't loan the impudent little bugger a farthing," said George.

"Not a crown," said John. "you scouser, you. 'By the by,' you never paid me back the last time *I* fronted your lunch. Quit bandying about. We're all hungry. Ringo, if you wish, go for the biscuits. That's using your loaf. Let's separate."

"Disunite?" asked Paul. "We always knew you'd be the first to go, John."

"Listen, lads, we're not trying to start a war here; I don't believe in war; we're just trying to get something to eat before the bloody concert. Come, George," said John. "Let's us spicy lads crack on and investigate that pungent food odor. You're fond of curry, now aren't ya? This smells almost as zippy. "

"Aye, I'm ready to order based on the odor."

"Yeah, and Ringo, me boy, let us pursue the more basic sustenance of mankind: butter and biscuits, hot from the oven. Maybe I'll write a song," said Paul.

"Right," said John. "You and bloody Ringo can become the new songsters. Bugger me and George." John and George marched toward the burrito stand.

"What did I say?" asked Paul of Ringo.

"I don't know, Paul. But it would appear that John is getting a bit peevish."

"Bloody cranky!"

"Irritable."

"Ill-humored, to say the least."

"Well, you know, he gets a bit disagreeable when he hasn't eaten."

"Or when you ask him for bloody money," said Paul.

Paul and Ringo sauntered over a few steps to The Holland House booth and lined up for biscuits. They made jokes that the "Butter and Biscuits" song Paul had in mind would have to be a Blues beat, rather than a Mersey melody.

Ringo sang, "Baby, pass me the butter; there isn't no other savory flavor that Paul and I favor . . ."

"On our hot buns," Paul added. They laughed at the innuendo.

"Look at them over there," said George. "I know that laugh; they're bashing you."

"Bloody ingrates," said John. "They would still be back in the bloody hotel if it wasn't for bloody me."

"Was bloody clever of you, John." he paused and looked around. "Any idea where the bloody hell we are?"

"The infamous hamlet of Golden, according to the taxi driver. I instructed him to take us someplace far from the madding crowd. Somewhere we wouldn't be easily recognized. And, I slipped him an extra fifty not to tell anyone where he'd taken us."

"Fifty! And Ringo says you're tight."

"Tight! Is that what he said?"

"Well, he didn't say thrifty." George pursued his advantage.

"Bloody tight!"

"I didn't hear—frugal."

"So, I suppose he thinks I'm stingy."

"I believe he does, John."

"George, you're beginning to peeve me."

"That's not my intent, John. Truly it isn't," he smiled. "May I buy you one of those burrito buggers? They look tasty."

"You boys aren't from around here, now are ya?" asked the man in the Morrison Inn booth.

"Actually, no, were not." answered John. "That's bloody perceptive of you. Was it the accent?"

"No, it was those citified clothes," he answered as he plopped a burrito into a long, red-and-white-checkered, cardboard, trough-shaped plate. "Red or green?" he asked.

"You don't care for our clothes, then?" asked John.

"Oh, I like 'um just fine. I just noticed they ain't like nothing you'd buy around these parts. Red or green?"

"So it wasn't the hair?"

"No, not the hair. 'Though I'll say, there is a lot of it. Red or green?"

"And not the shoes, I take it?"

"Nope, son, it wasn't the shoes; pretty and pointy as they are. I just noticed your suit didn't have no collar and no lapels, that's all. I didn't mean nothing by it. Do you want red or green on your burritos?"

"They're called Cuban heels, if you're curious," said John.

"Don't care much for Cuba," answered the man. "Castro and those commies tried to blow us up with a bunch of Russkie missiles. You boys ain't Cuban are ya'?

"No," said John.

"You ain't commies are ya'?"

"No," repeated John. "Why do you ask?"

"I'd have to dish you up a serious serving of wup-ass instead of these burritos," he said. "Red of green?"

"I don't believe I've ever seen wup-ass on a menu before," said John. "Is it a tasty dish?"

"It's something you don't want to partake of too often," said the man. "But I'm contemplating serving a side order right now if you don't decide pretty soon on red or green."

"Red or green what?" asked George.

"Chile, junior. It gives it a bit of spice—picata, a bite."

"Green—I guess," said George. "It reminds me of home."

The old man ladled the steaming gravy over the beef and bean burrito, nearly filling the cardboard boat. "So, you're from Ireland, are ya'?"

"Not bloody likely," said John. He watched George cut off a mouthful of burrito with his fork and take the plunge. "Well? How is it?" George could not move, but his eyes grew very large and moist. "Spicy?" asked John. George could not talk; he weakly nodded; it was still a somewhat ambiguous response as far as John was concerned. He turned to the old server and asked, "Is he all right?"

"Will be in awhile," said the Morrison man. "Guess a little wup-ass must have sneaked into this last batch of green. You boys must be here for that concert up Red Rocks way?"

"Yes, that's it. We're here to aid the lads with the concert." He watched George who still stood paralyzed and mute.

"Maybe you should try the red," said the man. "So that's why ya'll are dressed the way you are. You're part of the English crowd. Are you supposed to look like those Beagles or something?"

"Yes, The Beagles. We're here to show our support for . . . is my friend all right?"

"He's OK; he's still breathing, ain't he? Red?"

"I believe you're right. I'll try the red. Reminds me of my politics."

"Good choice." He generously covered the second burrito. "Wait a minute; I thought you said you wasn't no . . ."

"Just making a joke, Mr. Bloggs."

"Funny. Well, enjoy." He handed the heavy container to John. "Say you do sort of look like what's-his-name, the leader."

"John?" asked John as he took a bite.

"No, I think his name is Ringo."

John stood stupefied.

"I remember it 'cause it's a Western name. You know— Johnny Ringo, quite the gun slinger."

John's voice was a barely audible squeak, "No. I'm not *him*."

"Come to think of it, you actually don't look anything like him."

John smiled with déjà vu and nodded as the tears filled his eyes.

"Good, ain't it?"

Paul, across the street, in front of The Holland House booth, was eating his fourth hot biscuit. He had smothered each with butter and an oily rivulet dribbled down one side of his chin. Ringo feeling a tad more adventurous had two biscuits smothered in gravy. He tapped his fork in a staccato rhythm on the edge of the plate with delight after the first bite. They looked across the street for their friends at the burrito shack and raised their forks in a friendly sign of acknowledgment. Neither John nor George returned the gesture. Neither John nor George moved at all.

"Still peevish," said Paul with his mouth full.

"Forget them," said Ringo. "Let's eat 'till we pop." They turned back to the biscuit table, and Ringo held out his plate toward the server. With a pitiful Dickensian expression he asked, "Please, sir, may I have more?"

It was then that a group of young girls thought they recognized John and George. The girls threw a fist full of jellybeans to try to get George's attention. It was a misinterpretation of a ritual they had read about in a music magazine concerning English fans throwing jelly *babies* at the Fab Four. Jelly babies are soft chewy, translucent candies shaped like babies and bears. George had made the mistake in an interview saying how they were his favorite confection. Jellybeans, an American candy, are hard, opaque, sugarcoated, kidney-shaped projectiles with which the Beatles had been pelted since their arrival on colonial shores.

The damn things stung like bees and the group was getting downright gun shy. The painful sweets bounced off George's face, one catching him in his wide-open, watery eye. He finally moved. As he winced from the shock, he blew out the unswallowed mouthful of burrito con chile verde onto the chest of his partner. As a reflex action to the surprise of the unsavory sight of green chili coming directly at him, John involuntarily flung his *galleon* of red over his head. It floated over the crowd on the closed street and struck—plop—on Paul's shoulder.

Thinking the insult on purpose, Paul immediately flung a butter-laden biscuit in retaliation at John. He missed, but it did stick with buttery impertinence to George's face, covering the wounded eye in soft biscuit comfort. John took George's trough of green and threw it open palmed as one might pitch a pie. It went past both Ringo and Paul and smacked the man serving biscuits—whomp.

"That's it!" yelled the biscuit baron. "I've taken all the crap I'm going to from you, you burrito bandidito, you Mexican food barbarian, you Morrison moron." He picked up a huge serving spoon, dipped it into the chicken gravy, and flung it like a sling shot across the thoroughfare where it, of course, hit an innocent bystander, who immediately threw her coke into the air. He fired the biscuit catapult again. By this time the old man in the burrito shack had loaded his own heavy artillery: weighty bean filled burritos, and returned the insult to The Holland House booth.

The antics were infectious.

"Food foozle has filled the air," said John.

"The festival has exploded in vittles violence," said Paul.

"People are having great fun," said Ringo. "It's a flinging food fight."

The mayhem slowly migrated down Washington Avenue, consuming several blocks. At first, most people were laughing, a few running for cover. Ringo noted that the only serious combatants, who were by now entrenched in fist-a-cuffs, were the competitors from the Morrison Inn and The Holland House. They were better cooks than pugilists, and the physical damage thus far was minimal, but one did have what looked to be a bloodied nose—actually it was salsa. The sight of *blood* incited the surrounding spectators to take sides. It was not immediately evident whether their spontaneous allegiance was based on epicurean preferences or aesthetic assessment of sportsmanship. The Morrison contestant challenged their principles of fair play when in an unpleasant episode of momentary superiority he stuffed a burrito up the "bleeding" nose of the weaker gladiator. Disparaging insults based on differences in gourmet tastes and gamesmanship soon divided the crowd into contrary camps.

Things got ugly.

The young girls, undistracted by the food war, focused on George and John, convinced they were right: Those were two of the Beatles. When the other two mop-tops joined them and confirmed the foursome, the girls screamed to gather courage. Although the screams should have been drowned out by the crowd, it was a unique and familiar enough sound, edged with adolescent perversity, that it got the attention of all four fab fellows. They correctly read the eyes of the group of girls—windows to fervent souls—and instinctively fled in unison. The chase was on.

It was a Hard Day's dodge for the nearest building, which happened to be The Holland House Hotel. There was a ramp immediately inside the entrance running downhill and to the right. Stairs stared at them on the left. And the desk clerk, dead center, had a surprised gaze of his own. They took the path of least resistance, sprinting right. Unfortunately, the ramp led to the Holland House Cafe where the commotion from the street had spilled into the coffee shop. Three industrious girls had also anticipated the boys' move and were hustling through the cafe entrance and heading up the ramp. In a Keystone Cop pivot, the lads did an about-face and cleared the top of the ramp just as the rest of the female hunting party slammed through the hotel entrance.

"Suddenly," yelled John, "the stairs look more fortuitous."

Up they went. The hotel hallway was long and dark. They paused, trying to decide which way to go. Neither direction looked inviting. They considered returning from whence they came. They looked back; something had delayed the girls. They thanked the fates as they saw that the first lassie had stumbled on the third stair and caused a seven-colleen pile-up, momentarily blocking the stairwell. The boys didn't wait for the jam to clear; they ran into the dark.

The thunder of the Beatles' dash could be heard through the ceiling above the lobby. The sound of fearful flight energized the teenyboppers, as does the sound of a wounded bird induce play in a homicidal feline. It was just a moment later when the rumble of the gaggle followed the panicked footfall. To the confused clerk below, it sounded like the demoiselles were quickly gaining ground.

John and George made a perpendicular left at the end of the hundred-yard hall; Ringo and Paul disjoined, disunited, detached, divided, and turned right only to face a short hall that was obviously a dead-end. In an attempt to recover and rejoin, reunite, reattach, reassociate—they ran smack dab into the leaders of the sisterhood. Ringo's collarless, lapel-less suit coat was made sleeveless before he got to his feet. Paul lost a pocket off his pants. With a flush of adrenaline they escaped the frenzied subteens and actually sprinted passed their fleeing fellows.

"Ringo, no fair lightening the load by taking off your clothes," yelled John.

Both he and George looked at one another as the inspiration hit them. They paused only long enough to throw off their jackets. The diversion worked. The pride of adolescent cougars pounced on the coats and began fighting among themselves for the lion's share.

The lads ran out the southern, back entrance of the hotel and turned right, west on Fourteenth Street toward the School of Mines. They ran through the campus, at one time running onto an athletic field where several future engineers where playing a weekend game of rugby. A player came out of the scrum and pitched the fattened ball to a fast moving blur on his left side. It was Ringo. The percussionist crossed the end line untouched and spiked the ball in triumphant defiance. They continued to run, leaving the school and the ruggers far behind. They ran past several screaming Jefferson County Sheriffs' cars going the opposite way, probably in response to the food riot in downtown Golden. They ran up Nineteenth Street and onto a short north-south dogleg of Sixth Avenue where Anthony Hands of the Bear nearly ran them down with his pickup truck.

Tony swerved the truck onto the right shoulder of the road and fought it to a stop. He jumped out, angry that these idiots had almost forced him to participate in their suicides, but calmed when he assessed they were in distress. Who the hell are these guys? He looked to see if whoever was chasing them was still there. If it was the cops, the foursome had outsmarted them; they were going the opposite way. Operating from the unwritten charter of the fraternity of rapscallions, Tony did not abandon them. He waited and allowed them time to catch their breaths. They all leaned over with their hands on their knees, fighting for air. Finally, the one with the prodigious nose looked up. His large, sad eyes were imploring.

"Need a ride?" asked Tony.

It was not long until the truck ran into traffic heading for Red Rocks and the summer concert. Tony told his passengers that he, too, had to get to Red Rocks, and he knew a back way over the east side of Genesee Mountain, he turned off Ninety-three at Mount Vernon

Canyon. There was no traffic going up the road, it was all coming down, probably concertgoers. After a couple of fast miles he crossed the highway, turning southeast and raced onto Grapevine Road, a dirt thoroughfare winding its way through the foothills.

The back of the truck fishtailed as Anthony pushed the old pickup around the earthen curves. John and George were banged against each other in the cab. Paul and Ringo hung-on for dear life in the back while dodging Tony's toolboxes as they bounced from side to side. Within about twenty hair-raising minutes they ascended into the tiny town of Idledale, made a hard left onto paved Highway 74 and let fly down the canyon. It had been a while since Tony had explored Morrison, and he overshot his turn on the outskirts of the town. When he saw the traffic at the opposite end of the burg, all waiting to turn right to get to the road leading to the park entrance, he pulled a U-turn in the middle of the main road.

"Look," said George, "It's the bloody Morrison Inn."

"Well, that's nice to know now isn't it?" said John.

"So, you guys have eaten there, huh?"

"Not exactly," said George.

"It's more like we've been eaten," said John.

Anthony raced back the way they had come for about a quarter mile and turned onto another dirt road, which had the sign "PRIVATE" posted at the gate. He lied to the guard, well, stretched the truth, and said there was an emergency in one of the amphitheater's bathrooms.

"Who are those guys?" the Red Rocks Ranger asked.

"Plumber's helpers!" he yelled as he floored the truck. It was a short curvy sprint to the service area on the south side of the park. Tony pulled into the lot where he saw several lighting and sound equipment trucks and three limousines. Business types and park officials suddenly surrounded them.

"Where the bloody hell have you four been?" yelled a smallish man with an English accent. "We've had the bloody police searching all afternoon. You look like hell."

"Cheery-oh, Brian," said John. "We just stepped out for a bite."

"Look at your clothes. It's a good thing I had the foresight to bring up a change."

"Always the clairvoyant one, Brian Luv," said Ringo. "Is there some place I can wash up?"

He pointed toward the backstage entrance.

"Tah, Bri, old chum." said Paul as he passed by.

"Forward thinking there, Brian," said George. "Bloody well done. Gear."

"How soon are we on?" asked John, "and, could you be a dear and get us something to eat?"

"But, I thought you said . . ."

"No need to fuss. Something simple would be OK. Grilled cheese would be nice. Bloody room service at the hotel never did deliver our grilled cheese."

"Or biscuits," said Ringo.

The Righteous Brothers could be heard belting out *(You're My) Souls and Inspiration* on the other side of the flagstone wall. Jackie De Shannon and the Exciters stood in the wings, drawn between watching the pandemonium backstage and that in the audience. The Bill Black Combo appeared bored by the whole event.

Anthony used the distraction of the four entertainers to sneak away from the scene. He knew he was on the opposite side of the amphitheater from the tomb. He also knew how to get to where he wanted and avoid the crowds of concert spectators milling about the park. As he disappeared into the woods he thought: Well, that was lucky; everybody was paying a lot of attention to those lads. So that's the Fab Four. I read that little girls actually wet their pants over those guys. Frankly, I don't see the attraction.

TURTLE, COYOTE, RAVEN and RINGO: Mystical Journeys

Part Three: Three Rivers is the Future

"What you do today governs tomorrow."—Troy Three Rivers, Wyandotte

"The future belongs to those who believe in the beauty of their dreams."
—Eleanor Roosevelt, a Roosevelt

Chapter Twenty-three

Three Rivers

Fall, 1963

How different are the crevices and ravines created by Turtle, Wind, and Water to those canyons manufactured by humans. We use the sisters: sedimentary, igneous, and the most beautiful of all— metamorphic, and we use centuries. You mortals, perhaps because you're in a hurry (your lives are short) build your urban arroyos faster than Sapling grows juniper forests in my mountain passes, and you build your cities one upon another, new upon the old, generation upon generation. And ever since this inventor Otis created the elevator your canyons of concrete, glass, and steel have grown taller and higher, penetrating the very heavens in which you have placed our residence. Soon, you may actually be trespassing. Be careful, cities seem to invite folly.

Just such a place have you built, east of our setting, in the evening shadows of the foothills. You call it The Queen City of the Plains, a fitting title that references its location on the apron of the great Rocky Mountains. It sits in the sun—an inviting, vertical, and glittery signpost signaling the end of the horizontal trek across the endless prairie and the banal flatlands of Kansas or Nebraska. Beyond me, sings Denver from her elevated queen's throne, lay the Continental Divide and the indomitable snow capped peaks of legend. She sings my song. How Denver has grown, and quickly! I witnessed the small bands of Ute and other natives hunting buffalo, deer, and beaver on the parallel plains, among the gentle foothills, and in the pristine waterways converging where Denver was to sprout. Then came the miners. They found ore in Cherry Creek, established a campsite called Auraria, meaning gold, *on the west side of the creek that competed with a later camp on the east side named* Denver. *Denver won out, and streets snaked over the grasslands, buildings began to grow, and humans lit the night with electricity, debauchery, and greed. More gold, silver, lead, and molybdenum were discovered in the mountains, and the avaricious needed a base from which to launch their enterprises. The town grew into a city. You relished the quest for the skies and your queen city canyons grew taller and cast longer shadows—long shadows indeed.*

"Well, I love Denver," was the answer to the first interview question. "I think there is great potential in Denver. I was raised in the Midwest, but it was Denver that attracted me as a home and a professional locale. It's a boomtown, there is a lot of growth at the moment, there are the mountains, and the people. The people of Denver are great." *What a stupid answer—the people are great. Which people?: the rapacious bankers on Seventeenth Street, the bums on Larimer, the overzealous sports fans, the government lackeys, the ambitious lawyers for whom I work, and who put me in this stupid interview. I fear that I'm here only as a token. Wait, quit thinking negatively: I know some good people. Baines, the bartender at the Ship Tavern, he's good people. And that is exactly where I'm going when this inquisition is done. You better get with it, Rivers, or you could blow this interview and there would be hell to pay if you lost the account.* "Yes, the people are great, but it's the opportunities for growth and business that keep me here. I don't mind telling you, I'm an ambitious and proactive man. Denver provides me, just as it would for your organization, the opportunities for profit, and as I said: growth." *Way to go, blockhead; that was succinct. Come on, get with it! You're better than this.* "Look, Denver is also an advantageous location, geographically. It's got an international airport ten minutes from downtown—Stapleton—and it has two major interstates connecting her with the rest of the region. I-25 and I-70 make for an easy drive from north, south, east, and even west over the mountains. Denver is centralized. I would think *access* is important for your clientele. Most are Indians, correct? They will be traveling from all directions, right?" *Better, much better.*

"Yes, Mr. Rivers, we are very familiar with the positive attributes of Denver. You do not have to sell us on the Queen City of the Plains. We have already made our choice for the event. It's here; that's a given. Actually, we were breaking the ice, so to speak, by asking what brought you to Denver. We have a series of questions about you, specifically. Allow me to be perfectly clear—it's you we are interviewing. It's you—as an agent of the law firm Earl, Brownstone, Barber, and Delta—we are interested in hiring. Well, actually, the reputation of the firm is solid. We are ninety percent positive that we have made an appropriate choice of the firm. That said, lets be even more clear: it's you for whom we have questions. Although I must say, Stephan Barber was very complementary about your work; we are here to confirm his confidence and address the issue of your upbringing, well, your heritage, actually.

"As you know, our clientele, as you put it, is primarily Indian. That's true, all are Native American, but even more important is that the director, Mr. Kahnawake, of Mohawk decent, is adamant about working with fellow Native Americans, particularly in important positions of responsibility, such as the legal infrastructure of the event. I hope I've been clear about our intentions. Shall we proceed?"

"Thank you; you've been perfectly candid. I appreciate that. So, allow me to be frank. While I am indeed of Indian 'heritage,' I would hope that the fact that I am an excellent lawyer, with a proven record of accomplishment, would be your primary motive for hiring our firm. I specialize in facilitating large events such as the Pow Wow you have planned. I have provided legal services for Denver's annual stock show. It's quite famous. I've consulted on the planning for a new sports arena, and facilitated numerous political conventions and dozens of other professional conventions. . . ."

"Yes, Mr. Rivers, we are very familiar with your résumé."

"Of course. The point I was trying to make is that I have never used my heritage to advantage, or disadvantage, the work I do. To be honest; I've never used it to further any aspect of my life: school, scholarships, sports, taxes, or early jobs. It's not something I prioritize or promote."

"We wouldn't have it any other way. Shall we proceed? Although, I must warn you, a few of the questions do deal directly with your heritage and your upbringing. Are you comfortable with that?"

"If I become uncomfortable, I'll let you know. After all, I believe it is important that both parties be as open as possible if we are to create a productive partnership. Please, proceed." *Oh man, what have I gotten myself into. These guys want an Indian. Barber has really set me up on this one. If I blow this account, it's back to the reservation. Who am I kidding, I never lived on a reservation, I'm a spoiled city kid. I love the city. There's women in the city, good restaurants, and you can buy Italian shoes in the city. This city has great bars, and that is where I'm going when this fiasco is over.*

"Tell us, if you don't mind, what you know about your tribal connections."

"Sure. My knowledge of the Wyandotte comes from my grandfather and grandmother. I was raised by my grandparents. My parents were killed in a train wreck when I was twelve." He paused a moment. "Let me take it back a notch. I haven't thought about this for decades, but I have a Wyandotte name. My grandfather gave it to me. My Indian name is Trois Rivières—Three Rivers. It's French. My father changed it to Troy Rivers, for the birth certificate." He paused. "It's been a long time since I thought about such things."

"Tell us about your grandparents, if you don't mind."

"I don't mind. As I said, they raised me. I owed them a lot— everything, really." He paused again and ran his hand down his tie to make sure it entered behind his vest just above the buttons. He checked the knot—*impeccable*—and then asked energetically, "Have you ever heard of the Harvey Girls?"

"Entertainers? Singers? No, I can't say I have. Why?"

"The Harvey Girls were the staff women, the service people for a highly successful chain of hotels and restaurants owned by an entrepreneur named Fred Harvey. He specialized in hotels that catered to the railroads at the turn of the century. They were famous in the Southwest. Harvey built these elegant hotels and fine restaurants next to train terminals. Up until that time, train travel was horrendous. Bad food, con artists, uncomfortable accommodations, all the things that discouraged the public from traveling by train to the West plagued the railroads. Harvey saw an opportunity and changed all that. As I'm sure you can relate, Eastern banks and businessmen had invested a lot of venture capital in the West and in the railroads; they wanted to see some return on their money. So Harvey made an agreement with, for example, the Atchison, Topeka and Santa Fe Railroad which has routes through Kansas and New Mexico."

As an aside he asked, "Did you know the Atchison, Topeka and the Santa Fe Railroad does not go through either Atchison, Topeka or Santa Fe? Never mind. I was talking about the Harvey Girls." *Careful with the humor, Rivers. These guys are pretty stiff.*

"A Harvey Girl was not your typical waitress or hostess. They were famous for being prim and proper. Harvey dolled them up in full skirts with embroidered lace aprons—very distinctive. They had an old country charm. He insisted that they be very friendly, I mean, hospitable, great service, that kind of thing. There were no shenanigans." *Careful! No jokes and definitely no innuendo.* "They were very hard working and they lived in dormitories above the hotels. The Harvey Girls were a legend, the sweethearts of the West. Well, my grandmother was a Harvey Girl at the Castañeda Hotel in Las Vegas, New Mexico, not Nevada. Las Vegas, New Mexico was once the territorial capital and a cultural center of the Southwest, a major stop on the Santa Fe Trail. Back then, Las Vegas, Nevada, was a dry little burg in the middle of the desert, halfway between Los Angles and the rest of the world. The world that has passed by Las Vegas, New Mexico. Today, you can't even see the town from the Interstate, I-25."

"We're familiar with Las Vegas. You were saying?"

"My grandmother was one of the few Harvey Girls who was an Indian. She was a beauty with fair-skin, raven hair, and bright intelligent eyes. She looked the role of the Indian princess. Folks liked that; it confirmed some standardized image that was important to them. If it opened some doors, so be it.

"She was educated in white schools; so, she could speak *American* and *knew her place.* You know what I mean. She functioned well among the whites. Don't get me wrong. She was a strong woman, so was my mother. They just figured for the sake of their children, if you can't beat 'um . . . well, you know what I mean.

"She was so pretty everyone called her *Leen-da.*" He exaggerated the long "*e*" sound. "You know, *Línda,* Spanish for *pretty.* I didn't realize that her given name wasn't Línda until she died. I always called her *Nana.* I saw her real name on the funeral announcement. It was, of course, French—Éclatant. She spoke several languages, including English, Spanish, and French. She was unique, that was my grandmother. Harvey hired her as a novelty, but she was so much more." He paused. "I miss her."

"My grandfather," Rivers quickly buoyed the tone, "was the man-servant, a gentleman's gentleman, for a wealthy white railroad baron—a retired Army colonel who rode with Teddy Roosevelt's Rough Riders. Grandfather was a quiet man—a noble man. Not *noble* like that noble savage cliché, but a man of pride, maturity, and quiet compromise. He compromised for family, for my mother and for me. He raised us both; that's more of a commitment than a compromise. It takes a man who can make a commitment to raise two generations. My grandparents' house mirrored that of a typical American home. I suppose we were middle or lower-middle class. We didn't think then in those terms. Oh, maybe I did, as a teenager. You know, when I was trying to impress high school girls, after the old hormones hit." *What did I tell you about the jokes?*

"Anyway, athletics seemed to open the door to adolescent popularity; so, I really can't complain. I didn't suffer much because we weren't wealthy. My grand folks, both of them, worked hard. They never complained. They never dwelled on the difficulties of their lives, their childhood, their being Indians. In fact, in those days, one just did not talk about things such as race."

"Were both of your grandparents Wyandotte?"

"The last full blooded Wyandotte died in 1830 something. They were as Wyandotte as one could be at the time. The French were the first to start diluting the tribe, if you'll forgive me the risqué reference. Those old fur trappers were a long way from Provence." Troy noticed the interviewer jotted down a note after his little joke. *Well, that looked like a notation for a demerit. You know, to hell with these guys if they can't take a joke.* "Anyway, the French called the Wyandotte the *Huron*. It meant ruffian, or something, and referred to their head roach, the Mohawk hairdo, you know what I mean."

"Isn't there a Huron Street here in Denver?"

"Yes, imagine my surprise when I moved here. There are both a Wyandotte and a Huron street. And several states east of here there is a lake, which I am sure you know about." The interviewer made another note. *Boy he really does hate humor. Or, for some reason does he actually care about the streets? Next he'll be asking me to recommend a good restaurant.*

"Despite their fame and having streets and lakes named after them, according to my grandfather, the Huron were almost wiped out in a frontier war. The Huron made the mistake of siding with the French. . . ."

"The French and Indian War?" asked the interviewer.

"No, that was later. We chose the wrong side then, too. They allied with the French against the British in a conflict called *The Beaver Wars*. It was more about the economics of beaver pelts and trade goods in the New World than the cowboys versus the Indians thing. The Brits won; they had the Iroquoian Federation on their side."

"We are very familiar with the Iroquoian Federation."

I'll bet you are. "The surviving Huron had to split up into smaller bands, or join with other tribes, some were their ancient enemies, the Iroquois. My grandfather's people ran off to Canada, just northeast of Montreal, down the Saint Lawrence from Quebec, a place called Trois Rivières—Three Rivers. They became the Three Rivers Wyandotte."

"Then your grandmother is also a Three Rivers Wyandotte?"

"Actually, no. My grandmother suspected she was of Huron and Petun descent. Her grandparents were forced to flee west because of the Iroquois. I don't quite remember, but I believe she said as far west as the Chicago area. Then they were driven east again, fleeing from the Sioux. Later, the Iroquois pursued them again, forcing them out of settlements in what is today the Detroit area. They finally put down roots in Ohio—Upper Sandusky, and then came along the American Revolution. The Huron choose the wrong side in that war, too. The Wyandotte sided with the British. The Brits, after all, allowed them to keep their own Indian government and religion. The British were more interested in the fur trade and commerce. The Americans wanted land. George Washington had promised his troops land for service. Upper Sandusky was prime agricultural terrain. So it was the American government and the Father of Our Country who forced the Huron out of Ohio.

"Once again, Nana's people were forced to march from rich lands, over the rolling hills of the Mid-west, and onto the Great Plains—a trail of tears. It's one we don't hear about in our history classes. Anyway, they stalled the trek in Kansas for a while.

"America, white America, continued to grow westward. Eventually, reaching Kansas, where the Wyandotte lands caught the eye of settlers. Jayhawkers ran the Indians out. There was no place else to go. Homeless and lost, they were ultimately invited to locate in the northeast corner of Oklahoma, the new Indian Territories. However, our government didn't give them the land. The Feds never gave the Wyandotte any acreage to reciprocate for the land they took. Ironically, it was an ancient enemy from the Iroquois Federation, the Seneca, who offered them a home. I remember my grandmother saying that perhaps now they could end their long trek. If they were lucky, there was nothing worth killing over in the new territories."

Rivers remembered that his grandmother told how she and the other children were forced to go to Indian schools, but because she had lost her parents to small pox, she entered the white-structured world with practiced resignation. "She decided to show these white people that she was as smart as they. She would excel at these peculiar white endeavors. She had fewer problems adjusting than many of her classmates, particularly those who still had parents trying to teach them the *old ways*. Other children would go home periodically and be re-indoctrinated with tribal customs. She had no one; so, she stayed at the school. As per the rules, she was always well groomed. Her clothes were tidy and her hair cut in *a civilized* manner. Other children would sometimes rebel by not bathing or destroying their Sunday clothes. She chose her conflicts carefully, favoring those she could win. People who criticize my grandmother for giving up don't know what a spiritually strong woman she was. She was determined to be a survivor. As I said, she chose her battles. Perhaps that is where I inherited my interest in the law."

The interviewer made another note.

"Perhaps not." *I don't think these guys like lawyers.* "Regardless, Nana was a whiz at languages. On her own, she learned arithmetic and science. She borrowed the texts from young Indian boys who had no interest in *book learning*. The authorities, from both races, frowned on young Indian girls studying needless, impractical skills like mathematics, but she learned anyway. That's what I mean about her choosing her own battles.

"After grammar school she returned to the Wyandotte reservation in Oklahoma, where she worked as a servant in the home of the Seneca Indian agent, a Mormon. This man, contrary to most agents, was basically fair and sincerely concerned about the plight of, as he called them, his naïve native wards.

"There was just enough bookkeeping to trouble the agent, thus ingratiate my grandmother and her proficiency with numbers. The wife of the agent felt such tasks were beneath her. The government required records for foodstuffs, subsidized clothing, tools, and farm implements disseminated to the Indians.

"She was also given housekeeping duties at the agency. It was in the service of this bureaucrat that she first rode on a great iron horse. The train ride was a thrill. She was fascinated by the power and noise of the locomotive, the rhythm of the tracks, and the speed—the unimagined speed. She preferred riding in the open air; it was like flying. She eventually left the employment of the agency and sought work near the railroads.

"When Fred Harvey came up with the idea of using a few Indian *maidens* as Harvey Girls in New Mexico, at Las Vegas and Belen, grandmother was given a chance to fulfill a dream. Harvey was secretly disappointed in the stature of the local Pueblo women. Many, at least those interested in working for a white man, just didn't quite fit the Harvey Girl mold. To Fred Harvey's critical eye, most seemed short and portly. He considered dropping the whole idea. Besides, the local Hispanic girls were *que bonita* and eager to work. So, her sudden appearance on the doorstep proved advantageous for both Nana and Harvey. She was hired on the spot—Fred Harvey's quintessential Indian princess. She would allow herself a gentle laugh when she told the story, and in her laughter you heard her forgiveness of Harvey's stereotypical thinking. Ironically, Grandmother told me that most of the tourists and rail patrons never knew the difference between the Hispanics and the Indians. Nor did they care. She was taller than most Pueblo people. Perhaps it was her French and Huron blood. She told stories about a famous Wyandotte sachem, a chief, who was six-feet-four-inches tall and known as the *Crane*. I like to think it was her independence that allowed her to walk a little taller.

"When she proved herself experienced in the service trade, with excellent references, and mathematical skills, Harvey was ecstatic. She was placed in the opulent jewel of a hotel in Las Vegas. It had over forty rooms—no Motel 6, if you know what I mean."

The interviewer made a quick note.

Don't tell me he has stock in Motel 6. "She eventually became a staff trainer for the girls. Although many of the white girls resented being reprimanded by an Indian, she became a well-respected member of the Harvey family. Hotel Castañeda became her home. It was there people began calling her *Linda.*

"My grandfather was also an aficionado of the rails. His Rough Rider Colonel, a ruthless entrepreneur, parlayed some political favors and family inheritance with an abandon mirroring a charge up San Juan Hill," *Don't make jokes,* "and finagled the majority stock holdings in several businesses connected to the railroads. In New Mexico, he owned new lumber stands, silver and copper mines, and water rights. Water proved extremely valuable. Grandpa's Colonel traveled quite often into the Southwest. Business took them into Las Vegas. They always stayed at the Harvey House."

"So that's how your grandparents met?"

"For Grandpa, a descendant of the Three Rivers Wyandotte, it was love at first sight. He was making sure things were correct for a reception hosted by his employer. The dining room was elegant.

"The Castañeda boasted a $200,000 silver service, Turkish rugs, and terrazzo floors. I've seen photographs and read their old brochures. The tables were walnut with solid brass chairs. As I said: it was no Motel Six."

The man didn't make a note this time, but he also didn't laugh, not even a smile.

"Grandpa first saw Nana leaning across the middle of the main table, arranging a huge bouquet of fresh flowers. She wore a wampum necklace, telling him that she was possibly Huron or Iroquoian.

"He often told the story that his usual professional and stoic demeanor cracked. She often added that she looked up and saw this handsome man who had suddenly and obviously just been struck by *the thunderbolt*. What Nana called the *ooky-look* was a dead giveaway. She had captured the heart of this stranger before she ever spoke a word.

"Grandpa would confess that it was all true. The lightning bolt struck and knocked him off his feet. He said that it felt like he'd been eaten by a goose and made into pâté." *Will you stop with the jokes? You are killing yourself.*

"The romance progressed appropriately during several repeat visits. Two years later Fred Harvey himself hosted a lavish wedding reception and joyous good-bye party at the Castañeda for Grandpa and Línda.

"The newlyweds decided it was smarter to move into the servants' quarters in St. Louis, with Grandpa's Colonel, rather than stay in New Mexico. Besides, Harvey confessed to Línda one evening that the service business for the railroads was doomed. The government was talking about an interstate highway network, and if Henry Ford had his way, every citizen in America could soon afford an automobile. An emerging airline business was also stealing travelors.

"They rode away in a private sleeper car provided by the colonel—a wedding gift. The Atchison, Topeka, and the Santa Fe took them north to a new married life, leaving the land of enchantment."

He paused and after a long quiet moment said, "I've talked too much. That's probably a lot more information than you were looking for. I apologize. Are there any legal questions you have?"

"No need to apologize. You gave us the exact information we needed. You are very fond of your grandparents."

"Of course. But I'm confused. I thought you were interviewing me to assess my legal expertise. You haven't asked anything about my credentials."

"We've confirmed the credentials that are of interest to Mr. Kahnawake. He has, shall we say, unique requirements of employees. He is very particular with whom he teams. Business relationships with the Kahnawake Corporation, I assure you, can be extremely cordial and, of course, financially rewarding. What questions do you have for us?"

Troy addressed a list of potential legal needs, which they answered nonchalantly. Everything seemed manageable. He had done all this before. They avoided any direct questions about Mr. Kahnawake and said that if things go well, and as anticipated, Mr. Kahnawake will request a final interview. They thanked him for his time and closed by saying that he would be hearing from them soon. Troy left first and headed directly to his favorite bar in the Brown Palace Hotel—The Ship Tavern.

Troy Rivers entered the tavern with the confidence of a regular. He was early; the after-work crowd had yet to arrive. Casually dressed couples took up a few of the tables. Troy guessed they were tourists or hotel guests. He waved at the waiter, Baines, who was talking to the bartender, Adam. Baines acknowledged his gesture with a practiced familiarity; said, "Right away, Mr. Rivers," and ordered "Mr. River's usual." Troy paused just a moment to survey his surroundings. Rarely did he have this prime a selection for a table. The bar was usually crowded by the time he left work and wandered down Seventeenth Street for a little R and R. Regardless, he needed a drink—now. He didn't feel the interview went well; it was alien and atypical. He'd call the office later; right now he was going to get comfortable.

The Ship Tavern was a great place to relax. It was nestled stately in one of the triangular corners of the Brown Palace Hotel. Many regulars, Troy among them, bragged that it was the second home of Denver's elite. It could not be called a vacation home, however, because there was too much wheeling and dealing continuing past five. The Ship Tavern had maintained that gentlemen's elegance of the era when gold and silver were the royal couple of local commerce. Dark hardwoods, brass, and a selective use of polished stone gave the tavern a subdued masculinity. Each evening—but particularly on Friday afternoon—cigar smoke, lascivious laughter, and the smell of freshly shined shoes enriched the manliness of the bar. Troy's people: bankers, developers, CEOs, and of course, lawyers "worked" the bar: quietly making deals, enriching fortunes, laying political groundwork, hatching plots, bragging about sexual conquests, destroying careers—men's stuff. Troy loved immersing himself in the environment. He was astute enough to know, however, that one could not exhibit visible enthusiasm for the place. That would be too "underclassman," too novice. Rather, the appropriate behavior was a professional aloofness, a corporate detachment, yet inside he buzzed with economic energy and commercial ambition.

He decided to sit at a mast-table. There was extra width to the seat at the mast-tables, not enough for two to squeeze in, rather just a touch of throne-like luxury, and the sitter had his back to the huge, ship's mast in the middle of the room. It gave one an excellent view of the rest of the bar and a gunslinger's confidence by protecting one's back. The seat across the table from the mast chair was a traditional saloon chair, in which the sitter could not help but feel just a bit disadvantaged.

He thought about his friend Hawthorne and how he always took the mast chair. He consistently walked in front of Rivers so he could quickly occupy the seat that faced the room, leaving Rivers to face the wall—always, every bar and restaurant they attended. Not today. He spread out his arms along the back of the wide bench and allowed himself to relax for just a moment. Baines arrived and placed a coaster in front of Rivers. With a practiced chorography, Baines positioned an iced and elegant highball glass atop the coaster. "Your Scotch-rocks, Mr. Rivers." Troy appreciated the ritual. He sat to attention.

"Thanks, Baines. Why don't you start me a tab; I believe Mr. Hawthorne will be joining me soon. How are things with you?"

"Fine, sir. Looking forward to a crowd tonight. It's Friday."

"So it is, Baines. So it is. I've had a rough week; this Scotch is going to hit the spot. How was your day?"

"Right in character, sir. It will be a pleasure to see Mr. Hawthorne again. I'll bring over his drink when he gets here. Anything else for you, Mr. Rivers? A menu?"

"Not at the moment, Baines. I'm just going to sit here and relax before Hawthorne and the hordes arrive. Thanks." Troy wondered what in hell Baines meant by *right in character*. It reminded him of the odd tone of the interview. He thought about loosening his tie, but then remembered his often-professed axiom: "You think you look relaxed when you pull down and loosen your tie, but you don't. You just look drunk. And nobody likes an inebriated lawyer (let alone a drunken Indian)."

He touched the knot of his tie to make sure it was in place. The tie was silk, expensive, conservatively patterned, and even through he was off work, he kept it pulled tightly around his button-down collar. Very business like. He was comfortable in his Brooks Brothers three-piece suit; his shoes were Italian and well shined. He liked Italian shoes; they were stylish, lightweight, and looked expensive. His hair was short and immaculately quaffed. He rubbed his temple wondering if his hair looked appropriate for the interview. He rubbed his chin to confirm that his shave was presentable. He took pride in his well-scrubbed face. It had the translucent glow of good grooming, as did his fingernails. He looked at his manicure; the back of his hands were tan. He turned his hands over to check out his palms. He didn't believe in the occult, but was pleased that his lifeline was deep and long. Mr. Rivers, he said to himself, you're dressed for success, and then he thought about his colleagues soon to arrive. They all dressed for success. A handful of *The Brothers of the Fraternal Order of Seventeenth Street* had already entered the tavern and wandered toward tables. Troy assessed their suits: all were dark. Ties, none of them loosened, were the only hint of variant independence. None too daring, but each seemed to express a subtle, almost subliminal message about the man wearing it.

He allowed his disenchantment with the interview to creep back. Did I tell them Denver is on the verge of a financial boom? The tourist trade has always been good. We're building a new convention center. The skiing industry has, as they say on *The Street*, *legs*. Lots of potential legal entanglements, contracts to design, construction, whole towns like Breckenridge are being remodeled and revived. And then there's petroleum. The Arabs have self-destructed. Domestic oil is the latest lady of the economic evening. Things are good.

He surveyed his surroundings again. He loved the Brown Palace Hotel, an elegant ochre monolith at the south end of Seventeenth Street—*The Street*—the headquarters of the financial movers and shakers of Denver, the tallest and deepest corporate canyon of the Queen City of the Plains.

"So, how did the interview go?" It was Hawthorne. He was standing behind the saloon chair on the other side of the table. He looked around the bar, "What do you say, let's move to another table?"

Troy saw through his ploy. "Naw, this is good. I already ordered you a drink." He looked over his shoulder and signaled Baines. "Have a seat."

Troy watched Hawthorn look around the tavern, probably checking out who was there, but more than likely searching for an excuse to change tables. He gave up and sat down. Baines was there with his drink. "Cheers," he said and lifted his glass while continuing to peruse the room.

"I think I blew the interview."

"I'm sure you did fine. Why do you think it went badly?"

"It was like no other interview I've ever attended. They wanted to know more about my heritage and my grandparents than my legal expertise."

"I don't think you have anything to worry about. The firm probably thinks the new clients prefer someone with the same heritage. It's a coup of sorts." He paused to see if his witticism got a laugh. It did not. Hawthorn continued, "But seriously, this could be a big assignment—lots of potential. It's an honor that Barber and the boys trust you with it. Big contract, big deal. Do a good job, establish it as a major annual event, make EBF and D look good, and go for a partnership down the road. Troy, it's an investment in your career. Could be a big step up. Your folks would be proud."

"Yeah, you're probably right. I mean, I should at least give it a shot. Barber thinks it's a big deal. He thinks it could turn into an annual powwow extravaganza. Huge crowds. What the hell, what could go wrong? It's generally routine, cut and dry contracts. Building rental, insurance, licensing, typical stuff."

"Exactly, Chief. What could go wrong?"

"Don't call me Chief."

"Jesus, Troy—relax. I was just making a joke."

"Sorry, Clark, but this thing has me concerned. I'm starting to question why the firm hired me. I always assumed it was because I'm a good contracts lawyer; it never dawned on me that it might be to fulfill some affirmative action quota."

"I'm sure you're wrong about that, Rivers, and I'm sure you're unnecessarily paranoid about the interview."

"No, my instincts are usually good, especially about these kinds of things. I had the feeling when I first entered the room that things were amiss."

"Why do you say that?" Hawthorne's question had an edge; he was getting impatient.

"Well, as you know, contrary to my wishes, Barber nominated me for this assignment because I have an Indian heritage."

"You're an Indian? Should I be sitting with you? Do they allow Indians in bars now days?"

"Funny."

"No, seriously," Hawthorn continued to feign concern. "Considering who you work for, I always thought you were just another very tan Jew boy."

"OK, if you don't want to talk about it, just say so."

"Come on, Troy-my-boy, I'm sure you're worried about nothing, but go ahead. Tell me what happened and then let's talk about something else. Me—for example."

"I wouldn't bother you with this ordinarily, Clark, but I need to get it off my chest."

"Go for it, but first let's order another drink. Where the hell is Baines when you need him?" He signaled the waiter for two more. Baines gave him a thumbs-up. "Go ahead. You thought things went badly from the start. . . .."

"It was just a feeling I got. I entered the room and introduced myself before I sat down. They gave me a serious once-over, checking out my suit, my tie, and really giving my shoes a look. I stood there for what seemed like an eternity, waiting for them to offer me a seat. They kept looking around me as if someone was behind me, as if someone else was about to enter the room. When they finally asked me to sit down, I thought they looked disappointed."

"Disappointed? I don't get it. You're a snappy dresser. Why would they be disappointed?"

"Honestly, and I hate to admit this, but . . . I think they were looking for Tonto."

Chapter Twenty-four

Powwow

Fall, 1963

What's in a name? I have many. Indians nations are most
often known by names invented by others. "Huron," for example, is
a French appellation of the Wyandotte People. "Sioux," a term that
means "enemy," is how the Dakota People are known. And others
have named my old friends long gone from the Southwest. They are
called "Anasazi:" The Ancient Ones.
For individual Indians the polynomen ceremony was
nurturing and affirming. Names of individuals were the province of
the various clans within the tribe, and to maintain the power and
magic attributed to a name, the name would be handed down from
generation to generation or to a living tribal member if the owner
was killed. The new recipient, of course, already had a name, but
from that day forward would also be known by the clan name.
Therefore, Indians (a misnomer) often had several names within
their tribe: given names, nicknames, secret clan names, names of
respect and of affection, names from other tribes—friends and foes
alike. Names reflected great achievements and important events.
Often, tribal leaders, men of great accomplishments, would take on
the name of their tribe. To be allowed to do so was a great honor
bestowed upon the leader by his community. The clan name was
never spoken out loud. To do so was to invite folly. I am Turtle, clans
of the Wyandotte and the Iroquois carry my name.

"Sky cowboys, that's what they called us," said Orvis
Kahnawake. "Now isn't that typical of the white man. Ninety
percent of us were Mohawk, most from the Caughnawaga
Reservation, and in an attempt to be complementary about our skills

as ironworkers and riveters, the whites call us cowboys. Like John Wayne was *our* hero."

He caught Troy Rivers glancing again at his ponytail. He would have liked that River's interest was because it was a thick, healthy head of ebony hair—not bad for a man his age. He took pride in the two wide, silver-gray stripes, shinning like metallic ribbons that began at his temples, and in a gentle curving rhythm, undulated the full route to the middle of his back. He would have liked that to Rivers the silver-gray *feathers* looked distinguished and suggested maturity and wisdom, but he knew this was not the case. The younger man was nervous about being seen in the Ship Tavern, the bastion of the local corporate fraternity, with an odd, pony-tailed, old Indian.

He had hoped that Rivers would understand that the ponytail was a symbol of the resurgence of Indi'n pride. Well, I'll convert him or torture him, he thought.

Orvis was a proud man. He was over sixty years old, but possessed the body of a gymnast: average height, broad shoulders, narrow hips, flat stomach, and brawny guns. Modesty was not his strong suit, but he felt himself a patient and just man. He had the weathered complexion of a battered copper cooking kettle, which he earned from numerous days fighting the sun and winds on top of the steel armatures of skyscrapers.

"My brothers and I," he continued the one-sided conversation, "were in the iron trade, as were my father and his father. During our peak years skyscrapers sprung up on the bedrock of Manhattan like rhizomes. My grandfathers were among the first Mohawk to become *ironmen*. They helped to build the Canadian Pacific Railroad Bridge across the Saint Lawrence at Montreal. The south abutment was on our reservation land. That's how my grandfathers got their jobs and learned the trade. Jobs were part of the agreement giving the railroad and the Dominion Bridge Company access over the Caughnawaga lands. That is why my fathers and my uncles used to be called *bridgemen*. Before we started building skyscrapers ironworkers were called bridgemen. Everybody thinks it was improvements in strength from iron to steel that led to skyscrapers, but actually it was the invention of the elevator. Anyway, before we ironworkers started dancing around on those balance beams in the clouds, we became somewhat famous as daredevils in bridge building. Now we're *cowboys*."

He paused, waiting for a response from the mixed-blood sitting across from him at the small tavern table. The younger man was obviously only half listening. He was nervously looking around the bar. This guy is more nervous than a stuffed rabbit at a dog race, Kahnawake thought. He continued out loud, "Oh well, what's in a name? You say tomato and I say tomahto, potato, potahto, maize, corn and squash. That brings up another point about the whites . . ."

"It's awfully noisy in here," interrupted Troy Rivers. He looked around anxiously, obviously regretting that it was he who suggested over the phone that they meet at The Ship Tavern in The Brown Palace Hotel.

Kahnawake thought that Rivers probably wanted to be on familiar ground, his turf, and maybe show off a little. Did he think that I might be impressed with The Ship Tavern? I know the best of Denver's business bars. I might be an old Indi'n but I've imbibed in some of the best bars in the world. One of my favorites is the Kona Inn in Kailua on the Big Island. It's hard to beat the Dragon Bar in Santa Fe. Hell, I have tabs at Harry's Bar in Paris and in Rome. I have the baseball caps to prove it. Now that would have gotten a rise out of Rivers; I should have worn my *Harry's Bar Roma* baseball cap. If this was an attempt on Rivers' part to exhibit some kind of fraternal familiarity here among the high rollers, it's backfiring. It's obvious that it had never crossed Rivers' mind that his client would have a ponytail, and rather than wearing a tie, wore a silver bolo with a jeweled turtle, not your typical attire in The Brown.

"If it's too noisy, we can go to your hotel," yelled Rivers over the Friday afternoon dissonance.

"No problem, Mr. Rivers," said Orvis in a normal voice, not acknowledging the noise. "This *is* my hotel."

Rivers balked, "Really?"

"I always stay at The Brown when I'm in Denver. But I don't usually do business in the bar."

"I love The Brown; it's my favorite hotel," Rivers was scrambling, looking visibly shaken.

"Oh, do you stay here often?"

"Actually, no. I've never actually stayed here. I mean the Ship Tavern; it's my favorite lounge. In the hotel. I mean, it's my favorite bar—anywhere. Not just in the hotel. Everywhere. And the restaurants here are great, too." In what looked like panic Rivers raised his hand in an all-too-familiar gesture to order a drink. He pulled his hand down quickly, blushed with embarrassment and asked, "Mr. Kahnawake, did you want a drink? I mean, should we have a drink, or should we leave? I mean, would you prefer to leave?"

Kahnawake enjoyed having Rivers on the defensive. It was an ancient Mohawk custom to torture captured enemies. He thought about the term *Mohawk,* an English abridgment of the Algonquian term *Mohowawog*—meaning *man-eaters.* He was *Ga-Ne-A-O-No-Ga,* but *man-eater* seemed appropriate tonight. Rivers was coming unraveled.

The Iroquois, and other Northwestern tribes, were infamous for inflicting horrific pain to test the courage of a prisoner. The victim, still living, could earn great respect by acting oblivious while his captors stripped the flesh from his bones. Sometimes the Mohawk, the Ga-Ne-A-O-No-Ga, would consume the flesh, not because they were cannibals—they were not—but rather as a symbol of respect and to absorb the strength and courage of a brave victim. Fair is fair; the Huron would be more than happy to reciprocate with an Iroquoian captive.

"Yes, the restaurants are wonderful; great place to get a rare slab of meat," answered Kahnawake. "No, I don't prefer to leave. Look, I agree, it's a bit noisy to discuss legalities, but I had a savage trip (he couldn't help but smile) and a couple of rough flights; had to stop off for some quick business—to martyr a couple of colleagues in Chicago and St. Louis. A drink is a good idea." He leaned back in his chair, closed his hands together across his stomach and surveyed the crowd in the tavern. "My family tells me that I need to learn to quit torturing myself . . . with work. You seem to need a drink; I'll have one also. Later, we can go up to my suite; there's a conference room. We can order up a pot of coffee and get down to business."

Orvis noticed a group of four young corporate lions leaning against the bar, mumbling among themselves and periodically looking over. They chuckled with priggishness. "Tell me, do you spend a lot of time here?"

"Great idea. The coffee I mean. No, not that much time, actually."

The waiter suddenly appeared at the table, "The usual for you, Mr. Rivers and what would the other gentleman like?"

"Yes, Baines, the usual," Rivers' voice seemed to have an uncharacteristic resignation.

"A rough day, sir? Should I make it a double?"

"Oh, for Christ's sake no, Baines. I mean, no, thank you." He turned toward Orvis, "What would you like Mr. Kahnawake?"

"What are you having, Mr. Rivers?"

"Scotch, Mr. Kahnawake. Scotch or possibly hemlock."

"Rocks or straight up?" Kahnawake laughed.

"Usually arsenic straight and strychnine on the rocks, particularly after a great start like this," answered Rivers.

"You need to relax, Mr. Rivers. As I said, I could use a drink." Well there, he thought, is an appropriate response to a little good-natured torture. He looked up at the waiter standing above them, "I'll have a Scotch. McCallan's thirty-year-old, straight up and an ice-water chaser. And charge these to my room. Oh, Baines, give Mr. Rivers his double."

"No, really, Mr. Kahnawake, I don't need a double. Baines, charge these to my tab."

"Well, that's very generous, particularly for a guy that doesn't come here too often. I insist. Baines, charge these to my room."

The sarcasm caught Rivers off-guard and forced a pause just long enough for Baines to get away. "Well," he capitulated, "I mean, thank you—sir."

Orvis was pleased he had the younger man on the defensive. Psychotaxis was a strategy that served him well in business. In addition to making younger adversaries nervous, he was not above using white guilt, if he felt it could give him a slight advantage when negotiating. He was wondering if this young man could muster equal moxie. His Mohawk ancestors and the other Iroquoian people were excellent traders, as were the Huron, Rivers' kinsmen. Orvis knew that it was his bloodline and the other tribes of the Iroquoian

Confederacy that wiped out the Huron in the Seventeenth century, fighting over the beaver trade with the Europeans. If Orvis was going to place Rivers in a position of trust, he needed to know more about the man. Was he a believer in the resurgence of Indi'n pride? Was he politically oriented? Could his thinking be clouded by resentments toward whites or other races? Could he harbor resentment for their respective tribal histories? Orvis decided to pontificate about some controversial issues; thus, allow Rivers to expose himself.

"Yes, I never was conformable with that sky cowboy thing," Orvis began. "You know, they couldn't call us kings—Sky King was a white guy." He paused and looked for some kind of reaction in Rivers' eyes. Troy continued to peruse the room with trepidation. "Although I loved being up on those skyscrapers. Still do. My daughters try to tell me I'm getting too old. They don't understand. I've watched the sun set from eighty stories in Manhattan, Chicago, Los Angles, Seattle, Houston, Quebec, Montreal, all over the continent. Sometimes the sun sets unimpeded by clouds; it's giant orange neon ball sinking toward the arch of the earth, and there is a bright green flash, like a last good bye, just as it disappears below the horizon. It's a sublime experience, spiritual in that it makes you think about a power greater than ourselves." He paused again. No response. "Knowing that you played a part in the creation of that magnificent Manhattan skyline, well, it's hard to describe."

His tone suddenly changed, "The fact that the white man stole the entire island from our neighbors for a few trinkets, however, sort of taints the pride we took in the accomplishment. Well, what can you do? My brothers tell me I dwell on these things too much. But to be honest with you, it's my concern over the indignities suffered by our people that motivates me to volunteer as the coordinator of these powwows. It seems the least I can do under the circumstances. Have you ever been to a powwow, Rivers?"

"No sir, I can't say that I have. But I have facilitated the legal needs for several large events here in . . ."

Orvis interrupted. "You probably don't even know what powwow means?"

"Sure I do, sir. It's like a meeting or a confab, a conference, I mean . . ."

"See, that's what I'm talking about. America, you know, owes much of its contemporary vocabulary to Indian languages." He took a small handful of peanuts from the bowl in the center of the table and threw a couple into his mouth. Chewing quickly he continued to speak. "Not to mention cuisine—peanuts, tomatoes, potatoes, corn, squash; they were all originally our foods, you know. Tobacco, for crying out loud. And I am sure you're aware that the names of most of the states and hundreds of towns within their borders reflect the tongue of the original native inhabitants. All except the News, you know: New York, New Hampshire, New Jersey. Typically the Anglo-American society has mispronounced, misinterpreted, and misunderstood the Indian terms they freely borrowed in an attempt to add local color and attract tourists. *Powwow* is just such an idiom. Originally an Algonquian phrase, *pau wau* referred to a medicine man or shaman. But the Europeans watching the dancing of the medicine men attributed the phrase to the dancing. Maybe you already know this?" Rivers shook his head no and looked around the room. "And just as Indian tribes allowed the white man's name to stick—Huron, Sioux, Apache, Mohawk for example—modern Indians . . .," he paused; did not finish his original sentence and began a new thought. "Indian, now there is an example of what I'm talking about. Indians, can you imagine, it's a damn lucky thing Columbus wasn't looking for Turkey." Troy laughed out loud. "Yeah, it's a great line, funny, but it isn't mine. A guy named Vine Deloria, Jr. wrote it. I'm not much happier about *Native American*, but what can you do? Anyway, to get back to my original point, we Indi'n have allowed the Anglo connotation of powwow, referring to a meeting or event, to revisit our own language. Now even we use it incorrectly. Of course, and again this is typical, the revisited vocabulary words still mean much more than the Anglicized generalizations. A powwow is indeed a meeting, but it is much, much more. Today, powwows are celebrations about being Indi'n—Skins, you know. Ceremonies, dance contests, singing marathons, drum competitions, and family reunions are just some of the activities taking place at powwows. They are how we maintain continuity."

"I didn't know that," said Troy. "But listen, Mr. Kahnawake, there is something you need to know before we go any further. My

firm may have misguided you into thinking I was an Indian activist
or something. I'm not. What I am is a damn good lawyer with an eye
for details and a strong work ethic. It sounds ironic, and I definitely
don't mean for it to sound derogatory, but it's a strong Judaic-
Christian work ethic. I can do a good job for you here in Denver, but
if you were looking for someone with stronger ties to their Native
American heritage, sorry—I may not be your man. I plan to
approach this job as a confident and competent lawyer, not someone
on the warpath."

"Relax, Mr. Rivers, some of my best friends are Judaic-
Christians." He laughed. "I'm not looking for a radical, but I do need
a warrior. I need someone who is willing to battle, so to speak; battle
legally for my people and me. Negotiate for our advantage, you
know. But, no, I'm not looking for an Indian militant. That's my
job," he laughed.

Kahnawake appreciated Rivers' honesty. He had found over
the decades that lawyers, particularly white attorneys, assumed
negative stereotypes. They negotiated from a weakened position
based on those stereotypes. Rivers seemed unique. Kahnawake could
appreciate the distinctiveness—he and his brothers were rare among
many contemporary Iroquoian people. They were probably full
blooded. His family could trace their lineage all the way back to the
coming of the French and Dutch to the New World. Wars between
local Algonquian and fellow Iroquoian tribes decimated
communities. The wars that followed the arrival of the white man
and the new diseases immigrating with the Christians, to which the
native inhabitants had no resistance, devastated tribal populations.
Therefore, it was a common practice of the Northeastern Indian
peoples to adopt members from groups of defeated enemies to
replenish citizenry and replace loved ones lost to disease and battle.
Perchance, just such a prisoner had contributed to Kahnawake
heritage, but the family's oral history and written documentation,
which started about four generations ago, mentioned no such
member. What was documented in Canada and the States, however,
was the family changing their name from Walker, an Anglicized
name forced on them in the eighteenth century. Back then, nearly all
Indians thought they could somehow avoid or postpone the
inevitable constriction of their lands by appearing to assimilate the

white society, even to the point of taking on American names. In recent decades, however, the family was encouraged to take the name of Kahnawake, a derivation of their historical home, Caughnawaga. The Walker family, as part of the Turtle Clan, earned the privilege of the repatriated name. It was the community who invited the name change, in order to articulate the contributions of the family and a reemerging Indian pride.

Orvis' mother, grandmothers, and their female ancestors for numerous generations had served as tribal consuls. His fathers and their fathers had been well-respected warriors, spiritual leaders, and Mohawk representatives within the Iroquoian Confederacy. The Mohawk, Kahnawake would inform anyone who would listen, lived originally in the eastern most territories of the Iroquoian *Long House*, as the confederacy was known. The map of the Iroquois territories mirrored the floor plan of their Elm-bark enclosures. Each of the five tribes had a vertical, north-to-south, homeland adjacent and in line with the others. All five formed a long horizontal territory stretching from the Hudson River, south of Lake Ontario, nearly to the northeast tip of Lake Erie, then westward across what was to be New York. It was the beauty and fertility of these lands that eventually attracted the new Anglo-Americans and caused the destruction of the Long House, the Iroquoian League. The other four original members of the confederacy were the Oneida, residing just west of the Mohawk; the Onondaga, whose central and protected location made them the "Keepers of the Fire"—the fire which symbolized the kinship and perpetual peace of the alliance members. The Cayuga lands were west of the Onondaga, and the Seneca were the keepers of the western gate. Several other Iroquoian speaking tribes surrounded the five aligned houses. These included both enemies, such as the Huron, and friends, such as the Tuscarora, who later joined the alliance expanding the Iroquois League to six nations. Algonquian speaking tribes, most of them were enemies of the Iroquois, inhabited the lands surrounding the Long House—north into Canada as far as Hudson Bay; south into Pennsylvania, Ohio, the Carolinas; west to the Mississippi; and all along the East Coast.

The different member tribes taking opposing sides in the American Revolution accelerated the eventual devastation of the League. Those fighting for the colonists, the Oneida and Tuscarora, fared no better after the war than those siding with the British. Late in the war the soldiers of George Washington stripped and burned the pristine lands of the Seneca. It was America's first execution of a genocide policy. After the English were booted from the colonies, Indian farms and territories were quickly invaded and confiscated. Orvis' people escaped to Canada.

Orvis knew that the Wyandotte had suffered a similar, tragic story, much of it at the hands of Iroquois. He could not decide if the strange thing he did next was motivated by ancient regret or because he was at heart an incurable missionary. He questioned why he was trying to revive some sort of historical pride in this lawyer sitting across from him in this den of Anglo-American inequity. He paused for just a moment and reached into his coat pocket. "I've been rude. I should have given you this when we first sat down." Kahnawake pulled a beaded tobacco pouch from his pocket and set it on the table in front of Rivers. "As you may or may not know, it is traditional when soliciting a relationship of trust to present an honorable gift—tobacco, for instance."

Troy Rivers reacted with an expression that asked if this was some kind of a test. He then said, "Mr. Kahnawake, you've got me at a disadvantage. I am not familiar with the giving of gifts before a business deal is consummated. I have nothing for you. You wouldn't even let me buy the drinks."

"I didn't expect that you would be familiar, Mr. Rivers, and it is I seeking service from you, a fiduciary relationship; it is therefore appropriate that I begin with the presentation of tobacco."

"But the pouch, sir. It looks like an antique. It looks very valuable."

"Please, Mr. Rivers. It's appropriate that I do this. It does not obligate me to hire you, nor you to take the job. It's a tradition. It simply signifies that we are open in our discussions, that the things we say have importance and are truthful."

"But, Mr. Kahnawake." He examined the intricate pattern work. The beads were actual porcupine quill, whelk shell and quahog clam used in making wampum, "It must be of irreplaceable value."

"If it did not have value—and your assessment is probably high—if it did not have some value, it would be contradictory to the tradition. Please, you must accept it. As one Indi'n to another," He smiled, "Would it make you feel better if I let you pay for the drinks?"

Troy opened the pouch and lifted it to his nose. He inhaled deeply. "I sense a heavy aroma. Latakia?"

"Yes." Orvis was surprised.

"There is also evidence of a high quality Virginia. Am I right?"

"Right on target."

"There are a couple of additional tobaccos with which I'm unfamiliar. This is an interesting blend. It smells rich, as rich as the beadwork on the pouch looks expensive."

"It's a special blend I have made right here in Denver. At Jerry's Tobacco Shop in the Security Life Building. Do you know the place?"

"Yes, I do. I'll buy a good cigar there once in a while."

"Well, there you go. If things work out, you can give me one of Jerry's excellent cigars."

"Well, here is to things working out well," he took a large whiff of the tobacco, pinched out a bit, and set it in the ashtray. He lit it from above with his Zippo. A sweet smoke rose from the glass circle. Both men caught a handful of the smoke and pulled it toward themselves, washing their faces in the aromatic benediction.

Kahnawake thought to himself: He knows more than he is letting on. I like that. He's going to make me dig a little more. OK, I can do that. Orvis knew that although his motives were honorable, he had again manipulated the situation. The giving of gifts was indeed an honorable tradition; however, Kahnawake and his brothers had never actually initiated such a custom in their business dealings. The pouch was an antique, a priceless historical heirloom. He had rescued it when a famous collection of Indian artifacts, owned by an Anglo industrialist, was about to be sold to a foreign collector. The Caughnawaga Steel and Construction Company outbid the collector and donated the artifacts to a small Indian museum in upstate New York. The tribe insisted that he take the pouch for himself. The old sachem said at the time that the spirit of the pouch may someday redeem a soul. Something about Rivers' "warpath" comment motivated Orvis. He thought, I know this young man. He is one of my younger brothers. He is like so many of the young professional Indians I know. They have given up their heritage, thinking of it as excess baggage on their climb for success. The white man has always attempted to remake the Indian into their idea of the ideal man. In the last century it was the farmer. Hunters and warriors were transformed into 'civilized' agrarians. Today it's the corporate clone. Orvis spoke aloud, "Besides, Mr. Rivers, if we do end up working together, I may convert you into some kind of an activist. The ancient memory of the Huron still runs in your veins; we just have to remind you that the blood also runs through your heart." He laughed.

"If I didn't know better, Mr. Kahnawake," said Troy, "I'd think that laugh was to keep me confused—to make me think: is he serious or just kidding?"

"Well, Mr. Rivers, that kind of thinking is probably why you are a good lawyer, and being a good lawyer could prove financially advantageous. We'll see if there is something in all of this that proves advantageous for you—beyond the financial, of course."

"Why do I get the feeling I'm being set up?" asked Rivers.

"I can't set you up, as you say, Mr. Rivers. If there is nothing you want from me, then there is nothing that makes you vulnerable. Right? It is I who needs your services."

"Somehow that doesn't make me feel any less *vincible*. Perhaps now would be a good time to discuss my fee."

"I know your fee structure, Mr. Rivers. I knew that before I called your firm. Unless, of course, you are trying to charge me more because I'm an Indian. You wouldn't try taking advantage would you?"

"I think I just got put on the defensive again, didn't I?"

"You're doing better. Let me tell you a little more about the powwow."

"Please, I'd like to . . . I need to know more."

"To date most have taken place on reservations, in village plazas and school gymnasiums. A few we have organized recently have used city auditoriums, in Oklahoma for example. But this is the first large enough for a convention center. This Four Corners Intertribal Powwow is the initial step of a strategic plan to generate a national sense of unity, or at least common goals and analogous identity among all the various tribes. Denver is a good central location. And we have already made a small step toward our objectives. I was informed recently that the mayor and the city council are preparing a statement for the press apologizing for Denver's part in the Sand Creek Massacre and welcoming 'Our Native American Brothers back into the hospitable arms of the Queen City of the Plains.' It seems that the heroics of the 'Fighting Parson,' Colonel Chivington, have been reassessed."

Orvis paused to change thoughts. "I am amazed and continually flabbergasted, Mr. Rivers, at the power of commerce." He sat quietly thinking and then said, "Chivington in his unscrupulous, ambitious pursuit for political power, used as a rationale for his murderous campaign, the fear that the Indians may bring economic hardship to Denver. That and his basic, demagogic hate of the Indians led to the massacre. Oh, war and retaliation played a part, but the underlining motive for the complete annihilation of the Southern Cheyenne, Black Kettle's people, was gold. The Indians were stalling the run for gold and silver. And now here we are, one hundred years after the massacre, 1964, and it is the potential for profit that has Denver singing a different song. Today they want us here, 'nits and lice' and all."

"Nits and lice?" asked Rivers.

"I'm referring to the infamous quote from Colonel Chivington when he recruited and rallied the rowdies and local toughs from saloons, gambling halls and mining camps to, 'Kill them all, big and small, nits make lice!' The seven-hundred-man militia surrounded the Southern Cheyenne village at Sand Creek on a cool November morning, on the sandy plains of southeastern Colorado. Black Kettle raised an American flag to remind the soldiers that he and the other chiefs had just sued for peace and were following the instructions of the commander of Fort Lyon. The peace gesture was ignored and using rifle and pistol and four howitzer cannons, using sword and knife and rifle butt, the Colorado Militia bludgeoned, riddled, and impaled one hundred and twenty-three Cheyenne people, nearly one hundred were women and children."

Orvis thought of the death song of White Antelope, a seventy-year-old war chief, shot down at Sand Creek. He mumbled it aloud, "Nothing lives long, except the earth and the mountains."

"I'm sorry, Mr. Kahnawake, I didn't hear you."

Orvis shifted moods quickly. "It's ironic, isn't it? The power of commerce, I mean. The powwow . . . where was I? Oh, yes. Although the traditional Plains People have participated in powwows as far away as the East Coast, and in the Dakotas and Oklahoma, we have not yet garnered participation from the Pueblo Peoples of New Mexico and Arizona, the several Ute tribes here in the central Rocky Mountain area, and Apache people of the southern Rockies, Hopi or Navajo, or any of the West Coast and Pacific Northwest Peoples. We may even have participants from Mexico.

"As a volunteer, I have taken on the chairmanship of the nonprofit organization sponsoring these powwows. We have conducted much smaller multitribal gatherings in Canada and New York, along the East Coast from Maine to the Carolinas, and as far west as Saint Louis. If things go as planned, The Four Corners Intertribal Powwow could be the biggest event of this kind east or west of the Mississippi. We are talking an eventual attendance of several thousand—tens of thousands—maybe not the first year, but soon after."

"I had no idea they had become that popular."

"Yes, but the popularity can be a mixed blessing. When they become this large they lose some of the important historical elements, and tend toward being entertainment, mostly for white folk."

"So, with the increased profits, you can lose some of the art?"

"Yes, the art, I suppose—more the spirit. You tend to lose some of the spirituality, although these are by no means a religious event, as such. Of course, we Indi'n have always had a hard time separating church from state. In large events like this one, you have to search out the pockets, the more private places, where families and tribal members can socialize. It's OK. The balance is we educate people, both whites and our young brethren who have lost touch with their heritage. Come to think of it, it might do you a lot of good to participate in a powwow. Sounds like your spirit could use a little tune up." He laughed.

A shadow suddenly engulfed the table. "You look pretty thirsty there, Troy Boy. I know this can't be your father. He's deceased. Right? Your father I mean; not this old gentleman, of course."

Rivers blanched at the inappropriate joke and the intruder's flippant attitude, obviously fueled by too many drinks.

"Clark!" Troy interrupted quickly, "Allow me to introduce Mr. Orvis Kahnawake, Owner and Chairman of the Board of Caughnawaga Steel and Construction. Mr. Kahnawake is a potential client—the powwow event I mentioned to you last week."

"Oh, the powwow," answered Hawthorn. Orvis could see that he had no idea what Troy was talking about.

"Yes, the powwow—the Native American event that Barber was so optimistic about. You remember."

A latent recognition finally registered on Hawthorn's face. "Oh, the powwow!" He looked at Kahnawake's ponytail and the sacred turtle bolo. "Now I get it." Hawthorn sat himself in the extra chair at the table. "Say, Mr. Kahnawaga . . ."

"Kahnawa-ke," corrected Troy.

"Sorry. Say, Mr. KahnawaKE, have you thought about using a local bank to expedite some of your financial transactions?"

Rivers winced again.

"Actually no, I haven't. I'm sorry, I didn't get your name."

"Hawthorn, Mr. Kahnawake. Clark Hawthorn. I'm Vice President of. . . ."

"Why the hell don't you just sit down, Clark? I'm sure you're not interrupting or anything."

"Thanks, Troy Boy." He ignored the sarcasm. "So, Mr. Kahnawaga. . . ."

Rivers' hand went up instinctively. The thrust into the air accelerated by a chest spasm.

"None for me thanks, Troy," said Hawthorn. "I'm already a little snookered."

"Nor me, Rivers," Kahnawake added.

Troy began wildly waving his hand in an attempt to communicate to the bartender to cancel the order. The waiter, however, they were soon to find out, interrupted the gesture to mean: another round and hurry!

"So, Mr. Kahnawa. . . ." Hawthorn got a puzzled look on his face and turned toward Troy.

"*Kē*," answered Rivers. "*Kē . . . Kahnawa-kē*, Clark. Kahnawake. It comes from his family name. The people after whom the Caughnawaga Reservation was named. Hear it, Clark. *Caughnawaga*—the reservation. *Kahnawake*—the man to whom you are being rude." He turned to Orvis. "I'm sorry Mr. Kahnawake. Clark was just leaving." Rivers pulled on Hawthorn's left arm forcing him to rise.

The waiter suddenly stood next to Troy. "Sorry, these took so long Mr. Rivers. The bartender thought you gentlemen were starting the usual heavy FAC bash so I brought two full rounds instead of one."

"Put these on my tab, Bainey," said Hawthorn and sat back down.

Rivers collapsed into his chair holding his chest.

"Well, Mr. Rivers, I am a bit surprised you knew all that," said Orvis.

"Oh, Troy here knows a lot of that Injun stuff. Do you think he looks Injun? He's afraid he looks like a Jew. I don't think he looks like a Jew. He just acts like one most of the time. Right, Troy Boy? Anyway, we love this kid here on The Street." He reached over and mussed Rivers' hair, "This guy is a go'er, Mr. Kahn, you mark my words."

"That's it, Clark. It's time for you to leave. You have insulted my client and you have insulted me." Rivers stood and pulled Hawthorn out of his seat. He signaled for the waiter. There was no mistaking this gesture. "Baines, Mr. Hawthorn is leaving."

"Sir?" Baines was confused.

"Mr. Hawthorne isn't feeling himself right now, Baines. We need to intervene, I'm afraid. He is to be placed in a cab and sent to his apartment. Here's money for the fare. Give the cab driver a large tip; include one for yourself for putting up with this . . . aggravation. Make sure the driver understands that he is not to drop off Mr. Hawthorn at any other bars. Is that straight?"

"Troy Boy, what the hell are you doing? I'm not ready to go. Come on, let's have a drink. I'll buy, Kemo Sabe."

"Mr. Rivers is correct, Mr. Hawthorn," said Baines, surmising that Hawthorn was inebriated. "You know our policy, sir. We can't have you hurting yourself or any other patrons, sir. We can't allow you to be embarrassed by the police. I'm afraid we'll have to cut you off this evening, sir, and make sure you're safely home. It's policy, Mr. Hawthorn; I'm sure you understand. Please, sir, come with me."

"What the hell is this all about?" he yelled. "Who the hell did I piss off? Mr. Kahn, did I piss you off? Troy Boy, you know I would never do anything to piss you off, not on purpose."

"The cab is here, sir. Shall we go?"

"Troy," Hawthorn's face slowly transformed into an expression of sloppy sincerity. "I . . . You know I wouldn't . . . Oh, shit." He suddenly stood erect and straightened his vest. "You're right, Baines, it's time to bid adieu to this dump." He raised his open hand to his own mouth and mimicked an Indian whoop. He stumbled out of the bar on the arm of the waiter.

"He doesn't respect you, you know," said Kahnawake.

"Honestly, he doesn't mean any harm. He's just a spoiled rich, Yankee kid. He always has been. And I mean Yankee, real Mayflower stuff."

"He doesn't respect either of us. Chances are he's an anti-Semitic, but he is a definite horse's ass."

"That he is, Mr. Kahnawake. That he is. Well, I apologize that you had to go through that." Troy looked around the room, his thoughts seemed nebulous; he looked embarrassed and unfocused. The dubious glances from several of the customers, all wearing the same corporate uniform, seemed to bore into him. He looked as if he suddenly felt out of place. He reached to see if his tie was loose. He started to say something and then paused. Kahnawake waited. Rivers pushed the tobacco pouch across the table towards him.

Rivers' voice sounded genuinely disheartened, "Perhaps, I can suggest another firm, someone competent, someone you would like to consider for the powwow."

Chapter Twenty-five

Sky Cowboys

Fall, 1963

The Pueblo people of the Rio Grande valley dance each
spring to awaken Mother Earth. It is I, Turtle, who stirs. Recall
duality. The women of the pueblos instinctively know when it is time
to leave the kivas and parade into the dirt plaza. Several times they
initiate the dance, until the air and the earth tell them the task is
done. They wear evergreen fronds as a symbol of rebirth and some
wear headdresses with geometric steps depicting clouds. Their
gentle shuffle mirrors the rhythm of the heart. They dance
barefooted to keep contact with the earth and coax her, urge me, to
waken. And as long as I have had a say, their dance has never failed
to bring the rains. Great billowing, baritone clouds send music to
accompany the dance. The chorus is loud and thunderous, but Rain,
herself, has a mezzo-soprano voice. In harmony with Wind her range
slows to contralto and accelerates to soprano. Her talent is rich and
dramatic. Renewal is a partnership: men and women, Turtle and
Rain, song and dance, old and young.

Troy Rivers felt he had done the right thing by brusquely
sending Clark Hawthorn, banker and bigot, on his way. Paying
upfront for the cab was a smart move, as was giving explicit orders
to Baines, the trusted waiter, to expedite the expurgation. The more-
than-generous tip for Baines and the cab driver was the pivotal
element in the forced expulsion. However, he knew he had made a
major mistake the minute the cool Colorado air hit him in the face as
he exited the tavern to see why the taxi had not yet left. The plan was
expeditious, spontaneous as it was. Authority was appropriately
delegated; it was the right thing to do, but, no! He could not leave
well enough alone. Lawyers! He chastised himself. He had to go

outside and investigate the delay. To his chagrin, Clark was in rebuttal with the driver and Baines. Troy knew that Clark Hawthorn's submissive behavior in the bar was too good to be true. He instinctively looked around for witnesses.

"Thank god you're here," cried Hawthorn. "Would you tell these sons-of-bitches I'm not going home. I've got places to go and babes to see. What the hell are you trying to pull anyway, Troy Boy? You embarrassed me. A lot of those people are customers of the bank. They're friends of mine, and you embarrassed me."

"Clark, you could have cost me a very lucrative deal in there. You were insulting to Mr. Kahnawake *and* to me. You were way out of line. Now go home and sleep it off, I'll call you tomorrow."

"Bull shit, Troy Boy. If you two can't take a joke then. . . ."

"Thanks, Baines," Rivers said to the waiter, "I'll take it from here."

"The meter is running, bud," said the driver."

"No problem," answered Rivers. "We won't be long." He turned to Hawthorn. "Listen, Clark. You're drunk and you're making a fool of yourself. Everybody in the tavern is watching. We can talk tomorrow. The cab driver has already been paid. Go home."

"Don't get uppity with me, Troy Boy. A week ago you weren't even sure you wanted the damn powwow job. Remember? The poor misunderstood Indian crap you were handing out? So don't give me any shit about insulting you." He tried to climb out of the cab. Rivers blocked his way. "If anybody is insulted here, Troy Boy," he raised his voice, "it's me. You and that son-of-a-bitch Baines can't throw me out of *my* bar in front of *my* friends. I tell you right now, Mr. Three Rivers, or whatever the hell your name is. Nobody on *The Street* is going to put up with any militant Indian crap. If you are trying to do some bidnezz in this town, you better cool the political activist Injun ca-ca, Cochise."

"No, you listen, Hawthorn. I'm the one who isn't going to tolerate any more Indian crap—from you or anybody else. And as far as *The Street* is concerned, give me any more feculence and I will wipe your lily-white tush up and down several blocks of it. How'd you like to explain to that bank of yours what you've done? How'd you like to explain how you lost the account from Earl, Brownstone, Barber and Delta, Clark, *Lad?*" He leaned into the taxi and spoke firmly to the driver, "You've got his address and you got your instructions, right?"

The driver nodded in the mirror but did not turn around.

"Feculence!" laughed Hawthorn, "feculence! What a shitty thing to say. And don't you try to threaten me, Troy Boy. Maybe Barber and the boys will be getting rid of their token red man instead of. . . ."

"Then get this cab moving!" Troy pushed Hawthorn firmly, making sure he was clear of the door and slammed it. The door got the worst of the act. He yelled through the window, "Don't call me, I'll. . . ." The cab sped up Tremont Street, Hawthorn shot Troy the bird with his left hand and mimed an Indian hooping rhythm with his right.

Orvis Kahnawake was waiting at the elevator. "Get your friend taken care of?"

"Clark is a business, correction, was a business associate, Mr. Kahnawake, I mistakenly thought one day he might prove to be a friend."

"Can he cause you trouble?"

"Nothing I can't handle. Shall we order that coffee you were talking about? I'd like to hear more about the powwow."

The elevator doors opened, they stepped in; Orvis pushed the button for the top floor.

"A penthouse, Mr. Kahnawake?"

"It's a suite. 'Eisenhower slept here' is still scribbled on the bathroom wall. A little perk I permit myself. The company picks up the tab if I do some business while I'm in town. A few of the people from C. F. and I. will be driving up from Pueblo tomorrow to see me."

They stepped out of the elevator and traversed the open balcony and walkway. Troy looked over the cast-iron railing at the opulent lobby six floors below. The quiet vocals of the pianist, seducing a concert Steinway, placed between the entrance to The Palace Arms and the lobby lounge, drifted past the pair and gently echoed off the leaded glass of the skylight ceiling. Rivers stumbled a bit as he looked downward and when he followed the song upward and gazed at the stained glass, his dizziness became obvious.

"You're not scared of heights are you?" asked Kahnawake.

"Didn't think so . . . until just now," he answered.

"Hmm," Kahnawake hummed, "You never should have told me. It's always advantageous in negotiations to discover a weakness in the opposite camp."

"You're trying to put me on the defensive again, aren't you?"

Kahnawake just smiled as he looked over the railing and mumbled, "Nice view."

They crossed the thick carpet to a *Queen City* set of double doors. Kahnawake put a key in the lock and opened the suite. He went immediately to the phone on an antique desk. Troy strolled to a window across the room and looked down onto Seventeenth Street. He sighed, "A lot of traffic down there."

Orvis spoke into the phone, "Yes, room service. This is Mr. Kahnawake in room . . . well, *Ohayo, oai dekite saiwai desu,* to you too." He looked at Troy and grinned while shaking his head in what seemed to be familiar disbelief. "This happens all the time. It must be the way I pronounce my name. The damn Japanese are taking over everything." He turned back to the phone, "Yes, please send up a pot of coffee and two settings. Coffee. *Hai, onegai shimasu. Sonna hima ga attara ne.*" He turned to Troy again, "You want anything light to eat, sushi maybe?" Troy laughed and shook his head: no thank you. "Nope, just the coffee. *Arigato gozaimashita,* to you too." He hung up. "Now, where were we?"

"I take it then, we will be working together, Mr. Kahnawake?" asked Troy.

"Hai, Rivers-san."

They both laughed. Troy loosened his tie and opened his briefcase.

"I understand," he said, "that you may be seeking a gambling license for the event?"

"Nothing serious. It's more like games and contests. Some of the people like to bet on games. But there are prizes and some funds change hands. Family stuff."

"Family stuff?"

"Oh, you know, bingo is about as serious as the sanctioned organized gambling goes."

"Your powwow organization is non-profit, I assume?"

"Yes: 501-C-3," he answered. "Here in the States."

"What about liquor. If you want to sell beer and liquor it limits us on the places where we can hold the powwow."

"No liquor."

"No beer?"

"No, we have found that things go better if we don't sell any booze. The dancing is better, and there are no flare-ups of ancient tribal feuds. These are basically family events. Oh, a few of the people will have beer and whatever in their campers—just like regular folk." Rivers smiled to let Orvis know he was listening. "They will enjoy a drink with dinner, maybe some wine, you know. But we don't sell anything at the powwow."

"Well that should make it a little easier."

"Oh, later, after the powwow we furnish beer and wine at the picnic for the organizing crew, and I might provide a bottle of Kentucky sour mash. So we will need to lease a park or picnic area afterwards. A keg is usually a good idea."

"That's no problem. We just make sure it is kosher with the park people and we can have everything delivered."

"Back to the powwow. We do expect a percentage of the refreshment sales if we rent from the city. Here are copies of contracts we had in the past. We're not totally comfortable with these; I think they can be improved upon. Determine if they are applicable to things here in Denver and see what improvements you can make. You know.

"I meet tomorrow with the steel people from Pueblo, so you can get back to me on Monday. You don't mind working over the weekend, do you? I'm not, you know, taking you away from your family or anything am I?"

"No family, no girlfriend. Well, at least no serious girlfriend right now. No, I don't mind." Troy pulled out another business card from his pocket. He wrote on the back and set it next to Orvis' telephone. "That's my home number if you need to contact me."

"Good. It sounds like the coffee is here." He rose and walked toward the door. Rivers heard nothing. Orvis opened the door just as the bellman was getting ready to knock. The bellman and Rivers had the same look of surprise. "You can set it there on the coffee table, I'll pour, thank you," said Orvis as he took the ticket off the cart and signed it." He continued talking to Rivers as he handed the bill back to the bellhop. "We can get serious on Monday after you've read the old contracts and get a better idea of what it is we do. Let's talk a bit. I can start working on reviving that spirit. I'm sure it's no surprise, but I have done some research on you and your firm. And, of course, I read the transcripts from the first interview. You're Wendat?"

"Yes, my folks were Wyandotte." Troy closed his briefcase as Kahnawake poured the coffee. "You know the old pronunciation?"

"Since I took on organizing these powwows I have learned quite a bit about several tribes; so, my knowledge of the Wendat comes from personal curiosity. I'm sure you're aware of our respective tribal histories, and that the Iroquois Federation replenished their numbers with prisoners from other tribes—like yours. Wyandotte did the same thing. Considering the probable hanky-panky going on between Indi'ns, we might actually be related."

"All children of Falling Sky Woman, right?"

"Well, you do know a bit about your heritage."

"Sure, I know some history. It's not that I'm not interested, you understand. It's just that, as I said earlier, I'm not on the warpath."

"In the interview you talked quite a bit about your grandparents. I thought it quite interesting that your grandmother was a Harvey Girl. New Mexico is one of my favorite places; I'm familiar with the Harvey saga. I was sorry to hear that you lost your parents at an early age. What do you remember about them?" He paused and looked earnestly at Rivers. "I'm sorry. That was an inappropriate question. I apologize. My motive, however, was honorable. You see, my brothers and I are, as I said, somewhat out of the loop. Our family assimilated decades ago—the iron company, you know—and over the years, as a result of business and my travels, I have met a few Natives who have similar stories about how they struggled to live in both worlds. *Expatriates,* I'll call them. That's kinder than some of the things the traditionalists call us. These are very successful people; at least they are financially successful. All are aware of the paradox that traditional cultures do not always entertain change nor appreciate those of us who drift from the traditional conventions, the historical circle.

"You're a professionally successful man, educated, a respected attorney. You're knowledgeable about your heritage; yet you say your dicrotic heart isn't bothered, isn't concerned with the duality with which we others struggle." he held out his left hand, "You know: materialism," and then his right, "and idealism.

"Forgive me again, but I'm just curious how you made the balance, how you personally have come to grips, and I thought that perhaps your parents may have had something to do with it. I'm sorry. The query about your parents was rude."

"I was warned you were an Indian evangelist, Mr. Kahnawake, but if you're looking to convert me, I may disappoint you, or at least prove to be more of a challenge than you're used to. I'm proud of my parents and grandparents but I don't 'struggle,' as you say with the 'duality' of the red man being ambitious and seeking financial success. I hope that your motive for hiring me and Barber Brownstone is for our legal expertise and not some misplaced evangelical zeal. Honestly, I'm a damn good lawyer, but a questionable recruit. If that's a problem, maybe—again—you need to evaluate our collaboration."

"Let me worry about that," said Kahnawake with a wry grin, "You might not be as hard-shelled as you think. I've got time. Coffee?"

"Thanks," he passed his cup to Kahnawake. "You know, of course, sir, that I probably am not a full-blood Wyandotte?" asked Troy. "But I am kind of unique in that both my grandparents on my father's side, although from different groups within the tribe, were Wyandotte.

"Aunts, my mother's sisters, often brag that there was Indian blood in their family history as well, Chickasaw, they think—thank god, no Cherokee royalty—but only since it's become fashionable. There are no family records. So, I hope it isn't too important, but I never figured out how much Indian blood I have running through my veins."

Kahnawake interrupted, "As Will Rogers said, 'I never got far enough in arithmetic to know what that makes me.' "

"My grandparents moved back to Wyandotte, Oklahoma, after Grandpa's railroad baron passed on. That's where my father was born. My father played football for Commerce High School along with half-a-dozen of his brothers. It was a large family. They were all local sports heroes. Commerce was a small mining town in the northeast corner of Oklahoma. Wyandotte was the little settlement on the other side of the river. So you had miners and Indian kids, a tough lot, on the football team. They played high school sports alongside Mickey Mantle's brothers."

"Interesting," said Kahnawake. "That wasn't in the transcripts. My Canuck cousins would never forgive me if they knew, but I've always been a Yankee fan. Well, the baseball team, anyway."

"My father went to Oklahoma University on a football scholarship—fullback, never lost a yard, so the story goes. Mother attended O. U. a year later. They met, they married, and here I am."

"I've heard of your father. I harass my daughters with football trivia—*trivia* in the fun, competitive sense; not to imply that your father's football career was trivial. Didn't he play for the pros?"

"Dad had a five-year stint in the pros, played with Sammy Baugh and the Washington Redskins in the early Forties. Yeah, I know, some of you radicals are upset with using Indian people as mascots." He noticed Kahnawake come to attention. "But I'm too tired and it's too late to argue that particular issue tonight." Kahnawake relaxed and smiled at himself. "Anyway, the pro ball made my dad a kind of local hero in Oklahoma. Commerce named the high school stadium after him and his brothers. Unfortunately, he got hurt and had to retire from football. After that, he worked as a roughneck for Nobel Drilling. The owner knew him from college and liked him; loaned him the money to buy his own semi-truck. B. F. Walker Oil Field Transportation, a subsidiary of Nobel, gave my dad a shipping contract. Walker moved the home offices to Denver and my dad followed.

"Later, my folks were invited to a reunion of the Redskins. The owner, George Marshall, was hanging it up. They were killed in an Amtrak train accident between New York and Washington. They were in New York because my mom wanted to tour the Guggenheim Museum; she was an aficionado of art and architecture. My grandparents raised me, eventually sold the truck, and used the money to send me to law school at Denver University." He paused. Kahnawake remained quiet. "Well, as they say: that's all there is."

"I appreciate you sharing that with me, Troy."

"Oh, it's the least I can do, Mr. Kahnawake, if you're going to try to convert me."

"Keep thinking about the strength of your parents and generosity of your grandparents, and you may convert yourself. And call me Orvis. I'm comfortable with that, if you are."

"Thanks, Mr. . . . . Orvis. Thank you, I will."

"More coffee?"

"Just a splash. It will help keep me awake." He purposefully changed the subject. "I'd like to get a first-reading of these contracts tonight." He passed his cup to the older man. "I've done a lot of talking, and I really don't know much more about the powwow or you, Orvis."

"Sure, I can take a turn, but you know what I would really enjoy before I start boring you with all my palaver?" He pulled a beautifully aged brier pipe out of the desk drawer. "I think it's time to properly seal this relationship with some of that tobacco I gave you. And I don't want to hear any Indian giver jokes."

Troy placed the antique pouch on the coffee table. "Help yourself." He watched Orvis open the pouch and, with an intimate familiarity, use two fingers to pinch out the tobacco. "Mr. Kahnawake, really, I can't take that pouch. It is just too valuable a gift."

"We've gone over this, Troy. You must keep it. It's important to me that you do." He folded the pouch closed, leaned over the table, took River's hand and placed the intricate bag in it. He leaned back into his chair and lit the pipe.

Rivers looked down with some trepidation and slowly put the antique back into his pocket.

Orvis began, "By the time I was born my father and grandfather had revived their spirit—as bridge men. Oh, we were still poor, but their pride as men, contributors to their people, had been rekindled by becoming wage earners and providers—daredevils, actually. We never, in my memory, depended upon subsistence from the Canadian Government. So it wasn't until later that I learned that most of our fellow Indians had had a much rougher time of it, particularly here in the States. Our Dakota, Nakota, and Lakota brothers, wrongfully known as the Sioux, for example, did you know that they never accepted payment from the US government for the Black Hills? They have never acknowledged the sale of their sacred lands. It is for this reason, they are among the most poor and impoverished among the Indian people." Kahnawake sensed he was going off on a tangent. He continued, "Anyway, my maternal brothers and I seemed to have a knack for leadership, something we probably inherited from our great grandfathers and grandmothers. We became foremen of job crews all over the world. Early on, we helped organized the Mohawk ironworkers into a union. We eventually opened a construction company, financed by loans from Americans, Canadians, and Japanese. No good deed goes unpunished, however, because now we became the managers negotiating over wages and contracts with the very guys we helped organize." He laughed and re-lit his pipe.

"A few years ago several of our workers came to us talking about these powwows. A few participated in the dances, but they all spoke about a reemerging Indian pride evident at these events." He paused. His eyes seemed to well with moisture as he contemplated a distraction. "You know, my sons have had to battle all over again— fire guns, destroy property, threaten violence—to maintain some of their rights in Caughnawaga. They have had confrontations with the Canuks over fishing and hunting rights. The authorities actually fired bullets into their homes—their houses, where their wives and daughters slept." He paused again and obviously thinking it more prudent, continued with his original thought. "My brothers and I first became involved in the powwow movement as judges. We contributed a little money for prizes and startup costs and after a while they asked us to judge some dances. What did I know about Indian dances, although I personally can do a pretty nice Fox Trot." He paused to see if Rivers got the joke. Rivers smiled and Orvis continued.

"But I learned a lot about the dances and a lot about other Indi'n people at the same time. Eventually we sponsored some events and volunteered as coordinators. My brothers, in their usual fashion, let me do all the work. Actually, I don't mind. I like to travel, to learn new things, to meet new people, sometimes—to make a change. My daughters call me: 'The Missionary.' Ironic, eh?

History tells us that one of the most impactful things we got from the missionaries was small pox."

Rivers noticed Kahnawake's pipe had gone out. In a slow reverent move he pulled the Zippo from his pocket, leaned over the coffee table, and conjured a flame. Orvis leaned forward and puffed on the pipe. The tobacco glowed.

"Do you do snuff?" he asked Rivers, only half concentrating on his question.

"Snuff?"

"You know," he came back to full attention. "Snuff, powered tobacco. Kids stick it between their lip and gums. Baseballers use it."

"No, I can't say I do."

"That's good. I can't stand the stuff. I much prefer my pipe."

Rivers started to rise and reach for the pouch in his pocket.

"No, no," said Orvis. He rose and went to the desk and pulled out a plastic pouch filled with tobacco. Rivers could tell from the aroma that it was the same blend. Orvis returned to his chair and poured himself half a cup of coffee.

"The dancers, in the powwows, make bells out of snuff can lids. You know, they sound great. Dozens of them, the women in the Jingle Dress dance, will move in unison and create this enchanting, rhythmical sound. It evokes an aura over the whole proceedings, an enveloping dome of soft percussion, a mesmerizing tinnitus. I think it was originally an Ojibwa dance. Men also use the snuff lids on other costumes, but it's the numbers, the chorus of hundreds, *thousands* of bells in the Jingle Dress Dance that really makes you swear you hear the songs of ancestors. You hear them coming in the Grand Entry, a catered rhythm, but it's the dance that summons the spirit."

"What's the Grand Entry?"

"Sorry. It's when all the dancers in costume and total regalia parade in at the same time. Usually it's at the very beginning of the dance contests, but if the spirit moves them, they can do it anytime. It's a visual and audio delight—very exciting."

"What other kinds of dances do they do?"

"Well, the Men's Fancy Dance is one of the most athletic. And the native costumes are elaborate—double bustles, long buckskins, bone chest-plates, huge colorful roaches. All are based on authentic historical costumes, of course, but have now become much more ornate. Some of the first Anglo organizers in Oklahoma convinced the reservation dancers they could draw more tourists if the costumes were fancier. They started embellishing them at the turn of the century. It's OK. In fact, it's quite a spectacle. They wear makeup, too. You know, war paint, so to speak. It really does percolate the Indi'n in you."

"You said before that powwows aren't religious."

"Actually no, they aren't, not per se. Of course when you deal with a reemerging and common spirit it can't help but include some sacred elements. But it is not organized religion. No one is preaching hell fire and brimstone; there are no sermons. Once in a while you will hear an eagle-bone whistle. It's probably part of a ceremony, rather than part of a presentation the tourists see, and then you know a sacred thing is going on. It is often very private. It's a beautiful sound, too. But I really love those snuff bells."

"It seems funny somehow—using something modern like a snuff can to augment a historical event. It seems a little incongruous."

"I do need to work on you, Three Rivers." It was a gentle rebuke but nevertheless drove home the point that Troy must have made a typical Anglicized comment.

"Indians use whatever is necessary to get the job done. This is real life, Troy. It's not auditions for some Hollywood movie, or fulfilling some misguided romantic expectations. And it's not a museum exhibition. When you come to the powwow you're going to be surprised to see many of the participants using tape recorders. Lots of super-eight and we are starting to see video cameras. Why we even have telephones on some of the reservations around the country. I'm sorry, I'm teasing you. Most people think exactly the same thing. There is something inauthentic about Indians dressed in traditional garb using modern conveniences. To many, it's a paradox or at least a contradiction of some kind. But think about it, Troy. These are all modern people with contemporary problems: crime, alcohol, unemployment, student dropouts. Try getting a mortgage to build a home on reservation land—that's a contemporary problem. A powwow simply helps to bring historical memory into a real-life reference. It's all about affirming modern life and giving it purpose via our roots. But we are still living in modern times; we acknowledge that. So, powwows are not some maudlin romantic nostalgia, you know, that noble savage nonsense. They're about finding a modern identity based on a proud history. Powwow dancers drive pick-up trucks pulling Aero-Stream trailers. Sometimes they stay in modern motels and watch television, hang out in juke joints and jitterbug to Rock-n-Roll. But at powwows they also dance to traditional drums. They dance with the joy of living and sing about the sorrow of dying." He paused. "I know a few southern Baptists who do the same. The modern white uses books, movies, and television to study history. Well, we use dance, song, and drum. Our identity, our lives, our spirit are tied up in doing the appropriate thing—following the right path. As I tell some of my Anglo-American friends, you do it your way, and we will do it our way; we just want the opportunity to do it. That's when I usually hit them up for a donation."

He paused again. The older man's enthusiasm was obvious. "Once you see it happen. Once you attend a powwow, you will understand what I'm talking about."

"I think I'm beginning to understand—a little," said Troy. "You're right. I need to attend a powwow. I need to meet the people. Is there anything planned between now and the Denver event that I could attend?"

"Taos Pueblo is having a small powwow, a dance competition next week. Here's a plan: I have to meet with C. F. and I. this weekend; you can take Monday and Tuesday to clear your desk and we can drive down there on Wednesday. It's only about six hours from here. Have you been to Taos?"

"No, I've never been there. Even though my grandparents met in New Mexico; I've never seen Taos."

"If you don't mind driving, we'll take your car. I can't stay for the entire weekend, but I'll introduce you to a few people who can show you around. Once you're settled, I'll fly out of Albuquerque to Denver; I've got business in Wyoming, and then home. You'll have to drive back by yourself. Is that a problem?"

"Not at all. I think it's important I witness a powwow first-hand. I'll inform my office. I'll read these contracts this weekend so

I have a better idea of the logistics of the large event you're contemplating."

"Sounds like a plan. I haven't been to Taos for quite a while. I'll make the hotel reservations since I know the place, if that's OK with you, and I'll put together a loose itinerary."

"Sounds great. I'm actually a little excited about the trip. Friends in the office have for years invited me to vacation in Taos and Santa Fe. Never had time for a vacation. I'm looking forward to mixing a little pleasure with business."

"That's the spirit. That's what keeps me going."

Troy lifted his cup and quickly swallowed the last of his coffee. It was cool, but the heavy aromatic taste was still satisfying. "I should let you prepare for your C. F. and I. meeting. I'll take the contracts and be on my way. Wednesday it is. I'll call Tuesday and confirm a time to pick you up here at The Brown."

"I may be running a few errands early in the week, so I'll call you Tuesday just in case I'm not here at the hotel."

Troy felt a strange excitement he had not known for some time. The idea of the trip was energizing—exploring someplace he had never been. If there was time, maybe they could visit the Hotel Castañeda, where his grandparents met. He liked Orvis. He enjoyed his subtle sense of humor and his patience. He was pleased to see that the monosyllabic face that first sat down at the table in the tavern was, after all, only paint. The stone-faced Indian had not only cracked a smile but also a joke or two. The man had a deep sense of his heritage and a pretty sharp business mind. Troy actually enjoyed the old man's lectures. He somewhat eagerly, or at least with an unexpected zeal, anticipated the drive to Taos. He determined he would let, or if need be—cajole, Orvis into telling more tales.

He sprung from the elevator and quickstepped through the lobby, peeking half-heatedly, more out of habit than interest, through the door to the tavern, noticing but not wanting to partake of the pandemonium. At the huge brass doors to Tremont Street he suddenly ran into Clark Hawthorn coming in the hotel. Hawthorn was obviously drunk and draped over a young woman. She was struggling with his pliant weight. He spotted Rivers on the opposite side of the door and raised his right hand, palm outward, in a theatrical Indian greeting.

Hawthorn slurred, "How! Troy Boy."

"Legally. That's how, you putz," answered Rivers, "and swift as an arrow." He gave Hawthorn a war hoop, loud and shrill, that sent visual shivers down the spine of the drunk and got the attention of a few of the Seventeenth Street crowd near the door of the Ship Tavern. They laughed; Hawthorn scowled.

"Who was that?" asked the girl.

Hawthorn answered through clenched teeth, "Last of the fucking Mohicans, that's who."

Chapter Twenty-six

Taos

Fall, 1963

Animals exhibit instinctive wisdom when they choose the path of least resistance. Of course, animals simply migrate; *only when you humans personify them in your fables and films do they* journey. *In contrast, a mixed blessing bestowed by us immortals upon you transients is your inexplicable propensity to avoid the path of least resistance, thus partake of* odyssey. *The epic adventure can be a gift from the gods or the bane of misstep. Not only do we celebrate your passages, they are the essence of our very existence, for it is during the voyage, the pilgrimage you come to know us. So are you blessed?*

Troy Rivers was driving. He and Orvis Kahnawake had been on the road for about an hour when they sped out of Colorado Springs, out of the shadow of Pike's Peak, and away from the adamant military gentry of Cheyenne Mountain. Rivers seemed overly pleased how his "pretty little Beamer" took the curves and blasted past the semi's. Orvis made some derogatory comment about them being "pretty" conspicuous once they got south of Pueblo. The most common vehicles inhabiting the interstate would be pickup trucks, semi-trucks, and large American made sedans—General Motors, cars named after Indians and the European adventurers who exploited them.

According to Orvis, the landscape signals a change: geographical and sociological. No longer hugging the highway, the foothills and pinnacles rise far west of the road. From Colorado Springs, through Pueblo, to the highway fork outside Walsenburg things remain fairly flat and straight.

Orvis, anticipating the next two hours of prosaic views, gazed out the window of the car and with a voice heavy with reminiscence said, "It's too bad we didn't stop for ice cream."

"Do we need to pull over?" asked Rivers as he passed a sign saying a rest area was two miles ahead.

"No, let's keep going. We're making good time. I guess that's important. I was just thinking about ice cream."

"Michelle's!"

"You've been there?"

"One of my favorites."

"I thought the Brown Palace was your favorite?" As they passed through the Pueblo center of town on a brief roller coaster stretch of turnpike Orvis anticipated and eventually viewed the towering silhouette of the smoke stacks of Colorado Fuel and Iron, a company with which he had done a lot of business. The cold C. F. and I. profile dominated the eastern horizon beyond the town. He instinctively checked his watch. *Old habits, thinking about work.* "Ah, the oft visited hamlet of Pee-ebb-lah. It feels funny passing it by.

"Should I stop? You want to make a call?" asked Rivers.

"Oh, no, no. Funny is fine. I'll get over it. What I'll never get over, however, is how the locals pronounce *pueblo*."

"Pee-ebb-lah," said Rivers.

"Right, you're a Colorado boy; you've heard it before," said Orvis. "How the hell someone can butcher a beautiful Spanish word like *pueblo* into a nasal Appalachian spoonerism like *pee-ebb-lah* I'll never . . . oh, well." He resigned his disenchantment because he feared that launching into another pedantic lecture about Anglo abuses, linguistic and otherwise, might taint their trek. He knew there was much for Rivers to learn but figured he should learn most of it on his own, by observing, by listening. However, the one expository role he couldn't resist was tour guide, "Pueblo signifies a dividing line of sorts."

"How's that," asked Rivers.

"At Pueblo, and north is domesticated America: big cities and industry; south is less urbanized, more agricultural. Once out of the triplex, the landscape goes rural and uninhabited, flat and empty of landmarks. My business associates from the East Coast are flabbergasted by the wide-open spaces. They cannot fathom the miles and miles of undeveloped expanses. I have to admit it, but I too prefer some signs of civilization. I'm warmed once we approach the small Latino fincas, farms, and the aldeas montañas, mountain villages, the rancheros, and the Indian pueblos. They draw me back. Somehow, I'm more comfortable down here than in the metropolitan East. Although it's quieter here and slower paced, it seems more adventurous. Maybe it's that Old West mystique." He was quiet for several miles. Rivers did not interrupt his contemplation.

Orvis looked to the southeast and pointed out a familiar landmark: Huerfano Butte, the Orphan, an isolated volcanic neck, an inverted cone with a cropped top, the lone vertical pediment for miles around, a historical marker for the Ute and Arapahoe, and since the eighteenth century for those Nuevo Mejícanos and pioneering Anglos traveling to or from Denver on the Taos Trail. It also stood as the milepost between the province of the Hispanic and Indio south and the Anglo-industrialist north. The sight of the orphan animated his memories.

"Take the Walsenburg turn-off," said Orvis.

"Doesn't I-25 go all the way?" asked Rivers.

"To Santa Fe—yes, but not to Taos. If we don't turn at Walsenburg, we will have to exit after Raton. I want to go over La Veta Pass. It's much prettier than Raton and there's less traffic. We'll come into Taos through the back door. Autumn is beautiful on La Veta. The sage, the chaparral, the willows and scrub oak take on gold and pastel hues. "

Orvis, again taking on the role of tour guide, explained that a spectacular vista awaited them. After turning off the main highway and passing through Walsenburg, approaching the wetlands at the mouth of the valley of the Cucharas River, the full bosom of Tierra Madre soon rose into sight. Montañas Españoles, Spanish Peaks, dominated the horizon—twins, ample and enticing—more comely than the monumental monolith Pike's Peak. Long irregular fences of solid rock radiated from Spanish Peaks toward the travelers, although from the driver's viewpoint, the petrified walls seemed to flow away from the road and up the mountain, rising toward the ancient crown of the twin mountains. Orvis informed Rivers that the locals call the formations War Bonnet Ridge. The dikes were the remnants of molten magma that oozed into vertical cracks in the skin of Tierra Madre and cooled into resistant slabs. The surrounding shale subsided through thousands of years of erosion and today the vertical walls subdivide the terrain.

"We'll cross over the Sangre de Chisto Mountains via La Veta Pass, drop down into Fort Garland, turn south across Trinchera Creek and head for Colorado's oldest town, San Luis, pronounced by local Anglos as *Sand Loo-ee*."

Rivers said that he felt himself enchanted by the landscape and the sound of the landmarks: Huerfano, Cucharas, Trinchera, La Veta, and Montañas Españoles. Fort Garland, on the other hand, sounded out of place. "Fort Garland doesn't have the same ring to it as Koo-charrr-ess," he exaggerated the romantic Spanish syllables. "What's it named after?"

"It's an old army fort. Kit Carson was the commander there for a short time."

"I thought Kit Carson was a famous mountain man."

"That he was—mountain man and Indian fighter. Carson's an interesting character, typical of the Old West, more myth and legend than actual hero. How much do you want to know?"

"I'll tell you if and when I've heard enough. Sounds like the history books I was brought up on might have left out a couple things. Right?"

"It makes me nervous when you see my pontification coming. Am I that transparent?"

"Don't go shy on me. I like the history and local color. So, what about Kit?"

"Carson was actually the Indian Agent for the Tribes of Northern New Mexico. He lived in Taos. His house is still there; it's a museum. They also named a street after him and a park. At one time, Carson was married to an Arapahoe girl. Waa-nibe, *Grass Singing*. He actually fought a dual with another trapper for her. Kit and Grass Singing had a daughter; he named her Adeline, after a white niece. Waa-nibe died and he married a Cheyenne girl, Making-Out-the-Road. She later divorced the little cuss, you know, by throwing all his belongings outside the teepee. The house, museum and most the history books celebrate his third and Hispanic wife, Josefa Jaramillo."

"So, the stories about him being a friend of the Indian are true?"

"It makes historians comfortable to perpetuate that fable. You know what they say, 'history is written by the winners.' The Navajo and Mescalero Apache may have a different opinion. So may the Taos Pueblo people."

"So, what's the story?" Rivers prompted.

"There was a revolt in 1846 against the new American government in Taos. America had just won the Mexican American War and with victory claimed New Mexico territory, Texas, Arizona, and most of California. It was a dream-come-true for the Manifest Destiny boys. Carson served as scout for American forays into the Southwest and California. He knew the territory and the inhabitants. Except for some Hispanic and Indian resistance zealots, Kit Carson and Charles Bent of Bent's Fort fame were well-respected men in Taos."

"Bent's Fort? That old tourist attraction in southern Colorado?"

"Outside La Junta. Have you been there?"

"No. One of the firm's partners collects Western Art. He talks about it all the time. Every year he gives everyone in the office a calendar of pictures he's taken throughout Colorado and there is always a Bent's Fort image. It's usually August, I think."

"You should go; it's worth seeing, despite a few tourists. It's very authentic, lots of history, and if you like stories about mountain men, well, you know, that's the place where they were rendezvousing and raising hell."

"Maybe we can take a detour on the way back," said Rivers.

"Your way back," answered Orvis. "Anyway, Bent was married to a local New Mexican girl, the sister of Kit Carson's wife. Bent was the first American Territorial Governor and therefore a likely target for the angry rebels. A few Taos Indians and some local Mejícano sympathizers unsuccessfully tried to banish the Americans and in a scurmish, unadvisedly massacred Bent. America sent in the troops. The rebels hid out in the Taos mission chapel—sanctuary, you know. The American militia, with Kit Carson in charge, surrounded the old pueblo church with cannons and rather than waiting for a surrender, proceeded to bombard it. The cannon fire leveled the old adobe structure to the ground. All the instigators inside were killed. The pueblo never rebuilt that particular chapel. Today the grounds are a local cemetery."

"A cemetery? So they buried the victims right there at the church?"

"Yes. The rebellion and the severe punishment of the rebels was a major event in the history of the pueblo and the town. To the Taos Indians these friends and relatives were, you know, *canonized*."

"Oh, Orvis," said Rivers, "you deserve to be buried for that bomb."

"Sorry, Mr. Rivers; it just slipped out. If you think I'm bad, wait until I introduce you to my friend in Taos. He's driving up from Albuquerque to meet us."

"Who's that?"

"William Ho-Ho-Horace Green. He's an artist, a painter. He lives near Albuquerque but exhibits in Santa Fe and Taos. He's somewhat famous."

"Ho-Ho-Horace?"

"Ho is what his friends call him. He is a huge man and in giving him a nickname we sort of played off the fact that he's also an accomplished gardener; grows his own vegetables—famous for his chilies and tomatoes. He cans his own salsa and gifts it to friends. We, you know, the recipients of salsa, have always been amused by the image of this huge man bending over his cute little vegetables. And, think about it: his last name is Green."

"I get it," said Rivers. "Ho—Ho—Ho. Now I see where you get your ho-ho-horrible sense of humor."

"You're being a little critical, aren't you?" Orvis feigned hurt.

"How does he like being called Ho-Ho-Horace?"

"It's OK. Mostly we just shorten it to Ho. He likes 'Ho' because it often shocks nosy strangers, meddlesome people eavesdropping, trying to figure out who this huge, apparently famous, fellow might be. They think we're affectionately calling him a 'whore.' For some strange reason, it amuses him that Indi'ns would be speaking Black, street slang. He explained the incongruity once at a dinner party. I think I was the only guest who saw the humor."

"What did he say? How'd he explain the humor in being called a whore?"

"He said the absurdity is based on the fact that every white person we know claims an ancestor who is a Cherokee princess. Every hippy is an Indian wannabe, and here we are, real American Indians, using the affectations of American Negroes. There is an ironic contradiction in there somewhere that he thinks is humorous."

"Sounds droll," added Rivers. "And complex."

"Yeah, he's quite the entertainer. But, I don't mean to cast the wrong impression. He has a serious side; he is very serious about his art. He gets a little defensive if he thinks people don't even give the time to try to understand it. He gets a little prickly if viewers are blasé, just think the colors are pretty, and don't attempt to interpret a deeper meaning. All he asks is that you pay attention; open your mind. He refuses to be ignored. Now that is a more ironic circumstance than street talk."

"How's that?"

"The myth of the stoic Indian. That he 'ain't.' Considering his size and his impatience with uninitiated and uninformed art patrons—did I mention he was large?—it's difficult and unwise to turn a blind eye, so to speak, to Ho-Ho-Horace Green or his paintings."

"Is he violent?"

"Not as often as one would expect."

"You're kidding . . . right?"

"Yes, I'm kidding. He's very gentle for a bear. Actually, he's quite the diplomat; he's well respected in each circle of the New Mexican tri-culture . He maneuvers well among the Whites, the rich gallery owners and collectors, the politicos and average Joes. He's respectful of the Hispanic culture, loves the cuisine, has a great appreciation for the land and history of Nuevo Mejíco and, I almost forgot, enjoys good Country Western, Mexican Rock-a-Billy and historic corridas. Plays the guitar. For me and his Indi'n friends, he's an excellent apostle—very serious about the rekindling of Indian pride and the reverse exodus. I think that's why the paradox of Indi'ns wanting to mimic another minority by adopting affectations like 'Ho,' strikes him as ludicrous but entertaining—as if we don't have enough problems, you know."

"The reverse exodus?" asked Troy.

"It's a return to Indian ways. For some, even a return to the reservations, but knowing what we know now. The reverse exodus is an attempt to reestablish our identity with young people, recapture our spirit, and revive our connection to Mother Earth. Don't ask these questions if you don't want me converting you."

"No problem, Orvis. I'll let you know when you get too preachy. I probably shouldn't tell you this, but I actual enjoy your history lessons *and* your oration. So, tell me more about Mr. Ho-Ho-Horace Green."

"Well, as I understand it, his father, a Ute, was a miner in southern Colorado and named Ho after a William Green. The family name is Nighthorse. It seems Green was a famous labor leader from Coshocton, Ohio. He served as a leader of the United Mine Workers and president of the AFL, you know, the American Federation of Labor."

"Of the AFL-CIO fame?"

"Before the merger. In fact that's when Ho's old man quit the mines. Green is famous for a book called *Labor and Democracy*. The history of mining and conflicts with the unions is infamous here in southern Colorado. Ho's old man was quite the activist. I think Horace must have inherited a lot of that warrior spirit."

"And the Horace part of his name; was that William Green's middle name?"

"No, that came from Ho's mother. William, her son, Ho, was a rebellious youth. He was already large and difficult to discipline; so, whenever he misbehaved she pleaded with his father to punish the big horse's ass. 'hors' ass,' as she would say with her broken English. The Anglo principal of the reservation school misunderstood William's mother when he had to call in the parents for a disciplinary hearing. Just as she told the father, she gave permission to the principal to beat the: *hors' ass*. The administrator changed his permanent file to read William *Horace* Green Nighthorse. To hear him tell it, it was to keep him humble. He didn't even know it was part of his high school record until he applied for an art college. By then it was too late."

"And you say old Horse's Ass is an artist?"

"And very large. I wouldn't call him 'Hors' Ass' to his face. Only a mother—you know."

"No problem; *Mr. Green* it is until he tells me different."

"Ho coordinates the powwow participants from Arizona, Utah, New Mexico and southern Colorado. It's important that you meet him. He's my right arm here in the Southwest."

"I'm looking forward to it. He sounds like quite a character."

"Oh, he has his moments."

As they began the climb over La Veta Pass they were slowed by two halves of a double-wide mobile home, each on their own trailer, and accompanied by three pickup trucks—bow, amidships and stern—posting "Wide Load" signage, and forming a snail's pace parade. Orvis Kahnawake told Rivers that they were in no particular hurry; he should relax and enjoy the scenery; there will be a safe place to pass soon enough. If Rivers didn't mind, he, Orvis, might catch a quick power nap. He rolled his jacket into a cushion and placed it next to the car window. He could still feel the vibrations of the road, but the pillow comfortably insulated them. His youthful heart saw a crow with a white back racing next to the car. A raven, larger and darker seemed to be guiding the crow. A brief look, he wasn't sure what he saw, he wondered what spirits had joined them. He remembered, as a youth, he would conjure a great horse that galloped next to his father's car as they sped down country roads. Even as he dozed the landscape was familiar; he had traveled this "high-way" many times. The road over La Veta pass climbs to almost ten thousand feet above the seas. It meanders gently through forests of juniper and aspen tees. Half-awake, he saw the broad leaves of the aspen catch the sunlight and mountain breezes, shimmer in recurrent groves of silver, a dancing contrast to the gray-green carpet of pines. Alpine streams cut deeply into the terraces of the uplifted cordilleras. The fires of unseen cabins or campsites filled the air with the fragrance of piñon pine, or perhaps it was just a twilight memory aroma, a sweet-acrid dream. Semiconscious, he sensed they were near the summit. The trees became stunted and gnarled by the brisk winds; more black crows riding the winds, like spirits of the mountain, portent messengers, drifted down the river canyon running parallel to the road.

Troy looked toward his passenger; the old man had fallen asleep, his head leaning against a jacket he had rolled and set between him and the window; his exhale leaving a vaporous ghost of warmth on the window that quickly disappeared as the glass reclaimed its chill from the crisp air outside. Rivers drove on, following the crows down the Western Slope of the Great Divide. As the road leveled out, and the parallel hills diminished, allowing a more distant view, another huge pinnacle rose on the horizon to his right—Blanca Peak. Watching the road, but perusing the peak, it wasn't long until he spotted a gas station on the outskirts of Fort Garland. Trucks lined up for diesel; Troy pulled up to an empty driveway next to a gasoline pump. Orvis awoke when Rivers turned off the engine.

"Sorry about that," he said as he stretched his arms in front of him, toward the dash, and then rubbed his eyes. "I wasn't very good company."

"No problem. I enjoyed the drive. That really is much prettier than the Interstate. Sorry about waking you, but we need gas."

Orvis arched his back, sticking out his chest and continued to stretch away the stiffness sown by sleep, "Fort Garland! I must have had quite a nap."

"Where do we go from here?"

"Don't be in such a hurry. I need to make a call. There's someone I want you to meet."

"You're the captain."

Troy pumped gas while Orvis went inside to find a phone. When he returned, Rivers was waiting in the driver's seat. "Any luck?"

"Nobody home. Maybe I can set up a meeting for the return trip. This is my Fort Garland sweetheart, Patty. You'll like her. I think she'll like you, if you don't come off as a big city lawyer. You two need to meet. She'll help with the powwow. I left a message that you'll call on the way home. Don't forget. I'll give you her number. She's someone very special to me.

"So, are we all gassed up? Go left out of the station. The old fort will be on my side of the car. Do you want to stop?"

"Stop? At the Fort?"

"Yeah, we can take, you know, a tour."

Rivers expected to see tall palisades of thick tree trunks, a Lincoln Log fort with hewed green roofs on the guard tower at each corner. Instead, he saw several squat adobe buildings with flat roofs and chimneys that seemed too large for the small dwellings. There were no surrounding walls. The whole thing looked like a poorly planned subdivision of soddies. Some fort, he mumbled.

They both continued to stretch as they exited the car and walked slowly over a dirt embankment toward the nearest building. Troy cupped his hands against the glass of a dirty window. Orvis tried the door; it was locked.

"All I can see is a bunch of old knickknacks," he pulled away from the window and turned toward Orvis who was walking to the next building in the row. "Looks like original issue to me. Old Kit may have spit tobacco into one of those coffee cans."

Orvis ignored him and tried the next door. It too was locked. He turned and faced the compound; put his hand above his eyes to shield them from the glare of the late-day sun. "I don't think anyone is home." Rivers watched him stroll to the center of the compound and stared up at a tall mast in the middle of the tiny plaza, a lookout post and flag pole—forty feet high with a crow's nest platform near the top. He looked at the bottom where four crudely hand-hewed, four-by-ten, pine buttresses were wedged next to the mast. It was a frontier improvisation, seemingly designed by a disenchanted seaman suddenly assigned to hell—landlocked and covered in sagebrush—a prairie surrounded by mountain peaks and as far from the sea as an ill-fated sailor could wander. The entire impromptu apparatus was painted white and had telephone pole spikes sticking out of the side—a makeshift ladder for anyone fool enough to climb the swaying mizzen. "Shall we go up?" Orvis asked gleefully.

"Are you crazy?" Rivers responded.

"Seriously," replied Orvis. "It's not that high, and look," he pointed to an "L" shaped spike, "there's a ladder. Nothing to it. It'll be fun."

"We're a little too old for 'fun' aren't we, Orvis." It was a statement, not a question.

"You're never too old for fun, Counselor. Consider it an adventure, a rite of manhood."

"The bar exam was all the rite of passage I needed. This is a test of rejuvenated adolescent irresponsibility."

Orvis continued to tease, "Are you afraid of heights?"

"Not in an elevator."

"Look," he pulled on the ladder spike, "It's secure; you'll be safe. I'll climb below you, to catch you, to keep you from looking down."

"Why shouldn't I look down?"

"Oh, you never look down, you know," he laughed. "You never want to see where you might splat."

"It's getting late. Didn't we want to get into Taos before dark?"

"Nice try." He pulled Troy's hand and placed it on the iron rung. "See, it'll hold you. It's like life, Rivers, one step at a time. Come on, you can do it. I'll be right behind you."

"Something tells me this is another set-up and I'm going to regret this."

"You're right, Rivers. It's a test. We're going to find out where your spirit resides: Earth, Air, Water, or Fire. Despite your namesake, I think you're a landlubber. Get moving, pledge."

Rivers took the first spike in his hand and reached for the second.

"There, that's not so bad; is it?"

"Don't patronize," he uttered as he reached for the next rung and lifted himself into the air. As soon as he lost contact with the ground, he felt the panic surge.

"Keep going, I'll be right behind you," said Orvis. "And really, whatever you do, don't look down."

"Damn-it, Orvis, be serious!"

"I am serious. You never look down. Well, not until you get to the top."

Troy Rivers moved more cautiously and carefully than he could recall ever before in his life. More cautiously than his first climb up the ladder of the high dive at the community pool. That too was a dare, but he did it. The smacking sting of the water swam back into his memory. The pain and the embarrassing red singe from the clumsy flop gave him pause. The other boys teased him. "We thought you were trying to fly," they laughed as they lifted his arms and pointed at the crimson sting. In his mind, he heard their laughter below him. He looked down to confirm. "Oh, shit! What have I let you talk me into?" He felt dizzy and the sudden sweat on his hands, threatening his grip, nearly sent him into panic.

"Didn't I tell you not to look down!"

"I'm coming down, Orvis!" He descended.

"No way, Rivers. Get your chicken Indian ass up that pole."

"I'm coming down, Orvis! With you, without you, over you, or under you, but I'm down."

Rivers looked up toward the crow's nest. It seemed a lifetime away. "I can't do it. I'll get you for this, Kahnawake. This and those stupid jokes you told in the car."

"I know you will, kid. Believe me." He moved aside and allowed Rivers to lower to the ground. "I owe you one—a Scotch. You know."

"A bottle!" He brushed off his thighs. "Is this the kind of thing you and Ho-Ho-Horse's Ass do? If it is, I may head back to Denver tonight."

"If you don't mind waiting a couple of minutes, I'm going to climb up. It's kind of a tradition."

"Be my guest," said Rivers.

"I won't be long," said Orvis as he grabbed the first iron ladder rung.

Troy was astonished at the nimbleness of the older man as he nearly sprinted up the pole.

"Made my living in the air, remember Rivers?" he called down from the halfway point, leaning away from the pole and holding on with one hand. "Yeah, I think I'm definitely a sky spirit; live and die with the wind."

"Jeez-zus, Orvis, don't do that!" He backed away from the base of the mast; he wasn't sure if it was for a better view of the old, agile sky cowboy, or because he didn't want the old showoff to fall on him.

Orvis reached the platform and with the confidence of a circus performer swung over, paused, brushed white paint flakes off his hands, and stood admiring the view. "This is beautiful," he said as he looked around.

Rivers turned to see what Orvis was looking at. The sun illuminated the crown of Blanca Peak.

Orvis called down, "It shone like a gold temple of the fabled Seven Cities of Cibola. I half-expected to see conquistadors riding toward the fort."

The deep azul shadows of the southern San Juan Mountains filled the entire San Luis Valley and engulfed the base of Mount Blanca. The Sangre de Cristo range, on the opposite side of the wide valley, glowed as red as their namesake, in bright contrast to the blue-violet valley floor.

"You can't see what I see from down there on the ground." chided Orvis.

"I can see just fine, thank you," said Rivers. "The colors are beautiful, even from down here."

"Troy, are you going to view the world like a baby bird, stuck in the nest, or are you going to risk spreading your wings one day?"

"I like the turtle's point of view. Slow and steady wins the race. It's level-headed, close to the ground, armored, with four-wheel drive—got good traction." River thought he felt an ever so slight tremor below him.

"Don't tell me about the turtle's point of view, young man, you're talking to a sachem of the Turtle Clan." Orvis paused and looked at distant peaks. "Further south, just outside of Albuquerque," he yelled, "they call those mountains Sandia. It means *watermelon*."

"Interesting," Rivers knew now *he* was patronizing.

Orvis stood silently for a long time. The air began to cool. The near-evening breeze added sway to the perch. Then he said just loud enough for Troy to hear, "It's from difficult-to-get-to places like this that we Indi'n people have sought our visions, you know. Not pony soldier forts, of course, only in an emergency, but sacred places requiring a journey of struggle, a quest. From these visions we often find our animal guardians. And sometimes, if we are receptive, we see our future, but it takes a special effort. All my sane Indi'n friends have gone through some sort of odyssey or introspection, even in these contemporary times. It is a difficult balancing act—keeping your feet on the ground and yet having a majestic view, a vision, like this—is it not?"

"Well, it's getting late," interrupted Rivers. "I'm sure the view just keeps getting better, but right now, Orvis, you are getting preachy."

"You know, you're right," he sighed. "We probably should be going." He nimbly knelt and reached for the top rung and began his descent.

Rivers felt the adrenaline perc' mildly as he anticipated Orvis' climb down. To calm himself, he took another look at the grandeur of the aging sun and the glowing landscape from ground level. To his surprise, Orvis in what had to be a rare miscalculation missed the last rung and plopped onto his backside in the soft dirt at his feet.

"Well, I'll be damned," Orvis laughed. "It's been a long time since I took a misstep like that, you know!"

Rivers reached down and grabbed an arm, "Are you all right?"

"Of course, I am. I've jumped from greater heights and, god knows, taken longer falls than that. You know, it just caught me off guard."

"Serves you right," laughed Rivers, "serves you right for trying to teach a younger fool to fly."

"It *was* a nice trip, wasn't it." They both laughed as Orvis brushed himself off and Troy searched for the car keys. He found them on the second try in the same pocket.

They were quiet for several miles, through San Luis, along a straight stretch, speeding toward the Colorado and New Mexico border. Just after they passed a sign advertising White Horse Ranch, and the mountains surrounding a distant Taos came into view Orvis spoke of an alluring and enveloping light in the skies of northern New Mexico. It is as clean, crisp, and cordial as the mountain air. Perhaps, it is because Tierra Madre is so much closer to the sun. Regardless, in the daytime the blue of the sky is more saturated, the green of the pine more intense, the subtle chroma grays of the sage and mesquite are more velvety and rich. Painters and other artists have celebrated this light for generations. And when the sun sets, turning the sky crimson in other latitudes, it transforms the clouds, the air and mountains of New Mexico into the resonant red of Sangre de Cristo, the blood of Christ.

The ride through Costilla, Questa, and toward Taos remained quiet; both men absorbing the dramatic views as the miles and setting sun altered the scenery—the chaparral turning from green-grape gray to red wine, the mesquite becoming blue, the piñon growing as black as the pavement humming below them.

Climbing again, heading south out of Arroyo Hondo, nearer now to the Rio Grande; sprinting toward the flat terrain of the top of a great plateau surrounded on three sides by the Jemez and Nacimiento, the Sangre de Cristo, and the Picuris Mountains; they could see the faint glow of the hospitable lights of the town of Taos. The cook fires of the Indian pueblo were too small and too distant to view, but their piñon perfume permeated the night. The sacred, Blue Mountains hung from the sky like omnipotent curtains—harboring the deities of thunder, wind, and rain.

After parking in the plaza and crossing the *North-South Highway*, the road upon which they had just entered town, they walked less than half-a-block in the purple light of evening, feeling the warmth still radiating from the walls of the adobe buildings. Orvis led the way to the entrance of the Taos Inn. The heavy scent of burning piñon hung in a layer of air just above them.

"Orvis, you old reprobate," bellowed a baritone voice in the warm hospitable air of the bar. A titan with a bumper crop of huge shining teeth filling a Galligantus smile stood at the bar.

"Yah-ta-hey-Ho," Orvis exaggerated the syllables in greeting.

The two men hugged and slapped one another on their backs.

"How was your drive?" asked the Goliath, looking more at Troy than at his old friend.

"Great . . . scenic," answered Rivers acknowledging the very brief eye contact.

"Ho," began Orvis, "this is Trois Rivières, the young lawyer I was telling you about."

"Bonjour, Mr. Rivers," greeted the smiling man. "Well, it may be too late for *bonjour*, but it's nice to meet you anyway." He looked at Orvis, "You two want to wash down some of that road dust? I'll buy the beers."

"Sounds great, Mr. Green," answered Troy, "and it's nice to meet you, too."

"Mr. Green is my father, Troy. I'm Horace to any friends of the sachem here. Well, saddle up, pards. I've been saving a couple of stools for you at the bar. I expected you earlier." He turned back to Troy, "He didn't have you climbing the lookout pole at Fort Garland did he?"

Rivers noticed that Green's head almost touched the heavy, roughhewed pine logs running parallel across the ceiling. "As a matter of fact. . . ."

"You'll never change will you, Orvis?" They pulled three stools away from the bar. The aged pigskin squeaked as they sat down and the crisscrossed cedar frames groaned. It was obviously a sound to which the two Taos veterans were familiar.

"They're called *equipale*," said Horace. He had noticed Rivers checking out the stools. "Noisy, but comfortable. Very *Santa Fe*." He laughed loudly at his own joke. Orvis chuckled; Rivers didn't get it.

Troy awkwardly pulled himself closer to the bar. The other two men seemed much more experienced in maneuvering the earthy seats. It was, however, surprisingly comfortable for a wood and leather concoction imitating furniture.

"I'll never forget my initiation up that devil's tower," said William Horace Green.

"Initiation?" asked Rivers, giving Orvis an incredulous look.

"Sure it's an initiation; he just doesn't bother telling you before he prods you up that pole."

"Of course, for Ho here," interrupted Orvis, obviously not wanting his strategies exposed, "it was a lot shorter climb. Are you going to order those beers? What did your friend in Denver say, Troy, 'Hey, I ain't no camel.' "

"Mexican or America's Fine Light?"

"Excuse me?" asked Troy Rivers, glad Orvis had changed the subject.

"They serve some excellent Mexican beers here, and Taos just started stocking America's Fine Light . . . Coors. I thought you were from Denver. Doesn't everybody in Denver drink Coors?"

"Right, Coors. I get it."

"So, what's your poison?"

"Actually, I'll try a Mexican. What do you recommend?'

"Travis," Green called the bartender, "tres Negra Modelo, con límon, por favor."

In the silence that followed, as they acquainted themselves with the cold beer, Orvis reacquainted himself with the room. A cordial piñon fire crackled in a genial fireplace which was designed like an horno, the organically round, tear-drop, adobe ovens used for baking bread. A dozen tables, also equipale, and Butaca chairs were randomly placed around the room—two at this table, four at that, only three over here. Orvis liked the cavalier attitude of the place. The natural hide seats were well worn and darkened to a rich sienna from years of posterior polishing. He liked equipale furniture. He had a dining set on his patio at home, a souvenir of his travels to the Southwest. He thought about the construction: how wet pigskin or leather was stretched over cedar frames, and allowed to dry, thus lend strength to the crosshatched armature. It reminded him of how architects design strength into skyscrapers—triangles.

The walls of the bar were thick adobe, painted white at some time in their distant past. The floor was comfortably uneven, made of terra cotta tiles, the main traffic areas worn and colorless in comparison to the reddish brown tiles under the loosely organized tables. Latillas—thin, sapling-sized shafts—ran in diagonal herringbone patterns between the large rough vigas in the ceiling. A few small windows, framed in course pine sills with peeling aqua blue paint, allowed an amputated view of the sidewalk and street outside. Hewed vertical posts, the same size and surface as the vigas bracing the ceiling, were place along the walls and throughout the room in the most inconvenient places as far as easy traffic and views were concerned. Simple scrolled corbels topped the posts to better distribute the heavy earthen roof. It was obvious that all of the interior elements were where they were, and what they were, for functional reasons and not stemming from some sort of dubious decorative decision. The environment was definitely primitive, somewhat vexing, nonchalantly clumsy, but amazingly human, comfortable, inviting, and cordial; too rough and aged to be called *quaint*; rather, it was natural and organic. Orvis thought, It's no Ship Tavern in the Brown Palace, but it's comfortable. If these walls could speak. . . . He turned back toward the bar when he heard Rivers open the conversation.

"Orvis tells me you're a painter," Rivers asked Green. "Will I get a chance to see some of your work?"

"Do you like paintings," asked Ho

"Well, I don't know anything about art, but I know what I—"

"Whoa, don't say it, counselor," interrupted the large man. "Let me show you some art, maybe even clue you in about what I'm doing, then you can decide whether or not you like it."

"So, I surmise that tired old cliché bothers you?" Troy asked.

"Yeah, sorry, it's almost as irritating as being asked to match my painting to the color of the carpet."

"Well, there is another one I'll avoid," said Rivers.

"Actually, if you want to learn something about what I do and maybe a little something about contemporary art, even Indian art, I'm making a quick run to my studio in Albuquerque to pick up some paintings, and drive back up to Santa Fe to drop them at a gallery. You're welcome, if you'd like to tag along. Orvis, it would give us a chance to talk some details about the powwow."

Orvis said, "I can't. I have to make a quick stop in Wyoming to finalize some things with our group there. Then, be back in Manhattan ASAP. We have some people from Japan flying in to check out a project in midtown—eighty-six stories. But Troy planned to take an extra day or two before the serious work starts.

"You guys can take me to the airport in Albuquerque and I'll catch a flight to Denver, connect to Wyoming, and red-eye to New York. I think a run with the ol' Ho here will prove productive. A couple of days in Santa Fe, a couple in Albuquerque, you can get some business done, meet some people, and see the sights."

"Did you see Patty in Fort Garland?" asked Horace.

"No, her office said she was on vacation. Be back tomorrow or the next day."

"That's too bad. I know she would love to see you."

"I'd love to see her, and I want her to meet Troy. Maybe on the return trip," said Orvis.

"That's going to be difficult," said Rivers. "You're flying north. You're not on the return drive. How will I know her?"

"You're right, Troy. I guess some things you'll have to do on your own."

"I'd go, but I have to have the work in Santa Fe," said Horace Green, "for an opening Thursday night; they need time to hang the show." He took on an exaggerated posture of importance and smiled his huge beacon, *The First Annual National Invitational, Indian as Artist Exhibition.*"

"My, my, sounds *impo'tent*," joked Orvis.

"Actually, it is—important that is," Green was serious. "It could prove to be a *very* important show. Anyway the sales potential is huge, big crowds; the Scholder Gallery gets handsome prices. And, I don't mind telling ya', I need a new pickup.

"Troy, I'd like you to see my studio, and I promised the sachem here some good New Mexican cuisine. I told Jake, one of the owners of the M and J Sanitary Tortilla Factory, to work up a special batch of carne adovada, 'Orvis is coming to town.' "

"Carne adovada?" asked Troy.

"A local delicacy—pork marinated in a red chili sauce. Something you can't get in upper state New York," answered Ho.

"Why don't we take the high road out of Taos; go through Chimayó and stop at Rancho de Chimayó for lunch. Troy can get his first taste of carne adovada there. Then we can compare it with Jake's the next day, but don't tell Jake. Hey, I can handle two doses," bragged Orvis. "You know what they say—a dose a day keeps the white doctor away."

"Pretty spicy, I take it?" asked Troy.

"Sí, muy picante, pero dulce, también."

"Qué? Dulce?" asked Troy.

They all laughed at his unconsciously asking "what" in Spanish.

"Sweet," answered Ho-Ho-Horace Green. "The mountain road is a scenic trip. You won't get to see much of the Rio Grande, but we go through several old, Hispanic, mountain villages. I guess it's OK; you'll see the other *civilized* culture in New Mexico, besides the Indi'n."

Rivers laughed and noticed an old, Taos Pueblo woman drifting as silently as a ghost toward the threesome. She had her blanket, red and worn, pulled over her head in the traditional manner, her weathered brown face peering from below the woven hood. She carried a tray of handmade jewelry, some with small bits of turquoise, some looked to be silver. She held strings of beaded necklaces, a few of glass, most of colored corn. They hung from her fingers. She said nothing, simply displayed her wares to the three men. Troy, not wanting any of the naïve art and not knowing what to do, turned his back on her.

Ho smiled and said, "No, gracious, mamacita. I have no woman whom to bless with your talents." He offered her a cigarette, which she took silently; he lit it for her. He pulled a cigarette from the pack with his lips and lit his own. They stood quietly and smoked together. She bowed, said nothing, and turned to approach what looked like a group of tourists sitting at the opposite end of the room. "Vía con Dios, madre," he said.

Troy watched her go and said, "I hate being solicited like that. I'm surprised she approached us. I mean, you look like a local and Orvis is obviously no tourist."

"It's what she does, Troy. That's her business. Besides, locals need a little body decoration occasionally. And, no offense, Ol' Orvis, despite that full head of gray sachem hair, is a tourist."

"Right," laughed Orvis. "And as a tourist, I can tell you: this is a lot different than getting approached by a vendor on the streets of Manhattan."

"You're right," said Troy. "I let my urban paranoia get the best of me. Should I go buy something from her?"

"Not unless you want something," answered Green.

"Besides," Orvis said, "she didn't solicit us. That's why she stood a respectful distance from us. She didn't want to invade our privacy. Ho invited her into our space when he spoke to her."

"Now I feel dumber than before," said Rivers. "I've got a lot to learn."

"Don't we all, Mr. Rivers, don't we all," answered Green. "You realize, of course, she didn't have any trouble picking us out as visitors because the three of us are kind of misfits."

"Speak for yourself," said Orvis. "You artistic types have always been considered a little strange."

"What do you mean, 'misfits,' " asked Troy.

"We're Apples," answered Ho-Ho-Horace Green.

"Apples?" asked Troy.

"Sure. Red on the outside and white on the inside."

"That's insulting, isn't it?"

"Depends on the individual," answered Green. "Don't get me wrong, and I hope I'm not insulting Mr. Kahnawake, my friend and art critic, but she could see that we had assimilated."

"Assimilated?" asked Rivers. "Into what? Who?"

"Apples. That's what I'm telling you. She's old school—ancestral, traditional. I went to an art school—contemporary, nontraditional. Oh, I'm still an Indian, but going to the art school, off reservation, even though it was an Indian school, it changes you."

"She could see you were a graduate from an art school?"

"No, not exactly. She could see that we had, metaphorically speaking, left the rez."

"That's true, you know," mumbled Orvis.

"I went to the Institute of American Indian Arts in Santa Fe, but even though all the students were Indi'n, it changes you. You go home afterwards, back to the reservation, back to your family; maybe it's because you're full of ideas, you think you can help; you know that there are things that could change, but you're impatient with the traditional slow pace for change; for all the right reasons you want to take a leadership role and share what you've learned. For all the wrong reasons it doesn't work. They feel that you've lost touch with the land and with *the people*. You've drifted from the circle. Do you know what I mean?"

Orvis nodded his head, "I've given him this speech already, Horace. We're starting to parrot each other."

Rivers remained quiet, listening.

"Anyway," Ho continued, "you're changed, not a lot, but just enough that you sense something is different, and of course, your family notices. They're just too polite to say so. I saw it first among older Ute friends who went to Fort Lewis College in Durango—on BIA scholarships. They tried to come back into Ignacio and help, but grew disenchanted. Maybe it was that the reservation was not as exciting as the White world. Like I said, maybe it was the pace, the polite old ways in which change is very, very gradual. I saw it happen to Sioux friends. There was actually discrimination between brothers on and off the reservation. I even saw a growing dissent between full-bloods and *breeds*. I have—because of my livelihood—been called an Apple to my face."

"In the 1700's," said Orvis, "we Haudenosaunee, in response to white schools ruining several of our Indian youth for anything good—skinning beaver, hunting deer, ambushing enemies—offered to educate several of their English sons and turn them into men. They neither accepted the offer nor sensed the irony."

"Well, I hate to disagree, gentlemen," said Rivers. His voice tense. "Well, actually I don't. I am not going to apologize for being a materialist. I like my car, my stereo, my condo, my Brooks Brothers suits, and I spend a hell of a lot of money on Italian shoes. Excuse me—moccasins."

"Whoa, pard, don't get pissed." responded Green. "That's why I said, 'the three of us.' We're not saying you have done anything wrong. No one is telling you to cut the seat out of your Polo chinos. We are just saying: if you are going to work with us and, more importantly, with our friends and brothers, you need to be aware that this traditionalist philosophy rears its head occasionally. I'm not giving up my painting. And I'm not going to paint traditional tribal images to satisfy the elders. Neither do I paint the Hollywood Indian image that White "chiefs" are comfortable with. I don't do romantic or sentimental."

"What do you paint?" asked Rivers.

"Well," Horace paused. "Well . . . it's ineffective to talk about one's art when you're not in front of it. I'll show you some work. I'd like for you to see it. And then we can talk. The point I'm trying to make without looking at the work is that traditional Indian arts and crafts—pottery, basketry, carving—is an extension of our, of their, oral tradition; it's a way of passing on historical knowledge. Therefore, according to the tribal elders, it would be inappropriate for an individual to metaphorically take possession of that knowledge, try to own it, and through unique expression keep it from his neighbors or, worse, change the meaning. So, traditional ways of doing things tolerate little revision. It's the same with pottery, baskets, and, consequently, with paintings."

"The exception is entertainment," said Orvis. "Storytellers often enliven their oration to make it engaging, but the crux of the story is still there; the heart, the history, the lesson are all intact."

"Right," said Horace. "Anyway . . . Western culture celebrates individuality. In the arts, Western schools and connoisseurs demand singular expression. Yes, we work with universal themes, but we celebrate a unique translation of such experiences. The Western world rewards an artist who can take a subjective truth of an objective reality and make it recognizable to an audience."

"That's easy for you to say," said Rivers.

"Right . . . this isn't the first time I have had to explain contemporary Native art to non-artsy audiences. Sorry about the pedantic prose. Anyway . . . we nontraditional *indigenous* artists live and work in paradox: we celebrate our heritage while at the same time forcing change upon it. Some of our fathers, brothers, and mothers, like that abuelita in the corner over there, forgive us. Others do not."

"Sometimes," said Orvis, "it's a tough balance, an ironic and troubling path. I made my living balancing on precarious iron beams in swaying towers, but later, when seeking a bigger success, being ambitious, rather than adhering to an unspoken and innate modesty professed by my heritage; you know, being satisfied with the role of a sanctioned worker, I made a wrong turn in the eyes of the elders. I wandered from the circle. Even today, I still stumble."

Horace continued, "Don't get me wrong. I volunteer to help with the powwows because I enjoy them. And I enjoy the people. I don't do it out of guilt. I serve on the Board of Directors of the Indian School, but I'll be honest with you, sometimes it's a little disconcerting to be called an Uncle Tomahawk. Even if I'm tainted, and I say that tongue-in-cheek, not forked-tongued," he looked over at Orvis for confirmation of the low humor, "I'll continue to contribute to my people my way. I can't give up my art. That's who I am, as much as my ancestry. I'm both, and, like you, Mr. Rivers, I'm not apologizing. And no one is asking you to atone."

"Fork-tongue," chuckled Orvis. "And 'Italian moccasins', that was pretty good too, kid."

Rivers relaxing again, shook his head as if in disgust, but revealed a slight smile, "You two are just alike—you both tell terrible jokes, you're pedantic and preachy, you're misplaced patriots, helpless romantics, obviously a couple of *rotten apples,* and you tell the worst puns I have ever heard. You know what that makes you, don't you?—really bad pun-*ditzs*."

"Oh, my god," said Ho-Ho-Horace Green. "He's one of us."

Chapter Twenty-seven

The High Road

Fall, 1963

El Santuario de Nuestro Señor de Esquípulas, nestles in the heart of the Hispanic, mountain village of Chimayó. It is considered among the most beautiful adobe chapels in the Southwest. Only Saint Francis in Rancho de Taos, with its huge beehive buttresses, is photographed or painted more often. Like Saint Francis, El Santuario is the pride of the community that maintains its organic vitality. Adobe churches seem to be living things. They breathe and sing and grow old and need the loving touch of human hands to heal them. In turn, they heal their parishioners—spiritually, and in rare places—physically. El Santuario is the chapel of the healing earth: esquípulas. Symbols of manifest miracles—cast off crutches, letters of prayer and penance, fetishes of blessings and gratitude, photographs and portraits of the miraculously healed—cover the walls of an entryway, leading to the room (a walled-in transept) in which a hole has been dug from the center of the dirt floor, optimistic handful by handful. Skeptics are quick to point out that the priests are forced to fill the hole each night with earth from some nearby source, or else, considering the tens of thousands of eager hands, the hole would now reach heretic lands on the other side of the earth, thus Catholic prayer creating a void right through the heart of The Beast, piercing the corazón de Tierra Madre—wouldn't be the first time.

The trio of apple Indians entered El Santuario from a small door on the side of the nave. It was probably a transept at one time, but divided into two small rooms and walled off from the main chapel. One room, the entryway, was crammed with attributions, ex-votos, and votive milagros: silver legs, hands, torsos, heads, and eyes filled display cases and hung from photographs, letters, and poetry left by parishioners or family members vowing faith and praying for healing. Many thanked and confirmed miracles. Orvis Kahnamake, perhaps a believer in miracles, lingered and read a few of the letters and prayers. He focused on the photographs of the faithful, searching for evidence or omen of why these particular individuals were granted their wishes, gifted their needs.

The walls of the next room were also crowded with ex-votos, milagros, and personal celebratory anecdotes, but the floor of this tiny room was dirt, and in the center lay the hole containing the healing earth. Ho-Ho-Horace Green, unofficial local guide, hurried Rivers through the small room—perhaps a nonbeliever. He had seen holes in spiritual places before. Every ancient kiva contained a sipapu, the hole from which humankind entered the surface world, the world of light. A painter, he wanted Troy to see the altar. The entry was so low from the transept room with the dirt floor and the hand-excavated hole, filled with esquípulas; it forced Troy to stoop and Horace inadvertently to genuflect. Kiva designers, it dawned on him, weren't *that* clever. As Rivers stood erect he saw the apse wall covered by an altar screen as tall as the ceiling. A dozen charming but unschooled paintings of crosses, saints, and simple designs representing drapery rose behind a common table serving as the altar, but covered with a drape of hand-done needlework: white and pure.

Ho gestured with an expansive arm toward the alter, "Look how elemental; not bad for a bunch of farmers, eh." He leaned on the hand-carved, hand-painted railing separating the nave from the sanctuary and altar. "I love the simple designs the best, the living crucifixes—so instinctive, so natural, totally unpretentious." He looked back into the chapel; it was empty for the most part. They had entered through the devotional rooms because a crowd of churchgoers lingered in the atrio, the walled-in yard in front of the mission church, and blocked the large wooden, double-door entrance. El Santuario was known as well for the hand-hewn doors as for the esquípulas. They were a favorite subject of photographers and artists. Ho knew they didn't have the church to themselves for very long. A couple of clergy were conferencing near the famous doors. The younger padre nodded recognition toward Ho. "The paintings are called retablos, they're done on wood panels, usually local ponderosa, and the sculptures are bultos. They are carved from cottonwood, gessoed, and painted. Local women make the clothes for the bultos. All of these you see, with the exception of the bulto of La Virgin de Guadalupe in the very center of the altar, are as old as the village."

Rivers acknowledged the information but remained silent and reverent. A unique and ancient aroma whiffed over him. He unconsciously interpreted it as the odor of centuries: tragedy, contention, survival; of aged cottonwood and ancient timbers, of fertile earth and dried adobe, holy incense and prayer candles. The light was dim; the chapel was softly illuminated by a clerestory, out of sight, and a few frugal incandescent bulbs hung unceremoniously from primitive wooden fixtures. Even from the interior, Rivers sensed the thickness of the adobe walls. He recalled the elegant tombs of Santa Croce in Florence, Italy and thought: The villagers could bury the devout in those adobe walls lengthwise with their heads toward the congregation so they could hear the sermon, and their feet to the exterior, warmed by the sun. He regretted his sarcasm when Horace informed him that the petitioners did indeed bury the pious under the floor upon which they stood. For a few paces his steps were hesitant.

Horace mentioned that a mass was about to begin, so he suggested they quietly leave and make room for the local worshipers. As they politely exited along the edge of the chapel, to allow a smooth entrance, Rivers thought he had transported back in time. A group of elderly women entered first. All were dressed in black and had black sarapes, bufanda, pulled over their heads and shoulders. The old men followed, each dressed in a black suit, and meekly carried a farmer's hat; the white lacquered straw a bright contrast to the dark suit. Rivers remembered old photographs of immigrant ancestors—weathered faces reflecting hidden sorrow, stiff poses, artificially calm, hands like leather, and the requisite black clothes. They were small, ceramic men bent by decades of hard labor, fired by the sun. And then, much to his surprise, large men dressed in blue jeans, wearing cowboy boots and bright colored shirts followed, towering above their *padres*. The *vatos* removed their stylish cowboy hats as they entered from the atrio. Several nodded to Horace in recognition and looked at Rivers with curious disdain. An attractive Hispanic woman wearing a bright colored, floral pattern scarf over her head bubbled as she recognized Horace. They stepped out into the atrio. Horace introduced her as Tina; she was an artist. Tina asked if Orvis was with them; she screamed delight when he appeared out of wings next to the entering crowd. She hugged Orvis and kissed him on the cheek. She continued to hold his hand as she invited them to stay for the mass. Horace begged off; she didn't hear him. Tina was focusing on Orvis. She beamed.

Horace gently led Rivers through the gates of the atrio and toward the dirt parking lot. "Tina's an artist."

"You said that," said Rivers.

"She's up from Albuquerque, visiting friends, probably. She has a friend here—Gloria Cordova, a santera, a wood carver."

"Bultos?" said Rivers, proud that he had remembered and seeking acknowledgement from Horace.

"Right! Bultos. You're a good listener, Rivers."

"Orvis seems to be listening to Tina pretty intently right now?" He was fishing.

"Yea, I suppose he is." He paused. "They're old friends; haven't seen each other for a while."

"She's very attractive." He continued to troll for information.

"Very." Horace offered nothing. "Well, what did you think of El Santuario?" but before Rivers could answer, he asked, "Are you hungry? I'm starved."

Tina and Orvis joined them. She again invited the threesome to mass. Horace thanked her but gave his regrets. He explained that they were doing the sightseer thing and more important issues than religious confirmation awaited these tribal tourists—food. She laughed and said that Horace never confused his priorities. She would suggest to her friend that they try to meet after the mass and catch up with the men at Rancho de Chimayó. Orvis walked her to the entrance of the chapel; they stood in warm, bright contrast to the dark cavernous nave. He left her there. She kissed him on the cheek again, reluctantly released him and waved at Ho and Rivers as she entered alone.

Rivers tried to start a conversation about Tina; Orvis immediately changed the subject. He explained to Troy that the cuisine at *Rancho,* where they planned to eat, was as famous as the church, and for him personally, more palatable than Catholic doctrine.

"Oh, I don't know, Orvis, Tina looked pretty *palatable* to me." He gave it one more try.

"The restaurant," said Orvis with an adroit sidestep, "had at one time been the main house of the hacienda of Manuel Jaramillo and his family. The Jaramillos have warmly offered their picante comida for several generations to neighbors and to strangers, alike. Now, in the mid-sixties, they offer their geniality to the paying customer. It was our very own Horace Green who introduced me to the Jaramillo's Nuevo Mexicano culinary delight. After his first plato of carne adovada, he called his friend in Nuevo York—yours truly. I was on the next flight to Albuquerque; Ho met me at the gate; the drive to Chimayó took about two salivating hours.

"In New Mexico I have two particular weaknesses: one red and one green. First—properly prepared Carne Adovada, usually an appetizing pomegranate in hue, and second—a bowl of green chile purveyed from the fields near Hatch. Chile verde is not to be confused with the spicy sauce for smothering Tex-Mex burritos," he face showed contempt, "or the chili con carne stew one can buy in a can—with or without beans. This is a delicate soup, prepared only for the purist, filled with the sweet-fire of roasted and peeled capsicums, pork pieces and eaten by sopping up the liquid with a flour tortilla, and in an emergency, as when one gets to the bottom of the bowl, with a spoon. Hatch chilies have for decades had the reputation for a unique sweetness balanced with an energizing combustible flavor—perfect for chile verde. Chimayó is famous for its red chile. Red and green are my two great weaknesses, but menudo, a soup made with tripe and fabled as a hang-over cure, runs a close third."

"Off-hand, Orvis, I'd say," said Rivers, "you like the stuff."

"Well said, young scout," answered Orvis with an uncharacteristic verve. The idea of adovada seemed to excite him. "My infrequent visits to Chimayó were balanced by a strategy more convenient to Ho's habitat. For the past few years, we adovada aficionados have depended for our frequent spice and fire fixes on the *sanctuary* of traditional New Mexican cooking—The M and J Sanitary Tortilla Factory."

"What the hell is a sanitary tortilla?" asked Rivers.

"It's just what it sounds like—a hygienic and uncomplicated, delicious tortilla—usually filled with an epicurean masterpiece. By a true turn of good fortune, Ho's studio is right across the road from The M and J. It's heaven on Second Street, in old industrial Albuquerque."

In fact," interrupted Horace, "Bea Montoya and her husband Jake not only serve as warm hosts for me and my artist friends, they gave me my first public art show. Local artists, the famous and not so famous, considered it a privilege to *hang* at The M and J."

"Horace," Orvis continued, "actually printed up an advertisement bumper sticker that said just that."

"Just what?" asked Rivers.

"Artists Hang at the M and J."

"Oh my, another ho-ho-horrible pun; didn't we talk about this?"

"Anyway," Orvis ignored Troy's chide, "As far as I'm concerned, my two favorite places to partake of carne adovada are Rancho, where we're going, and The M and J, on tomorrow's itinerary for you two."

"You'll be pleased to hear, Rivers," offered Horace, "that Jake liked my bumper sticker so well, he had T-shirts and baseball caps screened with the same saying."

"I can hardly wait," said Rivers. "Can I get a cap at the Rancho?"

"No. Rancho de Chimayó is classier than The M and J. You know, table clothes and matching silverware, but you can probably get a cookbook. As I said, it's a restored hacienda: has a great rustic feel, a cordial old bar, and a multi-tiered patio for outside dining in the summer. The Rio Quemado runs behind the place and keeps the desert air comfortable. The waitresses all wear ethnic skirts and blouses, are cute and prompt, and can help you *turistas* read the menu. Although, I have to admit, Rivers, your Spanish is getting better."

"Gracious, jefe."

"Although the comida is as delicious, the neighborhood for The M and J is in direct contrast to Rancho. Rather than a nearby church, the most famous, infamous, landmark is the Santa Fe Rail Road water tower. It's an important symbol to us Indi'ns. Infamous because of the many tragedies—murders, knifings, robberies, and such—taking place at its base and in the surrounding vacant lot. The area is like Larimer Street in Denver; you know, small taverns and shot-and-beer bars. They serve the transients, bums, disenfranchised veterans, lost Indians, and toughs who roam the surrounding barrios. It's the same old story: our brothers, angry at life's misdeal, fueled by alcohol, insult and murder one another instead of organizing an effective revolt."

"Hey, OK, the neighborhood's a little disreputable, but the rent is cheap. There are several artist studios around, and, of course, The M and J attracts the bankers and suits, construction workers, blue-collar guys, even women's clubs. If you're careful, it's safe. But Orvis is right. You don't leave anything of value in sight in your car and you don't walk around in the vacant lot or under the water tower. Treat the panhandlers with a little respect and they'll leave you alone."

The hostess at Rancho de Chimayó recognized Orvis and Horace and gave the threesome a good table, open to the fresh air of the patio but covered. Orvis ordered for everyone—platos picante, extra sopaipillas. Horace suggested that Rivers try the prickly pear margarita. An innocent looking, pinkish drink as sweet and refreshing as a snow cone.

Rivers, wanting to be a good sport, immediately dove into the bright meat, an earthy crimson, glazed with a rich marinate, viscous with an aroma of danger. Stabbings, thought Rivers, were supposed to be the menace of barrio Albuquerque, not of charming Chimayó; however, it only took a second for the stab of the adovada to inflame his tongue and ignited his lips.

"Speechless, aren't cha?" asked Orvis, noticing Rivers' wide-eyed expression. "It's that good, isn't it?"

Rivers looked for his water. Before either Orvis or Ho could warn him, he took a drink to extinguish the sweet red-chile fire.

"Too late," hummed Ho, shrugging his shoulders.

Orvis, torn off a piece of sopaipilla and handed it to Rivers, whose eyes were now flooding streams. "Water just makes it worse; here, eat this, it'll help."

Troy grabbed the larger piece of the fried bread sitting on Orvis' plate and ignored the small piece the man tried to hand him. He stuffed it into his mouth. Relief was not coming fast enough. He looked again at his water.

"*Au contraire*," Ho waved his finger.

"Good, huh?" asked Orvis.

"Tender!" interrupted Ho.

"Troy?" asked Orvis again.

"Tender," he squeaked, finally feeling some relief from the ambush.

"Try some of the posole. But be careful, this batch is just a little spicy."

"I'll pass." Rivers heard his voice, in contrast to his earlier reply, drop several octaves.

The waitress asked if everything was fine.

"Perfect," whispered Rivers as he raised his hand in an affirmative gesture.

"Would you care for another order of sopaipillas, or perhaps some sour cream?" she asked, smiling at the change in the color of Rivers' complexion.

"Don't you dare order any sour cream," demanded Orvis. "This ain't Texas."

"Some more bread would be nice," said Ho to the girl.

"What the hell is wrong with sour cream?" asked Rivers, recovering.

"Sour cream is for cowards. It kills the fire, but also diminishes the flavor."

"Oh yea, I'd hate to 'diminish' the flavor," said Troy.

"No, really, don't you like it?" asked Orvis.

Rivers carefully lifted a much smaller amount with his fork. He tentatively placed it toward the front of his tongue, chewing cautiously, with temperance, using just his front teeth. "Actually," he paused and reached instinctively for his water. Stopped immediately after making eye contact respectively with both men, and said, "It is quite tasty."

"And tender," added Ho-Ho-Horace.

Rivers lifted a larger folk full and followed it with a piece of the deep-fried bread. "It's good!"

"Bueno!" exclaimed Orvis and raised his hand, signaling the waitress. "Tres más margaritas, por favor," he sung as she approached.

"Sí, Señor," the song of her reply was more melodic than the Kahnawake baritone. She turned toward the bar at the end of the large brick patio where the bartender had already taken the cue and begun mixing the prickly pear concoction.

The threesome feasted. They ate until they hurt.

Rivers felt it an ironic sight—the CEO of a major East Coast construction company, a high-priced corporate lawyer, and a famous American artist packed tightly onto the bench seat of a rather rustic, 1950 Chevy pickup, poorly painted in a peeling turquoise blue. It was Ho's truck and he was driving, of course. Their choice of driver was additionally appropriate because Ho's added bulk, thought Rivers, probably allowed a reduced effect of the three rounds of margaritas.

"I usually don't drink like this," rationalized Orvis, "but the food tasted sooo good and it was sooo easy to wash it down with those cooold mar-grrr-ee-taz." He smiled, satiated.

"Yes," agreed Rivers, "it wath good."

"It certainly 'wath,' " chided Horace.

"I din say 'wath.' "

"Yeth, you did say 'wath,' " rebuked Orvis. "And I'm ath-shamed you can't hold your tequila any better than that."

"Look, I'll admit I have a little buzzth on, but I am not drunk and I did not say 'wath.' "

"Wath that a 'buzzth' I heard?" asked Ho-Ho-Horace.

"I think it wath a buzzth," added Orvis.

"Just becuth it wath a buzzth duth'nt mean I can't hold me margar-ee-tuth," laughed Troy. "So there, Cuz."

"It's a good thing you're driving," said Orvis to Horace.

"Well, I feel OK. I had several cups of coffee. You guys just kept eating those sopaipillas with honey. Too much!"

"Well," Rivers jumped in, "it did all tasth so good." Hearing himself he added, "Oh Chrith, here I go again."

"We'll stop in Santa Fe for some coffee and then head on in to Albuquerque," said the driver.

"Good idea," answered Orvis.

"I'll drink to that," giggled Rivers.

They passed El Santuario; Rivers leaned forward and looked past Orvis at the view of the church out the passenger side window. A large black crow perched on the steeple watchcd them pass.

"Maybe we should stop for some of that magic dirt, I may need some for my head after I sober up," said Troy.

"I have some magic pills in my glove compartment," said Horace.

"Indian drugs? Mescaline? Peyote?" asked Rivers.

"Aspirin," answered Ho. "I never go anywhere without them."

Rivers laughed and watched the small village of Chimayó pass by. Ho's driving seemed fine he thought.

Turning left just past Ortega's weaving shop, pulling past Trujillo's tiny rug studio, they headed downhill toward the town of Española. About four miles out of Chimayó a metallic-red Chevy Impala pulled off a side road in front of them. Troy noticed the car seemed too close to the ground. He also felt the Chevy was going too damn slow.

"Why don't you pass 'um?" he asked Horace.

"We're OK. This is his neighborhood. It's cool."

"His neighborhood?" questioned Troy. "I don't get it. We're practically in the woods here. I don't see any neighborhood."

"Trust me. It's his neighborhood. Look around, you can see a few adobes through the trees. The local people like to get away from the road noise if they can. We're in no hurry. Sit back and enjoy the scenery."

"What's wrong with his car?" Rivers asked, surmising that it was indeed only a few inches off the road.

"It's something kinda' new the locals are doing to big sedans. It's called a low rider. They chop out the factory suspension, replace it with a hydraulic suspension, and put on those tiny tires. Some of them turn into real art pieces. He is probably going down into Española to 'cruz' the North-South highway."

"At this piddling speed?" asked Rivers.

"Yeah, in town they go even slower."

"I don't get it."

"It's cool, man child. It's a creative way of expressing themselves. It's a way the local *vatos* identify themselves— *expresión artistico, qué no?*"

"You know," said Orvis, "no Anglo is going to do that to their car. It's a way of declaring an association. Why do all you people in the Brown Palace wear the same suits?"

"That hurt," said Rivers.

"You know what I mean."

"Yeth, Orvith," Troy exaggerated the lisp. "I was juth teathing."

"That's a nice set of wheels," said Ho.

"So, are these low rider guys gangsters?" asked Troy.

"*Pachucos*? No, not really," answered Ho. "They're not hoods or anything like that. Most of them are our age, but they do have an accelerated idea of territory. You don't come into their neighborhood and act rude. Besides, it takes a lot of money and work to turn a car into a low rider, not many kids can afford it."

As the impromptu parade approach the town, the cherry Chevy slowly pulled into the right turn lane and the plain pickup into the left so Ho could turn south toward Santa Fe. All three Indians turned to look at the Chevy. The driver wore a black straw fedora, dark sunglasses, and was slumped so low in his seat, the glasses were barely visible above the car door. With the slightest turn toward the truck, he appraised his audience. It was quiet for several seconds as the two vehicles waited for traffic to clear so they could make their respective turns. A heavy voice came from the car.

"Hey, Horace, man. That is one ugly pickup troque. Why don' you part with some of that *fierros* you make, Señor Arte, and let me paint it for you?"

Ho responded, "Qué pasión, Margoles. I didn't recognize your wheels."

"This piece of shit. No man, I am just delivering this *ranfla* to a friend. I did the paint, man, it's a *camello*, no se."

"That's no Camero," said Rivers quietly, "that's an Impala. Even I know that."

"Who's the pendejo?" asked the low rider.

"Me abogado," answered Ho, telling his friend that Troy was his lawyer.

"Qué lástima, vato. Are you in trouble again?"

"Sí, jefe, siempre."

"Se, también. Well, I got to turn norte here, vato. Wouldn't want to hold up the traffic. Call me when you want to paint that *rata raite*. *Chutear* the *cherife*, man. *Al alba, vato, al ratón*." He slowly turned into the double-lane road, in front of a probable rental car, forcing the tourist to abruptly slow down.

"Rata raite?" asked Orvis.

"He called this fine piece of American engineering a 'rat ride,' " answered Ho.

"That 'wath' pisthy," Orvis joked.

"Pith-er!" Rivers tried to best him. "What else did he say?"

"He was cool. Suggested I shoot the sheriff, and told us to be careful, catch us later."

"Nice guy," said Rivers.

The drive through Española was slow. Several other low rider sedans cruising the main thoroughfare entrapped them. A few going the opposite way recognized the pithy pickup and gave Horace the "high sign."

Horace and Orvis were very familiar with their route, but it was all new to Rivers. They had driven through alpine forests and isolated mountain villages; coming out of Chimayó they drove down a cool cañon cut by an ancient stream and emerged adjacent to badlands—a dry, inhospitable moonscape, filled with crooked, perpendicular popple towers of gray and beige sandstone, the remnants of prehistoric alluvium. They entered Española and the flats near the Rio Grande valley. Pulling out of the low rider capital of the Southwest, they headed the truck south and uphill, and were quickly surrounded by a rolling, dry sagebrush desert, climbing toward the top of the great plateau, upon which perched the historical town of Santa Fe. Horace dropped off the highway just before it turns into Saint Francis, passing the huge National

Cemetery, a rolling sea of white crosses, at the fork of Guadalupe and Paseo de Peralta, turned left, taking the latter. Paseo de Peralta is a cozy semi-circular road that skirts the perimeter of Santa Fe—a paved horseshoe to the north, east, and south. A little past half way, Ho made a left turn onto an even smaller street named Cañon Road, where the proportions of narrow streets and low adobe buildings gave Santa Fe its charm and geniality—human proportions, manifest in hand-done buildings, rounded corners, organic materials—far from the over-designed, the neo-classic banks and the pseudo-Bahaus glass towers of Seventeenth Street in Denver. No human grandeur challenging the sky was here. It felt more like a village inhabited by homes celestially celebrating the earth, harmonious with the ground—terrestrial.

"Every time I come into Taos and Santa Fe," said Orvis, "it makes me feel that maybe I have been going the wrong direction in my attempts to get closer to the Great Spirit. Maybe instead of going up as high as steel and my brother Mohawks can carry me, I should be going down, staying close to the Earth, building my walls out of mud."

"Its very warm, cordial I mean," said Troy Rivers.

"It does have its charm," laughed Horace. "take a good look, 'cause it won't be long 'till the tourists and the Hollywood crowd *discovers* it and they *Californicate* the whole place."

"Always the optimist," said Orvis.

"I need to stop by the gallery and let Fritz know I dropping off the paintings first thing tomorrow, OK?" asked Ho.

"Take as long as you need," replied Orvis. "I'll walk Troy down to the plaza, we'll meet you at La Fonda."

"Well then I'll let you out here; shorten your walk." He pulled over just after the intersection of Peralta and Cañon.

In a short time the two men were walking west along Alameda Street next to the Santa Fe River, a trickle to their left. Two flat-topped, unfinished Romanesque church towers loomed above the trees to the northwest. Orvis guided them onto a side street, Cathedral, and they walked toward the sonorous song of church bells. Just before reaching the church they made another left onto San Francisco Street and continued for half-a-block.

The portal to La Fonda hotel was a large turquoise blue, double door, down a long hall, the floor of which was large irregular stone tiles. The bar was dark and small. So they chose instead to sit in a large interior patio, opened to the sky, soaked in sunlight, bordered with large plants. They took a seat at a table in the direct sun. Troy leaned back in his chair, basking in the warmth, feeling his cheeks and chin flush in just a few minutes. With his eyes still closed to the bright light, he ordered a Mexican beer, "Whatever you've got that's dark." Orvis ordered an iced tea, anticipating the drive to Albuquerque, his flight east, and doing business tomorrow. Continuing to drink would only exasperate jet lag, but he did suggest a *Dos Equis* to the waitress for Troy.

"Bueno," mumbled Rivers to the sun, acknowledging the recommendation. "Man, this sun feels great."

"You need to be careful there, Apollo. This Santa Fe sol can quickly bake you."

They sat quietly through the time it took Troy to slowly drink the first beer. He would lean forward periodically and take a sip and then return to his basking. Orvis enjoyed the quiet, the warmth, and reminiscences of past trips and past afternoons in the enchanted light of New Mexico.

Noticing his dark glass bottle was empty Troy leaned forward to the table and said in a contented voice, "Shall we order another?"

"Sure, but I'll stay with the tea. I don't want to have to sober up on the plane. You go ahead. Try some of this salsa." A basket of fried tortillas and a brown earthen bowl of red and green chopped vegetables had magically appeared on the table during Rivers' semi-siesta.

He shoveled the pulpy salsa onto a chip. "Umm, that's great!" As he reached for another tortilla the latent fire of the diced tomatoes, onions, and chilies hit him. "Wow . . . picante!" He looked at Orvis as his eyes suddenly watered.

"Yeah, but good, right?"

"Déjà vu!" He put down the chip and reached for his beer. The bottle was still empty. He looked around for the waitress; she stood stoically between two of the large palms near a busing station.

Troy waved the bottle in the air. She grabbed the pitcher of iced tea and approached the table.

"Would you care for another beer, Señor?" she asked as she filled Orvis', translucent blue tea glass. It made a deep ringing sound as the ice cubes ricocheted off the sides.

"Sí, señorita, uno mas cerveza, por favor, y muy pronto, por favor. La salsa es muy, muy picante." said Troy.

Orvis laughed at Rivers putting together a full sentence in Spanish. "Well I said it before, but your Spanish is getting better. It's amazing what you can do in an emergency."

Rivers continued to engulf chips. Once the panic was diminished, he lightly dipped another into the salsa, more carefully, selectively digging out only a piece of onion and tomato. "Tasty," he mumbled through a mouth stuffed like a chipmunk.

The waitress delivered two beers. "Señorita, muchas gracious, but I only ordered one cerveza," said Troy.

Sí, Señor. It is now Happy Hour—two for one."

"Orvis, would you like one of these?" he asked.

"No, thanks. I'll stay with the tea."

"Well, leave them, señorita. I'll save one for Ho." He took the nearest beer, took a sip to cool his palate. Risked another dunk of salsa, took a large gulp of the smoky sweet liquid and leaned back, basking again. He spoke to the sky, "This is great, Orvis, I'm really glad I came down here with you. I wish you didn't have to go back so soon."

"Duty calls, kiddo. We all do what we have to. It's a dirty job but. . . ."

"Somebody's got to do it." It was Horace. He walked up to the table carrying a beer in each hand. "Orvis, would you like one of these? I guess it's Happy Hour."

"No thanks, Ho."

"Hey, Ho, how did it go?" asked Troy in a sing-song rhythm.

"I see Mr. Rivers already knows it's Happy Hour."

"Have some salsa," said Rivers, remaining perched at a forty-five-degree angle, his face in the sun, his eyes closed.

Orvis and Horace talked quietly about the gallery and upcoming exhibit. Troy listened half-heatedly, treading that mid-ground between a sun induced sleep and comfortable consciousness.

Eventually his thirst brought him back to the table and the conversation of his friends.

"Man I feel great. I haven't been this relaxed in years." He raised his bottle in a toast. "Muchas gracious, amigos. I think I have found one of the fabled cities of gold. This just may be heaven."

"Careful, scout," teased Orvis, "when one finds heaven so easily, El Diablo usually is waiting just around the corner. Don't forget, Señor Turista, there is still some work to be done on this trip."

"Sí, jefe. Mañana," he laughed at his own joke as he took another drink of the Dos Equis, another tortilla spade full of salsa, and reached for his next beer. It was still cool and he felt a comfortable anesthesia ease over him.

"Jesus, Orvis," said Horace, "He's gone native on us. Have we created a monster?"

Orvis reached over and put his hand on Troy's forehead as if checking for a fever. "He's alive, he's alive." He waved his hands in the air in mock celebration. "But seriously," he said to Troy, "your head does feel hot. You *do* need to be careful of this sun."

Rivers took both hands and felt his cheeks, "I see what you mean." He leaned his elbows on the table. "Well, are we in a hurry, or should we have one last beer?"
He waved the bottle and the waitress acknowledged the gesture.

"As I recall, you had a pretty good night your first time in this patio, Uncle Orvis."

"Oh?" asked Rivers.

"Yeah, pretty good," laughed Orvis.

"Tell me about it," said Rivers.

"Well, we had a meeting of several of the organizers for the various powwows all over the Southwest. Ho invited a few of his artist friends, a few locals dropped in, and I guess we had kind of an impromptu party."

"I'm not much of a party guy, myself," Troy laughed as the waitress delivered four more beers.

"The patio was cleared of furniture for some reason. It wasn't set up as a restaurant—just a few tables, a couple chairs around, you know. Anyway, we all sat around on the terraced stairs right over there by the long hall. An artist friend of Ho's named Frank

McCullough magically conjured up a guitar and started singing these Mexican *canciónes* in authentic Spanish. You know, folk songs."

"Sure, *canciónes*, I think my high school Spanish is coming back," answered Troy.

"He looks like Don Quixote," said Orvis, "gaunt, lean, a goatee, balding—distinguished looking and talented as all get out."

"A lot of clueless folks," said Horace, "think he is Anglo— McCullough and all. He is, but his family comes from the earliest traders on the Santa Fe Trail hitching up with local landed Hispanics. His wife's family had an original Spanish land grant. He's got more history and kinship to New Mexico than any gringo, particularly the pretentious artists from *Tejas* and the tourists trolling the pottery galleries on the plaza, looking for bargains on trinkets, turquois and those obnoxious blue coyotes. As far as the historic American government and the old *comandantes de Nuevo Méjico* were concerned the early traders were outlaws and invaders. They'd lock 'um up in the hoosegow or hang 'um if they could for selling pots and pans. Frank, to his credit, has upheld, celebrated even, that desperado spirit . . . with vigor, I might add."

"That's *verdad*," laughed Orvis.

"He writes poetry in Spanish and plays the guitar like a *trovador*. But he also creates these atmospheric paintings that give sacrament to the mysterious landscape and light of New Mexico. Hell, he hangs next to Georgia O'Keeffe in the art museum. Sorry, I didn't mean to interrupt. Go ahead, Orvis."

"It's OK, you described him well. So, Frank sings several songs, putting everybody in a great mood. And then we all took turns. A couple of people tried to play the guitar and sing folk songs, but they can't entertain like Frank. But, you know, we are all having fun, nobody cares. So it comes to my turn. I don't play the guitar and sure don't know any folk songs. So I start this chant. Ho and the other Indi'ns in the group start drumming on anything at hand— tables, chairs, the floor, their chests, you know. Anyway, it builds and builds and leads into quite a ceremony. All of the sudden this gorgeous female Indi'n artist jumps up and starts dancing. Several of the other women join her in a line. All very elegant. And then," he took a drink of his tea. "Then this young kid named Alexie Grant jumps up and goes into his fancy dancing routine. The drummers instinctively adjust the percussion. And let me tell you, this kid is good. You'll meet him. So, anyway, the rest of the night we're all taking turns, I mean it was the only time I witnessed a true integration of the so-called tri-culture down here. The Nuevo Mexicanos singing songs and playing the guitar, the Anglos tickled the hell out of all of us by switching from folk songs to rock and roll and Broadway show tunes, and several of them act out some of the theater antics. We Indi'ns chanting and singing and drumming, and everybody dancing like crazy."

"You're not telling the best part, Mr. Modesty," chided Horace.

"What are you not telling?" Rivers asked.

"Ho is teasing. There was a young lady artist that took sort of a liking to me. But he's inappropriate."

"Took sort of a liking; that's an understatement," continued Ho.

"A young lady—I must say, Orvis, I'm surprised. A father figure such as yourself, a family man and all." Rivers teased.

"An authority figure, yes, Mr. Rivers, and don't forget who's paying your stipend. Always a family man. But it's not as bad as it sounds. You probably didn't know, but I lost my wife twelve years ago."

Rivers was suddenly serious, "I'm sorry, I didn't know. I didn't mean to jest."

"It's OK. You had no way of knowing. It's Ho who's acting like a horse's ass."

"Oh, Orvis, you know I only tease you because I'm jealous of all the attention the young ladies give you. It must be the gray hair. He is too modest to brag, Rivers, but the two most important women in Orvis' life are here in the Southwest. You met one, and just missed meeting the other. Right?" He looked to Orvis for confirmation.

"It could be that they sense a good soul, Horace. Something you could work on."

Horace made the mistake of taking Cerrillos Road away from the plaza and toward the highway to Albuquerque. He wanted to show Rivers where he went to school. Traffic was heavy; the going slow. A combination of the altitude, the warmth of the day, the heat on his face, the rhythm of the engine, and the several beers lulled Rivers to sleep. He dreamed of Times Square, of flying high above the bright Coca Cola sign and the noisy traffic jam; he dreamed he could smell Nathan's hot dogs and "street" pizza. And as he flew higher—above the sky scrapers, looking at the setting sun reflected in gold on the surface of the amber rivers and the pthalo-green ocean—a black, sable-eyed raven flew next to him.

Chapter Twenty-eight

Rios En Infierno

Fall, 1963

When the sun sets in Albuquerque, the western slopes of the
Sandia Mountains explode in a vibrant red, and while viewing them
from the west bank of the Rio Grande one can pick out small patches
of gold and silver vibrating with a solar rhythm within the crimson
curtain of stone. The jewels are the windows of homes and other
buildings hidden among the junipers and crevasses of the peaks. The
entire landscape seems to hum from the radiant energy of the
maturing day. All of the mountains in New Mexico ripen to red at
journey's end—The Sangre de Cristo, for example, darken in
consolation to the mournful maroon of sacrificial blood.

Troy Rivers' face was almost as red as the mountains in the
setting sun. Earlier, while peaking through the open roof of the
cantina of La Fonda, the sun had taken advantage of the thin air and
high altitude of the Santa Fe Plateau and seared Rivers' citified
paleness. He awoke, still sitting between Ho-Ho-Horace Green,
driving Ol' Blue, his trusty pickup, and Orvis Kahnawake, riding
shotgun.

"I feel like I've been eaten by an aardvark and shit on an ant
hill," mumbled Rivers. He reached to rub the sleep from his eyes.
"Ouch," he cried and rose quickly in front of the rearview mirror
investigating the source of the pain. "My god!" he said with surprise,
"who painted my face?"

"The Santa Fe sun, son," laughed Orvis.

"What tribe did you say you were?" teased Horace, "The
Brule'd Lobsta'?"

Troy looked around and somehow sensed they were heading east toward the Sandias and not south toward Albuquerque as he expected. "Tell me, you coyotes, are we heading east?"

"Well done, sleepy scout," answered Ho. "We had a little time before Orvis' flight so I ran an errand on the west side of town. Picked up a couple of framed drawings I had on loan. I want to put them in the exhibit. You slept through the stop. We didn't wake you. You looked so comfortable leaning on the seat with the sun on your face, figured you wanted a little more time to tan."

Rivers looked in the mirror again, "Thanks. I'm glad my pain is amusing. Why do I have white line on my forehead?"

"We laid my key chain on your forehead. It blocked the sun; left a pale silhouette. You know, like a streak of war paint—a chevron. Now we can call you Chief Chevrolet."

"War paint!" snarled Rivers. He looked in the mirror to confirm the chevron.

"You already had a good burn from Santa Fe," said Horace. "We were afraid it wouldn't show, but I think it came out, don't you Orvis?"

"It wasn't my idea, Troy. Horace has a mean streak. I have to tolerate him sometimes. Don't worry, it'll be gone by tomorrow. It barely shows." He wore a patronizing grin.

Horace said, "To me, it looks more like a pulsating vein in your forehead than war paint. I wouldn't want you mad at me."

"I am mad at you." Rivers looked in the mirror, turning left, then right, viewing his total scald. "I suppose I deserve this: immersing myself in the local color too deeply, too soon. But just remember, Horace Green, we lawyers don't stay mad, we get even."

"Orvis, did that sound like a threat to you?" asked Horace.

"I believe it was," said Orvis. "I can't tell you how pleased I am that you boys are getting on so famously. It makes a father proud."

Rivers joked, "Are we there yet, dad. I have to go to the bathroom and I don't mind telling you: my mouth tastes like I've been eating monkey droppings."

"Well tough it out, warrior, we're on our way to the airport." Horace exited Highway 40 and pulled back onto south Interstate 25. As they passed the exit sign for Coal and Lead Streets Horace mentioned that his studio was just below them, across the bridge. It wasn't long and Rivers noticed an exit sign for the airport.

"Well, Orvis I feel bad . . ." started Rivers.

"I'll bet you do."

"No, I mean I feel physically rotten, but I feel it's my fault we didn't get to talk much business."

"Not to worry, hijo. Ho here can answer any questions you might have. It was more important to me that we got you out of those awful striped ties, you know. And god knows, now you look a hell of a lot more like a red man."

Rivers ignored the joke. "Well, anyway. I guarantee I'll get on the job after you fly out."

"It ain't over yet," Kahnawake laughed. "Relax, Troy. It's been a good trip so far. It's been awhile since I enjoyed the sights and swapped stories at La Fonda. I miss it. You men should continue to enjoy yourselves. It's important that you experience the local color, and Horace will introduce you to some of the committee members with whom you'll work in Denver. Besides, you need to check out those wild paintings for which crazy people pay him money."

Horace suggested they walk Orvis into the airport. He parked the truck in a short-term lot. They lifted the bags from the back of the truck, putting Rivers' luggage in the cab and locking the doors. Each of the younger men carried one of Kahnawake's bags. They stopped at a redcap station on the ramp outside the entrance and checked the suitcase and the garment bag. Orvis carried his attaché. They waited as he checked in and got his seat assignment. All three strolled toward the gates.

As they passed an airport bar, Orvis asked Rivers, "Care for some hair of the dog?"

"Oh, man, I really shouldn't. I've had too much fun already." He raised both hands and pointed to his face.

"Ouch," said a uniformed stewardess walking in the other direction.

"It'll probably make you feel a little better until you can get something on that sunburn," answered Orvis. "Besides, it's too late to try and make a good impression on me."

Horace had turned and watched the flight attendant walk away, "Chief Red in the Face made an impression on that pretty lady."

"Ho," Rivers asked, "are you going to have anything?"

"Yeah, I'll have a beer. I don't want you drinking alone, Rojo."

"Well then, OK—just a beer to wash this simian coating off my tongue."

They sat at a small round table, too small for the three beers, and talked about business in general terms. After Troy Rivers took a large slurp of his beer and sloshed it around his mouth, he nursed the rest of the brew. He felt it appropriate to demonstrate to Kahnawake that he wasn't ordinarily the lush who acted like a college kid on spring break. Orvis gave no sign whether he noticed Rivers' temperance or not. Troy diligently took notes on a bar napkin. Horace had heard and done it all before; he watched the women walking the concourse. After half-an-hour, they strolled with Orvis to his gate.

"I hope you are not regretting this afternoon, Troy. I was serious, you know, when I said it was time to take off your tie and enjoy yourself."

"Well, I appreciate your saying so, Mr. Kahnawake. I didn't expect to enjoy myself this much. I'm glad we had a chance to travel together."

"Yeah, Mr. Kahnawake," chirped Horace. "I don't think you have anything to worry about. I'd say the kid fits right in. And don't worry, I'll be watching out for him from now on."

"Watch your back, Troy," said Orvis, "and don't forget why his mother named him."

"You didn't tell him that story, did you?" asked Horace.

"He told me everything, Horse's Ass," interrupted Rivers.

"Oh, Orvis, you know it's bad luck to speak a tribal name; you'll tempt the fates by talking about another Indi'n like that."

"Listen, Troy," Kahnawake's tone became more serious. "I'm going to claim a little privilege via my seniority for just a minute. I believe this is indeed, you know, an important trip. We can talk business anytime; I'm good at controlling an agenda when need be. As I've said before, I considered this more of a recruiting trip than a business trip. I'm wily enough to know that you are going to be more sensitive to the subtleties of our needs if you better understand our constituency. This rascal Green can set you straight on the powwow business. My mission is as the evangelist and I'm too old not to connive once in a while."

"Once in a while?" laughed Horace.

"Don't worry, Mr. Kahnawake, it wasn't a well-hidden agenda. I told you before, I enjoy your stories and your tutelage."

"*Turtlege*," said Ho.

"What?" asked Rivers.

"Turtlege—teaching from the turtle clan."

"Enough with the puns, already."

"Anyway," said Orvis, "as an old sachem and a modern CEO, I'm used to giving advice. You'll have to forgive me, but I could not forgive myself if I did not try to enlist you and your talents into the reverse migration, into the revival of Indi'n pride. Don't forget, Hijo Rojo, your drift from the sacred circle was different from us two sour apples. Forgive the *jeu de mots*, but you have always *traveled to a different drummer*. Your life's chant took an albumen course before you knew there was a cultural dichotomy. There is no fault in that. My concern is, and here's where I am taking advantage of seniority, now that you've learned of the two worlds, you have yet to acknowledge a need for a personal balance between your heritage and your vocation."

Rivers tried not to look like the chastised schoolboy, but judging by Kahnawake's change in tenor, he knew that he was unsuccessful.

Orvis' energy rose, "You want so badly to be a champion!" He paused, probably surprised by his sudden zealousness. He continued calmly, "So, if you continue with us, this old Indi'n and this reprobate artist, we will challenge your reluctance. We will tutor the warrior. I give you fair warning." He paused, Rivers tried not to but squirmed. Orvis looked to Horace for some sign of confirmation.

Green's eyes simply smiled. Orvis decided to go on.

"I'm not sure this is going the way I wanted." He looked again at Green.

"You started it, Monsieur Black Robe, Mr. Missionary, you finish."

"Thanks for your help. What I'm trying to say is—just listen to your soul; it's a good one and worth saving. I'm a pretty good judge of people, so trust me." He obviously decided the didactic approach was making people uncomfortable, so he concluded, "And stay out of the sun."

They all three laughed; Troy's chuckle just slightly patronizing—a courtesy laugh. Kahnawake recognized it immediately.

"You know, kid, I told you I was going to try to recruit you."

"It's not a problem, Mr. Kahnawake. Orvis. I appreciate your concern." Rivers was sincere. "I've enjoyed the trip. And as you said, 'It ain't over yet.' "

"Thank you for being patient, Troy," answered Orvis. "Well, that's last call to board the plane." He started toward the uphill ramp leading to the movable gateway. Noticing the steep ramp, he turned and said, "Just remember, hermano. You must climb before you can fly."

"Adios, Orvis," said Horace.

"Vaya con Dios, Ho. Hágoónee´." He paused. The red reflected light of the Sandia sunset shown through the end of the tunnel walkway. It rebounded over the fuselage of the airliner through the spaces where the accordion bridge was not flush against the plane. The white walls of the tunnel glowed crimson and the light from the interior of the plane created a bright spot in the middle of the red corridor. A dark silhouette stood in the doorway, waving a hand and beckoning Orvis to enter.

Troy and Horace waited until an airport employee closed the double doors to the ramp, cutting off the radiance.

"I need to get to the studio and load some paintings," said Ho interrupting the moment. "And I promised Orvis that I'd treat you to your second dose of carne adovada at the M and J Sanitary Tortilla Factory. We had best get going if we want to beat the crowd."

"The M and J it is, but I'm not sure about the adovada. I'm still hurting from Chimayó, and I have one hell of a late-day hangover."

"The adovada can cure that. Or maybe—say, have you ever eaten menudo?"

"Menudo? Orvis mentioned menudo. What is it again?"

"Tripe." He paused with a smug smile. "Pig intestines in chile verde. It's great for a hangover."

"You know, that adovada doesn't sound so bad after all."

They parked in a dirt lot just south of an old two-story building on Second Street, between Coal and Lead—both boulevards named after two of Albuquerque's fledgling commercial endeavors. The M and J glittered across Second like a misplaced Christmas package. The A T & SF water tower squatted at the northeast corner of the lot—an ominous silhouette. The lurking, silent giant was a famous landmark; made famous by local authors like Rodulfo Anaya, and harking back to the frontier history of Albuquerque. Made *infamous* because it was a homing beacon for bums and railroad vagabonds, disenfranchised Indians, or out of luck Mexicans, who ended up killing each other in planned larceny, drunken arguments, or spontaneous mayhem.

It wasn't unusual for seven or more murders annually. Horace had mixed feelings about the murders. He was averse to the violence, but the lethal reputation of the neighborhood kept his rent low. It also discouraged the urban renewal developers from invading with condos. He didn't ignore the violence—he chose to address it through his art. A street-smart Horace knew that if one didn't go out looking for trouble, one could usually avoid it. Besides, he was a large man, well-liked locally, and the tourists frequenting the M and J were easier pickings for the beggars and muggers. Ho felt right at home.

Aged green tiles created a checkerboard pattern on the front of the building housing his studio. The decor was dated, too old to discern. The color either had faded to *bile* or was in reality an extension of the architect's original bad taste. Troy peered through the large picture windows between two doorways. To his left was the main entrance to the building—a large, double glass door. Considering the neighborhood, it looked extremely vulnerable. In contrast, to his right was a solid, metal reinforced door at which Ho wrestled with a crowded key ring. Ho got the heavy door open and held it for Troy to enter. A narrow and tall, unpainted, poorly lit, claustrophobic stairwell greeted him. In his delicate state, the climb up the stairs was exhausting. He waited at the top of the straight, two-story staircase, wishing there had been a respite half way. Ho fumbled with his keys again, trying to lock the street door from the inside. Horace finally bounded up the stairs and wrestled with the keys all over again at another door at the top of the stairs. Hopefully this led to the studio; Rivers' legs were tired. Finally, it opened. Ho held the door and gestured for Troy to enter. The room was dark, but Rivers could see the faint glow of two walls of tall exterior windows. He could also see that the ceiling was high, probably fourteen or fifteen feet. The silhouettes of rectangular paintings sat on a variety of easels throughout the large room.

"Hold up," said Ho. "Let me get the lights."

"No problem," answered Rivers. He wasn't about to lead the way into a realm about which he knew nothing.

Horace reached around the doorjamb and in a familiar movement slapped the switch. Long rows of florescent lights suspended from the ceiling blinked in a spasm and eventually illuminated the room in a greenish glow. Even under this unnatural light, Horace's colorful canvases suddenly brightened the space. "This light is no good to paint by," he said as he rushed over to a vertical bank of aluminum scoop fixtures and pushed the toggle switch at each base. As the incandescent light flooded the nearest canvas the reds became *more* bright, the blues more saturated, the yellows more intense. Ho repeated the ceremony with five other paintings. The rich colors grew to full saturation once the florescence was overpowered.

"You do like color, I'll say that," said Rivers.

"Too much, you think?" asked Horace with sincerity and concern.

"Horace, you know what I know about art—nothing. I didn't mean it as a criticism. I like the color. It's just so much brighter than anything I've seen."

"Yeah, well you're right. I do like color." He ran over and turned out the ceiling fixtures. The paintings took a final step toward the pure spectrum.

Troy silently wandered from canvas to canvas. Even as a novice he could see that Green was celebrating paint. It was applied thickly, opaquely in wide swatches. The artist allowed drips of one color to spot and speckle a rectangle of another hue, each as intense as the other. "You like paint, too," said Rivers.

"Right."

"These aren't like paintings of Indians I've seen. They're huge and it looks to me like some are meant to be frightening? Am I right?"

"Absolutely."

Rivers waited for him to say more, but nothing came forth. He continued to move from painting to painting. After he had perused each, he stood in the middle of the studio and pivoted around, looking from a distance. "Well, Ho, you're no romantic—not as a painter anyway. These are not paintings of the noble savage. No one is going to accuse you of idealizing the Indian. I sense negativity here. Violence. Am I right?"

"Good eye," he walked toward a painting. It was of the upper torso of an Indian, wrapped in a blanket, pulled tightly over his shoulders, covering his neck and chin, creating a jagged diagonal across the subject's cheek. The head was tilted and not quite a full-face. The features had been simplified, almost into a skull, the large eyes vacant but burning. A single feather, as loosely and aggressively painted as the blanket and face, sat more like a dagger blade slammed into the crown of the Indian than a badge of honor slipped into the hair. The blanket resembled a dirty and bloody flag, stripes and stars barely discernible beneath the physical brush strokes. "A lot of people say I paint ugly Indians, that I hate Indians." He paused, waiting to see if Rivers would respond.

"Well, Horace, they *ain't* pretty." He looked again at a particularly disturbing canvas that seemed to have an anguished body slapped diagonally across the bottom of the format and a somewhat demonic dog standing above the cadaver. The paint drips in this one looked almost as if they represented splatters of blood. "But I don't think they are paintings about hate. It seems to me, and like I said, you know what I know about art, but it does seem to me that you are depicting what has happened to Indians—tragedy, not hate."

"You're doing okay, Rivers. A local critic called them *Indians as Aliens*. He was pretty close. Indians have been alienated—often violently. Homes have been destroyed; a way of life exterminated. I suppose that's as good an explanation as any. That one you're looking at is called *Canícula.*"

Rivers looked puzzled.

"*Dog Days.*" answered Horace.

"So, he's been murdered? And the *Dog Days*, I take it, refers to being struck down like a dog, or living a dog's life—a life filled with disappointment, unfulfilled, until finally it ends—unacknowledged? Or maybe even murdered by a dog soldier?"

"You got it better than a lot of people. See there, if you give yourself a chance, you do know more about art than you think. One just has to open one's mind in order to interpret artistic expression. Not bad, Rivers."

"What's this one called?"

"*Dancer.*"

The image was of an Indian in costume, but the figure was heavy, painted in thick lines and impasto, much too heavy to dance. Some gigantic weight obviously burdened the man, and he was forced to stand in the center of the painting, mired in a background of blood red, scrubbed with large brushes, each leaving the physical trail of the violent attack by the artist.

"They're frightening, Horace, but very effective. They make you think."

"That's good. Art is supposed to be a form of communication. It's supposed to express those ideas or experiences that are difficult to express literally—things too horrible or too important, or what the hell, sometimes too sublime, to trust to verbal language. Of course, *sublime* doesn't describe my paintings. As you noted, I'm not much into 'pretty.' I do think, however, they say something that definitely needs saying, even if the message is not *pretty.* A lot of the art you see in Santa Fe and Taos frustrates me. The most popular is by white guys painting these beautiful Indian maidens. Every Indi'n woman is Pocahontas or Sacagawea or some Cherokee princess. I get tired of all the guys copying the noble savage bronzes done a century ago by Remington and Russell. They haven't added one thing to art, haven't said anything about *their* time and *their* place. They perpetuate the romantic fable about the Old West, and the Hollywood nonsense about cowboys and Indians."

"Orvis and I walked by a larger than life bronze on the way to La Fonda. It was an Apache crouched over as if spying on the enemy. I have to admit, he was a pretty handsome guy."

"That's what I'm talking about."

Rivers spoke in an exaggerated Jewish accent, "Some of my best friends are Apache." He paused, waiting for Horace to laugh. He didn't.

Ho went on, "Yeah, well some of my best friends *are* Apache, and I can tell you, all are not good looking. Some of my Ute brothers fart once in awhile, and have B. O. They can't ride a horse for shit, let alone bareback in a loincloth."

Rivers laughed, "Talk about pain."

"Are you kidding me! Sorry, I preach too much. I should let the paintings do the communicating. But sometimes, you just have to speak out against the rampant commercialism cramming local galleries."

"It's not a problem. I asked. And I really *do* want to know."

Green walked over to a vertical storage rack filled with canvases wrapped in a translucent paper. "I'll show you a painting that actually got me in a lot of trouble. He pulled a canvas from the rack that looked to be four feet in height and six or seven feet long. He unwrapped it and the paper fell to the floor.

Rivers could see the painting was divided into three sections, each two to two-an-a-half feet in width. The center panel had a school of elegant black and white fish with long trailing ventral pendants flowing behind them. Rivers recognized them from a vacation in Hawaii.

"Do you know these fish?" asked Horace.

"Sure," he answered, "They're called Moorish Idols."

"Right. Do you recognize the guy in the left section?"

"Can't say I do."

"Well, there is no reason why you should unless you are involved in the Southwest art scene. He's an Indian painter who lives north of here. He's made his living perpetuating the myth of the beautiful Indian maiden. He sells like crazy, but he's also the local celebrity drunk. It's sad really. As a young artist, in my opinion, the guy had a lot of talent. But he hit on something that sold, mostly to Anglos, and now you see his stuff in every damn motel room and restaurant from here to Chicago. I'm talking posters, calendars, cookbooks, coloring books for kids, playing cards, you name it; his maidens are on it. There are rumors that he doesn't even do his own work anymore, that he has apprentices do it. Anyway, as you can see, it's a rather unflattering caricature of him. Do you recognize the woman on the other side?"

"Sure, it's what's-her-name, the sexy little entertainer who just married the rich guy. Didn't he buy a television station for her or something, so she could have her own variety show? Wasn't it a flop? Barely lasted a season as I recall, followed by a handful of disaster movies. Mia, Pia, Tia, Zia, something like that?"

"That's her. Anyway, this was my first painting accepted in a local Indian art exhibit. It was a big deal, lots of museum people, gallery owners, and rich collectors. Well, the Indian maiden artist shows up, blasted, of course, and at first he is real flattered that someone has done a caricature of him. Then he read the title and all hell broke loose."

"What's the title?"

"Well, you got the fish, you got the sex goddess, and you got the so-called famous *Indian* artist. The title is *Idols: Moorish, Boorish, and Whorish.*"

It was a moment before Rivers burst into laughter. "Obviously the guy had no sense of humor."

"Yeah, if he can't take a joke . . ."

"What's her name never saw it did she?"

"Well, it seems one of local mucky-mucks from the theater department of the College of Santa Fe knew her, or at least her husband, so they took a picture of it and sent the photo to them."

"What happened?"

"The museum received several threatening letters from both the singer and the artist. Their lawyers were relentless. They threatened to sue for slander, vindictive this and that, public humiliation, the works."

"Did you get sued?"

"No, but the museum eventually removed the piece under a threat from the local politicos that they would cut off funding. They tried to resist the lawyers, but the legislators were the straw that finally broke the proverbial back. It wasn't my intent to get the museum in trouble. I wasn't even trying to cause the huge censorship controversy that followed—creatives versus bureaucrats, first amendment clash. I was just trying to make a statement about crass commercialism."

"So, you allowed them to pull the piece?"

"Yeah, I put on my best martyr imitation and went up and pulled it myself. What the hell, I'd made my point and I got tons of publicity. I know what you're thinking, but this way the museum owed me."

"Kinda' manipulating the situation, weren't you?"

"Oh! He understands art and he has a conscience. That's ironic talk from a lawyer."

"Touché. So, what happened?"

"So, I decided rather than poking fun at other artists, I could better spend my time and energy finding my own voice, vision, if you will. But I did learn a lot about the politics of art, and that lead me to thinking about the politics of the victor and the vanquished, and that reminded me of my heritage, and that finally resulted in the *Indian As Alien* series."

"And?"

"And now I have had several shows in that same museum, as well as, every major museum in the region. And now my paintings sell for twice what the chubby drunk's sell for. And now I'm getting stinking rich and stupidly famous, and I don't have to do it on the back of other people. Now I feel I'm closer to finding a unique vision. And now, because I'm so damn wealthy, I'm going to buy dinner over at the M and J. What'da ya' say. Hungry?"

"Hungry and inspired, and you're right. You can pay."

The exit routine of turning out the lights and locking the doors went no quicker than the entrance, even through they were going downhill.

"A booth or a table, Horace?" asked Jake as Ho and Troy entered the M and J.

"A booth, of course, Jake," answered Ho. "Jake," he continued as they walked toward the last empty booth, "this is Troy Rivers, a friend of Orvis' and mine, and quite an art connoisseur. Troy, we've already given you all the dirt on Jake."

"Oh, I get it, Señor Verde, you been telling tales out of color." He turned toward Rivers. "Buenas noches, Señor Rio," He placed two worn and mimeographed menus on the Formica table. "Qué paso quemoso," he exclaimed as he looked at Rivers to shake his hand. "You must be Rio Colorado. You are as rojo as my adovada, Señor. I will pinch off a leaf of aloe vera." He pointed to a large plant near the window.

"Aloe vera?" asked Troy. "Por qué?"

"For an appetizer, burro," he laughed. "Horace, you tell him. Don't let him eat it. The food will be aquí, pronto. Dos cervezas, de siempre?" He didn't wait for an answer. Grabbed a waitress by the arm, pointed to the aloe plant and then to Troy. Her eyes grew large as she focused on his sunburned face. Her eyes quickly narrowed and arched into a smile, "Está lumbre," she laughed. She hurried to the plant and pinched off a large fat tentacle. She placed it on a napkin in front of him.

"Gracious," he acknowledged.

She looked at Horace and saw his huge smile. With a gentle hand she touched Rivers cheek, pulled away waving her hand in the air and chuckled, "Está 'orno!"

"Sí, señorita," said Horace, "está uno picante!"

She laughed and blushed almost as red as Rivers, "Sí, caliente; correrle caliente a uno."

"What am I supposed to do with this?" asked Troy, tolerant that he was the brunt of jokes he didn't understand.

"Take the sap and rub it on your sunburn."

"Get serious, Ho."

"Seriously," answered Horace. "It'll will cool the burn and help heal your face."

"You're not trying to make me into a bigger fool than I've already been are you? Is this an initiation you guys pull on tourists?"

Horace grabbed the leaf and squeezed out a large blob of the pale, syrupy gel into his hand. He reached across and slapped Rivers above the jaw. The aloe spread across his cheek. A nearby table of patrons laughed. "Well?" asked Horace.

"It may be too early to tell, thank you, Horace. My face still stings from the slap."

Jake arrived with the beers. He looked at Rivers with the big glob on one cheek. He grabbed the plant, squeezed out a mound and slapped Troy on the other cheek. "Un ungüento, sumamente Cristiano, you turn the other cheek," he laughed, "An ointment. Muy bueno, muy frío." He waited for Rivers to do something.

Troy sat, staring at them both, with the thick gel slowing oozing down his cheeks. He looked up at Jake. The old man was obviously waiting for Rivers to act, but Rivers did nothing. His ignorance of what to do with the aloe perplexed him, as did being slapped by a stranger. Jake waited a little longer. He reached over toward Rivers. Troy jumped back, expecting another slap.

"No problemo, fundillo," he laughed and rubbed the gel over Rivers' cheek. "Rub it in, silly boy. It's good for what ails you." He wiped his hand on his apron and laughed again as he turned and left the table.

Rivers slowly, and suspiciously rubbed the sticky translucent mucus over his face. Initially it stung, and he looked with vengeance at Horace, but soon the cooling qualities took hold. His tension melted away. He sat back and relaxed for the first time since he entered the legendary restaurant. "Nice place," he said to Ho. "Friendly people."

"The food's good, too," smiled Horace.

A small black-and-white television, inconveniently placed high in a corner, distracted Horace. Troy saw that the commentator was a stately looking Hispanic woman.

"I know her," said Horace.

Her large eyes were dark, sensuous, and glowed with intelligence. Her dark hair framed a fair face with high cheekbones and a chiseled chin that gave her a look of nobility.

"She's the newscaster I watch most often," said Horace.

"Because she's pretty?" asked Rivers.

"She is that," said Horace. "We met a couple of years ago at a gallery opening. The next month, after a few too many art-jug-wines at a museum event, I worked up the courage to flirt with her. She was cordial, but noncommittal. Later, she and her husband purchased two paintings for their Nuevo-territorial-Japo-techno-concrete-solar-Macmansion. She got the paintings in the divorce, and I have always retained an oozing aloe, cooling crush on the woman."

"What's her name?"

"Linda Oeste."

"Anything else I need to know?" As Troy focused on the newscaster the screen filled with a gruesome picture of an airplane crash. He read the words, "Longmont, Colorado" at the bottom of the screen. By the time he had asked a waitress to turn up the sound the attractive newswoman was back on camera. She was talking about a local Albuquerque softball team that had possibly perished on a connecting flight from Albuquerque to Denver to Wyoming. "It is feared that all on board the United Flight are lost as witnesses said the plane seemed to explode in midair. Actual numbers and identification of those on the flight are not available at this time, pending notification of next of kin."

Everyone in the restaurant sat numbed by the announcement. Three women and two men from a nearby table jumped up and ran from the restaurant, one woman very close to hysterics. Two of the men had their arms around her.

Troy and Horace looked at each other in disbelief. Rivers was the first to break the silence. "Didn't Orvis say he was going to Wyoming before his return to New York?"

Horace nodded. He stood and walked to the wall mounted television reached and turned the volume louder.

"We will continue the report as soon as we have further information," said Oeste. "To reiterate: it is feared a championship girl's softball team from Albuquerque was aboard a United airliner flying out Stapleton Airport in Denver. The DC-10 seemed to explode in midair according to witnesses near Longmont, Colorado, a town just north of the airport." She looked off camera and paused, composing herself. She continued, "On the National front . . ."

"You stay here and listen for more reports," barked Horace. "I'll go over to the studio and get on the telephone. If I know Orvis, he was on a different flight. He has a sense for these kinds of things."

"I hope you're right," said Troy. "Oh, god!"

"What?"

"The owl—Orvis saw an owl and made some kind of a joke about it being an omen. I only half listened. You don't suppose he did sense something was wrong and went anyway?"

"Now cut that shit out! This is the nineteen-sixties."

Horace looked as if he only half-believed his own rebuttal—1964 or not. Rivers felt a cold pang of doubt enter his bones.

"If you hear anything'" said Horace, "beat on the door, I'll have to come down to let you in." He ran from the M and J toward the studio across the street.

Rivers sat back down, but pushed away his food. Jake carried two beers with him. He sat down in the opposite seat and set one of the beers in front of Troy.

"Those people who ran out of here were good friends, neighbors. Their daughter was the catcher on that team. Dios mediante the news is wrong. Qué lastima, qué lastimada!" He sat quietly and watched the television.

Rivers took a long drag on the beer, oblivious to everything around him. He had forgotten his painful face. He did not even notice when Jake left the table to talk to another booth of friends. He was unmindful that the entire restaurant was subdued in fear. He did not notice that when his bottle was empty, Jake had replaced it with another. He drank nervously from the fresh beer.

The announcer came back after a commercial and said, "Breaking news tonight. This just in on the air crash near Longmont, Colorado. A spokesman from the Aviation Administration has informed the media that they are initiating a bomb investigation. Authorities have launched a manhunt for an as yet unnamed suspect. A relative of a passenger informed the police of the possibility of a bomb hidden in luggage. Unfortunately, we must now relinquish the air to the National News. As we learn more, we will interrupt the Huntley-Brinkley Report with pertinent local information. To reiterate . . ."

Troy cursed the lack of details and turned from the screen, unconsciously taking another long drink of beer. He looked across toward the studio. There was no sign of Horace. He finished the beer. Another appeared. It was Jake. "Gracious," he mumbled to the old gourmet.

"Por nada, amigo."

Troy looked back at the TV. A commercial was playing. Ironically, it was an airline pitch. He downed half the beer in his uneasiness. Suddenly an out of place movement near the studio building caught his peripheral attention. It was nothing, he thought. Some guy carrying a suitcase. Something made him look again. "That's strange," he thought, "That guy has luggage like mine." The man stopped in front of the building and appeared to call back to someone as yet out of sight. A second man appeared, he was carrying a briefcase. Problem was: he did not look like someone who owns or uses a briefcase. He held it with both arms, up against his chest, as if it were some precious object. "That's weird," thought Troy. Then it finally dawned on him. He stood and looked with determination. "Oh, hell, that's my briefcase!" He ran toward the door. He looked back at Jake who was standing with a surprised look on his face. "That son of a bitch is stealing my briefcase!" Rivers yelled as he ran out of the restaurant.

Jake immediately ran to the phone by the cash register. A worried patron was on the telephone trying to get news about the plane crash. Jake urged him to get off; he had to call the police.

As Rivers ran across the street, almost getting hit by an Oldsmobile sedan, he looked to where Ol' Blue was parked. Sure enough, there was broken window glass next to the side of the truck. Rivers caught up to the two thieves about midway between the studio building and the Santa Fe water tower. They were in a vacant lot, waist high in dead field grass.

"Hey! That's my luggage, you sons-of-bitches." Rivers had a bizarre flash that he was yelling at Lenny and George of *Mice and Men,* one man was large and slow, the other smaller, with a weasel's quickness.

The larger man threw the briefcase at Rivers and bellowed, "Chinga te!"

Both men looked Indian to Rivers. Their dark hair was matted and in need of washing; it sat dull and flat above their wide faces. A thought flashed through Troy's mind that they must be stoned on something. Their eyes were fire—demonic almonds of angry confusion. The briefcase missed Rivers' head by inches. He bent over to pick it up. It was a mistake to take his eyes off the pair of tramposos.

The weasel moved with a predator's quickness. In a flash he dropped the suitcase, pulled a knife from his pocket and lunged toward Troy.

"Suato," he hissed, "pendejo; Yo filereo, gaviota." Verbalizing his threat to cut the stupid white man gave Troy just enough time to react.

The blade, aimed at Rivers' chest, plunged into the briefcase, but the force of the attack knocked him backwards. As he fell he let go of the case, and in the smaller man's impatience to shake the knife free of the leather, he broke the blade. "Chinga," he cursed.

The Lenny character, large and lumbering, kicked Rivers so hard it lifted him off the ground and took his wind. He rolled trying to escape the next kick. His tumble was frantic enough that the huge Indian was a half-step off.

The Indian ended up kicking the air, the missed punt throwing him on his dirt-stained pants. The evil eyes narrowed in anger.

Rivers struggled to get his wind. The bruise to his ribs and the dust in the air choked him; he was suffocating. Looking up at the tower, the stories of violence rumbled through his mind; Rivers couldn't believe the irony. A fast flying form came between him and the landmark. Instinctively, he kicked upward. It caught the weasel in his crotch. The squeal he heard when his foot made contact gave him a fleeting pleasure. He could smell the filth and anger as the rabid simian collapsed on him. Rivers applied blind effort and lifted the small, imploding form over his own recumbent body. He rolled onto his stomach, trying to find a breath and wanting to view the damage he just inflicted. He struggled, trying to get to his feet. He caught a glimpse of the shadow of the huge man as he came up behind him. He was suddenly airborne, transported off the ground by the leviathan, grabbing the backs of his arms like a misbehaving child and levitating him. He held Rivers, pinning his arms against the large body.

The wounded ferret took a moment to recover, now that their prey was controlled. He caught his breath, straightened up and pulled on the top of his filthy britches in a vain attempt to gain another couple of inches; his hypothermic eyes focusing on Rivers. With mongoose swiftness his right hand slammed into Rivers' diaphragm.

He had no air but the hold of the huge man kept him from crumbling. He was harnessed and vulnerable to the next attack.

The giant's grip did, however, allow for Rivers' head to fall forward. Looking through the tops of his eyes he tried to anticipate the timing of the next blow. He instinctively snapped back his head, more in avoidance reflex than retaliation. The back of his head collided with the nose of his captor. Blood exploded over the large man's face and down Rivers' neck. Blood flew past his ears and splattered the rodent across his face—causing him to pause in surprise—where the hell was the blood coming from? The Goliath released his grip and grabbed his nose. Blood continued to gush between his fingers.

Rivers thought about striking out with his fists, but his arms were numbed by the vice grip he just escaped, so he kicked again, reacquainting his foot with the crotch of the stunned rat. One down. . . . He turned to likewise deal with the bloodied giant when the first nightstick crashed across his back. The second baton thrust into his stomach, point first. Without the behemoth to hold him up, he crumbled to the ground, a club slammed across his shoulders, he was drowning in quicksand, unconsciousness encroached, the world faded to dark.

The police jailed the three combatants in separate areas of their local hoosegow; they assessed that it was two-against-one as they approached the fight, thus did the sole fighter a favor and threw him into the drunk tank. He seemed to need less medical attention than the titan and was less menacing than the Tasmanian devil. The single perpetrator was unconscious and the other two were obviously on something and out of their heads. They smelled of Sterno.

In the tank, the quarantined residents of the judicial nether world, watched as the puercos hauled in their latest victim of police brutality. The inmates were an informal fraternity of sorts, loosely organized around a pecking order, enforced thorough violence and brutality. Common hatred for the bulls did not keep them from exercising jailhouse humor. One of the senior members figured an initiation, rather than camaraderie, was in order for the unconscious neophyte. Thus, the demonist took it upon himself to urinate on the lifeless form. Another, less landed among the satanic gentry, declared his displeasure of the repugnant act by regurgitating nearby and accidentally splashed on the haggard soul for whom he had wished to exhibit empathy. The Loki searched Rivers for anything of value. The dozen or more denizens in various degrees of drunkenness skulked around the boundaries of the abyss. All were either Indians or Hispanics—New Mexicans, Texans, Mexican nationals. They were bums, vagabonds, beggars, drunkards, wife-beaters, life-dissenters. Society had disenfranchised these men decades ago. Disappointment, anesthetized through abuse of alcohol, had robbed them of their esteem and any dreams they had were puked and pissed away a thousand inebriated nights ago. Their bruised and broken bodies manifested the destruction of their spirit and exit of their souls.

And here lay Troy Rivers looking like brethren, for all the local authorities cared. The cops—pressed uniforms, crew-cut hair, shined boots, wielding their batons—would contemptuously check from the periphery to see if Rivers was still breathing. They joked among themselves about the debasement his inmates inflicted. The sad irony of this journey into the depths of *Infierno,* was that the guards were also Indian and Hispanic. It was common for minority officers of urban precincts to cite their severe disappointment in their brothers and cousins with brutal tattoos from righteous batons. They warranted retribution: secure in their sanctity, reinforced by decades of arresting these dregs; they sanctimoniously inflicted accountability on their fallen kinsmen. *Embarrassment* is a violent motivator. Perhaps they would have been more lenient had they known that Rivers was the victim. They did not take the time to evaluate the circumstances. The scene was all too familiar. *Once again* they were summoned (from something more important) to quell a disturbance under the shadow of the Santa Fe water tower.

Unfortunately, Rivers looked the role of the local rabble. The aloe had made his face sticky; the dust of the arena covered his face. The blood from the wounded giant mixed with the dust to cover and soil his shirt. His pant pocket was tore away when one of the pugilists tried to grab his wallet. His wallet was lost; he had no identification on him. He smelled of beer and blood. He was dirty and disheveled. To the police, he looked derelict if not criminal.

They assumed the worst, perhaps the obvious, and ran him in, no questions asked.

     Cradling the phone between ear and shoulder, Horace Green sat on a paint-splattered chair in his studio. His ear was sore from the inordinate amount of time he sat on *hold*. He had heard the ruckus below his studio, but paid it little heed because an airline official had finally answered. Horace lied, telling the United administrator that he was family, the younger brother of Orvis Kahnawake; it wasn't too far from the truth.

     He had been trapped on the phone for nearly two hours—holding, hoping for the best, imagining the worst. He thought about running over to the M and J and getting Rivers, but he didn't dare put down the telephone once he got the United office, even if they did put him on hold. And, No! You can't call me back when you know something. Why the hell can't you just confirm whether or not Mr. Kahnawake was on that flight? I don't care if you don't like giving out that information on the phone. I need to know something before I come down to the airport. I'll hold.

     After two hours and six conversations with various supervisors a voice confirmed that "Mr. Orvis Kahnawake did indeed have reservations on the ill-fated flight." But, this did not guarantee that Mr. Kahnawake was on the plane. The voice asked, "It is possible that he changed his mind or took another flight. Could you please come to the airport?"

     He hung up the phone and sat quietly with his hands over his eyes for several minutes—disbelief and confusion making him inert. He looked across from the chair at the painting of the fallen Indian and the demonic dog. It seemed ghoulish in the green light of the fluorescent fixtures above him. Until today, death had been an abstraction. But now, he responded to the news by doing the thing he knew best. He grabbed several tubes of acrylic and squeezed the paint onto a palette. He opened several jars of paint sitting on a workbench. He attacked the painting with impulsive energy, unconscious reflex. He used brushes to spread the paint. He became impatient with the brushes and used his hands. After large areas were covered with violent, physical strokes, he returned to using the brushes for details. He stood back, toweling the paint off his hands. He paused and assessed what he had unconsciously created. Death fell from the sky in ferocious strokes of reds and yellows; greens and violets erupted in horror. The figure, prone on a saturated ground, lay diagonally across the canvas. Above it, violent splattered color; below it an impasto surface lay diagonally across the canvas. Flowing from the dead figure, more like a mist or essence than life's blood, was a calming, meandering series of rhythmic, overlapping organic shapes, culminating in a large visible circle. Loosely rendered within the circle, dozens of gestural figures danced in full-feathered regatta. A smaller concentric circle of drummers sat nearer the center, and emanating from the center, intersecting with the series of circles, was an abstracted, simplified skyscraper and a dark silhouette of a shaman standing on top of it lifting his arms to the heavens.

He hurried to the storeroom and opened the top drawer of an old bureau. He took out a cigar box; it rattled as he returned to the canvas. From the box he grabbed a bell made from a bent snuff lid and pressed it into the wet impasto paint. Twelve snuff bells created a new circle around the original. He flopped into his chair—exhausted.

Horace dozed, he wasn't sure how long. He awoke and glanced at the painting, but before he immersed himself in an appraisal the thought hit him: what happened to Troy Rivers? Was he still in the M and J? He looked out the window of his studio. The lights were on in the restaurant across the street, but it looked deserted. He figured he had better pick up Rivers and they should go to the airport and talk personally to the United people. He looked at his pants. They were covered with paint splatters; so was his shirt. Not a big deal, he would run by his place and get a change of clothes before they went to the airport. He took a last look at the painting and felt the sorrow welling up in his soul again. Solemnly, almost ceremonially, he turned out the bank of incandescent lights near the canvas. He locked the door and slowly descended the long narrow staircase. It seemed more claustrophobic than ever before. He exited and locked the street level door and strolled across Second Street to the M and J.

He was surprised that the door was locked. He put his hands next to his eyes and peered through the glass. Jake and a few of the staff were sitting at a table with their backs to the door, watching the television. Horace knocked. Jake jumped up and opened the door.

"How is your friend?" Jake asked. "The police were pretty rough, qué cabróns!"

"Police? What police?"

"You have not been to the jail? Un desmadre, a bad ending! Se lo llevó la perica; he was taken to jail,

"Jake, what the hell are you talking about? Rivers is in jail?"

"Sí, he saw somebody taking his things out of the troque, dos tramposos, Indios. There was a terrible fight. La Policia took all three to jail. I thought you was there when you didn't come back to the restaurant. Qué lastima. They thought your friend was cuete, drunk. Ramon from the kitchen went out to see if he could help, but the police was listening to ninguno y nada. He brought back the cartera 'e bolsillo, his wallet, but I think your other stuff is still out there in the field. The police didn't take nada with them. The pendejos just whacked everybody with their clubs and loaded 'um in the squad cars."

Jake dug out a flashlight from under the counter and he and Horace ran over to the vacant lot. The suitcase was ransacked. There was a pair of underwear and a torn shirt which looked as if somebody had fought over the remnants. They found a brown spot in the dead grass and dust where someone had obviously bled a lot.

"Jesus! Lo siento, me sabe mal, Horace. I couldn't get out in time to stop de police. I thought Ramon was there, está sebo, que sonso. I thought you was there, también. I thought Ramon said he saw you. Muy muy sonso!"

"Está bien, Jake. I appreciate that you guys saved the billfold. Está milagro."

Jake continued to yell apologies as he returned to the restaurant and Horace ran to his truck. He was in such a hurry that he drove three blocks before he realized he had not turned on his lights. He sat on the broken window glass and cursed the red stoplights at every intersection.

The desk sergeant was less than responsive. He judged Horace's clout by his paint splattered pants and shirt. He voiced particular skepticism that the filthy drunk they had thrown in the tank was a lawyer. He was piqued just enough, however, that he sent an officer back to see if the prisoner was conscious yet.

The cop entered the tank and being careful not to dirty himself in the puddles of urine and puke next to Rivers, he ordered two other prisoners to lift him off the floor and onto a bench. He had to bark commands three times before several of the inmates would clear a space. Rivers was only semi-conscious, but he could answer the policeman.

"Do you know your name, *amigo*?"

"What?"

"Do you know you name? Who are you?"

River instinctively reached for his wallet.

"You got no ID, man. Do you know who you are? Do you know where you are?"

Rivers looked around, he smelled and then looked at the mess on his clothes. "I'm in hell," he answered.

"Yeah, and you're in a lot of trouble. Now who in hell are you?"

"Rivers," he mumbled. "Troy Rivers."

"Who?"

"Troy Rivers," he said more firmly. "Troy Rivers, attorney-at-law."

"Right," chided the policeman. "Well, counselor, another one of your derelict friends is here to bail you out." He got up to leave, "Don't go anywhere," he laughed, "'till I get back." He exited the tank, being careful to step over the refuse.

"So, you're a lawyer?" asked the man who had helped lift him onto the bench.

"Yeah," he muttered as he rubbed the back of his neck, not believing how it hurt. The smell of his clothes distracted him from the pain. He felt as if he were going to throw-up.

"I hate shyster lawyers," growled one of the men who had to relinquish his seat. "Whew, qué jediondo, what a smell!"

Rivers sat and looked the man in the face. Several of the drunks jumped for the space created on the bench when Troy straightened up. They bumped and jostled him. He remained quiet, trying to remember how he ended up in this sewer.

"Yeah, ain't no lawyer ever done me no good," grumbled another man sitting one person away from Rivers.

"I'm not that kind of a lawyer," he replied knowing the minute he said it, it was a feeble reply and would probably cause him more grief than not.

"You're all the same—lenguónes, liars. You deserve to be covered in goma, pendejo. Pedorros, all of you."

"What say we beat this palomita?"

"You're right," said another, "he is a little prick. My lawyer was a palomita; didn't do me no good."

"Pase quebrada, give him a break. He didn't do nada to you. Cabróns!"

"Shut your jeta! He's a lawyer, ain't he? That's enough to kill the cabeza de caca."

"Calmantes montes, cool it. I ain't sticking around in this casa de putos for no murder investigation. Veinte y cuatro horas, del todo. Para entonces, vendo, vendo vendi."

"Correlón!" Someone called him a coward.

A pocked faced man snarled through yellow teeth, "I been rousted by the cops so many times—h' desmadrado, beaten to nothing—that I can caerle this llorón, this cry baby, and it will never show. The puercos will never know."

Three men grabbed Troy. The man grinned a menacing butterscotch smile. "Turn him around," he told the others. A crippling blow hit Rivers in the lower back on his right side. He nearly fainted from the pain. Another insult slammed him on the left side. The men had to struggle to hold him up. He felt his kidneys implode. From the back the man added insult to injury by reaching between Rivers legs and grabbing his scrotum. He yanked as he came up behind Rivers' ear and belched, "Oye la agua, chavalo mocoso. Don't take it too personal, snot-nose." Then he spat in the ear, "Gargajo, pendejo."

A dull debilitating pain spread through Rivers' lower body and stomach. The bile rose in his esophagus.

"Te gusta estar guardado? How do you like jail, maricón?" growled the man holding Rivers' left arm.

They turned him forward. With his finger the pocked villain slowly drew an *X* across Troy's solar plexus. He took a step back and with his right hand hammered Rivers just under his ribs as he wisecracked, "Equis marks de spot." The other men couldn't hold Rivers any longer. They dropped him to the floor.

"Fileramos the son-of-a-bitch," called out a bystander. "Anybody got a fila; anyone carrying a knife. Stab the son-of-a-bitch."

"I think he wet his pants," another cruelly quipped. "I think I smell chi." He kicked Rivers in the ribs.

"Kick him in the chicloso!" another yelled.

"No, man he'll explode and cuacha will hit everybody."

The man who had just kicked him snarled, "Gabacho!" as he lifted his leg to kick again.

"¡Ya basta!" a large man yelled, "Enough. He's no white man, está no gabacho. Look closely, he's Indio." He walked over and surveyed the quarry and said more quietly, "Ya estufas, it's finished."

Troy lay in the corner. He was semi-amazed that he could take such a beating and still think. He recalled as a kid being in a few push and shove matches but had never really been beaten up. He remembered that college boys talked about such things. There was a lingering fear in the back of a *man's* mind: can I take the pain? What immature nonsense, he thought. They could have killed me. He was glad, within some perverse contentment that comes from being a survivor, that they had not beaten his face. In the back of his mind the whole incident seemed to be some kind of savage initiation rite, "Welcome to the other side, Apple."

Although he knew that sleeping was dangerous, his body insisted on some recuperation. He dozed restlessly at first, and then his subconscious took over and sunk him into a deep healing stupor. The others left him alone. The large Pueblo man sat nearby, a guardian of sorts.

Two officers escorted Rivers into the judge's chamber. He was shackled and handcuffed. Horace was red faced and angry when he saw Troy. The police had not permitted him to shower or clean up. He guessed that they wanted to emphasize their point that he was easily mistaken for a derelict.

Horace was yelling at an officer standing in the chambers that he was glad he notified Mr. Rivers' law firm in Denver about this police fiasco. He was not apologetic that they contacted the judge and put their clout to bear on the Albuquerque authorities. He was happy that all hell had broken loose. He didn't give a rat's ass if they were embarrassed. Look what they've done to his friend—to his lawyer. He was personally *pissed* that he had gotten nowhere with the desk sergeant—just another Indian trying to get his pathological pal out of el bote. "I heard that *officer* right there say," he pointed at the cop to Rivers' right, "'All these químicos lie for one another.' He called me a liar, your honor."

"And then that one," he pointed to the other officer holding Rivers, "said, 'Verdad. Está uvas para uvas, winos for winos, man. Thieves honor.'" Horace knew he had to control his anger. He addressed the two cops. "This man is a well-respected lawyer from Denver, vatos. He is a friend of mine, and a *brother*. You puercos need to come out from behind those badges and remember who you are, where you are from."

The two officers looked to the judge to intervene. He sat behind a large desk, a court stenographer beside him. Rivers noticed that Jake and Ramon from the M and J stood against a wall.

"Mr. Rivers," asked the judge, "do you need a lawyer present?"

"Am I being arrested?"

"No, actually you're being released."

"Then why would I need a lawyer?"

"I understand you may have some complaints against us."

"Then, Your Honor, do you need a lawyer?"

"I can understand why you are angry, Mr. Rivers. I have already spoken to each of your friends, here on your behalf, and feel I understand the circumstances of your arrest and detainment, but I don't appreciate a flippant attitude. Not in my chambers."

"I beg your pardon, Your Honor, but to my recollection, I was never charged or booked for any crime. And as for my flippant attitude, I guarantee there is no carelessness in my actions. I am taking all of this very seriously."

The judge was quiet for a minute. He looked at each of the officers, but said nothing.

"He was unconscious, Your Honor. We couldn't book him if he was unconscious."

Horace blurted out, "You put him in the goddamn tank unconscious?"

The judge admonished Ho with the same look he gave the officers.

"You have some powerful friends in Denver, Mr. Rivers." He paused. "Where do you see this situation going?"

"With all due respect, Your Honor, I have some powerful *colleagues* in Denver. I have friends here in Albuquerque." He turned and acknowledged Horace and the others. "And as far as this going anywhere, all I want is out and away from your *judicious* hospitality."

"Take off those shackles, officer Gonzales. Officer Fuentes, please go get Mr. Rivers' belongings and file from egress. I think we can handle things here. Would any of you gentlemen care for a cup of coffee? Mr. Rivers?"

Troy did not answer. He was watching the policeman remove the cuffs. "Chíngale," Rivers grinned, shocking the officer with his Caló idiom—meaning *hurry up* but incorporating a derivation of the *F* word one does not use with cops. The insulted man looked at the judge.

"Hurry up, officer," acknowledged the judge.

Troy took the large brown envelope and poured the few belongings the police had taken from him onto the front of the judges desk—his watch, a ring, car keys. Horace handed him his wallet, he smiled. Ramon smiled.

"You're free to go, gentlemen," said the judge, "with my apologies. I take it Mr. Rivers, this issue is closed?"

As the others left through the door single file, Troy turned to the judge. "There is a larger issue here than my incarceration, Your Honor. Something happened while I was the guest of your establishment that opened my eyes, and that larger issue is anything but closed, Your Honor. I'm going to use my powerful colleagues, in

Denver and here in New Mexico—all over the country—and we are
going to address, with vigor, the larger issue of how Indians and
Hispanics are treated by you and *your* colleagues." He turned and
left.

The police started to follow Troy out; he heard the judge call
to them. "Officers, please stay a moment," ordered the judge, his
voice exhibiting a determined edge of retribution. "I'm not finished
just yet with you gentlemen."

Outside, the sun was going down. The four men stood in the
blood red atmosphere reflecting off the Sandia Mountains.

"I'm so sorry, Troy. Once I found out you were in there, I did
my damnedest to get you out, but these local marícon marranos are
determined to keep people for at least twenty-four hours. To make
the streets safe—pendejos!"

"Orvis?" was all Rivers said.

"It's not good, brother." The huge man seemed to shrink. He
stopped walking and leaned on a car. "According to the airlines, his
name is on the passenger list. In all likelihood, he was on the plane."

No one said anything. They watched Rivers for some
reaction, some sign of what to do next. There was nothing to do.
Troy felt ill and angry. He could not imagine why the fates had
forced him on a journey through hell and kept him from his
companions when they confirmed the loss. Although his eyes welled
with moisture, he tried to show no emotion. The stoic calm that
slowly enveloped him felt cool and numbing.

He was too self-conscious about his fetid state to hug the
huge man who had emotionally collapsed on the car across from
him; *always the lawyer* he thought, disappointed that this corporate
conditioning still influenced him. But he stepped forward and
extended his right arm and firmly gripped the man's right shoulder.
His own head, needing support, dropped to his shoulder. He
clenched his teeth to dam the emotion welling in his jaws and eyes.
A dark mass filled the area behind his eyes, a cloud—putting his
mind, his heart in shadow. Ho reached up and grasped River's
forearm. They clenched silently for a long moment. Rivers felt a
kind hand on his shoulder; he knew it must be Jake. Minutes later
River's quietly spoke, almost whispered, "I need to go."

They all walked quietly to Ho's truck. Ramon jumped in the back and the others squeezed into the cab.

"Your suitcase and clothes were ransacked. I've got some stuff you can have at my place. We found the briefcase but most of the papers had blown away. The power of attorney Orvis signed was still in a closed compartment. It's here."

"No problem. I have copies of all the contracts in my files." He watched the setting sun sink over the distant llano. He was distracted for a moment by the peaks growing deep burgundy behind them.

"You look like you could use a good meal," said Jake, visibly uncomfortable with the silence.

"No, gracious, viejo amigo," Troy answered. "Horace, I think I've had enough of the local color. It's important for me to get to work—for me, and for Orvis. Can you get me to my car? Do you mind driving back to Taos.?"

"Think about it, Troy—a change of clothes, some hot food. I can take you to Taos tomorrow, first thing. You need some rest."

"Please," he said with determination. "Drop Jake and Ramon and take me to my car. You understand?"

On Second Avenue, in front of a dark M & J, Jake and Ramon offered their condolences. Jake said something to Ramon in a quick Caló that Troy didn't catch. He leaned in through the shotgun window and told Troy to take care of himself and that he hoped his opinion of Albuquerque would not be based on those macana, blackjack, wielding puercos, pigs, and he understood, también, why he had to split, descontarse. Soon Ramon reappeared with two large Styrofoam cups of coffee, another styro container of chili verde and a sack of sopaipillas.

"Goddamn, I'm sad about Señor Orvis," Jake shook Troy's arm. "He was a hell of a guy."

"Me, too." whispered Rivers.

Horace pulled away. Soon they were heading toward Santa Fe. A thin red line to the west, cast by the dying sun, exposed the contour of the plain and the distant peaks. Ahead of them, flashes of lightning periodically exposed the silhouette of the high plateau. Thunder rumbled in a prophetic baritone. Storms were building to the north.

Chapter Twenty-nine

As The Crow Flies

Fall, 1963

Local scientists and educators in the college at Alamosa, Colorado, near Fort Garland, say birds fly toward thunderstorms because the squall line and winds stir up insects, and because the noise sends small prey scampering; thus, making them easy pickings. Atmospheric turbulence and upheaval, say the scientists, generates an ambiance making the local populace atypically vulnerable.

Poets and playwrights, romantics, elaborate on the mystical powers of a tempest. And the indigenous people of the Southwest, those who have lived here for thousands of years, poets themselves, vocalists of histories and singers of prayers, will also tell you that storm-seeking crows are actually the souls of lost brothers, properly mourned at last, and set free to journey, flying toward the thunderclouds to catch a ride into the next life.

"To what do I owe this pleasure, Turtle, old friend," Raven asked.

"I need a good flyer," I answered.

"A flyer? Turtle, I've seen you fly. In fact, for a denizen of the fertile earth, a land deity, you're not too bad."

"I also need your gift of subventive vision."

"You want someone to see through my eyes? Sounds like there might be a good trick involved. Am I right?"

"No one could ever fool you, Raven. You're too smart. Of course, there's the opportunity for some trickery, but there is also an important message that needs to get through, and you, Raven, are the messenger of the gods. At least that's what I've read. You're getting famous: novels, sculptures, movies."

"Don't try to trick a trickster, Turtle, you old reptile. I'm not Coyote; appealing to my vanity will only get you so far. I know folks

underestimate your expertise at trickery, considering your modest appearance and all. You get away with such mayhem. Look, it's solid, steadfast, plodding Turtle; how could Turtle cause folly? I with my shiny black robe, I am always suspect, never to be trusted. My human literary glory was a dark, macabre poem; yours a cheery fable, a race, a slow and steady victory. What a charlatan you are, a rogue really!" He ruffled his feathers and turned so that the sun would illuminate the hidden iridescence. He cocked his head and peered at me with his left, smiling eye.

"Oh, Raven, how clever you are, to turn the flattery ploy back on me with such agility. I will have to be careful asking you for a favor. It may prove to be too expensive. I'm not sure I would be comfortable being in your debt."

"Who is it you need to send a message?" he asked, revealing his interest. "Not a mortal, I hope."

"I'm afraid so; someone I have taken under my wing."

"Careful of the metaphor, Turtle. Being overly solicitous is not going to gain my favor. Which brings up an important point. Suppose I help you, or help this mortal see and understand; what's in it for me?"

"The potential to interfere, or enhance romance—the most fertile arena for trickery."

"Tempting. What is it you want me to do?"

"Well, I can conjure up a storm, but I need you to guide the furor to my ward, and I need him to see what you see as you fly above the Rio Grande rift and lead the turbulent clouds to him. I want him to see it coming, so to speak. I'll take over from there. Actually, I'm hoping he will take over and allow his visions. You're to prime the incubus pump, so to speak."

"And the potential Juliet, where is she?"

"She will be waiting on the ground. It is he who is to be perched on a swaying balcony."

"This could be fun, I'm in." He flew above the earth with a loud raspy caw. "I'm waiting, Turtle. Begin beclouding."

Troy Rivers pulled into the deserted parking area between the highway and the grounds of Fort Garland. The white mast stood erect, a light colored splinter against a darkening landscape, a perpendicular intrusion into both the flat floor of the valley and the blanket of cool air above, a liaison between earth and sky. He walked quietly to the base. Although he was determined to climb, his imagination broadcast the horrific result of each potential misstep. An inner need drove him upward. The night breeze was brisk and the pole swayed; swimming in thinner clouds than those building to the south, the moon sunk from sight, dimmed behind the atmospheric scrim, the dark quickly closed and became claustrophobic. Halfway up he clung to the mast and waited. The clouds migrated and he continued upward. The iron rungs felt cold and slick. He thought: What a primitive handhold; nothing more than spikes driven into the pole. The thick coat of white paint made them even more treacherous. The leather soles of his shoes slipped and the cold numbed his hands. Heeding the old axiom, he dared not look down. Knowing he was one step from panic, one misstep from paralysis, he climbed onward. His grip tired, his legs shook, and even though the air was cold, he perspired. The moisture exasperated his paranoia and his weak hold on the slick spikes. And then it was done. He was surprised to find himself at the lookout platform.

He cautiously eased himself over and onto the perch. He sat and buried his face in his hands rather than survey the view. Slowly, though, the moon drew him out. Sitting with his back against the mast, he perused the panorama. Blanca Peak had changed from the warm red of the earlier trip to a cold concrete gray. The skirt of pine trees looked black. The rock face above timberline was a giant canine molar—crooked and broken. It had evolved from a picturesque alpine backdrop to a frozen and foreboding curtain. He turned and looked down the dark, wide valley. The Sangre de Cristo range was to his left and the San Juan to his right. They seemed now like the walls of a great trough trapping the cooling cumulus drifting toward Fort Garland—spirits confined by the grave mounds of the mountains. It was as if the clouds shadowed his escape, trailing the road he trekked. They rose above Arroyo Hondo and oozed over San Cristobal. Cibola Mesa barely stalled them. Questa and Cerro were consumed. They filled the Rio Costilla Valley, like a pyrotechnic flow riding on a cushion of cold air a hundred feet above the valley floor, and volleyed over Garcia, Juroso, and the Melby Rancho. The flash flood was deep and wide enough to submerge Mesita and Manassa farther to the west. They crashed against the walls of the Rio Grande rift and spilled in an oxbow over Bountiful and La Jara, surging due east over Lasauses and Old San Acacio; both disappeared beneath the deluge. And then they stalled, reenergizing and reorganizing in a squall line above San Luis. Now, as he heard the thunder, they charged. He watched them bump and struggle. They rolled in huge, rhythmical somersaults, gaining momentum, growing taller, towering above, stealing away the sky as they rushed over him.

The clouds piled against Blanca Peak and let loose a pelting rain. Huge drops of cold frustration roared as they attacked the earth below, creating a raw wind. Troy stood to face the storm as the white pole pitched in the frigid breath. The tempest soaked his clothes, scoured his face, and beat him into a splashing numbness. The water ran in a flood from his eyes and brow, but he did not cry. He stood for hours until the incessant rhythm and the bone chilling cold deadened his consciousness.

Then they came. Out of shadows between the clouds, out of the haze as the rain diminished, came the faces of his fathers, ruffians, their bristly roach headdresses swaying in the wind. They carried beaver pelts and clubs, carved wood with lethal spheres at the end. They wandered—lost. Other spirits joined them: forest people, Indian farmers, people of wetlands, desert people, and plains tribes, all wandering up the valley toward Troy. As they came closer he saw that many had cut off their fingers and gouged their eyes in lamentation, and their voices mingled with the sorrow of the rain. Thunder rolled. Lightning echoed in a vertical cascade from Blanca to La Veta. And they were gone.

Slowly at first, and then building, riding on the giant acoustic ripple of a distant thunder crash, a stagecoach, rumbled toward him. A buckskin-clad wild man stood in the boot of the coach, cracked a whip as loud as lightning, and waved a broad cowboy hat. Rivers saw the coach chased by a war party of young braves, buffalo running beside them. One young brave sprinted past the thundering coach, rode adjacent to the team of crazed horses, almost outrunning the entire rig. The frenzied showman cracked his whip and the young

Indian tumbled from his pony. In a blinding flash of lightning and another crack of the whip, the entire scene disappeared.

Troy did not move. In an open area of the sky above Blanca Peak a small cloud twisted and grew into a huge tree. Ribbons of red, yellow, black, and white hung from the branches of the tree. From behind the tree, an aged medicine man, carrying a hoop, lifted the circle and it encompassed the moon. He looked at Troy and pointed to a figure sitting at the base of the tree. Here was an old man, more ancient even than the shaman. He smiled at Rivers, an ornery smile. The spirit seemed to have fangs, two beige crescents pointing downward, but suddenly he sucked one into his mouth and ate it. His cantankerous laugh filled the sky. The tree and the vision faded in the moonlight. The rain became a trickle. The clouds raced beyond the horizon. The moon sunk below the San Juans. The first herald of the sun broke the horizon.

Troy felt a chill and then unexpected warmth. Orvis Kahnawake stood next to him. His mouth did not move but Troy heard him say, "I don't know which I liked best up here: the sunset or the sunrise. You'll have to decide for yourself. This is my last gift to you. Treat her well, Three Rivers."

She watched him for almost half-an-hour. She had arrived in her government issue, Park Ranger truck just before dawn. She thought that the lights of the truck, or the noise of her parking it, would have gotten his attention. But there he sat, atop the white mast, like a nesting bird, oblivious to everything going on around him. She even had time to run his car license plate, check for outstanding warrants, get an ID, and determine that the car had not been reported as stolen. In all likelihood, that was Mr. Troy Rivers, of Denver, sitting on top of *her* flagpole in the center of the grounds of Fort Garland. She wasn't in a panic, but she was sure she wanted him down before her supervisor arrived for work. Her captain was hard-nosed and would definitely want to prosecute for trespassing. That meant she could spend her last morning-off doing paper work. Some voice in the back of her mind solicited empathy.

She had just returned from covering for a colleague who was supposed to open the gates at Sand Dunes National Monument. She unlocked the gate in the fading darkness and breathed deeply of the cool air, cleansed by the rains. A pleasant thought dawned along with the sun: *The stream that runs along the foot of the dunes would be high and wide and generating a bloom of bright mountain flora.* She knew that rains like the storms last night spawn a serendipitous appearance of a flow. *I'd love to take a look, maybe even wade for a while before the tourist show, but something tells me that Beamer is still at the Fort.* She liked where she was. She like her job. Life was *Shił t'áá'áko,* all right with me. She thought of the last decade, posted here in southern Colorado, and felt good about her life, isolated as it was. Mornings like this made the world *nizhóní,* as her Navajo friends would say—beautiful. She was heading home, south down 150, when that voice told her to take the extra forty minutes and run by the Fort. That was a hellacious thunderstorm last night, and she had spotted this car from Denver in the parking area. She thought she had better see if it was still there this morning, and considering the wind that came up, she needed to see if the flagpole was still standing.

"What are you doing up there?" She called to the man perched in the sky.

The trance was broken, the journey abridged. He acknowledged at last that he had heard her. He climbed onto the handrails and slowly descended. With his foot on the last spike, still above the ground, he looked more closely at the ranger.

Her face was in the shadow of her wide-brimmed hat and she worn sunglasses; the khaki uniform and jacket neutralized her physique, but her hair broke the androgynous regalia. Her hair looked like the rich fur of one of the animal denizens of the nearby mountains. It was thick and long and grizzled with sections of black, gray, and sienna. She looked as if a pack of winter-coat coyote pups had hidden under her ranger hat and lined their tails in unison behind her head. Her hair moved in the morning breeze as if it were indeed alive. Her nameplate read: P. Andrette.

He noticed that by standing on the last rung he was forcing her to look up and into the rising sun. He didn't mind the advantage. "Searching," he answered her question.

"Something you lost?" she asked.

"Lost and maybe found," he answered.

He didn't need another run-in with the law. He hoped that she interpreted his odd behavior as something important and not just a prank. He hoped he'd get a chance to explain. He hoped she noted that he hadn't given her a hard time after asking him to come down; he wasn't a drunk or a suicide attempt.

"I hope I didn't prevent you from finding what you were looking for, but the Head Ranger would have a fit if he caught you up there. Were you up there all night? You could have been struck by lightning"

"It's OK. It was time to come down." He lowered himself and the strangest thing happened as he touched Mother Earth. He suddenly became erect. He folded his hands shyly in front of his crotch and meekly bowed his head looking at the ground in a coy attempt to cover his surprising response. The pose was almost pious.

"What's that you've got there?" asked the ranger.

He blushed, misinterpreting her question, not realizing he had unconsciously reached into his pocket (needing something to do with his hands) and had pulled out the antique tobacco pouch.

"Ma'am?"

"It's Miss, I'm no 'Ma'am.' What's that you're holding?"

He looked, surprised to see the pouch in his hand. He squirmed, still somewhat determined to conceal his impediment. He was trying not to look guilty or crazier than she must think he already is. "Oh, this! It's just a tobacco pouch, a gift from a friend."

"You're not smoking marijuana up there are you? If you are, that changes things. I'll have to arrest you."

"No marijuana. It's tobacco: a tobacco pouch." He used both hands to open the purse and expose the ingredients inside. His hands hid the design of the pouch; he didn't need her thinking he had stolen an heirloom from a local museum.

The look that came across her face was difficult for Troy to interpret. The aroma of the tobacco distracted her. She looked him in the eyes, searching for something; Troy wasn't sure what. They looked at each other, her gaze quizzical, his trying to express innocence, for an uncomfortably long time. She finally broke off the contact.

"I need to see some ID," she said softly but with lingering authority.

He stuck the pouch in his front pocket with his left hand and reached for his wallet with his right, recalling he had pocketed it in front, his back, wallet pocket a victim of the attack. There was no hiding now. She appeared to follow his hand movement to his pocket (there could be a concealed weapon after all), he was sure she was staring at his embarrassment.

As he tried to hand her his wallet he noticed that she could not conceal a smile. She said, "Take it out, please."

"Ma'am?"

"Take it out of your wallet, please—your ID. And quit calling me Ma'am."

He stumbled a moment trying to juggle the wallet. With a tardy, coordinated effort, he removed his driver's license. Out of habit, he included a business card.

She took the card and first read the license, "Well, Mr. Rivers, I see you're from Denver. If I remember correctly, this address is in a fairly affluent neighborhood. I've also heard of your law firm; high rollers are they not? I'm a little confused by your appearance. You seem a little shabby this morning. Hard night?"

He noticed her demeanor had changed. She was more relaxed, less officious. He thought he actually caught the beginning of a smile. "It's a long story, Miss, but yes—a very hard couple of nights."

She was silent, obviously contemplating what to do next— run him in, let him go, continue the somewhat cordial reprimand. He wasn't sure why; normally, he would be anxious to exit a potential arrest, but he hoped she chose to continue a lecture. He wasn't sure why, but he felt drawn to her. What he was sure of; however, was that he wished he was more presentable. He was concerned about first impressions and worried he must be a bedraggled sight. He tried unsuccessfully to tidy his hair and straighten his tattered shirt, alternating his hands to groom and also hide his adolescent disruption.

"You look like you could use a cup of coffee," she handed back his license and watched him as he put it back in his wallet.

"Coffee sounds great. Only, it'll have to be someplace that takes plastic. One of the sad chapters of the long story is that I have no cash."

"Ahh, a vagrant. I may have to run you in after all." She was smiling, but Rivers wasn't sure if she was kidding or not. "We'll take my truck," she ordered. "I'm still not convinced you're in any shape to drive. And the coffee is my treat."

She removed her hat for a moment and shook her hair into place; put her hat back on, pushed the thick hair behind her shoulders and took off her sunglasses. She smiled and gestured toward her truck.

Troy returned the smile. He noticed that she wore no make-up. A *natural prettiness* wasn't a quite accurate description, he thought, *confident* is closer, perhaps: *comely.* Her hands were graceful and fingers long. She wore no jewelry. She moved athletically. She seemed uniquely feminine to him. She was a Native American. He was slightly surprised at his attraction. Women in corporate dress—heels, skirts, and a salon coif—were his *type.*

The ranger's boots were government issue, as were her dark olive pants (ordinarily not very sexy). It was difficult for Troy to pinpoint why he found her attractive—perhaps it was because she carried herself so confidently; she was so comfortable with herself. He took a quick inventory: her hair was licentious, her face was tan, her skin smooth, her eyes were dark and alert. They shown brightly in the shadow of the brim of her hat.

There's that voice again, she thought. Normally, she would never adopt a stranger like this, even for a innocent cup of coffee. Something about this guys said he was in serious need of a rescue. And he was Native . . . and good looking despite the obvious trauma he had recently been through. She was curious and a bit intrigued. They pulled a left at the main intersection, heading west through the town of Fort Garland: several gas stations, a truck stop, a few retail establishments, an old general store, and one dusty cafe. She pulled into the parking lot. Every head, every patron in the several booths and all along the counter turned to look. Of course, she knew each and every coffee sipping, huevos rancheros eating resident and also knew that each and every one was a gossip and scandalmonger; it was a small town, after all. *Oh look, Ranger Andrette has picked up another stray. Will that girl never learn?* They were right. *What the hell is it with me and lost souls?* She backed out and drove past the cafe. The patrons inside gazed through the windows at the retreating truck. Blanca, the town beyond, was even smaller, but the few locals lingering in the doughnut shop were just as curious about the ranger and her passenger.

"Is there a better spot for coffee?" he asked.

"I can't take you out in public in your condition, now can I?"

He paused and considered his condition. "Where are we going?"

"I have a small place just up the road. That is, if you don't mind. And, ahh, no offense, but you could use a shower, Mr. Rivers."

"No offense taken. But . . .," he paused again. "This is a small town. Everyone in the cafe has already taken notice that you have someone in your truck. I'm not somehow compromising your position here, am I?"

"We'll see."

She felt her face blush. She turned off the main highway onto State Highway 150. They drove for another five minutes and exited onto a dirt road. Piñons and junipers covered the surrounding terrain as it became more and more hilly. They came over a rise in the road and a small stream joined them in a parallel journey. About a half-mile away stood a stand of willow trees, their soft drooping branches flaxen in the morning sun. A small adobe house nestled behind the trees. Redwood buckets of bright geraniums hung from the beams of the pórtico and a dull red ristra swayed between the flowers. The truck tires crunched the gravel in the driveway and, as if on cue, an ancient golden retriever staggered around the corner wagging his tail. His coat near his belly had long ago turned from warm gold to cool silver. A weak "woof" announced that he was on duty.

"Guard dog?" asked Rivers.

"Roommate."

As he exited and stood next to the truck, Troy reached to pet the old hound, which immediately stuck his wet nose under River's erection. It had diminished in the truck, but re-emerged in the driveway.

Ranger Andrette pretended not to notice her dog's curious greeting. She strolled onto the porch and reached up to one of the swinging flower baskets and checked the moisture. She opened the door and held it while Rivers struggled to get past the affectionate pooch.

"You're sure he's not a guard dog?" he asked. "You know, nuzzling people into surrendering."

"He'd have to," she answered. "He has no teeth, but given time, he could slobber you to death."

He walked past her, into the house, the dog at his heels. The place appeared comfortable and the sun crept through several windows and warmed the interior. He noticed immediately that the ceiling was not enclosed. A cathedral open space gave the interior airiness. A half-dozen pine vigas ran parallel across the open space. The roof, visible from the interior, was corrugated tin. He stood looking up at the rustic covering.

"It sounds wonderful when it rains" she said noticing his attention to the roof, "but it's cold as Santa's workshop in the winter. I actually look forward to the first heavy snow that sticks to the roof—insulation."

He noticed she had put an airtight insert in the fireplace. "That should help keep things warm," he commented.

The house was small but cozy, rustic but comfortable. Santa Fe Opera posters hung in several places. The graphics informed him that the artist was Georgia O'Keeffe. An unpainted santo of the *Tree of Life* stood on a rough pine mantel above the fireplace. A chubby Adam and demure Eve stood shyly among birds, butterflies, pigs, raccoons, a raven, a coyote, and a turtle. The kitchen table sat halfway between the main room and the kitchen area. Chimayó rugs covered the floor in strategic spots. What looked to be an antique Navajo rug hung on the west wall. The aroma of piñon, mesquite, and incense mingled with the warmth of the sun coming through the kitchen windows. He was surprised to see pine, plantation shutters at the windows instead of cute curtains. The kitchen was an area in the southern part of the main room. The bedroom was separate; a door-less entrance, framed in rough wood, marked the way. He looked through the low, pine-sill doorway.

"The bathroom and shower are through there," she pointed. "Throw your clothes out, and I can wash them." Then she continued with a new pride in her voice, "I've got my own washer and dryer!"

"A pioneer woman like you. Isn't that a little citified?" he joked from behind the bathroom door.

"Hey, Mr. Rivers, don't forget. I'm still the one with the gun."

He looked down. He mumbled, "I'm not so sure."

"What?"

"I'm sure," he said aloud. "I mean, don't worry, I won't forget."

He threw his filthy clothes around the door. The bathroom was obviously an add-on to the house. The bathmat was a Chimayó rug, but he noticed a more typical "Monkey Wards" type bathmat folded on a shelf with towels and other linen. It was pink and out of character with the rest of the decor.

He stepped into the tub and turned on the water, waiting for it to warm. When he was satisfied with the heat, he pulled the plastic curtain, reached up and put his right hand over the showerhead to prevent the shock of the water from hitting his tired body, and with his left hand lifted the pedestal shaped valve on the top of the faucet. The water chugged through the pipes and soaked his hand and arm. When the initial shock diminished, he pulled his hand away and allowed the wet warmth to saturate his face and hair. The water was therapeutic; he began to relax. "It's about time," he looked down. "You're embarrassing me." He searched for soap.

Why don't you have a change of clothes with you, Rivers? she wondered as she gathered them up and instinctively smelled them. She pulled her head back quickly, assessing: beer, smoke, dirt, the paint from the flag pole, blood, a faint order of vomit, maybe jail puke, and if she wasn't mistaken—carne adovada. *I know you can afford a change, judging by your shoes. They're pretty expensive; no bum's shoes unless you stole 'um, and definitely no pole climber's boots. She paused. Are you going to tell me that long story?*

By then she heard the shower running. She looked at the clothes, although casual, they confirmed he was no transient. She walked into the tiny laundry room adjacent to the kitchen. Actually, it was an area of the back porch she had had enclosed to keep the elements off her precious washer and dryer. She noticed he had left his wallet in his pants-his front pocket. The rear pocket was torn.

What has this guy been doing? She removed the billfold and thought for a moment about looking through it. What the hell, she was an officer of the law and she did have arrest jurisdiction, if necessary. She decided against looking; it wasn't difficult to see that it was fat with credit cards. "He's no bum," she mumbled to herself. She searched for the tobacco pouch in the other pocket. It wasn't there. She swore she noticed him put it back in his pocket. Her suspicions instinctively perked, but only mildly. She heard the shower stop running and threw the clothes in the washer. She dialed the wash cycle, stealing the hot water.

"I hope you're out of the shower," she called out as she walked into the bedroom, "and not just between rinse cycles." She didn't hear a cold scream, so opened a large, pine trastera and pulled a sweatshirt off a shelf. It was an extra-large; she enjoyed the roomy and sloppy comfort of oversized sweats and tee shirts. She thought there may be a problem with the pants, however. She held them up. No way. She set them back on her shelf. She placed the shirt on the foot of the bed and walked into the kitchen to check on the coffee. It wasn't peculating yet. She went over to the washer and picked up Rivers' wallet, his keys, and the stuff that was in his pockets. Her police instincts clicked in again as she remembered the dark, familiar aroma of the tobacco. This is too much of a coincidence she thought. Two men, both pulled off that damn lookout mast and each using the same tobacco.

She thought back—was it a decade ago that she almost arrested that crazy Mohawk? It was her first assignment in the Four-Corners area. She knew she was taking a chance, but she didn't want the local authorities coming down hard on an Indian, not for such a minor transgression. Perhaps, it was misplaced empathy; perhaps, it was that he had such a charming sense of humor. He made her laugh. He was middle-aged, but full of life. He was knowledgeable about current musical groups, particularly some up-and-coming Native American entertainers. He didn't act older; he knew good dining, he taught her about wine and he loved to dance—Rockabilly and Country Swing. It was dance that solidified their relationship. If someone asked about their relationship, she would say they were dancing partners. He convinced her to participate in a powwow in Durango. She was hooked. She competed in every local powwow she could—Santa Fe, Taos, Albuquerque, and several in southern Colorado.

She remembered: one minute she was making coffee, he asked if she minded if he lit his pipe, she commented on the unique and pleasurable aroma of the tobacco, she held his hand—holding the pipe near her face, they looked across the smoldering embers at one another. A kiss had obviously crossed both their minds, but before it happened, a forlorn moan came from the front door.

She joked later that it was probably the steam of carnal tension that attracted the wounded golden retriever to her porch and rescued her from being the next victim of this *Kanien'kehake* Casanova.

They both answered the scratching at the door. The poor hound was matted in mud, sad eyed, and limping. His rear leg was bloody, the fur and skin torn revealing the bone. They took him in and doctored him together. They searched in an early autumn snow for plants to make a poultice to wrap around the dog's leg. They made a medicated tea that eased the pain of the poor animal and put him into a restless sleep. They both commented how the application and prescription of *medicine*—herbs and plants, attitudes and emotions, knowledge and experiences, Ute and Mohawk, were similar and confirming.

She decided to keep it—the dog. The man, she knew from their first moment together, was not to be domesticated. In gentle celebration, in remembrance she named her new furry friend after her new dance partner, her mentor, her spiritual father. She called the retriever: Orvis.

Troy Rivers stepped into the warm kitchen. He had found the sweatshirt and put it on. He took the clean pink bath mat and wrapped it around his waist. It was bigger than the towels. He was hoping the weight of the mat might help hide his embarrassment should it reemerge. Pink was not his first choice in color, but the size and weight made it advantageous. "That coffee smells good," he said.

She looked first at Troy, registered the humor in his appearance, and then acknowledged that the coffee was indeed percolating. "I'll pour you a cup," she stepped to the stove. "I see you found the sweatshirt." She reached for a cup in the cupboard above the sink. "You look good in pink."

"Well," he blushed, "the towels were a bit small."

"No, really, it's a great match. I wish I'd thought of it before." She poured the coffee. "Maybe I'll sew in a zipper later."

"No cream, no sugar, thank you." He tried to ignore her chiding.

"I have some artificial sweetener somewhere. Would you like that? It comes in a pink package?"

"Just black. Are my clothes in the washer?"

"They are, yes." Then she faked alarm, "Oh my god, I think I mixed the colors with the whites. It could turn your underwear, well, you can guess . . ."

"You're enjoying my discomfort, aren't you?"

"I'm sorry, I shouldn't be teasing you. The clothes are washing; it shouldn't be too long. Here's your coffee. Your things are over there on the table. I can sew up that pocket?"

"Thanks." He stepped into the kitchen from the bedroom doorway. He was standing on a woven rug, but the second his bare feet hit the bare floor of the kitchen he felt his penis begin to rise again. He looked down toward the floor. The heavy bathmat seemed to be doing its job.

"It's earth," she said. "The floor, it feels different because it's an authentic adobe, earth floor. They mix blood with the adobe mud. That's what makes it smooth and hard; otherwise, I would have to sweep it all the time and the whole place would be full of dust. Stand over here where the sun's been. It's warmer."

He moved to where she said and took the coffee. He held the cup for a long time, absorbing the heat through his palms. He took a deep drink of the brew and let it begin warming him from the inside. He became conscious of his quiet, looked at the woman standing across from him, "Sorry," he said.

"It's okay. You've obviously got something important on your mind. Does it have something to do with that long story you mentioned?"

He looked at her, but said nothing.

What sad eyes he has, she thought, *No way . . .* she hoped good sense would take a firmer stance against her emotions. *No way, not another stray dog. I can see he's hurt, but no way! I'm a Park Ranger; helping out people in distress is my job. Okay, I'm on vacation, my last day, but no way am I taking someone into my heart right now. No long distance romances; they never work. I know Denver is only four hours away as the crow flies, but no way!* She looked away.

"So, I'll, ahh, I'll check on those clothes," she said as she walked from him. "You know, I don't usually do this kind of thing."

"I appreciate your help."

"Well, you know, you looked like you could use a helping hand. Anyway, I really don't usually do this kind of thing—bring strange men into my house, but like I said."

"I understand. As I said, I appreciate your help. And you were right; I was feeling a little lost."

Talking more to herself than to him, she continued, "One time before. I pulled a crazy man off that tower. If I'm lucky, he'll bless me with a visit once a year or so. You don't dance by any chance? You know: County Swing, Jitterbug?" She didn't wait for an answer. "Anyway, I just didn't want you to get the wrong idea."

"Not to worry, Officer Andrette. Seriously, I appreciate the coffee and I don't think I could have driven another mile in those clothes, in my emotional state. The shower was great; the coffee is healing."

"Pat," she said. "I'm no ma'am, and *officer* sounds too formal. Call me Pat."

"Thanks . . . Pat."

He had a nice voice. It was polished, citified, not rural, definitely not *Alamosa*. She guessed he had done a fair amount of public speaking. She watched as he reached for the wallet and noticed that the pouch had reappeared. He's being awfully protective of that pouch, she thought. He opened the pouch, covering both sides with his hands, and breathed in as deep an inhale as his first drink of the coffee, as if seeking the same healing powers. The bouquet of the blend filled the tiny kitchen. She wasn't the only one who recognized that aroma. The old retriever reacted to the smell. He jumped from his guard post—lying against the front door—and hobbled into the kitchen. The dog lumbered in. She knew what was to come, but was too slow to prevent it. The old dog repeated his nuzzling, only this time it was under the pink bath mat. Rivers struggled to maintain his modesty and grabbed at the falling mat. The tobacco pouch spilled. The dark sweet worms of tobacco tumbled to the floor. The old dog shifted his attention from Rivers' crotch to the aromatic pile on the polished earth.

"Orvis!" she yelled.

The look that came across Rivers' face was unfathomable. A huge hurt suddenly consumed him. At first it looked as if he was trying to catch the tobacco, but it was soon obvious that he was collapsing with emotion, folding forward.

All three creatures posed over the spill. The dog lapping at the blend, Pat panicked. She shoveled it into a pile, anticipating a sweep-up. Troy tried to replace the bathmat, confused where he should pay attention: the spill, his exposure, the flush of sentiment.

She looked up from her task; Rivers was staring at her. His eyes welled with tears. A large drop plopped next to the spilled tobacco. She paused. *Don't do this, don't do this. You don't do these kinds of things. Comfort him, be sympathetic, but don't do this. I don't know what's devastating him but you are not the answer. Be smart; be cautious; he may be Coyote. He may be Bacchus; you are not Ariadne. Damn Orvis and his coaxing her into the Classics. For once, be careful.* The other voice was louder in her, overpowering her restraint. *It is men who are supposed by be struck by the lightning bolt. We women are the seducers. The old stories, the fables often tell of the braves being bewitched.* In an instant a Sioux tale of a maiden and a handsome magician, a seducer, and his snake brothers flashed through her memory. She wasn't sure but thought it ended sadly. No . . . maybe the Indian princess won the day. It wasn't clear, but she did remember that the maiden was proud. *She outsmarted them . . . right? Right? Be careful, foolish woman; remember who you are.* Was he using magic; was the deep hidden voice casting a spell; was it his voice? She heard thunder outside, but sun light still warmed the adobe floor. The dog licked his face, seeking a taste of salt or perhaps comforting his sadness. At first, she was hesitant, but then she saw the pain, the real pain.

Instinctively, she reached across and took him in her arms. *Hold him; just hold him, for just a moment.* The thunder repeated; she thought she heard the clap of distant lightening. She looked to the window again. A crow sat in the flower box under the eave, avoiding the storm she thought, but it seemed to watch them rather than the skies. It seemed to smile and only sun shone through the window, the shadow of the crow cast large in the bright rectangle of warmth on the floor. *What magic is this?* "Go to him," said the voice.

Troy searched in his mind for some reasonable explanation for his lack of emotional control. The coincidence of the dog's name was forced from his immediate mind and his shattered emotions flooded forward. Nothing made sense. He had heard stories about how an unmourned death can suddenly sneak up on you. He had never really grieved his parents; nor, had he, in the name of stoic young manhood, ever truly mourned the passing of the grandparents who raised him. Controlling sentiments was the appropriate, manly thing to do. But here he was: suddenly in an unfamiliar predicament, losing it.

Trying to think it through did him no good. The strange feeling over flowed. In a cleanse —Troy sobbed. All at once his emotional indiscretions attacked his self-control. He raised his face and tried to explain, but only pain filled his voice.

She grasped his face in her two hands and said firmly, "Don't say anything. You don't need to say anything."

He tried again to speak. She covered his mouth with hers. She must have sensed that he would try to explain, so she held his head more firmly and kissed him harder.

He sought the comfort of her kiss. He kissed back. How warm she was. He looked again at her face, her eyes green, her mouth just slightly crooked, her lips more full now from their kisses, the lips blushed ruby. No, he thought: violet. "You're beautiful," he managed to mumble. They kissed again.

The old retriever, probably uncomfortable with the emotion or possibly sensing the pain, licked across their tangled faces.

They separated just enough to laugh, tearfully to each other. Then slowly, deliberately, sensuously she moved toward him. She pulled the sweatshirt over his head. He helped her unbutton her khaki blouse. His lips traveled to her cleavage, his kisses continuing toward her neck. Her hair smelled of the sun and mountain flowers; he bit into it; it was silky and tasted clean. He rubbed his face in it, breathing in the bouquet.

She arched her neck and back at the pressure of his face and his chest. She stood and he untied her boots. She kicked them off as he undid the uniform belt, unzipped her olive pants, helped her step out of them and her panties at the same time. He buried his face in her warm down and breathed in her musk. As she knelt again to meet him, he pressed and kissed her body, kissing her belly, her ribs, each breast individually, the nape of her neck, and her lips, her violet, full lips.

The floor was cool next to the table and warm where the sun had charged through the windows. They took turns feeling the warmth as they changed places—top to bottom, controller, acceptor, initiator, receiver—sharing.

He rolled the sweatshirt and placed it under her hips. She reached for him, arms extended, inviting him. He began slowly, she responded. She took his face in her two hands again and he placed his hands on the floor on each side of her. His contact with the earth seemed to enhance his determination, no embarrassment now. In an animal attempt at escaping his newly felt mortality, he entered her— seeking life. In a celebration of living and joy he lifted her shoulders and rolled, horizontally pivoting her on top of him; she rose, the bright sun igniting her hair and face, she closed her eyes. Rapture.

The sun progressed west, its light meandering from the floor to the opposite wall in the kitchen, and their embracing bodies cooled in the shadow of the passing day. The golden dog, acting impatient with the quiet that followed their loving began to nuzzle them both. She pulled the dog toward her and ruffled its head.

They sat up.

"I probably owe you an explanation," said Troy.

"Not if it's going to spoil this," she answered.

"Actually, maybe you owe me an explanation about your dog's name."

"Not if it's going to spoil this," she repeated.

She unrolled the sweatshirt and pulled it over her head. It covered all but her athletic legs. She rose and picked up the coffee cups, filling them with hot brew. Then she walked into the bedroom and pulled a blue-white-and yellow quilt off the bed and handed it to him. He wrapped himself in it.

"I don't ordinarily do this kind of thing, you know," she smiled.

"I know you don't."

"Well," she started again, "I mean I'm no kid, no virgin obviously, after all I . . ."

"You're beautiful," he interrupted.

"Like I said, I'm no kid. And I also know I am not what you would call beautiful. Thanks, but I know who and what I am. Anyway, I don't usually do this."

"Maybe I should tell you what's happening—to me, I mean. And, you are beautiful; don't argue. I'm a lawyer."

She started to say something.

"Now don't interrupt," he said. He began the long story, "I lost a friend recently, a new friend, but once I knew him, I felt he was a part of my family, a missing part, someone I lost long ago. Losing someone like that, twice . . . well, it forced me to remember that I never said good-bye."

Troy went on to tell her of his first meeting with Kahnawake, of their trip to Taos, the television announcement about the fight and his arrest, jail, and his fleeing to the great white mast and the vision he had while aloft. He finished by trying to explain the sudden flood of emotion he experienced when he heard her call the dog *Orvis*.

She jumped from the blanket and searched for the tobacco pouch. It was her turn to cry. She covered her face. He could still see the tears fall from her hands. He moved next to her and held her. She mumbled through her tearful mask, "The tobacco, I should have known."

He held her, consoling her, when suddenly she looked up. "Why the hell didn't Horace call me?"

"Call you?" he sounded confused, "Horace? How do you know Horace?" And then it dawned on him.

"You're *Patty*. Oh my god! Orvis tried to call you on our way to Taos."

She broke into tears again.

"Oh, Patty . . ." He paused. "I'm so sorry. Things were so confusing." He unwrapped the quilt and enveloped them both, his arms around her shoulders. The last of the day faded; the room fell to darkness. They did not move. They did not speak.

He did not know what time it was when he quietly emerged from the blanket and searched for a light. The dog was scratching to get out. The house had grown cold. He couldn't find a lamp, but felt his way to the front door. He stood for a moment in the open space. Stars flooded the sky in undulating currents of sparkle. He had never seen this pristine a night. City lights had always diminished the stars. The moon softly illuminated the piñons, turning them pewter. The old dog disappeared into the forest shadows.

"I'll start a fire," she said from the darkness behind him.

"I've never seen a sky like this," he said as he turned.

"Part of the reason I live out here." Sadness still filled her.

He watched as a flickering light of kindling weakly illuminated the room near the fire insert. She was still nude; her smooth skin was the same color as the floor. She closed the fire door, and a soft radiance emerged through a small glass window as the wood took flame. She appeared darker, silhouetted in the enclosed light, her hair softly lupine, but her skin more fawn. She looked up at him, her eyes reflecting the fire's glow. He gathered her into his arms and carried her to the bedroom. "You don't need to say anything," he consoled her.

She knew better. Silence was inappropriate. She held his hand as they lay on the bed and began her story. "I am a dancer. I dance the jingle dress dance, and Orvis was my teacher, more than a teacher. He was like my father, but more than a father, and I was his daughter, more than a daughter . . ."

They took each other into their arms again and again. Each time he needed renewed energy he slipped one foot from under the warm quilt and placed it on the earthen floor.

The old golden dog howled hoarsely, harmonizing with their love song. The song was uninhibited, robust; crescendo filled the arroyo. A coyote on the piñon-covered hill barked a serenade, and set off every dog and hound in the distant town. Town's people walked from their dinner tables and out of the truck stops to confirm what they were hearing. South, past the San Luis Valley, toward Taos, they could hear a particularly haunting and more baritone canine voice. Most citizens assumed it was a large farm dog, but one old timer recognized it for what it was—a wolf's song.

A large raven with feathers of iridescent black and green perched on the sill of the bedroom window next to the crow, and peeked inside. It laughed a trickster's melodic, an old seducer's, caw.

"Let them be," said a silver-backed crow taking flight, riding the pre-storm wind. "It is I, not they, who needs your accompaniment."

"Coming, Sachem," cackled the raven.

Together, they caught a thermal and spiraled upward, out of sight as lightning pierced the summer sky somewhere between the small adobe house and the sacred high plateau.

Chapter Thirty

A Convention of Percussionists

Summer, 1964

Sometimes dreams are wiser than waking.
-Black Elk

      Ringo was the first to change into new togs and ready himself for the concert. Still feeling a bit peeved at the others for making him the frequent brunt, the bum-diddy-dumb-arse, of the jokes, still hungry, and needing a smoke, he wandered into a large back stage area that looked to be set up as a green room or cafeteria for the set hands. Long tables with *aluminium* serving trays covered in foil and heated with Sterno jelly tins sat orphaned along one wall. He almost let his mild hunger motivate an investigation under the foil but propriety and a more immediate need for the healing powers of tobacco averted him. He looked past the buffet. The architecture awed him. The room itself was rather plain and typical industrial, but at the back and on one side, the designers had allowed the natural red sandstone of the amphitheater to integrate into the room. The long, red, roughly textured walls dominated the space. Only a few of the ceiling lights were on; it was all rather eerie, cave-like, but the quiet and solitude attracted him. He entered, and sought the farthest corner, which was the junction of the two stone walls and which sat in the dimmest light. He lit his cigarette, his *fag*, took a long drag, leaned his head back and relaxed. The silence of the room eased over him. The hectic flight and frenzied travel drifted away with the smoke. He pushed away any thoughts of the others, any thoughts of the day, all other distractions, and let his mind slide into a warm, miasmic, dark purple emptiness. Time waned. Eventually he noticed heat between his fingers. When he opened his eyes and gave it a gander, he saw that his cigarette had burned close to his grip. He hadn't remembered taking another puff; how had the fag burned down so quickly? Must be the thin mountain air. He sat up to take a last drag, enjoyed the flavor of the tobacco and blew a long ethereal cloud into the air above him.

"We use smoke as the messenger to carry prayers to the Great Father," came a nearby voice.

Ringo was startled. He had not noticed a group of men entering and sitting at an adjacent table. There were dressed in Indian outfits. He thought they must be part of the show put on by the management, you know, for local colour.

"It relaxes me," said Ringo. "I'm told I shouldn't; it's bad for me, but once in awhile . . ."

"Who would say such a thing?" asked the largest of the men.

Judging by his stature and his weathered face, Ringo guessed he was the leader. Ringo thought he looked familiar, that he'd seen the fellow's picture somewhere. Perhaps he was a famous American actor. His features were sharp, chiseled. The lines under his cheeks were deep and led to his mouth—wide and frowning. The eyes were narrow and dark but sagacious. His hair was tied tightly in two long braids. For Ringo, he looked the quintessential Indian chief from the flicks. Ringo enjoyed American Westerns: the cowboys, the Indians, and the vast landscape. He had no idea how vast it actually was until he flew over it.

The other two were smaller but each had an immediate presence. The youngest, Ringo thought, reminded him of a clergyman. He simply had a pious and calming attitude, like a vicar he had known in his youth when his mother, Elsie, called out for "Little Richie" to dress for church. The third was the oldest codger Ringo had ever seen. He knew him from the plane. "Thought I might see you again." He smelled of yonks, the ages, and of cashews. "Are you gents part of the show?" he asked.

"Indirectly," answered the leader.

"Obliquely," said the pious one. He looked at Ringo with penetrating eyes.

"Don't tell me," said Ringo, "your lot plays word games, too."

The old fellow just smiled, laughed noiselessly, and slapped dust off his shoulders.

"Smoke," said the priest, "is an important part of rituals. It is used by storytellers when educating our youth, when telling the sacred animal stories. Smoke is shared when we tell of the animal people—Coyote and Raven, and of the clans: Turtle, Deer, and Porcupine. Smoke carries our songs and thanks to Wakan Tonka for the creation of humankind. Smoke is sacred."

"Yep," thought Ringo, "he's a vicar all right."

"Smoke is used by healers who treat the ill and infirmed. It accompanies . . ."

"Initiates," said the chief.

". . . our concerts and dances,"

"Judging by the aroma in the air outside in the theatre," said Ringo, "I'd guess the audience of this concert is initiating some heavy smoke, if ya' know what I mean."

"But, of the most importance," continued the holy man, "is that smoke is offered when opening a conversation, a meeting, and to inaugurate a friendship. You will meet others of us on this night— an associate . . ."

"An apprentice," said the old one, speaking for the first time.

"To offer him tobacco would be hospitable and beneficial."

"I've been rude," said Ringo. "Would you chaps care for a . . ."

"You have already shared with us," said the chief. "It was your smoke that called us from the rocks."

Ringo started to ask another question, but the priest interrupted, "You're the drummer?"

"Aye," said Ringo. "Are you fans, then?"

"We've been waiting a long time," answered the chief.

"Well," said Ringo, "we were almost late. The back way through these mountains is serpentine and treacherous. Trust me, I know. It's been a long and winding road. And the traffic clogged with teeny boppers; well, I don't have to tell you about the delirious danger there. Have you been watching the news? You need to watch the news."

"We know of long roads," said the oldest.

The priest asked, "Do you know of the importance of drums? Do you know of their symbolic significance?"

" 'Course I know," said Ringo, "but I wish you'd tell me chums," said Ringo. "They often think very little of the rhythmical contributions."

"The drum's round form represents the universe , the circle of the drum head is the circle of life. The drum beat is the pulse, the throbbing heart at the center of the circle," said the pious fellow. "As the voice of Wakan Tanka, it stirs and helps us understand the mystery and magical power of things."

"Like I said," said Ringo, "I wish you'd tell me mates. They think it's all guitars and lyrics."

"Songs tell our story," said the chief. "It is through songs that we communicate with the Great Spirit. Songs define us. Songs prepare us for death. But, the beat of the drum is the thunder that resonates, rattles, a man's heart out of despair, and the rattle is the rain drumming on the human heart. The voice in song is the lightening of the thunderstorm. The flute is the wind."

"From your lips . . .," said Ringo.

"The flute," said the oldest, "has six holes, one for each of the four sacred directions and one each for the earth and the sky. I play the flute. I am the wind and I hear the drums. A hundred deaths have I suffered and yet I hear the distant beat of the drums of my fathers. As do you Tatanka Iotanka, and you Wichasha Wakan. I feel our fathers' and their fathers' drums within my heart, and their hypnotic rhythm mirrors the beating of my heart, and because I hear the drums I shall endure a thousand more deaths if necessary to take coup upon Pahaska. This drummer before us has helped to bring together the magic."

"I couldn't have said it better meself," said Ringo.

"It is said that you four shall bring a new age," asked the chief. "Do you think this is so? Are you four seers, four prophets mindful of the four sacred directions and of the circle? Is an awakening to be driven by the rhythm of your drum?"

"I'd like to think I'm a part of the new movement," said Ringo, "but, honestly, we're all a bit surprised by the reception, and I'm only the drummer."

"The drum is the magic and the mystery," said the priest.

"Come to think of it, I have to agree: it's the drum beat that carries us along," said Ringo. "Anyway, things are moving pretty fast. We say we want a revolution, that it's about the music, and you're right: It's the drum and the song that's led us to this magical mystery tour."

"We know of magic and mystery," said the old grizzled man. "Don't forget, drummer, you must help, in any way you can, our initiate . . . the warrior."

The cigarette, finally consumed near the filter, began to burn Ringo's fingers. He looked down, concentrating on snubbing it out, unconsciously checking to see if he had burned himself rather than attending to his guests, Ringo cavalierly asked, "How will I know him?"

He looked up. No one was there, but he heard a departing voice say, "You will know him. He will come to you from the dark. Lead him to the light."

"Blimey," said Ringo. "Now that was abso-bloody-lutely Shakespearian, wasn't it? If I didn't know any better, I'd say I've taken role in fookin' Hamlet . . ."

"Ringo," a voice at the door startled him. It was Paul. "You're wanted, lad."

"Well," said Ringo, "that's nice to hear at last, en'it."

"What are you getting on about?" said Paul.

"Paul," asked Ringo as he exited the eerie room, "do you believe in ghosts?"

"Not likely," said Paul.

"What if I told you some spirits said to me in a dream, that we was initiating an era of magic? What would you say?"

"Well," said Paul, "there you are."

Chapter Thirty-one

Fancy Dancing

Summer, 1964

Come together, right now, over me . . .
-John Lennon

They are all coming together.
-Turtle

Rivers heard but did not see the arrow that whizzed past him. The, "Whoa, look out, Troy!" came much too late to warn him, came several seconds after the buzz of the aluminum rocket had sailed on toward the concentric circle target and pierced the bull's-eye with the smooching sound of a wet kiss.

"Damn, Horace! You almost killed me!"

Ho yelled from the opposite end of the convention center, "No, Troy, I almost wounded you. What the heck are you doing coming up *those* stairs anyway?"

"I wanted to look out the west window at the teepee city. How was I to know you guys were up here target-shooting?"

The convention center, was over two city blocks long and a city block wide. It was basically a large dome with a huge arena floor surrounded by a maze of halls and satellite rooms. There were suites of offices at the east end, several stories high, and around the entire interior perimeter of the huge oval was a balcony suspended about two stories in height. Most of the activities of The First Annual Intertribal Four-Corners Powwow would take place on the arena floor. The balcony would serve as a viewing platform and a quicker route from one end to the other should a pedestrian wish to avoid the huge crowds below.

Ho, Veloy Vigil, and several others had set archery targets at the west end of the balcony and were working their way backwards to the east end challenging one another to impossible shots with their bows and arrows. The seventy-meter competition distance quickly grew boring, and with creative minds: boredom breeds mischief.

The bows were not historical Indian weapons made of hardwood and sinew. They were not the rugged short bows shot from the back of a sprinting pony while plunging handcrafted, stone tipped arrows deeply into the haunch of a stampeding buffalo. These were fiberglass and carbon-body bows, with machine-tooled limbs and alloy handles, weighted with stabilizer bars, and strung with pulleys for plunging frail target arrows of carbon and aluminum into brightly colored circles. These were bows with sights and buttresses, and many were more valuable than the cars and trucks of their owners. The battle for the West was not fought with this technology. These were equipment for the Modern Olympiad—bows more from the realms of science than the hunt, aristocratic weapons which, in this case, found themselves in the hands of hooligans.

Ho possessed a prototype of the first compound bow created by Holless Wilber Allen. He had yet to apply for a patent. The model he loaned to Horace was based on an earlier design by Claude Lapp and artistically enhanced by Allen. Ho's reputation as an archer, and friendship with Fred Bear, of Bear Archery fame, made Horace a likely candidate to field test the bizarre bow. The design used six wheels, eccentric hanging metal brackets, and narrow fiberglass limbs. The bowstring crisscrossed in a confusing weave behind the riser. After a few warm-up arrows, Ho decided this was the best thing since Christmas.

Veloy had a beautiful handmade, recurve bow. He teased Ho that the machine he was using would take the romance out of archery. He needed to say something—Ho was consistently the better shot.

The latest volley from Ho, hitting a ten-point bull's-eye, and nearly impaling his friend, required of the archer that he arc the arrow from within an inch or two of the conference center ceiling in order for it to make the city block distance to the target at the opposite end of the building. In a game of Robin-Hood-Horse that had lasted the better part of an hour, Ho was: *H-O-R*, and Veloy was ironically: *H-O*. A couple of the other contestants were about to go out, *H-O-R-S* and an *E,* if they couldn't match the bull's-eye Horace had just scored.

"Do I have to shoot it past Rivers?" asked the next archer.

"Naw, just make the target, that's all," said Ho.

"How much is ridin' on this?" asked the other man, shooting to save an *E.*

"Twenty bucks," answered Veloy, already fantasizing how he was going to spend the money.

"Troy!" yelled Horace, "you may want to move on by, please. Roberto here is getting anxious to lose his money!"

"I'm on my way. Hold your fire." Troy hurried past the target to the huge picture windows on the west end of the dome. He looked out upon a small sea of teepees pitched on the large grass area between the convention hall and Speer Boulevard. Troy petitioned for special permission from the Mayor of Denver to allow many of the powwow participants to pitch tents on the grounds. The result was a teepee village of nearly a thousand tents running for blocks parallel to the boulevard and Cherry Creek. It was quite a sight for the Denverites driving down Speer, a main thoroughfare in the city.

Horace joked that it was probably bigger than the Sioux and Cheyenne village that surprised Custer when he rounded the bend of the Little Big Horn.

Troy Rivers was taking great pride in the view when a distracting "thunk" sounded above and behind him. Roberto had made a poor choice in using a fixed broadhead arrow; it stuck in the ceiling.

"That'll be twenty big ones, chump," said Ho. "Veloy, you're next."

Veloy did not hesitate. He placed his feet in a wide stance, loaded the arrow, and pulled back the cord against his cheek as he elevated the bow. The fourteen-strand string and the arrow sung as he released. His arrow flew precisely on the arching path he planned. What he did not anticipate, however, was that while Roberto's elevation was poor, his line was true. Veloy's missile careened off the hanging fletching, the feathered vane, of Roberto's arrow and ricocheted off the balcony about five feet from Troy.

Rivers waved at the group of contestants, "I'll move!" he yelled.

"Interference!" protested Veloy.

After a long argument, they decided to give him another try. But in order to expedite the situation and quell Veloy's complaints that Roberto's arrow impeded the perfect path for a winning shot, Ho pulled a squirrel arrow from his quiver. It had a blunt metal tip rather than a point; thus, should not stick in a tree limb when hunting squirrels. It was the concussion, rather than an impaling, that *whomped* the life out of the rodent. Ho took only a few seconds to aim, pulling the bowstring up against his chin and the tip of his nose. He lightly kissed the string and released. The flat-nosed missile hummed as it swiftly approached the arrow imbedded in the ceiling. The blunt end struck exactly at the base of the arrowhead, shattering the shaft. Both arrows fell to the arena floor, hitting Flora Florida, fondly known as *Aromatic Flower* by several of the archers (and a few others), who was setting up her booth and unloading a box of new toys from the Wham-O Corporation—bright plastic disks called Frisbees. With good humor she yelled up at the party of bowmen, "OK, you ruffians, this means war!" She took a red disk from a box of dozens, held it by the edge, pulled her arm across her body, and pitched the plastic saucer with a flick of her wrist. It flew in a straight line, forcing the band of merry men to duck.

They rose at different intervals, exhibiting varying degrees of surprise and risking a peek at the woman who had just performed this magic. "That was cool," said Ho, the first to stand up and fully expose himself to danger if Flora was going to fire another. Her arm was cocked and ready when he said, "Can you pitch one out over that way, away from us?"

"I can put one any damn place I please," she laughed. "Why?"

"I could use a moving target."

"Hey, I'm selling these things. They cost money, hermano."

"How much?"

"For you, Horace . . . two bucks."

"For a plastic pie pan?"

"For an original Wham-O Frisbee, you bet—two bucks, no tax."

"How about, if I hit it—it's free, if I miss it, I'll buy a half-dozen?"

"It's a deal. You other Ton-toes are my witnesses. Here goes!" She gracefully ran a few steps and with a twisting torso motion arched the red disk into the air. It gained altitude as it rode the still currents of the arena.

Horace strung a target arrow, judged the flight of the saucer, and kissed the string as he released. At the last second the rotating disk, as if sensing an impending jolt from the bolt, dipped slightly on the dead air. The arrow missed and flew on where it exploded off the steel girders just above Troy Rivers.

He broke into a self-protective run and screamed across the arena, "Maybe it's time you boys took your game outside—before somebody gets hurt!"

Veloy pointed at the running Rivers, "There's your moving target, Ho."

"Naw, no challenge." He leaned over the railing and yelled down to Flora, "How about double or nothing?"

"Sure, Horace. A couple of more shots like that and I won't have to work the booth tomorrow." She let fly with a blue disk, difficult to see against the windows.

"Clever, girl," he said as he pulled the bowstring and gauged the flight of the toy. The arrow left the balcony with a zing and impaled the disk forty yards away with a midair smooch. It pivoted to the ground with the asymmetrical loops of a wounded bird.

The band of braves broke into cheers.

"Damn," said Flora under her breath and then to the group of dancing adolescents on the balcony, "That's it, I'm not going to play with you bad boys anymore."

Veloy asked Flora to throw one for him. "No way, you hoodlums will ruin my profits."

Veloy offered to buy one if she would throw it. Just then the booming voice of Troy Rivers came over the intercom. He made it back to the offices without any wounds and went straight to the PA. "That's it Robin Hood. You and your gang of merry men take your games outside. Building Security is here; they're pissed and so am I. Horace Green, you and the others have plenty of work to do to get ready for the opening of the powwow tomorrow. Understood?"

They laughed and waved toward the office windows and began to pack up their equipment. Rivers was right; they had plenty to do to prepare for tomorrow's big events.

It was an explosion of color and rhythmic movement, over a thousand dancers entered the exhibit area in an undulating parade of feathers, beads, and bells. Fifty drum teams, in perfect synchronization, molded the sidewalk of sound upon which the dancers made their Grand Entry. To the ears of whites in the audience the reverberation was too loud; it sounded like the rumbling bowels of The Beast, but to the dancers, who felt the booming of the hundred drums surge through their bodies to their bones, it was the heartbeat of Tierra Madre.

Rivers thought that perhaps it was in response to the national announcement of the death of Orvis Kahnawake that brought the large numbers of participants. Perhaps it was also that the time was right for the powwow to stand as a symbol of the reemergence, and the populace wanted to be there. Regardless, two thousand dancers and drummers, twice what Orvis, Ho, and Troy had anticipated crowded the convention center. In total, there were nearly three thousand participants entered in the variety of competitions. The extensive list included the Senior Men's: Straight, Traditional, Fancy, and Grass; the Senior Women's: Cloth, Buckskin, Shawl, and the melodic Jingle Dance; Junior Boys and Junior Girls competed in the same categories as the adults.

An unofficial count placed over one hundred tribes and twenty-five states with representatives. Troy had to do some last minute fancy-dancing-fund-raising on his own to increase the prize money for the dancers. Over fifty drum teams from the hundred Nations of Indian people registered for contests. Hundreds of other drummers and kinsmen participated in the powwow but not the formal competitions. Estimates placed spectator crowds at fifty thousand. It was huge.

Troy had been troubleshooting, putting out small fires here and there; he took on the duties usually facilitated by Orvis as well as his legal responsibilities. Deliveries were late, conference staffs took too many breaks or were not at their posts, union guys were creating back-up at the loading docks, permits were lost.

Concessionaires had problems. Someone stole a case of Frisbees from Flora Florída. Most all the booths ran out of change—every visitor to the powwow carried only twenty-dollar bills and bought only one sixty-cent coke. Extension cords were hijacked, microphones went kaput; the Jingle Dress Dance needed another judge. He solved that problem by volunteering himself. He had an ulterior motive. Her name was Patty.

Rivers finally understood what it was that delighted Orvis about this particular dance. The hundreds of snuff can jingles on each dress, singing in harmony with the hundred other sister dancers created a choir of thousands of snuff bells, and the ten thousand bells in turn, in rhythm, in sync accentuated the soft simultaneity of the steps of the dancers. It was simple, symphonic choreography, a hypnotic prayer to awaken Mother Earth.

The Intertribals always needed another judge or score keeper. Ho Ho Ho finally cornered Troy and had him watch the current king of the Powwow Trail, a young athletic Fancy Dancer named Robert Adrian. He was covered in ribbons and yarn streamers. He wore a double bustle of eagle feathers wrapped in bright red, black, and white cords, fringed and beaded buckskins, a high fur roach topped off with eagle feathers, silk pendants, beaded cuffs, buffalo fur leggings, and bright moccasins. The moccasins helped the audience see the dazzling footwork.

When he danced he became fire—the long yarn and silk streamers trailing just behind and mimicking the flying arms, the twisting torso and pounding feet seemed to gain altitude as the dancer spun. He seemed to become vaporous, air born. Then, as the main auditorium lights dimmed and various colored spots danced over the frenzy, stopping briefly to focus on individual athletes, a blue light captured the young Adrian, moving like a stream of water. The surreal environment was transformed to that of the coral reef and the dancer undulated to the rhythm of a stormy sea. A golden, yellow light lingered, and he became air, a whirlwind, a dust devil of the American plains. A red spot, and he was fire again.

A dream state usurped the interior of the building. Spectators stood frozen. Pedestrians on the elevated walk halted and leaned over the railings to watch. The cadence of the drums captured each of the fifty thousand heartbeats and cajoled them into parallel rhythm. The auditorium became engulfed in a fog of song, a misty and colorful cloud of chant, pierced by undulating, swallow contrails of flute.

"Don't blink," yelled Horace above the thunderous artillery of the drums and shrill peal of the song, "they all must stop exactly on the last drum beat."

Rivers listened for some hint of the conclusion to the concussion of the drumming. He could hear only the redundant rhythm. "How do they know?" he asked.

"They know. Watch."

In a sudden silence as explosive as the drumming itself, the crowded auditorium floor changed from fire to flowers in a heartbeat. Every dancer stopped and posed as if frozen in time until, seconds later the audience erupted in their own congratulatory cheers.

Horace wore a grin as wide as the convention center. Veloy Vigil ran up to Troy and Ho and yelled, "Is that kid hot, or what?"

"Charged," answered Rivers.

"Radioactive," laughed Ho Green.

"Thanks for making me pay attention, Horace."

"Fancy Dancing is jolting," Horace answered, "but Traditional hits you here." He put his fist over his heart. "You need to quit working so hard and enjoy some of this, Troy. People will figure things out."

"He's right, you know, Mr. Rivers," said Veloy. "You have worked very hard for all of us. You need to loosen your tie and enjoy the brotherhood. This is a celebration, verdad, it's meant to make you happy."

"Well, you're both right, of course. It's just that the news media is supposed to show up today; I've been a little nervous, so I relied on old habits—the coat and tie. Thought I'd try to look good for the cameras."

"I think the media is going to be disappointed, Mr. Rivers, if they come looking for an Indian and find a banker."

Both Troy and Horace laughed. "You may be right, Veloy," said Rivers. "And please call me Troy, or from you I would be honored to be called by the name of my home: Three Rivers."

"It is I who am honored, Three Rivers." He backed away and as he turned and broke into a run he looked over his shoulder and yelled, "I'll catch up. There is something I have to get."

"Did I say something wrong, Ho?"

"Not at all. You extended him an honor. He's just going to get something, like he said. He'll find us."

"In this crowd?"

"Sure. After all, he's an Indian."

"Oh, Ho, I've really missed your rotten sense of humor."

"Good. Did you hear the one about the traveling trader whose wagon broke down and he had to spend the night in a hogan with an old Navajo and his three daughters?"

Just then the public address interrupted, "Mr. Troy Rivers, you are needed at the conference office. Mr. Rivers . . .."

"Saved!" said Rivers. "I'll catch up to you later." He began to jog away. "Hey," he said to Ho, "I recognize that voice."

"How is Patty?" Horace asked. "If I read the schedule right, she volunteered for office duty. I think," he looked at his watch, "it starts right about . . . now. We'll see you later."

"Are you sure you can find us in this crowd? After all . . .."

"Very funny. If I get lost, I'll have you paged."

He entered the office, giddy with anticipation. Patty had arrived just today from Blanca and they had not had a chance to talk. There she was, leaning on the front of the desk, dressed in her Jingle Dance outfit. He rushed her. They embraced. How he had missed her.

"Is that how you treat all your clients, counselor Rivers?" said Shirley Lauderbach, stepping into the office from the backroom. Shirley was one of the executive assistants from Earl, Brownstone, Barber and Delta. She was on loan for clerical and coordinator duties.

In his excitement to see Patty, he forgot that Shirley was on the clock. "Ms. Lauderbach, may I introduce you to Officer Patty Andrette, Park Ranger and dancer extraordinaire."

"Oh, Patty and I are already old friends. I think she is going to be a wonderful assistant. We need all the volunteers we can get, so don't go scaring one away by groping the help. Or is there something going on here that I don't know about?"

Troy and Patty blushed. "I'm sure you'll hear more than you need to," said Rivers, "if I leave you gals alone in the office for very long." The two women feigned an insult. But for now, Shirley, can you hold down the fort? Patty and I have some catching up to do."

"Actually, Mr. Rivers, I hate to be a wet blanket, but we just got a call from the City Manager's Office. There is some kind of trouble with the bus to the picnic."

"What kind of trouble?"

"There isn't one."

"What do you mean, Shirley?"

"They called and said there was a mix-up and that, although they know they owe you a bus to the staff picnic as part of the convention center rental, there is not one available. They want to talk about possible solutions, and asked that you call them, but you have to do it right away. It being the week end and all, they're about to close up shop."

"Who is they?"

"Actually it was the driver of the bus. He noticed on Friday that the work order was for the wrong day. He brought it to the attention of his supervisor, who was supposed to bring it up with *his* supervisor, who didn't contact his administrator, who has the authority to call another supervisor who should have talked to someone in the Mayor's office to clear-up the mistake and authorize a bus, and so on, and so on."

"It sounds like they took you through all the bureaucratic levels of inefficiency," he said. "Man, I hate dealing with civil servants." "Did *they* leave a number?"

She handed him a small, pink piece of paper. He took Patty's hand and walked into the adjoining office. He closed the door.

"There are things she could do while you are calling the city, Mr. Rivers. Things are stacking up," said Lauderbach through the door. There was no answer. "Busy with other things, I take it?" No reply.

As soon as the door closed, their kiss was long and tender.

When Rivers returned to Shirley's outer office after several minutes, he noticed Horace leaning on her desk. "Well, you were right," Rivers said to her, "I spoke to the driver who alerted his supervisor who told his other supervisor, and so on and so on. Of course none of the supervisor sons-of-bitches are available to straighten out things. Pardon my French."

"Merde," she giggled.

Rivers smiled

"What are you going to do?"

"Well, the driver is trying to call a charter bus company, and can you believe it, the company is owned by his cousin?"

"Yes, I can believe it," she answered. She turned away from him and faced her typewriter which clicked efficiently. "And I think that fucker is trying to screw you."

"I *am* feeling a little abused," he answered.

The phone rang. They both looked at it. "I'll take it," he said. "You keep working." He picked up the phone but covered the mouth piece before talking to whomever was on the line. "Shirley, I don't believe in the law office I ever heard you use that word?"

"Well, I don't believe I ever did. However, this is the weekend."

He laughed and spoke into the phone, "Rivers."

It was the woman in the ticket booth at the front entrance to the convention center. "There is a Channel Two News truck unloading their stuff in front of the building. Do I let them inside, gratis?"

"Of course, Beth. Tell them to take all the footage they want in the arena and if they need me I'll be out on the floor soon. I'll find them or they can have me paged." He hung up the phone.

"Seriously, Troy," said Shirley. "Is there something I can do to help with the bus debacle?"

"We'll wait awhile and see if the bus driver calls back with a contract for his cousin. If they do, remind him I've got a keg of beer chilling and a ton of hot-dogs to transport, along with about forty-six staff. They've got to take us to . . . what's the name of that park? By the way, are you coming to the picnic?"

"Paramount and probably not."

"Why not? You've earned a free meal."

"That I have and I'm going to get one—from you. But its going to be another night and it going to be in a very expensive and exclusive restaurant."

"I understand." He left the office in a hurry.

The news that a TV crew had arrived with cameras quickly circulated through the arena resulting in a strategic declaration from the MC, Russell Schemitzun, that another Grand Entry was being called. Two or more Grand Entries a day was not that uncommon.

"Stop what you're doing, Indi'ns," broadcast Schemitzun, "Get yourselves prepared. We're going to have another Grand Entry, brothers and sisters, so gather in the halls and make ready. Drum teams find those elk skin drums. Singers loosen up those vocal cords. You young dancers stop the snagging—get those hormones under control. You men get back to your wives and you wives quit flirting with your neighbors. We'll not take any responsibility for divorces or babies; let's concentrate on the business of dancing. It's time for a celebration. We dance and sing for life; we dance and sing for victory—we dance and sing because we're still here! Make ready for a G-r-r-r-and E-n-n-n-try!"

The palpable energy was vitalizing, everyone was hustling their bustles to line up for the parade. The camaraderie was contagious and invigorating. Troy stayed in the wings and watched the TV crew from a distance, they could see the energy without his help, and had their large video cameras humming, capturing the fever and the color. If they had questions, they could ask them later. He felt conspicuous in his Brooks Brother's suit. Horace and Veloy approached him, coming from near the cameras and the heart of the action.

"No wonder you're hiding, Rivers," said Ho, "You still look like a lawyer."

Troy ignored the jibe and looked past his friend at the gathering dancers and the TV crew but instinctively straightened his tie.

"Maybe I can help with that," said Veloy. He handed Troy a package wrapped in colorful paper. It had a small cottonwood branch tied to the top with a few dollar bills taped to the branch.

Troy accepted the package but had a serious question on his face. He looked at Ho.

"Open it!" Horace shook his head. "You don't accept presents any better than you accept compliments."

Troy held the package. It was heavy so he set it on the floor, untied the branch, set it next to the package, and pulled at the bright paper. People passing by smiled knowingly at Veloy and gave him various signs of approval. "Yá át ééh, buena idea!" said one man.

Still puzzled, Troy opened the cardboard box. From inside he lifted a bone vest, each parallel bone perfectly matched to its partner above and below. A line of four eagle feathers hung from the bottom, one for each of the sacred directions. Below the vest lay a beaded loincloth of delicate deerskin. Rectangular borders of bead and silk reinforced the geometry of the leather. A bright beaded circle filled the center. The top, bottom, right, and left apexes of the circle were the four sacred colors of the four directions and the four seasons. A diagonal "X" divided the circle into four pie shaped sections. In the top section was the profile of a black mesa in front of sacred blue mountains of the Pueblo People. In the right was a great green turtle of the Huron. The bottom depicted the silhouette of a skyscraper and a tall pine tree, and to the left was a white, beaded buffalo.

"I don't know what to say," Troy stumbled.

"I started the loincloth months ago thinking it was for Orvis. That's why I put in the skyscraper and the tree, you know. But last month I added the turtle; you are of Turtle Clan are you not?"

"Yes, I am, Veloy, but this is too much."

"So when we lost Orvis, I figured it was the right thing to present this to you. And when I saw you in your lawyer's suit again, I felt it best to do now, today."

"Veloy, I don't know what to say. This is beautiful."

"I am pleased, if you are pleased. Perhaps you will wear these humble things if you talk to the TV camera." He shook Rivers hand and walked into the crowd where several witnesses nodded with approval.

"Horace, what does this mean?"

"It means he wants to honor you for your deeds, but more importantly, he's announcing that you're 'one of us.' It means he wants to be your friend."

"What do I do, how should I respond?"

Horace shrugged: no help. His look suggested that the answer should be obvious and simple, but the gifts humbled Rivers. He was still ignorant of many Indi'n ways and stumbled to understand living within the Circle.

Horace finally answered, "Be his friend."

The drums began like thunder, the chanting chorus of voices rose in the air, otherworldly, alien to Western tonal music, like the songs of distant wolves. Troy Rivers, timid to expose his emotions, gathered his gifts, held them tightly, and walked shyly from the crowd toward a quiet stairwell. He sought the sanctuary of the conferences offices, but in his haste he accidentally bumped into an old man standing by the door. "Excuse me, father, I am clumsy." The old one only smiled and nodded in agreement. He held the door for Rivers. As Troy passed him, and he felt the breath of the old man holding the door with some obvious exertion, he thought he smelled cashews.

"Horace said it's a symbol of friendship. I didn't know what to do," said Rivers to Patty as he sat on the corner of the desk. She held the loincloth in the air, inspecting the detailed beadwork. "What should I do?" he asked her.

"Be his friend," she replied.

"I am his friend," said Troy. "You know what I mean. Should I give him something back?"

"Only if you want to complicate things. You lawyers! Can't you just accept a gift. It seems to me that he gave you this because you have already given him something. Didn't you say that Veloy told you the gifts were a token of appreciation for all the work you've done?"

"Sorta'. I guess. I just don't *really* know what to do."

"I'd wear them for the camera, as he suggested."

"Now that makes sense. Why didn't I think of that?"

"You would have." She lifted the vest from the box. "There are some nice leggings here, too." She set down the vest and lifted the crotchless pants. She inspected the beadwork along the seams. "This is beautiful work. I would guess both he and his wife spent a lot of time on this. They look like they sould fit. Try them on."

He went into his office. Getting caught half dressed in the front office with Patty could tickle a few gossips. While watching through the window that overlooked the arena floor, he took off his tie, suit coat, and pants. He gently lifted the vest over his head and onto his torso. He struggled putting on the leggings over his socks and boxers and then wrapped the ornate loincloth around his hips. He stepped out of the office and stood in front of Patty.

"The black socks are a bit much," she said.

He leaned on her desk again and pulled off the socks.

"Well, that's more natural, but it looks a bit unfinished. You're not wearing your underwear are you?"

"That's none of your business." He looked as his bare feet and thought about wearing his Italian loafers without socks. "I don't have any moccasins."

"I do," said Horace Green, standing in the doorway of the office. He set a pair of calf-high, orange deerskin moccasins on the desk.

"Horace, I don't know what to . . ."

"Just put the damn things on." Rivers did as he was told. "Looks pretty good, Troy. We're going to make a *Skin* out of you yet."

"Sexy," said Shirley Lauderbach as she entered behind Horace.

"Have you gotten us a bus for the picnic yet, Ms. Lauderbach?" asked Troy.

"Working on it, Mr. Rivers. Should I fail, it looks to me like you'll be OK walking. Nice legs . . . sir."

"I concur," said Patty. She moved next to Shirley as if they were teaming up.

"Thank you, Shirley. Thank you, Patty. I've always thought the same of both of you, or as the case may be—yours."

"I never thought you noticed, Mr. Rivers. God knows I have suffered these high heels for quit a while now."

"Oh, I noticed."

"You make your staff wear high heels?" chided Patty.

"Only the women," answered Troy.

"Shirley," said Patty. "We need to talk."

"You two mind if I break this up? What's this about needing a bus for the picnic?" interrupted Horace.

"The City screwed-up our bus," answered Shirley.

"Nice choice of words," said Rivers.

"I'm trying," she answered.

"No bus!" yelled Horace.

"Not at the moment," she said. The phone rang. "Conference offices," she spoke into the receiver. She listened and shook her head to the two men. She hung up the phone and said to Troy, "The TV newscaster would like to interview you on camera, if you're willing. They are down by the bleachers, under the announcer's booth."

"On my way. Horace, Patty, would you like to accompany me?"

"I'd much rather stay here and help Shirley find a ride to the picnic," said Horace.

"Thanks, folks. I'll be fine."

Troy and Patty watched as Ho, reluctant to leave, tipped his cowboy hat, his eyes took on an irregular tilt, one brow higher than the other, and his chin was set equally out of kilter with a thin lipped, lopsided, lascivious grin.

Rivers and the ranger could hardly keep from laughing.

"Your friend is very *legible*, Mr. Rivers," said Shirley.

"That's a coyote grin if I've ever seen one," said Patty. "I believe your administrative assistant needs a cavalry rescue, Mr. Rivers, sir."

"Too late," said Troy. He sang: "You should see by my outfit that I'm not a cowboy."

"What'd I do?" asked Horace, feigning innocence. "Miss Shirley, have I said something wrong?"

"Heal, Horace," said Rivers as he pulled on his arm. "We're heading downstairs."

Chapter Thirty-two

Womb De La Madre

Summer, 1964

I feel revived. The concert at Red Rocks awakens the connection between humans and me. For most concertgoers the connection is subtle and indirect. Their appreciation of the unique setting, the megalithic landscape, moves them spiritually, but few credit the sanctity to Turtle. They have a vague idea that some "intelligence," some creative force must be behind the geological splendor, but they do not name it. They speak of the beauty of Mother Nature; but few acknowledge: Turtle, per se. I don't mind. The important point is that they aesthetically and spiritually respond to the gigantic prisms of red stone that form the deep bowl of the amphitheater, and whether or not they utter a prayer or gasp in awe to Turtle is irrelevant. Their wonder vivifies me, as does the music.

The visual artists have Lascaux; I mentioned earlier that prehistoric cathedral to culture, but the musicians have Red Rocks. It is not quite a cave; the stars serve as the ceiling, but the hallowed envelope remains. The music creates a divine cavern. And there I nestle among the cliffs and caves and listen to the music enhanced by the perfect acoustics sculpted by The Turtle Trio: Wind, Rain, and yours truly—musicians in our own right.

This is why Red Rocks and the Front Range are among my favorite haunts. Of course, there are always a handful of discriminating souls who recognize my handiwork. One such devotee is Anthony Hands of the Bear, a connoisseur of the canyons of red stone and a rascal who reminds me of my sons: Sapling and Flint. It remains to be seen which ancestor will dominate his destiny.

The perpetual child in Anthony enjoyed "playing renegade Apache" in the canyons, bowls, and arroyos of Red Rocks. The child remembered that he was always a champion at hide-and-seek. He became the stone, the pine tree; he was invisible in the shadows, a phantom among the crevasses. He was one with the earth.

When he first moved to Denver, settled on Lookout Mountain, and claimed a fiefdom on the pool table at Cody's, he enjoyed double dating with his friend Delregis. Both were poor, so a typical date was an afternoon picnic in a hidden canyon at Red Rocks. A social afternoon, cooled with a case of chilled Coors, would turn into an evening of adult hide-and-seek in which only Delregis would worry about being found. Tony, the master, would steal kisses from both dates as he mystically appeared from out of the shadows. A kiss, a guilty giggle, and he would disappear. Eventually, Delregis would give up the search and call all in: "ollie ollie ox in free," never the wiser.

Their childish cowboy versus Indian games went so far as to use dime store bows and arrows, dart guns, squirt guns, and when they were really trying to impress their dates, they would "aqua ambush" them with water balloons. At the end of the game, with the girls shivering from the soaking, Tony would suggest that they could warm up by "catching rays" in the buff atop the huge pediments of red stone.

Picnics, however, had lately been few and far between. Delregis served time for trespassing on posted land. He thought, in trying to hide from the police, that he could become one with a blue spruce. Delregis was a good enough apprentice, but not yet the master. The Feds had no patience with the novice, rejected the idea of "do over's," couldn't have cared less about hide-and-seek, and roughed him up during the arrest. They had no sense of humor. *Well?* . . . Tony had to rethink that criticism. When they pulled Delregis from the treetop, they allowed their canine partner to teeth tattoo his rump. Tony saw the scars after a coed water balloon battle. What a boisterous, fun-loving bunch those federal cops were.

He missed Delregis. A serious girl staked a claim on his heart. He liked the attention; she became possessive; they both agreed that Tony was a bad influence—the games had become dangerous after all. Tony believed she was more worried about the post water balloon ritual than the danger. Regardless, she forced Delregis to continue his construction career in Fraser, Colorado, a

Continental Divide away from Tony and their rambunctious romps on The Rocks.

Tony liked working at Red Rocks. He did not mind remodeling concession stands, repairing thousands of wooden benches, hanging hundreds of lights, and laying miles of flagstone steps. He related spiritually so well to the sedimentary cathedral that he even tolerated repairing the bathrooms.

What he could not tolerate, however, no matter how warm he felt about The Rocks, was his boss—Henry Humboldt, Chief Supervisor in Charge, Red Rocks Rangers, the indigenous security "authority." Since Delregis was gone, Tony was getting all of Humboldt's attention. The unwanted scrutiny forced him to accelerate his skills at hiding. His two best hiding places were the dark canyons of The Rocks and the dim atmosphere of Buffalo Bill Cody's Bar Grill Trading Post and Texaco Station. He left Cody's a little while ago and ran by his place for a quick shower. He had new prospects in Red Rocks and he wanted to smell good.

Tony congratulated himself for disappearing after dropping off those four limey characters instead of hanging around back stage. As entertaining as they were, his instincts told him that Humboldt wasn't far away, and besides, he was on a quest. He decided to avoid the crowds filling the walking ramps to the amphitheater and slipped off the path into the rocks. He felt right at home. He emerged from the trees just a few yards from the bathroom where he discovered the Indian tomb. He knew he wasn't supposed to be there. Immediately upon informing Henry about the grave, he was rudely escorted out of the park by Humboldt's lackeys.

"This is far too important for you to be hanging around and screwing things up, Hard-hat," said Henry. "Get your ass out of here and don't breathe a word of this to anyone if you know what's good for you . . . if you want to keep your job."

Two things brought Tony back to the grave. One was his resentment of Henry, but this was not the first time he had risked his employment by disobeying Humboldt. It had become a game. The second motive, the real reason for his insubordination, was that while hiding out at Cody's he saw Olivia Hotchkiss, Lady Anthropologist, in a television interview. It was clear that she was alone in guarding the tomb. He was mildly curious about what happened to Henry and his subordinates; figured they were busy with concert security in the amphitheater proper, couldn't let anyone rush the stage or steal a coke. However, he was highly intrigued by the images of this woman. She was definitely worth a libidinal look see, Humboldt and the crowds be damned. He chose a spot near the entrance of the tomb but convenient to the shadows if he needed to disappear. Olivia was there; she looked better in real life than on TV.

Her hair was long and blonde, braided in a thick column. Pools of potential tears filled her earth brown eyes behind large round, lightly tinted sunglasses. Tony thought the circular lenses made her appear more vulnerable, animal-like, maybe like a large kitten. They kept slipping down her thin nose and she was having trouble pushing them back with her middle finger and keeping a hold on the shovel. She was swinging the shovel at bystanders who were teasing her about looting the tomb. Her plight and teary eyes and the way her breasts bounced as she swung the shovel at some marauder pulled at Tony's heart.

Several youths were amusing themselves by harassing Olivia with short feints. The hooligans always managed to jump just out of shovel reach and the whole crowd was laughing at the spectacle. Where was Henry and his ninnies? Probably on a coffee break. Tony's instinctive empathy for the underdog came to play. He pushed his way to the front of the crowd and stood a moment behind a longhaired young man who was taking special delight in tormenting Olivia. Her frustration only added to Tony's fascination. At least half-a-dozen swings by Olivia missed the boy by a foot, and the crowd roared as a mighty sweep threw her off balance and she nearly fell on a bottom Anthony thought was pretty cute in her tight jeans. But she came up swinging, and just as the lad jumped back, Tony subtly shoved forward. The shovel probably would have taken his head off but Olivia's bosom got in the way, her swing went low and the shovel made the sound of a pancake hitting a hot griddle. He folded.

"You've killed him!" It was probably the wounded lad's girlfriend. "Oh, my god, you've killed him." She rushed to take him and his palpable pain out of shovel range. He was obviously still alive; one could tell by his whimpering. "You've ruined him," the girl friend amended. An ominous buzz rose above the scene. It was apparent to Tony that the crowd did not think the hit, all things considered, quite cricket. He quickly decided this was the time to make a heroic move. He turned his hat around backwards and stepped forward, pivoted, and faced the angry mob. "All right, you bunch of wild-haired hippies, I think it's time for you to . . ."

Olivia connected.

Tony's yellow hardhat ricocheted into the tomb, bouncing around a corner like a missed pool shot. Tony dropped to his knees, pressing hard on his ears with his palms, trying to stop the ringing that dilated his eyes. He saw an out-of-focus crowd back off (now that Olivia was batting five-hundred).

Concert music suddenly blasted through the valley, and most of the people hurried away. Finally, only Olivia remained with Excalibur, the shovel. Tony's head throbbed; he was still on his knees.

"Are you all right?" she asked.

He could not hear above the ringing in his head but saw she was talking. "Why the hell did you do that, Lady? I was only trying to help."

Olivia did not know she had deafened him. She surprised herself when she broke into tears. "Oh, I'm so sorry, but you don't know what I've been through." She sobbed. "All these people, I'm not used to all these people. I've lived a quiet and gentle life lately. I think they wanted to loot this tomb; they're nothing but a bunch of souvenir thieves. This is too much." She fell forward into Tony's arms.

She did not know he could not hear, but he held her close and whispered softly in her ear, "I know, I know."

"Professor Antwerp is expected at any time. He's the world's greatest expert on the American Indian, you know?"

"I know. I know." he nodded.

"This tomb could be the anthropological find of the century. He knew it might be unguarded. He said I was the only one he could trust. He pulled me out of a place I loved and forced me to come home, to come here. It's madness."

"I know. I know."

"The police have been no help whatsoever. No one is in charge. They're buffoons. You can see; none of them are here. Don't they understand?"

"I know. I know."

"You're so understanding. I don't know how to apologize for hitting you."

"I know. I know."

"Is there anything I can do?"

"I know. I know."

"Sir, can you hear me?"

"I know. I know."

"Oh my god, what have I done?"

"I know. I know." He smiled a blank smile and slowly toppled over on his face.

When he awoke, they were inside the coolness of the tomb. A makeshift tent covered the entryway, draped over the hole left by the collapsed wall of the restroom. A damp cloth lay across his forehead. Olivia sat beside him, wearing his yellow hard hat and making strange sucking noises. He looked at her; there was a thin white tube between her lips.

"Here," she passed him the joint, "this will make your head feel better."

Tony shrugged his shoulders and took the hand rolled cigarette and inhaled. His eyes opened wide as the bitter taste burned his throat. "What the hell is that?" he coughed.

"Niopo. A kind of grass. Try it again. This time hold it in as long as you can."

"Come on, cut the crap! I'm a beer and Turkey man. No thanks." He sat up and felt a sharp pain in his temples.

"I'm telling you," she started rubbing his head with long soft fingers, "it will make you feel better."

He looked at her in the dim light weaving through the tent canvas. The sun would set soon. She seemed to glow. She had taken off her glasses. Her eyes were seductive, her lips full. Her breasts heaved as she sucked on the stick.

"Well, what the hell, why not?" He took the joint and inhaled, holding the heavy smoke long in his lungs.

"Better?"

"I don't know . . . not bad, I guess. Seems to improve my hearing." He took another drag.

They sat for a while in the dimness, passing the medicinal cigarette back and forth. Tony noticed the lights were out in the adjacent bathroom area. His toolbox, a kerosene lamp, and heater sat near the sink. He perused the tomb area. Stacks of Indian pottery sat in rows on the floor and lined the walls on natural stone shelves, so covered with dust they looked as if they were carved from the stone of the cave. More pottery and baskets lined the floor near the cave entrance. Ancient headdresses, bows and quivers, and buckskin leggings hung from bare pine boughs wedged into cracks in the stone. Tomahawks, shields and spears leaned against a stone slab on which lay the remains of the great chieftain. Part skeleton, part mummy slept in what must have been the finest of beaded buckskin, but green-gray moss and spots of fungal umber gave the aging leather a relic hue. Eagle feathers, enduring better than the natural hides, crowned his skull. Ceremonial drums sat at his feet.

"Wow," muttered Tony.

"Feeling it, huh?" said Olivia. "It more intoxicating, more spiritual than the 'rope' the local hippies toke."

"Yea, well, I'm feeling medicated, but . . . ahh, look at this place." He surveyed further, wide-eyed with a mushrooming mellow. "I don't know if it your wacky-tobacky or the vibe I'm getting from the vault."

"Intriguing, isn't it? I've been so busy repelling looters that I haven't had a chance to survey things. What a leader he must have been. I've never heard of the Ute or Arapahoe entombing their chiefs like this, and I've never seen any Indian grave site with this much tribute. Do you suppose he was a Sioux? I vaguely remember a legend about a prophet trying to unite the Sioux with the Ghost Dance ceremony. He promised the return of the buffalo and all the deceased Indians. He said he had seen a vision of the destruction of the whites. But the army squelched the Ghost Dance. If I remember correctly, this was the prologue to the massacre at Wounded Knee. The holy man disappeared, never to be heard from again. Was there some fable about a hidden tomb? You don't suppose this could be it do you? Oh, what was his name? Woo-woo-ka, or something."

"Hunkpapa."

"What? No. I don't think that was it."

"Hunkpapa. The designs on those shields over there are Sioux all right, but they were done by a Hunkpapa warrior."

"I don't understand. My expertise is South American indigenous people. The little I know about North American natives led me to believe this was a Sioux tomb. The buckskin, the war bonnet and all."

"No, you're right. It is Sioux, well, some of it. It's just that Sioux is a white man's term. I think it was actually a Chippewa word. It means *enemy*. I think the French screwed up the pronunciation, and it came out *Sioux*. This guy and his kin called themselves Lakota, and there were about seven or so bands within the Lakota. You've heard of Sitting Bull? Well he was a Hunkpapa. So was this old geezer, or maybe Oglala, judging by the beadwork on the moccasins. Anyway, he's Lakota. The strange thing is the jewelry—that's Navajo." Tony blew a cloud of dust off the squash blossom. "So's the blanket the old guy is lying on. And that looks like a stack of Navajo blankets over there in the corner."

Olivia took up the kerosene lamp and lit it. It hissed an eerie light as she approached the cadaver. "Nossa! I'll be damned, I think you're right. I didn't notice. There were already looters in the tomb when I got here. Who knows what was taken? There are footprints all over the place. Professor Antwerp is going to be irate. The Rangers chased some of the looters, but stopped and said something about having to do crowd control for the concert. No other police have shown. Chief Ranger Humboldt said the other police were called to Lookout, some sort of riot. I was the only one left to guard the relics—until you showed up." She smiled at him. "I'm glad Ranger Humboldt had to leave. He got a message that The Beatles had just pulled into the park; something about them riding in an old pick-up. One of his men recognized the truck. He got all upset all the sudden. Sounds crazy, I know, but I'm glad he's gone. I've been dying to toke-up."

She reached into her backpack and rolled another cigarette. She lit it, inhaled deeply, and handed it to Tony.

"This could be an even greater discovery than I imagined," she continued. "This old chief must have been an Indian Messiah.

Weren't there stories?" She scrutinized Tony. "You're him, aren't you?"

"Him?"

"You're the guy Chief Ranger Humboldt was so upset about. He warned me about you. You discovered the tomb. He said you weren't supposed to be here; you're not to be trusted. You're some kind of con man. I'm supposed to inform him if you show up. You're not a thief, are you?"

"If I wanted to rob the place, I would have done it the first night, and I never would have told Humboldt about it."

"I had a feeling you couldn't be the rat he said you were." She smiled, a very coy and alluring—long eye contact—grin. He looked to confirm that she was flirting. There was nothing overt; she was very cool. "By the way," he said, "the Ghost Dance messiah was Paiute. His name was Wovoka. And you're right: neither the Sioux nor the Paiute had graves like this, and it is certainly not Ute. I don't know who this man was, but he's someone important, and I'll be damned if I'm going to let Henry Humboldt steal his thunder. He's a racist little tyrant."

"He doesn't like you," said Olivia. "That's obvious. Is it because you're an Indian? I'm sorry—Native American. Is that why you came back? To help protect a Native tomb. Why did you come back?"

She gave him that long provocative look again. "You're obviously not a thief, not a souvenir thief, anyway."

"Just to piss off Henry, of course. Somebody needs to keep an eye on the little bigot; otherwise, artifacts could mysteriously disappear. Looters aren't your biggest challenge, not with the Chief Ranger working the backdoor." He smiled his best flirtation grin at her, but sensed it was more Cheshire Cat than Cary Grant. He thought the drug may be putting him off his game. "Why else would I risk an arrest or getting fired . . . coming back to a place where I'm obviously not wanted, been warned against? Why would I risk that kind of danger?" Now he smiled his best, and practiced come-on beam.

"Henry's not here. I'm the only one here," she smiled back. "You don't think I'm dangerous, now do you?"

"I don't know; where's your shovel?"

They both laughed playfully.

"I'd like to think," she said, "you sensed the tomb may be unguarded and you're right: I could tell Chief Ranger Humboldt might be a dubious character."

"Sure," said Tony, "that's it." He paused. Maybe it was the dope, maybe it was he sensed that this was a smart woman and he might make more mileage with something he rarely used in the past—honesty. "And, to be honest," he continued, "I saw your TV interview."

"Meaning what?"

"Meaning you looked a little vulnerable."

"Vulnerable?"

"Yeah . . . vulnerable . . . like abandoned."

"Not helpless?"

He rubbed his head. "Definitely not helpless."

"But *vulnerable*?"

"Yeah . . . vulnerable."

"Not impressionable? Not pliable?"

"I don't know what that means. I mean, if you're suggesting I noticed that you're attractive . . . guilty. But, really. You looked like you might be in jeopardy. As it turns out, it's the trespassers who are in danger." He touched his head again.

"Sorry about that."

"It's my own fault. Maybe my motive for returning wasn't totally honorable. You did look pretty good on TV. But, honestly, since witnessing your dedication to protecting the tomb and seeing the vault in daylight, my reasons for staying have amended."

"I thought you discovered the tomb?"

"I did, but in the dark, during a thunderstorm, and I don't mind telling you—it was spooky as hell. I panicked."

"You panicked?"

"I screamed like a little girl and ran for cover."

"You were vulnerable."

"Jeopardized."

"Scared?"

"Terrified."

"And yet, you came back?"

"Well . . ."

"I'm glad you did. I've been rattled, too. I don't like to admit it, but this is not my thing: playing policewoman, fighting off looters, tolerating chauvinists like Humboldt. Well, if the truth be known, I've experienced nothing but sexists since I left the jungle—cops, salesmen, taxi drivers, newsmen, trespassers, fucking Beatles fans. You can't blame me for being a bit suspicious of you, of doubting your motives."

"I plead guilty, Olivia. My motive may have been a bit carnal, but I really am concerned about the tomb and this old chief. I mean . . . I've learned in this short time that you're an intriguing woman—brave, smart, adventurous, and beautiful."

"You think I'm adventurous?"

"Look at you. I mean, the jungle and all. Coming here to Colorado to guard a tomb you knew nothing about, putting yourself at risk. That's pretty adventurous."

"You think I'm beautiful?"

"Look at you!"

"You know," she said, "I'm quite accomplished in my field. It's not easy for a woman in the sciences. Looks can be a detriment."

"Don't I know," he smiled.

She laughed and seemed to reassess him, taking a longer than decorous look to evaluate his appearance.

"Funny," she said.

"Witty?"

"Maybe . . . we'll see." She was definitely checking him out again.

She changed the subject, "I agree that Humboldt probably has ulterior motives. I haven't decided yet with you. You know, he couldn't look me in the eye. He kept talking to my chest."

Tony knew it was a test. He kept eye contact and said, "Well, now you've put me on the spot. I'm dying to look, but I don't want to insult you. But, I'll be honest. Thinking about you running around in the Amazon in your birthday suit is making me all warm inside. Or, maybe it's your dope."

"The drugs'll do that . . . make you all warm inside."

"You feeling warm?"

"Getting warmer."

He smiled.

"You can't insult me. I'm used to men undressing me with their eyes. But I'm comfortable being nude even when they think I'm naked." She smiled again.

This was a woman comfortable with herself, he thought. *That makes her even more beautiful.* "I don't know what that means: naked and nude."

"Seriously?"

"I mean I know what being in your birthday suit means. What are you saying?"

"*Naked* suggests vulnerability."

"Ahh, vulnerable. We're back there are we."

She ignored his comment. "*Nude* is a natural state. It simply means unclothed. A nude subject can appear comfortable."

"You seem comfortable . . . I mean, comfortable with yourself—confident."

"Oh, I have my unsure moments. Sometimes the male 'gaze' the 'stare' can get to you, can make you feel *naked.* Being naked suggests possible discomfort and embarrassment, an unnatural and vulnerable state. Artists know the difference. Degas' woman stepping into the bath is nude, Goya's *Naked* Maja is prurient. Purists, on the other hand, pedantics are judgmental and by saying you're naked they are suggesting an immoral condition. I don't think I'm an immoral person even when I'm nude."

"I'll be honest," he muttered. "All this naked and nude talk is putting pictures in my mind. I'm reviewing a library of paintings and sculptures I've seen, trying to figure out if they're naked or not. I know I don't want to insult you, but I'm doing that sexist thing and trying to undress you with my eyes. I'm sorry."

"Don't be. It's partly the dope and the power of suggestion. It's my fault; I don't mean to tease but I wanted to learn something about you, something beyond Ranger Humboldt's description of you. I'm finding out important things. I like you, I trust you, but tell me: you're obviously native. Are you Sioux? I'm sorry Lakota?"

"Ahh, no," he admitted. "Tohono O'odham."

She shrugged.

"Papago," he answered. "From Arizona, west of Tucson."

"What does Tohono O . . . mean?"

"Desert people. You know—Arizona. *Papago* is not what we call ourselves. It's sometimes considered a derogatory word. It's thought to be a derivation of a Spanish term meaning bean eaters. Kind'a makes secondary citizens of us. Natives suffer that judgement all the time."

"Well there you are," she said. "It's like what I was talking about—naked versus nude and how detractors force misnomers on us. They discriminate."

"I don't know of any tribe names in common use that aren't 'misnomers' as you say."

"I don't know anything about the desert. I'm a rain forest Indian myself," she laughed a hearty chuckle. "My people thought of me as a jungle cat—a puma, because of my blondness. They are all very brunette, very dark. You're a brunette. You have beautiful hair." She reached across and touched his coif.

He felt her hand graze his cheek and temple. It was fire. His body flushed with a sudden response. The delight of it generated an obvious inquisitiveness and he felt a ridiculously huge smile arched across his face like a neon banana. He saw that she saw that she got his attention. She didn't seem put out and he purposefully didn't look apologetic.

"You're starting to feel the magic," she said, "the niopo. Have some more; it's good for what ails you, or, maybe, for what ails me. And to answer your question: yes, I'm blonde allover." She re-lit the joint and passed it to Tony after taking a long drag.

Maybe she is a tease.

"No," she said apparently reading his mind. "I'm a botanist studying herbal spiritual practices of South American indigenous people."

He inhaled a prodigious hit and jerked a scatterbrained shrug, paranoid that either she was indeed a mind reader or he was mumbling his thoughts out loud.

"Hallucinogenic plants of the Amazonian Indians. Shaman practices. I was inducted into a tribe," she beamed with joy. "I was sort of an apprentice to a shaman." She went on and told him about her year among the Onça Parda.

Tony pictured her in the rain forest, nude and pale against the dark green jungle. He remembered a painting: a native girl stood next to a river in a tangle of foliage—a flat, exaggerated jungle, typical houseplants rendered gigantic. Primitive, unschooled, currently appropriate. She was playing a flute and snakes watched from the trees. The girl changed into Olivia. He saw an old shaman smiling at her from behind the bushes. He held a turtle. He offered the turtle to Olivia, and then the shaman turned into Tony and the turtle into a green tree boa. The snake's red eyes burned with reptilian sorcery. The piercing eyes below the mushrooming brows of the serpent's head seemed to hypnotize her. The snake grew rigid in the air, the eyes closed, the jungle darkened. The dream passed.

"I didn't know you could play the flute," he said.

She looked puzzled. After a moment she asked, "Are you thinking about a painting? Rousseau's *Snake Charmer*? So, that's how you see me." She smiled. "You're undressing me with your thoughts again, Tohono. That's not very chivalrous. If you think these blue jeans are bohemian, you should have seen me on the plane. I had just come out of the rain forest."

"I think I would have liked that," he grinned.

Changing the subject but blushing with the compliment, Olivia asked, "So, how do you know so much about the Sioux, the Lakota, I mean."

"Oh, I've got some friends, guys I work construction with. And I've spent some time near Pine Ridge and Rosebud. Hunting, you know. Doing some inipi, sweat baths, dated a couple of their sisters, you know."

"They let you date their sisters? Aren't these the wrong people to piss off? Compared to the Onça Parda, the Sioux braves I've seen are huge, although the Onça Parda have a dangerous reputation as head-hunters. Maybe you're the adventurer." Her smile was a tease. "So, you're a builder?"

Wasn't she coy, he thought, always changing the subject. "Yeah, I guess you could say that." He liked the sound of it, "builder," it had a nicer ring than *flunky*."

"You actually do something, construct things, you create." She averted her eyes. "I love people who work with their hands."

Tony felt another rush of adrenaline, "I like people for their brains. And! for their adventurous spirit. Living in the jungle . . . that took some courage."

"It was beautiful. Lush and green, well, that's obvious. But it wasn't really dangerous. The people live in such harmony with the rain forest, with nature—the animals, the birds, the giant trees, the earth, even snakes." She smiled. "It was such a balanced and spiritual life. So different from here. I mean, these hoodlums actually trying to rob this wonderful tomb. They are like the *bandeirantes* in Brazil, mining for gold, burning the forest, destroying habitat, stealing land from the Indians, from my friends. Why? To raise cattle—filthy, stupid beasts. To keep Rio in steaks and Burger Barn in patties. I get so angry."

Tony rubbed his head, "I believe you." He feigned very sad eyes.

"I'm so sorry," she walked to him and took his head gently in her hands. "The Onça Parda, the people with whom I lived, believed you can heal one through touch, by putting on hands."

Tony became kindling. He placed his hands atop hers, something ignited. "So do my people." He rubbed *her* hands on his temple, "I think our people are right. It's magic. I'm feeling better."

She pulled gently away.

"But, don't stop."

"Magic," she continued. "Our people, our friends don't seem that different." She looked at him coyly.

"Oh, they're not. They're not. I bet we celebrate life in many the same ways."

"That's it, isn't it—a celebration of life?" She paused. "I think my greatest memory, the most important event of my life so far, was when I was inducted into the Onça Parda nation. *It* was a celebration of life. It was a journey into the other life, the spiritual world."

"Ahh, the spiritual world. My people, too, believe deeply in the spiritual world. We celebrate becoming one with the earth." He picked up a pipe lying next to the old chief and blew off the dust. He was puzzled why it was together, usually pipes are stored in pieces, the bowl wrapped separately from the stem. It crossed his mind that perhaps the old chief had died smoking the pipe. If he partook of anything like that Olivia had to offer, he died a happy man. He looked for a clean cloth with which to wipe the pipe. There was none. Everything was covered in dust. He took off his shirt and rubbed clean the ancient relic.

Olivia watched as he pulled off his shirt and smiled at the cleaning of the pipe.

"These symbols on the pipe express the Indians' desire for harmony with Mother Earth. The buffalo calf here on the bowl symbolizes the Earth, the mother who nourishes The People." He moved closer so she could see the carved calf. She touched it gently with her fingertips. Tony stirred. "The bowl itself symbolizes the center of the universe from which The People emerged from the dark world to the light."

"The Onça Parda use pipes as well. Not as beautiful as this one, I'm sure. Although I participated in many of the spiritual ceremonies," she looked him in the eyes, "I never used one of their pipes."

Tony stirred again. He continued, "These four ribbons symbolize the four sacred directions. Their color is faded today, but when the chief was alive they were bright and represented the four quarters of the universe. This black one . . ." She took the ribbon gently between her fingers and pulled along its length. ". . . it symbolizes the west from which the thunder beings send us rain. The white . . ." She repeated her tug on the ribbon. ". . . is for the north and the great white cleansing wind. This, the red one . . ." Again, she toyed. ". . . symbolizes the east where the morning star lives and the light and the star give us wisdom. This last, the yellow." He pulled it up vertically. "It is from the south, the place from which comes summer and from where men find their power." She moved closer to him, almost in an embrace. "And this eagle feather, alone, symbolizes Wankan Tonka, the Great Unknown, the Great Mystery."

"What a beautiful word. Say it again."

"What? Wankan Tonka."

"Yes, it's beautiful," she seemed to purr.

"Sometimes it is said as one word," he placed his mouth next to her ear, exchanging the innate warmth of touching, his voice became breathy, "*Wakantanka, Wakantanka, Wakantanka.*"

"Tell me more."

Tony began searching his brain for every Sioux word he knew. "It is the holy men, *Wichasha Wakan*, who pray to *Wakantanka.*

She lay her head on his shoulder. "More," she whispered.

"*Hunkpapa*," he whispered, now definitely feeling high. "*Wakan . . . Tanka, Wichasha . . . Wakan, Shyelas. Lakota, Lakota, Dakota.*" He paused wracking his memory. "*Oglala, Oglala.*" he repeated too quickly. She started to drift out of the aural trance.

"*Chacun Sha Sha*," he couldn't remember what it meant: red willow bark or something, but it sounded good. "*Minnie Wakan.*" He knew it meant whiskey and was afraid something so base might break the mood, then remembered a more literal translation would be *Holy Water.* So he repeated, "*Minnie Wakan, Minnie Wakan.*"

"It's a beautiful language," she hummed.

And then his summer picnics with his Lakota colleagues, accelerated by Olivia's niopo, drove into his memory. "Tanyán wahi," welcome; "Tókheškhe yaúŋ he," how are you?; "Táku eníčiyapi he?," what's your name? "*Pahaska*," he muttered, remembering old Buffalo Bill. "*Wasichus,*" he whispered. And then he was on a roll; he remembered the names of the clans. "*Miniconjou, Brule, Sans Arc, Sihasapa, Hunkpapa, Oglala, Miniconjou, Brule, Sans Arc, Sihasapa.*"

He stalled again. She looked up at him. "*Waga Chun*," he blurted out. It didn't seem as spiritual, meaning cottonwood tree, but then he used his pièce de résistance. "*Tatanka-Iyotanka,*" he murmured. "He was the great chief Sitting Bull." He repeated it three times, "*Tatanka-Iyotanka, Tatanka-Iyotanka, Tatanka-Iyotanka.*"

A breeze filled the cave, but it seemed to come from the back of the tomb rather than the tented entryway. The movement snapped them both to attention. They peered into the darkness at the back of the cave. Goosebumps covered their flesh. Nothing moved. There was no sound other than the drip of the water, the hiss of the kerosene lamp, and the pounding of their hearts. They waited trembling in each other's arms. Nothing.

"Perhaps, I have summoned some spirits," he joked, a little concerned that perhaps the ancient chief lying next to them was also aroused.

Olivia pulled away from him and ran to her backpack. "I have something for the pipe. Is it possible to have a ceremony? Is it too sacred for a woman to participate in? Can you show me? I've studied with a shaman, after all. I want to be a shaman. Can we do it together? Can we celebrate life . . . the harmony, the oneness?"

"Yes, we must celebrate," said Tony, moving behind her as she dug through the pack.

"Here," she stood suddenly and turned to face him with a small plastic bag of dried leaves held between her bright eyes.

"What is that?" asked Tony, temporarily distracted.

"It's even stronger than the grass; even more sacred to the Onça Parda. Very strong medicine. Great, huh?" she purred. "For the pipe."

"To smoke the pipe is to become one," Tony smiled. "One with the earth and one with each other. Is that what you want?"

He watched her weigh the question. "Has it been a while since you celebrated the life spirit?" he asked.

"A while," she answered.

"And your sadness at having to leave the Amazon, you must be very sad?"

"I'm sad," she answered.

"The stress of travel, and having to leave in a panic—you must feel stressed?"

"I'm stressed," she said.

"Then the fear," he was talking softly, "the fear of the tomb being looted, the struggle outside, it must have been overwhelming?"

"Overwhelming . . ."

"Listen to the spirits. They call you; we are your people. You are to become one of us."

She gave him a look. It said either, "I'm wise to you; this has gone far enough," or "There's no need to go too far with the spiritual thing; after all, you are good looking and a carpenter; how much more holy can you get?"

He decided to push, "This could be a once in a lifetime experience. Look at this tomb. Why, it's nearly like a kiva. The drums, the earth, the rocks, the old chief to serve as our guardian, the shields, the bows, the arrows . . . all of it—can you feel it?"

She began to rub her body. "Mother Earth calls me to be initiated."

She can feel it. "It's traditional," he said aloud, "to cleanse ourselves first. To sweat."

"How?" she asked.

All of Tony's tools were there. He left them when he ran out of the tomb to call Henry. He busied himself: leaned a pair of two-by-fours against the rock wall onto the top of a work table, grabbed his roofing hammer from the tool belt, and with a single stroke drove a sixteen-penny nail through the first two-by-four and into the table top. He repeated the warrior like strike and bludgeoned the second nail. Her shocked but appreciative eyes gave him the compliment he sought. He then draped a canvas drop cloth over the boards and placed the kerosene heater inside the makeshift lean-to. He fired it up. He smiled at Olivia and then ran outside the tent. As he pulled back the flap covering the entrance to the tomb, music from the concert drifted inside.

You never close your eyes anymore when I kiss your lips . . .

He knew this song: The Righteous Brothers. He stayed on task and searched the bushes next to the walkway. He soon reentered the tomb with hands full of weeds.

"First we rub ourselves with these holy plants. You, ahh, you need to take off your clothes." He hoped that "holy" and "plants" and getting naked all fit together.

She turned from him and pulled off her T-shirt. She took several heavy strands of beads from the wall, shook off the dust, and put them over her head and around her neck. She turned and faced Tony. She held out her hands to him.

She was more beautiful than he imagined, more enchanting than Rousseau's jungle goddess. He recalled the ancient tale his Lakota friends told him of how The People acquired the sacred pipe. How a beautiful maiden, White Buffalo Calf Woman, appeared before two hunters. The first of the braves lusted for the maiden, but the second sensed she was a sacred being. She beckoned the first to approach her, reading his carnal thoughts. They were consumed by smoke. Only she stepped from the cloud. The first brave was left there on the plains—a pile of bones, burned white and picked clean by worms. The second, more spiritual brave, escorted the maiden to his village, and there she bestowed the pipe to his people. She explained the seven directives for acting human, the principles of community, and an understanding of their place in the great circle of being.

Tony looked at Olivia. At any moment he expected to burst into flame, his bones left on the floor of the cave. But then for the first time he sensed that this woman was nude, not naked. He couldn't articulate the difference; he simply sensed it, just as he sensed the healing benefit of touching. He stepped forward and began rubbing the sage across her shoulders. She took several stems from him and rubbed his shoulders. They both turned away and removed their pants. He took a loincloth from a branch wedged in the wall. He shook the dust off the deer hide. She pranced over to her pack and pulled out a loincloth of her own. It was brightly colored, woven of soft grasses, feathers, and handspun cloth. The design sung of a greener place, of colorful macaws, and smelled of the jungle cat.

"We don't have to sweat for too long," he said. "I need to keep my strength." He pulled back the flap of the makeshift lean-to and motioned her inside. The rock wall and floor were hot. They exploded in perspiration the instant they sat inside, and the aroma of sage filled the tiny tent. Tony was speechless. She closed her eyes and allowed the heat to penetrate her body. She leaned her head backward against the stone wall.

Tony reached across with the sage and traced the path of the beads on her breasts. She smiled, keeping her eyes closed. Her skin was tan from her time in the river country, the sage left tiny tracks of red where it rubbed against her. The tiny itching caused her to raise her hands up slowly and cup her breasts. She rubbed them gently, feeling the tingling of the sage and the hot dampness from her perspiration.

The sight of her caused Tony to sweat even more. He leaned toward her. Moisture trapped on the canvas and the walls dripped as he moved and hissed as it hit the heater. The sizzling noise caused her to slowly open her eyes. She saw him coming closer and remained quiet with her head against the wall.

The first kiss was restrained. His lips barely touched hers— an electric shimmer. As he pressed ever so gently, the taste of sweet perspiration dripped between their lips, and the smell of their aroused breath filled each of them. Large drops of sweat fell from the tips of their noses. Rivers of sweat flooded over their brows and off their cheeks, making the kiss slippery.

"Perhaps it's time for the pipe," she whispered.

He pulled back the canvas and the rushing coolness of the cave blanketed them. She responded to the cold with alertness, and again unconsciously placed her hands over her breasts. Tony wiped the sweat from his eyes, "We need a fire," he said and began picking up construction scraps and anything else combustible. He built a cone of wood. The fire was small. Shadows flickered on the walls of the cave. Olivia loaded the sacred pipe with Onça Parda primo.

She sat cross-legged by the small fire. He sat across from her and put a drum in the strategic area suddenly exposed in the fire light. He smiled. She pulled a burning piece of wood from the fire and began to light the pipe.

"No, no," he said. "First there is a song, a prayer."

She handed him the pipe across the fire. He watched her as the light from the flames danced on her glistening torso. As was appropriate, he stood.

There was nothing he could do now to hide his enthusiasm. Shadows made by the flames danced on his thighs like a kinetic sundial: one o'clock, now three, now seven, then noon, ten o'clock and on and on. Now she smiled. He waited for her to pay attention. "We must ask to be one with the four sacred directions, with the sky and with the earth." He stepped just out of the circle of light. When he returned he was wearing a war bonnet. "Each feather is a symbol of courage or wounds earned in battle." He stood for a moment, silent above the fire, then extended his arms full length with the bowl of the pipe closest to himself and pointed the mouthpiece to the heavens.

Olivia jumped. She was shocked.

"What is it?" he asked.

"I'm sorry, but I suddenly recognized you. I remember you."

He was confused.

"Standing there with the pipe, in that pose, you're the man in my dream on the plane." Chills shook her body, her eyes opened even wider. She starred at him in astonishment, her eyes glowing, reflecting the firelight, as do the eyes of a cougar.

"I don't know what to say." He paused.

"Go on, please. I think this was meant to be."

He was nervous. "I may not do this exactly right," he apologized. "This is a Lakota ritual, you know, and I'm O'odham. But I've been through it a few times with my friends." He looked at her, still shining from the sweat lodge, seeking confirmation that he mirrored her dream. Her look gave him goose bumps.

He began his song with mixed feelings. He felt he should be respectful of the spirits he was about to address, but he also wanted worse than potential damnation to continue to woo this, the most natural and beautiful woman he had ever touched. He began by using a limited vocabulary. He mixed the little Sioux he knew would lure her, some clumsy Spanish from his days in Arizona, and some long lost Papago—Yuman.

"Wakantanka, oyes this wichasha wakan. We have purified ourselves with the inipi. Now oyes this canción. I am not Tcu-unnyikita, the Coyote, the trickster. I am not the defiler of Wohpe, White Buffalo Woman, pero a mortal man struck by lightning . . . Ni-woji, Ahnih chu'ig shonikon ah wepgih." He knew his Papago was clumsy; it troubled him. "Mi taku oyasin, we are all related, oh, spirits of my fathers. Hemako, gohk, waik, gi'ik, hetasp, chuhthp, wewa'ak, gigi'ik, humukt, west-mahm (one through ten in Papago), Komkch'ed e Wah'osithk (Turtle Got Wedged—the Papago name for Sels, Indian Oasis, his home in Arizona), Waw Giwulk (Constricted Rock—Papago—one can only guess why this phrase came to mind.), Ahnih Ogolgam (I bear)." He then proceeded to name off the months of the year in his native tongue: "Giìhothag Mashath, Kohmagi Mashath, Chehthagi Mashath, Oam Mashath, Ko òk Mashath, Hahshani Mashath, Jukiabig Mashath, Shopol Eshabig Mashath, Vashai Gakithag Mashath, Wi ihanig Mashath, Kehg S-hehpijig Mashath, Ge è S-hehpijig Mashath."

The rhythm created by the repetition of *Mashath*, moon. He hoped it caused a reciprocal rhythm in the beating of Olivia's heart, an accomplished linguist herself.

And then the strangest thing happened. Tony forgot about speaking O'odham, or any other language, and a song rose and filled the tomb. He did not recognize his own voice; he did not know the meaning of the words; he did not know from where the song came, somewhere high in his throat; it was nasal and echoed the pitch of bone pipes, it sounded of the wind.

He sat down, stunned. He turned the mouthpiece away from the heavens and toward himself. Olivia leaned across the small fire and lit the pipe. Tony inhaled deeply. He felt a rush of euphoria almost immediately. Leading with the mouthpiece, he handed the pipe across to Olivia. She placed it in her mouth and waited for Tony to reciprocate with a light. He was lost in contentment. She sucked on the mouthpiece anyway. The sacred herb ignited and glowed in the bowl as Olivia inhaled. She let her head fall back and stared at the ceiling.

"An-thon-io," she cooed, drawing the syllables longer as in a chant.

"Hey-a, hey-a, hey," he sang as his ears buzzed with psychedelic energy.

"An-n-n . . . t-h-o-o-o-o-n-e-e-e-o-o," she repeated.

Other songs came from outside on a cool evening breeze. John, Paul, George, and Ringo were working their own magic. *She loves you, yea, yea, yea . . . .* Tony's state of mind combined the songs, "He loves you, hey-a, hey-a, hey." Soon other voices from inside the tomb joined in a necromantic chorus. His eyes drifted past lovely Olivia to the flickering shadows. Ancient faces in black and red paint sang as they dodged in and out of the dim light. The rhythm of tribal drums, accentuated by Ringo's Mersey beat, filled his chest and ancient chanting his ears. From the depths an ancient figure stepped forward. Without moving its mouth, it spoke to Tony.

"You have honored the sacred calf pipe well for a desert person, Hands of the Bear. And the white woman, she has great magic. You should honor her. She is not selfish like the Wasichu of my time. She has great courage in protecting the tomb from those who rob my brother. We know her guardian animal spirit, the puma. It is strong and has traveled far. You, honor yourself, though you have wandered from the true path, though you have never been part of the circle. You honor Wakantanka and White Buffalo Woman. There was nothing sacred before she brought us the pipe. But you must travel here in the dark world with care, my son. I, Tatanka-Iyotanka, sing you this warning."

Another figure stepped forward from the dark. "And I, Black Elk, must also beseech you, young Wichasha Wakan . . ."

Together they sang, "Do not dishonor this grave site of our brother. Only bad things can happen if you do not honor him whose grave you trespass." The song repeated but grew quieter, and the figures disappeared into the shadows. In the distance a herd of buffalo stampeded from rock to rock led by a great white beast who transformed into the loveliest of Indian maidens. And as she raced across the plains she metamorphosed into a sleek puma, and the puma leapt across a green river, and the puma changed into Olivia. His mouth dropped open and his eyes glazed. Tony began to wilt.

"I think it's hit you hard, Antonio. I mean, you feel it, yes?" Olivia swayed in the undulating fire light.

"Ummm," he tried to speak.

"It is good. But don't let it take you too far."

"Fathers have come to visit us. Their spirits inhabit the cave. They wish to thank you, Olivia, for protecting the tomb. Truly, I believe this man was a great chief, and you have saved him. The spirits of the fathers wish me to thank you, Olivia. You have become a Daughter of the Earth. But I believe the kindred spirits wish us to leave this place."

Like the gracile jungle cat she was, sleek and silent, in a feline dance, lovely Olivia leaned forward onto her hands and knees. She crept toward Tony. Like mist on a breeze she reached her hand toward his semi-erectness. Her hand was like smoke and silk. "Not before another taste of the pipe, A-n-t-h-o-n-i-o-o," she purred.

Chapter Thirty-three

The Warrior Awakens

Summer, 1964

I have spoken of the birth of my sons (and your fathers) according to the Haudenosaunee People who call them Sapling and Flint. To the people of Trois Rivières, the Wyandotte, they are also known as "Made of Fire" (Tseh'-stah) and "Made of Flint" (Tah'-weh-skah'-reh). In so naming the twins, The People of the Longhouse and of the Great Lakes explain the presence of good and evil. "Sapling" suggests growth, fertility, and the cycle of life, including "rebirth." His alias, "Fire," clarifies the importance of fire to the survival of humankind. Tseh'-stah, Fire, and Iouskeha, Sapling, are one and the same, signifying "good." Evil has but one name: "Flint."

Good and evil have many manifestations; thus, they are a part of us all, of all of you. The "warrior" is the role in which this paradox is most evident. The warrior is the destroyer of enemies; he becomes Tawiskaron and Tah'-weh-skah'—Flint—combatant, taker of scalps. While at the same time, he is the husband and provider, the father of sons and daughters, the builder and protector of communities. We have all heard stories of how sometimes it takes calamitous circumstances to awaken the warrior, to trigger the enigma of our propensity as evildoer and good person, hater and lover, destroyer and protector. The same is true of the People of the Plains. The same is true of the People of the Desert.

Anthony Hands of the Bear dreamt of great battles, carnal conquests, playing Apache, and hide-and-seek. He awoke exhausted and hungry. He had a splitting headache. He stood looking at Olivia, coiled in an innocent sleep. He felt a surprising flush of affection. He tried to force the alien emotion from his mind. He looked around the tomb, only faintly illuminated by irregular interruptions of light from lanterns along the walkway when the breeze, *Hewel*, struggled to enter. The song of *Juhki*, rain, seemed to fill the tomb. He risked a peek outside; the sky was clear. Concert music bounced off the rock walls and the low, harmless clouds of the cool summer night. People were still milling around on the ramps. The sound of water, he concluded, was coming from inside the cave. He turned and let the canvas shut off the exterior world. He contemplated the artifacts. A spasm of conscience bubbled across his mind: I am standing here in the tomb of one of the great fathers and my nakedness exposes the falseness of the hero disguise, a sham that helped me accomplish my quest. I am seducer, not hero, not even warrior.

Something stirred. He checked: It was not Olivia. Juhki's song, the trickling water, changed pitch. The babble seemed to acquire voice, and the voice was fathomable. He questioned whether it emerged from the cave or in his rattled mind.

"It is righteous, brother, that you admit your inadequacies," uttered the voice. "I lived ten thousand moons and died a hundred deaths. My hero's quest unfulfilled."

It seemed natural to Anthony, considering his state of mind, to respond to the spirit he assumed was that of the messiah. He felt it necessary to explain. "I take no pride that my quarry is mil-gahn, white, and yet, I have this giddy feeling about her. I take no coup from this, and yet I am elated, I rejoice, I am exultant. I chirp like a damn cricket, chuckle like a teenager. This is too weird. The irony is that I don't plan to brag about this to anyone, particularly any of those *locote* at Cody's."

"To do so would be inappropriate, my son. Thus, your path, while not pious, nor virtuous, is fitting. Both Sapling and Flint dwell in our hearts; in mine decades ago and in yours this consequential night, and so it is that I shall dwell also in your heart."

The voice faded, the tenor returned to splashing water, "I have need of you, my son . . ."

Olivia stirred and brought him out of his scrutiny, but she did not awaken. His head throbbed. He asked himself, Is it the drugs? He scrutinized Olivia. Is she some kind of a ho'ok, a bruja, a witch?

His hunger pangs reemerged. In the closed acoustics of the cave his stomach made a guttural, animal noise that belonged, he thought, in a zoo. He looked down at his stomach, somewhat proud of the prehistoric rumblings, and again noticed his nakedness. His momentary bumptiousness had disappeared, and he wondered if he had what it takes to be the *hero*, truly to guard the tomb. An ancient and distant chant echoed off the deepest walls of the cave. Anthony stood silently, staring into space, listening to the distant drumming, the thought rippling in concentric circles on the quiet pond of his mind, until finally his stomach repeated its bovine complaint. He remembered that he usually kept a bottle of aspirin in his toolbox. He checked. It was empty. He spotted Olivia's knapsack, tiptoed over, and began rummaging through it, searching for something to help. He moved over to the canvas curtain where the light was better. All he found was plastic envelopes of dried plant leaves, berries, vials of powder, some dried mushroom caps, beans that resembled pea pods, and small fruits about the size of cherries but looking more like small persimmons. He pulled out a plastic bag of dried mushroom buttons and the fruits. He looked over at Olivia; she was still asleep. He was embarrassed at rifling through her things, but hunger and pharmaceutical desperation clouded his judgment.

Sparrows chirped outside, disturbed by the rock-and-roll and the unnatural lighting. He looked out. Another creature, more nervous than the birds, one Chief Ranger and Superintendent in Charge, Henry Humboldt, was limping up the path, heading for the tomb.

Foreboding crept into his mind "on little cat's feet." It was dark and cold as flint. Yet, it warmed his insides. A fever rose from his stomach to his heart and filled his brain behind the ice at the frontal lobe. His senses became sharp as the rush overtook him. He felt the texture of the canvas and the rocks. His hearing was acute. His vision—like that of the eagle. He could smell the fear on the approaching quarry. Was it the drugs, he wondered, or the hatred of Humboldt fueled by adrenaline? Could it be that his predator instincts were responding to wounded prey? His "Apache" skills clicked in gear. He slipped on the backpack to avoid making noise, glided past Olivia, picked up a tomahawk, and slunk into a shadow. There, in the darkness, he planned his attack. He visualized the dance, his ferocity, and the sequence of the assault.

"What the hell is going on in here?" choked Chief Park Ranger and Superintendent in Charge, Henry Humboldt, when he pulled back the tarp and viewed a prostrate Olivia Hotchkiss at his feet—naked.

One with the darkness, Hands of the Bear could see Humboldt's expression: Henry was confused; his thoughts were racing. With near panic in his eyes, he crouched in a gunslinger pose, his hand at the ready to quick draw a pistol he wasn't wearing. Bear watched as Humboldt flinched from the pain of the sudden move. Henry's foolish exhibition fused Anthony's sinister intentions. Henry had no gun. Rangers were not allowed to carry revolvers. Henry straightened up to cover his bonehead move. Ol' Henry, always trying to save face.

"Hardhat, you murderous son-of-a-bitch, I know you're in here. You were seen. Give it up. More Rangers are on their way. So are the Denver Police. You haven't got a chance."

There was only silence. "You Indian pervert! If you raped and murdered this girl, you're going to pay. No one gets away with this on my watch. I'm going to enjoy seeing you hang."

It dawned on Tony that Colorado no longer hanged criminals; the wrong-minded tirade was only bravado. Smelling Henry's fear increased the intent. The thought of the "sparrow" anticipating the cat's pounce gave Tony devilish delight. He had already let his prey talk too much. He stepped from the shadow. "Hello, Henry, I've been expecting you."

At the sound of the demonic voice, Humboldt again snapped into a gunslinger crouch, arm cocked in the empty air. He grimaced again, almost grabbed at the source of the pain, but thought better of it.

"Feeling a bit impotent are we, Henry?" He jumped from the shadow into the dim light. "No gun? New stitches?" He mimicked Henry's flinch, only *his* hand held the tomahawk. They stood opposite each other, like toy soldiers, cowboy and Indian—frozen in a plastic, melodramatic pose. Henry went pale. Hands of the Bear smiled as he eased into the next step of his plan. Humboldt was bald, and this was his greatest vulnerability. Tony had often made fun of the pretentious rug, and Henry responded vehemently. This was his opponent's weak spot. *It's is going to be an easy scalping, clean and quick, and the pain will be Henry's humiliation. I couldn't ask for a better circumstance.*

"What are you doing with that?" Henry asked as he eyed the tomahawk.

"A symbol, Henry, for taking coup, for taking scalp. You've insulted me for the last time."

Henry's empty gun hand moved to the top of his head. "You wouldn't?" he dared.

"Oh, yes, I would." Tony grinned.

"You're under arrest, Hardhat."

"Nice try, Henry."

"You're trespassing. I'm firing you for insubordination, and I'm arresting you for suspicion of murder. Killing me won't help you. They'll hunt you down, you son-of-a-bitch. You can't go around killing cops and get away with it. You can't kill an innocent anthropologist on my watch and expect we won't get you. I always knew you were no good, you devil. You're going to rot in hell."

"Shut up, Henry. Your whining could wake the dead. It's you who are trespassing. This is an Indian tomb, and I'm going to punish you for entering it uninvited."

"This is my turf, Hardhat. You're the one to be punished. Don't forget who's in charge here."

"I know you, Henry. I can read your mind. You're scheming to sell off these relics. Well, I'm here to stop you, and after I'm through with you, they'll never catch me. I know these rocks, just like I know the catacombs of your dark heart."

Olivia stirred at the moment Tony said, ". . . sell off these relics . . ."

Her movement got Henry's attention. He looked a moment too long.

Tony saw he was distracted and pounced. Adrenaline (and remnant niopo) rocketed through his brain as he became the predator. Like the bird of prey in attack mode, his field of vision became a focused tunnel, his coordination sharpened, the world outside his actions disappeared. Henry was a frozen target.

Olivia rose as Tony leapt. Vestige sleep (and remnant niopo) prevented her from clearly comprehending the attack. In her mind, she saw Tony scalp Chief Ranger Humboldt. The tight tape Henry used to keep his hair secured made a Velcro-tearing sound as Tony separated hair from head. To Olivia it was the echo of skin coming away from skull. She fainted.

Henry also fainted. Tony wasn't sure why: perhaps it was the shock of the attack, perhaps it was Henry losing his hair, perhaps it was the screams, or perhaps it was seeing Olivia's naked beauty.

The screams were three-fold. Hands of the Bear let out a loud war cry. Olivia screamed at the violence. Henry screamed at the scalping. The wails were nearly simultaneous. They got the attention of another Ranger approaching the tomb. "Is everything OK in there?" he called out as he broke into a run.

Tony, himself unnerved by the screams and the responding unexpected surge of adrenaline, knew there was no way he could explain to the approaching officer why he had de-rugged his boss. There was no time to revive Olivia for a getaway. He panicked. He heard the Ranger coming, so he grabbed for his pants. He missed. He grabbed for the loincloth that was closer. The strings had tangled with a strap of Olivia's knapsack. The next closest thing was an old bow and a quiver of arrows. He grabbed them too, not knowing why, other than a vague thought that he might need a weapon. By now the flush of crisis and chemicals took over his thinking.

The warriors awoke. The ghost of the ancient cadaver sang out. Tony heard himself let out a bloodcurdling war cry, "Die! Invading son of the white eyes." He ran toward the shocked Ranger who froze in his tracks. Hands of the Bear touched the Ranger on the shoulder with the handle of the tomahawk to count coup and disappeared into the darkness.

Later, when interviewed by the police and the press, the shaken Ranger said, "At first I thought he was a streaker. But then I saw the purse, and I thought I had interrupted a tryst between a couple of fags. So's, I yelled, "Stop, pervert!" He didn't stop; so's, I went looking for his partner in the tomb. That's when I found Chief Ranger Humboldt and the naked lady."

"What did you think then?"

"I thought she was pretty good looking."

"No, what did you think had happened?"

"Oh, I get it. Well, I thought it was a double murder. The queer had killed both of 'um."

"What did you do then?"

"I took another look at the naked lady and said, 'What a shame.' She's real pretty."

"You didn't feel for a pulse or anything like that?"

"I guess not. I didn't feel good about touching no dead folks."

"What then?"

"Well, I ran down to my radio car and called for help."

"To whom?"

"To the Ranger's office. I told them some sicko-son-of-a-bitch had killed Chief Ranger Humboldt and this pretty lady. I mentioned that she was real pretty, too. I said the perpetrator was dressed like some queer Indian. Well, undressed like an Indian, anyway. I thought maybe it was an Indian terrorist thing, or a fag thing, you know."

"That's all?"

"Naw, then I told Earl—he was on dispatch—that I might be insane, but I could have sworn that the homo running away looked like that crazy mother: Tony Hardhat. He's an Indian, you know? But I didn't know he was a sissy boy, if you know what I mean.

"Earl, he's the dispatcher, immediately radioed all our fellow Red Rocks Rangers; he called The Jefferson County Sheriffs Department, The Colorado Highway Patrol, The Parks Service, The Golden Police, and The Denver Police. We done launch the greatest manhunt in history, each department betting they was the one to bring in that blood-crazed Indian terrorist faggot. And, you know, it was kinda' funny."

"What's that?"

"Every one of the chiefs of each police department said, when he heard the news, the same thing."

"What was it they said?"

"Ya' don't kill cops, not on my watch! Funny, huh?"

Anthony Hands of the Bear—warrior, fugitive, and specter— sensed he was but a movement in the corner of one's eye as he dodged from shadow to shadow, from tree to rock, from crevice to cave. He counted on concertgoers shrugging off the glimpse of something moving in the trees as their imagination.

A vague decision transported him back toward his truck. From a high vantage point above the parking lot he spied on the bevy of Rangers and police surrounding his pickup. He settled in and waited for an opportunity to present itself.

In the quiet moment his hunger returned. He had the shakes. He searched Olivia's knapsack for anything edible. It was then he noticed that he had stuffed Henry's toupee into Olivia's satchel. He set it aside and continued his search. All he found was her passport, some personal items, a lighter, cigarettes, and gum. The backpack contained books about Indian art (no wonder it was so damn heavy), a canteen of water (useful), and more of her samples (dangerous). He was suspicious of the dried mushroom buttons. He took a delicate bite off the edge of one. It tasted musty and earthy and unappetizing. He put the remains back in the bag. He took out one of the mini-persimmons and smelled it. It had a ripe, sweet aroma. He peeled off a crown of tiny leaves and smelled them. He touched one to his tongue. Nothing; no minty flavor or anything. He released the leaves into the wind. He touched the fruit to his tongue. There was a slight fuzzy texture like peach skin and an obvious sweetness. He took a nibble. It tasted odd, but OK. He took a bite. The interior was fleshy and full of small seeds, reminding him of a strawberry or kiwi. He ate the rest of the small fruit. Not bad. He ate another. Sweet. He ate a third, and then decided that the entire bag would be but a morsel, and he had better leave them for Olivia.

He sat in his hiding place, contemplating his plight, and trying to forget his craving. He smiled recalling Olivia's hunger. He smiled even larger remembering Henry Humboldt's two recent humiliations: the truck accident and the one he had just inflicted. I don't regret it, he thought. I'm glad I embarrassed the little ass. "Little ass," he repeated. The largest smile in Hardhat history crossed his face as he remembered Henry's most public humiliation, the one that left scars on his posterior. He was going to fire me anyway. There are other jobs. Then it dawned on Tony that the consequences might be more serious than dismissal. Henry was vindictive. He still blamed the wreck on Tony, and he would surely press assault charges for the physical theft of Henry's hair, faux shag that it is. "I guess I'm a renegade now, but it's worth it—my first scalp. I wish I'd hit him with the tomahawk, just a glancing blow, just enough to give him matching scars—one on each end." He held up the hairpiece and almost let out a whoop. Thinking better of it, he looked over the ledge to see if any of the Rangers had noticed his perch. They were still talking among themselves. It appeared that they had devised a plan. They broke up into groups of three or four and headed off in different directions. A figure in a darker uniform, probably a Denver cop—he was wearing a gun—was giving orders and pointing off in the opposite direction of Tony's ledge. One guard remained, leaning on Tony's truck.

Slowly, almost imperceptibly, his emptiness went away. Numbing warmth filled his tummy. Olivia's voice called out. It was a siren's song. He thought about her being grilled by Humboldt and he wanted to protect her. It's unfair her having to listen to the little autocrat, maybe he should go back and face the music. The music— he listened to the concert for the first time. *You think you've lost your love; well, I saw her yesterday-ee-ay. It's you she's thinking of, and she told me what to say-ee-ay. She said she loves you, and you know that can't be ba-a-ad. She loves you . . .* and then came the adolescent screams. They were thunderous and overwhelmed the music.

As he bent over to gather up his booty, another warm sensation plopped into his head. He stood up and looked around. The rocks reflected the color of the stage lights: cyan, yellow, and magenta. The sky became electric. The clouds seemed to sprint across the sky. The screams became the songs of his fathers and meandered in his skull. He lay where he was and raised his hands toward the moon. He made a circle with his hands and placed the glowing disk in the center. He stared at the corona. He held the moon in awe as clouds, mysterious in the night, raced past his hands. In his heart he howled, the ancient lupine song reverberating in his soul. The moon echoed a radial rhythm. An hour passed.

Finally, it was Anthony's thirst rather than his hunger that broke the trance. He picked up his thoughts right where he left off before his lunar communion. "I will go rescue Olivia from old Henry." He leaned over and checked to see if the guard was still there. The incessant chanting continued in his head. He watched as the cop put out his cigarette on the upholstery of Tony's truck. And then he had the audacity to strike a match on the door, leaving a mark, and lit his next smoke. He threw the match into the back of the pickup. Something ignited. A small fire flickered over the gunwales. The vandal had to hurry to the cab and grab Tony's fire extinguisher. He sprayed the fire. It went out in a cough and a cloud.

Tony felt his adrenaline rise as the bluecoat, who was visibly pleased he got the fire out, looked around to see if there were any witnesses, and when he thought no one was watching, he used the fire extinguisher to smash a tail light.

A century long index of historical abuses and an inventory of current insults added up and sum-totaled in Tony's heart. Under the soft light of the summer moon, toniabkam mashath, in the shadow of the ogre's cave, ho'ok cheho, Tony Hardhat, rascal and fugitive, transformed from venery and flight into Ahgachug Nowi—Hands of the Bear—avenger and warrior once more.

Olivia was losing patience with the officer questioning her. If he wanted a straight answer, he could take his gaze off her chest and look her in the eye. Several uniformed men were surrounding her, crowding the entrance to the tomb. Reporters crowded behind the officers. They filled the air with their testosterone tug of war as the various police tried to take charge and assert their particular authority. She noticed only the Red Rocks Rangers hung back. A couple of them looked as if they wished they could disappear. She surmised their reticence was the result of the brilliant police work done earlier: declaring the tomb a murder scene.

As soon as revived, Henry Humboldt tried to disappear. She knew it was to avoid the embarrassment. He said he needed to coordinate the search for Hardhat, but he acted exhausted and in pain. She could tell he was dying to sit down, but for some reason did not. He was incensed that a newspaper reporter got a picture of him without his toupee. The cavern was in chaos. Before Henry could beat a hasty exit a TV crew forced its way past the other reporters and interrupted Humboldt's chastisement of the nearest Ranger.

"What the hell is going on?" yelled Henry above the melee. "How long was I out?"

"We all thought you were dead," answered the confused officer.

"Dead! Dead!" Henry yelled. "Do I look dead?" He spun around trying to make sense of the crowd. It pained him. "How the hell did all these people get up here? Oh, god, is that Chief Sweet over there?"

"They all responded to the APB. We all thought you'd been murdered."

"Murdered! Murdered! Do I look murdered? Oh, my god, that is Sweet, and there's the Jeffco Chief Sheriff and the Sheriff from Golden." Henry tried to hide; he was too slow. He forced his way between Olivia and the gang of cops interviewing her. He tried to exit through the defunct bathroom, but it was blocked. "Oh, no," he said to Olivia as if she cared. "They're coming over here. I could die of embarrassment. I'm dead. Do you hear me? Dead. Do I look dead?"

The crowd parted and Sweet stepped through. "Looking for the bathroom, Henry?" He smirked. "Glad to see you're feeling better."

"Yeah, Henry, good to see you up and at 'um," said the Jeffco Sheriff. "You look pretty spry for a dead guy. The all-points bulletin said you'd been killed."

"Killed?" Henry laughed weakly, "Killed? Ha, ha . . . do I look killed?"

Their smiles revealed the same satisfaction as when they caught a suspect in a lie.

"As disappointing as that may be, Henry," said Sweet, "there is the matter of you're being assaulted. And no cop is assaulted on my beat." As he finished his sentence, he looked at Olivia's bosom.

The others nodded emphatically. The TV crew barked out questions.

"Where is the body of Chief Ranger Humboldt?"

"Are you Chief Ranger Humboldt? Weren't you in an accident earlier this week? What were the injuries? Are there injuries tonight?"

"Who was the murderer? Did you know him, Ranger Humboldt? Who is the woman? Were you men fighting over her?"

"Are you married?"

"Does your wife know? Are you having an affair with this woman?"

Olivia answered, "Over my dead body!"

"Where's the body?" repeated a reporter.

"How long have you been Chief of the Rangers?"

"What are the Red Rocks Rangers," came a voice from the back. "Is this a real police force?"

"Who let these reporters in here?" bellowed Sweet. "This is a crime scene, gawdammit. Officer Carson, front and center. Where the hell is Carson?"

"You assigned him to guard Hardhat's truck, sir, just in case the Indian tries to get away."

Well then, Officer Simpson, let's implement some crowd control, son. Sheriff, your men can assist."

Henry pulled his Ranger aside and whispered. "I'm going to check out Cody's Bar Grill and Texaco. That's Hardhat's favorite hide out. Don't tell anyone where I'm going. Got that?"

The Ranger nodded. Sweet pushed a reporter and Henry took advantage of the ruckus that followed.

After two of the Denver Police took charge of the reporter and escorted him out of the tomb Sweet asked the Ranger, "Where did Henry slip off to?"

"Sorry, sir, he said not to tell."

"Look, Ranger, you don't want me to pull rank on you, now do you?" The Ranger squirmed. "Where did Henry run off to, son? We're all in this together." The Ranger remained silent. "Gawdammit, officer, do you know who I am? Now where in the hell is Humboldt? Is he hiding?"

"No, sir!" the Ranger seemed incensed. "He is not hiding. He is after the terrorist that caused all this." He realized he may have said too much and added, "He's not feeling well, sir. He left to get some rest. This has been a trying week for the Rangers."

"Right, officer, Henry's off resting. I get it. You know, this Indian may not be alone. Henry may need our help, officer. We don't want him getting hurt again, now do we? This is two for two.

Think about that. You'd feel terrible if the third time was charmed, and our boy Henry was seriously injured. Now . . . for your own good, for the good of your Chief Ranger and Superintendent in Charge, where did he go?"

"To someplace called Cody's Bar and Grill," said Olivia, "but you didn't hear it from me."

The Ranger looked at Olivia as if she'd stabbed him. He turned his back in anger.

"You did the right thing, son. And mum is the word." Sweet turned to his colleague, "Sheriff, Humboldt thinks the perpetrator is hiding out at Cody's on Lookout. What do you say we head over that way? I could use a drink, how about you?"

The Sheriff gave a clandestine nod.

"Leave the woman and the others here to distract the press. Officer Carson can drive us over in his black-and-white. Where the hell is Carson? We can sneak out through the bathroom."

Olivia had had it. The reporters and TV crew were barking out an avalanche of stupid questions.

"Are you acquainted with the assailant?"

"What started the fight?"

"Tell us about this tomb. Is there a connection between the tomb and Humboldt and the fugitive?"

"Are you related to the Colorado Springs Hotchkiss family?"

"What do you estimate is the value of the artifacts here?"

"Why was this Anthony Bare Hands here? Was he helping you somehow? How are you related?"

"What do you think of The Beatles?"

She tried to respond. "It's *Hands of the Bear*, and he was here to help protect an important archeological find. In fact, he is the person who discovered it. He may be an Indian patriot or a shaman. I personally witnessed a most remarkable ceremony."

"What sort of ceremony? You mean he is a priest?"

"Possibly. Who knows what would have happened if he hadn't been here? He saved this tomb, and he probably saved my life."

"Saved your life? How?"

"We didn't know who Humboldt was. For all we knew he was an attacker, a rapist."

"Humboldt is a rapist?" asked a short reporter on the periphery.

"One never knows, many of these ancient tombs carry an evil curse with them," Olivia decided to dupe the reporters, if for no other reason, just to vex the police who were standing nearby. "Only a shaman or holy man can remove such a curse."

"Humboldt is cursed?" asked the confused newsman.

"You got that right," mumbled a policeman, apparently disgusted with the whole event.

The reporter jotted down some notes and yelled from the back of the crowd, "Has anyone died from this curse?"

"Not yet," Olivia answered demurely, "but, as I said, one never knows."

The news reports were conflicting and confusing. They took two basic tones. Most were pro law-and-order. They misreported the seriousness of the crime, ranging from assault on Chief Ranger Henry Humboldt to murder of both Humboldt and Olivia. Reports stated that Anthony Hands of the Bear was everything from a common criminal to an Indian shaman/terrorist. Several called him an assassin. Neighbors were encouraged to report any suspicious persons in the area to local police. The suspect was described as above average height, dark hair and complexion, and probably nude or wearing a traditional Indian loincloth. The reports urged caution: the culprit may be armed with a bow and arrow. Stay tuned to this station for further developments; bla, bla, bla....

Other stations, however, took a more anti-authority approach. Tony was a Native American medicine man who "scuffled" with police in an attempt to protect a recently uncovered anthropological site in Red Rocks Park. Witnesses confirmed a confrontation between an AMERICAN Indian shaman, they emphasized *American*, and a security guard at the park. Henry was called a rent-a-cop who overstepped his authority and tried to force an anthropologist and the American Indian holy man off the sacred site. The American Indian protector was forced to flee into the surrounding rock formations. Local citizens are asked to stay out of the area as several police forces have seized the public park and are enforcing marshal law despite the ongoing concert.

Although the city and suburbs of Denver were tuned in, the only people in Red Rocks who heard the news were in the Green Room. None of the audience was aware of the conflict; they were listening to The Beatles. Neither Tony, nor Olivia, nor Henry, for that matter, had heard their ordeal as reported by the pack of *professional* radio journalists. A few stagehands and entourage members were among the *informed.* Someone, however, told Brian Epstein watching his lads from the wings. When George stepped to the wings to grab a blast of oxygen from a hidden tank Brian instructed him that they should cut things short and get off stage.

The Fab Four had played for only a half-hour, but an exit was timely because poor George had been pelted again with a bag of jellybeans as he stepped toward the mic. He was injured. John signaled the others. They promised to return as they left the stage.

"Have you lost an eye, George?" asked Ringo

"I'll live," answered George. "It seems we have bigger problems, what gives, Brian?"

Epstein informed them of the alleged assault and the trouble at the tomb. He thought there was potential for a riot. He was worried about their safety if things got out of hand.

The boys seemed more interested in the tomb than personal safety. They wanted to see it. They began negotiating with management for a tour. Brian and the Red Rocks staff said it was impossible; they would definitely have a riot if anyone saw The Beatles amongst the commoners.

While John continued to harangue for a guided tour, Ringo, once more, felt the urge of tobacco. He slipped away and with a shufti saw the Green Room, where he'd smoked before, was full of people. So, he sauntered past the others again, still unnoticed and stepped outside for a cigarette. He prided himself that he had become expert at sneaking a smoke in the alleys and shadows of arenas throughout Europe and the American East. Red Rocks was a perfect venue for hiding and stealing a few moments of peace. He was furtive as he exited backstage through large, metal, double doors. He immediately spotted a likely hiding place a few paces from the loading dock. A stealthy glide moved him into the dark. Although it was summer, the air at this high altitude was cool. He pulled the Carnaby Street cap he was wearing lower for warmth. Only when he lit his cigarette was there fleeting evidence of his presence. "I doubt they'll even miss me," he thought.

He noticed a group of policemen approaching another officer standing next to the pickup truck in which the lads had hitched a ride from Golden. A heavy-set and loud individual said something about disabling the truck, gawdammit, just take the distributor cable, and hurry up, "We got to get to Cody's on Lookout, Carson, before Humboldt nabs Hardhat and gets all the glory." They continued to mull around as the bobby lifted the bonnet on the truck and reached in.

Ringo thought it great games to spy, unseen from the shadows. He realized his voyeuristic delight was similar to the titillation when hiding from childhood friends and siblings in forbidden places like his parents closet. He was amusing himself with memories of the shenanigans in the tunnel from the Brown Palace Hotel, bragging that if he wished, the others could never find him here next to the rock cliff. They could stand in the light a few paces away and never know he was there. "See what I mean. None of those coppers buzzing around that truck even know I'm here. They couldn't find me if they was looking."

From the depths of the dark came a voice. "Too many for one warrior. Cursed white-eyes. Cowards."

Ringo nearly soiled himself. Fight or flee flashed through his mind, but in the same instant he concluded he was not a fighter, and his feet were frozen to the ground. He stood, wide-eyed and helpless as a face appeared. It was startling, but not menacing. "Here we go again," he said. "I wish you blokes would quit popping up like that. You're going to give me a coronary." After his initial panic subsided, Ringo recognized the ghostly figure as the driver of the pickup, the man who had rescued them outside Golden. "Bloody hell, man. You nearly scared the shite out of me!" He looked the fellow up and down, noticing he was nearly naked. "Clever outfit," he said. "Very fashionable considering the setting. Care for a fag?"

The man gave himself the once over, didn't seem concerned about his uniform (or lack of it), and cast an angry look toward Ringo. His eyes went demonic.

"Fag?"

"Cigarette," said Ringo. "Care for a cigarette?"

"Tobacco?" asked the man, his demeanor returning toward calm.

Ringo smelled the stick he was smoking. "I believe so; Marlboro," he answered. "Filtered. American. Satisfying. A manly smoke. I've been told it's proper etiquette to offer a smoke when one is inaugurating a friendship. You are friendly, are you not? "

"Sure," answered the dark figure. "Tobacco is peace. Important to start a parley with tobacco."

"Gear," said Ringo. He flipped a cigarette from the pack and offered it. The man took it, and Ringo searched his pocket for his lighter. "We were in such a hurry whence last we met, I didn't get your name. I'm Ringo, Ringo Star, percussionist. Drummer?" He lit the man's cigarette, and waited as he took a long draw. The man paused and eased the smoke slowly from his lips. He seemed calmer. He raised the cigarette in thanks and nodded. Ringo waited.

"Ahgachug Nowi," said the man. "Warrior."

"Ah," said Ringo. "That explains the outfit. I was told you were coming." They smoked together in the dark for a few minutes, enjoying the quiet. Then Ringo said, "You're him aren't you? The bloke everyone is looking for? The Indian? They say you've murdered some police fella and a lass?"

"No," answered Anthony, "I only scalped him." He held up a fist full of hair.

"Well," said Ringo, feeling a bit vulnerable. "The bugger probably deserved it." He looked toward the stage doors, hoping someone had missed him after all. No one came. He looked toward the truck, but the police had piled into a sedan and were heading out of the parking lot.

It was more a snort than a laugh. "Bugger? Ha," the man said. "Bloody bugger! That's a good one."

Ringo waited, expecting the Indian to say more. He didn't. "The hair looks rather neat?" asked Ringo. "I'd a thought a bloody scalping was a bit, you know . . ." He really didn't want to know, ". . . bloodier."

"Rug," answered the warrior.

"Beg your pardon?"

"Rug," said the Indian, and placed it on his head for affect. Misplaced, it covered his cranium and forehead.

It reminded Ringo of his own hairdo—long bangs "Ah," he mumbled. "Much ado about nothing."

"You betcha. But, it scared the 'shite' out of *him*."

George pushed open the doors and stood on the elevated dock. "Ringo," he called out, "Ringo! I know you're out there. Don't go getting lost. Brian thinks we should leave. John's still arguing. I know you can hear me. Where are ya'? Have you got a fag?"

Ringo and Anthony looked at each other.

"Do you want one?" asked Ringo as he stepped into a circle of light.

"Tar," said George as he walked down the short flight of stairs. "Me eye is killing me. Brian's in a panic. Things have gone bonkers. Yes, I need a smoke." He rubbed the bruise on his brow and stepped toward the dark. "It's nice out here. Quiet like."

Ringo handed him a cigarette. George put it between his lips and continued to rub his wound, waiting for a light. Two hands came from the dark. They cupped a lit match. George leaned forward, accepting the flame. Only then did he notice that they were not Ringo's hands. No rings. He looked up.

"Bloody hell!" he coughed.

"That's what I said," said Ringo. "Spooky, ain't it?"

The spook tipped Henry's wig as if it was a hat. "Nice to see you again. Which one are you?"

"George ..." said George in a weak response. "Guitar."

"This is . . . well . . . I can't really pronounce his name," said Ringo. "but he's a warrior."

"Groovy ..." said George, still weak. "Thanks for the light."

"My pleasure," said the warrior.

"Tobacco's important," said Ringo. "It's a friendly gesture."

"I see," said George. "I agree," he added. He paused, looking over the fellow, noting the nakedness. "Do we know each other?"

"He's the bloke what gave us a ride," said Ringo.

"Oh," responded George. "Sorry, I didn't recognize you with your clothes gone."

"Spooky, ain't it?" Said Ringo

"Very ethnic," answered George.

"He's the bloke what everyone's looking for," said Ringo.

"Groovy," said George, sounding doubtful.

"I think he's better at hide-and-go-seek that me even," said Ringo.

"Groovy."

"He scalped a copper." Ringo grinned.

"Very groovy?"

"That's his hair, there," Ringo pointed at Tony's forehead.

"Looks gear," said George.

"Rug," said the warrior.

"Groovy," said George, visibly confused.

He handed George the wig. At first George was shocked, but then he deduced it was not a real scalp. "Posh," he seemed relieved.

Paul came out the double doors and onto the dock. "George, Ringo! Where are you? You're out there smoking again, aren't ya? You know it's bad for your vocal cords. Oh, what the hell; have you got a fag?"

"You might say that," answered George.

"Don't start any rumors," said Ringo. "He's got enough people pissed already."

"Sorry," said George. "No offence, but your outfit's a bit dubious. You've got nice legs though."

"You've always been a leg man, George," said Ringo. "Not me."

Paul had by that time joined them. "Nice legs," he said to the Indian. "Ringo, lad, gim'me a smoke, won't cha?" He continued to check out the Indian while Ringo lit him. He paused, questioning Ringo and George with a look. Neither said anything.

"Are you with one of the bands?" Paul finally asked.

"He's a warrior," said Ringo.

"I don't know them," answered Paul. "What label are you on?"

"You don't get it, Paul," said George. "He's a bloody warrior. You know, Attila, Alexander, Cochise, Geronimo, Genghis bloody Khan. A bloody barbarian for chris'sake." He looked at the Indian. "No offence."

The Indian answered, "It's groovy."

"Oh, The Bloody Barbarians," said Paul. "I've heard of them. Didn't know you was playing tonight. Nice outfit."

"Thanks."

"What instrument?" asked Paul.

"Tom-tom."

"Ahh," said Paul, "you're like our boy here, Ringo, then?" He paused and enjoyed the cigarette. "To be honest, however, I don't think the Indian outfit thing will ever catch on. Next thing ya' know bands will be dressing as cops and cowboys, or painting their faces with spooky make-up. It'll be a bloody carnival. I hope we never see that. No offence."

"None taken," said the Indian.

"Lads!" called out Brian from the dock. "You need to come back inside. We've got a short press conference, and then we need to bugger off."

Just as he said it, a group of reporters, accompanied by a handful of police, came around the corner from the amphitheater. The ramp they were walking on was down hill; the slope quickened their step.

"You better stay with us," said Ringo to the warrior. "Give me your jacket, George." He helped George remove his coat and he gave it to the Indian. "Put that on, and the wig; put it back on like you did before. Lots of bangs. Here." He took the Carnaby cap off his own head and placed it low toward the back of the Indian's head. "Let the bangs show," said Ringo. "Gear! You look like a bloody Beatle."

"I thought he was a Bloody Barbarian," said Paul. "What's with the getup?"

"He's *the* bloody barbarian," said George. "The bloke the coppers are looking for. Don't you recognize him? He's the chap that rescued us. We owe him one."

"Oh," said Paul. "Sorry, I didn't recognize you without your . ... Well, I never bloody liked the Barbarians anyway. Too much like the Stones." He yelled toward the loading dock, "Coming, Brian." He turned to the Indian, "Let us walk in front; try to hide those legs."

Brian held the door for them. He immediately noticed the stranger among them. "Who's he?" he asked.

"He one of us," said Ringo. "A drummer for the Bloody Barbarians."

"The Barbarians?" asked Brian. "Who the hell are the Bloody Barbarians?" Brian looked at the stranger's legs. His eyes brightened.

"He's one of you, Bri," said George. "Dying to meet you. Seems you're reputation precedes you. You're bloody famous. Thought we'd do you a favor; give you an introduction. Sort of a *thank you* for all the hard work."

The Indian looked at Paul, confused by George's statement.

"Don't ask," said Paul. "Just keep walking."

They entered the back door with the reporters and police close behind.

Chapter Thirty-four

The Gospel According To John

Summer, 1964

Social behavior is a part of culture, and, as I have said before, "culture" is an interest of mine. I have, during my research, often been intrigued by the White race of Americans' superior attitude toward my red venerators and their social customs. Irony prevails. Take for example the differing attitudes toward social intercourse. Calm down, I am referring to verbal communication and social exchange.

My old friend Luther Standing Bear (now deceased), an Oglala chief, exemplified the Indian point of view when he said, "Conversation was never begun at once, nor in a hurried manner. No one was quick with a question, no matter how important, and no one was pressed for an answer. A pause giving time for thought was the truly courteous way of beginning and conducting a conversation. Silence was meaningful with the Lakota, and his granting a space of silence to the speech-maker and his own moment of silence before talking was done in the practice of true politeness and regard for the rule that: Thought comes before speech."

As they set up for the press conference, John joined the others in the Green Room. "There's going to be hell to pay for a short concert," said John. "I hope they don't blame it on us, like we're some kind of dodgers."

"Bamboozlers," said Ringo.

John noticed the stranger. "Who's he?"

"A friend of Brian's," said George. "A local."

"Gear," said John. "Bri's been working too hard." He turned away and seemed to be reviewing some hand written notes. He turned back. "There's quite a little excitement going on with this

Indian tomb thing. I'd love to get a look. You lads up for it? Perhaps your local friend there can distract Brian and we can get away."

"Maybe he's not Brian's type," offered Ringo, trying to deflect the direction things were taking.

"Why not?" asked John. "He's got good legs."

Paul attempted to come to Ringo's aid, and said, "He's a Bloody Barbarian."

"All the better," said John.

"Lads," interrupted Brian. "They're ready for you."

"Just a moment, Bri," said George. "John," he took Lennon aside, "There's something I need to tell you."

John kept looking over George's shoulder at the *local*. Ringo figured that George was informing John about the stranger's true identity. John looked at Brian, who stood nearby in a confused posture. John smiled, one of his infamous devilish grins.

Brian remained confused. "Lads?" he interjected. "It's time."

John and George parted. John walked to the Indian and whispered, "It's you is it, Anthony. I thought you looked familiar. George tells me we owe you a favor for the rescue from the near fatal clutches of the ingénues in Golden. Indeed we do. Well . . . stay close." They all walked from the Green Room to the press area.

Anthony stood a few paces behind the Fab Four. They sat at a long table with microphones. The crowd of reporters and a few police sat and stood opposite, bustling among themselves. Ringo watched as Brian eased next to Anthony and smiled, trying to check out the Indian's eyes under the exaggerated bangs.

"So, you're from around here I take it?" Brian asked.

Suddenly, Tony's eyes shone large.

A reporter impolitely barked out the first question. Ringo watched to see Brian's reaction.

Brian, upset at the false start, stepped forward to take control. As he moved down stage, he turned and gave Tony a wink. By that time, John had already begun.

"Before we answer any questions," said John into a microphone. "There's something I'd like to say—a statement, if you will."

"Gentlemen," Brian jumped in, "By way of an introduction, I offer you Mr. John Lennon. As you all know, Mr. Lennon, John, as he is affectionately known, often serves as the impromptu," he turned and reproved John, "spokesman for the group. After Mr. Lennon's, John's, brief," he turned and looked again, "statement, the lads will be glad to take questions. That's why we're here." He gestured with his extended arm, and backed away, giving John the stage.

"Thanks, Bri," said John. "Gentlemen and ladies, pillars of the press, local gendarme, I find myself in an awkward position."

Brian returned to the back wall and stood again by Anthony. "We make a good team, the lads and I, don't you think?"

"Groovy," said Anthony and tried to avoid eye contact.

Ringo amused himself by switching his focus from John's pontificating to Brian's inveigling.

John continued. "I don't need to tell you that The Beatles are big. The States have embraced us with open arms. You have been more than hospitable and kind. Our records are selling in the millions and as you can see from tonight's concert, we are selling out arenas wherever we go. All of that is good and wonderful. It's gear, believe me. However," he paused, "with fame comes responsibility. You can't just take the booty and run off, and buy cars and fancy clothes."

Several reporters toward the front pointed out Anthony's legless outfit and laughed. "Who's the fellow behind you, John? He could use some clothes," called out a reporter.

"An intern," said George.

"A Beatle's pledge," said Ringo.

"A bloody apprentice," said George again.

"A friend of Brian's," said Paul.

"He's one of us," said John. He turned and gave Anthony a look of support. Turning back to the audience and restoring order, he continued. "As you may also know, we—The Beatles, have begun exploring the world beyond entertainment. We have concerned ourselves with global issues, spiritual investigations, violence to our brothers and sisters, and human rights. I have already made statements about the evils of war. Sometimes the things I've said were unpopular with the establishment, The Man. But I'm declaring here tonight—it's just the beginning. So . . . here we are. I want to take advantage of this gathering and the events going on outside in the park to take a stand. We've already refused to play for segregated audiences here in The States, anywhere really. We've had it put in our contracts. Both the Florida Gator Bowl and San Francisco have done the right thing, shown love, which is all we need, accommodated us and integrated audiences. Well, seems to me this local Indian issue likewise needs our support.

"As you all know, an American Indian tomb has been discovered just up the way. As I understand it, there's some sort of dispute about who should be in charge. Who owns the tomb, and the like? Well, it seems to me, and the lads here, in the name of what is right and proper, that if it's an Indian tomb, the bloody Indians should be in charge. It's theirs.

"And what's all this about a local shaman trying to murder a cop? The one witness, a lady anthropologist, has already reported that that's bunk. The bloke was just protecting his ancestor. Why is *The Man* trying to insert himself and muck things up? If we Beatles had known this sort of Gestapo thing was going on behind the scenes, we never would have agreed to play in the bloody place, beautiful as it is. You've got to stand up for who you are and what you believe. If I was an Indian, I'd be jumping in me cars and, what do you blokes call 'um—pick me up trucks—and, as you Westerners say, hauling ass up to Red Rocks."

The police in the audience went red faced. Brian nearly fainted. Ringo cheered. George shouted out "Love! Peace! Power to the forgotten people!" John eased back in his chair. He wore a smirk and crossed his hands on top of his belly as if very pleased. The reporters surged, screaming questions. Riot consumed the room. Paul leaned forward, put his chin in his hands, and mumbled, "Well, there you are."

Anthony, honorary Beatle, took advantage of the bedlam and snuck away. As he exited the doors backstage he ran into a lone reporter who had the same thought. They bumped going out the doorway.

"Excuse me," said the reporter. He was excited. "It's nights like this that make me love my job. I've got to get to our remote truck and file a story. We're on the air in five minutes. Sorry, didn't mean to mow you down. No offence."

"None taken," said Anthony as he held the door for the reporter.

The newsman sprinted off the dock and up the ramp toward a white panel truck parked at the end of the lot. Tony slipped from the light to the darkness, the shadows, as his new friend Ringo would say, "from whence he came."

Five minutes later, those listening to KIMN, a local rock-and-roll station, heard the following report. The reporter had the pitch and pace of a hyena.

"Mania continues in Red Rocks Amphitheater. The evening's extravaganza was led off by Jackie De Shannon and the soulful ballads of a little known California duet called *The Righteous Brothers*. However, police and security forces continue on duty following the historic Beatles concert at Red Rocks. A Native American activist and Beatles fan, stirred on by the inflammatory music of the Fab Four, challenged authorities at the site of an ancient Indian burial tomb just discovered in the park. Concerned about the drama, taking place just around the stone corner from the stage, the Beatles entertained the crowd of seven thousand screaming teeny boppers for only about a half-hour. When asked to comment, spokesman John Lennon was pleased that their rock and roll renditions could ignite such patriotic and rebellious action on the part of a fan. 'It's only Rock 'n' Roll,' he was quoted as saying. 'But then I don't understand all the screaming, either.' Well, screaming there was, and I can tell you Denver, this reporter needed an extra dose of aspirin to maintain his position in the *pandemonious* front row. Police were actually putting bullets in their ears to muffle the noise. Teenage girls were fainting to the left of me, to the right of me. This kind of adulation has not been seen since the crooner Frank Sinatra sung at the Elitch Gardens, and Frank, take my word for it, could sing. Stay tuned to this station for further developments and the continued coverage of the Beatles' saga as Beatlemania continues to take America by storm."

Before the technician had shut off the sound, he was heard saying to the reporter, "I didn't know Sinatra sung at Elitch's?"

"You might be right . . . maybe it was Glenn Miller. Are we off yet?"

"Don't light up the bubble gum machine, Officer Carson," said Chief Sweet to his driver. "We don't want to attract undue attention. I figure most of the automobiles approaching the park are full of reporters and TV people."

The Jefferson County Sheriff knew it was a courtesy for Sweet to allow him to ride shotgun. Sweet, a much more rotund man, rode in the back seat of the Black and White.

"It's kinda crowded back here," Sweet observed out loud.

"Right, Chief," said Carson. "As you have said many times, 'It's our job to arrest criminals, not make them comfortable.' "

"Thanks, Alan for letting me sit up here," said the Sheriff. "I'd move the seat up, but I don't think I can." He reached under the seat and acted as if he was searching for a lever that both he and Sweet knew didn't exist.

"No problem, Sheriff. I was just commenting, not complaining."

"You mentioned earlier that you knew this Hardhat character, Chief," said the Sheriff, purposefully changing the subject, knowing the man in the backseat well enough that when he said he was just commenting—he *was* complaining.

"When I was Chief in Golden, he was just some punk Indian kid who had moved onto Lookout to work construction. He would get in a few fights at Cody's and harass a few of the local bimbos; otherwise, I never expected anything like this from him."

"You know Henry pretty well, too, don't you? Could he be exaggerating the circumstances?"

"Yeah, I know Henry, and you bet your ass he's exaggerating. Regardless, you don't assault a cop, even one of Henry's caliber, and get away with it, not on my beat. Besides, Red Rocks is owned by the City of Denver."

"So Henry would blow things out of proportion to save face?"

"Is a frog's ass watertight?"

"What about the tomb, Chief?" asked Carson. "If I may interrupt."

"Well, Carson, my boy, the way I see it, it is just like I said. Technically, Red Rocks is owned by the City and County of Denver. The tomb is on our turf."

"It's also in Jefferson County, Alan. I hope you see that the Sheriff Department has some level of jurisdiction, and can be helpful to you."

"You're in the car, aren't ya'?"

"I'd love nothing better than to nab this Hardhat guy and make an example of him to all those hotheads who want to punch out a man with a badge."

"That's an affirmative," said Carson and drove on toward Cody's.

"Turn on the regular radio, officer," asked the Sheriff. "I'd like to hear what the news station is saying about all this."

Carson turned the knob and the PBS station gently filled the car with classical music.

"What the hell is that?" barked Sweet.

"PBS, Chief. The Public Broadcasting System. The classical music keeps me calm, but alert, if you know what I mean."

"No, Carson, I don't know what you mean. Turn to the news station and see if there is anything on there. 'Calm but alert,' that's why I like you, son; always on duty."

Just as Carson reached for the tuning knob an announcer came on, "This just in from our editorial desk. It seems Chief Alan Sweet and his Boys in Blue are in hot pursuit of an American Indian patriot in Red Rocks Park, bringing to the forefront another possible confrontation with local minority constituents. This station has well documented Sweet's aggressive posture toward minorities and his punitive handling of grape protesters and pickets in the produce departments of local grocery chains. That the Denver Police have little patience for human-rights advocates is well known."

"Leave it, Carson," ordered Sweet.

The editorial continued. "In order to squelch the touchy situation at the famous amphitheater, the site of a recently discovered ancient Indian, Native American, gravesite, Sweet has called in several fellow police groups including the Jefferson County Sheriff Department, the Golden Police, and The Red Rocks Rangers. It would appear that it was trespassing by one of the Rangers that led to the confrontation and subsequent vigorous involvement by Chief Sweet and the others. The Native American was aiding in protecting the tomb from potential looters at the Beatles concert. He became allegedly militant when confronted by The Chief Ranger and Superintendent in Charge, one Henry Humboldt. To use Humboldt's words, 'A physical confrontation broke out.' Humboldt is not available at this time to answer allegations of police brutality, and the victim of the confrontation has been forced into hiding, somewhere in the famous rock formations of the park . . . "

"What kind of bullshit is this!" Sweet screamed from the back of the car, grabbing the metal screen between the seats. "I have always hated this liberal, commie, damn radio station. Carson I can't believe you listen to this pink-o crap."

"The music, sir. I just listen to the music. I have never liked the news . . . "

"Can it, Carson, I can't hear that faggot son of a bitch."

"Should I change the station, Chief?"

"Nah! I may as well listen. It will all come back at me sooner or later. I may as well hear what I am going to have to rebut. What I'd really like to do is get that pink-o S. O. B. in a cell and kick his little, liberal fanny."

"That's an affirmative," said the Sheriff.

The radio announcer continued. "Although the exact nature of the tomb has not been determined, our research department has suggested that since we know local and neighboring tribes of the Great Plains do not ordinarily entomb their dead, there is a good chance that such a tomb could be of ultimate importance as the last resting place of an Indian messiah such as the Paiute medicine man, Wovoka. Wovoka, as many of you may know, was the holy man responsible for reviving the Ghost Dance in the late 1860's, a last heartfelt attempt on the part of the Sioux to survive the Plains Indian Wars. They believed that wearing the Ghost Shirts would make them impervious to the bullets of the soldiers. They believed their dead would rise from their graves, and the buffalo would return. This may explain why the tomb is reportedly filled with so much tribute—things the messiah may need upon his return to the physical world.

"Sadly, the reality of the situation was that the authorities used the Ghost Dance as an excuse to execute Sitting Bull and instigate the infamous massacre at Wounded Knee. Wovoka went into hiding and was never heard from again, although there were fables that he and representatives of several tribes were secretly trying to reorganize. It is possible that Wovoka was hiding here in the foothills of Colorado and, unfortunately, passed away before he and his compatriots could launch a coup d'état against the cavalry. If the tomb at Red Rocks is indeed that of Wovoka, it could prove to be the most important archeological find of the century in North America. Is it any wonder that a local Indian patriot chose to protect this tomb from the inept and ineffectual security of Chief Alan Sweet and his confederates in blue from Golden and the Sheriff's Department?"

"Summm—offa—BITCH," shouted Sweet.

"While the Beatles continue their British Invasion and assault on classical culture, yeah—yeah—yeah, the various police organizations concentrated on getting cars parked and teenyboppers into their seats, leaving a major part of American history vulnerable to adolescent souvenir hunters. And when someone finally decided to take a stand and protect the gravesite, a Native American mind you—protecting his heritage, he and his scientific colleague were accosted by the local constabulary. Typical.

"How many policemen does it take to apprehend a single protester? One may just as well ask how many cops it takes to screw a doughnut. It's been a long hot summer and this may prove to be another in a long hot series of events illustrating our over-energetic law enforcement and their continued inept police performance."

"Son-of-a-bitch," echoed the Sheriff.

"Stay tuned to this, your public information station, for further developments as we continue to follow the saga of a local Native American activist and his attempts to save a fragile part of his ancient culture. As always, I must close by saying, the opinions expressed in this editorial do not necessarily reflect the opinions of PBS and sponsoring institutions. Remember our membership drive will begin tomorrow. It is through your memberships that we can bring you the alternative voice of . . . "

"Turn that son of a bitch off, Carson," bellowed Sweet. "If I find out you're donating to that communist clap-trap, I'll put you back on the streets. I have always hated that guy. This is all Henry's fault . . . a double murder! Can you imagine? What the hell kind of police work is that? Well . . . we're in too damn deep to get out now. We have to bring in this Hardhat character and make him the focus of all this; you know, find out every questionable and criminal thing this guy has done, and kill off this Indian patriot crap. We've got to make him look like the radical he is, get the public back on our side, shut up the motormouth on PBS. Somebody is going to take a fall for all this, and I guar-AN-tee it is not going to be me!"

Together, Carson and the Sheriff said, "That's an affirmative, Chief."

Troy Rivers, Patty Andrette, Ho Ho Horace Green, Veloy Vigil, Flora Florida, and Shirley Lauderbach sat in the convention office and listened to the news-breaking announcement on the local rock-and-roll station. An Indian priest at Red Rocks was trying to protect a tomb.

"Why does it take five police forces to arrest this one guy? There is something going on they're not telling us," said Ho.

"Was that Ranger killed or not?" asked Veloy. "Turn to another station, see if we can get any answers."

"Turn on the TV," said Flora. "See what they are saying."

"Do we have a TV?" Troy asked Shirley.

"I called AV to bring one up so we could watch your interview. It's on the way."

"Great idea, Shirley. You're always on top of things," said Horace.

"Call them and tell them to hurry," said Rivers. "Veloy try to get another station on the radio."

While waiting for the television set to arrive, the group listened to several other reports, each more sensationalistic than the last. One station had already had to broadcast an apology, "Further investigation has clarified that Chief Ranger Humboldt and the anthropologist, Olivia Hotchkiss of Colorado Springs, were not, we repeat NOT having an affair."

"Well, that's good news," said Flora. "Really—who gives a shit?"

The announcer continued, but no one heard the first part while Flora was talking. They all heard the last sentence, however: "A conflict ensued and details are sketchy whether or not there are fatalities."

"Fatalities!" screamed Flora. "They killed the holy man!"

"Whoa, Flora, we don't know that for a fact," said Patty. "I know the Rangers. They don't even carry guns."

"Well, what are we going to do about it?" asked Veloy. "We can't just sit here and let them execute him, now can we? Troy, isn't there something we can do? We need someone to take charge here."

They all looked at Rivers.

"Troy?" asked Horace.

It was quiet for a long moment.

"Where the hell is that television?" asked Rivers.

"Yeah, where the hell is it?" yelled Ho. "I'm a visualist. I need pictures."

"Quiet, I got another report here on the PBS station. Listen up!"

"Shirley," asked Ho, "can you put this on the public address system?"

She flipped a toggle switch on the large console, "With just a push of a button."

"Whoa, I'm not so sure that's a good idea," said Patty, but it was too late. The PBS editorial blasted into the convention center.

Troy took Patty's hand as they listened. Dread filled their consciousness. Rivers' thoughts moved from friend to friend. He read their concern. He felt their anxiety. When Patty stood and looked him directly in the eyes, he saw her support. It warmed him. Something, not yet lucid, awoke.

Although the crowds had departed, the organizing crew of over forty Native Americans stopped their activities and listened. They looked toward the office windows high above the floor of the conference center. A lone figure walked up to the huge glass rectangles and returned their empathetic gaze. The lights of the office were brighter than the worklights in the auditorium; thus, the figure stood as a broad-shouldered silhouette. And even though none could see his face, all on the floor knew the man who stood above them was their leader, Trois Rivières, Wyandotte.

The brothers sat at the bar. Talks Softly was enjoying what he felt was authentic Western ambiance. He was amused that the bartender of Buffalo Bill Cody's Bar Grill Trading Post and Texaco Station was embarrassed that he didn't have fresh mint for his request—a Mint "Tulip."

"I'm afraid I'll have to use a julep mix," he said. "I think I've got some in the back room, partner. I don't get many requests for that drink around here. Will that do?"

"*Certainement,*" answered T.S.

"And you, partner?" the Bartender asked Red.

Talks Softly could tell his brother did not like being called, "partner," despite the Old West character of the place.

"What beers do you have?" asked Red Stick.

"Coors is our most popular. You know, America's Fine Light."

T.S. saw regret on the bartender's face right after he gave the unsolicited advertisement. Red looked even more impatient.

"Ahh . . . ," the bartender stumbled for something to say, "You boys aren't from around here are you?"

He looked like he regretted his second statement even more than the first.

"I mean, I don't recall seeing you in here before?"

"Is there a problem, punaise?" asked Red suddenly growing larger.

"No, no, of course not," stuttered the bartender. "I'll go get that Tulip mix." His voice squeaked on the *T*. "You gentlemen make yourselves comfortable." He turned and quickly sought the sanctuary of the storeroom.

"I told you," said Talks Softly "people are friendly up here." He looked around and gestured, throwing both arms wide open, taking in the expanse of the place. "I knew you would love it."

"I don't love it," said Red Stick.

"Now don't lie to me. You ate enough of those biscuits and gravy at the Holland House this morning to choke an alligator." He waited for his brother to react. Red sat . . . stoic. "I know you're disappointed that the Beatles only played a half-hour, but wasn't Jackie De Shannon fabulous?" He waited again—no comment. "OK, so I got lost on the way back to the hotel. So, sue me. This is serendipitous; what a fabulous place. What a fantastic find. It's just like the Old West. You can't fool me; you love it."

"The biscuits were good, but I thought the desk clerk was rude to us."

"Well they don't get many of our kind very often."

"Our kind? What the hell is 'our kind,' T.S. "

"You know."

"No, I don't know. Tell me."

"You know—Indians."

"This is a trading post and it looks damn near like an Indian museum, T.S. Are you trying to be funny?"

"Yes, Red, I am. You have been a grump ever since you left Louisiana."

"He called us, 'boys,' T.S. Doesn't that bother you?"

"No, Red. Not here. He didn't know any better. He's not from the South and these Colorado folk call everyone *boys*. Hey, boys, what'cha doing? Hey, boys, want a drink? Hey, boys, see the girls? Hey, boys, want to snuggle in the hay, boys?"

Red smiled.

"Well it's about time, you big lummox."

The bartender returned with a squatty can, reading the instructions. "Got it, men" he said and held it up. "Did you decide on a beer, sir?"

"Coors will be fine."

The barman continued to chatter, "Is Tennessee OK for you, sir?"

"Tennessee?"

"Bourbon. I'm afraid I don't have Kentucky for your Tulip."

"Oh," Talks Softly giggled, "Tennessee will be fine. That's why we call them a *Tulip* . . . when they're made with Tennessee Bourbon instead of Kentucky. Get it?"

"Got it," he said. "The drinks will be right up."

"I just love this place?" chirped T.S. "See, he didn't call us *boys*. Mr. Buffalo here knows a man when he sees one."

A man in a police uniform burst through the door. He was bald. His face and forehead were as red as a spanked bottom. He sprinted toward the bar, but stopped dead-short in his tracks when he focused on the brothers. He looked around the bar as if to confirm he was in the right place.

T.S. said, "Sorry, we're the only two customers." He doubted that he was heard.

"My god, things are changing too damn fast," the officer mumbled. "Billy," he leaned over the bar and grabbed the old man. "Billy," he repeated, "and don't lie to me. Have you seen that son of a bitch Hardhat?"

"Take it easy, Henry." said the bartender.

"So he's a Mr. Billy, not a Mr. Buffalo," T.S. said quietly, somewhat disappointed.

Billy pulled away from the lunatic grip of the officer. "I haven't seen him since you ran him off the other night. What's this all about?"

"Then you haven't heard?"

"Heard what? Henry," Billy the bartender seemed sincere, "You've got to calm down. You're going to give yourself a hemorrhoid."

Henry, the officer, paused in silence. He appeared to be trying to figure out if Mr. Billy had just given him a shot.

"I haven't seen him, Henry. What's going on?"

"He tried to kill me; that's what's going on. That Indian son of a bitch tried to murder me!"

Red tensed at Henry's choice of words. T.S. could see that he did not care for the man's uniform or his demeanor. "T.S.," he whispered, "I'm not sure, but for some reason that cop looks familiar."

"Kill you?" Billy asked credulously. "Come on, Henry. Anthony likes pissing you off once in a while, but I don't think he'd actually kill you."

He served Red and T.S. their drinks and gave them a look which acknowledged that all three were thinking the same thing—that this guy in the uniform is crazy.

Talks Softly smiled and said to Red, "I told you. It's the Wild West. Indians trying to kill cowboys, shootouts, old bars, and we're about to have a barroom brawl. It's like a movie, right here in front of us. Now, don't you just love it?"

"Quiet," said Red.

"I'm telling you," continued Henry, still agitated. "That crazy, red son of a bitch tried to chop my head off with a goddamn tomahawk. I caught him porking some blonde in the Indian tomb at Red Rocks, and he tried to murder me."

"Here, Henry, have a drink. On the house. Now calm down and tell me what happened."

"Indian tomb?" asked Talks Softly of Henry, but his voice was too quiet for the aggravated man to hear.

"What," he yelled, his face expressing his confusion as to why this stranger was trying to take part in his conversation.

"I don't think he likes black folks," T.S. said to Red, and then turned back to Mr. Henry, "You said there was an Indian tomb at Red Rocks. We were just there for the Beatles concert. Did you go? Don't you just love 'um?"

"What!" he yelled even louder.

Red stood up. "He asked you about the Indian tomb at Red Rocks."

Henry stood dumfounded for a moment, grabbed the drink Mr. Billy was putting in front of him and downed it in one gulp. "Huh?" he asked more quietly.

"The Indian tomb. We'd like to see it," said T.S. "It sounds very interesting. We're Indians, you know."

Both Mr. Billy and Mr. Henry looked bewildered.

"Huh?" repeated Henry.

"Tchoupitoulas," said T.S.

"Huh?" asked Billy.

"Oh, Christ," said Henry. "New Orleans! Well, there goes the neighborhood."

Talks Softly looked to see how his brother reacted to the insult.

"I'm trying to figure out why this clown looks familiar," he told T.S.

"Turn on the TV, Billy," said Henry. "I need to see what the press is saying about this."

"The TV is on the fritz. I'll turn up the radio. It's on PBS, I like listening to classical music when things are slow."

"And jazz," said T.S.

"Huh?" asked Henry.

"And jazz. The PBS station is the only channel where you can get good jazz."

Both white men strained to listen. Talks Softy assumed that neither had heard him. Both looked at each other for clarification. There was none. Both looked to Red for forgiveness.

Before his brother could respond, the PBS editorial interrupted. They all listened.

"Oh, Christ, I'm dead," mumbled Henry and collapsed on a bar stool, slumping over the counter. "Give me another drink, Billy. I'm dying here."

"And another for us, please," asked T.S. "This is getting good."

Red continued to scrutinize Henry. "New Orleans," he mumbled several times.

T.S. recognized the consternation. Red looked submerged in deep deduction, but nowhere near enlightenment.

"I'm fucked," moaned Henry. "Butt fucked."

The slightest gleam of recognition made Red squint his eyes.

"And you think that was Anthony?" asked Billy of Henry.

"I know it was," answered Henry. "I know it was that Indian son of a . . . ," he paused and looked at Red still standing and staring at him. "Neither of you boys are construction workers are you?" he asked.

Red stiffened; T.S. patted his hand, "Costume designer," answered T.S.

"No," said Red, glaring.

Henry turned back to Billy, "I'm sure it was that carpenter, that toilet fixing, dry wallin', nail drivin', Snickers stealing son of a bitch."

They all heard a car pull up outside. Henry jumped from his stool and hid behind the door to surprise whoever walked through.

The others remained where they were and waited to witness the pending excitement.

T.S. was visibly disappointed when another cop came through the door. He recognized him from newscasts. It was Chief Alan Sweet of the Denver Police. He was followed by a smaller man in a Jefferson County Sheriff uniform and a younger Denver officer.

"Billy," said the Chief.

"Sweet! Long time no see," said Billy.

"We're looking for . . ."

"I haven't seen Hardhat, Chief. I don't know . . ."

"So, Humboldt's been here, has he? Where did the little cadaver get off to?"

Henry slowly pushed the door closed, and revealed himself.

"Henry, is that you?" asked Sweet, "Or the ghost of Humboldt past?"

The Sheriff laughed.

"Any sign of Hardhat?"

"None," Henry said sadly.

"Well, he'd be a fool to show up here. It was a long shot. Anyway, I had to get away from those reporters. I could use a drink, and where better to imbibe than my favorite rustic bar, eh, Billy?"

"It's good to see you again, Chief. Still got your tab back here somewhere."

"That's great, Wild Man. Set 'um up. Henry, need another drink?"

"Nothing for me, sir," said the younger officer. "Thanks, but I'm still on duty."

"Well, that's good, Carson. You be on duty for the rest of us. Set 'um up, Wild Billy."

T.S. registered that the young virile officer's name was *Carson,* and the bartender was now "Wild Billy!" Oh, he just loved the frontier flavor of it all.

"What will you have, officers?" asked Wild Billy.

"Bourbon?" asked Sweet of the Sheriff.

"Tennessee, OK?" asked Talks Softly.

"What?" asked Sweet, sounding surprised that T.S. would interject.

"Tennessee, OK?" interrupted Billy and brought the bottle and three glasses around the bar. The law enforcement troika followed their host to a round, heavy pine table.

Carson, *he's very tall*, remained standing, looking out the door as if something may happen outside.

"Billy, bring us a pitcher of water and a bucket of ice; I may hide out here for a couple of drinks. Carson, go hide the car, just in case Hardhat is foolish enough to show up. And turn on the TV, Billy, but keep the sound low. I'll turn it up if I see there's anything worth listening to."

"It's on the fritz, Chief, but the radio is working. It's on PBS right now."

"Never mind, Billy."

Chapter Thirty-five

Rivers of Doubt

Summer, 1964

I have a unique perspective on history. I am fortunate—I live it. In the late 19th century, the "Great Indian Wars" were going badly for The People of the Plains. As he stood on the verge of battle, I commented to a Cheyenne chief, Wooden Leg, that I thought his buckskins were handsome. The beaded images of turtles were particularly beautiful. I asked if they gave him strength.

He answered, "The idea of full dress in preparation for a battle comes not from a belief that it will add to the fighting ability. The preparation is for death, in case that should be the result of the conflict. Every Indian wants to look his best when he goes to meet the Great Spirit."

Troy Rivers, lawyer, knew that the reflection in the office window was a gift. There, looking back, stood the image of Trois Rivières, Indi'n. Through their generosity and faith, Patty, Veloy, Horace, and the others had transformed him. He searched the transparent group portrait for the likeness of his mentor. He sought the specter there in the proper place, among his friends, between Patty and Horace. The old sachem did not appear, but Rivières could see that the others were watching him as he came to the window. He stood at the large glass, looking down upon *his* clan, the conference team, dressed in tribal regalia. He feared that his image was but a semblance, his vestment was but a costume.

They had all heard the herald from John Lennon. Had he alone heard the soliloquy from Orvis Kahnawake? When did they decide that he would lead them to Red Rocks? When did he accept? What did they see? He searched his reflection again. It was appropriate that they were dressed for battle. The tomb of their father called.

"Who knows the way to Red Rocks?" Trois Rivières asked. He spoke into the glass.

The small group behind him looked among themselves for an answer.

Horace Green finally asked, "Don't you? You're from Denver for crying outloud."

"You live in New Mexico, you ever been to Carlsbad Caverns?"

"Several times."

"OK, you even been to the State Capitol?"

"Several Times."

He turned to face Horace. "OK, you ever been to Los Alamos and the atomic place?"

"Yes."

"And the Natural History Museum?"

"Of course."

"Well, screw it. I've never been to Red Rocks."

"How far could it be?"

"Not far. I don't know exactly how far, or its precise location, but I do know it's not far. It's just out of town; over by Golden, you know, where they brew Coors beer."

"Yeah, I know. Can you get us to Golden?"

"Probably."

"What's that mean?"

"Well, contrary to popular belief, everybody who lives in Denver does not tour the Coors Brewery. I know where Golden is, but I've only been to the Court House—the Jefferson County Court House."

"Can you get us that far?"

"Yeah, sure I can. Red Rocks can't be far from there."

"What about the bus driver? Will he know how to get us to Red Rocks?"

"What about the bus, Horace? We don't know yet. Shirley is still on the phone trying to get the bus the city promised us."

"Sorry, Three Rivers. You're right. We need to calm down and make a logical plan. Sorry, it's just my blood is boiling at the possibility of that tomb being looted and something happening to that shaman fellow."

Rivers knew the plan was his job. Was he, or was he not, going to be a leader? He stepped from the window, back into the office.

"I know exactly how you feel, Ho. I feel the same way. Last year I would have been thinking about how I could put that Hands of the Bear guy in touch with a good criminal lawyer. Today, all I want to do is kick some bluecoat ass."

"That's an affirmative," said Veloy Vigil walking in from the adjoining office.

"Any word on the bus?" asked Rivers.

"Nothing yet. Boy, that Shirley can go on the warpath when she needs to. You should hear her. I'm amazed a roar like that can come out of a fine feline like Shirley. And the language!"

"Keep your mind on the task at hand, Vigil. You can plunder the white women after the battle," said Horace.

Veloy looked at Troy, "What'd I say?"

"Nothing, Veloy, nothing. Don't worry about it. Patience is thin; tempers are flaring—having to wait, you know."

"Well, you had better say something to the others, Troy," he pointed at the crowd of forty or so men milling around on the conference floor. Several bottles of alcohol had suddenly appeared. "That booze they are passing around is no good—especially under these circumstances. It ain't no good, never. Take my word for it. I been sober for four years now, and this ain't no good."

"You're right, Veloy. We better talk to 'um."

Rivers slid the large window and leaned out the opening. Veloy and Ho stood to each side. Troy yelled. Veloy whistled. Horace banged on the adjacent window to get their attention.

"Men," yelled Rivers, "Men! Please quiet down for just a second. We need to talk."

The crowd quieted: somewhat.

"And the booze, you guys. You know that's a bad idea!" yelled Veloy. "Ain't no good going to come from the booze."

"Ahh, put a cork in it, Vigil," came a rebuke from the crowd.

"Yeah, just 'cause you're on the wagon don't mean the rest of us . . . "

"Veloy is right," yelled Horace. "The last thing we need is to get drunk before we get to Red Rocks."

"We know you're concerned." said Rivers. "We're all angry at what's going on, but we have to keep our heads about us if we are going to help our brother at Red Rocks. We've got to get smart, not angry. Our goal is insuring that the tomb remains untouched. So, please, put the liquor away. Save it for the celebration. By the way, who here knows the way to Red Rocks?"

"He don't even know the way," grumbled a voice from the floor.

"Give me a hit off that bottle," said another, but most of the men had stopped and conversed quietly to one another.

Shirley Lauderbach entered the office and whispered in Troy's ear. She looked red in the face and blurted out, "Damn it!"

"What's wrong?" asked Horace.

"No bus?" asked Veloy. Shirley nodded with angry vigor.

Rivers reminded himself that he was a problem-solver. He didn't have a solution at the tip of his fingers, but he would think of something. He regretted prepaying in full, but the charter was with the City. They didn't accept partial payment, and if you can't trust the city, whom can you trust? He regretted not going to a private bus company, but the City gave him a reduced price as part of the rental fee for the conference center. It was a bargain. Well, damn it, he should have known better; you get what you pay for.

"The guy at the bus barn said they can't get another driver until after the football game." said Shirley. "That could be four or five hours minimum. Everybody is working; they are all on duty. Anyone who was off came in for the overtime; it's Sunday."

"Football? This isn't football season." said Veloy.

"It's some kind of exhibition game, a big deal, veterans versus rookies, meet the players, marching band competition, cheerleader contests; they were hoping The Beatles would stick around for one more day and make an appearance. The whole city is there. It's a big deal for the mayor; this is an election year. That's all I heard before I lost my cool and blasphemed the City, the mayor, the Broncos, and the pinhead to whom I was ranting. Sorry. I don't think I made any new friends." Shirley heard the phone ring; she crossed her fingers in the air, and ran back into the adjacent office.

"If that's not the transportation department calling back with good news, I'm going over to the depot myself and rattle some cages. You guys try to keep the spirits up, but put a kibosh on the drinking. We don't need that."

"She runs nice," said Veloy.

Horace took his arm and spun him face to face, "Put a cork in it, Vigil."

Rivers followed Shirley. The incoming call proved fruitless. He tried one more time to call the depot. The phone rang more than thirty times before Troy slammed down the receiver. "That's it!" he yelled, "I'm going down there!" Shirley mumbled "Give 'em hell," but Patty tried to calm him. He gave her a fleeting kiss and said he had to go. He ran out of the office and down the stairs, looking for Horace. He found him talking to several others. "Come on, we got an errand to run."

"An errand . . . now? What kind of an errand?"

"I'm going to teach a public employee some manners, and pick up a bus if I have to drive the thing myself. Coming?"

"Right behind you, Troy, but shouldn't we change our clothes first? Aren't you going to look a little silly thrashing some clerk in an Indian outfit?"

"There's no time. Maybe it'll scare him. Maybe he'll figure that if we don't get our bus, we're going to scalp him."

"Like I said, Kemo Sabe, I'm right behind you."

"Veloy," Rivers grabbed Vigil's arm. "We are on our way to get a bus, you stay here and keep these guys focused. No booze. We'll be right back. If you need help, Shirley and Patty are up stairs. Listen for more information about what's happening at the tomb. Ask everybody again if they know the way to Red Rocks. Wish us luck. Adios."

The two braves ran the length of the convention center and exited onto Fourteenth Street. "Lets' grab a cab. Maybe the driver will know where the bus depot is," said Rivers.

"I wish you hadn't said that."

"Just wave down a cab."

"Do you know the way to anyplace in Denver?"

"My office, my apartment, my favorite bar, the Convention Center, and the zoo. OK?"

"No problem. Look there's a cab." They both waved frantically; and watched helplessly as the cab swerved to pass them by. The same thing happened several more times. "I told you we should have changed our clothes."

"Desperate times—desperate measures," said Troy as he stepped off the curb in front of an oncoming taxi. When the driver tried to swerve into the next lane to pass, Rivers again jumped into the way. He was not to be denied.

The first few chapters of his life flashed in front of his eyes as the taxi screeched to a halt. Before the cabby could bark an insult out the window, Rivers and Green were in the back seat.

"I could have killed you, ya' crazy idiot," yelled the driver. "Don't they have any cabs on the reservation, Chief? Ya' never seen a moving car before?"

"What the hell has happened to this city? Where's the hospitality. This used to be a friendly place. What happened, can you tell me that? A dozen cabs passed us. If I hadn't jumped in front of you, you would have kept driving, too. Right?"

"Look, Chief, that was a pretty stupid stunt you pulled. I can't afford no trouble. Killing an Indian would look bad on my record. Here in the city we got laws against that sort a' thing."

"Don't call me *Chief*. And don't preach to me about laws. I know the law. I'm a lawyer, damn it!"

"In that case, I should'a hit ya'." the driver turned to face his passengers. "Where to, Counselor?"

"The city bus depot, and step on it. We're in a hurry."

"I can see that. The central office or the bus barn?" asked the driver.

"Hell, I don't know," said Rivers. "Where can we get a bus?"

"If you wanted a bus, why did you step in front of my cab?"

"No, I mean, where can we pick up a bus that's been chartered? There are more of us. We chartered a city bus and we're in a hurry to pick it up."

"More like you? I thought the powwow was over. All you Indians walking and gawking everywhere, didn't help my business. I didn't get one decent fare, not to mention tips."

"Just get us to the bus garage," said Rivers.

"You wouldn't happen to know the way to Red Rock Amphitheater?" Horace asked the driver.

"You guys new in town?" he asked.

"I am, but the Chief here is a native," answered Ho.

"Because it's too damn far to walk," continued the driver. "Could be a pretty hefty fare. Twelve or fifteen bucks. Not including the tip."

"The fare," gulped Rivers.

"What?" asked Ho.

"Yeah, what?" asked the driver.

"I didn't bring my wallet," said Rivers. "Did you?"

"I'm not wearing any pants here, Troy. I told you we should have changed clothes."

The cab screeched to a halt. "Now look, Chief. This ain't no charity. If you and Tonto here ain't got the fare, you should have told me."

"I told you, don't call me *Chief.*"

"Tonto?" asked Ho. "Tonto? Do you know what Tonto means?"

"Look, you guys, if you haven't got the fare, you're out'a here. I don't care if you are a lawyer or what your names are, Chief. You're just another couple of deadbeat Indians as far as I'm concerned. Out'a my cab."

"Look, we can pay you after we pick up the bus. You can follow us back to the convention center. We'll pay you double," pleaded Troy. "Keep the meter running."

"Tonto?" repeated Horace.

"No deal, Chief. Get out of the cab."

"He told you—don't call him *Chief.* You been listening to traffic noise too long, Bub?"

"Bub? So that's how it's going to be is it, Pocahontas. Get out of the goddamn cab before I call a cop."

"Pocahontas? Pocahontas was a woman, you jerk. Don't you know anything?"

"I know I'm calling a cop." The driver reached over the back of his seat for the handle to the back door. "Now get out." His hand tangled in a long strand of rawhide hanging from Rivers bone vest. It snapped and several of the sacred bone beads fell on the floor and in the street. "Sorry, Chief, but I want you out of my cab."

"That does it!" said Troy and slapped the drivers cap in retaliation. It flew out the window. He exited the cab still angry, but concerned about the bone beads, left the door open, and bent over to pick up some he saw on the pavement. He notice the driver jump out his door; he assumed to retrieve the cap.

Horace got out and was moving around the back of the cab. He watched the driver focus on Rivers, bent over searching for beads, his buckskin clothed backside exposed and vulnerable to attack. The driver raised his right foot in the air, preparing to kick Rivers.

Out of the corner of his eye, Troy noticed Horace rush past him. He heard an *oomph* and a thud, and turned to see the driver spread-eagle on his back in the street.

Laughing, his anger somewhat quelled by the sight of the driver, Rivers tried to help him up by taking one arm. The driver pulled away. His shirt, however, remained in the River's hand. The sleeve tore away at the shoulder.

Rivers and Horace laughed together. The driver paused for a moment, contemplating the destruction of his shirt. Judging by the expression on his face, he blamed Horace. He took a swing at Ho, but missed.

"Now hold on!" yelled Troy as he tried to grab the irate driver. The driver responded by spinning in the opposite direction and tried to hit Rivers. Troy grabbed the other shirtsleeve as the momentum of another missed swing spun the driver past him. It tore away even more easily than the first.

"Oh, hell," laughed Horace. "Let's just finish it." He stepped forward and grabbed the collar of the man's shirt and pulled down. The white cotton ripped away exposing the man's pale chest.

The driver stepped back and looked at his predicament. He glared at Horace. "I'm not afraid of you, you big sona' fa bitch. Jus' 'cause you're bigger 'n me. I fought a lot of assholes bigger 'n me. You've made a big mistake, Tonto."

Horace stopped laughing. "Well, I'm waiting, tough guy. Make your move."

The driver slowly pulled his belt from the pants loops around his waist. He expertly wrapped the leather strap around the fingers of this right hand, clenched his fist, and tested the hardness of the impromptu bludgeon by smacking it against the palm of his left hand.

"You shouldn't have done that," said Rivers from behind the man. Troy reached with both hands and took the respective back pockets of the man's pants and with a single motion pulled the britches to the startled man's ankles.

The driver stumbled as he tried to turn and smack Rivers who was kneeling far below the unbalanced swing. Horace pushed the off-balance taxi tough, and watched as he tripped over his pants and tumbled to the street, face first. Horace then, rather ungraciously, grabbed the man's cuffs, pulled the pants off the owner and into the air.

The man rolled over and feigned unconsciousness, lying there in the street. Troy figured he was playing opossum and hoping these wild Indians would not injure him any further.

"Which way to the bus depot?" asked Rivers leaning near the man's buried face. "I'm in kind of a hurry, Chief," he said.

The man's right arm came up slightly. The belt had unraveled and hung loosely from the hand. A single finger protruded from the confusion. "Two blocks up Lawrence Street," mumbled the driver from under his other arm.

"Oh, yeah," said Rivers. "I remember now. That's where they park the busses. Thanks."

"Now you remember?" asked Horace.

"Yeah, it's not far. We can walk."

"Why not take the cab?" asked Horace.

"Pantsing a guy is a misdemeanor," answered Rivers. "Stealing a taxi is a felony."

"Hold on a second," said Horace. He reached into the taxi on pulled out the microphone, tossing it down the block. "What'll destroying Yellow Cab property get me?"

"They got to catch us first, eh ya, Tecumseh."

The driver remained lying face down in the street until a stranger came up and asked if he were hurt.

"Do you see any Indians?" he asked with his face still buried.

"Is this some kind of a joke?" asked the Samaritan.

The driver jumped to his feet, looked around in case the stranger was wrong, and reached for some phone change where his pocket should be. He had no pants. He ran to the cab and pulled open the ashtray where he kept spare change and dug out a fist full of coins. He ran half a block to a pay phone and called the police. They told him to get back in the cab and lock the doors. They would send a patrol car.

The desk sergeant at the Curtis Street station patiently listened to the taxi driver's tale. It was getting rather long and animated, so he took the opportunity to send another officer for a sobriety kit. He planned to administer the test on the driver, who was going through his story again, embellishing his heroism even more. The sergeant stopped him half way through and acknowledged a patrolman entering the precinct with the driver's pants. The driver continued his story while he dressed as best he could. The patrolman whispered to the sergeant, "We didn't see any Indians, Sarge. So—what'da you suppose this is, some kind of a joke?"

Troy and Horace beat on the door and the windows of the depot. They thought they saw someone move inside, but no one came to the door.

"I know he's in there," said Rivers.

"I can smell the fear," joked Green.

"I could smell it on that driver," laughed Rivers. He thought he saw movement inside the building again. "I saw something. He's in there." He beat on the glass door and yelled, "Open up, you coward. We've got some business to settle. I want my bus! You recognize my voice, you pendejo? I know you're in there! Open up, you chicken shit!"

"Eloquent as that was, Troy, you may want to try some other wily lawyer tricks. Maybe we can find a brick and you could just put it through the window."

"Thanks for the advice, Horace, but we're in kind of a hurry. We need to get that bus and go ASAP because I don't think that driver you pants'd is going to take too long to summon the police."

"Open up you little chicken shit," Horace yelled through the glass. "I've got a brick here, and I'm going to bust out your window."

"You silver-tongued devil, you."

They heard sirens in the distance.

Horace jumped off the stairs and ran toward the parking lot in which a couple of lone busses were parked. He jumped onto the chain link fence and began climbing. "I'm going over the top, Rivers. You can stay here and face the troops or follow me."

"See if you can find someone in there to open the door. I'll wait here."

The sirens got closer. "Oh, well," sighed Rivers with resignation, and joined Horace on the fence. "The taxi was funny, Ho, but if we get caught in here it's trespassing." They dropped to the ground inside the fenced lot and sprinted toward a side entrance next to a huge garage door. It was unlocked; they ducked inside. A radio was playing somewhere in the dark interior of the warehouse-sized building. They followed the sound.

The door was open to an office in the back where they found the radio. On the desk, next to a phone, were a page of scribbles and doodles. Several had Rivers' and Shirley's name written below them. "Asshole," was legible below Rivers' name.

"This must be the place," said Troy.

"And you thought he didn't like you," said Ho reading the graffiti.

"Where do you suppose he's hiding?" asked Troy

Horace pointed toward another open door through which they could see a sink and a urinal. They both walked into the latrine.

"Who's there?" came a confused voice from a toilet stall. "Edgar, is that you? It's about time. Those Indian assholes have been screaming at me on the phone about their bus. Boy, did you guys screw up that contract. I think one of them is an asshole lawyer. Edgar?"

Troy took one cuff and Horace the other as they reached in unison under the stall door and with practiced coordination jerked off the man's pants.

"Boy, did you screw up," said Troy.

"Who's Edgar?" asked Ho.

"Who's there?" screamed the man in a panic.

"The asshole," said Rivers. "Now where is my bus? Is it one of those outside?"

"Where are my pants?" the man was still screaming. "Give me my pants. You're not supposed to be in here. This is trespassing."

"In a public office. I don't think so," said Rivers. "I should know. I'm an asshole lawyer; remember?"

"I'm calling the cops. I know the door was locked. You guys broke in. That's trespassing. I'm calling the cops."

"I just got one question," said Ho. "How you gonna' get down that hill?"

"What?" asked the voice.

Rivers rolled up the pants into a ball. "How ya' gonna get down that hill, amigo?" He echoed Horace. "Don't you go to the movies? Didn't you recognize Paul Newman's best line from his best Indian role?" He looked at Horace, "*Hud*, right?"

"*Hombre*," answered Ho.

"What the hell are you guys talking about," asked the man in the stall.

"How you gonna get out of there and call the police, hombre, is what were talking 'bout, bub." said Ho.

"Now listen. All we want is our bus and we'll leave you alone. No cops, no problem. No one needs to know we *pants'd* you, and I'll write a letter to your boss telling him what a cooperative and helpful little shit you are. Is it a deal?"

The stall door flew open, a pudgeon, trying to pull his boxer shorts up, stumbled out. He was red with fury and embarrassment. His rotund stomach jiggled in spastic convulsions as he tried to force his way from the stall.

The door barely missed Horace. It bounced against its hinges and was flying back toward the man. Horace helped it along with a hard shove. The door should have hit him on the bouncing belly, but the man had lost the grip on his boxers and was looking down adjusting his underwear. The door made a horrible sound as it clonked him on the top of his head. He hit the floor like a dropped tomato.

"This is progress," said Horace. "What do we do now?"

"Make sure he isn't having a heart attack and you didn't break his neck, Horace. What where you thinking hitting the door like that? Here, help me roll him over."

"Troy, get serious. First of all, I didn't mean to hit the door. It was a reflex. Secondly, that is one of the ugliest white men I have ever seen. I'll be damned if I going to touch that piece of blubber, heart attack or no."

"Horace, help me. We just wanted to scare him into giving us a bus; not kill him!"

"Just when I think you're enjoying becoming an outlaw, you go and get all serious on me."

"Horace!"

He knelt down and grabbed the opposite arm from Rivers. "Call me Ishmael," he said as he took hold.

"Other way. Roll him onto his back." Rivers knelt over the man and put an ear near his mouth. "He's breathing, that's a good sign."

Just then the loud rattling noise of a large, metal garage door going up echoed into the room. The two trespassers looked at each other to make sure each had heard the noise. They jumped to opposite sides of the door, ready to surprise whoever entered. No one came in. They waited.

"I'm gonna gas up Number 13 and head back out to the stadium, Fats," yelled a voice from the garage.

They peeked around the doorsill. A bus had just pulled in and sat idling near the door and a pair of diesel gas pumps.

The driver was walking toward the pumps and the rear of the bus. "Fats, you hear me. I'll only be a few minutes. I'm gassing up Number 13; don't wan'na go dry mid-run."

"That's a good idea," said Horace as he came around the front of the bus.

"Sweet, Jesus!" brayed the man. "Who the hell are you?" He looked at Horace's outfit. "What the hell are you?"

"We're not going to hurt you," said Rivers.

The man spun around when he heard Rivers' voice behind him. He checked out Rivers' costume. Confusion creased his brow. "What is this, some kind of a joke?"

By that time, Horace was right behind him.

"Do you see something funny?"

The driver turned back to Ho and was forced to look up. "Well, do you?"

"No. sir," said the man meekly. "I ain't got no money to speak of. This is a chartered bus. I haven't been collecting no fares. So, there's no money."

Rivers could see the man's legs were going weak. He helped him to the bus entrance where he sat back in the doorway, plopping on the stair, gasping for air and grasping for reality.

"The fat man inside's got the money, but being Sunday, I bet there ain't much."

"We don't want your money, Pilgrim," said Horace.

"Can you drive this bus?" asked Rivers.

"Duh!" said Horace.

"OK, OK," said Rivers, "that was a stupid question. I'm just a little disconcerted here, Horace; thank you very much." He turned from his companion and faced the driver. "What I meant to ask was, do you know the way to Red Rocks? Can you drive this bus . . . to Red Rocks?"

"Huh?" asked the man still trying to grasp his predicament. "Red Rocks?"

"Yes, Red Rocks."

"Red Rocks Park?" asked the driver.

"Duh," repeated Horace.

"You're not helping, Ho. Yes, Red Rocks Park and Amphitheater."

"No," the man meekly shook his head, looking back and forth between the two Indians.

"You drive a bus and you don't know the way to Red Rocks. What the hell kind of a bus driver are you, anyway," yelled Troy.

"He probably has lived here in Denver for the past fifty years, Troy. Why the hell should he know the way to Red Rocks?" He turned to the driver. "Do you know the way to the zoo?"

"Yeah?"

"Well there you go, Troy. He's a native."

Rivers stood for a moment in deep thought and then said, "It's OK. I've got a plan."

"Great," said Horace to the driver. "Everything is OK now; he's got a plan."

"Go get the fat guy's pants."

"That's your plan. We're finally going to change clothes. Well, if that's the plan, you get Moby Dick's outfit."

"No, Horace, that's not my plan. I can drive this bus. Have this guy fill it up. Then we pull out all the phones so they can't call the police. We take this guy's clothes, too."

"Why are we taking their clothes?"

"Because I'm tired of killing." He looked menacingly at the driver. "And I don't have any rope to tie them up. We'll lock him in the bathroom with the fat one. I saw bars on the window. Besides that, it's too small to climb out." He looked at the driver, "Right?"

"Right," said the driver. "Old Fats, he can barely fit through the door."

"Besides," Troy repeated, "would you run naked into this neighborhood if you didn't have to, even to summon the cops?"

"Not me," said the driver. "Curtis Park is one mean-ass neighborhood. I'll just sit here and be quiet. I promise."

"OK, Troy. It's worth a shot. Come on, Sterling Moss," he said to the driver, "let's gas up this buggy."

Rivers ran back into the office and began pulling the phones from the wall jacks. He looked to see if the fat guy on the floor was still breathing. He was—sort of. He was making whale noises, guttural burps, gasps, and coughs from the depths. Troy interpreted them as harmonics he probably always made when trying to wake up. Rivers grabbed the collar of his shirt and tried to pull it off. He asked himself why these chubby jaspers insisted on wearing knit, golf shirts. Was it pride in the rotund, masculine, well-fed, beer belly, or was it comfort—the stretchy, soft cloth feeling supportive and accommodating? Regardless, it was a struggle pulling off the shirt. It stretched to five times its normal length by the time he jerked it from under the burden. He rolled the shirt with the pants, listened one more time to the song of the humpbacks, decided he'd live, and for some unclear reason, checked to see if the man was wearing a wedding ring. He exited the suite mumbling, "I ain't touching those boxers; they're all hers."

It took several minutes to fill the tank with diesel. The rotary meter spun around and around. Horace paced as it spun. Rivers familiarized himself with the gauges, pedals, and gearshift of the bus, in case he had any questions of the driver. It all seemed manageable. He'd learned multi-speed transmissions and double-clutching as a kid.

"That's a lot of fuel," said Horace.

"It sure the hell is," said the driver. "Now that I'm a little more confident that you Indian fellers ain't going to murder me and Old Fats. I don't mind tellin' ya', this is robbery as well as hijacking. The city is libel to take the fuel costs out of my paycheck. Where should I send the bill?"

Rivers listened through the open door. Horace paused but a second, and answered the codger: "Send it to the Seventh Cavalry."

They waited impatiently for the driver to strip, and escorted him to the bathroom, where the fat man was finally sitting up, rubbing his head. It was difficult for Rivers to tell if the shocked look on his face was in again seeing his Indian assailants, or in viewing his colleague, the driver, pale, embarrassed, and shivering in his nakedness.

The bathroom door locked from the inside; so, Rivers wedged a chair up against the doorknob. He admitted to himself that it probably wouldn't hold them long. He hurried back to the bus, threw the busmen's clothes into the second passenger seat, and jumped into the driver's seat.

Ho pushed the button to open the garage door, which rattled loudly as it rose. He jumped into the bus and settled into the seat behind the driver. The chain link gate opened by itself as soon as they drove over some buried trigger. They watched it close behind them and chuckled at their ingenuity.

"Red Rocks or bust," yelled Horace. Troy did not acknowledge the humor.

At the end of the block they saw two speeding police cars racing down a perpendicular street, but heading their way. Troy had Ho throw him the driver's cap, which he pulled low on his head. Horace ducked out of sight below the windows. From his high vantage point Troy could see that the taxicab driver, with whom they had brawled, was in the first cop car. They sped past the bus with only a cursory look. Rivers slumped in the seat so that from their low vantage in the cars, only his face and hat showed. He watched in the rearview mirror as the sedans screeched to a stop in front of the bus depot, now two blocks behind them. Horace peeked over the last seat and yelled forward that he thought they made it. Troy stuttered something about their having to hurry and about which way was it to the convention center.

The police were getting impatient and concerned that no one was answering the door. They beat on the glass repeatedly.

"I'm telling you, it's Sunday. Nobody is going to be here on a Sunday," said the first officer.

"Sure they are," said the second. "They got to service all those busses for the Bronco game—even on Sunday."

"Hey, how about those Broncos?" said a third.

"Can we concentrate on arresting some Indians, please," barked the cab driver. "I mean, this is where I was taking them. I know the murdering savages are in there."

"OK," said the first cop, "I've had it. I'm going over the fence."

"Come around and open the front door," said the second. "We'll wait here."

He jumped the fence, drew his service revolver, and ran toward the building. He found the garage door open, and peeked inside. The coast seemed clear. He hurried his way through the building to the front door. He pushed on the horizontal lever and let the others in.

They searched the building trying to find any signs of skullduggery. They were cautious. Each covered for the other as their search took them around blind corners. Their deliberateness was consuming vast amounts of time.

Finally the cab driver lost patience and stomped into the office. He noticed the chair wedged up against the bathroom door. "Officers," he yelled. "Come have a look at this."

Hearing the cab driver's voice, the fat man and the bus driver decided it was safe to yell for help.

The police cautiously opened the door, one officer kneeling down and pulling the knob from a low stance, the others standing just behind him with guns drawn and pointed at the doorway.

Inside, the two naked men cowered at the site of the revolvers aimed at them. The fat man soiled himself. The police jumped back, flabbergasted at the sight of the two men.

"Well, there's something you don't see every day," said the first cop.

"It's frickin' Laurel and Hardy—naked," said the second.

"What is this," yelled the third policeman, "some kind of a joke."

Troy pulled the bus into the loading dock at the convention center. He was somewhat pleased with himself because in the short trip from the depot had stalled only a half-dozen times.

"I think I'm catching on to this, Horace," he said as the bus lurched to a sudden stop.

Ho kept himself from falling into the aisle by catching the back of a seat, "Seems like it."

"Tell me honestly, Horace. Do you think we've gone too far with this thing? Sooner or later, there is going to be hell to pay. Should we turn ourselves in before we involve the others?"

"For a lawyer, yeah, you've gone too far. As an Indian— maybe it's about time some of us take a stand. As far as hell to pay . . . I think your credits good with the rest of us. Anyway, there is one thing I'm certain of—it's too late to go back now, so I say, 'Full speed ahead.' Just, learn to use the clutch will ya'."

"It's good to have you here with me, Ho. I was thinking on the way back—I wish Orvis was with us."

"He'd have gotten a chuckle or two watching the lawyer go renegade. That's for sure."

"I miss him."

"So do we all, Three Rivers, so do we all."

"I actually thought once when I looked in the rearview mirror to see if the cops were following that I saw him sitting in the back of the bus."

"Naw, if Orvis were here, he would insist on sitting up front."

"He'd insist on driving!"

"No, Troy, you're the perfect driver; I mean with your excellent sense of direction."

"Funny, Ho. Since I'm driving would you please go inside and get Veloy and the others. Tell Shirley we got the bus, no problem once we presented our side of the argument, and that she should go back to the office and keep apprised from there. No sense in both of us embarrassing the law firm. Have Patty go with her. No sense in a government employee being arrested as an accomplice."

"Shirley and Patty are good people, Troy. They'll be there if we need them."

"I know they will, Horace. And you're right, but there is no sense in them taking any more risks than necessary. And besides, we may need someone in Denver to bail our Indi'n asses out of the fire if things continue going as well as they have thus far."

"Good point, Chief."

"Horace, don't . . . "

"I know. I know." He ran from the bus into the convention center.

The other braves, most in powwow regalia, had already realized the bus was there. They hurried out of the center before Horace had a chance to open the door. Veloy led them, and Shirley held the door. Horace seemed to be giving Shirley a rather lengthy explanation and she almost fell to her knees in laughter. She waved at Troy, standing beside the bus door urging the others to load quickly. Rivers noticed that several of the men were still carrying bottles and their archery equipment, but knew there was no time to deal with it. He looked at Veloy for an explanation, who simply shrugged his shoulder in exasperation and apology. Veloy was also carrying what looked to be his and Horace's long, canvas archer cases.

"Did you get directions to Red Rocks?" Troy asked Veloy.

"No, I thought you were going to do that at the bus barn."

"We got distracted," he answered. "We'll figure it out." He yelled at Horace, still talking to Shirley, "All aboard, Ho! I think I hear sirens."

Patty ran from the dark entrance, skipping stairs as she left the loading dock, and rushed to Rivers' side.

"Did I hear Horace correctly? You stripped every white man you encountered?" She hugged him.

"We didn't want to kill anybody. We hoped they'd die of embarrassment."

"Troy!" She kissed him on the cheek. "Doesn't this go beyond the covenant of the contract?"

"Well," he answered, "I guess it's our turn to break the treaty." He kissed her back. "I don't want you coming with us. You and Shirley can do us more good here, in Denver. You may have to notify the partners that we need legal help. Somebody may need to tell the press our side of the story." He looked to see that she agreed. "This isn't how I planned our long weekend together. I had a room reserved at The Brown Palace—the Honeymoon Suite. Had the champagne ordered and room service alerted."

"I can wait," she said. "The wine will still be chilled, and I'll be there when you get back."

The men on the bus hooted and cheered at Troy' and Patty's embrace and the Hollywood kiss that followed.

"Hey-soos, why don't you kids get a room," yelled Veloy.

Rivers gave Patty another quick peck. He waved for Horace who watched with Shirley as he and Patty entertained the others.

Horace took the cue. He leaned forward and grabbed Shirley, bent her over in a romantic dip and kissed her. He stood her up straight, smiled and sprinted to the bus. She stood in the open doorway, stunned but also smiling. She waved. Ho jumped aboard, and Troy pulled the chrome pivot lever and slammed the door closed. He gunned the engine and popped the clutch. The bus lunged forward. Horace fell into the front seat next to Veloy. Rivers looked in the rearview mirror to make sure Ho was OK.

Veloy seemed somewhat perturbed by what he had just witnessed on the loading dock, "Who the hell do you think you are—John Wayne?"

They had proceeded a few blocks when Ho stood up behind Rivers and asked, "Do you know where you're going?"

"No talking to the driver, sir. Please return to your seat." said Troy.

"Seriously, do you?"

"Not exactly, but I know where we are not going; so I'm optimistic."

"A positive attitude is important."

Rivers was trying to get onto Colfax Avenue, but the turn off 14th Street was a tight angle, traffic was heavy and he stalled the bus twice when the rear tires jumped the curb.

The passengers, his friends, brutally and in unison chastised his driving.

"Whoa, check out this guy," yelled Veloy, pointing out the window to a pedestrian.

A longhaired, young white was trying to wave down the bus as it struggled through the sharp intersection. He wore a Navajo hat with a snakeskin hatband. He had on a fringed deerskin jacket and the most corpulent turquoise necklace seen in the Americas since the fall of the Mayan kingdom. He wore Levi jeans and had on Apache legging-type boots, which were elaborately beaded. There was a ring on almost every finger and his belt had another huge piece of turquoise on the buckle.

"Should we stop for him?" asked Veloy.

"Hell no," said Troy. "This bus does not stop for musicians, hippies, and pseudo-Indians."

"The cop is watching, Troy" warned Horace.

"Oh, hell," said Rivers and pushed the door handle.

"Cool," said the young man as he entered the bus. "I saw the outfits from the street, and knew I had to ride this bus, man. So, what's happening?"

Horace answered, "I'd say your outfit is what's happening."

"You must be some of the powwow guys, at the convention center, right?"

"Right."

"Hang on," said Troy. "I'm clear. We're heading down Colfax."

The busload of Native Americans cheered. The horns stopped honking, and the cop applauded as he waved on the traffic.

"Like, I tried to rent a sales booth at the powwow," said the new passenger. He held up both hands and turned them backwards to display all the rings. "I make, like, Indian jewelry. Cool, huh?"

"Cool," said Horace and nudged Troy's shoulder.

"Well, some bitch named Shirley something said, like, I had to be an Indian to sell my wares. Can you imagine? Like, I could tell from her voice, she was no Indian, man. Besides, I am part Indian, really. True. Like my great-grandmother was a Cherokee." He looked around to see if any of the other passengers acknowledged, like, knowing her.

"A princess, I bet," said Ho.

"Yeah. Right. So I really missed not being able to, like, be a part of the powwow, man, but I went both days. It was the coolest. I actually sold some of my rings right off my fingers. I had pockets full of them. Like I made some serious green."

"Groovy." said Ho.

"Oh, man, you probably been on the rez too long. Nobody says 'groovy' anymore. Hey, but that's cool."

"So, you know Shirley, do you?" Horace said. "He says he talked to Shirley, Veloy. Did you hear?"

"I heard."

Veloy seemed to be thinking the same thought as Horace. Rivers pictured them stripping this pretender and throwing him off the bus in the middle of downtown Denver. "How do I get to Sixth Avenue from here?" asked Troy of the youth, giving him a momentary reprieve.

"Turn left at the next light, on Kalamath. It'll take you straight there. You're not from around here I take it. That's cool. So, where are you cats going?"

"Do you know the way to Red Rocks?" asked Horace.

"It's been a while, but, yeah, I think I know the way. Cool place." He paused. "Oh, I get it, man. You're going up to that tomb thing I heard on the radio. You cats must have listened to Lennon. Long Live the Beatles. Cool. Like, is there going to be a rumble?"

"Is that a problem?" asked Ho.

"Like, no way, man. It's cool. Like, I would join you. I'm deeply into protest, man. Civil disobedience, right on, man. I'm there."

"Groovy," said Troy.

The youth looked at Troy, surprised that he repeated the cliché. "Like, I get it, man. He raised his fist in a protest gesture. "Right on, man. Power." He looked around for confirmation, but saw none. He leaned toward Rivers, "Cold, man." He looked out the windshield, "Like, get in your right lane. It automatically turns into Sixth Avenue. Red Rocks or bust, eh, man," said the young mannerist.

"Cool," said Troy.

They passed several major exits: Federal, Sheridan, Wadsworth, Kipling, and as they approached Indiana, the young guide said, "You need to work your way over to the left. I think this is where Sixth and Highway 40 come together. You want to take Forty."

Troy looked in the rearview mirror to see if he was clear to change lanes. What he saw gave his heart a pause but created an involuntary push from his foot on the accelerator. A line of four police cars was racing up on the left. They prevented him from changing lanes. The light was green, he sped through the intersection as the police made the left onto Highway 40.

"That was our turn, man. You missed it," said the kid.

"I saw a Colfax sign," Troy lied. "I didn't see anything that said Forty."

"Colfax is Highway 40, man. That's OK, we're cool we can go on around on Sixth and turn around in Golden."

"Golden!" said Horace. "That sounds familiar. Is there a zoo there?"

"No, like, I don't think so, man."

"Troy, there is a cop car behind us. No lights."

"We're cool," Troy tried to sound encouraging.

"Yeah, man," echoed the hippie youth. "We're very cool."

"The cop is signaling right," yelled someone in the back.

"Then we'll go left," said Troy as they approached a stop light and signal. A sign on the side of the road had an arrow pointing to the right with the words, "City of Golden," beneath it was another pointing left and the words, "Lariat Loop, Buffalo Bill's Grave." He turned the ponderous vehicle left and made another immediate left. Ahead was a large stone gate with a sign again announcing Buffalo Bill's Grave. He also found himself on a narrow residential street, and realized it would be impossible to turn around and backtrack to Highway 40.

"It's cool, man. We can get there this way. It's a little longer, but it's a cool drive, real curvy."

"How curvy?" asked Horace as Troy sped the bus around the first curve and through the stone gates, throwing everybody over on their left sides.

"Oh, man," said Rivers. "I know this road. It's a nightmare. I'll try to turn around." By this time the shoulder of the road on the right side of the bus had already dropped off into a steep mountainous slope.

"Where?" asked Ho, concerned.

"Like, no where, man. Not on this road. It's like this all the way to the top of the mountain, man. There is no going back now. Full guns ahead."

"Speed," corrected Horace.

"Like, yeah, man. I'm already on it. Two hits, pure amphetamine, White Crosses, man. I've got more. Want some?"

"Groovy," said Ho as he shook his head—no.

"You, man?" he asked Troy.

"What are you talking about?" asked Rivers.

"We're climbing in altitude, Troy, but our Indian guide here is already several clicks above us."

"He's high?"

"As an eagle, man," grinned the youth. He thrust both his arms out, imitating wings and cawed several times.

"Cool," said Veloy.

"Jesus, Troy!" yelled someone in the back. "Keep the bus in the middle of the road, will ya'. Have you seen the drop off?"

Rivers was stressed, but it was still an amusing choreography he checked out periodically in the interior, rearview mirror. He recalled how his grandparents shifted from side to side in the car the first time he took them up Lariat Trail, as if shifting their weight could keep them from going over the edge. His Indian friends tried the same strategy. The dance was loosely synchronized, an informal and ineffectual ballet shifting their accumulated weight to that side of the bus opposite the sheer drop off. Each curve changed the side at risk. He allowed himself a brief reprieve from the events of the day. Their hokey-pokey dash from side to side would not save them if he missed a turn. If their number was up, if the spirits of the mountain wished demise, their cha-cha could not prevent the disaster. He fought the unwieldy machine as it crawled up the ribbon road, and stole a peek at his friends when the road permitted. Entranced in their fandango, they were missing the spectacular views of the steep slopes of Lookout Mountain, of the City of Golden below, far below, and the Queen City of the Plains beyond.

Two cars pulled up behind the creeping bus, then three, then five; before long it was a slow parade of a dozen vehicles. Troy noticed them and felt his stress return. About half-way up the mountain the meandering line of autos was thirty strong.

He knew the switchbacks were going to spell trouble. Sure enough, as he tried to maneuver the bus around the tight U-shaped curves, the cars, most full of tourists, coming down the mountain were forced to stop. If they didn't stop soon enough, there was no room for him to complete the turn through the switchback. Impatient drivers tried to hurry through the curve before the bus took possession. He alternated between anger at the impatient drivers and guilt for clogging the downward artery.

Finally, just as he had feared, an intolerant driver, trying to outrun common courtesy, got himself wedged in the center of the switchback with the bus blocked both uphill and downhill. Dread that he initiated the largest traffic jam in the history of Lookout Mountain took root in Troy's troubled heart. The cacophony of angry auto horns put an end to the Indian dance inside the bus.

It would take several minutes for enough of the downhill traffic to stop, back up, one car at a time, starting with the last car, to let the discourteous idiot squeeze into their lane just far enough to get passed the bus. Troy knew that not since a teamster convention at the Robin's Nest bar on top of Lookout had the local granite cliffs echoed with the language being thrown at him from disgruntled drivers.

As the Indians, exhausted and bored, retrieved their bottles Veloy said to Rivers, "You can only return the gesture of shooting-the-bird to these irate tourists so many times, Troy. It's getting monotonous."

"Man, this is a drag," said the white kid

"I thought you said Colfax was the slowest street," said Horace. .

"Are we there yet," whined a voice from the rear of the bus.

"I have to go to the bathroom," said another.

"Me, too!"

"Me, three!"

"You shouldn't be drinking!" yelled Veloy.

"I got to. I'm dying back here. I'm tired of people crawling by the bus and casting aspersions on my mother."

"Me, too!"

"Me, three!"

"What can we do?"

"We need something to do, Veloy."

"What can we do?"

Veloy answered, "Let's kill the hippie kid."

"Like, not funny, man," said the kid.

"Oh, I don't know," said Troy, waiting for a car to clear the switchback so he could proceed.

"Like," imitated Horace, "do you know the way to Red Rocks from this side of the mountain?"

"Like, no," said Troy with the same exaggerated mimic.

"Then, like we need him." He changed to his own voice, "At least until we get there."

"Like, still not funny, man," the hippie repeated.

A voice came from the back of the bus, "Then can we scalp him?"

Chapter Thirty-six

Massacre at Mount Vernon

Summer, 1964

Hinmaton Yalatkit, known as Chief Joseph the Younger,
before he led the Nez Percé in the historic evasion of the cavalry,
before his famous speech of fighting no more forever, before he died
of a broken heart, said of freedom: "The earth is the mother of all
people, and all people should have equal rights upon it. You might
as well expect the river to run backward as that any man who was
born a free man should be contented when penned up and denied
liberty to go where he pleases."

Troy Rivers had traversed the Lookout Mountain high road
on the back end of the Lariat Loop and they were proceeding
downhill. There were a few curves in the road, but it was nothing
like those while climbing up Lariat Trail. Once in a while, on a more
genteel curve, they could see across Mount Vernon Canyon to the
mountains behind Red Rocks Park.

"We're getting closer now," said the hippie kid in the faux
Indian garb. "We hit Mount Vernon Canyon Road just up ahead,
turn left, downhill a couple of miles to 93, take a right for a mile or
so and we-are-there! Like, cool, huh?"

"Did you get that, Horace . . . Veloy?"

"Got it."

"Loud and clear, chief."

"Veloy, don't call me chief."

"Sorry, Troy."

"You thinkin' what I'm thinking?" Rivers asked.

"I'm thinking the boys are right. Now we can kill him." Ho
grinned an evil smirk at the hippie.

"Still not funny, man."

As they came to the bottom of the downhill section, Troy noticed a fork in the road. To the right was a large gate. Just around the curve to the left he could see an out-of-place adobe building with a neon sign in the front. From his angle, the words were difficult to make out, but *Buffalo Bill's* and *Bar Grill* were legible. He thought that this may be a good place to dump the hippie, but then he noticed that the parking lot was filled with police cars, and several officers were milling around in front of the building. The sight of the bevy of uniforms triggered a panic avoidance response. Rivers took the right fork, dropped the bus into low, and pulled through the large stone-pillared gate crowned with a rustic, arching wooden sign. Carved letters informed him he was trespassing: "Mount Vernon Country Club, Private." He gunned the bus up the winding road.

"Like that was weird," said the hippie. "I never saw so many different kinds of cops in one place before. Think they saw you?"

"No, I don't think so."

Veloy rambled forward, stood next to Troy and peered intently out the windscreen. He concentrated on something unseen by Rivers and turned to extend his rubbernecking along the side windows as the bus lumbered onward.

"Whad'da ya see, Veloy?" he asked.

Veloy was silent for a moment but then answered with an unexpected reverence, "This is sacred Ute land."

"Ute land?" He paused and looked out the windows, searching for some hint of confirmation to Veloy's declaration. "It's a private club, comrade. Rich White folks. What makes you think it's sacred to the Ute?"

"We just passed a Ute prayer tree," he answered.

"A what?"

"A Ute prayer tree," said Horace. 'Veloy . . . you sure? That could be a good omen. We Ute used to hang out in these foothills and mountains in the summer. Too damn cold in the winters but there have always been paths to sacred sites along these valleys. A prayer tree could symbolize that we are on the right path, the honorable path, that what we're doing is *kosher.*"

"*Kosher*?" said Troy.

"Hey," answered Ho. "Fables of lost tribes, man. If the moccasin fits . . ."

"Veloy," asked Troy, "what are these prayer trees you're talking about?"

"Utes would tie off sapling ponderosas, sometimes aspens and other pines, to manipulate the growth, to cultivate sacred trees. White men build churches and put up crosses; we Natives marked hallowed spaces with modified trees as signposts of consecrated ground, burial sites or to give directions. I think we also passed just such a navigation tree, signifying that there may be a spring or some important landmark to the southeast. Maybe Red Rocks. I'm not sure; it's dark and hard to see, but I know we passed a prayer tree. Their distorted growth is unmistakable. A trunk that parallels the ground for a few feet before it resumes its skyward trek, horizontal where no winds exist to contort growth, an altered, bent tree standing singularly in a bunch of typical vertical pines, signifies a sacred plot. These are Ute."

"I didn't see it," said Rivers. "I didn't know such a thing existed."

"Well," answered Veloy, "Like I said: It's dark and you gotta know a thing exists before you can see it. You gotta know something is, in order to grasp its essence."

"Ya know," interrupted the hippie, "the native people of the Caribbean didn't 'see' the Spanish ships of Columbus anchored right there in front of them until the conquistadors came ashore and they recognized them as funny dressed humans and, of course, by then it was too late."

Rivers and Veloy starred at the hippie.

"I mean," he continued, "I'm agreeing with Mr. Veloy, here. The Caribe People had no concept of Spanish galleons, so mentally didn't see them, couldn't comprehend them, get it?"

Rivers and Veloy continued to stare. Rivers admitting to his surprise that the dope head was saying anything intelligent.

"Or maybe," said the hippie spoiling the moment, "it was the Mayans hanging in Veracruz didn't realize those unrecognizable objects floating on the gulf was invaders. I tell you one thing, though. The horses scared the piss out 'um. Horses scare the poop out of me."

"Sit down," barked Rivers. "A historian, you ain't."

"I'm feeling good about this," said Horace. "Prayer trees could be a symbol of our ancestors talking to us. You know it took generations of attention and anticipation to get the trees to grow just the way they wanted. Near Colorado Springs we have discovered trees hundreds of years old. Now that's a spiritual commitment. Yes, indeed, this is a good omen. This is symbolic of us connecting with our past. This could mean protecting the tomb of the old one confirms we are in the sacred circle."

"Kosher," said Rivers. He followed the winding road for about a mile and found himself and his band of patriots in front of a large clubhouse.

"I'm going to go inside and confirm where we are." He pushed the hippie down into a seat. "Horace," he said. "I think I know a bartender in here. He used to work at the Brown Palace. He bragged about moving to the mountains and working at Mount Vernon. Let's see if he's on the clock."

"See if they've got a bathroom!" yelled several of the passengers.

A young boy in a white, valet uniform ran up to the window and asked, "Park your bus, sir?"

Troy opened the door and jumped from behind the wheel and stomped toward the clubhouse entrance followed by Horace and Veloy. "Naa, we'll only be a minute; just keep the damn thing running." They hurried through a glass enclosed foyer.

Troy bounded up a series of stairs and tried to walk past the receptionist to the restaurant and bar.

She called out, "Sir, do you have reservations?"

"Yea," he answered, "we have plenty of reservations—in Oklahoma, New Mexico, Arizona, the Dakotas."

A man in a three-piece suit strolled confidently through an office door behind the receptionist. "What seems to be the trouble, Tootie?" he asked.

Troy immediately recognized the brand of the suit and had a pretty good idea where it was purchased—a small exclusive haberdashery just off Seventeenth Street. The tie was also familiar. It wasn't so long ago Troy bought half a dozen similar patterns. Troy guessed that the well-dressed man was the manager. Troy felt a sudden dip of confidence. How alien he must now appear in his Native American attire.

"I'm sorry, sir," said the receptionist. "but if you are going into the Club, you need reservations, and you will have to wear a tie. That is Mount Vernon policy, sir." She looked to the manager for confirmation that she had said the right thing.

The manager gave Troy and his braves a quick once-over and said, "She's correct, gentlemen. I'm sorry, but the club is for members only."

"A tie!" barked Rivers. "Girl, I'm not even wearing pants."

The young lady leaned over the counter and confirmed Troy's statement and a question rose in her innocent blue eyes.

"The same thing a Scotsman wears under his kilt, sweetheart." said Troy.

Stan the Man Manley found great satisfaction in pulling the cold metal lever on the junction box. Let there be light, and with a downward pull—let there be dark. The tennis courts at Mount Vernon Country Club went dark. An after image of the green concrete and the white grid lines lingered in his mind's eye. This also gave him satisfaction—a detailed, fading image of his turf. Ordinarily, such duties would be delegated to tennis staff and the local pro, but Stan enjoyed exercising his authority despite overheard comments about him being a control freak. He had sent the latecomers home, cleared the courts, shut off the lights, and as soon as he locked up the office and pro's shop, he was going to walk up the hill and sign for a congratulatory cocktail in the club lounge. He planned on taking his favorite seat at the east end of the bar, turning on the plush stool and surveying the picturesque view of the foothills and the lights of Denver far below. Once satisfied that his country club perch remained superior to the urban backdrop, he would survey the interior of the lounge with an equally critical eye. He'd look for some of the regulars, and particularly any fellow executive board members, smug in that he had the arrogance to show up in the lounge after sunset in his tennis whites. Such casualness was against the rules, but, of course, he wrote the rules. Who better to flaunt them than Stan, the Mountain Man, Head of the Tennis Committee,

Head of the Swimming Pool Committee, Head of the Equestrian Committee, author of the Club Constitution, Chair of the Club Bylaws Committee, Director of the Decoration Committee, Coordinator of the Social Committee, and Editor of the Yearbook. Stan was also looking forward to taking over the presidency of the club.

Stan stumbled on the flagstone path to the clubhouse. The misstep interrupted the mental review of his résumé. He noticed that this section of the walk was uncharacteristically dark. A light had burned out. Someone is going to pay dearly for that negligence. I could have broken my leg. He made a mental note to bring up shoddy maintenance with the club manager.

He was looking forward to emerging into another of his favorite views—coming from the tennis courts on the warm, but dimly lit path and the dark woods to the brightly lit clubhouse. The Mount Vernon Country Club main building was an elegant, sturdy structure that perfectly complemented its mountain setting. Large granite boulders anchored the pioneer edifice to the ponderosa crowned peak, ruff-hewn pine framed the large picture windows below the shake shingle roof. It was handsome design, a balance between its Alpine source and Americanized luxury. And it was Stan the Man's main haunt. This is where he proudly showed up with Mrs. Manley but, often times to his regret, Stanley Manley, Junior. For just a fleeting moment, he had the ever so slight disappointment that he couldn't bring lovely Fleeta, his mistress here. She was something to show off, a trophy gal. Fleeta would drive the old conservatives to green-eyed madness. *Oh well, it's best to keep things separate. For now. What's this . . . ?*

He was surprised and peeved to see a large bus sitting in the driveway, blocking the view and the entrance. I'm not aware of any group events this evening. What the hell is that bus doing here? He hurried to investigate. He gave the valet a look to scorch the earth. "Shouldn't this leviathan be parked in the auxiliary lot?"

The youngster made two mistakes. First he spoke to Stanley, and second: he said something insipid, "It's a General Motors, Mr. Manley. A Supercoach, I think. I never heard of no Levi thing."

"Be here when I get back," said Stan. "We have some protocols to discuss." He dashed into the clubhouse. He couldn't believe his eyes. The receptionist appeared to be conversing with three Indians. She was giggling—another protocol ignored. Don Crow, the manager was emerging from his office. *Now this is quite a sight. What is going on? The place is falling apart.*

Stan knew a gate crashing when he saw it. The Indians were obviously trying to buffalo their way past reception and into the lounge. Despite Crow's presence, Stan interjected his authority. "What the hell is going on here? Tootie, obviously these men are not members." He focused on the fellow who seemed to be the leader. "Are you people lost? Or is this some sort of an ill-advised joke?" He didn't wait for an answer. He focused on the manager. "Crow, are you aware there is a bus full of wild Indians parked in the driveway and I think I saw some of them urinating in the trees next to the clubhouse. Tell me, Crow, have you lost total control?"

"Your name is Crow?" The leader asked the manager.

"Yes, sir, it is."

"A brother," cried the Indian, and hugged the manager.

"Oh my god, Crow," said Stan. "They think you're an Indian. Now that's rich. You're probably one of the few Americans who would never claim to have even a fraction of heathen blood; well, you and me." Manley was aware of Crow's background: years managing Italian restaurants in North Denver, a historical and notorious neighborhood rumored to be controlled by the local mob. La Cosa Nostra rarely claims any heritage other than Sicilian.

"Sorry, Mr. Crow," said the leader fellow "but some of my best friends are . . ."

"He's *Paisano* not Paiute, you cretins. Now enough is enough. I'm out of patience. Crow, throw these interlopers out."

"Allow me to introduce myself," said the leader. "My name is Troy Rivers, attorney at law." He offered his hand to Crow.

"Ute," mumbled the smallest of the tribe.

"Oh, heaven spare us," said Stan. "Just what the world needs, another lawyer, and quite the sense of humor you have, counselor; judging by your outfit."

"Bug off, Bobby Riggs," said the Troy ruffian.

"Crow, are you going to let him talk to me that way? Crow, I'm the president-elect of this club, if you get my point."

Everybody got his point, but there were differing interpretations.

"And this rather large gentleman, Mr. Crow, is Ho Ho Horace Green, an internationally acclaimed artist."

"And who's the other fellow?" asked Stan. "Not a famous tinker, I hope. This is starting to sound like a nursery rhyme—tinker, tailor, Indian chief." He smiled with self-amusement.

"Ute," the 'tinker' muttered.

"You want I should take care of this twerp?" asked Ho Ho Ho, purposefully exaggerating the menace of his stature.

"No, no, no!" said Crow. "Thank you, gentlemen; let's keep things cordial." He turned toward Manley, but was speaking to everyone present, "I prefer to deal with things myself."

"Crow, why are you talking to these primitives? Throw them out."

"Yes, gentlemen, I'm sorry, if I cannot be of some assistance, I'm afraid you must leave. Tootie, show them the way to the exit."

"Now wait just a minute. We are not trying to cause a problem, Mr. Crow. We have lost our way among the mountain roads and . . ."

"Got lost on the way to a costume party, I take it," interrupted Manley.

"Got lost on our way to an important engagement and I remembered that your bartender once worked at The Brown Palace. He's an old friend of mine, so I thought I would ask . . ."

"We don't serve your kind," Manley interrupted again. "And I know The Brown Palace; they don't think this kind of thing is clever, nor do we find your sort amusing. Going to the bar is out of the question. We have a dress code; I know, I wrote it."

"So I thought I would ask directions and use of a phone."

"Hey," said Ho, "a drink doesn't sound like a bad idea."

"Forget it," barked Stan the Man. "Didn't you hear me when I said this club is for members only. We don't serve . . ."

"Ute," interjected the smaller intruder.

"Yeah, I heard you," answered Horace, the giant, as he leaned his great height over white clad Manley, "but I'm not through here," He grinned at Troy. "Maybe you don't know who we are. We happen to represent N. A. Z. I. and we've had reports about this private club of yours."

"What!" asked Troy.

"No Nazi," repeated the third mouseketeer. "Ute."

"N-A-Z-I, NAZI," answered Horace, "The National Association of Zealous Indians. You may not have heard of us, Mr. Crow, but we are an important militant Indian organization and frankly, we have had our eye on your little establishment for some time now. For instance, what percentage of your chummy membership is of Native American descent? If one of you gentlemen would like to offer me and my companions a drink, I'm sure we can talk this over in the bar."

"Oh no, you don't," yelled Manley.

"Nice try," said Crow.

Tootie giggled.

The smaller member of the trio seemed put out with the larger "NAZI" flim-flamer.

"You see," said Manley. "Even your third stooge here doesn't believe that NAZI nonsense. Only Tootie is amused and I'm going to have a serious talk with her as soon as you leave."

"Did he just call us stooges?" asked the giant.

"Yes, I did," said Manley. "Larry, Curley and Ho . . . or Horace or whatever they call you."

The titan moved closer.

The leader stepped in front of him but growled, "Wait a damn minute, you tennis turkey. I was just about to leave, but now you've annoyed me. Let's get something settled. Are you saying this club is too good for me and my friends?"

"Imminently. Just take a look at yourselves."

"He doesn't like us, Troy?" said the large fellow. "And he's a rude little runt. He needs to be taught some manners."

"He doesn't like us, Ho. And he doesn't like your sister either."

"I'm gonna fold, mutilate, and spindle him, Troy." The Ho character again moved toward Stan. Both Troy and Crow stepped between them.

"Now you see what you've done," said Troy. "You've hurt his feelings. He could do you and yours great harm. Maybe you should apologize."

"Apologize? Oh, that does it. Crow, for the last time, throw them out!"

"Mr. Manley, would you let me handle this, please."

"Aww, Troy, let me spindle him, just a little."

"Ute," the nonthreatening fellow said.

"What the hell is he mumbling?" asked Manley.

"He's reminding you that these lands were originally Ute territory," said Horace. "Ute ... an indigenous people of Colorado and Utah. My people. Today our presence has been reduced to Southern Colorado—Ignacio, Durango. Seriously, Stanley you need to get off this mountain more often."

"I know Durango, you primitive. I couldn't understand the interloper; I thought he was hooting like an owl. Typical Indian trick to distract from the point. The point being: It's time for you savages to leave."

Crow asked, "Why does he think this is Ute land? What's he know we don't?"

"We passed several Ute prayer trees on the road," answered the Troy leader.

"Prayer trees?" barked Stan the Mountain Man.

"Prayer trees," asked Crow.

"Prayer trees?" giggled Tootie.

"Veloy?" Troy looked at his smaller cohort.

"Horace," he said, "we don't need to invent some nonsense organization with a dubious title, Brother. As you know, this establishment is on sacred land. We Native people often tied off young trees to distort their growth in order to create sacred spaces, give directions, tell stories and mark burial sites. I saw several off road from your entrance and gate. They are twisted or grow parallel to the ground for a ways or are otherwise misshapen."

"I've seen these twisted trees," said Crow. "I never thought much about them.

"We have one in our front yard," said Tootie. "And several on the back slope of our acreage. I never knew they were sacred. I have a favorite. I call it the Valentine Tree. Every year I . . ."

"I know the trees you're talking about," said Manley. "They're all over the place and as the chairman of the Landscape Committee it's my recommendation that we cut them all down. They're unsightly."

The Veloy character looked as if he suddenly felt a bureaucratic bullet pierce his heart. "You're right, Ho," he said. "We need to culturally modify this pendajo."

The Horace behemoth grinned and looked to the Rivers leader for a go-ahead. He was still conversing with Crow.

"You know," said Veloy. "Some of those trees may mark burial sites. You'd be desecrating graves.

"That's a lot of Sitting Bull-shit," countered Stan the Mountain Man.

Horace looked as if he was about to come unglued.

"One other thing, Cuacha," continued Veloy. "Some of those trees are prophecy trees. Look for intertwined trunks. We no longer know the prediction. We suspect they are optimistic: continued love, future alliances, unbroken respect for the Great Spirit. But, respect is an important concept here. You sir," he addressed Manley directly, "show us no respect. Nor do you respect the historical sacredness of this land. You invite folly. You're asking for it, Bub. You cast a dark shadow on your future. No tree will honor your progeny. No sacred living tree will mark your grave."

"Well said, Veloy," chirped Troy.

"Another threat! Crow how long do I have to tolerate these insults?"

"As I was saying, we have an intertwined tree on our property," said Tootie. "I've always thought they looked like lovers hugging each other. My sister had her wedding picture taken in front of it. I leave flowers there every Valentine's Day."

"That's nice, young lady," said Veloy. "You honor the spirit of the tree . . . of the land."

"Animism," said Crow. "This is interesting. I had no idea these . . ."

"Animism!" yelled Manley. "What the hell does 'animism' have to do with anything right now?"

"It means that a spirit has been attributed to the trees," answered Crow."

"To all living things," said Veloy. "And the rocks and the mountains . . ."

"If you find this interesting," said Horace to Crow, "maybe we can discuss all that *animism* means in the bar."

"I know what the hell 'animism' means," interrupted Stanley. "And no one is going to the bar. Crow, for the last time: do your job. Tootie, sweetheart, butt out if you value your job."

"Say something mean to her one more time and I'm going to teach you some respect," threatened Veloy.

"Veloy!" chirped Horace in an echo of surprise. "I'm liking this animated side of you, Brother."

"Thank you," chirped Tootie in another echo.

"What the hell is happening here," howled Manley. "Is the world turned upside down? Does anyone besides me see the absurdity of all this? These clowns are trespassing; they're breaking the law, not to mention club rules. And I'm being physically threatened."

"No one is threatening you physical violence," said Rivers. "at least not at the moment. Horace, Veloy, let's pull it back a step. Manager Crow and I can come to an understanding. But you are a disrespectful ass, President Manley, and as a lawyer I can promise that we will be back. We'll be back to address your disrespect of the land, your disrespect of people as evident by your membership criteria, I suspect, and your disrespect of your employees. There are laws, you know. Maybe," interjected Rivers, "as a lawyer I can help change current, loose laws and predict a future where callus assholes like Stanley here cannot just come in and desecrate sacred Native sites. There is a burgeoning movement to protect such sites from developers. Keep being rude, you rube, and my first act may be protecting these trees Veloy is talking about. How'd you like to tie up your landscape plans and any other club improvements in the courts for a few decades and membership blames you?"

"Threats! Threats! I hope you're listening, Crow. You're my witness. Tootie, you heard him threaten me, right, girl?"

"What?" said Tootie, still apparently admiring the legs of the gate crashers. She looked to Crow for some sort of clarity and simply smiled at Veloy.

Manley suddenly pushed from between them and retreated down the stairs to the glass-enclosed foyer where he blasted the parking attendant for allowing the bus to park near the entrance. He wasn't finished chastising the boy, but he noticed the large Indian and the *tinker* coming down the stairs into the entryway.

"Where's the other one?" he asked.

"Your manager was kind enough to let him use the office phone, Malcriado." And then he said under his breath, "Ya' rude little prick."

"Madrazo," said the other fellow, and they both slapped a high-five.

"Right on, Veloy," said the big one. "You're right; he is a blowhard."

"Thanks, Horace," answered the other.

"So," said Stan. "I can confirm names for the police. We have a *Horace* and a *Veloy* and counselor Troy Rivers upstairs, trespassing still. That will be important information for the authorities." *HA! That gave these hooligans pause. Let's see how tough they are when the police get here.* "Sticks and stones, you indigenous buffoons."

Stan noticed that the Indians inside the bus had their faces pressed against the windows. Several stood in the bus doorway. They probably heard the derogatory comments he made about them to the parking attendant. They heard him threaten the boy's job if, upon his return, the bus and the derelicts inside were not gone off the club property.

The boy stood dumbfounded. Either he had not understood his orders or was choosing to be cautious about approaching a bus full of Indians dressed for the warpath.

The large man named Horace stomped past Manley and the cowering car caddie. He seemed to be calling the busload of his companions into council. After a few moments and some loud mummers the large fellow stepped down from the bus and went directly to Manley. He was carrying an arrow.

"We decided, ya' little tennis gargajo you. It's war." He broke the arrow in front of his face, and threw the broken remnants at Stan's Adidas.

"I'm calling the police," Stan said. He turned to reenter the clubhouse, but saw the third Indian, the leader, coming down the stairs. There was anger in his eyes. Crow stood at the head of the staircase. He was trying to hide a stupid, rebellious grin. Stan stormed off to phone the police from the tennis courts, his home turf.

He regretted not getting the license number of the bus, but when he turned to look back, all logic left his thoughts. He saw several of the Indians slip from the bus into the dark just past the lights of the clubhouse. Their actions were stealthy and menacing. They were heading his direction.

He walked with a determined stride down the path he had so recently ascended. The dark section lay ahead. It seemed more ominous than before. He tripped again on the same irregular section of sandstone. To catch himself, he quickly planted his hand on an adjoining tree trunk that was growing horizontally for a few feet, a natural pine handrail. "You've got to be kidding," he growled aloud.

Soft bird sounds and coyote calls began to rumble down the slope on both sides of the path. He looked around for a moment in the darkness and sensed there was something alien watching him. His apprehension slowed his pace; he became cautious. Stanley whistled while he walked, to muster some confidence, but it was not long until he got the uneasy feeling that whatever was watching him was getting closer. He had lived in the forests of Lookout Mountain for years and had seen mountain lions and even a few wayward bears, but this unseen presence seemed more menacing. His tune became choppier as he drifted further from the lights of the clubhouse. Stanley Norman Manley, Stan the Mountain Man, with tennis racket in hand, broke into a terrified run.

His adrenaline fueled the last hundred yards to the courts. The sprint left him breathless. He jumped inside the cottage adjacent to the locker room because it was the closest building. He cursed himself for not going into the pro shop where there was the phone. Once inside the cottage he slammed the door and slid down out of sight with his back on the wall, and fought to catch his breath. Squatting on all fours he peeked through the window at the shadows beyond. He could not be positive, but he thought he saw movement between the trees. A faint eerie coyote call broke his skin into goose flesh. He felt his forehead go hot and his palms cold. He could not believe the Indians had the gall to pursue him. *I thought Indians never attacked at night.* He was chewing his bottom lip and suddenly noticed how parched his lips were. "I'm thirsty. Probably just the nervousness." *No problem, they can't flush me out because of hunger or thirst—I made a pig of myself at the club buffet.*

He heard a twig break. His head snapped toward the sound. He saw no one. *Oh, god,* he thought. *What if Crow didn't notify the police? Hell, even if he did, they'll never get here in time. They'll arrive just in time to find my body—mutilated, broken, spindled by that giant ignoramus. It would serve the members right if I'm gone. They've never acknowledged what I've done for this club. If the savages don't kill me, then the weight of all this responsibility will be my end. And do they appreciate it? Hell no, they make fun of my backhand.* He began biting his fingernails. After spitting out a couple of the trimmings he unconsciously began flossing with a long nail remnant. *How pissed off could these guys be? Are they just trying to scare me, or do they mean to really hurt me? That was one big son-of-a-bitch that threatened me. Why the hell didn't Crow call the police right away? Crow? You don't suppose he is an Indian? I always thought he was Italian. Where the hell is Security? Why the hell didn't I vote the money for a new phone system down here? So, OK, I thought I was saving money by limiting the members-only phones to outside by the courts and inside the Pro Shop.* He pictured himself in the sanctity of the Pro Shop with its larger locks and thicker glass windows. He figured, if need be, he could hide among the racks of tennis clothes, but then remembered none of the clothes displays reached the floor since most were men's shorts, tee shirts, and lady's short skirts. His bare legs would expose him. He tried to think of other possible hiding places in the Pro Shop, and cursed his obvious vulnerability in the towel cottage. How could he hide in here; bury himself under the dirty linen? He said out loud in a panic. "How was I to know?"

Images ran through his mind of the gang of huge Indian thugs beating him and laughing as they took turns trying to volley him over the tennis net—let serve, first fault, second fault, 'My turn.' Other more painful and degrading images soon accompanied his fears as he confused historic Japanese tortures with the torments of "B" Western movies and their Indian villains.

Considering the entire membership of this Club, I ask you, (the "you" was himself) *where the hell is someone else exhibiting a little leadership, a little backbone? Where are people when you need them? Who else concerns themselves with the overwhelming problems involved in an organization like this? No one that's who. Not Crow, obviously; where the hell is Security? You know I'm right.* He nodded in agreement with himself. *I don't know, but maybe I should consider not letting them take me alive,* he joked, thinking a bit of levity may lessen the seriousness of his predicament, but only half-believing it was a jest. *How would I do it? Cut my wrist with this goddamn piece of fingernail that's stuck between my teeth? Or I could beat myself to death with my tennis racket—not with my service stroke. Hold my breath 'till I die? No, that would never work. I know, I could stuff a tennis ball down my throat and suffocate myself. No, that's crazy, I mean, that's what those criminals are trying to do to me.* He peeked again through the window into the ominous night.

No, I'm not going to just give up. Not me. Not Stanley Norman Manley, not Stan the Mountain Man, not Stan, President-elect. If they want me, they can come and get me and, by God, they are going to have one hell of a fight on their hands.

He stood and yelled out the doorway, "You hear that out there? You got one hell of a fight on your hands. Indians? Renegades! Trespassers! You hear that? You hear me? I'm going to call the cops on you. The police are on their way," he lied. "So, you better get going, if you know what's good for you. You hear me?"

Silence.

Stanley decided to make a break for the phone in the next hut. He jumped to the side of the cottage and threw the large breaker switch. The sudden stadium lights surprised three braves on the edge of the tennis courts.

For Manley, the lights made everything appear familiar again. Now he *was* on his turf, "I thought I told you sons-a-bitches to clear-out!" His voice quivered with adrenaline.

The three warriors grinning with malice confidently approached the Mountain Man.

"Now stay where you are," Stan ordered.

They continued to stalk.

"OK, you bastards," screamed Manley, "take this." He reached into a grocery cart filled with practice balls and gently arched a green luminous orb into the air. The racket cocked behind his head and then with lightning speed flashed forward and down across his body. The green bullet shot over the net and slammed one of the braves in the groin. The insulted man moaned and slumped over the foul line. Fifteen, love. Manley tossed a second ball in the air and a second brave dropped. Thirty, love. He arched his third ball and prepared to fire it; however, just as it reached its apex, a gleaming arrow impaled the ball and it dropped at Manley's feet. He screamed. Thirty, fifteen. The next serve decided the match. The Horace thug, going out of turn, let his second arrow fly, and cut the strings out of Manley's racket.

Stanley dropped to his knees in tears. That was a new racket.

They came out of nowhere. He was surrounded. It was over. They had him. The Horace bully ordered them to tie "whitey" in the referee's chair towering over the court. He didn't know if whitey referred to his outfit or his skin. It didn't matter. All was lost. What devilish thing are they going to do now?

They blind folded him with a dirty towel. Who the hell didn't toss their towel in the wash bin? He heard them break into the pro shop. "That's private property," he yelled. He listened as they gathered things from the shop. Are they looting the merchandise? Then he heard them stacking stuff under the chair.

"Anybody got a match?" he heard the Horace guy ask.

"What is this," Manley challenged them. "a joke? You're not going to get much of a fire. Most of those tennis rackets are aluminum."

"Oh, there's plenty to burn," answered Horace. The sign-in book is good kindling, so are the posters: Laver looks flammable, and all those monogrammed shirts, they'll burn just fine."

"Not Rod; not the Mount Vernon Wapiti Team jerseys?" Manley felt he was about to cry. It never dawned on him that the corruption of the term *Wapiti*, Shawnee for elk, was enough to get him burned at the stake. The irony escaping Manley was that *wapiti* literally translates as "white rump," an appropriate descriptor for the pickle in which he found his lily-white posterior.

"That's right, Mr. Club President, all your precious logo outfits are about to go up in flames."

"You monsters. I hope you burn in hell. And, oh, by the way, I'm not club president yet, but I can guarantee you, when the members get wind of this outrage, they'll elect me in a landslide."

"Not if you're charcoal, Sonso."

Stan began pleading. He offered them anything.

"Drinks in the bar?" someone asked.

"On my tab," he answered.

"Tennis lessons?" another called out.

"Group or private—whatever you want."

"Do you have daughters?" asked a deep voice.

"No . . . a son, a worthless son. He's been a great disappointment to his mother and me." And then he recovered for a moment, "You can have Tootie, the receptionist. She's cute."

"Too bad. Light the fire you Comanche. Get ready to dance the night away."

Manley heard someone new run onto the court. It was the leader, the Troy character.

"Horace," he heard him yell. "I thought we agreed—no violence. This is not funny. OK, it's funny, but it's going to get us in a lot of trouble."

Horace answered, "How much more trouble can we get in, Chief?"

"Right," said Troy, "we're already in a lot of trouble. But, I told you. Don't call me chief." It was silent for moment. "Well, I can see the excitement on your faces," Troy continued. "We haven't killed anyone for a day or two. I know how hard it's been on all you guys, the long journey and all. What the hell, burn the bastard, but I get his scalp."

Stan the Man passed out.

Chapter Thirty-seven

More Best Laid Plans

Summer, 1964

"Come Raven, come Coyote," called Turtle, "Mischief is afoot."

Wild Billy, proprietor of Buffalo Bill Cody's Bar Grill Trading Post and Texaco Station, had no qualms about eavesdropping on the conversation of the leaders of the various police forces. He was pleased that his bar was the unofficial headquarters for their manhunt. Natural inquisitiveness elevated his impropriety for a couple of reasons. Okay, he was snoopy, but he had good reason. He was concerned that the manhunt focused on his friend, Anthony Hands of the Bear, good ol' Tony Hardhat; although, he had to admit: Tony was not his highest priority. More to the point, the situation had presented a potentially profitable opportunity. If he was clever, he could parlay the recent events into financial advantage for his establishment. As he walked the tray of drinks over to the table, he listened to Chief Sweet's familiar bray.

"No offense, Chief Superintendent Humboldt, Henry, old chum," said Chief of Denver Police, Alan Sweet, "but you, and your Rangers are more of a hindrance than a help. Why don't you leave the police work to some genuine police-*men*. Your little posse is under-trained, under-equipped, under-manned, and under-led. Understand? And reporting that that Hotchkiss dame was murdered, now that was a brilliant piece of detective work, and that's an understatement."

"My Rangers and I are going to be a part of this, Sweet, whether you like it or not. Red Rocks is still my jurisdiction, and besides, it was me that savage tried to murder."

"Murder, murder, do you look murdered?" the Jefferson County Sheriff laughed. "Listen, for all we know, Hardhat has skedaddled over the hill and out of the park. That puts him in Jefferson County and my jurisdiction."

"The crime still took place on the property of the City and County of Denver, and thus far I'm the one taking all the heat from the news media. As far as I'm concerned, that gives me priority, authority, and superiority. Regardless, my instincts tell me the perpetrator is still in the rocks."

"Then he is mine," said Henry with surprising determination.

"Then he is ours, Henry, and you had better let us take the lead here. I want to make sure we apprehend the culprit, no slip-ups, and no one doing something half-assed, no offense, Henry."

Wild Billy, leaning over to serve drinks, inadvertently made eye contact with Humboldt at the instance of the insult.

Humboldt twitched, an apparent anal spasm, his inflatable doughnut cushion smooched on the his chair, and then, in as menacing a voice as Henry had ever uttered in the hallowed halls of Cody's Bar and Grill, while maintaining eye contact, growled, "If I get my chance, Hardhat will not leave those rocks alive."

Wild Billy had listened to Henry's threats against Tony for a thousand nights, most had proved impotent, but the vilification in Henry's voice gave Billy pause. He paused just long enough for his entrepreneurial fervor to push his concern for Tony out the back of his brain. A cash register rang in his head, and he heard himself say, "I tell you what we would have done in the old days." He waited until he was sure he had everyone's attention. "The authorities would call in a specialist, an Indian tracker, an expert like the great Buffalo Bill Cody, may he rest in peace. Well, I hate to brag, but I'm something of an expert myself. The very Indian you are chasing hides out in here all the time. No one knows him better than I do. I know every corner of his wily mind. I know all his tricks. I know how he thinks." *Besides, I've got to get to Tony before crazy Henry finds him.* "You're going to need someone who Hardhat trusts, someone who can talk to him, someone who can get close to him. No offense, Henry, Chief Sweet, Sheriff—but Anthony Hands of the Bear, Tony, ain't going to allow himself to be shackled by no bluecoat."

Billy watched as they mulled over his idea. Henry did not respond but remained looking down into his drink as if some answer would emerge from the dark liquid—bubble, bubble, toil and trouble.

"And you'll never find him in those rocks," Billy continued. "He can hide in there for days. He knows every nook and cranny. Why . . . he actually takes dates up there and plays hide-and-seek, peak-a-boo, and who knows what kind of grab-ass. No offense, Henry."

"Will you guys cut the crap with the 'ass' jokes," said Henry. "This is a serious injury. OK, there may not be too much actual physical damage, a few stitches, but I'm bruised up worse than a bull rider. Believe me; the pain goes very deep, very deep indeed."

"Sorry, Henry," said Billy.

"Yeah, Henry, we didn't mean to offend you, make you the butt of humor," said the Sheriff. His smile was unsympathetic.

"Quit your whining, Henry," said Sweet. "You're always putting your ass where it doesn't belong. That's why you should back away," he looked around the table to see if anyone got his inference, "and let us handle the arrest."

Sweet took charge, "How about another bottle, Wild Man? Give my colleagues and me a chance to hash over your idea. Crazy as it sounds, it just might create the diversion we need to nab that would-be murderer."

Billy knew Sweet would expect the liquor gratis, but it was a sound investment if they went for the idea. He remembered Doogan's advice, "You got to advertise." Being a hero, the local businessman who helped arrest an Indian assailant—alleged—could prove to be inspired advertising. He would damn sure get a photo in the paper. He would wear his Pahaska outfit. Now that would make a picture.

Billy also knew that Sweet was anxious to distract the news media. And he knew, all things considered, that Sweet was the man in charge. Things were in Sweet's hands. Wild Billy felt he had made a good pitch. He was confident his plan would work. It was only a matter of time until they invited him back into their circle. He walked to the bar to give the police some privacy and to check on the only other customers, the two black men. Billy wasn't sure why, but the two men seemed to greet his return with some hidden animosity. Perhaps they felt he had ignored them while he schemed with the police. He couldn't imagine why, but perhaps they resented his plan as some kind of collusion. Oh, what the hell, I'll buy them a drink, too.

Slowly emerging from the Louisiana swamp of Red Stick's long lost memories, the image of Henry Humboldt's bare butt came into focus. The fat chief's comment, the one they called 'Sweet,' finally forced the synaptic connection. This was the little honky at Mardi Gras who insulted T.S. a few years ago with a blatant bare-ass and a crude homophobic joke. It was this ass being "where it doesn't belong" upon whom Red had extinguished a cigar. "I know that Ranger clown," he said to his brother.

"How could you?" asked Talks Softly.

Red wasn't worried that T.S. could be heard by the others. T.S. did not have to whisper, he lived in a whisper.

Red, on the other hand, whispered, "Trust me, I just do."

"Oh, this is getting delicious."

"What?" asked Billy, standing nearby. "Get another drink for you fellows?"

"*Absolument,*" tittered Talks Softly.

"Leave them on the bar," instructed Red. "T.S. can I see you in the bathroom for a moment?" He stood and walked toward the back of the saloon. He looked to see if his brother was following. T.S. was grinning at the bartender and quivering with the excitement of intrigue. He was about to say something to the barkeep. "T!" Red said loudly. "Let's go! Vite!"

From the table Sweet barked, "You're going to lose my business if Cody's is turning into that kind of a place, Wild Man."

Red ignored the insult and waited for T.S. just out of sight of the bar, near the bathroom.

The bartender, Billy, carried over a new bottle of Bourbon, "I'll sell the place, if that happens."

"Friends of yours?" chided Humboldt. "No offense."

Billy laughed and said, "Anything else you gents need? I've got to get back to the bar and mix another 'Mint Tulip.' "

Red burned as he closed the bathroom door and leaned against it to prevent anyone from entering uninvited. "We can't let these *porces* get away with this," he said. "We need to help this

Indian over in the park. I mean, after all, it sounds to me like he is just trying to protect his heritage, our heritage. And I know that Ranger asshole. I knew there was some reason I hated him the minute he walked in the bar, something besides his uniform and that squinty look in his eyes. You probably don't remember, but I put out a cigar on his butt when he mooned you and the Tchoupitoulas at Mardi Gras. It was what—four or five years ago? He's got less hair, but I recognized him. Seems to me, T.S., it was providence that I came on this trip and we ended up here."

"Oh, I agree, Red. It's magic. You must act. I must. We must help. What should vous do? Get it? Magic—voodoo?"

Red ignored the joke. "I feel right now like going in there and kicking some Ranger butt." He paused, "But, I think those other cops would shoot us, just for sport. We're no help to our Indian brother if we're arrested. We can't do this alone. You think Terry and the other guys you work with will be willing to help?"

"Oh, I'm sure they would. They love an adventure; they love bugging the police. Terry is still at the Holland House waiting for us. Oh, I've got a wonderful idea. Why don't we go pick him up; we can all put on our Indian outfits, hurry back up here and kick some croupe de flic.?"

"What's Terry doing with the costumes? I thought you had to make several more for the New Orleans party at the Hilton. Isn't that why you borrowed my outfit?"

"Yes, of course. Terry wants to show them to Lonnie H. at the Ornamental Resources Bead Company in Idaho Springs. They are going to help us with the other costumes. They have the rarest beads and baubles. Terry has them in his room. We didn't trust leaving them in the car."

"You're right. You should go get Terry and also call your other friends to meet us at Red Rocks. I'll stay here and listen in on what that ânon is planning. You two pick me up here and we will meet the others at the park. Bon?"

"Oui! Oh, this could be fun. I haven't worn my Tchoupitoulas costume for ages."

"Maybe the costume is not such a great idea, T.S., after all, we may have to be inconspicuous."

"Oh, spoil sport, I am not sure I can keep Terry from dolling up. After all, this is to support Indian pride. I'll hurry. Meanwhile, you don't start any fights."

Red and Talks Softly walked out of the bathroom together. All eyes in the saloon watched them approach the bar. Red loved his brother and his theatrics; so, he was inwardly amused when T.S., in a rather ineffectual masculine and Hollywood gesture, tried to throw down his drink in a single gulp but failed. He slammed it down on the counter, splashed most of it over the bar, wiped his mouth with an exaggerated swipe of his forearm and asked, "Do you have a doggy cup?" Before the shocked bartender could answer, T.S. looked over at the table of police and hummed, "Just kidding." He purposefully exaggerated his sashay toward the exit.

Just as he reached for the door another policeman, his cap said Golden Police, walked through. The cop paused and assessed the small man suddenly in front of him. He appeared dumfounded, and looked at the bartender for an explanation. There was none. He held open the door and allowed T.S. to pass.

"Merci," said T.S.

"What?" asked the cop, but T.S. was gone.

He approached the table of policemen, "I thought I'd find you guys here. Wild Billy, bring another glass."

"Chief Sheriff," acknowledged Sweet. "Where did you park your car?"

"By the door. There was plenty of room."

"We're trying to be somewhat subtle, Art. Hardhat may be dumb enough to show up here."

"Hardhat is hiding in the rocks. He was seen not too far from the tomb, but then disappeared. We found his truck in the south lot. Somebody had disabled it. He isn't going anywhere."

He looked toward the bar. Red knew they were checking him out. Red was tickled that this latest frontier *cochon*, still visibly confused by his encounter with T.S., must be really miffed that a couple of the brothers had the audacity to drink in his neighborhood bar. He hunched over his drink as if oblivious to the police convention, but periodically risked a covert peek in the dirty mirror; otherwise, he remained innocuous.

"You starting to serve greens and watermelon, Billy?" the newest cop asked.

The old bartender cringed, but said nothing.

The others chuckled.

Red acted as if he had not heard.

"So," continued the Chief Sheriff, "do we got a plan? Count me in."

"Why the hell not," cursed Sweet. "Maybe the frickin' Royal Mounted want in on the action. The more the merrier."

"Be careful what you ask for, Chief," said the Sheriff.

Two Rangers and a Sheriff Deputy came in the front entrance.

"It wasn't me that told, sir," said one of the Rangers to Humboldt when he noticed the crowded table. Henry ignored him. This group sat at another table near the association of their superiors.

"Where did you guys park?" asked Sweet.

"In front. Why?"

"It doesn't matter anymore. Carson, you may as well get our car and move it in front while there is still prime parking available."

"Right, Chief. I'll be right back." The younger, fit policeman hurried out the door, obviously delighted.

"He's an attentive little puppy. Can't do anything without him," said Sweet.

As Carson left the bar, two more Rangers entered.

"Is there anyone left at the park?" asked Humboldt.

"The Denver Police forced all the reporters and the TV crews into the lower parking lot. There are several guys with them—cops, sheriffs, Rangers. We're all represented."

"What about the tomb?"

The other Ranger spoke up, "We left Clyde guarding the tomb. We're just going to grab a bag of burgers-to-go and we'll head back."

"Kind of lax, isn't it, Henry?" said Sweet. "I mean, officers using their own initiative to decide to go off and buy burgers, or did he say to bag some burglars?"

"I'm getting a little tired of your witticisms, Pickles. Maybe we should concentrate on arresting the assailant instead exercising our arresting wit."

This got Red's attention. He looked in the mirror. Even through the dust he could see that Sweet was beginning to smolder at the Henry character calling him . . . what was it—*Pickles*?

Sweet was red-faced, but his voice was calm, "It's been quite a while, Henry, since anyone has had the foolish courage to call me that."

Sweet stood, pushing his chair back with the backs of his legs, his palms flat on the tabletop. The others eased away from the table.

Red thought: Damn, T.S. would have loved this. It's a scene right out of a "B" Western. He turned to watch. He felt himself smiling, hugely, anticipating the thrashing that his old nemesis, Humboldt, was about to receive.

Just as Sweet began to circle the table, and Henry, wisely, circled in the opposite direction, another cop burst through the door. "Chief!" he cried.

"What?" answered Sweet—angry.

"What?" answered the chief of the Golden Police at the same time.

"What?" answered Henry, foolishly looking around to face the door and turning his back on Sweet, who continued to advance around the table.

"All hell has broken loose," said the officer. He addressed the Golden chief. "A gigantic food fight has started up again in Golden. The downtown is a war zone. The owner of the Holland House and the Morrison Inn are resisting arrest. They've barricaded themselves on the roof of the cafe and are pelting us with chimichangas. A huge traffic jam has Lariat Trail locked up from the top of Lookout Mountain all the way to the brewery; road rage is rampant. Fights are breaking out up and down the mountain, and we just got some crazy call from Mount Vernon Country Club. Some hysterical person said that the club is under attack. Chief, we think they said, 'from a bus load of Indians.' Chief, what the hell do you want us to do? We're under-manned. A lot of the guys are still at Red Rocks, everybody else is trying to break up fights. We've got officers down."

"Officers down?" interjected Henry Humboldt. "Is there gun play?"

"No, sir," answered the Golden cop. "They were chasing perpetrators and slipped on burritos."

"Mount Vernon under attack by Indians?" commented the Jeffco Sheriff. "Is this some kind of a joke?"

"It's that goddamn PBS editorial," said Sweet as he reached Henry's side. "That commie bastard DJ has incited a riot. I'm going to lock away that little anarchist, right after we get that crazy son of a bitch, Hardhat."

"You're joking, right, Chief?" asked the Sheriff.

"I don't joke," Sweet answered as he took Henry's arm and turned him to stand face to face. "And I don't like jokers. Do you, Henry? Like jokes? Like being the brunt of jokes?"

"No, Chief Sweet. I don't," answered Humboldt. "And under the circumstances, it seems to me that we all need to work together. It's obvious that the Golden Police could use some help. My Rangers and I are willing to do what's necessary. Don't you agree?"

"Now there's a team player, Henry. You bet I agree, ol' buddy," and he emphasized his renewed camaraderie by swatting Henry on the butt.

Humboldt collapsed into his chair. He was speechless, but the butt doughnut squeaked loudly.

"We need a plan," said the Golden chief. "I appreciate any help you and your men can offer."

Sweet took charge—again. He *suggested* that against his better judgment, the Denver Police and the Reds Rocks Rangers should return to Red Rocks and focus on bringing in Hands of the Bear. And, contrary to his professional instincts, they should go along with Wild Billy's plan to pull a Judas surprise to get the drop on the "heathen."

Sweet's plan was simple in its complexity. The Golden Police couldn't cover both the riot in the city and the uprising at the country club, so the Jeffco Sheriff Department agreed to: 1) take on the Indians at the club, and 2) cover the mountain roads west of Red Rocks just in case Hands of the Bear tried to sneak out the "backside" of the park. The Golden PD could attack their task from two directions: take the upper Lariat Loop to address the traffic jam on Lookout from its "backside." Sweet would lead the caravan to the Red Rocks.

Everyone was delighted with the plan.

"I can't see bringing anymore manpower to bear on this," said Sweet. "I mean, with the police, the Rangers, the Golden Police, and the Jeffco Sheriffs, seems to me we got all contingencies covered. My worry is the governor. It being an election year, he is bound to try some grandstand move. If I know Governor Lyon, he will be itching to call out the National Guard for an inch-by-inch search of the park. That is just going to attract more media attention. He would love nothing better than to steal my thunder . . . our thunder, right boys?"

They all mumbled in agreement.

"No, we need to work fast, kick some Indian ass, and lock up a few crazies," said Sweet.

"Are we going with Wild Billy's plan, Sweet? If we are, we should hide a gun on Billy; he could get the drop on Hardhat, and then we can show up to make the arrest. As a team, you understand. It just might work," said Henry.

"How we gonna' get Billy up into the rocks? No offense, old timer, but it could take days for you to climb high enough to find Hardhat"

"I could call Stanley Manley," said Henry. "I'm sure he would loan us one of his horses. Billy, don't you ride that palomino of his in the Buffalo Bill Day's parade?"

"Sure I do. That pony and me are old friends. I'm positive Stan the Man would loan it to us."

Red tried to act as if he was disinterested in the policemen's planning. He turned away from the gathering and stared out the window. He was surprised to see what looked like a city bus stop in front of the bar. A passenger exited the bus, but from where Red sat, it looked as if he was ejected rather than departing of his own accord. He was a small white guy, dressed like some kind of a hippie Indian. Red watched as the hippie perused all of the cop cars. He acted paranoid, and skulked off into the trees, out of sight.

"So, Henry," asked Sweet, "you're willing to organize things here, call Ol' Stan?"

"It's the least I can do."

"Then it's settled. Henry, you call about the horse. The sooner they can get it down to Red Rocks, the better. We will all reconnoiter at the lower parking lot of the amphitheater. Officer Carson, let's go, boy. Gentlemen, start your engines."

"Was that a pun, sir—engines, Injuns?"

"I don't do puns, Carson. "

"Rangers, make ready!" yelled Henry.

"We'll be right behind you, Chief Sweet," said a Ranger. "We're just waiting on our bag of burgers. Henry, sir, we'll get a head start on you, sir. We'll be outa' here in two shakes of a . . ."

"Shakes!" interrupted the other Ranger. "We forgot to order shakes."

Sweet gave Henry a look of pontifical confirmation.

"Can we get anything for you, sir?" asked the Ranger. "A malted milk, maybe?"

"You can get your asses moving," said Henry.

"Nice choice of words, Henry" said Sweet as he led the procession out the door.

"Billy," said Henry, "can I use your phone to call Manley?"

"You know where it is. You make the call, I need to change."

Henry walked behind the bar and reached for the phone. He gave Red an inquisitive stare. Red thought for a moment that Henry recognized him, but before Humboldt could figure things out someone on the other end must have answered.

Henry turned his back on Red for privacy, and said into the receiver, "Hi. Junior. Is your old man at home? I need to speak to Stan the Man. Oh. Well, that's too bad. Hold on a second, Junior. Maybe you can help. I'm up at Cody's with the Denver Police Chief, Alan Sweet, and the Sheriff. We need to borrow a horse for Wild Billy to ride into Red Rocks and search for Tony Hardhat. I'm sure you've heard on the news about what's going on. You don't listen to the news? Well, never mind. What are the chances of borrowing that horse? That's right. The one that Billy rides in the parade will do just fine. Can you get him in a trailer and bus him up to Cody's, A-S-A-P?" He paused. Red continued to listen, but look disinterested.

"Sorry, Junior," Henry said, "It means: as soon as possible; it's military." He looked at Red. "You're right, Junior, I should have just said we're in a hurry. No, Junior, I wasn't in the military. Yes, Junior, I've always been a police officer. Yes, Junior, the Rangers are real policemen. Junior, we can talk about this later; how 'bout the horse?

"It's pronounced 'A-sap, Junior, not 'ass-apt'. Yes, Junior, it's a funny sounding word. I'm sorry if the old man calls you an ass. I can empathize with being called an ass, Junior. No, Junior, I was not making fun of being called an ass. I was just being self-deprecating. No, Junior I'm not making a *shit* joke. I'm sorry your dad calls you a little shit sometimes. I promise I'm not trying to insult you. I know he insults you, but trust me, I understand that you don't like being the butt of jokes." He looked again at Red for a reaction. Nothing. "Junior, we're running out of time here. No, I'm sorry I really don't have time to explain the humor. You're right; it wasn't funny. Junior, what about the horse? You say the trailer is already hitched to your dad's new Chevy Suburban, but he doesn't like you driving his new truck? Listen, Junior, I'll vouch for you. I'll tell your old man that it was an emergency, a police emergency. That should keep you out of trouble. Thanks, Junior. I'll be sure to tell Stan the Man how helpful you were. You're a chip right off the old block, kiddo. The acorn doesn't fall far from the mighty oak. No, Junior, I wasn't making another joke. If you could come by Cody's and pick up Billy, as-soon-as-possible. Right: A-sap; very good, Junior. That way I'll have time to get things organized at the park. Billy can fill you in about what's happening."

Henry hung up the phone, and turned to face Red. He poured himself a shot and threw it down. He set the glass on the bar in front of Red, stared for a moment, and then asked, "Don't I know you from somewhere?"

"I don't believe so," said Red. "I'm not from around here. Just passing through. He avoided eye contact. "Sounds like you police have a little excitement on your hands."

"Nothing we can't handle, boy." He looked at Red intently.

"Just doing the tourist thing. Came to see the Beatles and visit some friends. Wanted to try some beer brewed with pure Rocky Mountain spring water," he held up the Coors and flexed his broad shoulders and took a deep breath to show the expanse of his chest. He crushed the can, "If you know what I mean."

Judging from his expression, Henry got the point. He seemed to acknowledge Red's huge size, and moved around the bar toward the exit.

"Well, I think we understand each other. That's good. I'd love to stick around and chat, but there's some crime fighting to be done. Tell Billy, the bartender, I had to go. Tell him that 'Junior' is on his way with the palomino. Could you do that, please?"

"Oui," said Red, almost hoping Henry would make the connection. It would be much simpler to thrash him now that they were alone in the bar. In fact, he wouldn't mind paying back the bartender for *his* inappropriate humor, if Billy should interrupt the drubbing of Humboldt.

"Merci," said Henry, oblivious as ever. "Help yourself to another beer. I'm sure Billy won't mind, but stay out of the cash register, if you know what I mean. Just joking, big fella. But seriously, we don't want to have to launch another manhunt, now do we?" He grabbed his doughnut cushion off the chair and left in a hurry.

Red felt conspicuous sitting in the bar alone; so, he wrote Billy a note on a bar napkin. It said, "Junior is hurrying his ass to arrive with the horse; the other horse's ass just left."

Red Stick decided to wait for T.S. and Terry in the parking lot. The last thing he needed was to be accused of taking anything while the place was empty. He looked down the mountain and saw the last of the police parade. The exit of official cars looked like the end of a double feature at the local drive-in; the second film taking the teenagers past curfew.

He sat under a tall Ponderosa pine, the top of which looked as if it had been cropped by lightning. He looked toward the western, jagged horizon to see if any storm clouds were building. There were no clouds of concern, but he thought he felt a rumble below him, rising from the depths of the mountain.

Red saw the hippie kid checking him out from his hiding place in the trees. "Yo," he said.

The hippie emerged shyly. "What's happening, brother?" he said. "What the hey was going on inside, a cop convention?"

"I ain't your brother, hippie boy. What's the matter, don't you like the poleese?"

"I like 'um just fine, particularly when they are going the other direction."

"I hear that."

"Any left inside? I, ahh, kinda' need to use the bathroom."

"It's all yours. Le porcelet a' vite."

The hippie went shyly inside.

It was not too long until Red heard the familiar hum of the Volkswagen engine struggling up the incline. Soon it rounded the curve into sight. T.S. sat in the driver's seat of the tiny convertible. Even from a distance Red could see that the two small men were wearing their Tchoupitoulas Indian costumes.

"It's a good thing the police have already gone, little brother. You can't be doing any fighting in those outfits, and I thought we were going to stay inconspicuous."

"Inconspicuous, is my middle name," said Terry as he jumped over the car door and onto the parking lot. He shadowboxed an invisible opponent. The heavy costume bounced and the sequins danced as he exaggerated his footwork. "Which way did they go, George? Which way did they go?"

"Yes, I can see that," said Red. "Well, the costume looks good, Mr. Inconspicuous. That portrait on your loin skirt is great. Who is that, Geronimo?"

"Exactly. Do you like the monochromatic color scheme? I'll bet I bought every shade, tint, and tone of blue beads and sequins in the Rocky Mountain region. And, each one is individually stitched."

"Looks nice, Cassius Clay. Perfect outfit for fighting."

"We brought your old outfit, Red. I'll bet it still fits. Do you want to try it?"

"I'll wait 'til we're out of sight in the rocks. I want to surprise that asshole Humboldt. I want him to remember who put that scar on his white butt. I want to be in costume when I put another whoop on his honky ass—and when he gets that look of 'why me?'—I'm gon'na tell him it's for Indian pride, and then I'm gon'na punish him for insulting our mother."

"Red, Terry says he knows Red Rocks Park like the back of his hand. Maybe we can find the Indian fellow before the authorities catch him."

"That's great. I'll explain what the cops are up to on the way. We've just got one quick stop to make. Terry you think you can get us into the park unseen."

"Do salmon swim upstream?"

T.S. giggled.

"Of course, I can get us in—and out!—without being seen. I mean, after all, I'm from Denver. Everybody in Denver knows Red Rocks. I'm a native."

"Wait just un' momento. I'm in serious bladder panic here," said T.S. "Red, you said all the police are gone?"

"All gone, but . . ."

It was too late. T.S. was hurrying through the door and out of earshot.

The hippie was toking up in the bathroom. He thought he was the only one in the bar. Suddenly the door burst open and a feathered apparition pranced into the room and saddled in front of a urinal. He said something, but the hippie couldn't make out what it was. The spirit's voice was too soft. "What?" he mumbled, not sure if the image was real.

"I said, always shake twice and your britches stay nice."

The hippie, in pure reflex, looked down at his own crotch. Then he looked at the joint in his fingers. By the time he looked again for the feathered mirage, it was gone. He remained frozen, posed in front of the urinal, staring at the wall, contemplating reality and the potency of his weed.

Wild Billy Swarz, proprietor of Buffalo Bill Cody's Bar Grill Trading Post and Texaco Station sat in the dim light of his bedroom. Billy pulled an antique trunk from the depths of a dark closet. It looked as if it belonged in the boot of a frontier stagecoach and smelled of dusty roads. His mood was melancholy and his movements indecisive. He contemplated whether he was doing the right thing in aiding the authorities to nab Anthony Hands of the Bear. He looked around his room in search of a sign to relieve his pensiveness and thought how the room reflected the paradox. It was obviously a bachelor's quarters—comfortable but unkempt, smallish but packed with important man stuff, aged rather than old. Hunting paraphernalia hung from the walls or leaned in corners. Three Pueblo Indian pots perched on a shelf above the dusty mirror on his chest-of-drawers. One was the black-on-black vessel done by Maria Martinez and purchased (what seemed to be a century ago) by his Uncle Max. It was the black pearl that initiated Billy's, Mischa's, adolescent exodus from the confines of his European ancestry and the quest for adventure in the Old West. To the left of the *Maria* was an equally enthralling *Lucy Lewis*, a Santa Clara legend. The third was an ancient polychrome, probably Anasazi, a seed pot, its Neolithic patterns were hand-painted three centuries ago by a genteel hand using yucca brushes and black slip clay. They sat adjacent to one another, three very special mementos, not for sale, symbolizing the ancient frontier and a reminder of his long journey. He looked at several framed pictures hanging next to the bureau mirror. There was Uncle Max in a faded black and white photograph; the twinkle in his eyes still evident and the proud posture obvious. There also was Doogan in another framed memoir, looking tired, and old Rudi dressed as Buffalo Bill, looking drunk, both standing in front of the palomino that hurled them through the drugstore window, subtracting the sum total of local color by two.

Billy rationalized, "Otherwise, if I don't do this, it could get worse. Tony could get hurt. The cops are plenty mad." He sat on the edge of his bed staring at the trunk. "Yeah, yeah, I know, he's a friend, I shouldn't be helping to arrest him, but damn-it." He paused. He looked again at Doogan. "The business is crashing around my head. I've got bills to pay." He spoke directly to the photograph, "We need the publicity. It'll be great for the business. Remember— 'local color?' If anyone should understand, you should." The smile in the photo did not change. He continued to plead for some sort of sign confirming his weak convictions. "Reviving the Old West, crazy ol' Billy, Buffalo Billy—a potential hero, I'll be on every TV channel in the city. There may actually be national coverage—great, great, grandnephew of Buffalo Bill nabs Indian radical."

"Ligner," a voice with a Cuban-Hebrew accent seemed to come from the wall. He looked quickly, but Max didn't move. "Emmis, Uncle Max. You should understand—it's business. Everyone will know my name!"

He looked down at the floor. A bearskin rug was bunched and wrinkled next to the trunk. "One of the best trades I ever made. The poor grizzled drunk traded it for a couple bottles of booze. Cheap booze. He was an old black powder hunter, a geezer who authentically lived the way of the pioneer, a modern mountain man, not a contemporary impersonator, forced to trade by hard times. He wandered out of the woods looking for Doogan. The story was that Doogan had bankrolled the canyon hermit through many a hard time in the past. I saw him crumble when I gave him the bad news— Doogan and Rudi had taken their last ride on the pale horse. I don't know if he deflated because of grief for an old friend he obviously hadn't seen in a long time or the probable loss of a barter and swap. But if there is one thing I learned trying to keep this business alive; maybe I learned it from my curmudgeon father, not from Uncle Max, I don't think—but jump on a deal when you see one, particularly when you sense an advantage. It didn't take much haggling and I also got the hunter's freezer full of bear meat, venison, antelope and elk. The kitchen man, my cook, in the café grill ran lunch and dinner specials for a month featuring 'Exotic Game Steaks, Frontier Fillets and Backwoods Chili.' "

A floating, ganef regret briefly twittered toward consciousness, but Billy quickly grounded it with mercantile flak. What did almost reach awareness, however, was another episode of his periodic confusion about mortality. "Wish I knew some answers 'bout dying. Not looking forward to it. Scared as hell. 'The great emptiness.' Doogan, if you can hear me, I'd appreciate some comforting advice here. Rudi, you got any pontificating to contribute. Not like you to be this quiet this long." He paused, trying to assess his life so far. "Ahh, why would I ask you White guys; you're no better at philosophizing or *religiousizing* than this pale face. Wasn't it Porthos or Aramis, one of those musketeer types that said, 'Gentlemen don't concern themselves with such questions? Philosophy is for the unwashed … on guard, *fuker* de mére?' He was right . . . drink and fight, that's a proper man's legacy. 'Profit, don't ponder.' Now there is a relevant bumper sticker authored by a Wild West Jew boy running a bar and trading post about to go under.

"I know who I should have asked. Willie Wolf Song, that old Indian nut thief. Indians dwell on that afterlife, Happy Hunting

Grounds mumbo jumbo. Willie, if you're out there, I could use some guidance. Ahh, Willie, Willie, Willie; it's weird but I've missed you."

Billy thought he heard a rumbling coming from the bar . . . a soft rolling thunder. "Must be a construction truck going by . . . some large vehicle, like a bus. That's odd, neither is supposed to be up here on Lariat." He looked at the bear rug, "You hear that, Yogi?" The rug did not answer. "What you grinning at? Does Boo-Boo know what happened to you-you? Sorry, bruin, didn't mean any disrespect, I'm just a little confused right now and it's making me cranky."

As was the custom, the head of the bear was intact, fully three-dimensional, eyes wide with anger and maul agape with a toothy snarl. But the body was flattened and spread out like a . . . well, like a rug. He thought about the animal when it was alive— fearsome and venerated.

The bear was once revered for its bravery, strength, and defiance; now it decorated his floor—a trophy to misplaced machismo— robbed of its essence, deprived of its potential greatness. He asked himself, was he doing the same to his maverick friend, Hands of the Bear? "It's not the same thing, Mischa," he said to himself. "Can't you tell the truth to yourself even?" He looked back at the photo of his uncle. "Ix emmis, truth is, I should have stayed in the hotel business with you, Maxey. Then I wouldn't be thinking about turning on a friend, even if he is a rascal."

His fallacious mind allowed him the thought that he had talked himself out of the collaboration, but he continued to open the trunk. "For the first time since I was a rebellious kid, a kolboynik, no! a bumpkin, I'm having to admit that maybe becoming a frontier huckster was a mistake." From the top of the trunk he removed a box bound in twine. He moved in a ritual sequence, becoming numb to the idea that he was not going to do this dubious thing. He cut the twine, lifted the top off the box, and unfolded the brown wrapping paper. The beaded yoke of a buckskin jacket shown inside, and he thought how the sudden enlightenment never failed to surprise and please him. He lifted the historic garment. It was heavy, gratifying, and weighty like a leather-bound book. The ornate beadwork swirled in organic patterns from the collar to the belt line. The symbols suggested grandeur and nobility. He recalled the resplendence of the coat, and remembered leading the numerous parades through the streets of Golden. Any regrets flushed from his consciousness.

The matching pants nestled in the box, under a bright scarf. He removed them and set both on the bed next to the magnificent jacket. He walked into the closet. Stretching on his tiptoes; he pulled an ornate, leather hatbox off the shelf. A cowboy sombrero nestled inside, a Stetson with more gallonage than a keg of Coors. And coiled inside the bucket of the hat was a fall of silver hair, a wig— the capital *accoutrement* to becoming Buffalo Bill. He'd paid good money for this fall; story was, it once belonged to the old scout, himself. There was no bartering here, no good trade; it was too rare an artifact. He had to have it.

Cody was a vain man; he celebrated his luxurious quaff and the ladies loved it. So, even before the celebrity of the Wild West extravaganza he worried about losing his fine filigree—his symbolic plume of virility. As the great showman got older and his hair indeed thinned, over the decades, he would save remnants, natural sheds and barbered trimmings, and have them woven into a wig that perpetuated the potent image of frontier adventurer and Indian fighter—The, one and only, Buffalo Bill.

Wild Bill Swarz leaned down and placed the long hair atop his own white crop, and when it felt in place, flipped his head, the heavy hair making a great arch and falling over his shoulders. He felt himself change; he was drifting into character.

He ceremoniously removed the sombrero from the box, admired it for a moment, used his cuff to burnish an imagined blemish, and augustly crowned himself. He looked in the mirror, stepped back, and addressed the reflection and the family pictures at the same time, "Damn, I look good. Doogan, Maxy . . . . I'm probably going to Hell; well, we Jews actually don't believe in Hell but I'm screwing up a lot of karma. Well, we don't exactly believe in karma; we're more concerned with our comeuppance. What do the Indian's call it . . . 'Magic? Coup? Well, since none of you guys will answer me, I guess I'm going to do it; I'm gonna double-cross my old friend Anthony. I figure it's worth it, for the sake of the business. Hands of the Bear, I'm coming for ya." He dressed in the buckskins.

Chapter Thirty-eight

Prodigal Sons

Summer, 1964

I, Turtle, am in a quandary as to whether it was Steinbeck or
Custer who best typified Robert Burns' parable "Of Mice and Men."
Regardless, Buffalo Bill, both the actual and the impersonator, well
exemplify the challenge to best laid plans.

The fly on Wild Billy's buckskin britches was opened and
closed with intertwined rawhide strings, like a cod piece tennis shoe.
Billy knew it was a "pain in the crotch" to appropriately "free the
little fireman" when he had to take a piss, which was often. So, with
fly open to the breeze, he strolled into the bathroom, mumbling to
himself, "Never eat at a place called Mom's, never pass up a
bathroom, and . . . particularly in these tight buckskins . . . never
trust a fart." He was surprised to see a hippie posed over a urinal.
    "Sorry," said Billy, "I thought the place was deserted. How'd
you get here?"
    The hippie, still staring forward, not acknowledging another
male entering a bathroom, as was proper Musketeer etiquette, did not
turn toward the speaker, not when posted at a urinal. "Man. You
wouldn't believe it if I told you," he said to the wall.
    "Try me," said Billy, a little miffed that a dubious and
suspicious "long hair" had entered his bar without him knowing. No,
the irony that he was biased against a flower child because of his
long hair, while he himself was dawning a luxurious ersatz fall,
didn't register.
    The hippie seemed to sense the zesty edge to Billy's
question; so, he risked a social faux pas, one with which Billy was
imminently familiar, being a bar owner, and turned to answer. If
Billy had known the truth, the hippie was still shook from the last

apparitional visitor to the adjacent urinal—a soft spoken elaborately hackled specter. He watched as the hippie, slowly and with apprehension, turned to face him. The hippie went pale and his knees seemed to weaken.

Billy thought the hippie's sudden astonishment was due to the splendiferousness of his costume; after all, the hippie, too, seemed to appreciate buckskin.

The hippie reluctantly offered the joint he was smoking to Wild Billy.

"Oh, why the hell not? This is Junior Manely's thing; time I see what all the fuss is about. If it'll help me deal with the saddle sores this caper is going to cause, then it's worth a try. He's beautiful, but that fuckin' horse can be a rough ride." He looked at the hippie, "Get it? Rough Rider?" The kid didn't appear to get it. He took a long *hit* and passed it back to the hippie.

"No, no, sir . . . You keep it . . . I'm trying to quit."

"Thanks, I don't ordinarily do this sort of thing, but I'm under a lot of stress—Indian problems." said Billy. He noticed the hippie risked a look. The look was confused coincidence. Bill tight-lipped the joint, blinked as the smoke drifted into his eyes and made him tear-up as he laced up his fly. As he exited he looked back at the hippie, but the lad simply stared forward, back in the urinal pose of no acknowledgement. "Can I buy you a drink?" asked Billy.

"No thanks," said the kid. "Probably should try to quit that too. You go ahead, I'll just stay in here for a while . . . you know, think about things. What I've done with my life . . . gotta put some things behind me. Wondering what's next. You know."

"Do I! You said it, kid. From your lips to . . . if you know what I mean." Obviously the hippie did not know what he meant. "Never mind, but you're right. That's the truth. I can relate; I'll drink to that. In fact, I'm going to do just that . . . right now." He took another long drag on the joint and tossed it into the urinal. "Strong stuff," he growled. "Isn't that what you're supposed to say? I'm in the bar if you change your mind about a drink."

Costume intact, fly laced, wig in place, Stetson properly tilted, Wild Bill ambled from the bathroom and made a promenade into the bar; sad, he thought, that there was no one to appreciate his theatrical entrance. The hippie in the john seemed out of it. "I don't think he appreciated the quality of this outfit. The lighting in the head is bad. I don't think he got the full affect." The light in the bar was even darker, a purposeful miasmal affectation.

Four ethereal figures, however, sat at the bar. Billy did not see them; expectations, or the lack of it can blind a fellow. It is said that the Taíno, the indigenous people of the Caribbean, did not "see" the Niña, Pinta, and Santa María as they approached the islands because the natives had no visual or mental references to such otherworldly inventions or sights. *Now that!* thought Billy, *that hippie bobo might appreciate.* How our mind plays tricks—the prevue of Turtle, Raven and Coyote, who, as it happens, were the trio accompanying Willie Wolf Song at the bar.

Oblivious, Wild Bill turned to the back wall and took a moment to investigate another photo of Doogan, this one with his arm around the shoulder of a familiar young schlemiel, Mischa Wild Billy Swarz, himself, as a naïve novice—Little Billy Goat. "Look at that face, that stupid smile. It has shmontses written all over it." He looked past the pair—mentor and apprentice—future partners. Old Willie Wolf Song, like a phantom, lurked out of focus in the background. "Doogan," he muttered, "had his bane—that old thief, Wolf Song, and I've got mine—a young renegade, Anthony Hands of the Bear. Tony fricken Hardhat; it's better I bring him in."

"Better for who?"

"Whom," whispered Turtle.

Billy, surprised that there was anyone in the room, turned and faced the last person he ever expected to see. Willie Wolf Song sat before him. He was as ancient as the forest and as pale as the winter moon. "Willie! My god, you scared the bejesus out of me," Billy took a moment. "I thought you were dead?"

"Good thinking."

"No kidding around now, Willie. I mean, you look like death warmed over, but you always did and I ain't that drunk—not drunk enough to be seeing ghosts. I told that hippie kid I wasn't used to his ganja shit? Is that really you?"

"Good question. But it was you who summoned me." He looked down the bar at the other three astral patrons. "Who summoned us."

"It's stress," said Billy. "The business is getting to be too much—all this craziness at Red Rocks. The smoke, it's the smoke; all this smoke, cigarettes and dope. And that fercockta fireplace. It killing me. And booze. And pickled sausages, it's finally fermented my brain. 'You may be an undigested bit of beef, a blot of mustard, a crumb of cheese.' If I close my eyes, you'll be gone." He closed his eyes and opened them after a moment.

"Good try."

"Dickens, right?" said the figure next to Wolf Song. "Ever the performer, Billy."

"Am I dying? Have they sent you to guide me to heaven? Heaven! Sure, that's likely. Oh, hell!" he became despondent.

"Good guess."

"Stop it, Willie. Tell me—what's this all about?"

"I've been gone long time, searching. Wandering, unfulfilled, never caring if I saw this house of daft men again. But, something brought me back. Something important. My companions," he looked again at the trio sitting next to him. "They told me there was something here waiting. Who's hair is that?" he pointed to the wig Billy wore.

"I need a drink. You want anything? Sorry, I can't offer you cashews; I got rid of the nut machine not long after you disappeared. What happened to you anyway?"

"Long story. Little Billy Goat, the long hair you wear—it is not yours?"

"Naw, this ain't mine. You know that. It's . . . no, you wouldn't know, would ya'? You were gone by then. I forgot. It's been such a long time. How long has it been, Willie?"
"Time not important. Rejoining the circle important. Retaining coup important. Fulfilling purpose, accomplishing vendetta important, finding peace. Tell me, Billy Goat, where you get that hair?"

"I use this hair, Willie, for parades and such. You know I never could grow the long trail of locks that Buffalo Bill had. Even Rudi could grow a better head of hair. So, I bought mine. I don't wear it all the time, once or twice a year or so, you know, special occasions. Too bad too, 'cause it cost a pretty penny. It's part of the costume: the hat, the buckskins, the boots, the *hair*. It's famous hair. Of course, I could never tell anyone. I thought about selling it, you know me, make a trade, make a sale if it's profitable. But I decided to keep it. I don't know, something told me to hang on to it. It might get even more valuable. After all, it is the actual, authentic, bona fide hair of himself: William Fredrick Cody, Buffalo Bill—namesake of this here establishment and my historical mentor."

Wolf Song broke into a chant, a frightening wail that gave Billy the chills. The ancient Indian began thanking Wankan Tanka, and he seemed to gain stature. "This is the scalp of Pahaska? How did you come by this relic?"

"How do I acquire anything, Willie? You should know that? I traded for it."

"How was this done?"

"I need a drink first, old scout. I forget, did you want anything?"

"I'd take a margarita," said Coyote. "With extra salt."

"Two of those," said Raven. "If you're buying."

"Quiet!" said Turtle.

"You haven't introduced me to your friends, Willie," said Wild Billy. "I didn't catch your name, gents."

"Impolite to ask Indians their name, Billy Goat. You should know this," said Wolf Song.

"I didn't mean to be rude, Willie. You just got me out of sorts here. It's a real surprise seeing you. I'm sorry . . ." He looked at Turtle. "But you, sir. I've seen you before. You've been in here. We chatted a while back. I never forget a face and I never forget a name. Mr. Turtle, isn't it?" He addressed the others at the bar. "And, yes, gents, I'm buying. Mr. Turtle would you like a margarita as well?"

"Well," said Turtle. "I wouldn't say no to a margarita, but I have very particular tastes and, I'm proud to say, my own recipe. Grand Marnier is the secret, never Triple Sec. But I allow a digression, Wolf Song has business. Important business."

"I'm a little short of Tequila, but I'm sure there's enough for a round," said Wild Billy, ignoring the declaration of both business and Grand Marnier. "Let's all have a drink in celebration to Old Willie's return here. What do you say, Willie, can I offer you a toddy? Scotch, if I remember right. You always had a fondness for good Scotch and, of course, cashews. Fresh out of the nuts, as I said."

Out of the corner of his eye, Billy noticed the hippie had by this time worked up the courage to exit the bathroom; however, he took pause as he entered the bar area. He quietly tried to tiptoe past the conversation at the bar, thinking the participants another hallucination but, nevertheless, not wanting to disturb them. Just as he reached the exit . . . the ancient Indian bellowed.

"Tell me how, Wasichu!" Thunder filled the bar room. "How did you come by this scalp?"

"Now calm down, Willie. I'm gonna' tell ya'. But you got to admit, this is a pretty discombobulating visit, Old Salt. I never thought I'd see you again. Just give me a moment. I'll be glad to pour one for you; that is, if you'd like."

Turtle clicked his fingers. The chants of a thousand Indian souls suddenly swirled around the room. Paper blew off tables, menus off the bar, the curtains floated upward, the lights flickered and the door rattled an ominous quake.

The hippie, apparently with a flush of adrenaline and haunted panic, forced the door open and ran past the gas pumps, through the parking lot, back to the limited safety of the tree and rock that served as a bus stop earlier in his wacked-out odyssey.

"Man, the service in here sucks," said Coyote. "I don't blame that hippie for leaving."

"Yeah," said Raven, "Are we going to get those drinks you promised?"

Wolf Song's voice came from the depths of the earth. "Foolish man, do not risk further folly. Tell me how it is that you wear the scalp of my greatest enemy, Pahaska."

"Greatest enemy? I'm confused, Willie. I thought you and Buffalo Bill were pals. Didn't you used to be in the Wild West show?"

"Tell him what he needs to know!" The voice was an earthquake. It was not Willie's voice. It seemed to come from all directions at the same time. It knocked Billy back, against the counter behind the bar. His Stetson and the wig went flying.

Billy was shaken, but not hurt. He picked up the sombrero and brushed off the hairpiece. "This? Is it this hair you're asking about, Willie, old soul?"

Turtle raised his hand to click his fingers again.

"No, No! Hold on there Mr. Turtle. I'll tell ya'. Just, please . . . let me have that drink." He grabbed a beer mug and a bottle of Bourbon from the bar well. He spilled more than he poured in the mug, but an inch or so found its mark. He threw it back in one gulp, and quivered as the sweet heat of the cheap liquor settled in. "Like I said, Willie, I traded for it. A fella' sauntered in one night at closing, looking for Rudi. You remember William Rudolph—Doogan's pal? Of course, you do. Well, the fella' said he had something special to sell. I told him Rudi was dead; killed at Buffalo Bill Days; drunk as a skunk, rode a horse to hell; didn't make it back.

"The man obviously needed a drink; so, I offered him one— on the house. He drank whiskey, Kentucky, neat. The good stuff, not this cheap crap I just swallowed. The gent looked to be down on his luck. I gave him another. It loosened him up a bit. I asked, 'What's so special you got to sell?' I'm a businessman, after all. He dug deep into his coat and pulled out this fine fall of hair."

"Pahaska's hair?"

"That's what he said."

"How is this so? Pahaska had his hair when he was buried. I saw. I was there."

"You and half the country." He reached toward the well for the house Bourbon. Changed his mind and reached behind him to the shelf of "the good stuff." This time he neatly poured three inches and took a long chug then said, "But you were all fooled. Well, according to this fella' you were hoodwinked."

"How is this so?"

"Buffalo Bill was, how should I say it? Sparse . . . thinned on top the night before they moved him to the Capitol rotunda. Well, nearly bald. He had a good trim."

"Not so. I saw."

"He was wearing a wig, a woman's wig, when he went to greet his admiring public."

"Say more."

"According to this fella'— who should know, 'cause he put the wig on Old Bill—the Widow Cody, Louisa, and his sister were the culprits. They hated the owner of The Denver Post, Harry H. Tammen. They blamed him for much of Bill's financial bedevilment. Buffalo Bill's money woes put them all in dire straits.

Tammen offered Louisa a tidy sum if she would go along with burying Bill above Golden instead of at Cody, Wyoming. Financial desperation forced them to take Tammen's graft—he bought Ol' Bill's remains, ya' know, and determined to bury 'um on Lookout. The ladies took his money, but that don't mean they forgave him. They hated him even more and they wanted to show the world what a contemptuous S.O.B. he was. So, while this fellow was making Bill presentable, the widow and the sister placed a little bribe of their own and, in the dark of night, cut off what remained of Bill's luxurious hair, intending to keep it for themselves and mortify Tammen. Louisa had been weaving Bill's sheddings into this fall since their honeymoon. She felt that the public Buffalo Bill, not her William, had been callously bought and paid for by Tammen. It was her intent that Buffalo Bill—who had been reduced to an advertisement, a tourist attraction—would be remembered in perpetuity with a crew cut. Everyone would know that whatever it was Tammen was burying on Lookout was not The Great American Hero. It was a symbol of Tammen's skullduggery. Louisa and the sister would keep his beautiful hair as their remembrance of the man they both loved—William Frederick Cody, brother and husband."

"This is true?"

"According to this fellow, it is. Moreover, as I said, he should know. He worked for Olinger Mortuary and let the ladies in that last night before they put Colonel Cody on display. Well, Tammen and some of his henchmen showed up just as Louisa had bid her last farewell and she was about to sneak off with the hair. Of course, Tammen was suspicious, and when he got a look at Bill, all hell broke loose. The ladies had slipped the hair to the mortuary fella' who feigned surprise and shock equal to Tammen's. They knew Tammen would have them searched, but even a scoundrel as dark as Harry H. had to send for a woman to do the pat down. Seems the nearest woman they could find who Tammen trusted was the madam of the Navarre whore house across from the Brown Palace. It took a while before she showed up; business was brisk, all the folks in town to see Buffalo Bill and all. Meanwhile, in Tammen's panic, he sent the mortuary fella' back to the shop to get a wig and make Bill, as I said, presentable. The fella' hid the real hair, and found a lady's wig near enough to the same color as Bill's. Tammen was pacified, but warned the fella' that if any of this ever got out, he would disappear more mysteriously than Bill's hair. He gave him whatever cash he had in his pocket and told the fella' to take the next train out'a Denver. And that's how he escaped. He left Denver, hair in hand—so to speak—and never returned. He was petrified that Tammen would keep his threat. He tried to contact the ladies a couple of times, but it proved too dangerous. He kept the hair, and when financial straits forced him to do the wrong thing; he tried to look up Rudi who was the most famous Buffalo Bill impersonator at the time. Well, you can deduce the rest. If you don't believe it's Cody's hair, touch it."

"I cannot."

"Not to worry. It can't hurt ya. It don't bite. I mean, I was a little reluctant when I first tried it on, it being kinda macabre and all, but you get used to it."

"You don't understand. This is the wrong time and the wrong place, but soon I will hold it, soon it will hang in my lodge. Thus, will I disfigure the spirit of Cody. Thus, will he have to wander for all of eternity, misbegotten and disgraced."

"One of you fellas, would you like to touch it?" asked Billy. "I tell you what I'd like," said Raven. "I'd like that margarita that you offered. That's what I'd like."

"I'll drink to that," said Coyote. "I'm parched."

"You were about to ride to the tomb discovered in Red Rocks?" said Wolf Song. "You must go there, and you must take Pahaska's scalp with you. I cannot do this. The magic is too great. But, once inside the tomb, you must lay the relic on the body there, and the tomb must be sealed. You must not fail. Do you understand?"

"So, was this Wovoka character a friend of yours? What's he need with the hair? Honestly, old chum, I'm trying to figure out what's in this for me. I'm trying to understand, Willie, but as I said, this here hair piece cost me a pretty penny. What you got to barter with?"

Turtle answered, "Perhaps your soul, Whiteman. Weren't you concerned earlier about mortality and . . . what did you call redemption? Karma."

"Okay, you guys, I'm gonna need some more information. Who are you, really?" Billy perceived the anger in the eyes of the trio. They obviously didn't like the question. "Okay, let me think about it. Meanwhile, I'll fix those drinks. I keep the margarita makings in the back with the Mint Tulip mix." Billy put on the wig and pulled his sombrero tight on top. "It'll only be a second." He turned and left. On the way he mentally calculated what it would take for this strange tribe of hooligans to purchase or trade for his prized adornment. When he got back with the mix, Wolf Song and the others were gone.

"Just as well," he said to himself. "Grand Marnier is damn expensive . . . my own recipe, my ass. Get him. And I tell you, Mischa, my man, you old Jew, those three looked like heavy drinkers."

The hippie instinctively felt he needed to hide so he sought the dark shadows between the pines; however, considering his recent manifestations and the recollection that marijuana causes paranoia, he confirmed that he was indeed afraid of the dark. It was a quandary—the safety of hiding versus unseen incubi haunting his delusory sanctuary. He was concerned that the large unfriendly Black man might still be lurking in the woods. He could tell the big guy didn't like him and was obviously capable of doing someone great physical harm. He also feared the potential consequences—reservations for the padded room—if he experienced a reappearance of the brightly feathered and life-sized kewpie doll, Buffalo Bill, the ancient Indian at the bar, or the anthropomorphic critters accompanying the Indian. He wasn't entirely sure that the bus load of surly Indian braves wouldn't return for his scalp. Every time he worked up the courage to leave the forest and try to thumb a ride to the safety of the city, a swarm of police cars buzzed him back into hiding. Finally, a pair of headlights approached that weren't crowned with flashing cruiser beacons. He waited as long as he could, making sure it was a civilian vehicle (and that it was real) and he jumped from the woods and tried to wave down the buggy. His timing was off, probably the drugs, perhaps a hesitation induced by paranoia; regardless, he was a lot closer to the rumbling truck than he planned.

He sensed he could be crushed and almost soiled himself. Almost, "Thank god," he said out loud, "I spent so much time in the bathroom hoping that Buffalo Bill would not come back and that I heeded the advice of the feathered apparition and shook twice."

Stanley Manley, Junior, was jumpy as hell. He had been passed several times by a parade of cop cars speeding in both directions. An ambulance, which seemed to be heading for the country club, nearly forced him off the road. He felt he was inviting disaster by taking this battleship, his dad's Chevrolet Suburban, without permission, but it was Henry Humboldt, an authority of sorts, who instructed him to do it. The boat was hard to maneuver when he was sober, let alone after toking a ton of his own home grown. Hauling an unruly horse trailer occupied with "Pop's prized palomino," while stupefied was putting them both in peril and, he noticed, was causing him to speak in alliteration. If one of the cruising cop cars pulled him over, witnessed his verbal string of wanton wacky words, it would be obvious he was stoned. His father was nowhere to be found; so, the police probably would arrest him and throw him in the pokey for pilfering the horse. At least he didn't say, "pony." Just as he was regaining some confidence, a crazed hippie, hair and fringe flying, jumped from the forest, waving his arms in apparent fright, right in front of the Chevy. Junior swerved the titanic truck and nosed it into a shallow rain gulley on the other side of the road. He spit out his joint, bit his lip, bumped his head on the steering wheel, knocking off his cowboy hat. He panicked when he heard the horse stumble and bounce off the wall of the trailer.

"Sorry, man." The hippie suddenly appeared at the driver's window.

Junior pushed the button to open the glass. "Man, you could have been killed. We could have been killed. I hope you haven't killed my horse!" Smoke rolled out of the cab via the open window. It drifted past the hippie.

"Wow, man, I smell primo . . . you been imbibing, dude. Me, man, I'm trying to quit. You wouldn't believe where I've been and what I've seen today, man."

"My father is going to kill me," said Junior looking around the cab for the dropped roach, finding and settn' his hat, as if that would restore order, checking for blood, and fruitlessly searching for some abstract solution for his predicament. Finding no remedy, nor the joint, he repeated, "No question, he's just going to kill me."

"Sorry again, man," said the hippie. "I was just trying to flag down a ride. I didn't mean to fuck things up."

"Oh, they're pretty fucked all right. I'm killed." said Junior as he tried to restart the Suburban. It growled to life. He shifted it into reverse but knew right away that because the trailer was jackknifed at an odd angle, he was not going to be able to back out of the ravine. "I gotta check on the horse, man. Le'me out." He pushed on the door.

The hippie stumbled back. "Oh, fuck, man. There's a horse?"

"In the trailer, dumb ass. If he's hurt and I'm definitely killed, I'm killing you first."

"Here we go again, man. People wanting to kill me, that's why I was hiding in the woods."

Junior rushed past him and opened the back. The palomino was struggling to stand upright in the tilted trailer. He turned and looked back at Junior with an expression in his eyes that said: What the hell, human, are you trying to kill me. Stoned again, aren't ya'?

The trailer was a deluxe double-wide with room for two horses. When the palomino saw that the doors were open and he had an escape route, he struggled to turn himself around and exit the echoing tomb. His hooves kept slipping and sliding on the aluminum walls and slanted floor. Junior tried, but couldn't calm the horse to give him time to figure out how to extricate it without hurting the horse more. But, somehow the animal turned, bounced around the enclosure, struggled for balance, ricocheted and recoiled off the walls, rebounded and fell again, finally got his feet under him, and half crawled, half rebuffed his chest and forelegs out the trailer, up to his withers. He sat on his dock, butt and tail, with his rear fetlock and gaskin folded under him, taking a breather, apparently, feeling a little more secure with at least two feet on the ground. Again he looked at Junior and seemed to be saying: What the hell, kid; you were a big help. And by the way, this fucking saddle didn't make things any easier. Junior gently pulled forward on the reins and helped the palomino slide his back half out of the trailer. Junior immediately knelt and ran his hands up and down the gaskin, hocks, cannon and fetlocks, checking the horse's legs for injury. He was amazed but the palomino seemed unhurt.

"My father's still going to kill me," he muttered.

"Yeah, well if he doesn't," the horse seemed to be communicating, "Give me a chance and I'll stomp the living shit out of you."

Junior straightened the saddle and tightened the cinch. "I'm gonna walk Isham here down to Cody's Bar and Grill. Try to calm him a little. See if he's walking alright. Then I gotta come back here and separate the truck and trailer so's I can get some traction and pull the Suburban out of the ditch and tow out the trailer a' for re-hitching it. I'm gonna need some help if you ain't too stoned and don't feel the need to go off hippie-dancing in the woods again."

"Sorry," said the hippie. "I'm glad the horse seems okay. Whatever I can do. If you're going in the bar, you might want me to come along anyway, you might need some help in there, I think the fricken place is haunted."

"Has been for decades," said Junior. "Ghosts can't hurt you, but you best disappear before my pop shows up. He's gonna kill us both."

Junior led Isham, the palomino, down the road in a slow walk. The horse was still acting skittish. The hippie walked along side but kept his distance from the horse, which he swore to Junior was giving him the evil eye.

Junior tied Isham firmly to an old hitching post that served as a frontier-ambience-headboard for the handicap parking space. He held the door for the hippie and strolled inside. There was no one in sight. "Billy," he yelled into the smoky saloon, still funky and fumy despite being empty, "Billy, you here?"

"Hey, Junior," came Billy's voice from the dark doorway of the backroom. "How's it hanging?"

"The horse is outside, Billy, but I fucked up and ran Pop's Suburban and trailer into a gulley. My father is going to kill me."

"Anybody hurt?" Billy yelled from the dark. "How's the horse?"

"Nobody's hurt yet," said Stanley Manley, Junior, "but wait 'till my father finds out. You're gonna have to ride Isham to the park from here. The trucks stuck. It was this fucker's fault." Junior pointed at the hippie.

Still in full Buffalo Bill regalia, Wild Billy stepped from the dark to behind the bar. "I know him. Uses the pisser without buying anything, Refuses a drink when offered by a gentleman; breaking the code of The West. Looks like a snot nosed citified Indian pretender. I think he's a troublemaker, Junior. Probably, fucked up your dad's Chevy on purpose. Want me to relieve him of that long head of hair?" he joked. "Seems that I may be donating mine."

The hippie jumped from his stool, yelled, "I told you the place was haunted. That fricken ghost haunts the bathroom!" and ran in a panic out the door and into the night.

Billy watched the abrupt exit and said, "You know, Junior, that weirdo might be right. This has been the strangest night. That old Indian thief Wolf Song paid me a visit. He's got to be a hundred years old by now; he looked like a ghost. Maybe Cody's is haunted. Wonder if people will pay to see that kinda thing? He paused as if doing an accounting in his head, but then said, "You know, it could have been the wacky weed that hippie weirdo gave me. That stuff's dangerous, Junior, I don't know how you tolerate it. I'm sure it had me seeing things."

"It's an acquired taste, Billy. "I swear it sharpens your senses. Well, at least until a hippie jumps out of the trees in front of your truck while you're coming 'round the corner. Actually, I'm right. If I hadn't been high, I probably would'a hit the fool. Besides, you get used to it. I like it better than booze. I've got some right here," He searched his shirt pocket and brandished a new joint, "if you need a little boost before your midnight ride."

"Sharpens your senses you say. Well, maybe a little hit, that's what you call it, right? Maybe a little hit wouldn't hurt. You know, keep me alert, on my toes. Give me the keen eye while I peruse the rocks for Anthony Hands of the Bear."

"Tony Hardhat?" asked Junior. "I like Anthony. He's teaching me to play pool. Don't tell my dad; he'll kill me. What is happening with Anthony? Why are you in your parade outfit?"

"I'm trying to save Hardhat from a beating by the police. That and getting a little publicity for the Bar and Grill."

"Well, tell him Junior says 'Hello,' when you see him. Does this have something to do with all the cop cars on the mountain?"

"That and I heard that a busload of Indians attacked Mount Vernon Country Club."

"Really, Billy . . ." He paused and thought about the news. "Are you sure you're not already a little blitzed? Visits from ancient Indians, modern Indians attacking country clubs . . . next thing you'll be telling me is that Anthony has gone renegade and scalped old Henry Humboldt."

"That's about the gist of it, Junior."

"You mean the jest of it, Billy. This is all too weird." He took another toke of the joint and passed it to Wild Bill. "I better call my dad and face the music. He's gonna kill me."

"I really appreciate you doing this. Maybe we can get some good publicity for the ranch. You know, stud fees for the stallion and all."

"Oh," said Junior, "ever since the propane accident, we don't worry much about that sort of thing any longer, Billy. But thanks, anyway."

"Well, I better get going. They'll be waiting for me at Red Rocks. Help yourself to another drink, Junior, but I don't think I'd be drunk when your pop gets here. He's likely to be in a foul mood. And I don't think I'd let him know you been smoking hemp. That's likely to set him off worse than putting the trailer in the gully.

"I'll check back with you later, Junior. See if I can help smooth things over with your dad. Do me a favor while you're here waiting. Let me know if you see anyone hanging around."

"Like who?"

"Like that old Indian who used to camp here. Maybe you were too young. Do you remember Willie Wolf Song?"

"I remember stories about him, but I thought he was dead."

"Me too, but there seems to be life in the old fart still." He looked around the bar, searching in the dark corners, sniffing the air for the aroma of cashews. "Well, I'm out'a here, Junior."

"I'll walk out with you. Make sure the horse is okay." As they exited the bar, Junior flicked the roach into the air over the paved parking lot, figuring that was safe. Out of nowhere, a large crow swooped by and snatched, midair, the marijuana butt in his bill, gliding silently into the trees, leaving a contrail. Junior looked to see if Billy had witnessed the avian snatch-and-grab. Apparently, he had not. Billy was busy primping himself. Junior decided to let it go, doubting Wild Billy would believe him anyway.

Billy checked his reflection in the mirror of the truck. His buckskins looked tailored. The beadwork and his white hair sparkled in the light, and his showman Stetson tilted perfectly to one side. The red scarf shown like a badge of courage as it caught the breeze in a choreographed tribute to heroic flamboyance. He was Buffalo Bill.

The silver on the saddle mirrored the splendiferousness of the equestrian outfit. The palomino pawed the ground in anticipation. The auteur strutted to the left side of the steed.

"Be careful, Billy," said Junior, "He's still a little shell-shocked."

"Isham and I are old friends," Bill bragged as he mounted the horse, which Stanley Manley, Senior, named in honor of one of Buffalo Bill's favorite equines. "We've been through many a parade together, eh boy," he said as he firmly patted the horse on its neck. Isham jumped, kicked the air with his rear legs, and almost bounced Billy out of the saddle. Wild Bill hung on to the saddle horn with surprising strength. "I see what you mean, Junior."

The horse rearing startled Billy more than he wanted to admit. He was concerned that Isham seemed rattled. He tried to sooth his mount by bringing its attention to several routine elements.

"What's the problem, old sport?" he whispered in the horse's ear. "You like people. You're going to be surrounded by an admiring audience. Remember how they idolize you? You and Ol' Buffalo Billy. You know me. I'm a familiar weight. Are you trying to tell me I've put on a few pounds? You're a strong boy; you can take it." He risked patting the horse on its neck again. He held his hand and sleeve near the horse's nose, hoping it was smelling the redundant odor of the ancient buckskins. He exhaled, blowing his breath toward the snout, assuming that the enhanced, tainted actually, liquor-aroma of the rider would bring back nights of mutual frivolity. He wanted the animal to remember the good times, the parades, the parties before the unfortunate propane explosion.

The horse reared again. Billy interpreted the action as a spontaneous gesture of remembrance. "I know, old friend. That must have been a horrible experience. I know since then you ain't been doing much more than eating hay and dropping prairie pie. I'm sorry, Old Paint, that it's been a while since you laid pipe."

Billy tugged on the reins, testing for control and communication. Isham looked back at his rider. Billy saw a reacquainted synapse fire in the horse's expression, a neurological celebration of sorts. He felt a familiar quiver under the saddle, and assessed a reemergence of the old stallion's bravado.

Billy again raised his sombrero in a salute, "That's more like it, Isham. Let's go give these yokels a show." Billy spurred his steed toward the dark valley, his mighty palomino prancing, forelegs lifting high in an Andalusian allemande.

Just as Junior yelled, "You still got it, Wild Billy!" a raven buzzed past his ear and cawed next to Isham, who took off in a spooked sprint, the panicked sound of his hooves fading down the highway. Billy was right, thought Junior, this has been a weird night. He swore he saw jet smoke trailing that obnoxious bird.

Chapter Thirty-nine

Red Rocks Rendezvous

Summer, 1964

Buffalo Bill Cody's Bar Grill Trading Post and Texaco Station was deserted at last—an invitation for Turtle and his mischief-makers to host their promised margarita party.

"I'm buying," said Turtle. "My treat."

"You're buying; that's a howl," said Coyote. "We've never paid for drinks here."

"OK, if you want to split hairs," answered Turtle, "but we'll use my recipe. Poor Wild Billy is too cheap to use Grand Marnier and he still can't figure out where all his tequila has gone."

"Ghosts," said Raven. "Wild Billy now has a higher appreciation for the phantasmal world thanks to us and his visit from old Willie Wolf Song.

"Frozen or on the rocks?" asked Turtle.

"On the rocks seems appropriate," answered Raven. "We have a rendezvous on 'The Rocks' for some continued mayhem, eh ya."

"Actually," said Turtle, "I have a different plan. If you don't mind relaxing and having a couple of rounds, I thought we'd watch the next chapter on television."

"I thought Billy said the TV was on the fritz."

"For Wild Billy it is, but I'm Turtle." He reached up and turned on the set above the bar.

"Color!" said Raven. "When did Billy get color?"

"He didn't," answered Turtle.

The credits came on first.

The Lone Rider:
A Situation Comedy for Television

Episode 10: Rendezvous At Red Rocks

A Wolf Song/Gaia Production

Turtle, Raven, and Coyote: Co-Producers

Assistant Directors: R. Crow and C. Lupine

Directed by T. Gyan'-wish

"Nice touch," said Coyote. "How 'bout one of those famous margaritas?"

"I notice you got top billing," said Raven.

"I'm making the drinks. That, if nothing else, deserves recognition."

"OK, OK, don't go all hard case on me. And don't forget the salt."

"I'll drink to that," said Coyote. "Love salt."

"What's a margarita without salt?" said Raven.

"So?" asked Coyote, "who did you get to play me in the sitcom?"

"Actually," answered Turtle, "we all play ourselves, but for the rest of the characters I borrowed a cast from our old friend Stanley Kramer."

"That's mad," said Raven. "Just mad, mad."

"And mad" added Coyote.

"You got it," said Turtle. "So here's how I see the cast, taking into consideration Kramer's stable. Spencer Tracy goes from stoic bad cop to lawyer hero in our production. We use the magic of makeup to make him look younger; he plays Troy Rivers."

"No offense, Turtle," said Raven, "but as co-producer, that seems a bit of a stretch. Don't we have anyone younger?"

"We need the strong silent type for Rivers," said Turtle, "the one sane character in a mad world, trying to make sense of an insane dilemma. Who are we going to use: Buster Keaton? He's in the original cast, but . . . Jack Benny? Talk about old. Milton Berle? You see my problem?"

OK, OK, don't pull into your shell. I'm just asking. Who else? Wasn't Phil Silvers in Kramer's movie? He is one of my favorite rascals."

"Right you are," said Turtle. "He's bald; so, I figured he'd make an appropriately manic Henry Humboldt, Superintendent in Charge of the Red Rocks Rangers."

"I'll drink to that," said Coyote, more interested in another margarita than the casting process.

"Go on," said Raven.

"Now remember the limitations I'm working under here, but I do have a role for Milton Berle."

"Yes, what is it; who is he?"

"I see him in a quick cameo spot as John Lennon."

"I like it," said Raven. "Give him a wig, some pointy boots, a guitar. Berle is a natural ham; Lennon loves being the center of attention; got a bit of the ol' *jambon* himself. It could work. And the other Beatles?"

"Again, this is just a short cameo, for continuity and back-story so we can take some liberties. Buster Keaton plays George—quiet, reserved contemplative. Peter Faulk plays Paul—innate charm, crooked smile, innocent looking but shifty at heart. Ringo is played by Jimmy Durante—it's the nose thing and good humor. What do you think?"

"I think it's going to take a hell of a lot of that makeup magic," said Coyote. "Pass the salt."

"It's a quick scene; nobody will notice. Anyway, the main characters are the important issue. I've planned to use Jim Backus as the governor, Mickey Rooney as the hippy, Buddy Hackett as Veloy, and Eddie 'Rochester' Anderson as Talks Softly. It'll take some coaching, but I think he can pull it off. We just have to get him to whisper a lot. I thought about doing something extremely experimental. How about having Rochester play both of the brothers: Talks Softly and Red Stick? Again, it would take some coaching, clever makeup and some radical camera angles and editing tricks."

"Tricks," said Coyote, "isn't that our business?"

"I'll drink to that," quoted Turtle.

"I can live with it so far, Turtle," said Raven. "It's good for some laughs, but who do you have in mind for Wild Billy? Hurry, the show is about to start?"

"Don't you think Sid Caesar will look good in long hair, beard, and buckskins? I'll bet he has always wanted to play Buffalo Bill."

"I like Sid Caesar," said Coyote. "I like that he appears to be right on the edge of reality and psychosis, even when he isn't acting. What about Ho Ho Horace Green? He's a big guy."

"Big guys are hard to find, but I think Dick Shawn can do it, if, and this is a big if, we pull him back a little. Talk about over the top."

"You've left out one of the most important characters," said Raven. "Who plays the Denver Police Chief, Alan Sweet, aka Pickles?"

"That's my pièce de résistance," bragged Turtle. "There is only one cast member from the Kramer stable who has the mean personality, who is belligerent, combative, quarrelsome, and bellicose enough for the role. Pugnacious Chief Sweet is played by Ethel Merman."

"There's no business like show business," said Coyote.

"And his over-eager ward Carson is acted by the cute little blonde Dorothy Provine. They're a team, old Ethel and young Dorothy, mother and daughter, and now master and apprentice. I'd hate to break them up. Brilliant, if I must say so myself."

"Never a lack of confidence, Turtle, old man," said Raven. "I'll save comment for later. Let's watch."

An announcer's voice, sounding a lot like Tuttle, began the program: *In the previous episode, the bus load of Indians departed Mount Vernon Country Club after wreaking vengeance and leaving the president-elect a broken man. They were racing to Red Rocks Amphitheater, but not far behind, the police are caravanning back to Red Rocks as well. Wild Billy—costumed as Buffalo Bill—was riding a borrowed, but skittish, palomino to the park in order to help the police capture his friend, Anthony Hands of the Bear. The haunted hippy ran off into the woods (with Mickey Rooney hamming it the whole way); Talks Softly, dressed in his finery, and his brother raced toward Red Rocks just ahead of the bus and the police parade, driven by their determination to aid the renegade. We see Raven flying above while Coyote races alongside the bedlam.*

"Amusing," said Raven.

"Shh," barked Coyote. "I'm watching."

Turtle narrates, "As you can see, the opening scene is a brief flashback . . ."

Raven, in the guise of a dark menacing fowl, buzzes the palomino. The horse spooks and stampedes, out of control, down the mountain slope.

"I love this next shot," says Raven. "It's my aerobatic POV." The camera briefly follows the horse and panicked rider slaloming between the trees, but then pans into an aerial view high above the forest and the mountain road.

"Nice work, Raven," said Coyote. "I love the bird's eye view."

"Just good direction," said Raven. Giving a nod to Turtle.

From the high point of view, the headlights of the various vehicles: the Volkswagen convertible, the long city bus, the line of police cars, and Henry Humboldt's Dodge *bringing up the rear*, each separated by ample dark road, meander down the forested hill in a serpentine dance.

"Looks to be a plumbed serpent," uttered Raven, "with the big feathers at the head and the rattler on the tail. You're not interjecting symbolism are you, Turtle?"

"This is TV, Raven, ya' old demigod," answered Turtle. That would be too high-hat. Wouldn't it?" He grinned. "Now watch."

The long traffic snake, banded by dark shadows and patterns from headlights, was intersected by a fast moving and tiny white spot—the palomino. It cut across the ribbons of road from cluster to cluster of trees. At a dimly lit intersection the two trailing police cars leave the caravan; turn right and head up Mt. Vernon Canyon. The announcer explains: *They're covering the back roads behind Morrison Mountain and Lookout in case Anthony Hands of the Bear tries to sneak out the backside of the park. If he is foolish enough to try to escape in that direction, they'll be waiting. Sweet and Carson continue toward Red Rocks.*

Repeating Raven's aerobatic athleticism, the scene cuts to a steep descending pan, swooping from the bird's eye view to the windshield of Sweet's black-and-white, showing both cops' intense looks of determination in the exaggerated and melodramatic light of the car's dash.

Interior of police car fills the screen. Close-up on Sweet.

"Faster, Carson," ordered Ethel Merman in character.

Turtle noted, "We had to let-in Sweet's uniform a bit for the queen of showbiz, but, as it turns out, we needed very little makeup."

"I can't, Chief," said Dorothy Provine. "There is a bus in front of us and I can't pass here."

"She's cute," said Coyote, "even with the fake moustache."

"A bus! What's a bus doing up here? What kind of bus?" barked Sweet.

"Well, sir, I'll be dog'on if it doesn't look like a city bus."

"Now what in the hell would a city bus be doing on the Lariat Loop?"

"Maybe we should investigate it, sir."

"You're damn right we'll investigate, Carson. Hit the siren."

There is a cut to the interior of the bus. A youthful Spencer Tracy checks out the rearview mirror. The pacing is quick; it cuts to the mirror; shows the flashing lights; then cuts back to Rivers in close-up. He wears a panicked expression, "Jeepers, boys, it's the cops. Hide."

" 'Jeepers,' " asks Raven. "Who wrote the dialog?"

"You know actors," said Turtle. "They are always ignoring the script and adlibbing."

Sweet and Carson exit the car; approach the bus.

Inside the bus, the braves are ducking behind seats, jumping onto luggage racks and covering each other with anything handy, and a handful of Indians volley out through the side windows opposite "the cops."

Carson is tapping on the door with the muzzle of his drawn revolver. Sweet stands in support.

"Open up!" ordered Carson.

"She is just smoking cute," interrupted Coyote. "I'd love to muzzle her . . . him . . . ah, her."

"It's nuzzle, you hound dog," said Turtle.

"Muzzle, nuzzle, potato, potaato. You do what you want, I'll do what I know best," answered Coyote.

"Guys," said Raven, "do you mind."

The bus door opens. POV over Carson's shoulder. Rivers pulls the stolen cap low over his forehead and stares straight ahead.

Carson enters bus, Sweet stands in doorway.

"What's going on here?" Carson demands. He nudges the driver with his gun.

The scene cuts to the dark side of the bus: Indians are sneaking below the driver's window; Carson and Rivers are visible through the lit window above.

"What are you doing in this bus?" repeats Carson. He peruses the outfit of the driver. In a close-up, Carson's expression changes from confusion to disgust at the driver being half-naked. "Where is the regular driver? What have you done with the city driver?" Carson turns toward Sweet but says to the driver, "Stay put, bub."

Sweet looks both forward and backward along the bus. Sees nothing.

Carson also looks down the aisle of the bus, which from his POV is empty except for two more Indians who appear bent over and asleep.

In a slowly animated dolly shot down the aisle, the camera finally settles beside the Indians. In a dramatic low shot the trio can see that the Indians are pulling their tomahawks from under the bus seat. The braves, on screen, sneak co-conspirator looks at each other.

The three deities sneak confirming peeks, anticipating the ambush. "I purposefully slowed the pace of the dolly," said Turtle, "and shot it from the floor to enhance the suspense. Hitchcock, eat your heart out."

Carson looks confused; scratches his temple with the barrel of his revolver. He steps backwards onto the entry stairs of the bus, ever mindful of the driver, peering at the suspected perpetrator rather than watching his backward footfalls.

Sweet stands below his protégé.

"Chief Sweet," says Carson. "Chief, there is no one in the bus except for some Indian guy with the driver's cap pulled suspiciously low on his head and a couple of elderly . . . ."

As Carson turns to face his superior, to his shock he finds Chief Sweet surrounded and muffled by a war party of Indians.

"Now," said Turtle, "check out the fast pace of this next dolly down the isle of the bus from the POV of the two Indians who were playing possum. It's contrast, slow versus fast; it's the little details that take the episode from entertainment to art."

"Possum," says Coyote, ignoring Turtle's self-aggrandizing. "Many times I've tried to rouse and get rowdy with the old grey rodent, but he's either hissing his displeasure or rolling onto his back with those knurly, tiny legs pointing toward the sky, never to move. What a bore."

"Quiet," barked Turtle, "You're too old for those puppy shenanigans. Watch the show."

From inside the bus, the camera sprints with a fast-follow, trolley shot as the pair of "possums" race down the aisle and capture Carson.

Sound track: wild war hoops of several rampageous Indians.

The screen goes into a fade out; there is a brief dark screen. As the image fades in, several Indians are pushing the black-and-white off road. The car lingers at the edge and with an extra push, plods into the darkness, screaming defiance with a mechanical profanity.

Carson's confused and embarrassed face fills the screen, "I don't know how it could have happened, Chief. I thought I had things under control. I had my revolver pointed right at the heathen."

"Don't worry about it, son," answered Sweet. "Those damn savages can hide anywhere."

"That's much too much uproarious laughter on the sound track," says Raven. "You're trying to manipulate the audience, Turtle."

"That's an odd criticism, considering it's coming from you, Raven," said Turtle. "It's kind of the pot calling the kettle . . ."

"Now, now, you two," interrupted Coyote. "Artistic differences aside; frankly, I kinda liked the destruction and don't mind manipulating situations for a good laugh. Speaking of laughs," he pointed at the television, "I directed this next scene. After all, Turtle, you said in the beginning that we were co-producers and fellow directors. I think you'll be amused about what I've done to poor Carson and Sweet?"

The camera pulls back from the walk-the-plank execution of the police car and shows Sweet and Carson in their underwear. Carson's outfit is sexy and tight. Sweet's undergarments are huge, grandma type bloomers. Sweet stumbles as he pulls up his girdle in a feeble attempt to regain composure.

The laugh track echoes with hysterical laughter, cow-calls, hoops and whistles.

"Where did this idea of taking the victim's clothes come from?" asked Turtle. "I've been inducing folly with this bunch for some time now, and I never suggested stripping the quarry."

"They've got to take something," answered Raven. "Fans would never tolerate some savage scalping Ethel Merman."

"Don't forget, my friends, that's not Ethel, that's Chief Sweet. Besides, stripping them slows down the enemy," said Coyote. "I'd like to slow down Officer Carson."

"Think of the humiliation," said Raven. "Seems appropriate to me. I guess it just another example of *artistic differences*, eh ya, Turtle"

"I'll drink to that," said Coyote.

"I suppose there's some humor in it," said Turtle.

"It's especially funny when it's a uniform," said Raven. "Sort of puts the pompous in their place."

"Humbling," said Coyote.

"Pay attention, pilots," said Raven. "I'm inserting another acrobatic aerial view here."

The point of view is above the bus and the humiliated cops; a car is speeding around a dark curve toward Sweet and Carson.

The view cuts to the interior of the speeding car. Three Red Rocks Rangers sit inside. They are played by: Terry Thomas, Jonathan Winters, and Arnold Stang is driving.

From the POV of the Rangers, the shot is over their shoulders through the windshield; lights illuminate the road ahead, but only within a small semicircle of visibility and assumed safety. Otherwise, the mountain darkness ominously encroaches on everything else.

Suddenly, the semi-circle of light is invaded by two over exposed, semi-nude pedestrians.

Inside the car, Arnold Stang screams.

Cut to a low shot of his foot hitting the brakes.

As did Sweet's cop car squeal in protest as it lumbered over the steep shoulder, so does the Ranger's car wail as it screeches to a halt. All three occupants are thrown forward. Winters bumps his head on the dash. Thomas is thrown from the backseat in between the other two. All three curse.

Bright lights fill the screen. Sweet and Carson are temporarily lost in the glare.

Soundtrack: screams and gasps.

Inside the car, the three Rangers exchange confused looks. Winters rubs a bump on his head; Thomas struggles to return to the back seat; adlibs exasperation: "What the bloody hell?"

Stang exits the driver's side. He appears to be pointing a gun at the cowering couple in the lights. The audience, however, can see that he is only mimicking a gun with his clinched hands and extended fingers.

Laugh track: restrained laughter and subtle prophetic comments.

Stang: "All right you two perverts, pull over, I mean: Don't move. Stay where you are. Hands on your head."

Winters exits shotgun side of car. "George, you keep 'um covered. I'll frisk 'um."

Dorothy Provine, aka Officer Carson, reacts in anticipated aversion at the idea of being "frisked."

Laugh track: loud laughter, wolf whistles.

Head shot of Sweet: "Carson, "I'll get those red devils. I don't know when, I don't know how, but I'll get them. Do you hear me, Carson, I'll get them."

Duplicate head shot of Carson. He nods, shrugs shoulders, displays surrender and loops his hands onto his head.

Repeat the head shot of Sweet. As he puts his hands on his head, he says, "I'd rather swallow my tongue than let these bozo Rangers see me like this."

Laugh track: loud guffaws.

"I guess you're right, Raven," commented Turtle, "about taking the uniforms. It's the humiliation."

Back on screen, Jonathan Winters yodels, "Chief Sweet, is that you?"

"You're damn right it's me."

"Sorry, sir, but I didn't recognize you without your badge."

Laugh track: starts loud; diminishes as screen fades to black.

"You're not going to a commercial are you," chastises Raven.

"No, no," says Turtle. "I just figured we needed a cocktail break. Pouring from a processor pitcher, Turtle refreshed his cohorts' margaritas. "Well?" he asks.

"The margaritas are good," said Coyote.

"Raven?" said Turtle.

"I agree; the margaritas are good."

"You two know that's not what I'm asking. What about the sitcom?"

"When am I on screen?" asked Coyote.

"Coyote, you old camera hound, you're on screen soon," said Turtle.

Coyote continued, "As I understand storytelling, there has to be a minimum of believability for the audience to relate. It worked for me, but for a general audience, do you think stripping Sweet and Carson was believable? Not that I mind seeing Carson in her delicates, as I've said, she's a foxy little thing."

"Speaking of believability, haven't you gotten passed seeing Carson as a vixen and accepted her acting as an over enthusiastic rookie policeman?"

585

"Of course I have, but we're in Margaritaville right now; so, it's easy to fall back to carnal canine thinking. Besides, Turtle, I like what's happening. A little risqué can't hurt. Don't ruin it for me."

"Sorry, you're right," said Turtle. "I've never been comfortable in critique. I've always been a little sensitive to criticism. You'd think after all these centuries . . ."

"A little sensitive," screeched Raven. "Someone says something negative and you get steamed and cause earthquakes. But that's not the point. You asked Coyote if disrobing the enemies of the Indians was believable or not. Of course, it is. The Indians have to humiliate their adversaries somehow. It wasn't that long ago they would have mutilated their victim to make sure the vanquished opponent walked the afterlife in disgrace. A precedent was set with the cab driver and the bus driver. A pattern has been established; hopefully, for a comedic payoff later. Mortifying a few bad guys, instead of cutting off their hands and feet or gouging out their eyes with burning sticks seems almost merciful and somewhat restrained to me."

"Ahh, no offense, Turtle," said Coyote, "and none to you, Raven, but restraint doesn't seem to be your forte in these shenanigans; nor should it be. Me . . . I like classic screwball. Give me tacky excess every time. You're talking to an old dog who watches cartoons, for crying out loud. I mean consider the cast of characters, both casts, the sitcom and the characters they represent. Restraint?—boring. If my vote counts, I say let's play. I'm a quintessential trickster after all."

"Thanks, Coyote," said Turtle. "Someday soon the entertainment business will come to their senses and they will base a classic cartoon character on you, and," he gives an aside to Raven, "wily as you are, you'll probably take it as a compliment."

"Quiet, you two," said Raven. "The show's starting again."

The opening shot is of Ethel Merman, as Chief Sweet, still in her underwear, addressing the troops. "Men, there is the need for some serious police work afoot, here and now. It could be dangerous, but danger is our middle name; right, Rangers?"

Winters, Thomas, and Stang look confused and unconvinced.

Dorothy Provine, playing Carson; however, looks inspired.

"Don't say it, Coyote," interjected Raven. "We know she's cute."

"There is a bus full of red vermin just down that road," says Sweet. "They are thieves, hooligans, and they assaulted local citizens and your fellow officers. Besides that, they have a perverted sense of humor."

Carson modestly covers her bust.

"They must pay for the indignity thrust upon the uniform of the Denver Police Department," continued Sweet, "and the Denver Transit System. Let's go show them what policemen are made of. Driver, give me your gun."

"Sir?" Stang looks toward the others for support.

"Give me your revolver, boy. Your sidearm, officer. You drive; I'll shoot."

"I don't have a gun, sir."

"No gun?" Sweet's frustration grows. "What the hell did you have me covered with back there when you apprehended us?"

Stang holds up two fingers mimicking a gun profile; Winters and Thomas sidestep away from him and coward their way out of the video frame.

"And I didn't run," mumbles Sweet, "for fear of being shot."

Sweet and the others pile into the car. Sweet bullies Winters out of the shotgun seat.

There is a low shot of the rear tires spinning and kicking up gravel and dust as the driver punches the accelerator.

Over the trunk of the car, the point of view rises into an aerial shot. At the apex, it cuts to a close up of Raven soaring above mountain road in a wide shot.

"Nice," said Raven.

Raven, still flying above the meandering road focuses on the Ranger car racing downhill and from his high vantage point, he also spies the bus snaking slowly a half-mile ahead.

When the Ranger car, passengers bouncing back and forth, speeds around a mountain curve and catches up to the bus, Sweet tells the driver to hit the lights and the siren.

Raven shares his aerial point of view and begins a dive; in a fluid sweep, descending and smoothly flying behind the flashing lights. The bus is visible via a long shot through the lights.

"Alright, boys," says Sweet in a close-up, "this is it. I've got a plan. Since we have no guns and these crazed Indians will probably not stop anyway, I say let's pass 'um. We'll get a couple of miles ahead and on a sharp and dark curve we can set up a surprise road block. They won't see the car until it's too late. The Indians will have to slam on their brakes to avoid a collision. In the panic stop, we'll rush the bus and take control. What do you say? Is it a ten-four? Are you with me?" He looks around for confirmation. "What say you, soldiers; we board the bus and arrest the heathens, bare-handed and heroic?"

Winters and Thomas look at each other, exhibit doubt and concern; shrug shoulders.

"We're with you, Chief," chirps Carson."

"Great, boys." Sweet looks demonic. "Let's go get 'um. Driver, pass 'um now. Go for it, son."

The car screams past the bus; dust and gravel, hectic reflections of flashing lights, and a bouncing camera enhance the pandemonium of the maneuver.

In a reaction shot of Rivers through the bus driver's window, it's evident that he can't believe what he is seeing.

The occupants of the Ranger's car are cheering and bouncing as they pass the bus: Winters and Thomas yell: "Go, Arnold; go, Arnold; go, Arnold!"

"Nice going, son," says Sweet. "Now let's get far enough ahead of 'um to set the trap."

"That's a ten-four, Chief."

Raven's point of view returns. The camera pans from the side window to the rear of the car and then smoothly rises to an aerial shot of the curvy road with the car speeding ahead and the bus slowly following.

"Nice aerials, Raven," said Coyote as he set down his drink. "Well, I need to get primed for my entrance." He shook his whole body as if dispelling rain.

"Thanks," said Raven. "But I've got another good pan coming."

In the next scene, the Ranger car is stopped and parked in the middle of the road in the shadow of a dark curve. From behind the car, the Rangers and police watch up hill. Sweet speaks: "Driver,

stay behind the car, let them see you. The rest of us will hide in the trees. When the bus stops, they'll be focusing on you. You can do some of that professional pantomiming with your hands faking a gun (You clever little SOB, you) and that's when we'll jump 'um."
Sweet and others disappear into woods.

Enter Coyote.

The driver POV pans from watching the others to looking down next to his leg. Coyote is nonchalantly sitting at his feet. He alternates looking at Coyote and into the woods to see if the others have noticed his new companion: "Hey. You guys . . . did someone bring their dog?"

The video frame is slowly illuminated by the glow of the approaching bus lights.

Stang hasn't as yet noticed the approach of the bus; he is concentrating on the wild looking dog hunched but grinning up at him. Suddenly, the animal speaks, "This should be good."

Stang panics, as only Arnold Stang can panic. Well, maybe Jack Lemmon.

Coyote chuckles to himself and watches the driver run into the nearby trees. Coyote calmly saunters over to the opposite side of the road and sits to watch the impending action.

"Now where the hell is the driver going," asks Sweet rhetorically. "We need him behind the car or the Indians will think it's abandoned." He and the trees he is hiding among are silhouetted by the approaching bus lights.

Cut: return to an aerial shot. The bus can be seen approaching the dark corner and the car very slowly. However, from this high vantage point the audience also notices two sheriffs' cars with lights flashing, and sirens screaming, speeding into the video frame on the opposite side from the bus. The sheriffs' cars are charging uphill toward the darkened parked car.

The point of view changes in a fast diving pan from the aerial view to a close-up of the leading sheriffs' car. The passengers can be seen through the windows. They are facing the opposite direction within the video frame as were the Rangers and the Indians—uphill versus downhill; how's that for contrast?

Rivers facing right to left in the video frame, can see the flashing lights and hear the siren of the cars speeding up the hill. He cautiously proceeds downhill and around the curve.

Sweet, still hiding in the trees, finally notices the sheriffs' cars speeding uphill toward the Ranger's road block. He bolts into the road, waving arms, trying to flag down the sheriffs. As he runs toward the dark and parked Ranger's car, he is suddenly caught in the headlights of the zooming sheriffs' car.

At this tense moment, Coyote runs across road between the sheriffs' cars and a panicked Chief Sweet. Laughing and pleased with his own well-timed and athletic contribution to mayhem, Coyote disappears into the darkness on the opposite side of the road.

The screen image cuts to the POV of the driver of the lead sheriffs' car. It's obvious that he focused on the coyote running in front of car. At the last minute he looks up and sees a half-naked figure thrust into the headlights. The ghostly figure dives for the side of the road and out of the video frame.

The first Sheriffs' car smashes into the improperly parked Rangers' car; the second sheriffs' car rear-ends the first.

Sound track: horrendous crash noises.

Laugh track: gasps and moans intermingled among dubious laughs.

Rivers witnesses the crash through the bus windscreen. He immediately sees Sweet, Carson (in their skivvies) and the Rangers running about hysterically. A couple of the sheriffs struggle from the wreckage. "Now there is something you don't see every day," he mutters.

As the camera pans along the full length of the exterior of the bus, each of the Indians, in line, in turn, does a take reacting to the ghastly horror and ghoulish humor of the wreck below their windows.

There is a cut back to the POV of Coyote, sitting on the shoulder of the road opposite the wreck. He is watching the bus, almost in slow motion, definitely in nightmarish, apocalyptic lighting, as it moseys past the tangled cars, unnoticed in the pandemonium by the police. It continues downhill. Rivers looks outside the window as the bus gains speed. He sees Coyote racing along the shoulder of the road and Raven flying just above him. "I take it back," he says to himself. "That is something you don't see every day."

Fade out; screen goes dark.

"Well, that was exciting," said Coyote.

"I look good on camera," said Raven. "Love the aerials and swooping pans."

"Ready for another round of drinks?" asked Turtle.

"Does a coyote love it doggy-style?"

"Easy, Moon Dog, this is television. Ricky and Lucy, Rob and Laura still sleep in twin beds. I don't think Ozzie and Harriet even have a bedroom."

"C'mon, Turtle," said Coyote. "It's time to come out of your shell. All this violence and a little loving makes you nervous?"

"Speaking of violence" asked Raven, " as victims of most of the mayhem, I take it that Sweet and his boys are temporarily out of action?"

"We can watch or I can recap what comes next," said Turtle.

"I'm all for a summary," said Coyote, "that way I can concentrate on my drinking. Do you suppose Billy has any bar snacks?"

It was the irony that the various police forces were knocking themselves out of the game that amused Turtle and his trickster cohorts the most. They gave each other congratulatory toasts celebrating their subterfuge. Raven complimented Coyote on his waggishness and in return was congratulated on his stealthy aerobatics. Both praised Turtle's directory prowess. Once they had fresh drinks, Turtle confessed that there was still some theatric irony to be had.

"Seriously?" asked Coyote.

"I can't believe that you seriously asked Turtle if any of this episode was serious," countered Raven. "Wasn't it you who bragged his love of slapstick?"

"Hey, Crow! I'm just saying . . ."

"Easy, gents," said Turtle. "I know it's been a long ride but we need closure here."

"So," asked Coyote. "What additional ironic burlesque have you conjured?"

"I'll keep it short," said Turtle.

"I'll drink to that," said Coyote.

"Obviously, Troy Rivers and the Mount Vernon marauders made it to Red Rocks before Sweet and Carson and the rattled Rangers."

"And the sheriffs," said Raven. "By the way, I'm sure Sweet chastised the sheriffs and asked why they were rushing up Lariat in the first place."

"Well," said Turtle, "the irony of which I spoke is that they were responding to an emergency call from Mount Vernon Country Club that the club was being attacked by Indians. Only we and the audience were privy to the fact that it was the very Indians in the stolen city bus who also invaded Mount Vernon.

"Now that's funny," said Coyote.

"It gets better," said Turtle.

"Tell me."

"Sweet and the others thought they might apprehend the Indians after all when, of all the people serendipitously passing by the wreck, Henry Humboldt came upon the scene. Sweet again pulled rank, despite being out of uniform, and commandeered Henry's Dodge. He added insult to injury by criticizing Humboldt as always being the last to the party. 'However, Henry, in this case, better late than never . . . move over, I'm driving.'

"The covey of cops piled into the truck. There was no room for both Henry and his inflated butt pillow to sit comfortably. Sweet suggested that they strap him to the roof. Henry's little girly screams could serve as a siren. They actually considered it. Instead they laid him on the extended tailgate. Pain and humiliation curled him a fetal position reminicient and equally as medullary as Leonardo's famous fetus drawing. Winters and Thomas, two of the Rangers, were curled behind the last seat, like Leonardo's fetus drawing, that is: right side up and curled into an uncomfortable cannon ball, and assigned as Henry's lifeline—each holding a different part of their superintendent so as to keep him on and in the truck.

"Henry cautioned, 'Watch where you're grabbing, Ranger. I'm still damn tender back there.'

"Although no one said so, but everyone in the truck interpreted the grin on Chief Sweet's face as vindictive pleasure as he apparently and purposefully hit every pothole and bump on the road.

"Henry wailed with each jolt. 'Tighter, Rangers. Hold me tighter! Not there, Ranger . . . Oh. God, not there. Sweeeeeeet, for the love of god, pleeeeeeeease!'

"Just as Sweet had the distant taillights of the bus in view," continued Turtle, "and thought he might catch them, the last of my choreographed ironies took place. Out of the forest shot an apparition of doom: our white-haired horseman of the apocalypse. His mount panicked and spurred on by the lusty attack of a large black demon of a bird."

"Nice work, Raven. Once again you're given a central role," said Coyote, "and fly to the occasion."

"It's what I do," said Raven. "It's why I'm in the business and love it so. When one loves what they do, one can only excel." He bows—a deep, theatrical, full sweeping genuflect.

"Easy," said Turtle, "If your birdbrain remains the same while your head swells with conceit, your noggin will clatter like a baby's rattle. But Coyote is right, you've done some fancy flying for this farce. Well done."

"Hey," said Coyote. "What about my stunt. I was, after all, risking life and limb. Well, limb, well . . . OK, I can't be hurt, but Sweet didn't know that."

"Right again, Old Dog. As you know, Wild Billy's and Asham's cross from the woods, stage left, and exit through the pines, stage right, distracted Sweet but it was you sitting in the middle of the road, center stage, that finally generated his panicked swerve, which, coincidently followed right behind the horse."

"Another exit—stage right," barked Coyote.

"Why did the palomino cross the road . . .?" cooed Raven.

"When the Dodge hit the dip of the shoulder, Henry was launched like a plagued and venomous cadaver sent catapulting over the castle wall under a medieval siege."

"Isn't there a scene like that in Monty Python?" asked Coyote.

"Perhaps," vexed Turtle. "Regardless of your suggested plagiarism, it's a damn funny image and totally apropos. Besides, who are you to be accusing anyone of thievery?"

"Don't get your turtleneck all in a bunch. I was simply asking if . . . "

"Pots and kettles," cawed Raven. "Pots and kettles. Go on Turtle. I love the idea of Humboldt trying to fly. Maybe I could teach him a few tricks."

"Brown beak," mumbled Coyote.

Turtle ignored the hound and continued, "Even though the truck was lighter sans Henry, it was not as thin or agile as the horse, and soon came to an uncomfortable and sudden rest between two large ponderosa.

"Rattled, bruised, and confused, the gendarme all struggled up the mountain to the road to begin their long hike toward Red Rocks. Only the rangers searched for Henry. They found him via their keen sense of hearing rather than sight. Henry's moans were a dead giveaway. Had he been playing hide-and-seek, there would be no ollie-ox-in-free for noisy Henry. He was: It.

"But, of course, Henry wasn't intentionally hiding in the scrub. Events had long ago stopped being a game for the Chief Superintendent of the Red Rocks Rangers. If he had a sense of humor, it was extinguished via embarrassment and pain. No, hide-and-seek was far from his mind. However, what he was wondering about, in his current state of semiconsciousness, was if all this distress was covered by workmen's comp.

"He was quite a sight indeed, when they found him. He looked like an ancient Norse forest gnome. No, he looked more like an ogre from The Brothers Grimm. Which one is it that lives under a bridge and is covered in moss and lichens?"

"Ya got me," said Coyote. "I don't believe in those things. All that fairytale nonsense, frankly, I find it hard to swallow. Filling children's heads with such fantastic fabrications; they should be ashamed. "

Raven choked on his margarita. Turtle, ala their cast of wild-wild characters, blew an agave spritz. Both Turtle and Raven gave each other a comedic "take:" a momentary pause and a silent look through the fourth wall, directly at the audience, and then a slow turn, with a mask of disbelief, back to Coyote.

Coyote appeared oblivious. "What?" he shrugged.

"Nothing, Cerberus you ol' dog you. Just stunned me for a second."

"Cerberus who?" asked Coyote. "Oh, yeah . . . I get it. Please, Turtle, quit showing off and get on with the episode."

"Well, that does it. Sweet is done for. He has to give up the chase now," said Raven.

"Henry's done for, but Sweet is still determined and as luck would have it, they spot yet another set of headlights drifting down the mountain road. This time, Sweet stands firm in the middle of the lane. He figures he'd rather be hit and killed than suffer any further humiliation and setbacks. Again, as luck would have it, the vehicle stops just in time. It's Stanley Manley Junior driving his Pop's Power Wagon and pulling a horse trailer.

"Junior answers, 'Yes, Ma'am, there's room for everybody in the truck and the trailer. I ain't got no horse in there just yet, but I'm heading for the park to pick 'im up. My Pop's pissed that I loaned him out, but I got a plan to make things better. You ain't seen Wild Billy by any chance, have you? I need to find him pronto. He'd be riding a palomino.'

"Sweet, finally acknowledging the irony answers, 'As a matter of fact, Junior, I have.'

"Well, long story short . . ." continued Turtle.

"That'll be the day," mumbled Coyote.

"The cadre of lost boys filled the cab of the truck, the pickup bed and there was even room for Henry to ride prone in the horse trailer. 'I'm heading for Evergreen, eventual-like,' Junior told the rag-tag hitch hikers, 'but sure, I can drop you at the North Entrance to Red Rocks; specially if you say Wild Billy was heading that-a-way. I need to get that horse back.'

"New shot," said Turtle. "Fade in, if you will, as Troy Rivers, still at the helm of the bus, finds a parking place in the South Entrance bus lot, which is deserted, and on the opposite side of the park and amphitheater from the convening corps of cops. The warriors wander out single file, gazing open-mouthed, like typical tourists, at the splendors of the park. They break up into smaller groups and disappear into the woods and walkways surrounding the amphitheater. 'Search for the tomb,' says Rivers.

"It's here, as director, I would cut to an aerial view of the lower, north side parking lot in Red Rocks. The scene looks like a police convention. Dozens of cop cars have formed a huge circle in the center of the lot. Police and soldiers man their posts behind the wagons. A caravan of National Guard trucks lines the road near the entrance to the lot. And parked smack dab in the middle of the defensive circle is a long black limousine.

"Billy approaches with the horse, entering the circle of cars. Although, he had a head start and inadvertently delayed the progress of the Chief Sweet gang via unknowingly aiding in our choreographed wreck of Henry's truck, Sweet and the boys arrived first. Actually, Billy never realized he played a part in the mayhem. Oh, he heard all the crashing and grinding behind him but dared not look back. He only knew the noise was terrifying his mount and they were making damn good time. Unfortunately, the palomino was so panicked it ran right past the park, nearly all the way to Morrison. Only after it was exhausted could he halt the sprint, turn the horse around and walk him back toward Red Rocks.

"That poor horse has been through a lot," said Coyote.

"Billy sauntered into the circle of cars, leading a spent Asram. He noticed the guardsmen and the police were giving him confused and bewildered looks. 'What," he mumbles, 'your lot never seen a true-to-life Indian fighter before?' Their stares motivate him to get back in character. So, he straightens his posture, brushes the borrowed hair out of his face, and adds a swagger to his walk. He approaches a confab in the middle of the circle.

"Here, Billy recognizes the governor. He and a bird colonel are chastising the dickens out of some fat noncom in ill-fitting army fatigues. It takes a moment, but Billy finally recognizes the NCO. It is Denver Police Chief, Alan Sweet, in what obviously are borrowed threads. Officer Carson, also in fatigues, is standing next to Sweet. He looks like Nellie in South Pacific. "I'm gonna wash that man right out of my hair," drifts through his memory's song library. He hums as he listens in on the intense conversation.

"Sweet is bellowing something about not needing the National Guard. His police can handle things.

"The governor keeps repeating the same questions: What happened to Sweet's cruiser? What happened to the sheriffs' cars? Where was the city bus? And why was he, the governor, still getting calls from constituents at Mount Vernon about an Indian attack? How many Indians are we talking about? 'And why the hell are you out of uniform?'

"Wild Billy notices the Chief Jefferson County Sheriff, a couple of deputy sheriffs, and the Chief of the Golden Police standing in the periphery. They are trying hard not to laugh. He asks if anyone has seen Chief Ranger Henry Humboldt. They all shake their heads—no, but mention there's young cowboy, hippy kid looking for him. Seems he wants his horse back. Billy continues to watch Sweet and the governor argue.

"The governor, ignoring Sweet, notices Wild Billy standing nearby, holding a horse. 'Hey, Chief,' Billy says. 'Hey, Governor. What's up? What's with the circus?'

"Unadulterated hate fills Sweet's eyes. 'Whoa,' says The Wild Man. 'I haven't seen that look since the last time I asked the Chief to pay his bar tab.'

" 'And I suppose this rodeo clown,' asks the governor of Sweet, 'is part of your plan to apprehend the Indian?'

"Evolving from fuming to conciliation, Sweet answers, 'Well, sir . . . actually, yes, he is. Wild Billy here is a good friend of this Hands of the Bear character and we, the other police chiefs and I, figured Bill here might be able to talk the perpetrator out of hiding. We didn't want anyone else hurt, and we figured a ruse might expedite things.'

"The governor is not swayed. He asks, 'Did it dawn on you, Chief Sweet, that he's a civilian? And what's with the get up?'

"Here, again," points out Turtle, "I would cut to a reaction shot for Sweet: 'That was Billy's idea, Governor Lyon. I didn't know he was going to go all Halloween on us.' Sweet appears to de-evolve back toward fury, 'Billy, you didn't bother to mention you were going to play dress-up in your parade costume. Governor, I didn't know anything about it.'

"Billy, somewhat offended, says, 'It's Buffalo Bill, Governor. I'm dressed like the great Indian scout, Buffalo Bill Cody. Colonel William Fredrick Cody.'

"The governor growls, "I know who the hell Buffalo Bill is.'

"Billy tries to explain, 'I just thought the costume and the horse would add to the celebrity of the event. You know, a renegade Indian, Buffalo Bill, Red Rocks, Lookout Mountain, and all. It's great PR. Solid advertising. You understand good publicity, Governor. It's like my old mentor Cactus Face Doogan used to say . . .'

"At the mention of Doogan, a haunting legend in the foothills, and a fabled antihero with whom he is all to familiar, the governor interrupts, 'Sweet,' says the governor, "is this is some kind of a joke?'

"Once the laugh track fades," said Turtle, "I'll have a national guardsman run up to the group. 'Sirs,' he'll bark, 'Sirs, we have just received information that the Indian has been spotted near the tomb. In fact, Sirs, we have just received confirmation of several sightings. There seems to be more than one Indian.'

"This will motivate the governor to say, 'I'm sending up the Guard.'

Turtle digresses a moment. "Motivation, action and reaction, is the core of dynamic dialogue, you know. I don't mind reminding you two that . . ."

"Look whose head is in danger of swelling now," said Raven.

"Okay," answered Turtle, "Point taken. Anyway . . . the governor, motivated by the news says, 'Sweet, Wild Bill, with all due respect, my guard can make a sweep of the rocks and make a quick arrest. Colonel, prepare your men.'

"The colonel salutes and snaps to attention, 'Glad to, Governor. It's about damn time, no offense sir.'

"Of course Sweet would not like the turn of events, and motivated by his recent embarrassments and failings he would try one more time to control the situation. 'Hold up just a minute there, Colonel,' says Sweet. He takes the Governor's elbow and walks him just out of earshot. 'Listen, Lyon, don't think I don't know what you are trying to do here. I know it's an election year, and you would love nothing better than to steal my thunder for bringing this crazy mother in. Nevertheless, this is still a police matter, and activating the Guard is going far overboard. Don't think I won't expose your motive here, and don't think I won't announce the cost to the tax payers.'

"The governor's calm reply is: 'Are you threatening me, Pickles?'

"Sweet is again moving into attack speed for fuming, 'You bet your sweet peanut-butter-loving ass, and I'm telling you, Governor Lyons, sir, there is going to be political consequences if you try to embarrass me and pull rank.'

"Still calm, the governor says, 'You're so damn transparent. Everybody in the state knows you have political ambitions. What they do not know is that you are one pitiful excuse for a police chief, and you'd be an even worse politician. I'll be damned if I'm going to stand by and watch you make a mockery of this situation and of our state government. Look at you, you egomaniac. Your guts are hanging out under that borrowed shirt. Your pants are too short. What the hell *did* happen to your uniform? Oh yes, you're quite the picture of the local public servant, all right. By the way, Pickles, not only did I bring the National Guard with me, I also brought the local television news folks and their remote truck. So . . . you listen, you dumb Gherkin. I'm not your immediate supervisor, I'm not the mayor, but I do have some influence, even in the city government. If you want to keep your current job, you better get with the program. And whether you like it or not, I'm taking charge. I'm exercising my authority as the governor of this state to . . ."

"Here I have cute Dorothy as Officer Cason rush into frame, 'Sirs!' she, 'um, he yells, 'Wild Buffalo Billy is heading up the hill. What do you want us to do?'

"Billy saw his chance. Everybody was distracted. He mounted Isham and made his move. He reared the horse and waved his wide Stetson, the lone rider rides again. The TV crew spun the camera to catch the action. Billy was pleased at first when he noticed a flashbulb going off, *this will be a great still shot; I bet I can get a copy,* but the flash spooked Isham, who took off faster than Billy had planned. He tried to guide the horse between two cop cars but the horse had his own ideas, as usual. Billy felt them both leave the ground as Isham leapt over the hood of a car.

"In the silence of the glide Billy could hear muffled cheers, and the Sheriff, who was closest to the car being jumped said, 'Dang if that crazy old Jew can't ride.'

"Before any of the authorities could react, horse and rider were galloping into the valley of red stone and their promised rendezvous with destiny. Screen fades to black. Finis, as they say.

"Well," asked Turtle, "whad'ya think?"

"I think I need another margarita," said Raven.

"I'll drink to that," said Coyote.

Chapter Forty

A Place of Refuse

Summer, 1964

From a clearing near the peak of the climbing valley, Anthony Hands of the Bear watched a mounted figure ride toward him. As soon as the rider was out of sight of the crowd gathered in the lower parking lot, far below, he began scratching his crotch. He acted as if his buckskins were driving him to distraction, and he mumbled something to himself about how the horse had nearly bounced him "to oblivion." The rider called out, "Tony!" into the valley above. "Tony, it's me, Billy. Tony, I'm alone." He paused and searched the high rocks. "Tony, I know you're up there. Let's talk. They're willing to make a deal . . . Tony?"

Judging the pace of the palomino, Anthony Hands of the Bear still had time to continue his investigation of Olivia's backpack, desperately hoping for something to eat besides the tiny fruits he had already consumed. He looked again at the mushroom buttons. Out of curiosity, he poured a few into his palm. He smelled them. Too earthy. He picked a few of the bean like vegetables from their pea-like pods. They were reddish-brown in color. He smelled them. They smelled like dry beans. He ate a couple of them. They tasted like bitter legumes, nothing filling or appetizing there. He opened a plastic flask of powder, poured a small amount into his palm, and touched it with the tip of his tongue. Bitter. He smelled it and again touched it with his tongue. He wet his finger tip and dipped it into the talc for another small taste.

"Looks like we can add illegal drugs to the charges we're going to file against you, Hard Head." A pale and weakened, bald but smirking Henry Humboldt, Superintendent in Charge, Red Rocks Rangers, stepped out of a crevasse. He was holding a gun.

In an automatic response to the surprise, Tony licked his palm clean. He tossed the other items back into the pack.

"You should have known you could never hide from me. You forget, I too know every nook and cranny in this park, this is my turf, and I know all your favorite hiding places, you fuck-monster. Did you think all your little hide-and-seek games with those whores from Lookout went unobserved? I've got you now, Hardhat, and you're going to pay."

Suddenly, the voice of the rider came from the other side of a large boulder. "Cut the crap, will ya, Tony? I'm dying up here. This goddamn stupid horse is trying to kill me and these fucking buckskins are about to eat me alive." Billy and the horse came into the clearing just below Tony.

Henry backed into the crevasse but kept the revolver on Tony.

"There you are," said Billy. "Come on, Tony, will ya? Look I've come to make a deal. If you'll give yourself up, return to the reservation, so to speak, they'll reduce the charges. Tony, I had to do some fast-talking. If it wasn't for me you'd probably been shot by now." He scratched his chest with a vengeance. "What do you say, how about the deal?"

"There'll be no deals today," snarled Henry Humboldt as he stepped from the shadows.

"Henry! What the hell are you doing here?" Billy sounded surprised. He stood in his stirrups, trying to get a better look. "This was to be my capture. You police agreed."

"I never agreed to anything, you publicity hound. This is my arrest. If you want to help, ride back and get the others. Better yet, tell them Hardhat resisted; tell 'um I had to shoot him. Trust me, Billy, you better get going while the getting's good. Hard Head is mine."

As encumbered as Tony's mind was, he figured that Henry was ordering Buffalo Billy down the hill to eliminate him as a witness. The potential for danger accelerated his thinking; perception heightened. He was reading Henry's every move, searching for an edge, anticipating a mistake from his would-be assassin.

"Get out of here, Billy," said Henry. "Last chance. All you have to do is confirm to the others that Hardhat tried to jump me. It was him or me. You owe me, Billy. I'm going to end this here and now. You're either with me or against me. Don't make me hurt you, too. This is between Hardhat and me."

"You're crazy, Henry," said Buffalo Bill. "You can't go through with this. I know you hate Tony; you're angry. But you can't shoot him. It's not in you, Henry."

"You'd be surprised what I got in me, you phony cowboy clown."

Tony watched for an opening. He remained silent.

"Don't be stupid, Henry. They'll figure it out. You'll go to prison. Ain't no place worse than jail for a cop gone bad. If you got to fulfill this vendetta, then maybe a flesh wound would satisfy your anger, or maybe a good old-fashioned pistol whipping? What do you say, Henry?"

"I say it's too late to turn back now. I've got more than one bullet in this gun, Billy. Don't make me use one on you. I'm sorry, Billy, but this is you're own fault. You had a chance to leave. If I have to go through you to get Hardhat, I'll do it. I don't want to hurt you, Billy, but I will. I'll just blame it on the stupid Indian. You found him; he resisted; there was a struggle. I arrived too late to keep him from shooting you, but I got him in retaliation, avenging your death, saving the day." He turned the gun toward Wild Billy. "What's your decision, Buffalo Bill—live confederate or dead hero?"

"Tony, you've got to believe me," said Billy. He stood in the saddle, "I had no idea that Henry was . . ."

Suddenly, from the crest of a tall reddish pillar of stone an apparition appeared. Billy could not see it because he had his back to the trio, but to Anthony it looked like three dark spirits, one huge, two much smaller on each side of the central figure. His mind spun like a roulette wheel trying to locate some memory of an ancient triptych of colorful Indian specters or a fable about such a spectacular threesome. The white ball of memory plunked into a red cup: Art History Survey 101, required course. He interpreted the hallucination as a carnival Laocoön group: father and sons struggling, tangled in serpents. Only these vipers were the plumed cousins of Quetzalcoatl. The colorful feathers undulated in the wind. The headdresses were over four feet tall, one pink, the middle one red, the third blue. Rhinestones, sequins, and intricate beading covered the jackets and loin clothes. They shimmered in a psychedelic glow. Anthony thought for just a second that he recognized a beadwork portrait of Geronimo on the front skirt of the blue spirit.

The large red phantom launched an oblong green globe that appeared to float in slow motion as it arced toward its target. And then, suddenly, in a perceived contradiction to its flight, dipped its round nose and with the lethal accuracy of a guided missile, descended, gathered speed and exploded in the middle of Wild Billy's back. The watermelon knocked him off the palomino, and he hit the ground with a splash in a puddle of melon debris.

"That cracker son-of-a-bitching-cowboy was setting you up, brother," said the black bushwhacker with a slight French accent. Another green globe, launched at Henry, was half-way to its target.

Tony refocused on his foe. Judging by Henry's expression, the haunting demons were all too familiar. "Not again you don't!" he yelled and pointed the gun at the trio. "I knew I recognized you, you son of a . . ."

This was the distraction Anthony needed. When Henry turned, Hands of the Bear launched himself.

Henry must have sensed the attack. He turned back, but panicked and pulled the trigger too soon.

The bullet missed, but showered both with pellet-sized, rock projectiles as it smashed into the stone wall. A sharp piece of flying rock hit Tony in the same place a hailstone had bruised him a day earlier. Blood trickled down into Tony's eye. He touched the red dribble with his fingers and looked at the darkening plasma; the sight of it initiating rage. He concentrated his rage on the gunman. Henry cowered at the sight of blood and ducked from the exploding watermelon; Hands of the Bear knocked the gun from Henry's trembling hand.

At the sound of the shot the colorful apparitions ducked for cover.

"Humboldt, you crazy little asshole, you almost killed me." Anthony towered above the Ranger who was still hiding his head beneath intertwined arms. Henry's blatant cowardice gave him pause.

One of the joys of intoxication, thought Anthony—his mind racing, is knowing that you are intoxicated, but recognizing that you are functioning despite it. You rationalize your actions skewed from the inebriant—a complex thought—but you're still there watching via an out of body experience as you distort reality, and yet the scene is sensible. The unreal is real. Tony, thought, this is not like booze, it's much more electric, but I recognize the feeling. *Sentience*, he thought; we give it such credence. I'm aware; despite the abstractness of my thoughts, I am aware. Cartoons, he thought. Cartoons have at their heart some abstract realism—simplification, exaggeration, distortion. That's what makes them funny. A good joke has just a touch of the serious. A cartoon thought flashed across his mind, too ludicrous to give serious consideration, but then there was the history of Henry's prejudice against Anthony, there was the chronicle of malice, the litany of insults. He began to sum things up. A tally of injury grew, accelerated by intoxication, of which Tony was aware, and exasperated by circumstance. Anthony felt an unexpected empathy for Wile E. Coyote. He understood the plan: the bombs, the catapults, the rockets, and the roller skates, but he felt sadness that none had ever reached fruition. He commiserated the cartoon result. Cartoon became real, while the niopo and the hallucinogenic fruit anchored his frenetic thoughts. What would have been farcical became believable. Beep, beep.

Had not Henry cringed in such a cowardly posture; had not his cowardice been such an obvious consequence of his indiscretions; had not he tried to shoot Anthony; thus take the feud beyond past confines, had he not presented his posterior in such an obvious manner, Anthony may have taken a more mature action. But Henry did all of those things, and the consequence was that Anthony, aware of what he was doing—as far as his intoxication would allow, in a vaudevillian act, shoved an arrow up Henry's ass.

"I heard a shot," barked Chief Sweet. "Spread out, men." He hurried around the rock wall, followed by several police. A movement caught his eye. It was the heathen Hands of the Bear; he had picked up Wild Billy's wig and was holding it up in the air as if in prayer.

The image of an Indian, raising a scalp to the heavens gave Sweet pause. It was just too otherworldly. For just a moment, the sight of the savage, the surrounding prehistoric rocks, the smell of gunpowder in the air, the eerie light, seemed to warp time. Sweet knew he was not one to believe in ghosts, but a transitory coldness overwhelmed him. Ethereal images flashed across the stone screens. Buffalo and buffalo hunters riding bareback on painted ponies raced across the rock walls. A speeding stagecoach followed them with a screaming band of Indians in hot pursuit. Before he could focus, it was gone. So was Tony Hardhat. A noise, above on the rock pillar, caught his attention, but, again, before he could comprehend it, the flash of bright red disappeared.

"What's going on, Chief?" asked Carson, behind him.

Sweet sensed he was blocking the way. He stepped into the clearing wishing that they would find Billy holding a gun on the Indian. Instead, Chief Sweet stood over the unconscious Wild Billy, gagging in the melon pond. The angry Chief bellowed, "Now how in the name of Deputy Dawg would you explain this mess in a police report?"

"Sir, sir!" motioned young Officer Carson, "You better have a look at this." He stood over another unconscious clump. It was Henry Humboldt with an arrow standing perpendicular in his prostrate body.

"Now that crazy Indian has done it," barked Sweet. "Spread, out men. He can't have gone far. Shoot that son of a bitch on site. I don't care how big a putz Henry Humboldt was; no one, and I mean no one, assaults an officer of the law on my beat.

"Get that ignoramus and that nincompoop down the hill, out of sight." Sweet knew that it was a quarter-mile hike to the theater entrance and, depending on which way you go, either a steep and exhausting two hundred yard climb, or a dangerous descent on irregular stone stairs to the backstage and the office area. The closest place out of view was the bathroom and adjacent tomb. "They obviously need medical attention. Put the nitwits in the Indian cave." Carson, you run down and get on a radio to call for an ambulance. Tell the Governor what's happening. Show him to the tomb. I need to sit down a minute. I'm not feeling so good."

Olivia Hotchkiss and her mentor, Professor Edwin T. Antwerp had barely begun touring the tomb when the Governor and a colonel entered.

"There's been a shooting," said the Governor. "Someone is hurt. They are bringing them down. I'm sorry, Professor, but we're going to have to lay them in here briefly, at least until the medics arrive."

"Who's shot?" asked Olivia. "It's not Anthony, is it?"

"My dear," said Antwerp, "you seem genuinely concerned about this ruffian. Is there something you need to tell me?"

"It's a long story, Professor, and I don't think this is the time or the place. Well," she said, "it's the place, but the story can wait."

The police arrived carrying another officer and, it appeared to Antwerp, none other than Buffalo Bill. The tomb was becoming crowded.

The Governor and the Colonel said something about sending the Guard into the rocks, and that they were waiting for a report. A young man, who identified himself as Officer Carson, he was however not wearing a police uniform but was dressed in army fatigues, said to the Governor that it was quite a struggle getting "Wild Billy and Chief Ranger Humboldt" down the valley to safety. Although four or five men carried each, every step caused, "Henry considerable pain and Wild Billy was slippery as hell."

The two white men were laid on the cool floor beside and below the skeleton of the chieftain, Buffalo Bill to the left of the burial bed and the other, on his stomach, to the right. It was then that Antwerp noticed the arrow. He looked to the Carson lad for an explanation, but none was offered. Antwerp noted the make of the arrow by inspecting the feather fletching. He looked at a quiver of arrows hanging nearby in the tomb. They matched. He looked to Olivia for an explanation. None was offered.

Carson continued his report to the Governor. "We are all just thankful," he said, "that Chief Humboldt has passed out again and is finally quiet. All the way down the valley he was either pitifully whimpering about 'another damn scar' or raving about 'that sick son of a bitch, Hardhat.' He was hallucinating about 'some niggra-Indian devils.' Well, frankly, sir, a couple of the guys don't appreciate his language, arrow or no arrow."

The Buffalo Bill character awoke for just a moment. He looked up through off kilter eyes at the professor. "Hello, Teddy," he said. "Long time no see," and he passed out again.

It was a reaction the professor was used to. He considered himself a robust man despite his small stature. He was well aware of his resemblance to Teddy Roosevelt in his Rough Rider days. In fact, he cultivated the semblance. He had the same mustache, the same glasses, the same gleam in his eye, a khaki jungle jacket, and even a similar swagger stick with which he had again begun probing the artifacts.

"Come, Olivia," he said. "I've little time." He warned Olivia as she almost tripped over Buffalo Bill. Antwerp maneuvered over and between the human additions to the display as if they were part of the natural surroundings. He had little concern as to why they were there, why the place was filled with police, or why someone had obviously used or handled some of the items.

He briefly studied the skeleton, bending over and inspecting the remnants of the deerskin jacket and britches. Much of the intricate beadwork had fallen through the rib cage and lay on the stone bed and spine like sprinkles on a banana split. The war bonnet lay askew where it shifted position as the flesh of the old Indian dried and decomposed. Loose feathers lay here and there. The moisture that had entered the chamber had over the years accelerated the disintegration of the human remains. Sadly, thought Antwerp, there were no sands or soils or arid conditions to help preserve and naturally mummify the cadaver. Gray-white fungus grew in various depths, throughout the deathbed. For the most part, the organic decay was in its final stages. All that remained were the hard parts— the bones, the bead work, still on its fiber warp and interlacing, the feathers in the headdress. The leather of the war bonnet and the buckskin had surprisingly suffered less deterioration than the human remains.

As he investigated the grave, the professor hummed and slapped the swagger stick on his thigh when he had made an assessment. He looked often at Olivia with a quizzical expression, wrinkled his brow, and wiggled his mustache. When he had finished, he stood in one corner above the melon-soiled face of Buffalo Bill, calmly lit the stub of a cigar he had been chewing, and summed up the totality of the tomb's magnificence with one word—"Fake".

"What?" cried Olivia.

"Fake, the tomb is a fake." The professor noticed that the fellow in the Buffalo Bill outfit stirred as Olivia wailed and the police present began barking questions. "This," he said, "is a conglomeration of a variety of semi-historical and contemporary Indian craft goods—most are perhaps fifty or sixty years of age. A couple of items may be a century old, and there are a few antiques, probably Anasazi, Mesa Verde, Chaco, and some Mimbre, Mogollon. Nothing spectacular. There are probably more important pieces just south in the Colorado Springs Fine Art Center, or here in the Natural History Museum. Millicent Rogers in Taos has better contemporary work. This is more like a warehouse than a tomb. As far as being an Indian grave: Wovoka or whomever—no. It's a fake."

The Professor could see that Olivia's world went into a spin. She seemed light-headed. She struggled to remain standing.

Everyone began moving at once in a helter-skelter scrambling, which seemed to go nowhere but simply added to the bedlam. The shuffling filled the cave with dust. The Governor's cursing could be heard above the scuffling of feet. Someone named "Sweet" joined the fracas. He cussed louder than the Governor. They seemed to blame each other for the fallaciousness. The police seemed confused by the declaration of the hoax. Reporters became unruly. They mumbled statements about being duped. Their comments focused on Olivia.

"Olivia, my child," he said. "I am very disappointed. The merit of this collection, this concoction, should have been obvious. You should have notified me immediately. I made a mistake. I ignored the fact that *North American indigenous people* is not your forte. I should have sent you home—directly. That's what your grandmamma asked me to do. My affection for her, for you both, misled me. It was an error in judgment having you stop here on your way home, but I needed someone I could trust, someone in whom I had confidence to do some preliminary investigating. Instead . . . well, I'm very concerned about all the news reports. We work quietly in this business, Olivia, you know that. And it's very political. This embarrassment may create a blemish on your professional credentials. I hope you love the jungle work, Olivia, because the Amazon may be the only place where you can continue your research. Certainly not in the Southwest, or North America for that matter. It is a shame. I'm very disappointed. I'll do what I can to appease the authorities. If I were you, however, I would leave as quickly as possible. Go home. Please give my best to your grandmother."

Wild Billy Swarz began moaning and rubbing his sore head. It took him a moment to focus his eyes. He was a little surprised to find himself in an Indian tomb with Teddy Roosevelt. He sat up and tried to make sense of all the confusion. The scrambling figures remained slightly out of focus in the dust. Shaking his head to clear his mind, he noticed the skeleton's hand inches away from his face. He studied the hand with a shocked slowness, and surveyed the rest of the cave. He looked back at the hand. It had a macabre familiarity.
"WILLIE!" screamed Billy.
Everyone in the tomb appeared to jump out of their shoes.
Wild Billy was too excited to apologize. He leaped to his feet and pointed at the skeleton. "It's him—Willie Wolf Song. The old devil, I finally found him. Look!" Billy dug into a small pile of refuse and pulled out a dirt-covered vessel. He also lifted the skeleton's hand and placed the neck of the vessel into the clutched, bony fingers. The dusty scotch bottle was a perfect fit. "This is it. My best Scotch. It was Willie's favorite." He surveyed the cave. "So this was his hiding place. I knew he had some hideaway like this. That old rascal robbed me blind, hid all the booty in here, got drunk one night, and died on the spot." He shook the bottle and listened for any remnants. "Boy!" exclaimed Billy, "I could use a drink!"
"That makes two of us," said Chief Sweet. "I move that higher rank exercise its privileges and take advantage of the generosity of Wild Billy and resume our administrative conference in the authentic Western ambiance of Buffalo Bill Cody's Bar and Grill. Billy's buying.
"You men gather up poor Henry there and carry him to the parking lot. I think I heard the ambulance pull in down below. Let's

get everyone the hell out of here; I can't see a thing I'm doing with all this dust. I don't know about you, but I don't like breathing cemetery remains. I've got allergies. Clear out, boys. Why don't one of you Rangers stay here on guard, after all, this is your jurisdiction. If you need us, the chiefs will be at Cody's."

Troy Rivers, full time lawyer and part-time bus driver, remained hidden in the rocks with Horace Green. Veloy snuck away to tell the others as soon as they overheard the Professor's announcement.

"I can't believe it's a fake," said Rivers to Green. "What are we going to do now?"

"I think we better get everyone back to the bus, Troy. It's a long way to the convention center. The guys are going to be disappointed. This kind of takes the fun out of things, if you know what I mean. Maybe you could say something to them. It won't take long for it to dawn on them that we could be in a lot of trouble with our political rationale gone. Kind of makes you wonder why, you know what I mean, what all the fuss was about."

"What can I say?"

"You can tell them where they can get a good lawyer."

When they arrived at the bus, the others were waiting. Someone asked where all the police went.

"They all left in a big hurry, once the tomb was declared a fake," answered Veloy.

"The whole thing is a sham," someone said.

"It was a thief's stash," added Veloy. "It was the hideout of some old guy named Willie Wolf Song."

"I feel as if one of those huge red cliffs has just fallen on me," said someone next to Rivers.

Troy saw the life go out of his band of cohorts. The deflated group sat in a quiet circle and listened on a transistor radio to the local disc-jockey joke about the latest news on the tomb. A few individuals drifted from the circle—lost. Suddenly, they all looked tired and hung-over. Someone mumbled that he wanted to go home. A few sauntered into the bus and slumped into seats. Several buried their heads in their hands. Someone else mumbled that they had better get out of there before security showed up, or worse, if the police came back. The last thing they needed was more jail time, especially for some old thief none of them even knew. The magic was gone. The earth beneath them was cold and inhospitable, the rocks— overwhelming and remote.

Rivers reflected on his outfit. He felt alien in the Indian attire, a pretender. He subconsciously sought some sort of verification and reached for the tobacco pouch that Orvis had given him some many months ago. He often used it in times of stress, just holding it, smelling the tobacco, which he carried despite being a nonsmoker, perhaps to remind him of his old friend. The weight of the small turtle shape was pleasing, substantial for its size, like a book. Without opening the pouch, he raised it to his nose. The heavy, sweet Latakia, dark and earthy, permeated the pouch. The bouquet calmed him. And then the unmistakable aroma of tequila wafted across the air. *Are they drinking again?* A raven cawed loudly above him, and he thought he caught the glimpse of a coyote hiding in the ponderosa pines near the walkway.

A strange voice seemed to come from the earth below him. He looked to see if anyone nearby heard it. No one acknowledged it; they continued to brood. He listened again.

"Sorry, I'm late," said the voice. "They must never forget."

He sat, waiting. Nothing. He bounced the pouch in his hand, responding to the weight and the rhythm of the pitch and catch. Listening, wanting more, opening himself to the setting, the cool night air, the nocturnal clouds, and the past day's warmth still radiating from the huge monoliths.

He cast the turtle pouch a little higher than expected and reached for the catch. It plopped in his hand just as he heard the raven call again. And then another unexpected voice rang in his ears. It was his voice. "Wait a minute, come back here," he heard himself say. "Where do you think you're going? Listen to me. Listen. I ask that you hear me and give counsel to what I'm about to say."

Reluctantly, they gathered around.

"So what, so the hell what if it isn't the tomb of an ancient chieftain." They continued to gather—confused but curious. "It is the grave of one of our fathers. So what if he was a drunk. Tell me this—how many old drunks are going to die lonely and pitifully like that? We know what it is to lie dying in the dark, in the vacant lots, in the alleys of Albuquerque, Gallup, Tucson, and Oklahoma City. Our kinsmen know what it is to lie dying in the cold city canyons of Denver. I know—just like all of you know—what it means to dwell in hell; to lie hurt and ashamed in the drunk tanks of New Mexico and the Dakotas.

"It is only because of the friendship of Horace Green that I rose from the depths of hell to join you, brothers. Each of you has ascended—beyond your own house of demons—to join together here. Somehow you've done it; somewhere you found strength. But everybody does not make the ascension. Not all of our brothers survive.

"I have never, face to face, met this old man, but I know *him*. It frightens me to know that in seeing him, I may be looking into my own face. It should frighten you; I am looking at your faces, and I see him there. I see him now in each of us.

"He is our father. How many old Indians have to die, stripped of their pride, before we—their sons—do something about it?"

He looked around at the costumes of his companions. They were exaggerations of authentic clothes worn by their ancestors, but the excess of colorful feathers and snuff can bells did not bother him for he knew that they were created as a celebration of their heritage, as a loud cry of things past. He knew also: they were a symbol of renewal. *Renewal*, how Orvis had tried to drill that concept into him.

"I tell you this," he continued. "The party is over. We had some fun, broke some rules, stole a bus, and deflated a country club blowhard, but the party is over. Are these clothes we wear party clothes, costumes only—of the fancy dance? Outsiders try to make us believe our clothes are clown costumes, but we know that this clothing contains magic and lends us power. Each costume comes from the war bonnets of our past, and it is time we wore them in pursuit of coup and honor. If need be, the blood of enemies should christen these costumes."

He reached under the wheel well of the bus and found the dirt and grease he sought. He wiped a dark swatch across his forehead and down each cheek. "A father has died; he needs to be properly mourned." He hoped a paraphrase of Chief Joseph of the Nez Perce, the Nee Me Poo, would have relevance. "To do the right thing, we may have to fight some more, forever."

He hesitated. They stood listening, but silent. The silence confused him. He had one last thing to say.

"In the short time I knew Orvis Kahnawake he became like a father to me. That old man, Wolf Song, was our grandfather. Orvis is gone now, like the old man in the tomb—cold and alone. Would Orvis quit? I ask you, would he quit? Hell no, he wouldn't. Horace you know that. Veloy, you know it's true what I say. He would remind us that this is a call for respect and for renewal.

"The memory of my Wyandotte grandfather and my grandmother haunt me now. They reach into my chest and twist my heart to make me feel the pain and they ask me, 'How can you abandon him?' The spirits of our grandfathers sing out, 'We cannot be forgotten.' "

Horace cried, "No one, you hear me, no white must touch that old one's grave. He was Haudenosaunee, or Lakota, or Anishinabe. He was of *The People*. That's all we need to know. He was a father within the hoop. How can we allow them to take him from the circle? We are his sons."

The braves rallied in war hoops, among them Rivers could hear a coyote howl and raven caterwaul. The call to arms echoed off the red canyons, the rocks thundered in a rolling, baritone rumble.

Chapter Forty-one

On The Rocks

Summer, 1964

Anthony Hands of the Bear sat picket in the shadows opposite the entrance to the tomb. He had two uninvited and unexpected guests—Raven and Coyote.

"So, Hardhat," asked Raven. "Are we having fun yet?"

"I'm not talking to you, bird; to do so would admit I'm flighty as you. You're but a myth, a figment of Olivia's juju fruits."

"That Olivia," said Coyote, nestled at Anthony's feet, tilting his head, enjoying Tony's unconscious scratching behind his ears, "she's a fox."

"You're cheeky for such an old dog," said Anthony, miffed at Coyote's familiarity.

"*Cheeky*, you learn that from your four foppish English friends?" asked Raven. "I noticed that when the going got tough; they flew the coop, or is it: when the coup got tough; they blew?"

"I told you, crow, I'm not talking to you."

"Well, check it out, renegade. I believe that's sweet Olivia approaching the tomb as we don't speak. Who's that with her?"

Coyote stood and peered over the rocks. "He looks familiar."

Anthony tried to appear calm to his spectral companions, but was concerned that the fellow striding up the path with Olivia was Teddy Roosevelt. "I don't see anyone," he lied.

"Come on Hands of the Bear, this is Raven you're talking to. Don't try to deceive a deceiver. You should have learned by now, you can't dupe the mesmerizer? And I suppose you didn't see Chief Sweet and the boys carry Buffalo Bill into the tomb a few minutes ago? And that arrow sticking out of Superintendent Humboldt's ass, I suppose that was illusion, too?"

"Like I said; I'm not talking."

The rock upon which Anthony was sitting sprouted a long neck and a volley ball-sized head—a turtle's noggin.

"Don't you rascals have some chicanery to do?" it said, blinking at Raven. Distending its long, thick neck, it curved round to face Anthony, "Don't let them bother you. You're safe for now, here on the rocks. But, soon you need to leave, borne this lithic womb with lovely Olivia. To stay would to become embittered and cold as Flint. We have other plans for you. But first, tell me, you do still have the hair you took from Wild Buffalo Billy, don't you?"

Speechless, bewildered by the animation of the rock, Anthony held up the silver fall of hair.

"Good, hang on to it for now. It's important. You'll know what to do when the time comes."

"Speaking of *good*," said Coyote, "things are going to get good. Excitement brews, Turtle. Watch and listen."

"Fake?" they heard Olivia scream from the tomb.

"Willie!" they heard Wild Billy yell not long afterwards.

And then began the exodus. Sweet left in the middle of a curse. Most of the police followed him. A few reporters lingered, questioning Teddy Roosevelt. Finally they left. Only Olivia remained, the sound of her tears floating faintly on the night breeze.

"The coast is clear at last, my son," said Turtle. "She's waiting for you. Go to her. She needs you." He turned slowly to Coyote. "You two, get to your posts; it ain't over yet."

"We know," said Coyote. "Oh, hoooow we know." His howl rose like a thermal above the Permian turrets, and Raven rode the howl to the heights.

When Tony entered the tomb he saw Olivia standing as if she were in shock and staring at the skeleton. She turned, her surprised look transformed to relief. They read each other's minds. Theirs was the sweetest embrace. They loitered in the warmth until Anthony finally said, "We can't stay here, Olivia. There are strange goings on. I think the police are still after me, and I've got to free myself from these rocks."

She noticed the knapsack. "You've got my things," she said.

"I owe you an apology, Olivia. I was starving, so I ate a couple of the little fruits."

"Oh . . . Anthony . . . how do you feel? Do you feel . . . enlightened?"

He shrugged his shoulders.

"Edified?"

He shook his head.

"Psychedelic . . . electric?"

He frowned.

"Illuminated?"

"Lit up like a roman candle, Olivia. You wouldn't believe it if I told you."

They heard voices down the walkway.

"We need to go now," stressed Tony. He peeked out the canvas curtain. "It's clear, but hurry."

They slipped out of the tomb and circled above, away from the pedestrian walk and the voices. As they disappeared into the rocks, Anthony turned to see who was talking. He couldn't be sure, considering the latest threesome with whom he had a conversation, rocks, ravens and rascal canines, but these intruders walking the path looked like a pair of Indians—historical, quintessential Sioux braves, war paint and all. They were conferring over a map. The paradox of ancient and contemporary images merged. *Now there's another sight you don't see every day.*

They had climbed but a short distance when Anthony realized he still had a tight grip on the hair the turtle rock told him to leave with the cadaver. He also forgot his hardhat.

"Olivia, I have to go back. I've forgotten something."

"Go back? Where?"

"To the tomb. There's something I forgot."

"Anthony, it's too dangerous."

"I'll be careful. It's important. You stay out of sight. I won't be long."

"Anthony, be careful. I . . . I . . . just be careful."

"I love you, too." He kissed her. "I really do. It's not the drugs talking."

She stood, momentarily stunned. He was amused that he made her blush. He watched as she ducked into a crevice and he bounced down the mountainside in a rhythmical saltarello, retracing their path, jaunty from their kiss.

It was not long until Anthony skulked above the entrance. He saw no one, but could still hear voices just beyond. From the tone of urgency in their utterances he surmised that they were concentrating on the group of cars speeding out of the lower parking lot. He used the action below as a distraction to slip unseen into the tomb. He took a moment and stood above the skeleton, half expecting it to speak. Why not, everybody and everything he encountered seemed to have a voice . . . and an opinion?

Something told him not to place the hair like a wig on the brown skull. He laid the fall across the chest and rib bones, and crossed the hands over the fall and wrapped one end around them so that the old one took possession of the hair. "Looks like you finally took a scalp, grandfather."

He was only half-surprised when a torrent wind suddenly eddied inside the tomb. An ancient chant swirled with the current. An echo sang in his ears. At one point he thought he recognized the voice of the turtle rock, but then the song changed to that of an elder, "You have done well, my son," it whispered over and over until it faded to silence. And then Olivia's song filled him. He turned to leave.

The yellow hard hat sat on the floor of the cavern near the entrance. When he bent over to pick it up he saw a shadow on the ground gliding toward the opening. Anthony stepped backwards into the deepest darkness of the tomb.

The shadow entered and transformed into a human silhouette against the light of the cave entry. It moved toward the old remains, away from the backlight, and took form. Anthony could not trust his vision. Were Olivia's gifts still influencing his perception? Was he hallucinating again or was there indeed an Indian warrior standing over Willie's skeleton? The figure stood surrounded by darkness, theatrically lit, posed over the fallen elder in an eerie, Baroque holiness. Anthony gasped at the vision. The spirit heard his breathing. It calmly turned toward Anthony and stared through him.

As far as Troy Rivers was concerned, the tomb was spooky as hell, and he was not sure whether he heard something, but he was going to do his damnedest to appear calm. He stared in the direction of the breath, waiting for his eyes to acclimate to the dark. It seemed an eternity, his vision reluctant, when, slowly, silently a form emerged from the darkness. Was this an apparition or was he actually seeing the spirit of this dead Indian standing before him? At first, he instinctively wanted to introduce himself and explain why he was here disturbing the deceased and risking a trespass on sacred ground, but his embarrassment kept him silent.

Anthony recognized the costume as Lakota and he knew it would be impolite to ask this spirit, if it was a spirit, his name, but he instinctively felt he should explain his presence. Somewhat paranoid that he had been caught or that the image may think him trespassing, he finally heard himself say, "I work here."

The other essence took an eternity to respond.

Troy Rivers still was not sure that he was not trespassing, so in an effort to explain *his* presence in relation to what the other had just said he blurted out, "I have work to do here." In assessing his statement, he figured it was okay. Any spirit worth a haunting would understand that he and his comrades were here to help.

Anthony wasn't sure what that meant, but was getting anxious to shorten this visitation, so not knowing what else to say he said, "I forgot something."

Again, thinking there was more to what the specter was telling him, Rivers answered by saying, "It took me a long time to remember." If this was indeed a guardian, he would understand that Troy had with appropriate economy and traditional brevity just summed up his life and opened himself to the power of the specter. He stood, waiting for a sign.

Horace called from outside, "There's trouble brewing out here, Troy!" Rivers turned ever so briefly toward the voice, but it was all Anthony needed. He moved in a singular silent arabesque to pick up the hardhat and exit the tomb. He was up, over the rocks and away by the time Rivers turned back to where the Indian spirit had stood.

Rivers interpreted the vanishing of the figure as confirmation that he had just visited with an ancestor. It enhanced his firm resolve that he was on the proper path.

He spoke to the reclining skeleton, "Don't worry, old one; be at rest, father. Your sons are here to make sure you are appropriately honored." He walked from the tomb into the circle.

The Golden Police, leading the exit, were the first to receive the return call to duty. Like a line of dominoes, either via telegraph or telepathy, the message proceeded down the queue of cars. Profane responses could be heard filling the valley from each initiate as the dispatch reached them, " You gotta' be putting me on . . . Damn-nation . . . Damn, damn, double damn . . . Shit, shit, holy, shit . . . Seriously—seriously, are you serious? . . . Well, kiss my blue-uniformed patooty . . . Jeezus H, you are serious aren't you? . . . Is this some kind of a fucking joke?" Like a team of synchronized swimmers the caravan pulled a sequence of U-turns and sped back toward Red Rocks.

"What's up, Spartacus?" asked the governor of his driver as his limo joined the procession.

"Somebody just called in a panic from the amphitheater, seems a band of Indians in war paint have just been spotted infiltrating the park—maybe a hundred or more; it's hard to tell, they're hiding in the rocks. The park folks fear violence, probably a hostile occupation."

"Tally-ho," shouted the gov as he reached to open the sunroof.

"We cannot stay here, Anthony," Olivia resolved. "The police are coming back." While he was gone she had rolled and ignited a joint. "Do you know the way?"

"I thought I did, Olivia, but now I'm not sure. I used to be sure, but, frankly, this whole night has got me a little confused." He looked down the mountain toward the theater. If he could believe his vision, he thought he saw a parade of police cars and National Guard trucks speeding into the lower parking lot and circling-up as if they were a line of covered wagons under attack in an old Western movie. A long black limousine, with a John Wayne type standing up through the sunroof waving a white cowboy hat, was racing past the cars to lead the parade.

"Olivia," said Anthony, "I know it's the dope, I know none of this is real, but I feel like I'm in a Howard Hawks movie or something. There's an electricity rumbling my stomach and buzzing my extremities and scrambling my brain. It's entertaining, but there are things I want to tell you . . . real things and my mind keeps coming up with lines that sound more Shakespearian than John Ford. I'm feeling all poetic and I don't know if it's the enchanted fruits or being high on love. There I said it—love. I've never talked like this. Do I dare risk your laughing at me and my clumsy poetry? Do I dare remind you what you risk in accompanying me in this escape . . . an escape from reality, an escape from consequences?"

"Go on . . . you know I love languages, the sounds, the rhythm . . . tell me what you're feeling. I want to hear it. Seduce me."

"Fair Olivia, because of you I have dwelled in a different world. Our communion, your just desserts have cast me . . . cast me . . .," he looked at his costume, ". . . naked, Olivia. As have your sweet desserts" He surveyed the surrounding monoliths, "Upon these naked red and sacred rocks, fair lady . . ."

"Anthony, I would upon the chance that my persimmons have sparked this poetry, keep you supplied and sated." She was a little wacky herself, now that she had a chance to toke up, and with the aid of primo niopó, she fell immediately into an analogous role.

"Olivia, you little romantic you—a delicate flower. When first we met, we did not banter . . . *is* it the drugs?

"The drugs can only open doors to treasures that dwell already within a heart, Anthony. At our first meeting, your sights were aimed at a simpler quarry."

"A carnal vision . . ." He felt apologetic.

"But not unwanted." She restored his esteem. "Don't underestimate the intoxication of that prurient narcotic, Anthony. It too opens long closed doors . . . doors too long closed."

They kissed.

Tony was thinking how enjoyable their relationship had turned, how good she felt in his arms, he thought of laying her down on the bed of a smooth red boulder, warmed by the day when a handful of the Indian braves stood up from behind their rocks to see who was reciting. Olivia did not see them, but Tony caught a peek before they ducked out of sight.

"I think it's time we journeyed over the peak, Olivia. I might have another of those prickly things."

"If you like those, Anthony, I know a place where the lotus life blooms daily."

"I'm yours, Olivia. We climb to greater heights."

"We have a long trek in front of us, Anthony Hands of the Bear. But I'm optimistic and enchanted." She took his arm between hers and hugged him. "Lead on."

"I believe we're on the right path, Olivia."

"So?" asked Horace. "How did the tomb look? Is the old guy resting peacefully?"

"He's there," answered Troy Rivers, "and I think he's glad to see us. That's what I thought I heard, anyway."

"He said that to you?"

"In so many words."

"Then you think we're doing the right thing?" asked Horace.

"I believe we are, Ho. I truly do. Something just now happened to me in the tomb. It's convinced me that this is our righteous path."

Veloy Vigil scuffled up the walkway, "Looks like the pō-lease are coming back, Three Rivers. So, Chief, how do we let them know we're here, ready to protest, and itching for a fight?"

"Veloy," said Rivers, "how many times have I told you—don't call me chief. We are all in this together. One for all; all for one; get it?"

"Sorry, Troy," said Veloy, "Got it." He looked at Horace for an explanation. He didn't get it. Alexandre Dumas was not required reading in rural New Mexico. "But, Troy, sir, you are our leader. If it wasn't for you, we never would have stayed together. It's the leadership of both you guys that's going to get us through. You made us believe we can make a difference tonight. You are chiefs."

"I'll drink to that," toasted a voice from the back of the group.

Veloy turned to chastise the joker.

"Easy, Veloy," said Rivers. "He was just kidding. But I'm serious—we are all equally important. That is why we must stand together . . ."

Tensions were high in the bulwark circle of authorities, quaking behind their vehicles. The rumors of a hundred or more crazed Indians hiding in the rocks with who knows what on their savage minds peaked their adrenaline and blue-coat dread. Only Officer Carson seemed focused on reconnoitering the canyons above the defensive coterie of cops and sheriffs and soldiers.

Chief Ranger Henry Humbolt's moans of pain and regret, rectal remorse, only exasperated the tension.

"Can't we shut the little zealot?" asked Chief Sweet to no one in particular. "Can't someone pull the fricking arrow out of his meddling ass?"

"The arrows out, Chief," said Carson. "A medic from the National Guard did it, but we still need to get him to the hospital. He insists on staying put until we capture 'Hardhat,' Sir. The morphine seems to have little effect. He keeps mumbling something about the wound running too deep. He wants to witness the battle and keeps calling for his butt pillow so he can sit up and watch."

"Well, get him the damn pillow, Carson. His sniveling is driving me over the edge. Why the hell don't a couple of the Rangers take him to the damn hospital? Get him the hell out of our hair. Seriously, that whimpering is giving me the heebie-jeebies."

"As I said, Chief, he refuses to go. And, besides, we wrecked the Rangers' cars.

A couple of the Denver police, less sympathetic than Carson, found the pillow in a squad car on the perimeter of the circle. One flung it sidearm to another, but rather than tossing it on to the cruiser in which Humbolt loudly lamented, the second cop, in a moment of spontaneous frivolity and trying to break the tension, winged it back to his compatriot. It took on the flight characteristics of the Frisbee that Flora Florida was selling at the powwow, which neither officer got to attend; so, they never witnessed the new toy; this was a serendipitous discovery. Art historians and anthropologists call it "simultaneous genesis"—parallel creativity at two distant locales, like pyramids or archery. Who knew cops could be so creative?

Out of the corner of his eye, Troy saw a curious movement below in the parking lot. A police officer flung what looked to be a large, flat, orange doughnut toward another cop. The odd object flew flat and true, like a pizza-sized saucer. He noted that the quizzical flight caught the attention of several others. He went from amusement to horror when Horace drew an arrow and shot the peculiar pie-shape out of the air. It fluttered to the ground like a wounded duck. The cops dove for cover. Several gunshots rang out and bullets ricocheted off the rocks. The Indians *ducked* for cover.

"Horace!" yelled Rivers. "What the hell are you doing?"

"Horace," yelled Veloy. "That was one hell of a shot."

"Sorry, Troy. It was a spontaneous leadership decision. Damn you, Veloy, making me out to be a chief. Maybe I didn't think it through. On the other hand, we got their attention. They know we're here."

"What now, Troy? Do you think they'll attack?"

"No," he peeked above the rock. "I think Horace put the fear of Crazy Horse in them. Looks like they are staying put. I think we should also hunker down. No more arrows. We don't want them any more panicky than they are. We don't want anymore shooting." He called out, "Is everybody okay?" No one was hurt. "I think we should take a nonviolent approach. If we have to, if they don't want to listen to our side of the argument, we'll stage a sit-down in the tomb, and they will have to carry us out bodily. Then we can fight, like caged cougars, but before that, I think we should talk. I'll signal that we want to negotiate."

"How are you going to do that?"

"A white flag. Anybody got a white flag?"

"Left all my flags in my pants at home," said the same clown from before.

"You're not helping, Guillermo," yelled Veloy.

"Anybody got any ideas," asked Rivers. "I can't think of anything else. I know . . . anybody wearing white underwear?"

"Guillermo?" asked Veloy. "You got on white BVD's. I seen them when you was getting dressed. And man, you are an extra-extra-large. Fork 'um up. It's for the good of the cause."

"No way, man," said Guillermo. "No one is gettin' my skivvies."

Every Indian in earshot chided Guillermo.

"It'll make for a great story, Guillermo, if we ever live through this," said Ernesto, cowering in the rocks next to him. "I'll buy the drinks, and you can tell the story. You're a funny son of a bitch, *Palomita*. Now quit making jokes and do something for the cause."

"This is harsh punishment, man, for jus' trying to introduce a little levity. *Lodo!*"

"Guillermo," said Rivers. "Once we get their attention, I'll give them right back. I promise."

"It had better be some damn good tequila, Ernesto. None of that *gasolína* you usually drink . . . and several rounds, man, for me and all my friends here—eh, *borregadas*?"

They cheered as Guillermo began to pull off his underwear.

"I need some music, *carajos*." He joked. "And I'm going to kill anyone who tells my wife."

"Sweet," asked the Governor. "What's that they're humming?" He looked toward the Indian hideout.

"You got me, Governor," answered Sweet. "Maybe some kind of a war chant."

"Sounds like *The Stripper*, Chief. You know, Mancini?" said Carson.

"I don't think Mancini wrote *The Stripper*," said Sweet. "You're thinking of *Hatari*."

"What?" asked the Governor.

"You know. John Wayne, Howard Hawks. They're catching animals for zoos."

"No, I don't know that one and I don't give a . . . what's that?" the Governor asked, pointing toward the rocks.

"Is it a white flag, sir?" said Carson.

"I believe you're right, officer, or some kind of an Indian insult." said Governor Lyon.

"What do you suppose it means?" asked Sweet. "Waving around a huge pair of briefs on the end of an archer's bow?"

"Are they surrendering, sir?" asked Carson.

"If they are," said Sweet, "there's going to be some serious Indian ass kicking while we arrest them."

"That's why I'm taking charge, Chief Sweet. As far as I'm concerned, it's your short sidedness that has put us in this situation.

"Officer Carson, I believe you're right," he continued, "that's a flag of truce. I think they want to talk. Give me your handkerchief so we can signal then back."

"Sorry, Governor, but the Indians took my uniform. I don't have a handkerchief."

The Governor looked at Carson and recalled that he and Sweet were wearing only the fatigues loaned by the guardsmen. "Well get me something I can wave." He looked at the impaled cushion lying at Carson's feet "How about Ranger Humboldt's butt doughnut—the one they shot out of the sky?"

"Wrong color, sir," said Carson. "They might misinterpret our intent."

"Sweet," asked the Governor. "What color are your underwear?"

"No way, Dicky," grumbled Sweet. "I'll shoot myself first."

"Don't tempt me, Pickles." He paused for effect. "Although yours are probably the only ones large enough to be seen from the rocks, I've already made a citation for you being out of uniform. No sense rubbing salt in the wound." He hoped his smile didn't give away that that was exactly what he'd like to do. "Besides," he added, "we don't want to insult them with your apparel before we've had a chance to talk. Oh, that's right. They've already seen your briefs."

"Very funny, sir," said Sweet. "Officer Carson, find the Governor a flag."

Rivers recognized the Governor as he walked cautiously out of the circle of cars toward the rocks. He saw him refuse a revolver an officer tried to hand him as he walked past. Troy thought he heard the entire circle of uniforms, blue and green, hum in admiration.

"What's that they're humming?" Rivers asked.

"Sounds like *The Battle Hymn to the Republic*," answered Horace.

Troy appeared from his stone hideout waving Guillermo's underwear. He wasn't optimistic about the impending confab; he has been through many meetings and events when the Governor spoke. Calling him *loquacious* was kind, *garrulous* and focusing on the trivial was closer, *gas-bag* pretty much summed it up. He knew from late nights at the Governor's Mansion with his bosses Barber and Brownstone, discussing strategies over cigars and Bourbon, that the Gov liked to be the center of attention. He amused himself by emphasizing issue points with quotes from popular music, movies and television, as if entertainment sources were eloquent intellectual insights "Governor Lyon, it's good seeing you again; I wish it were under more pleasant circumstances".

"Injun," said the Governor. "I think we should powwow. Allow me to introduce myself. I've found it expedites negotiations if we polemicists know something about one another."

"Governor, it's me . . . ," Troy started to speak, but the white man interrupted him.

"I'm Governor Richard Lyon—call me Dick. Are you from these parts? Never mind, it doesn't matter. Old habit . . . always assessing whether or not the situation is going to get me some votes. I'm always a bit leery when I enter negotiations. I ask myself, does my opponent really want to reach an understanding or exercise the fact that they're a political enemy? Is my contestant really just trying to embarrass me somehow? I hope you're serious about getting some consensus here because, Injun, this situation is ripe with potential embarrassment. Speaking of embarrassment, you and your war party have adroitly embarrassed the hell out of one of my political enemies. He is down below pointing a gun at you as we speak.

As we speak, thought Rivers. *You're doing all the talking . . . as usual.*

"I believe you have met Chief Sweet," continued the Governor. "I understand you have his uniform; congratulations on that, by the way. But tell me, Injun, what is this all about? What are you fellows trying to accomplish here? Can you explain what's going on?"

"Governor . . ." pleaded Rivers, but was interrupted again. I don't think he recognizes me. How many times have we met? Fifty? How many committees have I sat on, representing the firm, doing some kind of gratis consulting for this guy? We've even golfed together. I've held the pin for him. Why the pompous introduction? He's acting like we're in an old "B" Western. Of course, there's a TV camera crew setting up down by the police cars. "Governor," Rivers tried to interrupt. "It's me, Troy Rivers. You know me, sir."

"Holy crap, Rivers. I didn't recognize you without your Brooks Brothers and those loud ties you wear."

Rivers instinctively reached to straighten his tie. It wasn't there. He felt the sacred bones; it gave him a renewed resolve. "Don't let the costumes fool you, Governor. They are part of a celebration of Indian heritage. Things got a little out of hand; events happened so quickly we didn't have time to consider what to wear before we made our protest. Regardless, underneath the feathers and war paint we are citizens, taxpayers and voters. And, yes, sir, we do have something that needs airing.

"You're a smart lad, Rivers—a good lawyer. I'm sure you realize, trespassing, kidnapping, commandeering city property, threatening violence, assaulting police officers, stripping one dumb son of a bitch . . . OK, I'll give you that one, I personally owe you something for humiliating Sweet; so, tell me . . . what's the point of this carnival?"

"As I said, sir, I'm afraid things got a little out of hand. We apologize for that. It was never our intent to hurt anyone. However, Governor, we do have a definite goal in mind. I assure you that this is not some stunt. And it is not our intent to embarrass you, sir. Sweet? It might be worth the legal consequences to deflate that duplicitous ass. But, as I said, that is not our goal."

"What is your goal, seriously? Because honestly, Rivers, I'm having a hard time taking you serious in that outfit."

"We are very serious, sir, despite the costumes. You need to get past that. And another point of contention: You called us 'Injuns.' Not a flattering term, Governor. It's demeaning and I have witnessed you at enough negotiations to know that you do not start off insulting your opponent. We're Native Americans, Natives, sir; oh, I'm sure Chief Sweet has a few other names for us, but there are two sides to this story, sir. Sweet's is not the only important point of view. There are extenuating circumstances beyond the kidnapping, kidnappings, the trespassing . . . ahh, foray at Mount Vernon, the sortie here in the park, the bus hijacking and the assault . . . ahh, assaults." He noted that his confidence dwindled as he repeated the list of offences. He hoped the governor didn't hear the diminishing dauntlessness.

"I'm sure there are, but to be honest, and take it while you can get it—the honesty, I mean—to be perfectly frank, you boys got yourselves between a rock and a hard place." He looked around at the setting and chuckled at his witticism.

Troy surveyed the surroundings and the view of the police-packed parking lot, "Tell me something I don't know, Governor."

"Well what in the name of Marion Robert Morrison are you doing here, Troy? We're a little old for cowboys and Indians."

"My friends and I are here to protect the dignity of that old man buried in the cave. We know that his identity is not as exciting or important as was first believed We know he's not John Wayne," Rivers wanted the governor to know he got his movie reference, "or Jay Silverheels, or Sitting Bull, or anybody famous, but the point is that he was a man, an Indian elder, a metaphorical grandfather. He serves as a symbol—not only of our common heritage, but also as a symbol of our current quest for a bourgeoning Indian pride and a revived dignity."

"'*Metaphorical, bourgeoning?*' take it down a notch counselor. I've heard your potty mouth on the golf course. When did all this Cochise consciousness take hold of you, Troy?"

"It's recent, Governor, but I had to go through Hell for it to sink in. Trust me . . . there are some serious injustices we Native Americans still have to survive. My point is that there is a new dawn, a new Native awareness, and our continued tolerance of unjust issues is going to be challenged—with vigor, Governor. The challenges are coming whether we here in Red Rocks accomplish our goal or not. It would behoove you, as a politician, as an elected official, to anticipate this movement and decide on which side you will take a stand."

"I don't like threats, counselor. I get enough threats from Sweet and his cronies."

"This isn't a threat aimed at you, Governor. I'm just trying to warn you, to advise you as I have so many times in the past. Just because I'm not wearing my three-piece suit doesn't mean the message is any less important, the potential for wrong sidedness any less grim."

"Troy, I'm sure you realize I've made a bold stand on civil rights—for all minorities. It's a matter of public record. But let me be honest one more time. There just aren't enough of you here on the rocks to be of any consequence, and you know that this is no way to make your point. As a lawyer, you understand that we have a system, a system of laws that, by following the proper channels, deals with injustice. You also know that we cannot allow people to take the law into their own hands. You men have had quite a little romp the last few hours. You're going to get enough media attention to make your grievance very well known. But, now I think it's time to put a halt to all the shenanigans, put your pants back on, and face the criminal consequences. You don't want to go to jail dressed like that."

"I'm hoping to keep my men out of jail, Governor, but we are prepared for the worst. We've gone too far to abandon our quest; too far to allow another indignity, to suffer another scurrility by the makes of Sweet and his kind. Trust me. We pledged nonviolence, but if push comes to shove, I'm not sure I can keep tempers from flaring. We're prepared to go to jail, if necessary, but we're going to raise a stink, we're going to cause a scene for those TV cameras you set up below. We're not going quietly."

"See, there you go using supercilious words again, Rivers. What do you say, counselor, can I tell them down below that you and your men are coming out?"

"Not just yet, Governor. We don't want any violence, but I can guarantce that we will not rest until that old one has been given proper rights and the tomb resealed. We are prepared to stage a sit-in at the least . . . resist if need be."

"Look, Rivers, you're not a bunch of college kids protesting curfew. You guys are adults," he looked at the several powwow dancers lingering in the entrance of the tomb. "Well, most of you, even if you're dressed like a bunch of Cub Scouts. As adults, as 'citizens, tax payers, and voters,' you know the system can't let you get away with all this. How big a sit-in are we talking here, Troy? Count heads. We've got enough police and guardsmen to assign each of your guys a dozen escorts. It's no contest. Look, you lads have had a few laughs, but if you stage a sit-in, some cop is going to push too hard, some Indian is going to resist too much, somebody is going to lose his temper, there is going to be a fight, and someone is going to get hurt. Now do you want that on your conscience? I can only control Sweet and his boys for so long." There was a pause. "If you see another way, I'm willing to listen. I have waited a long time for something like this to embarrass that old peanut butter filcher." He paused again and looked down the slope to the parking lot. He could see the TV truck was broadcasting. "We got a hell of a mess here, Troy," he sat down on a rock and ran his hands through his silver coif. "You've put us in a situation that is potentially embarrassing to me, not ol' Sweet Pickles.

"You know Barber and Brownstone have been good friends of mine for some time now?" He continued his aloud thinking and did not wait for a response. "They raise a hell of a lot of campaign funds." He looked at Rivers. "Does the firm know you're up here? Are they part of what's going on?"

"No, sir, they know nothing about what has happened in the last couple of days. I take full responsibility for the events that got us here."

"What did get us here, Troy? I mean one day I'm planning my upcoming campaign and the next day a bunch of English hooligans have Denver in an uproar and have almost single-handedly destroyed the Brown Palace Hotel. My daughter has gone sillier than snake shit, and a group of adults dressed like dime store Indians have hijacked a city bus, attacked a country club, and assaulted a variety of citizen, including police officers.

"Did you know I had to delay setting up my campaign headquarters in the Brown Palace because those Beatle bums took *my* rooms. Did you know Eisenhower had his campaign headquarters in the same rooms? Can you imagine that? I'm the Governor of the State of Colorado for Christ's sake. A bunch of piss-ant entertainers—foreigners, Limeys . . . can you imagine? How do you explain that?"

"I can't explain it, sir. I just . . ."

"I don't expect you to explain it, son. All I'm saying is one minute I'm planning reelection and the next I'm having a picnic at Red Rocks with a good lawyer gone radical and attacking the police and staging a sit-in in an unfinished bathroom, a cave for Christ's sake, in a concert park, then tells me that he wants to bury and honor some old thief from goddamn Golden, Colorado. Did I tell you I hate Golden? It's a serpent's nest of conservative vipers, and that old Indian was not Robin Hood. The only good thing in Golden is the biscuits at the Holland House. Now they're *golden*. Why can't Denver get a good breakfast joint?"

"Golden, sir?"

"Never mind, It's nothing that concerns us right now, counselor." He paused, taking in the panoramic view of the city lights far to the west. "It's pretty up here, isn't it? I'd forgotten. It's been a long time since I've enjoyed the mountains and the park." He sat, absorbing the surroundings.

Rivers thought it best not to interrupt.

"So . . . how many votes can you and your back-lot Indians muster? I mean, do you guys have any political clout? Is there an organization? What's the membership?"

"I'm not sure that's the point, sir."

"I know it's not the point, Troy. I'm just thinking out loud here. But while we're talking, I do have a point, a political point, if I may be so bold. That law firm of yours has some clout."

"I told you, sir. They have nothing to do with this."

"The powwow in Denver, you say? That's the Four Corners Powwow, isn't it? Orvis Kahnawake's shindig. Right?"

"Yes, sir. How did you know?"

"I've known Orvis Kahnawake for a long time, son. I considered him a good friend. I was torn to tears to hear he was lost in that plane bombing. That's right I cried, but that fact stays here with us. I sure the hell would not want Sweet and his political cut-throats to know I cried."

"To know what, sir?"

"Thanks, counselor. Maybe we *can* find some common ground," he said. "I met with Orvis and the people from C. F. and I. not long ago. We were putting together a deal. Did you know we are going to build a new airport just outside of Denver? Well, we are— the first new airport in the country in decades. C. F. and I. and Orvis' company may be among the players. So might your law firm. It could be a very big deal." He digressed and suddenly barked, "Holy

Lindbergh's limp-one, all we need is to find some Indian graves out there on the prairie. Can you boys help with that kind of thing? Now that might influence me to pardon your asses."

"Governor, I not sure what is going to happen tonight, but I guarantee it should have nothing to do with Earl, Brownstone, Barber, and Delta. I'm not representing them."

"That's too bad, Troy. It could help. Let me be honest one last time. I'm a superstitious man. Three is my lucky number. Good things happen to me in threes. I do everything in threes: three good meals a day; I take vitamins A, B and C; sun, moon and stars; earth, wind and fire; Father, Son and Holy Ghost; Patty, Maxine and Lavern; Huey, Dewey and Louie. And, Troy, you're about to spoil things for me. If things go badly here, the press is going to partner me with Sweet and Humboldt, and I can tell you right now—Larry, Curly and Moe is not a threesome I want to consider. If you can give me three good reasons why I should intercede in this fiasco, I'll give it my best. You're being part of Earl, Brownstone, Barber, and Delta—there's one."

"I already told you, Governor. This has nothing to do with Brownstone and Barber. It's inappropriate to bring them into this."

"All right, then we're back to zero."

"It academic, but four is the sacred number for Native Americans—the four directions and the four seasons."

"Then give me four good reasons, Rivers. Give me something."

"Governor, I am reluctantly speaking for a group of Native Americans who are determined to begin a trek, a quest, if you will, to regain some plundered pride, to reestablish some small, positive element to their stolen identities. We are willing to make a stand here-and-now. It's an insignificant payback when you consider all the pilfered land and abused spirit. These people have suffered at the hands of this government for the past two hundred years. Hell, for the past *four* hundred years. Here is number one: we are doing the right thing. Two: this government owes us; three, Orvis would do the same thing; and four—four hundred years of genocide.

"Sorry, son, but one doesn't count. Every constituent group I deal with says they are doing the right thing. A few of them actually are, and they don't attack country clubs. But this is politics. It has nothing to do with 'truth,' righteousness, morality, or justice. Even if what you say is true, even if you are doing the right thing—you went about it the wrong way. People have been hurt and property has been damaged. Somebody has to be held accountable.

"And as far as your number two, 'owing you,' I'll tell you something, Troy. I wasn't there. I never stole any land or shot any Indians. Even my grandfathers avoided that inferno. I never did any of those things. And I'm not willing to be crucified for sins I personally did not commit. I ain't *Spartacus*, he's my driver, and I sure the hell ain't Kirk Douglas. Speaking of Kirk Douglas, you're asking me to do a Colonel Dax in *Paths To Glory* defense thing here. Now, Kirk Douglas, there is an actor. Did he ever play an Indian? Never mind; it doesn't matter. The point is I'm not cut out for martyrdom, Mr. Rivers. And I'm not willing to suffer or take on the guilt because of all that historical injustice. Here's something you and your Indian rebels don't know. Did you know it was my office that got Colorado to apologize for the Chivington and Sand Creek debacle, not the Mayor, although it was the Denver militia that instigated the massacre. Me. Do you see that ham-fisted Mayor at this little picnic? Hell no, you don't. He's off sunbathing in the nude in Hawaii at some damn mayors' convention. I hope he sunburns the mayoral jewels. The apology for Sand Creek, that little touch of public relations, was for my old friend Orvis. It was he who suggested it. I'm afraid you're still batting zero, son."

"We are not accusing you of those things, personally, Governor. But, ask yourself: What have you and your governmental colleagues done to alleviate the historical inequities that continue to plague Indian people? The apology was important, but those victims are dead. There are thousands of brothers suffering today, and there's no rainbow road in the future.

"Here is something to think about, Governor. Just because you don't see the drunks collapsing and dying in the alleys, just because you don't have to tour the decrepit reservation towns, just because you don't see the unemployment and the depravation it creates, just because you don't witness the humiliation and the suicides, doesn't mean it's okay to ignore them. Just because most Indians don't vote, doesn't mean that when you accept the responsibility of your office, you can ignore the apolitical constituent. It doesn't mean we are holding you responsible for the past, but damn it, in the name *courage*—Governor Lyon, it does mean you have a part to play in the things that happen from now on. We're forcing you to look. You can't ignore us any longer."

The governor sat quietly again. He continued to look at the luminous shimmering on the plains. "OK, that's one. I tell you what I'll do; for giving me a chance to embarrass the shorts off Chief Sweet, I'll give you your second hit. You're still one short if you won't use the law firm—two short if we're going after the sacred four. Got any ideas?"

Troy looked toward the tomb and his friends, waiting for inspiration. A chill wind blew down the canyons of stone. They sat quietly as Lyon surveyed the scenery.

Troy sensed a presence. He looked to the top of a distant rise in the walkway. The peak sat under a street light. The sidewalk glowed like a Fellini set-up; *the Governor would appreciate this.* A gracile figure, dressed in white, rose in a Bergman emergence into the light. *Obviously, I see artier films than the Governor does.* The demilune (was it Buffalo Woman?) opened her arms in an ethereal gesture, palms out, arms gliding away from her, coaxing Troy to view the entirety of the setting. She moved toward them. Just as Rivers almost convinced himself that a divine intervention was taking place he recognized her walk. It was Patty. She was trying to get him to look around. He stood and looked toward the stage.

The Governor noticed his change in focus and turned to investigate what had stolen Rivers' attention. From their higher vantage point, they could see most of the park, most of the stage in the amphitheater, and all of the east-side roads leading into the park. During the debate, neither man had noticed that there was a flurry of activity in and near the park. The circle of police and the guardsmen did not seem to notice; the lower parking lot was a bowl with limited views, and they were concentrating on the confab above them in the rocks.

The men near the tomb, led by Horace and Veloy wandered toward the two debaters, trying to focus on the ridge of flatirons opposite the park and on the horizon backlit by the lights of Denver.

"Troy, your eyes are better than mine, you're an Indian after all." Lyon laughed. "What is that on the performance stage down there? Are those musicians setting up for a concert?"

Rivers squinted. It was something tall and light in color. Half-a-dozen people were milling around the conical object. Suddenly, as several other similar forms began to rise, recognition brightened Troy's face. "It's a tepee, Governor."

"A tepee?"

"Actually, there are several of them." He pointed to the other parking lots, south of the amphitheater, empty when they began their conversation. "And there are more over there." He looked to the open fields to the north of the park, stretching from the police parking lot to the highway. "And there, Governor, I see more over there. Beautiful aren't they?"

"Look!" said Ho. He pointed to Dakota Ridge, opposite the park on the east side. Standing along the entire length of the ridge was a line of silhouettes—men in Indian regalia.

Through the inverted-triangular cut in Dakota Ridge, the pass for the road, came a line of headlights. In the dim illumination, the guardians of the grave and the Governor could make out a slithering serpent of dozens of busses. To the south, illuminated caravans of pickup trucks, campers, and motor homes snaked toward the park from the Morrison route. And racing through the park entrance on the northern side, the entrance which led to the lot filled with police cars and troop trucks, came a caravan of cars being led by a Volkswagen convertible.

Soon tepees were being set up around the circle of police cars, and on all of the other parking plateaus. The tall, cone tents filled the stage, and several drum teams sat among them. An ominous rhythm began to fill the red rock bowl of the amphitheater. A shrill song, sung by a thousand voices, joined the pulsating drumming and drifted beyond the amphitheater, flooding the valley, rushing over the parking lot and Sweet and the other officers. The guardsmen ran for the security of the circle of police cars. The Indian camps to the north and to the south joined in the chant. A thousand more Indians began unloading from the busses and the tributaries of their voices joined in the Niagara cascade of the sacred song.

"Well, son, that looks like three," said Lyon.

"Closer to four, Governor. Four thousand, that is. I believe it's the whole damn powwow."

"Five."

"Five?"

"Yes, I would say by the time they all unload, it's going to be closer to five-thousand-strong. Trust me. I'm a hell of a lot better at estimating crowds than you. I'm starting to feel a bit like General Custer here." He escorted Troy to where they were under one of the streetlights and within sight of the crowd below. He put his arm around the Indian's shoulder and turned to face the TV camera truck, "The light and time are fading, son, and I need the news people to see this. You'll have to forgive me for manipulating the situation to my political benefit, but if I'm going to keep you and your friends out of jail, and if you're going to be available to explain to me how I can become more supportive of your—quest, did you call it? If this is not to be my Waterloo, then I'm damn sure I'm going to get some mileage out of this. You need to tell me right now if we have a deal. Can you compromise, just a little?"

"Compromise? What do you see happening, Governor?"

"I am sure we can come to an understanding," he paused. "I see turning this *Flintstone* latrine into a sacred tomb, if that's what you want. I see me embarrassing the hell out of the Chief of Police and loving it. I see me in the Governor's mansion for another full term. I see the potential for a hell of a lot of voters here. What do you see, counselor?"

"I see an extraordinary opportunist, sir, a robber baron from the past. I see a politico as potentially ruthless and tainted with skullduggery as your favorite director, Orson Welles."

"You see good, kid. Wouldn't you hate to have me for an enemy? You with me, or again' me; we gonna' do this or not?"

"Actually, sir, I would be much honored to have you as an enemy. We Native Americans measure our worth by the strength of our enemies. It would mean I was a man of great power. But, I would much rather have you as a friend."

The governor stood and smiled, his teeth reflecting the sky, "I'll take that as a compliment, Chief Rivers." He took Troy's hand, made sure they were in an appropriate camera angle for the TV crew, and shook it vigorously. He raised both of their hands and arms high into the air, as does an exuberant referee acknowledging the winner of a prizefight.

Troy spoke as he allowed the Governor to pose, "I'm really not a chief, sir. It makes me uncomfortable when you call me that."

"What in the name of the Wizard do you want to be, Rivers? Not the governor, I hope."

"No problem there, sir." He turned and greeted Patty. "You're a heavenly sight."

"We thought you might need some reinforcements," she said.

"Your timing was perfect—female intuition or Indian instincts?"

"Whatever works. Are you finished here?"

"One last thing." He turned to the Governor. "Sir?" he said. "May I introduce you to my fiancée. Patty, this is the Governor of our fair state, Richard . . . Richard the Lionheart."

"That was quite an entrance, young lady. You ever think about getting into politics, or maybe the movies?" He didn't wait for an answer. "Troy, I'll have the police and the National Guard pull out. I'll make a statement to the press. It'll explain my decision about the tomb and the conditions of your gubernatorial pardon. It's time you give the old man his due. You know what I like? I like those Viking funerals. That Kirk Douglas, now he knew how to make an exit." And he sauntered down the path, passing more and more Indians coming up the walk to the tomb.

Troy excused himself to Patty for just a moment and ran down to catch the Governor. "We will do our best to repay everyone for any damages we may have caused."

"Now, now, Troy, don't fret about that. That's only money, son. Right now we need to concentrate on getting me reelected." He took Troy's hand and shook it vigorously again. "I'm hope I haven't turned you into a political cynic, Troy. I hope I have not disillusioned you. I *am* a bit of a Charles Foster Kane, but I tell you, son, once in a great while I actually do some good. Once—it's been so long I'm having trouble remembering when—but once *I* actually did 'the right thing.' "He smiled a wry, sarcastic grin. "I'm personally glad we could have this little chat. I'm sure we'll be talking again—soon."

A huge local TV audience, several score of uniformed men, and thousands of occupants of the largest tepee village ever to occupy the slopes and meadows of Red Rocks Park watched, awestruck, as the two leaders of opposing peoples shook hands—proud men, parting peacefully on the rocks.

The Governor returned to the circle of interested spectators. He gave a brief press conference, the crux of which can be summed up by his first sentence in a long, very long series of many sentences. Quote: "After much carefully worded discussion I have personally convinced this large band of sincerely dedicated . . . what word shall I use to describe these dedicated men? Activists! American Indian advocates . . . to disband soon and cease their part of this difficult and hazardous conflict with authority. And I have personally suggested a token atonement that I am also personally sure will be to the benefit of all concerned. Their desire to appropriately honor and dedicate the gravesite of one of their fallen fathers is a minimal and decorous request, and it shall be honored. It shall be honored with respect and appropriate protocol from us authorities. We will be exiting this beautiful and rustic setting and leave our Native American brothers to their ceremony. This successful termination of a touchy situation reminds me of the time when I personally negotiated the strike between teachers and the school board of Denver Public . . ." And so on, and so on.

The parade and crowds of enthusiasts were led up the ramps by three of the most colorful characters Rivers had even seen. One was dressed in red; he was a huge man, and with his four-foot, ostrich feather war bonnet he appeared twelve feet tall. Two smaller men flanked the giant, one in blue and one in pink.

"They call me the jolly green one, but that is a truely large fellow," Horace said to Troy.

"Large indeed. And I don't believe I'll criticize his outfit."

They all began shaking hands and slapping one another on their backs. The jolly red giant approached Troy.

"I'm Baton Rouge, Toupetoulous. We've come a long way."

"We sure the hell have," he laughed. "And we've got a long way to go."

"We'll be there with you," said Talks Softly.

"I heard *that*," said Troy, "and I'm going to hold you to it."

"Did you hear, Red. He heard me!"

"I heard, T. S., I heard."

"You see, you big lummox. I told you you'd like it here."

"That you did, little brother, and that I do."

Patty finally had the opportunity to corner Troy for a quiet moment. "Don't you think it's appropriate to inform your bride-to-be before you introduce her to the governor as your fiancée?"

"I kind of got caught up in the moment," he said. "You seemed to appear from the heavens, and when you continued to look angelic; it just seemed the right thing to do."

Horace slapped his back and yelled, "Do you believe it. Patty got these busses and filled them with the powwow people. Isn't that great?"

"How did you do that?"

Horace continued, "Yeah, there must be thirty of 'um. Filled—standing room only. Is that great or what?"

"How?" Troy asked again.

"You're starting to talk like an Indian."

"Patty, my love?"

"The cousin called back."

"The cousin?"

"The cousin of the terminal guy you accosted. Remember, he said he had a cousin with a charter business."

Troy nodded, but was still somewhat confused. "What about us assaulting his relative?"

"He didn't mind. Business is business, and thirty charters seemed to interest him."

"You're beautiful, Patty."

"Don't we have some unfinished business?" she asked. "Is there somewhere we can talk?"

Troy smiled and gently kissed her on the cheek. He turned and wandered toward the darkness and quiet of the tomb. "I don't think the old one will mind. This could be the first romantic action he's witnessed in decades."

As they walked arm in arm and entered the tomb, they both searched for the source of the raspy laughter of a raven.

The view from their perch on the northern monolith, high above the amphitheater, inspirited Three Rivers and Patty. Below them, the procession of their comrades, like rivers of light, flowed toward the tomb. Partisans carried torches. Others carried stones with which to seal the vault. Scattered celebration fires united the surrounding ridges, the park, the meadows, the valley, and the theater. Lines of torchbearers connected the glowing cones of the tepee camps. The fires sparked and spit necklace strings of embers, looking like embryo stars, into the blue-black sky. Silhouettes of ravens, hundreds of ravens, circled like planets, as swift as swallows, within the celestial swirl.

The high pitch whelps of packs of coyotes joined the funeral chant of the celebrants, but one deep, throaty, and doleful song howled among them.

"There are no wolves in Colorado—are there?" Rivers asked Patty.

"Not for decades, I believe." She laid her head on his shoulder.

And the earth vibrated with the plangent rhythm of a hundred tom-toms.

The largest fire, in front of the tomb, cast dancing shadows of warriors on the walls of the maroon stone corridors. And on a ledge, in that transition area from fire light to dark night, screened from sight by the smoke, ethereally stood Black Elk, Sitting Bull, and Wolf Song.

"You have indeed earned the title *Wihili*, Brother Wolf Song," said Black Elk. "Truly, you have become the coyote, the trickster, a spirit of wit."

"Thank you, Wichasha Wakan."

"You have become one possessing great medicine, Little Brother," said Sitting Bull. "It has been a long journey. You have done well to be thus honored as the hero."

"As should you have been honored, Tatanka-Iyotanka," said Wolf Song. "But I find it ironic, my kinsmen, that in our lives, here in the physical real world and in the real world of dreams, that we have such little control over the most important things we do."

Each specter nodded in agreement.

"Yes, brothers, my spirit has finally taken coup. It was as you foretold, Wichasha Wakan, that I would redeem myself as the opossum. What do you think, my friends, those mortal remains we see being sealed in that tomb, are they truly dead or only sleeping?"

All three vaporous shades laughed heartily. Their smoke curtain was forced by their laughter into an eccentric path, exposing them to the watchers above on the rocks: he who was destined to become a sachem and she who was truly an Indian princess. And as they watched the three spirits rejoice, a fourth chimerical being, probably attracted by the joviality, drifted into view and stood behind the loving couple. The mortals seemed aware that the spirit was there.

"What's all this laughter, uncles?" called out the specter of Orvis Kahnawake, his hair long and loose in the rising smoke. "Have I missed a joke?"

Chapter Forty-two

Reunion

Some years later . . .

"It's been a while, Turtle. I'd forgotten how good your margaritas are. I'll have another; don't forget the salt."

"Yes," cawed Raven, "great party. I'm flying high."

"It's good to see you tricksters. How long has it been since our collaboration at Red Rocks?"

"Time means nothing to us, Turtle. You know that," said Coyote, "Not when we are remembered, not when we are vivified, not when there are pranks and tomfoolery to perpetuate."

"We'd heard you went on vacation, Coyote. Not true?" asked Raven. "What have you been up to?"

"More salt, please, Turtle," Coyote paused. "Well, it's true I went west after Red Rocks. I sought the sea air, some good wine, seafood, California girls; you know the routine. I was worn out. Red Rocks was a lot of work—fun, fulfilling—but exhausting." He sipped his margarita. "Perfect, Turtle," His tongue cleaned his wet muzzle. "Anyway, I simply couldn't resist the action. Wicked work is never done." They all chuckled. "I'm hanging out in San Francisco for a time. Living in a section called Haight Asbury. Raven, you would love it. There's parties every night and day. And drugs! That stuff Anthony Hands of the Bear was fooling around with, the niopó that gave us materiality, was rural and primitive compared to the manna of modern chemistry. The music is sensual. The Beatles we heard here at Red Rocks have led the way. They've evolved from pop to psychedelic, from rock to razzle, from mania to mantra. It's a groovy scene, man: a rebirth, a quest for the miraculous.

"And talk about music and philosophy reflecting the heartbeat of Mother Earth—Turtle, old friend, your persona as Gaea, Tierra Madre, has never been more celebrated."

"True," said Turtle. "but I'm afraid, as we all know, it's temporary."

"Then we'll have to cause a little havoc when they forget again, eh Turtle," said Raven.

"Ooooh, Raven," continued Coyote. "You won't believe the women. They're girls, really. Eager and electrified, creative and uninhibited, musky and aromatic . . . I've never had so much tail. I howl, man, oh—hoooow I howl." And he howled.

Turtle and Raven stood wide-eyed as Coyote recovered.

"Well," Coyote coughed, "I'm, ahh, dominating the conversation. Sorry. Hey, it's a reunion. What have you cats been up to? What ever happened to that Papago Indian and the lady anthropologist, and the lawyer and that beauty with the coyote hair?"

"Raven" said Turtle, "why don't you go. I'll fix another batch of drinks."

"I'll be glad to," said Raven. "Although I haven't been getting as much congress as old Coyote, I've stayed active.

"Maybe it was for old time's sake; I don't know. You remember," he joked, "even in the old country I was always accused of picking the bones of the peasantry. Maybe, now I'm trying to be a bird of another color."

Coyote looked at Turtle, seeking confirmation to the change in the old crow's character. Turtle shrugged his shoulders and continued mixing margaritas.

"Anyway," said Raven, "I've been accompanying the Native Americans for quite awhile. Well, while Turtle took Hands of the Bear and lovely Olivia under his wing—he can tell you about them. I helped him out by sticking around here in the foothills.

"You remember the lawyer, Three Rivers, and that pretty park ranger Patty?" Coyote nodded while he slurped the last of his first margarita and licked the rim. "Well, they came up with the brilliant idea to take some of the tribute in old Willie Wolf Song's tomb, sell it, and use the proceeds to start a nonprofit organization for the benefit of Indi'ns. They call it The Wolf Song Foundation.

"The governor loved the idea and put his influence behind it, but Wild Billy Schwarz came unglued. He wanted his booty back. It was his contention that Willie had stolen it from *him*. His feathers were ruffled until lawyer Rivers reminded him that he had collected the insurance on the loot. He had no claim, and if returned, he would have to pay back the insurance company.

"Seems the governor also influenced Billy's decision when the state discovered that the Wild Man had been negligent in renewing his liquor license. But, as the fates will have it, it all worked out."

"Well," interrupted Turtle as he served the next round. "Despite what appeared to be an amicable solution for all, Wild Billy suffered in the end. What the governor didn't tell him was that a major interstate highway, I-70, was going in just below the Mount Vernon Canyon Road. It's a six lane super highway, and in essence killed off Billy's traffic. Only the most curious or lost tourists found their way to Buffalo Bill Cody's Bar Grill Trading Post and Texaco Station. That's why we're here tonight. It's the last hurrah for Cody's. Billy is closing. I heard that he is moving to Florida and going into business with the illegitimate son of his Uncle Max, a Judeo-Cubano cousin. They think they can revive the Miami Beach area. They have a plan to refurbish art deco hotels and attract the beautiful people back to South Beach. Keep an eye on Wild Billy, Coyote. If things get dull in San Francisco, you may want to prowl for pun tang in Miami."

"A real estate company bought the building," added Raven. "They're turning it into offices to deal with the booming housing market that's cropped up on Lookout Mountain and Genesee. Million dollar mansions are sprouting up on the slopes like ragweed. The place is starting to look like an infestation of California suburbia. No offense, Coyote.

"The frontier spirit of the foothills has suffered a serious setback, except in Golden where one can still have their picture taken under the rainbow-shaped sign on Washington Street, which proudly states, 'Where the West Remains.'"

"I think it says, 'Where the West Begins,'' Raven," said Turtle. "They changed it."

"Oh, caw-rap. See what happens when you turn your back for a minute."

"Buffalo Bill Days," said Turtle, "is still celebrated, Raven. It gets boisterous."

"What about the Holland House?" asked Coyote. "In the old days, I could smell those biscuits baking all the way from Santa Fe."

"Closed," Raven cawed, it seemed to catch in his throat. Abandoned and now affectionately known as *The Haunted House.* There are plans to remodel it into an upscale hotel, looking like an adobe pueblo from Santa Fe or Taos. Maybe that crazy coot Doogan and Wild Billy had an influence on the area after all."

"You started out talking about the lawyer," Coyote reminded Raven. "I hope his is a happier tale."

"That remains to be seen," said the bird. "He proved to be a good lawyer and seems to have found his niche running the foundation. First thing he did was convince Mutual of Omaha, the insurance company that technically owned the tomb stash, to donate it to the Wolf Song Foundation. He reminded them that their logo was an Indian, and that a lot of Native Americans considered that sort of allusion as an affront to their heritage. Would not it be a smart public relations move to affiliate themselves with an Indi'n run foundation? The governor is rumored to have helped with that strategy, seems the state buys a lot of insurance. The insurance company earned a huge tax write-off because the worth of the pottery and artifacts had appreciated to astronomical levels. In fact, none of the pieces had to be sold to finance the foundation; rather, a certain bank on Seventeenth Street in Denver was glad to lend the start-up funds, listing a few of the pieces as collateral. It was a peace offering, presented by one Alexander Hawthorn in an effort to maintain the accounts of the local law firm—Earl, Brownstone, Barber, and Delta."

Turtle interjected, "It's who you know, you know."

"I'll drink to that," said Coyote. "A toast to my ancient friends."

They each raised their glasses.

"Anyway, the foundation eventually outgrew the Red Rocks location. So the function of the Red Rocks office was much simplified—serving as the main gallery for the Wolf Song Collection and a retreat site for cleansing and purification ceremonies. Indian wannabes pay big bucks to go through a sweat lodge and then spend hours in the hot tub drinking wine and telling ghost stories about old Willie. I get 'um going. My best trick is to pilfer a pound of nuts, gorge myself, and break wind above them. They all swear that around twilight they hear laughter emanating from the depths of the sealed tomb, and smell the distinct aroma of roasted cashews."

"And I was worried," said Coyote, "that you we're getting old, Raven. I should have known better. Tell me, what happened to the big Indian, the artist?"

Turtle answered, "Ho Ho Horace Green exhibits in galleries in Scottsdale, Santa Fe, Aspen, Los Angeles, Tokyo, and San Francisco. I'm surprised you haven't been to an exhibit."

"I've been a little busy. You know hooooow it is."

"He has never had a New York gallery exhibit his work," added Raven. "He jokes that if he changed his name to Ho Ho Horace Greenburg or Lachen Lachen von Grün he could get a show. Regardless, he was recently invited by the Smithsonian Institute to be one of six Native American artists to exhibit at the Corcoran Museum of Art. He annually donates the sale of several paintings to the Wolf Song Foundation. Three scholarships have been created from his generosity: The Green Award, which provides four years of full-carry for a Native American youth to study art at any art school in the country; The Three Rivers Scholarship which provides full tuition, room, board and books for any law student of Native American decent; and The Kahnawake Fund which provides a renewable four year scholarship for an Indian youth to attend college anywhere in the world. We firmly believe that knowledge is power."

"And," Coyote asked, "how about Humboldt, the guy with the arrow in his ass?"

"Henry Humboldt, Ex-Chief Ranger and Superintendent in Charge of the Red Rocks Rangers, did not fare as well. He was forced to resign from the Rangers. He became the Head of Security for Cinderella City, a large shopping complex in southwest Denver. I heard it's closing. He did, however, marry another Rent-a-Cop and together they raised a fine son—a doctor, specializing in proctology.

"Chief of the Denver Police, Allan Sweet, in case you're curious, retired from the police force to give full attention to his political career. Four years after the infamous *Indian Uprising at Red Rocks Park* he ran against the incumbent, second-term Governor, Richard 'Dick' Lyon. Governor Lyon handily defeated ol'

Sweet Pickles and served an unprecedented third term. The local papers reported that the minority vote carried Lyon in both his second and third election victories. The only precincts won by Sweet were two small communities just west of Denver—Morrison and Golden. I see you're not surprised."

"And his little sidekick," asked Coyote. "What happened to him."

"Officer Carson was recruited by the Treasury Department where he excelled as a Secret Service Agent and bodyguard for the wives of presidents. He served proudly until he was forced into retirement because of rumors of an affair with one of the First Ladies. Obviously that D. C. crowd does not feel that what is fair for the goose is fair for the gander."

"Well, Turtle . . . what of Anthony Hands of the Bear and lovely Olivia Hotchkiss, Daughter of the Earth? I always thought she was special."

"To conclude their tale," said Turtle, taking on a mystical tone, "we must return to Red Rocks Park and Amphitheater, August, 1964. I'll take us back."

"I love it when you do that voodoo that only you do so well, Turtle."

"I'm a god. It's my job."

Anthony and Olivia were climbing as fast as they could up the straight stone scar on the east slope of Mt. Morrison. They struggled on pumpkin-sized, irregular stones, which Tony knew— had heard one night at Cody's—were stacked as an incline in 1911 for the Mt. Morrison Cable Railway, an incredibly steep ride which carried one hundred passengers per car from Red Rocks Park to the top of Mt. Morrison. Anthony cursed the inventiveness of the cable engineer, who, from the looks of things, simply laid a ruler on a topography map of the mountain, drew an unwavering line as straight as pencil and ruler will allow, and declared, "That looks pretty good. We'll put it there." How Tony and Olivia wished the ride was still available, but they figured that speed was of the essence in their escape, thus risked being seen from the amphitheater below. Tony said they could traverse from one patch of pines to the next, staying in cover. He was an expert at moving in the shadows.

But Olivia said the open path allowed them to check and see if there was anyone in pursuit. The strategy seemed to work, for in about an hour or two, they were on the summit of the mount. One last look at Red Rocks, no one was behind them. But they were curious about what appeared to be a party to which they regretted they hadn't been invited.

Tony thought he saw remorse in Olivia's expression, despite how pretty she looked. The distant city lights of Denver formed a halo around her head; her face glowed with perspiration; her arms had the same glow of exertion; her eyes seemed to shine. A breeze skirting over the top of the mountain brought her perfume back to him. He turned away from her; he could not face her and articulate the thought that was twisting his heart. "It's me they're after, Olivia. You haven't broken any laws. I can make it from here; you don't really have to stay with me, if you don't want to. Maybe you should turn around here and go back down. It's a lot easier going down. You could tell them I forced you to come along—a hostage thing. I threatened you, but you got away."

She turned to him and looked into his eyes for an answer, "Don't you want me to come?" She sounded hurt.

"Of course, I want you!" he said. "It's just that, I got you into something difficult and I never really asked—do you want to be a part of all this?"

"I'm here, aren't I?"

"That you are . . . "

They kissed at the peak of the mountain. They tasted each other and felt the breeze surround them. She tasted of perspiration and tears; he feared he tasted of sweat and the dust of the red rocks. They took each other's hands and made the short jump off the rocks of the summit onto the other side. Tony directed the downhill romp through the pines to the southwest, the opposite direction of Cody's, Golden, and Lookout. Soon, Bear Creek Road, Highway 74, snaked below them. It was the road between Morrison and Evergreen.

When they reached Bear Creek it was totally dark: a deep, midnight-mountain, no-street-lights kind of dark. The cascading waters of a cool stream separated them from the road; a twenty-foot bank supported the highway above the creek. It was August; the water was fast but not dangerous, not anything like the torrent of a spring runoff. Despite the late hour and temperate air, the water felt invigorating. They found a calm eddy and floated on their backs, staring at the stars through the Ponderosa ceiling. Olivia eventually became chilled and Anthony hugged her in the shallows and on the bank, to help warm her.

He was the first to climb the boulders to the deserted road above. He stood on the shoulder, ready to jump back into cover, alert for the sound of an approaching car. Nothing. "It's okay. Come up." She struggled, her shoes still wet and slippery, her cold muscles just a bit uncoordinated. He reached down to help her with the last few steps, ignoring the road.

The bright headlights hit them. They froze—vulnerable as a pair of surprised deer. Anthony could tell, despite his panic, that the lights were large and tall and from a four-wheel drive truck. The Sheriffs' Department drove four-wheel drive vehicles on these mountain roads. They stood there like statues in the intrusive light. Suddenly, the air felt cold. Olivia shivered, Anthony put his arm around her shoulder to help stop the shivering and to gesture *thanks*; he appreciated the risks she had taken. "I wish I hadn't gotten you into this," he said. "But I'm glad you're here."

"I love you, Anthony." She whispered and waited for the occupants of the truck to burst forward and squelch the escape.

"Tony, is that you?" came a somewhat familiar voice. It had the edge of inebriation.

"Junior?"

"Yeah," said Stanley Manely, Junior, matter-of-factly. "You guys been skinny dipping?"

"Not exactly. What brings you down this road?"

"Oh, I was up at the Little Bear in Evergreen getting shit-faced. I'm pretty pissed at my pop. I got drunk and decided to run away. I stole his truck. Isham is in the trailer in the back. You know awhile back Pop almost beat the poor horse to death 'cause he couldn't stud anymore. The funny thing was that Fleeta Meeker reminded dad that he was having a little trouble, too. Pop smacked her around pretty good. You know Fleeta don't you, Tony? She's right here with me." He opened the door of the truck so that the interior light came on. Fleeta meekly waved from the passenger seat. "So we decide to go get plastered together. So we decided we really liked each other. So we decided to run away together. You guys need a ride?"

Michael Patrick Shane had long ago retired from coaching basketball at Wheat Ridge High School west of Denver. He moved in with his brother Patrick Michael, P. M., the nocturnal sibling, on their small ranch just east of the Papago Reservation and Sels, Arizona. A gang of thugs, wise guys, forced P. M. off the land because they coveted his marijuana crop, but eventually got themselves incarcerated. The Shane brothers reclaimed the rancho and rekindled their agrarian skills. In fact, the new crop was so large that Farmer Shane, P. M., sought the aid of a "farm" hand. Stanley Manely, Junior fit the job description perfectly. P. M. and M. P. had plenty of room in the ranch house. And M. P., the better looking of the pair, *purely* loved having a woman around, since admiring the attributes of womankind was second only to shooting hoops. Lovely Fleeta fit *that* job description to a tee.

Isham, it turns out, loved the desert. It was dry and hot and very, very quiet. Two years after the five of them left the foothills of Colorado, Isham sired a pack of palominos, numerous enough to fill a Shriner's parade.

P. M., M. P., Junior and Fleeta all remained very modest and low key despite their eventual outrageous wealth.

The Papago People, Anthony's Tohono O'odham kinsmen, escorted the two tachchutham, lovers, across the rez and into Sonora, Mexico. The Southern Pima, cousins, continued to chaperon the couple through Sonora and into the State of Chihuahua where the Mountain Pima took over. They traveled through the lands of the Tarahumara and the Northern Tepehuan and into the State of Durango where the Southern Tepehuan served as hosts. The search by the authorities was always cavalier, and when they lost tract of the loving couple somewhere in Nayarit and a small Huichol village, they gave up. Chief Sweet often made jokes that he would probably run into "Hardhat" in Acapulco if he could just get enough time off to take a vacation. It never happened.

Meanwhile in the River of Doubt region of Brazil, the old Onça Parda shaman, Olivia's adopted father, dreamed. And while he was dreaming he thought it was peculiar that the people and places of which he dreamt were not of the Xingú region, nor were they of Rio da Duvida, the hidden river that white men still think does not exist. They were not Amazonian, these astral inhabitants. He dreamed of a giant turtle, a snapping turtle, and the people who lived upon this turtle, between the crags. He knew that the great turtle of his dream was the northern sister of the giant turtle upon which the many rivers flowed that were his home. Only this was a colossal snapping turtle and not the long-necked, soft-shelled river turtle of his world. He sensed that the people who lived upon the snapping turtle were cousins, although they looked very strange. They wore too many clothes and their hair was too long. Their clothes were made from the hides of animals and their hair was tied back like rope. And these people depended upon a beast that reminded the shaman of the cattle of the Brazilians, only these beasts were as large as a hut and had great humps on their backs and they wore long coats to keep them warm for they lived in a land where the rain froze in the air and turned into white stars.

It was this image of the hard rain that piled into deep troughs as does the sand on the banks of the river after the spring flood that convinced the shaman that these were images of great power and should be taken seriously, although in his dream he laughed and laughed at the beast of sustenance and the clothes of the people. They did not cut their hair into the beautiful black, inverted-bowl shape of the Onça Parda. They did not put the juice of the red urucú seeds into their hair to make it as bright as the feathers of the scarlet macaws of the rain forest. The feathers they wore were but black and white. And they painted their faces in stripes and chevrons, not in the beautiful black masks of the Onça Parda.

And one of these strange kinsmen of the land of the snapping turtle came forward and spoke to the shaman. "I, too am a dreamer," he said. "I, too am a holy man for my people. And I have had, as you shall have, a vision of the future of our people. Only I was not able to transform my vision from the real world of dreams to the other world of solid things. I was not able to save my people. You must do better than I. And we people of the land of the snapping turtle shall help you of the rain forest and of the river turtle by sending to you one of our brothers; he who comes from the land of no trees and searing heat and the desert tortoise. He who wears the hat of the turtle." The shaman laughed at the idea of a land with no trees, but again the incomprehensible vastness of such an idea made him give credence to the celestial messenger. "Am I to know how you are called?" he asked the specter of his dream. The harbinger answered, "Brother."

And on into the deep night the shaman continued to dream. He dreamed of the jungle panther, the totem of his people, and he saw her running from the jagged back of the snapping turtle along the long neck and onto the soft shell of the river turtle and along the banks of the blue water river and into his village and up to his maloca, the men's hut. And he saw that she was accompanied by a bear. A bear had not been seen in the river country of the Onça Parda since before his father and his father's father. But he knew of such an animal, and being a worshiper of ancestors, he interpreted the bear as a messenger from his father and his father's father. These were spirits that should not be driven from the village into the jungle. These spirits brought with them knowledge and gifts, not bad luck and illness. These were spirits blessed by his brother from the land of the snapping turtle. This was the totem of his people and the messenger from his people before him. And as he dreamt, the bear raised itself onto its back legs and the legs grew long and he ran swiftly on two legs and as he ran he metamorphosed into the turtle man. And the jungle cat lifted herself erect and continued running on two feet and her legs grew long and lithesome and she jumped the width of broad rivers and flew over the ground, and the feline's hair grew long and more blonde and she transformed her front paws into long arms and graceful hands and when she had run the length of the blue water river, and upon entering his village, she turned into his adopted daughter. And just when this happened in his dream, he awoke and sat up in his hammock and looked to the north edge of the village and saw Olivia and Anthony enter the world.

The children of the village ran and grasped her by her arms and hands. They also pulled Anthony to the center of the village plaza. His bright yellow hard-hat fascinated them. After the long greeting, Olivia and Anthony finally seated themselves next to the shaman in his hammock and he told her of his dreams.

"He says that he knew we were coming," she translated for Tony. "He was told of our coming by one of the people who was not of this village and wore too many clothes and whose hair was a rope." She shrugged her shoulders but continued to listen. "He says he has been dreaming of turtles. They speak to him. He knew that you would come and as the man who wears the turtle shell on his head you would lead the people in great battles against the whites who have arrived in the land of rivers and want only to destroy the trees." She made a loose fist and wrapped on Tony's Hard-hat. "So, I guess your new name is *Turtle Man,*" she laughed.

The old holy man reached across to Tony and took both his hands. He held the huge right hand up against his own diminutive hand. "He says," continued Olivia, "your name is: The-Turtle-Warrior-With-Hands-of-the-Bear." She smiled and took the old man's tiny hand and rubbed it on her face. "I have missed you, father."

"I have been waiting for you a long time, daughter. You have kept me waiting for many days and many nights. But now you have returned, as you should, and now I can die, as I should. These are appropriate things."

"No, father! That is not why I have returned, so you could die!"

"This is not of your making, foolish girl. This is the way of the world. It is proper. But before I go, I have much to teach you, for you shall become the holy one of this village. I also have much to tell the people, so that they will see that you and Turtle Warrior-With-Hands-of-the-Bear were sent from the dream world to lead the people and make them safe."

"What is he saying?" asked Tony.

She did not answer, but listened to the old man.

"And when the time comes for you to be the holy one, I will give you a new name, appropriate of your station. I will base your name on this: for nine months you stayed in the womb of the village of the people and then when it was time for you to be born in the village, as is the tradition, you were taken by the black, stinging wasp that beat the air into submission. And you were not born. But, you were taken to the nest of the wasp where you died. Your spirit, the spirit of the Onça Parda, the jungle cat, escaped from the nest of wasps and carried you back here to the village of the people, where upon entering the village, you are born again.

"So your name shall be: *She Who Is Born Feet First.* And you shall be known as the Holy One Born Backwards. It's important for a shaman to have an affliction. Yours is a good one. It should carry with it great medicine."

It took some cajoling for the old shaman to convince all the men of the village that a woman should take his place. She would not be allowed, however, into the men's maloca. She would never be able to behold the giant magic flutes. But he talked of his vision and his dreams and as each came true, his side of the argument gained merit. For example, Anthony did indeed lead the people on raids of the construction camps and those cutting roads into the blue water area. More often than not, the raids were clandestine games of hide-and-seek in which he sabotaged the heavy-duty equipment in such subtle ways that the Portuguese-whites credited the breakdowns to evil spirits. The other perplexing mystery was the consistent disappearance of hard-hats. The Portuguese knew that no Indian could have that thorough a knowledge of the sophisticated machinery. Thus, their superstitions about forest spirits, plus the historical reputation of the Onça Parda as headhunters, kept the encroachers at bay.

Olivia's knowledge of hallucinogens and the jungle medicine cabinet eventually exceeded even that of the old shaman. Slowly the people became convinced that this woman who had the same coloring of the jungle cat, who possessed extraordinary knowledge of the sacred niopó, was indeed a supernatural being. They eventually took great pride in that this magical being was part of their tribe. Their neighbors had no such blessings. And although the thought of kidnapping the blonde specter crossed the mind of the Kalapalo, the Yawalapití, the Waurá, the Kamayurá and the other more violent tribes, they knew they dare not risk the wrath of *The Holy One Who Is Born Backwards* and her consort, *The-Turtle-Warrior-With-Hands-of-the-Bear.*

Village warmth and hospitality incubated the newcomers for nine months. All the while Olivia agonized over the old shaman's prophecy. At the end of nine months, Olivia and all the Onça Parda saw that the shaman, her father, had planned the day of his death to coincide with the birth of her first child.

He was a wily old holy man, for he knew that if he timed things exactly right, his spirit would not leave the village and join those of his fathers' in the rain forest; rather, it would float smoothly from the wrinkled and broken body that was his home for so many spring floods, and it would enter the pink, new body of his daughter's child, exactly at the moment the baby gasped for air to fuel his first cry.

It was not selfish magic. His soul did not ascend over the baby's. They were one, as the people were one. And it was the adverse times in which the people found themselves that demanded such magic—that and his love for his daughter, Olivia.

He would grow strong and smart under the love of she who was now his mother. He would learn to hunt again from the Turtle Warrior and together, his father and he would become warriors of legend and protect his people. He would become a village chief and for generations he would tell his people of his vision and his dreams, and he would instill in them the knowledge that to survive and keep the old ways they must do heroic things, and to be the hero one must be born and die and be born again. "This I know, for Turtle has made it so", he whispered as his last breathe left his ancient body. A mist danced on the clean, humid air of the world. A baby, fresh and frightened, entered a new world and gasped in wonder, pervaded by the promise of life. And he saw in the reflection of his mother's loving eyes that he was the culmination of a long odyssey. He was the first-born son of Olivia Hotchkiss, a holy woman, and Anthony Hands of the Bear, known as Turtle Warrior—a hero, at last.

The End

About the author

Lon Seymour's parents, a jock and a homecoming princess, were both University of Oklahoma grads. Later, Lon was born in our nation's capital, his dad playing fullback for the Washington Redskins. Lon is the second son. While a toddler, the Seymours moved back to America's Wild West, residing in California, Oklahoma and Texas, finally settling in Colorado. Growing up, Lon was  typically imbued with the tall tales and myths of the frontier, country music, Tex-Mex, and Pueblo-deco. He exhibited an affinity for drawing and painting. He earned his BFA in visual arts from the University of Colorado Boulder and MA from the University of Northern Colorado. Lon pursued a PhD at the University of Denver and has spent his professional life as an art educator and arts education administrator. Lon taught art in public and private schools, served as the arts coordinator for Jefferson County Public Schools, Colorado's largest district, chaired the art department for Metropolitan State University of Denver and was vice president for academic affairs at Rocky Mountain College of Art & Design. After decades in the visual arts, he decided to exercise his love of parlance and graphic story telling. His venues for self-expression expanded to include fiction writing. Old interests, like the heritage of his father's family, the Wyandotte People of Oklahoma, and new issues like the controversy surrounding sport team mascots—think the Redskins—motivated this his debut novel which addresses innate human folly, focusing on Native American social justice. His style marries humor and heartbreak, irony and historical imprudence. An artist, an author, an astute observer, Lon Seymour brings his insights and experiences to the novel: TURTLE, COYOTE, RAVEN and RINGO: Mystical Journeys.

87891697R00372

Made in the USA
San Bernardino, CA
09 September 2018